THE BEATRICE STUBBS SERIES
BOXSET ONE

BEHIND CLOSED DOORS
RAW MATERIAL
TREAD SOFTLY

JJ MARSH

TRISKELE BOOKS

Cover design: JD Smith

Published by Prewett Publishing.
All enquiries to admin@jjmarshauthor.com

First printing, 2012

ISBN 978-3-9524796-3-6

Contents

BEHIND CLOSED DOORS

JJ MARSH

Chapter 1

Utrecht 2007

"Howzit? You got here, then?"

"Yes, Joop. I got here. At last."

"Uh oh. Delays?"

"Right now I'm in a taxi from the airport. Not only did we leave Jo'burg three hours late, but I missed the transfer in Frankfurt and now we've just circled Schiphol for forty-five minutes, waiting for a slot."

Only an asshole like Joop would think it a good idea to whistle into a cell phone.

"Joop, listen. I need to take a shower and eat something. After that, I want to crash."

"Shit, man. That's all you want to do? Friday night is jol night, but if you're creamed…?"

Creamed? Where the hell had this guy learnt his English?

"There's just one other thing I need."

"No sweat. An SMS is on its way with the number of that agency I mentioned. It's not cheap but you can feel the quality."

"I appreciate that. Meet me in the foyer at ten on Monday, OK?"

"Don't wanna do anything tomorrow?"

"I got plans, Joop."

"See you Monday then. Sweet dreams."

Asshole.

He watched the scenery, such as it was. Grey, flat and bleak, with the occasional windmill to make sure you were paying attention. The hotel was a pleasant surprise. The first of the day. Street noise left behind, he glanced up at what looked like some sort of institution in its own grounds. Classy and quiet. His kind of place.

"*Goede avond en onthaal.* Welcome to Utrecht, Sir. We have good news for you. You have an upgrade today, to one of our Empire Suites. Please follow the porter."

A second pleasant surprise. Plenty of space, working area, two TVs, and most importantly, a vast bed. He palmed the kid a coin, who left him to explore the room in peace. Throwing off his coat, he sat on the bed. Heavy linen, an excess of pillows and a firm mattress, which would be seeing some action in the next twenty-four hours, if Joop wasn't exaggerating about that agency. The bathroom was massive, well-furnished with towels and little bottles of wife-pleasing potions. He made a mental note to throw some into his case. And a wall of mirrors behind the bath. Better and better. His mood started to lift. There was a message on the flat screen at the foot of the bed.

Mr van der Veld
Welcome to Grand Hotel Karel V
We hope you enjoy your stay.

Flicking to Bloomberg, he started to undress, while checking the screen for any significant currency movements. As he kicked off his shoes, he noticed the ice bucket and chilled Krug Grande Cuvée. There was a card.

With compliments of D'Arcy Roth.

That explained the upgrade. Nice touch. Unnecessary, as there was no one else in the running, but it certainly put their potential client in the right frame of mind. So, a shower, a glass of Krug, order room service and put a call through to this agency. All needs met.

As he unzipped his case to find his toiletries bag, he heard a discreet knock at the door. He frowned. Unexpected visitors, including hotel employees who wanted to 'turn down' his bed, were not welcome. He yanked open the door and his frown lifted. The neat grey suit, official clipboard and pulled-back sleek blonde hair told him she was a hotel employee. The pale skin drawn over fine bones and a high forehead, grey-blue eyes and cherub lips told him she was more than welcome. He checked the name badge. *Annelise Visser.*

"Good evening, Mr van der Veld. My name is Frau Visser and I ..."

"Good evening, Annelise. Nice to meet you." He offered his hand. A momentary flush before she recovered herself to shake it. He was well aware that conventions in the Netherlands dictate that one should use surnames in formal situations. He didn't give a shit.

"I am the Senior Hospitality Director, sir. I am here to check that your suite is satisfactory."

"The suite seems fine, Annelise, but I do have one concern."

The smooth dome of her forehead contracted.

"A concern? What would that be, sir?"

"The champagne." He pushed back the door and indicated the ice bucket. "Can I be sure this is top quality? You see, I'm used to drinking the best."

"Sir, the champagne is a Krug Grande Cuvée, and was specifically selected by your company ..." a glance at her clipboard. "D'Arcy Roth."

"They are not yet my company, Annelise. They want me as their client. But if you'll consent to taste the champagne with me, I guess we can agree that the suite is satisfactory."

A proper blush now. He loved a blush on a blonde. Pink cheeks, creamy skin reddened with warmth. He wanted to turn her over, pull down those panties and spank her right there. Raise some heat in *those* cheeks.

"Sir, I thank you, but I am on duty right now. Drinking alcohol would be inappropriate."

"This is the hotel that 'exceeds your expectations', right?"

"Yes, but ..." She laughed. "OK, I will taste the champagne. But then I am afraid I must go. I have to consider the needs of other guests."

He didn't reply, but gestured to the sofa. She sat, knees together, the grey skirt riding up slightly. The lamp behind her created a halo effect. An angel. He smiled as he twisted the cork. She was going nowhere. As the cork popped, he caught the overflow in a flute, with a loaded glance at her to see if she picked up on the image. She returned his smile, politely. He slid beside her and handed her a glass. Before he could propose a toast, she set her glass on the table.

"I'm sorry, sir. Champagne always gives me the hiccups. Would you mind if I take some water? I can get it."

He placed a hand on her knee. "Sit still. You're my guest."

She jumped at the touch of his hand. And he still hadn't made skin contact, as she wore pantyhose. He hated pantyhose.

In the mini-bar, there was an array of different waters. He grabbed a bottle of Evian and showed it to her. She nodded. Returning to his seat, he placed the water in front of her and raised his flute.

"To a very pleasant stay in Utrecht."

She tipped her glass to his and looked at him. "To a pleasant stay in Utrecht." She sipped at the fizz and closed her eyes. "Mmm. I don't wish to prejudice your opinion, but in my view, that's lovely."

Her voice was soft, intimate and breathy. He wanted to hear her say those words again. *Mmm, that's lovely.* Preferably as she drew her fingernails down his back. He hadn't even registered the taste, but his glass was two-thirds empty.

"I don't know, Annelise, the jury's still out. Maybe the second glass will clinch it." He refilled his and she didn't stop him replacing the tiny sip she had taken. A good sign.

"Now, what time do you finish tonight, Annelise?" His tongue felt thick and his speech sounded slow.

She swallowed some water and caught a stray droplet with the tip of her tongue. Shit, he wasn't sure if he could wait till later.

She avoided the question. "Why are you in Utrecht, Mr van der Veld? Is it just business, or pleasure?"

He took another slug and leaned towards her. He felt hot, horny and even a little drunk.

"Until five minutes ago, strictly business. But now, I'm not so sore."

That struck him as funny, because he wasn't sore at all. But he was as sure as he'd ever be. He started to laugh, but her eyes were looking into his, with intent. Was it too soon to …?

She smiled and reached for the bottle, refilling both glasses. Her voice was low, full of suggestion. He watched her lips.

"Have I satisfied your concerns regarding the champagne, sir?"

That was flirting. No doubt at all. His body felt warm and heavy and soft, with the exception of his cock, which hardened as she placed her hand on his thigh. She lifted the flute to his lips.

"Satisfy my champagne yet." His lips buzzed and he seemed to be slurring. It didn't bother him. He felt euphoric, completely relaxed. This was turning out to be quite a hotel. Who needed an agency when room service was laid on? She dropped her gaze to his crotch and up to his eyes. Pupils dilated. She wanted him.

"I guess you wanted to freshen up before I arrived?"

He nodded, and managed to mumble the word, "Shower."

"How about I run you a bath? More fun."

No mistaking that. She moved to the wardrobe and opened the door. He tried to tell her the bathroom was behind the other door, but she'd already found it. He laughed again. You'd think the staff ... He reached for his glass, barely able to lift it to his lips. His arms were leaden as hell and he felt fantastic. No idea if he'd be able to perform.

Here she comes. Pulling him to his feet, helping him undress, just like a nurse, what with the gloves and all. Easing him into the bath. Beautiful; soft hands, warm water. He sinks up to his chin, smiling. He can't recall feeling better in his life.

She's smiling too. And singing. He recognises the tune and tries to join in. He wants to touch her face but he can't move. He's happy, stroked and caressed by this beautiful woman.

The patterns are hypnotic. Crimson clouds twisting and swirling in the water. He watches as clear water loses the battle, dominated by red. She reaches for his other arm and turns his wrist, as if she's trying to see what he has hidden in his hand. It's funny and it makes him laugh. She's not laughing. Her face is sharp with concentration as she draws the razor blade along his vein, from wrist to elbow. More red joins the fray, and the clear water doesn't stand a chance. Now she smiles and puts the blade in his right hand. He can't hold it and it falls into the redness. He watches it fall, helpless. He heaves his head up to look at her reflection in the mirror and attempts a smile.

It's not working. He looks like an old dog with wind.

Chapter 2

London 2012

As the theme tune faded, Beatrice was not surprised to hear the doorbell ring. Family and friends knew that little couldn't wait until after The Archers. So her bright greeting into the intercom was in expectation of a welcome, familiar voice.

"Hel-lo?"

"Stubbs?" The voice was familiar, but as welcome as gout.

"Yes, sir."

"Need a word."

"Yes, sir." She buzzed him in. Hamilton visiting her at home? There were several explanations, and none was positive.

"Evening, Stubbs." He came straight into the flat and sat at the dining table.

"Good evening sir. Can I get you anything? Cup of tea? Glass of wine?"

Eyeing her half-empty glass of Chablis, he shook his head. "I never drink alcohol during the week. Now, I want to discuss a possible project for you. Highly confidential, see, hence my decision to come all the way out here."

Beatrice smiled. One would think that Hamilton had struggled through hail and wind to a remote Hebridean island rather than enjoying a chauffeured drive from Westminster to Shoreditch. Although it *was* raining, to be fair.

"I see. Must be something difficult in that case, sir."

"Look here, Stubbs, would you be prepared to leave home for a while? Work on a secondment sort of thing?"

"Without knowing the exact terms of 'for a while' and 'second-ment sort of thing', I'd have to say no, sir."

"Right. Good. So if the terms suit, you'll do it."

Beatrice did not respond.

"Need to identify someone to leave London in a week or so, possibly to remain in another location for some months. In addition, must be able to lead an international team, deal with a complex cross-border case, and crucially, remain discreet. I thought you might fit the bill."

"Thank you for considering me, sir, but …"

"I will have that tea, thank you. Wouldn't say no to a biscuit, either. Nothing fancy."

Sacrificing her last three ginger nuts, Beatrice placed the tea tray in front of her boss. He made her wait; he always did. Round and round the roses. She gazed out at the rain. Rush hour over, Boot Street enjoyed the lull before people headed out to the pubs, the galleries and the attractions of Hoxton. Warm lights in windows opposite reminded her of Edward Hopper paintings. Glimpses of other lives.

Hamilton sniffed, before taking a cautious sip of tea. His large nose and side-swipes of grey hair evoked an American eagle. He was ready to speak.

"Thing is, a series of cases may, or may not, be related. Remember Brian Edwards?"

Beatrice scanned all her mental filing systems for a match. A classic Hamilton technique. No clue as to whether the name was a colleague, criminal, or hurricane. She shook her head, allowing Hamilton's grin to spread.

"Sorry, sir, I don't think I do. Not unless you mean the Brian Edwards of Watermark, committed suicide in France, 2009?"

Hamilton's smile dissolved.

"2010. And the suicide part is suspect. No note, you know."

"Is there a connection between Edwards and this sensitive case?"

"Possibly none whatsoever. Fact is, Stubbs, we need to know if the evidence of the Swiss police has any bearing on the Edwards incident. Your job is to establish whether there's a case to open."

"The Swiss police, sir?"

Hamilton ate a biscuit. "Indeed. The Swiss police have worked closely with the force in Liechtenstein on the death of Jack Ryman."

This one Beatrice recognised immediately, but Hamilton got in first.

"American banker. Plastic bag ... oh, you *do* remember. Given the chap's position, the investigation was jolly thorough. Some DNA found at the site could indicate that his death was not accidental."

Beatrice considered.

Hamilton continued. "Search of Switzerland's DNA database threw up a connection. You may recall the Australian newspaper magnate who froze to death in St Moritz?"

"Dougie Thompson. Of course. The 'death by misadventure' hoo-ha. A major news item and much controversy over the coroner's verdict."

Hamilton sipped more tea and sniffed. "And rightly so. Not only in my view but that of the Swiss police. Foreign DNA on his flask, you know."

"They kept *that* out of the papers. Two deaths in a similar region, the chances of the same DNA ..." Beatrice muttered.

Hamilton nodded, and polished off the second ginger nut. Only one left.

"The combined opinions of the Swiss and Liechtenstein forces saw it as an unusual link, so they put it through Interpol."

"And the DNA was registered?" Beatrice asked. "Not with the Brian Edwards case?"

Hamilton swallowed some tea. "Not only Edwards, but a South African diamond dealer, name of van der Veld, who topped himself in a Dutch hotel. The key issue, see, is that all these deaths were apparently self-inflicted. Yet no suicide notes and now the same DNA at each incident? Bottom line, Stubbs, Interpol want to open a non-investigation. They're putting together a team, based in Zürich, to find out if this leads anywhere. Discretion is essential. As far as anyone else knows, we're simply tidying up loose ends."

"I see. Hence the foreign job you mentioned. Can I ask, sir, why you described this as a secondment?"

"Fair enough, good question. Situation here is, you'll be on loan.

Answerable to the General Secretariat in Lyon. This is not one of ours."

"And the time-frame is presumably as precise as the case itself."

"Quite. Well put. My rider was that we can spare you no longer than a six-month. If you've got nowhere by then, you might as well come home."

"May I have some time to consider, sir? I have various ongoing projects I would like to assess before deciding."

"Regarding your work assignments, all bases are covered. As for your personal life, that's up to you."

Typically, he didn't meet her eyes. Both points skirted dangerously close to a topic which made him most uncomfortable. Naturally her work was covered; she'd had nothing more than light administrative duties for the past eight months. That reference to her personal life was clear. He wanted reassurance she was stable enough to take this on. There was a certain irony to the situation. Less than a year after she'd attempted to take her own life, her first major investigation would revolve around a series of suicides. Offering her such a case was a sign Hamilton trusted her once more, and he wanted confirmation of her capability. She remained silent, unsure of the answer herself.

Hamilton spoke. "Very well, Stubbs, think it over for the weekend, but Interpol want someone top notch, and if you really feel you can't step up to the crease, you'd better have some damned good ideas of who can."

Beatrice nodded once, aware of both compliment and threat.

"I'll get back to you first thing on Monday, sir."

"Make sure you do. And you are aware that one can listen to Radio Four anywhere in the world these days?"

Any suggestion of a smile was hidden as he swallowed the final biscuit.

"Good evening to you, Stubbs."

"Same to you, sir."

"By the way, those ginger nuts were stale."

Beatrice checked her watch before dialling Matthew's number. On Thursday afternoons he usually had a faculty meeting on campus, which could drag on into the evening. Academia was notorious, he'd told her, for enjoying the sound of its own voice.

Thankfully he was home and she launched into her explanation without preliminaries. Predictably, he did not react at all how Beatrice might have expected.

"What a marvellous opportunity. Not only will you take on a fascinating case, but what a location in which to do it! You can climb mountains, boat round lakes, visit chocolate factories and the Swiss have some impressive collections of art, you know. In Gruyère, there's the H.R. Giger museum. Gave me nightmares for weeks. You'd love it."

"Thank you. That would be worth a trip. But I'd be going there to work, Matthew. My chief concern, rather than how I might spend my weekends, is whether I'm up to the job."

"Yes, of course, naturally. Hamilton is notorious for selecting utter incompetents to represent Britain in European investigations."

"Sarcasm is lazy."

"Insecurity is boring. So, do you intend to swot up the entire weekend, or are you coming down? I would understand perfectly if the former held greater appeal."

He really could try and sound as if he would miss her. No need to gush, but ...

Beatrice made up her mind. "Swotting can be done on the train. And seeing as I have no idea when I am likely to see you again, you may meet me from the eight-fifteen tomorrow evening."

"Ooh, you sound awfully Celia Johnson."

"Not quite yet, darling. Not quite yet. Will your girls be there?"

"Not this weekend, we're on our own. Regarding dinner, would sausage and mash suit?"

"Oh definitely. With red onion gravy?"

Matthew chuckled. "I thought so."

"Perfect. We'll eat sausage and mash, drink red wine and light a fire. And on Saturday, we'll walk, and buy scallops from that stall by the beach. Eat them flash-fried, with home-made chips. On Sunday, let's read the paper and have a pint at The Toad, before I catch an afternoon train back. That should give me some ballast to weather the week ahead."

"Sign me up for all of the above. Have you spoken to James?" he asked.

"Not this week. I only see him every fortnight now. Why?"

"Just wondered how you'll manage the dogs while you're away."

"The dogs are under control. Don't worry. Meet me at quarter past eight tomorrow. If you forget again, my revenge will be hot and furious. Do you want me to bring anything?"

"A smile?"

"See you then."

"Can't wait. Don't forget your wellies."

Chapter 3

Zürich 2012

The taxi emerged from another tunnel into dazzling sunshine. Looking up from her notes, Beatrice absorbed her first view of the city. To her right, a river ran beside the street, with a park beyond. Bright clumps of snowdrops and primulas dotted around the green space made her smile. Tall apartment buildings in shades of sober grey rose to her left, whose austere architecture was softened by scarlet geraniums on the balconies. Zürich presented itself with discretion and charm. The city's spires ahead stood out sharply against blue sky and distant mountains.

Like a film set, she thought. Odd how the power of Nature at its most impressive could only be compared to its imitator. None of the people striding along the streets seemed to notice the awe-inspiring backdrop. Business people, tourists, roller-bladers, students, and lots of dogs. The taxi driver, who had answered her initial German enquiry in English, looked in the mirror.

"This is the *Hauptbahnhof*. The main train station, late-night shopping, emergency doctors. But be careful, keep your wallet safe, huh?"

"I will. Thank you. How far is the apartment from here?"

"Only two minutes. But the street is one direction, so we make a loop."

They turned away from the station with its enormous rack of bicycles to drive alongside another river. Beatrice liked the look of this. Lots of greenery, water and a compact city centre. As they stopped at the traffic lights, a blue and white tram clattered past at surprising speed. A cheerful bell rang out. The feeling of a clean, efficient, friendly place calmed her nerves as they pulled up in front of the pale yellow building housing the *Apartments Züri*.

The apartment was twice the size of her own flat. It had a living area complete with balcony, a kitchenette with a proper coffee machine and a huge bedroom, with enormous amounts of storage space. Beatrice cautioned herself against becoming over-excited. Instead, she washed her face and brushed her hair and stared into the bathroom mirror, going over it once again. The intranet photograph was clear in her mind. Dark hair, thick moustache and bright blue eyes. The man looked like one of the Gypsy Kings' grandfathers. She knew this speech by heart.

"Good morning, Herr Kälin. I apologise for my early arrival. I know the team are not due to meet until lunchtime. But the truth is that I wanted to meet you first. A thorough reading of my notes tells me that this whole investigation arose out of your own work. I respect that. I also respect that the Kantonspolizei cannot release you to work solely on this investigation. But I wanted to come here to say that I have a great deal of admiration for what you and your team have achieved. Therefore, I would like very much to lean on your expertise, up until the point where it encroaches on your daily responsibilities. Herr Kälin, I have been given a role. Which is to lead this team. I am here to ask you to help me to do that, as I fear I will be less effective alone."

Grab the goat by the horns. All unpleasantness washed, aired and dried. And if she wanted to catch him before the meeting, it would be wise to leave now.

"Grüezi?"

A serious young woman sat behind the reception desk at the Zeughausstrasse police building.

"*Grüezi*. My name is Beatrice Stubbs, from Scotland Yard, London and I am here to meet Herr Kälin."

The woman did not answer, but turned to her computer screen. After some tapping, she nodded.

"Yes, Frau Stubbs. You have an appointment at 12.30. You are too early."

"That's true. But I hoped to speak to Herr Kälin before the meeting. Would that be possible?"

The girl looked dubious. "I can check. Please sit yourself."

Beatrice smiled her thanks and manoeuvred her little wheelie case beside her. She studied the various posters on the walls, attempting approximate translations. In such a country, the graphics naturally spoke louder than words. Translating each hard-hitting slogan into three or even four languages would strain the most creative ad-man. The woman tapped on her glass window.

"Frau Stubbs, Herr Kälin is at lunch. Do you wish his assistant?"

"Lunch? Already? Oh. I suppose I could talk to his assistant, yes. Thanks."

Lunch at half past eleven? Or was this a deliberate rebuff? Don't be so negative and suspicious, she reprimanded herself. Positive, co-operative and effective, remember? And it's your own fault for not calling first.

"Frau Stubbs? My name is Xavier Racine. I am joining your team, I hope."

Beatrice's spirits lifted. Well dressed, with strawberry blonde hair and an open, enquiring look. And freckles. Beatrice liked freckles.

"Nice to meet you, Mr Racine. I'm sorry to disturb you. I had hoped to meet Herr Kälin for a preliminary chat. But it seems he's already gone to lunch."

A blush. All the proof she needed this was indeed a snub.

"Oh, yes, of course. Herr Kälin wanted to have an early lunch in order that he is ready for you."

But Beatrice was tenacious, and would say her piece, whatever it took. "How very thoughtful. Tell me, Mr Racine, is he in the police canteen? Perhaps we might join him there? I would very much like to speak to him before the briefing."

"No, no, Frau Stubbs. He always eats in one of the local restaurants. I cannot say exactly. He changes every day. I am sorry. Maybe you would like to have lunch here? I can arrange it."

Don't get at him, he's only the messenger. "Thank you. But it's a little early for me. Do you think we could have a cup of coffee and then you could show me the briefing room? I would like to set up before the others arrive."

"It is a pleasure."

Nice lad. Even bought the coffees. As Xavier departed to get some food, Beatrice paced the briefing room. It was a setback, but a minor one. So she would do the briefing first and talk to Kälin later. The important thing now was to be prepared. She opened her wheelie case and withdrew her materials.

By 12.35, no one had turned up. The projector hummed quietly, the first slide glowed blue and every chair stood empty. Heat began to rise up Beatrice's throat. This was not Swiss. She'd read all about the cultural habits of this country, and in particular, this region. Lateness was extremely rude. But why all of them? Kälin may have wanted to make a point, but all four of the others? Including Xavier Racine? She stood up, furious, and dug in her bag for her mobile.

"Frau Stubbs!" Xavier burst through the door. "This is the wrong room. Everyone waits for you upstairs."

"But ... you showed me this room. I thought ...?"

"Yes, I am sorry. Herr Kälin changed the room. He thought it would be better if we meet in our working room on the top floor. He sent me an SMS and left a notice at reception for everyone else. I just realised you would not see it. You are here since 11.30. I'm sorry. But we have to go. Everyone waits."

Lugging her wheelie case up the stairs, Beatrice felt wrong-footed and harassed. She intended to speak to Herr Kälin about this. It was most unprofessional and if she didn't know better, she would suspect him of doing it deliberately to unsettle her. Xavier, carrying all her handouts and charts, tripped on the top step and scattered her presentation across the landing. Her breathing was laboured as they collected everything, especially as she had to repeatedly assure Xavier it didn't matter.

Xavier opened the door to silence. Feeling itchy, warm and

out of breath, Beatrice entered to face her new team. Two women, two men. The black woman with the erect bearing and deep blue suit would be Interpol's forensic DNA scientist. The relaxed long-limbed individual to her right must be the Dutch chap, information technology genius. So the psychologist had to be the delicate blonde in the white shirt. So young! Stony faced and sitting apart from the team was Herr Karl Kälin. Beatrice's image of him evaporated. The sparkle in his eyes she'd seen in the photograph was absent, replaced by a cold antipathy.

She heaved a deep breath to apologise, but he spoke.

"Ms Stubbs. It is unfortunate that you did not get the message intended for the team. All the others received the information without difficulty. And it is always a good idea to make an appointment when you expect to meet someone. I would like to make one thing quite clear. I am not a member of this team. I am a consultant, advising on any case that might arise. I have many other responsibilities in terms of my daily police work. So I would appreciate it if you treated my time with respect."

An awkward silence hung in the room, amplifying Beatrice's heavy breathing.

Chapter 4

"M'sieur? Bad weather comes. It can be dangerous. Maybe you prefer to wait for tomorrow?"

Dougie found the chair lift attendant presumptuous. "Maybe I prefer to go now. Cheers all the same."

He pulled the bar down over his hips, lifting his skis clear as the chair moved upward. The attendant shrugged and turned to the other couple behind him. Dougie twisted over his shoulder and saw the gloom-monger had persuaded the others to turn back. One girl gesticulated at his own ascending form in enquiry.

"Why me? Good question. Because I can."

He threw back his head and laughed, out to the open sky. The idea of tackling the run alone, with no amateurs to limit his manoeuvres, shot adrenaline into his system. The weather was a stroke of fortune. A rare opportunity to pit his skills against a hostile environment. And Dougie took every opportunity, in nature as in life. He smiled, recognising the bad habit of writing his own epitaph.

Of course, he shouldn't waste time. As that lumpen idiot had observed, it could be dangerous. The mountainside rushed up at him, as his poles and skis dangled below. The sharp edges, the blacks and whites, the geographical clarity challenged him, and he began to twitch like a hyperactive child. Going off piste accounted for only a part of his excitement. After almost a week of persuasion, Ana-Maria had finally agreed to a date. In fact, it was she who suggested this run; '*only advisable for the truly talented*'. They had arranged to meet at the tree-line; it would not do to be seen leaving together. Opportunities, yes; risks, no. The reservation at the lodge was made in her name. After they'd checked in, he would send a text message to his wife. Julia would understand his decision not to take on the storm, and accept his stay in a mountain lodge as an example of her husband's good judgement. Win-win.

The car ratcheted up to the platform and Dougie disembarked with grace. Another jobsworth advised him against taking the run; 'one must respect the weather', but Dougie dismissed him with a look. The scene was undoubtedly dramatic. The valley below reflected late-afternoon sunshine, while the blue sky and various pointed roofs completed a ridiculously cute Alpine village setting. Yet behind him, the remainder of the mountain sat; dark, huge, and unassailable. Grey, violet and yellow clouds – the colours of a bruise – moved to obscure the white tip, and a flash of fear stopped him. He had nothing to prove; his prowess as an expert, all-terrain skier was established. There was no need to take on millennia of ice, stone and snow. A second's decision would take him back down to Julia and the kids. He knew Rui and Katia would be ecstatic. They could have a raclette, play some games and he could do this run in the morning with fresh snow. The girl could wait. He hesitated.

No.

Dougie Thompson never backed down in the face of a challenge. He checked his boots, surveyed the piste, and with a glance back at the threatening storm, took off.

The snow was firm to hard. After adjusting to the terrain, his first few slopes were pure pleasure. *Only advisable for the truly talented.* She was right. He would never have known about this run had she not let him into the secret. The luck of the devil, his mother used to say, while his brothers called him a jammy bastard.

As he approached the trees, his route became less evident and he slowed to assess each stage. The sky darkened and the landscape became monochrome. It was an increasing challenge and he balanced pace with diligence. A mistake would be unacceptable, possibly lethal. A previous skier's trail indicated a sharp turn toward the edge of the forest. He followed, his pulse a bass-line in his ears. Something lay under the tree. The ski-suit was white, with blue and pink flashes; Ana-Maria. Prone, skis detached, surely not a fall? She was an instructor, for God's sake!

Dougie slowed and drew up beside the body. Her goggles covered half her face and a ski-mask took care of the rest. He crouched and watched her chest. No movement. He removed his gloves and lifted her goggles. Her eyes were closed. Convinced she was already dead, he reached his right hand to her neck for a pulse. Her eyes opened and he jumped.

"Hello. I've been waiting for you."

He exhaled, fear turning to irritation. "That was a damn silly thing to do."

"Sorry. I didn't mean to scare you. It was a joke."

"I wasn't scared. And I'm not laughing."

Sitting up, she reached for her rucksack. "Don't sulk. I brought us some *Kaffee Fertig* to warm us."

"Café what?"

"*Kaffee Fertig.* It means 'fixed coffee'. The Swiss version of *Kaffee Schnapps.*"

"No thanks." He pulled on his gloves. "We should move on. The weather's getting worse. Get up. Let's go."

She didn't argue and put the flask away. Dougie waited impatiently, surveying the slope through swirling flakes of snow. Silly bitch. If she thought that was funny, she had a bloody weird sense of humour. A shadow crossed his vision and as he turned, her hand hit his neck. A sharp prickle pierced his ski-mask in addition to the blow. He stumbled sideways, snatching at the place she'd struck him. She ran off into the trees, leaving her rucksack behind. Christ! Another stupid game? What the hell was she playing at? He attempted to chase her, before tripping over his skis. Releasing both clips, he lurched after the girl. The snow was hard-packed and as firm as concrete. But his legs seemed to think they were in deep wet slush. One of the fittest men in his empire, with a sportsman's thighs, he could move no faster than a turtle. He stopped and fell backwards, onto his arse. As he stared into the shadowy forest, he saw her emerge. She waved. Dougie's attempt to wave back toppled him over.

The figure in the white suit worked at speed. After heaving him across the snow, she propped the man against the trunk of the tree where he'd stopped to 'rescue' her. His head fell back, and she tipped a little of the liquid from the thermos flask into his mouth. He swallowed. Unzipping his jacket, she struggled to pull his arms free. Between giving him sips of liquid, she removed all his outer clothing, folding it in a neat pile beside him. The flask empty, she replaced the stopper and retrieved the lid from a plastic bag in her rucksack. She set it beside the pile and crouched to stare at his face. Nothing.

She glanced upwards. The sky loomed lower and blacker, as if it disapproved. Snow flew across her goggles. But the pastel-trimmed figure took several risky minutes to explore his mobile phone, before switching it off and placing it on top of his clothes.

Large white flakes floated onto the body and settled on his eyelashes, his hair and his cheeks as the figure replaced her skis. She smiled at him and whispered, "It's all in the public interest, you know." With one last glance at the scene, she skied with great caution down the mountain, her pale suit disappearing into the landscape like winter ermine.

Chapter 5

Zürich 2012

Placing her bag at her feet, Beatrice allowed herself a slow scan of the room while she regained her breath. The two women appeared bemused and looked to her for a reaction. The Dutchman raised his eyebrows with a small grin of sympathy. Xavier did not meet her eyes, but his high colour gave away his discomfort. Only one way to go, she decided. A cold stillness settled on her and she walked directly to Herr Kälin, extending her hand.

"Beatrice Stubbs, Scotland Yard. Pleased to meet you."

His face hardened still further, yet he stood and gave her hand one brisk shake.

"Detective Kälin, Swiss Federal Criminal Police."

Beatrice smiled as if she had received a polite welcome and turned to the team.

"I apologise for having kept you. I'd like to thank Herr Kälin for that reminder on how important it is that we use our time efficiently. So rather than my using more valuable time by restarting my presentation, perhaps we can kill two birds with one blow. I would like you to introduce yourselves, tell us why you were seconded to the team and give us your thoughts on this case." Kälin was looking out of the window. "You all received a briefing pack, and I have no doubt you have read it with care. From what you have read, does anything strike you?"

The uncertain silence of a new team stretched out. Beatrice let it continue.

The tall man spoke. "OK, I'll go first. Detective Chris Keese,

Europol, The Hague. I specialise in e-crime and IT forensics." He leaned back in his chair. "The obvious thing is what these guys have in common. We don't need to bother with the question *Did they have any enemies*? but instead we should be asking, *Did they have any friends*?"

Beatrice acknowledged the comment with a smile. The Dutchman's attitude was relaxed to the point of indolence and she was aware of the contrast he demonstrated to the rest of the team.

"You're right, Mr Keese. All the men in question had either made highly unpopular decisions, or were involved in morally dubious business. Identifying those who may wish to harm them would be time-consuming and, in my view, unlikely to prove fruitful. If we are talking about homicide rather than suicide, suspects will be legion. I am inclined to agree with Mr Keese. We need to be searching for the links between these individuals. Who indeed were their friends? This is certainly one line I would like to pursue. Any ... yes, Ms Tikkenen?"

The three men in the room took full advantage of the opportunity to stare at the speaker. Cheekbones as sharp as ski jumps, white-blonde hair and strong eyebrows arching outward, she reminded Beatrice of a Russian model. A lovely creature; just the type who might cause all sorts of unnecessary tension.

"Sabine Tikkenen. Central Criminal Police, Tallinn, Estonia. I am a crime analyst. I agree that we have some background to research, but we already have the most concrete lead to finding out how these men died. My question is this – how far can we go with the DNA?"

Beatrice was puzzled. "I'm not sure what you mean. We will exploit any available information we can glean from the samples we have."

"Yes, that I already know. But can we test this DNA for features that are not standard? For example, where does he come from? Does EU protocol allow us to find out everything we can about this person?"

"No, Ms Tikkenen, it does not." If Sabine Tikkenen drew all eyes, this voice commanded all ears. The lightness of a Portuguese accent coupled with West African gravitas, the black woman spoke with a voice you could never interrupt.

"European law dictates that ethnic group profiling could be counter-productive on several counts. We can only assume so much from these samples."

Sabine frowned. "That is disappointing. Having some information on this person's cultural background could make a psychological profile much more informed. But as the Interpol representative, you are telling us that we have the same investigative powers as the local officers; which is to say, none."

Kälin stared at the young woman in evident disbelief, but said nothing.

"Ms Tikkenen, I must explain. My name is Conceição Pereira da Silva."

Beatrice allowed a sigh of relief to escape. Now she knew how to pronounce the woman's first name; Con-say-sow. Rhymes with cats-say-miaow.

"I am a junior DNA advisor, supervised by MEG, and have no authority in this situation. My contribution could be on the side of how to extract all the information we can from a strand of DNA. And to consult on the legal issues relating to such a case. If we were to identify a suspect through legally questionable processes, we would be wasting our time. And I want to clarify: I am not an Interpol mole. We're all simply advisors here."

Beatrice spoke. "Thank you, Ms Pereira da Silva. Your attention to correct procedure whilst handling forensic evidence of this kind is essential. Ms Tikkenen, I appreciate that the more information you have, the better criminal profile you will create. I hope we will be able to contribute much more evidence to assist you. Personally, I would like to add that it is of overriding importance we follow the letter of the law, particularly now. The harsh truth is this. Despite the fact you are each a brilliant asset to this team – otherwise you would not be here – our job is going to entail a lot of dull, everyday police legwork. And we must be beyond reproach. Herr Racine?"

"Thank you. My name is Xavier Racine. Herr Kälin and I are both members of the Federal Criminal Police. Herr Kälin is our main Zürich investigative officer. I am on loan from Task Force

TIGRIS, a specialist operations unit. My opinion on this case is we may only scratch the surface, with what we know. I believe it would be worthwhile checking any other similar 'suicides'. High-profile men who left no explanation or indication as to why they chose to end their lives. We may find a bigger pattern."

"Fair enough." Chris Keese replied. "Makes sense. So how are we going to start on this?"

"By playing to our strengths. I suggest that you, Mr Keese ..."

"Ms Stubbs? I don't mean to tread on any toes, but I'd feel a whole lot better if you called me Chris."

Beatrice winced internally, in the sure knowledge Kälin would hate the idea.

"I see. Does everyone else feel comfortable using first names? It's quite usual in Britain. But I can understand other countries find that rather informal."

"For me, it is no problem." Ms Tikkenen raised her shoulders in a tiny shrug. "You can call me Sabine. We will have to work closely together, so we can be relaxed with names."

"How do you feel, Herr Racine? Ms Pereira da Silva?"

The young Swiss officer gestured toward his colleague to go first. She smiled.

"I have a feeling that although Conceição will be harder for people to pronounce, it is the right approach. I'm happy with first names."

"Me too. You can call me Xavier. It is the modern way." His smile spread more slowly than his blush.

Kälin shook his head. "No. I'm afraid that's completely unacceptable to me. Herr Racine and I work together on a professional basis. We use formal address. This team is operating in Switzerland, and Swiss prefer formality. Not because we are old-fashioned, but to indicate respect. We are forced to speak English as it is the only common language. However, I fail to see why you should impose your cultural habits on us."

Beatrice took a deep breath. "So, Chris, it seems you have your wish. First names are fine with everyone except Herr Kälin. My first name is Beatrice. However, equally acceptable forms of address would be Boss, Ma'am and Your Ladyship."

Chris led the laughter and Beatrice had a feeling the chap could well prove to be the team glue.

"Now let's get to work. As I understand it, the Kantonspolizei have given us equipment and space on this floor, in preference to downstairs. Is that right, Herr Kälin?"

"I have my own office. You can work downstairs or up here. I don't care."

Xavier jumped in, face aflame. "I think Herr Kälin means he doesn't mind. We often make this mistake in English."

Kälin turned his scowl on his colleague. "Herr Racine, my English may be inadequate. But I will not accept corrections from a non-native speaking junior officer. As I said, Frau Stubbs, I don't care where you work."

Beatrice moved on to spare Xavier's embarrassment.

"So upstairs it is. All those stairs might help keep me fit. Xavier, I'd like you to work with Chris on looking for links. We need to know if there was anything at all which might connect these men. Did they use the same bank, airline or masseuse? Who were their golf buddies? Was there any connection between their wives? Did the companies have any dealings with one another? Had these chaps ever met? Fine toothcomb, cross-referencing, your sort of thing, Chris.

"Sabine, here are all the at-the-scene details. You may wish to liaise with Chris and Xavier on details of the deceased. Your task is to profile the kind of person who could and would want to perform such efficient disposals.

"Conceição, all the forensic equipment you need is provided. You will need to check all the samples and ensure there's no possibility of error. I'd like us to be thorough. No stone unturned. But first, Xavier, could you show everyone where the canteen is located? I would like a word with Herr Kälin."

The room emptied surprisingly fast.

Beatrice closed the door and fighting her instinct to put the briefing table between them, took a seat beside him. She half turned to him and opened her palms.

"Herr Kälin. I had a speech prepared for you. I arrived an hour early so I could say my piece and clear the air between us. My plan did not work and it seems we got out of bed on the wrong foot. Would you like to tell me why you are so angry?"

"Ms Stubbs, if we are to have any kind of working relationship, I must ask you not to patronise me. This is not a conciliation meeting with a badly behaved junior. I am the Fedpol senior detective here. The case, such as it is, arose out of my report. From the work of my officers. However, Interpol find it appropriate to use me only as a 'consultant' and to bring in a foreign woman to lead this investigative team. A woman who seems to have little respect for the demands on my time."

"I see. If I understand you correctly, you are unhappy about the fact you are not in charge of the team, because your work has led us this far. You are displeased with me because I did not go through the correct channels in terms of arranging a pre-meeting with you. Is that right, or have I forgotten something? Are the words 'foreign' and 'woman' in any way relevant?"

He stared at her for a beat, then glanced down at his watch.

"Is there anything else, Ms Stubbs? Because I cannot see us making any progress."

"Nor can I, Herr Kälin. You'd better go."

He wrenched open the door and left, his footsteps thumping down the stairs. Beatrice closed her eyes and tried to stop shaking. She repeated the mantra James had taught her: Convert defeat into opportunity. Every failure carries the seed of success. Kill negativity.

She dwelt awhile on the last.

Chapter 6

Flight LX 728 to Amsterdam began its descent to Schiphol airport at 13.45. Chris skimmed his notes once more.

Jens van der Veld, (57). South African (Afrikaner) based in Kimberley, South Africa. Married to Antjie Heese (34), two sons Uys (5), Henk (3). Active in South Africa, Europe and the US.

Business interests: breweries, real estate, and diamond dealing.

Died in Utrecht, Feb 2007, suicide. Slit wrists in bath.

Forensic assessment: Victim unclothed in bath. No evidence of struggle or forced entry. In main room, two champagne flutes, one with victim's fingerprints and DNA. The other with no fingerprints and unidentified DNA. Do Not Disturb *sign on door, thus body undiscovered until Monday.*

Mobile call log as follows:

Friday 27 Feb

21.50: Outgoing call. Amsterdam. Call traced to Joop Kneppers, associate and colleague. (duration, 2 mins)

21.56: Incoming SMS. Amsterdam. Business card from Kneppers, with tel. no. of escort agency.

22.59: Incoming SMS. Kimberley, RSA. Message from wife, checking victim's safe arrival.

Van der Veld had confirmed meetings for the Monday morning, and according to colleagues, expected to finalise two significant deals in the Netherlands.

Kneppers came to hotel for a pre-arranged meeting at 10.00

Monday, and raised concerns when van der Veld could not be reached.

No visitors registered at reception.

Chris folded the papers into his briefcase and tucked it under the seat in front. So van der Veld drank champagne with someone before getting naked into the bath, and slitting his wrists. The champagne drinker. Someone he knew? Or wanted to know? Was it possible his visitor had provoked such an almighty attack of conscience? Wheels hit tarmac, and a powerful reverse thrust tilted him forward. He looked at his companion. Absorbed in *The Financial Times*, she gave no reaction to their landing.

"I checked out the meaning of your name, you know," he announced.

Conceição folded the paper. "Really? I didn't check yours. How rude of me."

He laughed, pleased she had a quick wit. Yet her face was unchanged.

"The meaning of Chris? I'll tell you myself, one of these days. But I've never met someone called Conceição before. I'm naturally nosy."

"Well, if you checked the name Conceição, you only know half the story. My full name is Maria do Conceição Pereira da Silva. Now what does that tell you?"

"You come from a Catholic country which likes long names."

"I can see why you became a detective."

She rose from her seat and reached for the overhead locker. As they exited the aircraft, a cool breeze caused Chris to hunch his shoulders.

Conceição. Weird name. Conception. Weird female. Seemed intent on slapping him down every chance she got. With some relief, Chris left her at Paardenveld-Kroonstraat police station, and wove a path through the crowds of shoppers on Catherijnebaan. As he walked, he replayed each curt conversation in his head. Had he overstepped the mark at all? He couldn't recall. She had no need to be so hostile, when they were both chasing the same goal. Yet he sensed a faint tone of disapproval from the whole bunch. Beatrice seemed to appreciate his humour and gestures of friendship, but even she was pretty uptight. Maybe it was a language thing. A local cop attitude. What would be the best way to handle it? Change nothing. Do your job, be yourself, and to hell with the rest of it.

Hotel Grand Karel V sat back from the street, in expansive grounds. To claim this much land in the heart of the city, it had to be something special. Entering the magnificent lobby, Chris managed his expectations. The incident he was here to investigate was over five years old. The staff would be worse than the Utrecht police; no one wanted this dragged up again. The chances of his finding anything useful were as likely as his cracking Conception. Still, go through the motions and you never know.

"Milk or lemon?"

"I'll take a little milk, please, Ms Zajac."

The housekeeper was an unexpected surprise. Her thin, steel-coloured hair was drawn back in a tight bun and the black frames of her glasses added to the severe image, but her face folded into a homely smile. She went out of her way to make him feel comfortable. Pouring a touch of milk into the tea, she continued.

"Back then, I was assistant. Now I am Head Housekeeper. I arrange all cleaning, laundry and maintenance." The grey uniform underlined her serious tone. "I found body of Mr van der Veld. The police came and took all they wanted. After that, we cleaned. Surprising, but it was not too bad. The bath needed work, but for a suicide, he was quite tidy. I have seen worse." Her dark brows dropped into a frown.

"You have?"

"Not here. When I was housekeeper in very good hotel in Rotterdam. We had two suicides. One with gun. That room – oh! It took us weeks to clean all blood, little pieces of bone, hair. Very bad."

Her reproach seemed directed at the inconsiderate shooter.

"And the other?"

"Pills. Terrible smell, difficult stains and some vomit. But if I compare to way some guests leave rooms, not so bad."

"So Mr van der Veld had a relatively neat death."

"Death in hotel is always problem. Police come, staff try to keep quiet, and we need extra cleaning."

"Of course. Ms Zajac, was there anything else unusual about that weekend? The Saturday in particular?"

"I have day book. We make notes in day book. Guests to be careful, staff problems, maintenance update, like diary. Like diary of hotel."

"You still have the day book from 2007?" Chris sat up in anticipation.

"Yes, I say already. I have here. 2007. Mr van der Veld died in February, no?" She flicked through her pages.

"That's right. Around the 27th February. Any notes about guests, or anything unusual for the week before?"

"Wait please. Yes, here. February 24th; two porters reprimanded for smoking in sight of guests. Fire alarm control. February 26th; complaint – Room 670 regarding noise from Room 671. One special request for upgrade to Empire Suite. Note van der Veld as VIP. Also, good bottle champagne required. 27th; Ballroom out of bounds for perfume convention. Two complaints – Room 670 and 672 about noise in Room 671 – occupants: Mr and Mrs Schmidt. Manager suggested room change. Offer refused, guests promised to be quiet. 29th; Visser given verbal warning. Police called – body in Empire Suite. I think you know the rest, Mr Keese."

"Yes, I'd say I do. Can you go back there, Ms Zajac? The fire alarm check – was that scheduled?"

She didn't need to check her ledger. "We always have control, February and November. Same company for last nine years."

"OK. Is Room 671 anywhere near the Empire Suite?"

"Different building."

"Hmm." Chris scanned his shorthand. "Visser? One of the smoking porters?"

"No. Receptionist. Let me look. Yes, on 23rd February, Annelise Visser reported uniform missing. She was told find or replace. She failed. So verbal warning. One hundred forty people attended perfume convention for launch of new fragrance, *Wish*. Horrible smell."

Chris smiled at her wrinkled nose. "And no one saw or heard Jens van der Veld until Monday morning?"

"He had *Do Not Disturb* sign. So we did not disturb. His friend arrived on Monday, and insisted checking room. And we found him, in bath."

"You said you found him, Ms Zajac?"

"Yes. I authorise opening rooms when guest is absent. I checked living room, bed and bathroom. I saw him in bath. Dead, no question. Up to his neck in blood."

"You worked the weekend?"

"No. I work Monday to Friday. Is enough."

"Who requested the upgrade for Mr van der Veld?"

"One moment." She flicked back a page. "His company, D'Arcy Roth. They booked room, not him. The porter told he was mean. Tipped only two Euros."

"Does that porter still work here?"

"No, no. Aard only worked here during studies. He left since two years."

"Is there any chance you could get me a list of guests who stayed here that weekend, Ms Zajac?"

"I think is possible. I ask."

"And does Ms Visser still work here?"

"Yes. Senior Receptionist. You want to speak with her?"

"That would be great."

"Mr Keese? Annelise Visser."

Chris stood to shake her hand. Her open and confident smile gave her a vague air of amusement. Her dyed-black hair was cropped short, gelled into perky spikes and her grey eyes were heavily made-up.

"Sorry to disturb you, Ms Visser. I'll only keep you a moment. Just a question or two. I'm here to clear up any details relating to the death of Mr van der Veld, February 2007."

"Yeah, I know. The suicide."

"Did you meet him at all?"

"No. At that time I didn't work weekends. So I knew nothing until his colleague arrived on Monday. He was impatient and rude, and insisted we check the room."

"You lost your uniform that week, is that right?"

"That's right. I change my uniform once a week. On Monday evenings, I always take the dirty one to the dry cleaner's and pick it up on Thursdays. I left it on the coat rack in the staff room on Thursday morning. When I went to pick up my things that evening, it had gone."

"What do you think happened?"

"I guess someone took it home, thinking it was theirs. I didn't worry too much; I thought they'd bring it back. It had my name badge on it, so they had to know it was mine."

"Did you get it back?"

She rolled her eyes. "No. I got a verbal warning for losing hotel property, and had to replace it. I learned a lesson. Now everything goes into my locker."

"And just out of interest, where were you that weekend? Do you remember?"

She smiled. "I remember. Same place as every weekend. I used to be a DJ in Rotterdam. So I left here on Friday evening, did my set till 5am, slept all day, did it again on Saturday night and slept on Sunday till it was time to come home."

"You're not DJing anymore?"

She shook her head. "Too old."

Chris raised his eyebrows at this sharp, articulate girl. "Oh God. If you're too old, what does that make me?"

Her grin widened. "Way too old?"

Chris laughed at her cheek. "Thanks Ms Visser. You've made my day."

"You're welcome." She rose, still grinning and slipped out the door. Chris headed back to his hotel, unsure as to whether he'd got anything more than a reminder of how much time had passed.

Entering the hotel dining-room, Chris noted he was not the only admirer of Conceição's posture. The woman held herself upright and moved with a hip-rolling gait which caught the attention of several diners. The waiter led them to a window table where they could observe the passers-by. She ordered sparkling water and he asked for a beer.

"Strange to arrange a hotel for us. I am sure there would have been flights back to Zürich tonight," she said.

"You're probably right. But maybe if we chat things over this evening, we might find something we need to take a look at before we leave tomorrow."

"Such as?" Her cold look expressed disbelief.

"I have no idea."

She picked up the menu and read in silence. Chris scanned the specials and made up his mind to try one of the classic Dutch sausages. With fries. To hell with it. If he had to sit opposite Sniper of the Year, he could at least look forward to his food.

A waitress arrived. "Two gin tonic?"

"I think that must be for someone else. We ordered one beer and one sparkling water."

"Oh. Sorry." The kid looked stressed.

"It's no problem." Chris gave her a friendly grin and returned to the choice of sausages.

Conceição folded her menu and met his eyes. "Chris, I should apologise. I have been most unfriendly to you and I think it is undeserved."

A waiter arrived with the right drinks and Chris's mind hurried to catch up. He had no idea why she'd changed tactic. But if she wanted to stop with the sour stuff, it suited him fine. Her speech seemed over, so he raised his glass.

"OK, so let's toast. A positive working relationship."

She hesitated, before raising her water to him. "A positive working relationship." She sipped. He slugged. Nothing else was forthcoming. Chris stopped trying to second guess the woman.

"Tell me about the *politie*," he said.

"Well, you were right. They were not pleased to see me."

"But they gave you what you needed, did they?"

"Yes. I spoke to the attending officers and the coroner. The DNA sample was taken from a champagne glass. Perfect procedure, so I can see no way it could have been contaminated."

"Good news for us. Isn't it?"

"Yes, I suppose it is. The body gave little away. The time elapsing between Friday evening and Monday morning meant that testing for substances was almost worthless."

Chris sighed. "Found in the bath with a razor blade, slit wrists, and he had no plans to meet anyone till thirty-six hours later. A verdict of suicide seems like the only possible choice the coroner had. Can't blame the guy."

"The coroner is a woman. Did you make much progress at the hotel?"

The judgemental tone returned. Maybe that was it. Did she have a chromosome chip on her shoulder?

"Yes and no. They were helpful all right. But I don't think I found anything significant. He checked in, tipped the porter and that was the last anyone heard."

After delivering their order to the waiter, Conceição leant forward. "Chris? What do you think is going on here?"

He stared back into her huge earnest eyes. Candlelight flickered across the planes of her forehead, cheeks and jaw, illuminating the tones of her skin. He cleared his throat.

"The way I see it, there'll be a simple answer. Like in the case of *Die Frau ohne Gesicht*. The woman without a face. Series of crimes across Germany. Turns out the DNA samples were all taken with a certain kind of cotton bud, contaminated by the factory worker who packed them. Or, much less likely, the same person was present at the suicides of four powerful men. The truth is, Conceição, I think we're probably on a wild goose chase. What about you?"

"Interesting. You think this case is pointless, but you still want to turn all the stones."

"If in doubt, stone-turning is all I've got."

"You might be right. There could be a prosaic explanation. Yet for me, there is something more. This man was a father, a husband. He was successful. His business was suspect, but it had never bothered his conscience before. Why would he end his life just then? My instinct tells me there is something wrong."

"Right. In the face of all the evidence, you're going on instinct?" Chris knew he sounded sarcastic.

"If in doubt, instinct's all I've got."

"I can see why you became a detective."

A smile broke across her face, revealing startlingly white teeth, and she began to laugh. Chris smiled back, feeling an odd swell of warmth towards this prickly peach.

Chapter 7

Belanov closed one eye as he looked through the Schmidt & Bender sight of the TRG-42. The Mil-dots in the cross-hairs enabled him to calculate range and height precisely, so that the man in the blue suit could be determined as just under two metres tall. The rifle was designed for accuracy at 1400 metres. The suit was less than 100 metres from his perch. Wouldn't stand a chance. He stroked the trigger and with a satisfied smile, removed the gun from his shoulder.

"Beautiful."

State-of-the-art design, and easily customised to the end user's purposes. It had .338 Lapua Magnum chambering, which could be adapted with a 254mm twist rate for the heavier stuff. He raised it once more to look at the people milling around the stands below. The black stock was two kilos lighter than the camouflaged version and had detachable muzzle brakes. A sniper's dream weapon. He played with the variable magnification as he swept the dull greys, blues and blacks of the crowd. Some colour caught his eye.

The redhead from yesterday. He trained the sights on her, placing her trade fair badge in the centre of the cross hairs. She stood in front of the chemical warfare protective clothing display, her head bent as she read some brochures. He calculated her height as 1.6 metres using the telescopic sight as a guide. A slim figure, with average tits and boyish hips. Her vibrant hair stood out against a pale green trouser suit, with a dark stain on the left shoulder. He returned the sight to her face and jolted as he realised she was looking right at him. Her head tilted and she raised her eyebrows. He removed the weapon, placed his hand on his chest and mouthed the word, 'Sorry'. She waved a hand as if to dismiss the apology and turned into the crowd.

It took him under three minutes to find her, in front of IDET's orientation board and map of the site.

"Mluvíte cesky? Ukrajinśkoju? English?"

She looked at him over her shoulder, suspicious. "I speak English."

"I wish to apologise. That was me, up there." Belanov indicated the gallery. "I was trying out the sights of a rifle. But I should not have pointed it at you."

Her face cleared and she turned to face him. "Oh I see. It's OK. There's just something weird, you know, about having a gun trained on you. Demo model or not."

"Of course, I understand. I guess I got carried away with such a piece. I am sorry if I alarmed you." On closer inspection, her tits were a little above average.

"No, no. Not at all." She hitched her handbag strap up her shoulder.

"I noticed your jacket. Did you have an accident?"

"Oh yeah. It certainly wasn't accidental. The protestors outside? They were throwing eggs at the attendees. One of them was a pretty good shot. I had to wash it off in the bathroom."

"They threw an egg at you? That's very bad. Yes, they have the right to express their opinions, but using missiles? No. That is dangerous. The police should stop this. You could have been hurt."

"Well, you know, it was only an egg." She looked around, obviously planning to leave.

"Even eggs can do damage. My name is Symon Belanov." He offered his hand.

She took it. "Caroline McKendrick. Nice to meet you."

"Are you exhibiting, Ms McKendrick?"

"No, no. Just browsing. And you?"

"Likewise. These kinds of things fascinate me. I am like a little boy in a sweet shop. But I was going to take a break for a beverage. I would be pleased if you consented to join me."

"Well, just a quick coffee. I have a meeting at five."

Belanov acknowledged her point and guided her towards the café.

"So what do you do, Mr Belanov?"

"My profession is much less exciting than what we see here. I sell used cars."

"You work in Brno?" She pronounced it 'Ber-know'.

"No, I'm based in Ukraine. But I do business in the Czech Republic, Slovakia, Poland, everywhere." She stirred her cappuccino, looking completely uninterested in his answer.

"And you?"

"I'm from Montreal. My company sent me here with a shopping list."

"And did you find what you wanted?"

"Not really. You're right, this place is quite a candy store. But what I'm looking for is a little different; handmade specialty chocolates, if you like."

"Perhaps you are looking in the wrong place?" He did not meet her eyes, observing the other customers.

"Well, yes and no. I won't get what I want right over the counter, that's true. But I was lucky enough to meet someone here yesterday who might be able to point me in the right direction. That's why I have to leave at four. I'm going to meet him in the city centre to talk it over."

"Be careful, Ms McKendrick. I hope your meeting is arranged in a public place."

"Sure. I'm not stupid, Mr Belanov." She flicked a glance at him and put down her cup.

"I apologise. I had no intention of suggesting you were in any way naïve. Yet I know many of these 'helpful' people, and therefore I have concerns for your safety. Is this man a reputable dealer?"

"I don't know if he's reputable. I only met him yesterday. And he's not a dealer. He described himself as a 'fixer', someone who can introduce me to the dealers. It's important to get a personal recommendation with those people, you know."

Belanov sipped his tea, watching her as he mulled it over. She drained her coffee and glanced at her watch.

"Ms McKendrick, may I make a suggestion? Call your contact and tell him you have already made personal contact with one of 'those people', so you have no need of his services. Then you and I can have dinner somewhere, you can tell me exactly what you're looking for. And if I can't help you, I will certainly know someone who can."

She stilled and looked into his eyes for the first time. He gave a small nod.

"Used cars?" she asked.

"And sundry other items. Shall we go?"

Pressing the fob, Belanov registered her expression as the Porsche Cayenne Turbo S flashed into life with a beep. The basalt metallic black beast sat in the spring sunshine, exuding class. His stomach still thrilled each time he saw it come to life at his fingertips. Sometimes, he had the same feeling while shaving. Running the blade across his jaw, watching the shape of his lips, exploring the planes of his face, he knew he was good looking. Coupled with his self-made wealth, there were times when he felt omnipotent. This was one such moment. He helped her in, before taking his seat. Her eyes took in the leather seats, the black interior and olive silk-wood steering wheel.

"This is not what I'd call a used car." Her smile flashed appreciation.

He gunned the gas, and sat back as the engine gave its big cat growl.

"A man should treat himself, sometimes." He drove out of the exhibition area, itching to get on open road and show her what 550 horsepower could do.

"Mr Belanov, where are we going?"

"That's up to you. You're staying in the city centre, I suppose?"

"I'm at the Holiday Inn. But I'd be happy to have dinner downtown."

"That's a possibility. Or, I have rented a small cabin in the forest. It is useful for me to have a place to entertain clients. I would be happy to cook dinner for us, and drive you to your hotel later this evening."

"I appreciate the offer, Mr Belanov, but as you said earlier, a woman in my position should be careful. If it's all right with you, I'd prefer to eat in public. And I haven't yet gotten the opportunity to see the sights of Brno."

"Of course, and you are quite right. To tell you the truth, I have very little food in my cabin, so eating out is a much better idea." He gave her a wide smile and could see her relief. Such fine bones, she was a pleasure to observe.

"However, I would like to collect some printed material in order to better demonstrate what I can offer. Would it bother you if we drove by my place quickly for me to pick up a few things? You can stay in the car, if you feel safer that way."

She laughed. "That's fine with me. And I get to see a little of the countryside."

The Porsche thundered through the trees. Belanov steered with his left hand, allowing his right, complete with TAG Heuer, to rest on the gearstick. Her colour was high and he could sense her exhilaration. He allowed the vehicle a four-wheel slide as they arrived at the cabin.

"OK, Ms McKendrick. I'll be five minutes. Would you like me to leave the music on for you?"

"You know what? I think I might be safe enough to come in while you get your stuff. Apart from anything else, I could use the bathroom."

Belanov repressed a grin and bowed like a gentleman as he opened the passenger door and offered his arm. He ran through his list. White wine and snacks in fridge, vodka in freezer. Fire laid, clean sheets, camera charged. And in the bedside drawer, a high-quality twist of cocaine. Czech.

After shoving a selection of brochures into his briefcase, he returned to the living room. She leant back on the sofa, arms behind her head.

"Cosy."

"Can I offer you anything while I prepare myself?" He maintained the pretence that they would be leaving soon. Maintained his style.

"I guess. What do you guys drink as a pre-dinner aperitif, Mr Belanov?"

"'Us guys' enjoy vodka, before, after and even during dinner."

He had no objection to playing to the stereotype, so long as she played into his hands.

"But can I ask you to call me Symon? In Ukraine, a good working relationship is based on friendship."

"No problem. I like that. And you gotta call me Caroline."

Like taking candy from a baby. In the tiny kitchen, he selected two shot glasses and poured a decent measure into each. The sound of whistling reached him, but he brushed off his discomfort. How could a Canadian be expected to know it was bad luck? He chose to focus on the moment rather than outdated superstition and headed back to the living room. She still wore her coat.

"Are you cold, Caroline? I can light a fire."

"No, we won't be here all that long, will we? This is such a cute cabin, Symon."

"For me, it is perfect. I am not the businessman to sit in public bars talking loudly. I prefer discretion and privacy. So do my clients. Now, *na zdorovia!*"

He threw back the vodka and felt a sense of achievement as she did the same.

"*Na zdorovoia!*" Her eyes widened and she coughed as the liquor hit her throat. She pressed a napkin to her mouth.

"Strong stuff, huh?" she wheezed.

"A Ukrainian special. It works well with small fish snacks. Would you prefer to go to the city directly, or shall we have another, accompanied by an *amuse bouche*?"

"Why not? Let's go local."

He poured another good measure in each glass.

She touched his arm. "And you know what? I think a lighting a fire might work pretty well right now."

It was sealed. No woman, not one, had ever drunk his vodka, sat with him in front of a crackling fireplace and left. He placed a match to the kindling in the grate and watched the flames grow. As he turned, she slid forward to hand him his glass.

"*Na zdorovoia!*" she smiled. They both threw back the vodka and locked eyes. Belanov was struggling. It would be wise to get the business settled before the inevitable, but he didn't want to appear rude.

"Caroline? Do you still prefer to go to the city or would …"

She moved onto her knees, pulled his head towards her and kissed him. Her tongue slipped into his mouth and touched his. His hands reached for her, but she pressed her palms to his upper arms, pushing them behind his back. His dick danced and twitched as she confidently drew his tongue into her mouth. She moved forward, kissing him, nibbling his lower lip, pressing her body until he relented and lay back on the hearth rug. She straddled him and sat up, grinding her pelvis over the swelling in his trousers. Her blue-grey eyes, dark with lust, never left his as she reached for his groin.

He stretched his arms above his head and let her get on with it. She surprised him, unbuckling his belt, whipping it loose from the loops, and fastening it around his wrists. Just the kind of dirty slut he liked. This could be a lot of fun. She tied the end of his belt around the leg of the armchair. He yanked at the leather to see if it would give, but he was trussed like a hog. His thighs spread as she undid his flies. He grunted and pushed his hips towards her. Suck it. Take it in your mouth. Do it.

She stopped moving and he realised he'd spoken aloud. His vision was blurred, but he could see her intense eyes focused on him and the only sound was his laboured breathing. She stood up and walked away.

"Caroline! Come back! I didn't want to …"

She was back. Out of focus, but she was back. She laid some-thing on the sofa, and slid both hands up his thighs, meeting in the middle. His dick pulsed and strained to get at her. She clasped him and he groaned. Smooth, soft hands, rhythmic upward jerks. His eyes rolled backwards in his head. He was going to come, right there. She let go and spoke.

"Suck it. Take it in your mouth. Do it."

He couldn't even see what she was forcing between his lips. But it was cold, hard and had a familiar smell.

Something went off.

Chapter 8

Zürich 2012

"Beatrice, can I interrupt you?"

"Of course, Xavier. Take a seat. Have you found something?"

"Maybe it is nothing. But I wanted to discuss about it."

The team had quickly adopted a routine, guided by Xavier's diffident insights into how the Kantonspolizei worked. So they started between 07.30 and 08.00, and worked till at least 18.00. Lunch was early and they usually ate together. Beatrice found these sessions an excellent way of discovering more about her team. In the first few days, a rapport grew which seemed strengthened rather than shaken by the occasional unpleasant appearance of Herr Kälin. He attended the daily update at eight with almost theatrical impatience, before disappearing into his own office, only communicating by email. Suited Beatrice just fine.

"Sorry." Xavier picked up the files he'd knocked from Beatrice's desk.

"It's no problem. Sit down, Xavier. It's safest."

He shrugged. "Sorry. I'm a ... how do you say that ... *ein Tollpatsch*?"

"Accident-prone, I imagine. Or failing that, clumsy."

"Clumsy, yes. It drives Herr Kälin crazy. I wanted to speak with you about the business connections between the dead men. Something keeps coming up. D'Arcy Roth."

Beatrice recognised the name. "The auditors?"

"Yes. They offer all kinds of financial services and consulting. One of the Big Five. Each man had a connection. The meetings van der Veld planned for the Monday after he died. One of them was with D'Arcy Roth. He was looking for a firm to handle his compliance issues."

"That's one of the best euphemisms for money-laundering I've heard yet, Xavier."

He grinned, and a hint of pink warmed his freckles. "I'm learning to be diplomatic, Beatrice. Now, Thompson and Edwards were also clients of the same company, but were a little more than average customers. They were personal friends of Antonella D'Arcy, the CEO."

"Mmm. That is interesting. You said all the men had a connection. Was Ryman a client too?"

"No. And this was the one that really made me think. Ryman's bank didn't use D'Arcy Roth at all. But the day he died, he was on his way to a polo tournament in Switzerland. To play against a team from Zürich, which included Antonella D'Arcy. They knew each other through the polo circuit and had previously played one another on several occasions."

"That is curious, you're right. So what do we know about this woman?"

"I already prepared a file. Details on her company, clients, and perception in the media. Also, information on her own background, hobbies and connections. This is not comprehensive, but I thought it would be helpful as an introduction."

"You're several steps ahead. I am grateful for all this. Perhaps I should go and have a chat with this lady."

"Good luck. She does not have a nice reputation. Nor does the company."

"Oh?"

"D'Arcy Roth are known informally in the business world as having the slogan; 'No such thing as dirty money'. Apparently, they deal with anyone; dictators, pirates, drug cartels. All that matters is that you have the cash to pay their bill. People also say that she …" He puffed out his cheeks.

"What do people say?"

"They say she has balls, Beatrice. Balls of steel."

"Really? That would be unusual. Yes, I think it's best if I check."

Xavier looked uncertain. "Do you want me to come with you? She speaks English, but you know, if you need me …"

"No, I don't think that will be necessary. I appreciate your bringing this to my attention and doing so much groundwork. But I believe the best person to assist me in interviewing a woman with steel balls would be Herr Kälin. Don't you agree?"

A wide, guilty smile of complicity spread across the young man's face.

As the BMW accelerated, Beatrice gazed at the late afternoon sunshine playing on the water. She wanted to look at the properties overlooking the lake, all leafy gardens and imposing architecture, but that would involve looking past Herr Kälin. She settled for an interesting enough view of the *Zürisee*.

"The 'Gold Coast'. So called because of the wealth?" she asked.

"Money, yes. And sunshine. The sun sets on the other side of the lake, so this coast gets the last of the light." He seemed slightly more forthcoming once out of the police buildings.

"I see." The BMW cruised past high walls and security gates, allowing glimpses of green lawns, French windows and occasional sculptures.

"These places must cost the earth," she said.

"They do. Similar to a town house in Kensington, I imagine. But in the area of Zürichberg, above the city, property costs even more."

"Good grief."

They sat in silence for several minutes, Beatrice absorbing the sense of privilege around them.

"How do you want to play this, Herr Kälin? Shall we do interviewer and observer, or would it be more effective to work as an interview team?"

"You're the boss."

"I am aware of that. But it doesn't answer my question."

He was quiet for a long time. He slowed to allow a dog walker to clear a zebra crossing. The retriever was dripping wet and carried a Frisbee in its mouth. It occurred to Beatrice that seeing as the road markings were yellow and black, a *zebra* crossing was rather a misnomer. A wasp crossing?

"She's a Swiss-American. Bilingual. I think it would be better if you ask the questions and I watch. Good cop, bad cop. I will add something if necessary," he said, eyes fixed on the road.

"I agree. That should have the right effect." Herr Kälin's skill as glowering, malevolent presence was beyond doubt. She hoped it was powerful enough to rattle steel balls.

The security guard examined their IDs and waved them through. The drive led up to a huge pink villa, sun reflecting from every window. The terraced gardens were well tended, with neat paths winding through blazes of yellow forsythia. Before Kälin had even switched off the ignition, the front door opened and a young woman waited to greet them. Beatrice observed the black high-collared dress, the court shoes and the serious face. The girl's hair was neatly tied back in a bun. How marvellously old school.

"*Grüezi mitenand. Mein Name ist Dina, Sekretärin und Tochter von Frau D'Arcy.*" She stood back to allow them in.

"Did she say she was the secretary and the doctor?" Beatrice whispered to Kälin.

"Secretary and daughter." His tone was dismissive, although he too was whispering. Beatrice attempted a friendly smile, but the girl's gaze remained fixed on the floor. She offered to take their coats, giving them a moment to assess their surroundings. It reeked of money. The floor was mosaic and probably depicted some dramatic image which could not be seen while standing on it. The optimum viewing point would be the landing of the grand curving staircase which arced upwards, from right to left. Despite most of the doors leading off the hallway being closed, light poured onto a variety of thriving giant plants from a cupola far above. A chaise longue upholstered in green leather sat beneath the staircase.

"*Frau D'Arcy wartet im Wintergarten. Bitte, kommen sie,*" the girl mumbled and led the way through an elegant reception room.

The décor was gold and green, with a fireplace and grand piano, wooden parquet flooring and several oil-paintings clearly chosen for their colours. Few photographs, Beatrice noted. More like a hotel lobby than a family room. Beyond the piano, French windows opened into a conservatory, filled with fig trees, succulents and indoor palms.

"Herr Kälin, Frau Stubbs," the PA-daughter announced.

Antonella D'Arcy rose to meet them. Black hair swung over her shoulders like watered silk. Her grey cashmere dress managed to convey sobriety and professionalism while making you want to reach out and touch its softness. Her face had that barely there make-up which took hours to achieve, highlighting her strong bones, dark-blue eyes and wide smile. The hand she offered was pale, manicured and free of adornment, apart from the silver Patek Philippe wristwatch.

"Ms Stubbs. Herr Kälin. I am happy to welcome you to my home. Please, take a seat and allow me to offer some refreshment." Her eyes, still smiling, flicked over Beatrice. "Ms Stubbs, it is a foolish hobby of mine to try to guess a person's nationality. I am often wrong, but I flatter myself I am improving. My first guess would be that you are British, more specifically English. Am I terribly wide of the mark?"

In a second, Beatrice became aware of her own hands. Whilst clean and tidy, they were also dry, wrinkled, and her fingernails echoed her name. The Marks and Spencer suit seemed provincial and style-free. Her shoes needed a polish.

"Correct first time, Ms D'Arcy. Well done."

The smile widened. Her teeth were perfect, reflecting light with as much sparkle as the diamond at her throat. "Thank you. Dina, bring tea. I presume that you are also a tea-drinker, Ms Stubbs? Or is that as much of a cliché as the Americans surviving on burgers? Herr Kälin, is tea acceptable to you?"

He nodded and Beatrice realised she was not required to answer. The girl left the room without a sound.

Antonella indicated the well-cushioned chairs and sat. "I must express my gratitude to you both. It was very kind of you to agree to meet me here rather than my office. I'm sure you realise that financial markets are immensely sensitive, and even the faintest breath of police interest in a company could sound the death knell. So I am genuinely appreciative of your taking the time to come out here. From what your officer explained on the phone, I understand your enquiry concerns the suicides of some high-profile men."

Kälin gazed around the room while Beatrice responded. "And we want to thank you for meeting us. We are simply tying up loose ends in these cases of suicide. All these men had significant enemies. We are trying to establish if they did indeed choose to end their own lives."

"Really? I am shocked. You don't think someone else was involved, surely?" D'Arcy's concerned expression seemed synthetic, like that of a wealthy politician extending sympathies towards victims of a poor nation's catastrophe.

"At this stage, we cannot say. We're investigating exactly what happened. Obviously, we need to explore any links between the individuals concerned. It seems one of those connections is you."

"Excellent police work. To find a connection between all these individuals to me is quite remarkable. However, perhaps we should make a distinction, just for clarity. There is Antonella D'Arcy, the woman, and D'Arcy Roth, the company. Now, the woman has been successful, and therefore mixes in certain circles. The company provides services to forty-three countries and every kind of business under the sun. It is natural that in one guise or another, I have crossed paths with most of the biggest animals in the jungle."

"Of course. And we are here for two reasons. Firstly, to eliminate you from our enquiries. That will be quite simple. If you can tell us where you were on those key dates, we can move on. Secondly, we hope to achieve some insight into the men who died. As someone who knew them professionally, or socially, your views could be most helpful."

A clinking of crockery announced the arrival of tea. D'Arcy's daughter placed the tray on the table and began distributing cups and saucers. Beatrice noted how the girl's awkwardness grew under their silent observation.

"Thank you, Dina. That's all right. I can be mother." D'Arcy flicked her eyes at the girl and at the door. It was the briefest gesture, but no doubt a curt dismissal. Dina fled, apparently grateful to get away.

D'Arcy's voice, however, was light and pleasant. "Ms Stubbs, how do you take your tea? Herr Kälin?"

As the woman observed the niceties, Beatrice observed her. She was a player. Smooth, urbane and polished, not only in appearance, but in small talk. She had prepared for their visit; Beatrice noted the laptop, Blackberry and desk diary on the table beside her. She devoted all her attention to Beatrice, barely giving Kälin a glance. She knew who held the power and how to get at it. Small wonder she had done so well. It would take a specialist kind of arrow to pierce this finely wrought armour.

"And here is the sugar. I serve it in lumps, the British way. I hope you approve, Ms Stubbs. These are Luxemburgerli, by the way. Similar to macaroons. But they may not appeal unless you have a sweet tooth."

Beatrice accepted one, but was urged to take two. The shiny little thing looked like a Disney hamburger. Pastel-coloured halves of meringue sandwiched together with matching cream, and small enough to fit between finger and thumb. It was delicious, danger-ously so. Kälin refused the cakes, but added several sugar lumps to his teacup and stirred vigorously. He gave D'Arcy a humourless stare, as she took a pink cake and popped it into her mouth, wiping sugary fingers on a napkin.

"Oh dear. I just cannot resist Luxemburgerli. An extra twenty minutes in the gym tomorrow for me. Now, you asked about my diary. Would you like to give me the dates and we can check?"

Kälin detailed the days in question and D'Arcy found the relevant pages or screens while making pleasant small talk with Beatrice.

27 February 2007: ski weekend in Davos. Six companions. Left Friday morning, returned Sunday evening.

Did Beatrice live in central London, or further outside?

21 March 2008: Brunch with friends in Feusisberg. 10.00 to 13.00. Then they took a walk around Einsiedeln, the monastery.

Had Beatrice been there yet? It was an absolute must. The home of the Black Madonna.

Home at 16.00.

D'Arcy had done her MBA through the London School of Economics and used the opportunity to improve her British accent. She aspired to speak cut-glass British English.

Beatrice nodded. "R.P."

"I'm not familiar with that term."

"What they call 'BBC English'. It stands for Received Pronunciation." Beatrice felt a childish delight in scoring a point.

12 September 2010: Flight back from New York. Attended a remembrance service for victims of 9/11. Twenty eight D'Arcy Roth employees had perished in their World Trade Centre office. Very sad.

Last time she visited London, she'd found a Swiss restaurant, had Beatrice ever seen it? Wardour Street, or somewhere near there?

"I live in the East End, Ms D'Arcy, so I tend to eat closer to home."

"The East End! Good decision. It is a growth area; the Olympic investments have made this highly desirable in terms of real estate. You made a wise choice."

Beatrice smiled. "You credit me with excessive foresight. I bought my little flat in 1982. I would like to get back to Herr Kälin's point. Jack Ryman. You played polo together?"

"Not quite correct. I played opposite Ryman. Let me top you up. Herr Kälin? Do you know anything about polo, Ms Stubbs? No? Well, I'll assume you have enough intelligence and research capability to appreciate what I say. I usually play number one in our team. Ryman played number four in his. We met often on the field and were direct aggressors. Nevertheless, with my track record, he had more reason to wish me dead than the other way around."

"Would you say Mr Ryman was a popular man in his social circle? I know he was disliked by the media," Beatrice asked.

"The media dislike anyone who takes tough decisions. Ryman was respected by those who understood his business. They are fewer than you think."

"That is becoming apparent. Most people who invested in these debt obligations seem to have found themselves holding a piece of worthless paper. Or are you referring to his company's so-called 'vulture funds'? The ones where the rich get richer by trading on Third World misery. I find it surprising you consider Ryman's strategy to be 'tough decision-making'. I am not a financier, Ms D'Arcy, but it looks like the man lacked any kind of moral compass and was selling hot air at a premium."

"If you can sell hot air at a premium and financial regulators see nothing wrong with that, you sell hot air at the best price you can get. That's what Ryman did, and he did it very well. Hence his impressive bonuses and profits. I actually admire someone who plays the game to win."

"Despite the disproportionate amount of losers?"

Kälin shifted slightly and Beatrice sensed it was a signal. She reminded herself of the reason for their visit and decided not to wait for a reply.

"Let's talk about van der Veld."

"There, I'm afraid I will not be able to help you. I never met the man. He was a potential client, but it seems he changed his mind."

"Did you know anything about his business, Ms D'Arcy? About the provenance of his diamonds?"

"He had a range of interests besides diamonds and needed some help with staying on the right side of the law. It is not my job to investigate the ethics behind his money. I am a professional, Ms Stubbs, which requires me to be neutral and unbiased. Anyone has the right to be a client of mine, if they can afford it."

"So I hear. But you did know Dougie Thompson and Brian Edwards personally, didn't you?"

"I knew them as social acquaintances, yes."

"And despite their unprincipled activities, you retained them as friends. That didn't bother you?"

D'Arcy folded her hands together and gave Beatrice a kind smile.

"I can see you feel quite strongly about certain issues, Ms Stubbs. And I admire you for it, I really do. However, it appears we see the world differently, so let's leave it at that. As far as I'm aware, it's not my ethical perspective which is under investigation, is it?"

Kälin's voice rumbled into the silence.

"The fact remains, Ms D'Arcy, you knew all these men. Why do *you* think they died?"

She turned to face him for the first time. "Do you think it possible they may have discovered a conscience?"

Beatrice cocked her head. "That's certainly possible. In which case, when you discover yours, will you do the same?"

Kälin's spoon stopped stirring.

D'Arcy's face smoothed. "It seems that we have gone past enquiry and into judgement. Is there anything more I can help you with, officers, or would you like to beat the traffic back into the city?"

The girl fetched their coats.

Beatrice's view of the lakeside buildings was unimpeded. Cyclists, joggers, picnickers, couples, groups of friends wandered through the spring sunshine towards the water. An inspiring evening, into which she carried her own little rain cloud.

Kälin kept checking her with sideways glances. "Where do you want to go?"

"It's late. Let's de-brief on Monday. I'd prefer to go home."

If only she could. A wild thought grabbed her. If she checked the flights as soon as she got in, it might be possible to fly to Exeter tonight, spend a weekend in Matthew's calming company, allow him to fuss over her and puncture her paranoia … Or not. Or she could stay here and work. After her outburst, jetting off for a weekend with her lover seemed to lack gravitas.

Traffic on Bürkliplatz held them up. She watched the tourists; he kept his eyes on the road.

"Herr Kälin, I am sorry I handled that so badly. Purely through my own aggressive attitude, I turned a friendly witness hostile. Maybe we should have worked as a team after all."

He didn't answer. Beatrice watched the west coast darken, while the sun's rays continued to bless the golden east. The weekend stretched ahead, full of nothing but shadows. The dogs were restless.

Kälin stopped in front of her apartment block but did not turn off the ignition. He turned to look at her as he spoke. "We did work as a team. My mistake was to think *I* was playing the bad cop. I wish you a good weekend, Frau Stubbs."

"Same to you, Herr Kälin."

His moustache lifted in an unfamiliar way. If Beatrice hadn't known better, it could have been a smile.

Chapter 9

Zürich 2012

"So what would you like to achieve from today's call, Beatrice?"

"The usual, I suppose. To explain how I'm feeling, and check with you that I'm still on course."

"OK, good. I'd be interested to hear how you're feeling. And when you say, 'still on course', what do you mean exactly?"

"That I'm still going in the right direction. I felt we'd made a lot of progress before I left London, but here, I feel more wobbly."

"Right, I see. Should we start with 'wobbly'? Is that the word which best describes how you're feeling?"

"Yes. What I mean is that I have very little self-confidence. Sometimes. I'm afraid I'm out of my depth. I ballsed up an interview yesterday because I let my temper get the better of me. And I did it in front of the Senior Detective here. He doesn't have much belief in me anyway, and now his respect has reached rock bottom. The thing is, James, I'm not at all sure I'm up to this. Maybe it's too soon."

"That's a possibility. But only one of many. I'd like to hear a bit more about what happened."

Beatrice explained, trying to rein in her urge to exaggerate D'Arcy into a monster and paint Kälin as a pantomime villain.

"So, you're saying you may have created hostility with the detective by being judgemental with that interviewee?"

"Exactly. I upset her, and him by behaving badly."

"Funny you should use the word 'bad'. Didn't you just tell me you had agreed to play 'good cop, bad cop'? How should a bad cop behave?"

"Oh, you know. Intimidating, aggressive, maybe showing obvious dislike of the witness. Come on, James, you've seen *Life on Mars*."

"I have. And isn't that exactly what you did? So I'm puzzled by why you think your behaviour upset your colleague. Tell me again what he said in response to your apology?"

"He said that we had worked as a team, and he just hadn't realised I was the bad cop. But he was being sarcastic."

"How did this sarcasm manifest itself? Did he say anything else?"

"No. Apart from wishing me a good weekend. You think I'm exaggerating."

"What I'm hearing may be a magnification of a negative moment, yes. What are the other factors that make you say you're not up to it?"

"It's a complicated case, the team are very young and whizzy, Kälin thinks he should be in charge and I'm homesick." Heat rose in her face, as she felt tears tickling her nose. She sniffed, her sudden self-pity followed by sympathy for James. How many times had the poor man sat listening to her grizzles?

"Sorry, James."

"I believe we had an agreement by which you did not apologise for your feelings?"

"Yes, you're right. I'm not sorry then. But it has been bloody tough."

"That I don't doubt. And I'll come back to that in a second. But first I'd like you to remind me of some of the recurring patterns we identified when you are under stress."

Beatrice sighed deeply. "I am selective. I remember events with a focus on the negative. And I magnify the bad things, so they become far larger than the good. I also tend to nurse a grievance, so that I feel hard-done-by for longer and more often than is necessary."

"You mentioned how tough you find your circumstances. Have you noticed any of these thought patterns happening as a result?"

"A bit. Yes. But I have been trying to make something positive out of it."

"Can I ask for an example?"

Beatrice considered. "By not showing myself to be rattled by Kälin, I think I'm earning more respect from the team. And even, perversely, from him."

"So his level of respect is actually increasing, you think?"

"It may have been until yesterday."

"Is there any chance you are projecting your own frustrations with your performance onto this man?"

"Possibly. But he can be quite horrible, James. I'm not making this up."

"I know that. Just remember that quotation; 'no one can make you feel inferior without your permission'. You are in control of how you feel. If you feel you made a mistake, it's fine to be angry at yourself. Let's remove this one step. If one of your 'young and whizzy' team had lost their temper with a witness, how would you feel? I'd like you to think about a specific individual, please."

"I would feel annoyed at his lack of professionalism. But if he recognised the mistake, apologised and learnt from it, I would forgive and forget."

"Good. Might your colleague do the same for you?"

"He might, I suppose. I did apologise."

"People make mistakes, Beatrice. It's how we deal with our mistakes that takes us forward. Now, a couple of practical questions ..."

"Yes, and yes. I am taking the Depakote without fail. And I have kept a diary. Not religiously, but noting any low symptoms."

"Good news. That'll be useful for charting lows, highs, and middle bits, so I'd like it if you made a daily note of your general outlook. Now, shall we turn to the positive things that have happened since our last call?"

After a session with James, Beatrice always needed time to digest and test her recalibrated outlook. She felt like someone who'd just discovered the reason why walking hurt was because she had her shoes on the wrong feet. A stroll by the river did wonders, especially as she watched people cycling, jogging, playing football and enjoying themselves. Wandering as far as the Allmend playing fields, she realised her feet now hurt because she'd walked so far and made up her mind to take the train back into the city. But first she stopped at a little cabin-café in the park and spent half an hour watching dogs and replaying James's words. Wagging tails, the sunshine and a good idea for a jaunt the next day lifted her into almost glad to be alive.

The S-Bahn delivered her back to the city and she returned to her extensive, empty quarters. She'd just put the kettle on when the phone rang. She skipped to answer it, keen to talk to Matthew.

"Hel-lo?"

"Good afternoon, Frau Stubbs. This is Herr Koch at reception. I'm sorry to disturb you. A young man just handed in a mobile phone. He found it outside in the street. I checked through the address book and I have the impression it might belong to you."

"I don't think so. One moment." Beatrice rooted through her bag. Her phone was indeed missing.

"Herr Koch? It seems you're right. I had no idea I'd lost it. I'll come down now."

"There's no need, Frau Stubbs. I'll send someone up to your room."

"That's very kind of you. I'll be more careful in future. Have a nice afternoon."

"Thank you. I wish the same for you. Goodbye."

People in this country were so nice, so honest. Very civilised.

"Zürich calling. How's the weather in Devon?"

"Outdoors, fine with a light breeze. Super washday weather. However, indoors we have thunder, lightning, black clouds and the strong possibility of torrential rain."

"Oh dear. Is Luke having a tantrum?"

"No, no. He's right here in front of the television. We're watching something rather sinister called *Teletubbies*. His mother, on the other hand, is prising open the yawning pit of Tartarus with a nail file. An alimony payment has failed to arrive."

"Poor Tanya. Send her my love, and sympathy. How's Marianne?"

"The second of the Eumenides is winging her way here as we speak. From Crediton. It may be wise to take young Luke out for a pint tonight. Too much female vitriol can put a chap off his food."

Beatrice laughed. "There may come a time to share advice and ale with your grandson, but you cannot take a baby to the pub. And your local hostelry is quite strict about under-eighteens," she said, envisaging the mismatched pair in a corner of the snug.

"Yet no laws exist on under-ones accompanying me to the shed for a pint of home-brew, as far as I know."

"True. Wrap him up warm and give him a kiss from me."

"Enough of my domestic low pressure system. How's the high life?"

"Nothing to write home about. I lost my temper yesterday and have been in a fug ever since."

"A fug?" She could hear his disguised concern.

"It's perfectly all right, Matthew. I should expect these insecurities, everyone has them. And I've just talked it through with James. I confess to having more perspective now."

"I'm happy to hear that. Would it help if I were to visit for a couple of days? I should very much like to see you."

Beatrice's smile broadened, but she hesitated.

"And I'd like to see you. Can we discuss this later in the week? I just feel a need to ... manage. Does that make sense?"

"Absolutely. I said exactly the same thing to my father. Three days in a row I came home with bloodied knees, raw elbows and grazed hands. He offered to put the stabilisers back on my bike, but I stood tall in my short trousers, looked him in the eye, and said, 'Thank you, Father, I can manage.' So manage away, my dear one, but if you need an extra wheel, you may summon me at a moment's notice."

"Thank you. It's good to know my stabilisers are in the cupboard under the stairs. It's peculiar, you know. I always rely on systems at work. They are there to make sure I don't miss anything, that I follow best practice, to keep me on the straight and narrow. Where work is concerned, I know I am fallible, so I adhere to my systems, my stabilisers. Now I have to learn to do that in my private life."

"We all have them, Old Thing. And some of those systems, which I prefer to see as habits, can become obsolete, outdated and counter-productive. Your life has just had an overhaul, and you're in the adaptation phase. A few scabby knees are part of the learning process."

"I know. But I'm an awful old dog to be learning new bicycle tricks."

"Had anyone else referred to you as an 'awful old dog', I would have offered him outside. Talking of tricks, when you come back, I thought we might try learning to juggle with that circus group in Totnes. Learning new skills keeps you young, so they say. Oh Good God!"

"What is it?"

"The television programme is over and the sun has gone down. It had a baby's face, and as it sank below the horizon, it gurgled. That is one of the most disturbing images I have seen since *Chucky*. Right, I am taking Luke to the shed and shall read to him from Rudyard Kipling, which will soothe us both."

"Excellent idea. Off you go. Just don't read him astray."

His laughter was rich, like gravy. "Was that deliberate, or one of your Bea-lines?"

"I rarely manage to be so apt by accident. Your turn to call me tomorrow."

"It will be the highlight of my Sunday. Apart from *Antiques Roadshow*. Enjoy your Saturday, my love."

"Matthew? After you refused your father's offer of stabilisers, did you stop falling off?"

"Yes, eventually. Although the day after that conversation, I broke my nose."

Smiling, Beatrice dug her laptop out of her bag and typed the word *Chucky* into a search engine. Sometimes, her contemporary cultural knowledge had the most appalling gaps.

Chapter 10

Zürich 2012

An unusual level of excitement hummed through the top-floor room. Sabine set up her laptop and projector, apparently oblivious to the louder-than-usual banter from her colleagues. Even Kälin's arrival failed to bring the buzz down. Sabine picked up the remote control and looked to Beatrice for permission to begin. It was 07.58.

"OK, folks. Sabine's ready so I'd like to get started. Just a reminder, this session is likely to generate some significant steps forward. So today's meeting is scheduled to run till eleven. It may not last that long, but if it does, I hope you'll understand why." Beatrice made eye contact with each individual, lingering no longer on Kälin than anyone else. Despite the fact that everyone in the room knew whom she was addressing.

"Sabine, over to you."

"Thank you, Beatrice. And thanks to all of you for being so patient. I have taken quite some time over this profile and demanded much of your attention and time with my questions. Cases reported as suicide tend to involve less evidence than homicides. So there were a limited amount of photographs, crime scene reports and witness statements to analyse. In other words, I have been filling in the gaps.

"Slide One. My method. I am a fan of the deductive system of profiling. That is to say, I want to find out everything I can about this individual before making comparison to statistical data. What do we know? For certain?"

The question was not rhetorical. Beatrice went first.

"The only thing we know with any certainty is that four men are dead. And that what appears to be the same DNA was found at each scene."

Conceição spoke. "In my view, we can drop the 'what appears to be' the same DNA. It's him. Since 1989, EDNAP – European DNA Profiling, and ENFSI – the European Network of Forensic Institutes have standardised procedures across the continent, setting the benchmark for short tandem repeat analysis. The vast majority of laboratories agree on STR testing for the European core loci. Some countries test for more, some for less, but all include the basic four. My checks show that the samples taken were large enough and handled with textbook care. It's the same guy."

Sabine nodded. "Thank you, Conceição. But even taking the DNA as a given, my point is we cannot be sure that these deaths were homicides. So let us work on premise one. These four men killed themselves and the same individual was present before, during or after the death. Could this person have triggered the desire to end their lives? If so, how? Blackmail? Coercion? That is an intriguing possibility. Yet something bothers me about this theory. These deaths were carefully orchestrated. Personally, I have a feeling these methods were purposely chosen. I will come back to this in a moment or two."

"Frau Tikkenenn. Is much of your presentation today likely to be based on your 'feelings', or do you plan to provide us with something of concrete value?"

"Herr Kälin, do you mind if we leave questions to the end? As I think you will see, my work is to a professional standard."

Beatrice froze at the girl's curt dismissal of a senior officer and steeled herself for the slamming of a door. Kälin didn't move. But no one dared look at his face.

"Premise two. If these events were intentional killings, serious questions are raised. The perpetrator is a serial killer. These were organised, meticulously planned and perfectly executed crimes. To leave a trace of DNA looks a little clumsy. Was it done on purpose? I'll come back to that, too. Let us focus on motive and method.

"Motive: Why kill these men, and in this way? This is where

Chris and Xavier's research proved very useful. All the dead men had a reputation for a lack of ethics.

"Van der Veld's wares came from mines known to violate working practice codes, and three out of these five mines were in litigation for abuse, inhumane treatment and corruption.

"Dougie Thompson. Thompson and family owned mainly right-wing newspapers and television channels all over Australia and New Zealand. They had a majority stake in two key US TV networks, both of which represent the 'Real American Family'. Every broadcast contains some reference to the abuse of the American system, by foreigners, kids or Democrats. They also own several of the worse gossip tabloids. The ones which feature stars with cellulite or Photoshopped romances. In the UK, the approach was more subtle. They claimed the middle ground."

Chris nodded. "The middle ground of Middle England."

"Yes. His papers laid claim to the morally righteous position, while whipping up anti-immigration, anti-gay, anti-intellectual, anti-teenager sentiments. Their trademark was exposing the youth leader as drug-pusher, the pregnancy consultant as baby-killer, the asylum-seeker as cynical sponger and so on. Every week, the front page 'exposed' some liberal or humanitarian cause as waste of the good taxpayer's money."

Beatrice twitched. "Sabine, can I ask you to stick to the factual side? Your personal bias is distracting, to be honest."

Sabine acknowledged the point with a twist of her head.

"Brian Edwards, whose company, Watermark, was found guilty of contaminating the water supply of a large area in the Peak District of Britain. Edwards resigned, accepting a four million pound pay-off. Lawyers are still seeking reparation for over three hundred brain-damaged babies and several hundred infertile women.

"Jack Ryman, used to be key client-manager for Mendoza and Schwanhof, investment bankers. Sold collateralised debt obligations at inflated prices, thus bankrupting the company, and dragging down several others. Fortunately for him, he saw it coming and jumped ship with his enormous bonus, mid 2008. Set up RAM, Ryman Asset Management, which specialised in buying up debts in war-torn countries. After those countries made peace, RAM sued for repayment. So rather than rebuild their infrastructure, they were legally obliged to hand over anything they had to investment vultures like Ryman."

"Sabine," cautioned Beatrice.

The girl sighed. "Sorry, Beatrice. I shouldn't get carried away. Although do keep in mind this is how these stories were reported and could therefore influence public perception."

"Carry on."

"In the years they died, these names were in the top ten of everyone's most hated. International press reported their deaths with a sense of justice. This, I believe, is our first pointer. Very few serial killers, or spree killers, continue to pursue this activity without an eye on their own 'fifteen minutes' of fame. I suggest the person responsible did this either because he felt it was the right thing to do, or that it was seen to be the right thing to do."

Chris offered his uncensored opinion. "So an extreme left-winger? Anti-capitalist who sees it as his duty to shoot fat cats?"

Sabine clicked to the next slide, which showed a pie chart of statistics. "This is where comparisons to similar cases can help. The vast majority of serial and spree killers tend to have more political affiliations with the right. That is not to say a left-wing vigilante is impossible. Simply unusual."

Kälin pressed his fingers to his forehead and looked down. Either he was crying or laughing. Beatrice attempted to give Sabine a sharp indication to continue and ignore his theatrics, but there was no need.

"Modus operandi. He made each death look like suicide. As Chris points out, one can see why. He assumes the role of their absent conscience. Our man is performing a 'cull' of those seen as malignant to society. Murder motivated by a political agenda? This is not unheard of, but as I say, rare for left-wing causes."

Xavier raised a finger. "Sabine, you said something about methods being specifically chosen. I know you were talking about your 'assisted' suicide idea, but I wonder what you meant?"

"This is not relevant at this point, and I did ask if we could keep questions until later."

Beatrice intervened. "That is usually the way I prefer to present, too, Sabine. However, we should be flexible to interruption and diversion, especially in an international team. Not all our thought processes work the same way. Answering Xavier's question may well make him better prepared for the remainder of your input."

"That's fair enough. Sorry, Xavier. It's just because my slides will now be mixed up."

"No problem. I can wait." The poor lad's complexion gave everything away.

"No, I will answer." She clicked forward to a table detailing how the victims died. "The first death. Van der Veld. Apparently slit his wrists in the bath. Found up to his neck in his own blood. Does the expression *blood diamonds* mean anything, anyone?

"Thompson froze to death, drunk on schnapps, while on a skiing holiday. The man who made his fortune by bugging cars, taking long-lens photographs and dragging his targets onto the front page, died of exposure. If I were a vigilante, I couldn't think of a more appropriate way to dispose of a media mogul."

Chris grinned. "Well, not unless he was hacked to death."

Sabine groaned but even she seemed to have difficulty suppressing a smile.

"Moving on, Edwards, poisoned by carbon dioxide in his car. Are the parallels clear?"

"And Ryman?" Chris asked. "Bag over his head? How does that figure?"

Sabine rifled through her notes for a moment.

A deep voice spoke. "The man achieved his fortune by selling something that didn't really exist. Maybe someone forced him to inhale his own toxic assets."

Like the others, Beatrice turned to Kälin. He stared blandly back, giving no clue as to whether his comment was sarcastic or contributory.

Sabine gazed into the middle distance. "Yes, that actually makes sense. I focussed on the fact that the killer left the top of the car down and therefore the body open to the elements and nature's scavengers."

"Both interesting thoughts," Beatrice agreed. "However, I feel we have only just started exploiting what we know. Can we continue with that and return to hypotheses later?"

Sabine snapped back into efficiency. "Yes, of course. Personal risk. How far did the killer jeopardise himself? So far, the deaths were seen as suicide or misadventure, thus no one was hunted. But in order to know where, when and what was going on in these men's lives, this person must have done serious research. In each case, there are signs of acceptance, welcome and co-operation with the other individual. Why?"

Chris threw in an idea. "I'd make a guess at some kind of service provider, obviously under-the-counter. He's a rent boy. Perhaps we should examine the sexual preferences of these four individuals. Or he's a drug dealer, high class, only deals with the top brass. Maybe he decides that enough is enough and wastes them while they're wasted."

"Good ideas, with plenty to support them. Anyone else want to offer something?" Sabine asked.

Conceição spoke with deliberation, thinking aloud. "With what you have given us so far, Sabine, I have to lean towards a professional hit man. There is no motive, apart from cash. He murders to order, and is either instructed, or chooses to add the poetic justice element. He may have different employers. This guy knows how to gain access, knows how to subdue and kill, and to depart leaving no trace."

"Apart from the single sample of DNA," added Xavier.

"Exactly." Sabine gave a satisfied smile, like a cat. "Now I offer my picture from such data. This person is a professional. He knows where to find his victim and can do enough preparation to arrange an 'appropriate' death. I suggest the killer was in place before the arrival of the victim and arranged circumstances to suit. I will offer the following theories. Firstly, the dead men knew, or wanted to know, the person who orchestrated their deaths. He had access to the victim, he had knowledge of the victim's movements and he must have appeared benign to each individual.

"Conceição's forensics lead me to believe if these men were killed, as opposed to performing the act themselves, they must have been drugged. It is near impossible to take a healthy man, force him to sit in the bath and bleed him to death with no signs of struggle. Edwards sat peaceably in his vehicle and allowed the carbondioxide to poison his blood with no attempt to leave. Which leads me to the idea that our man has access to narcotics. Legal or otherwise. Conceição?"

"Taking the deaths chronologically, Van der Veld's coroner's report showed no suspicious substances. Thompson, same thing. Bear in mind they were found around thirty to thirty-six hours after death. Nothing there." Conceição raised a finger. "But Edwards's body was retrieved quickly. The autopsy showed traces of GHB, gamma hydroxybutyric acid, in his urine. GHB works much like Rohypnol, a benzodiazepine better-known as the date rape drug. You need add only a few drops to liquid, and the effects of muscle relaxation, sedation and a lack of anxiety can happen in less than twenty minutes. At which point, you are free to do whatever you want with that person for the next four to six hours. Another key factor is that GHB metabolises fast into carbondioxide and water. It's difficult to detect, but easy to make, if you have some knowledge of pharmaceuticals."

Chris looked up from his notes. "And Ryman?"

Conceição shook her head. "It was late April, but that weekend Swiss meteorologists recorded summer temperatures. His body had been out in the forest for three days in 28-degree heat. So that must have been one unpleasant, and fruitless, autopsy."

Sabine smiled. "Thanks for that, Conceição. So what can we tell about this person so far? He has a conscience, and a need for attention. So does half the human race. He knows details about these men, their movements and crucially, their preferences. Each scene shows all the elements of a professional hit. He is organised, prepared and very well researched. He is not in any way weak with blood, violence and death, but coldly professional. Just look at van der Veld."

"Why van der Veld in particular?" asked Chris.

"The killer slit his veins open. That is not an easy task. I know. I have killed chickens," Sabine assured them with great solemnity.

Beatrice caught her lip between her teeth to avert a smile. Kälin exhaled sharply and Beatrice saw his moustache twitch once more.

"So to profile. Gender we know," Sabine said.

Xavier shifted forward in his seat. "Do we? If the DNA is planted, it could be a woman."

Sabine managed her annoyance more smoothly this time. "Possible, but unlikely. A tiny percentage of serial killers are women. And those that do kill more than once usually have a personal reason, like vengeance."

Xavier cleared his throat. "Yes, I understand that. But in theory, we could be talking about a vengeful woman, who leaves traces of male DNA, possibly on purpose, to implicate someone?"

"In theory, Xavier. But you don't need to make this so complicated. Look at the statistics. He is most likely to be white. As for social class, I'm divided. He could be a working-class hero, maybe a drug dealer who serviced these men. Or a medic, someone they would meet socially, but who had access to debilitating drugs. As for age, that's a tricky one. Received wisdom is that serial killers tend to start their 'career' around the age of thirty-five. The first murder we know of was in 2007. And it was perfectly planned. Five years later, our killer is most likely early forties."

Chris picked up a marker pen and noted the details on the whiteboard.

"He is more than likely to live alone. He works in some kind of pharma-related industry. Or deals with less legal pharmaceuticals in his free time."

"Sabine?" Xavier had another question, while Chris added more data to the mind-map. "Why do you say he lives alone?"

Sabine sighed. "Most serial killers do. Or possibly with someone infirm or elderly, who cannot check up on them. I believe he prepared the ground for these killings in detail, which means being away from home for some time. So I cannot imagine he has an invalid at home whom he can abandon for days."

"Although if he did, that might explain access to sedating drugs," Xavier replied.

Sabine thought for a moment and nodded. "OK, I'll take that into account. Thanks, Xavier. Either way, this guy has an 'in'. He's a professional, someone respected, someone they want on their side.

"We can't test his DNA for any markers of ethnicity, but one thing we should note. These kinds of crimes usually start close to home, in an area the killer knows well. The incidents we know about occurred in the Netherlands, Switzerland, France and Liechtenstein. He may be Swiss, or a Dutchman living here."

"Have we checked *your* alibi?" Conceição looked sideways at Chris.

Chris feigned realisation. "Of course! It all seems so obvious now. Everyone knows the Dutch are all drug-crazed left-wing hippies. I think we should take me in for questioning."

Conceição released a deep laugh.

Chris continued. "But seriously, this profile does tend to point more towards some kind of businessman. The hotel in Utrecht is the sort of place where people stand out if they're not wealthy professionals."

Sabine nodded. "Exactly. This guy is a chameleon, fitting in easily to his environment. As for his psychological make-up, I'm still struggling to piece together the motivation. This kind of world view where he believes he alone can rescue society from, in this case, capitalism and greed, is not uncommon. He is an avenger, a righter of wrongs, and sees himself as a very intelligent person."

"Not forgetting a meticulous planner," added Chris.

Sabine agreed. "Definitely. From what I have assessed, I see this man. He works, or maybe used to work, in the world of pharmacology. There may be some moral indignation in his world view. His trajectory was thwarted somehow and he now resents the 'proper way' of doing things. He may have been disappointed by the law, or his career path. He wants to correct what he sees as wrongs. I would guess that he brewed these plans for many years, and as explained before, he's likely to be around forty to forty-five years old.

"And finally, the dates are significant. We know of four suspicious suicides; 2007, 2008, 2010, 2011. No connected death in 2009. Did something major happen to our man in that year, so he took a sabbatical? Or did we miss one? And as Xavier mentioned many weeks ago, can we be sure that the first 'suicide' was in 2007?"

Chris looked at Xavier. "You suggested this before. We have to do that trawl for any similar kinds of deaths in 2006 and 2009."

Xavier's eyes shone bright. "Got it."

Sabine continued. "He's unlikely to be any kind of team player, with a strong conviction in his own beliefs. If this person is operating this way, his confidence and belief in his own power is increasing proportionally. He will be very attentive to any investigation and potentially become involved, whether that is observing, or attempting to hide himself behind a witness. We must all be very aware of any external interest in this case."

The girl was rising like a hot air balloon in Beatrice's estimation. Her presentation crystallised so many vague thoughts which had bothered Beatrice since first reading Hamilton's notes. Sabine came to a close.

"My views are based on both this particular person, and any parallels he may have with a similar MO. And while his operational strategy is one thing, his calling card is another. The DNA is not a mistake. Judging by the meticulously clean scenes of crime, I believe this person quite deliberately leaves some saliva, or hair for the police. His own, or someone else's. I think he must know this DNA is not registered on any database. Why?"

Chapter 11

Zürich 2012

Kälin's suggestion that Chris might like to accompany him to a second interview with Antonella D'Arcy was casual to the point of indifference. It caught Chris on the back foot. On one hand, he definitely wanted a close-up of a platinum-coated rich bitch. On the other, he wondered why Kälin hadn't asked Beatrice. Curiosity overcame courtesy and he accepted the invitation.

The foyer of the D'Arcy Roth building, classy and intimidating, warned that herein moved serious money. Grey marble flooring surrounded the receptionists' island in the centre of the vast entrance hall, giving way to pale blue tiles the other side of the glass security doors. Chris was impressed. He was supposed to be.

Suits came and went, often throwing curious stares in their direction. Chris sat at one of the visitors' tables while Kälin paced. At first, Chris put it down to impatience; D'Arcy was still in a meeting. But then he observed the detective's behaviour more carefully. Mobile to his ear, rattling away in Swiss German, Kälin frequently pushed back his jacket and rested his hand on his hip. The gesture allowed glimpses of his holster and police weapon. Unmistakeably, Kälin was announcing to everyone he was a cop. D'Arcy would be delighted.

One of the identikit ponytailed receptionists called over. "Frau D'Arcy is between meetings and will see you for five minutes. Here are your security passes and board level is on the sixth floor."

Passing the glass doors, into the lift, through another set of security gates at board level and they were finally admitted to the inner sanctum. Visitors to senior management level enjoyed deep-blue plush carpeting, leather armchairs and a selection of soft drinks. D'Arcy kept them waiting another ten minutes before a secretary showed them to a meeting room, complete with golf and yachting magazines to browse. The woman liked to remind people of her status; that much was clear.

She entered the room, closing the door behind her and sat at the head of the table. Her eyes swept over Chris and fixed on Kälin. Her black hair pulled up into a knot complemented her displeased expression. She wore a white shirt with a sober navy skirt and looked just like the headmistress of a private girls' school.

"Frau D'Arcy, can I introduce Herr Keese, my colleague. Thank you for giving us a few moments of your time."

She didn't acknowledge Chris at all.

"You gave me very little choice. So let's get to the point. How can I help?"

"When we spoke last week, I omitted to ask you how long you'd known each of the men in these cases of suicide."

She gave a disbelieving laugh and shook her head. "What possible relevance does that have to your investigation?"

Kälin's expression was regretful. "I'm afraid I can't possibly divulge why we need to know, Frau D'Arcy. It would be unprofessional to share our approach with suspects."

She sat quite still, her voice dropping lower. "Are you telling me I'm a suspect, Herr Kälin? If so, perhaps I should contact my attorney."

"I think calling your attorney, or lawyer as they say in *British* English, is possibly premature. But of course, it's your decision."

Chris wasn't sure exactly how, but Kälin had got under her skin in a matter of seconds. D'Arcy's pinched expression and grim jaw was testimony to that.

Kälin must have seen it too. "Let's just say we have not yet eliminated you from our enquiries. So to my question."

"I'd be happy to provide you with all the dates, times and locations where I first encountered these people, but it will take me some time. And this afternoon, I'm flying to Kiev. Had you called ahead rather than just turning up, I could have prepared all the information and saved us both the inconvenience of your visit."

Kälin shook his head. "I always prefer the personal touch. Could you confirm the duration of your relationships with these men …"

"More acquaintanceships, I think."

"… by tomorrow afternoon? It would be most helpful."

She didn't reply but stood and looked at Chris for the first time.

"So you've sacked that British woman already? I can understand why. Her interview technique was barbaric."

"Detective Inspector Stubbs, of the London Metropolitan Police, continues to lead our team most effectively. She's currently working closely with our psychological profiler and making impressive progress."

"Really." D'Arcy's voice exaggerated her lack of interest as she opened the door to leave.

"Yes, really. We're closing in on the perpetrators. It won't be long, Frau D'Arcy. The wheels of the justice may not turn quickly, but once in motion, they cannot be stopped. Rather like a train."

"A train?" She gave a dry laugh. "Yes, the image is apt. Slow, steaming and cumbersome, not to mention expensive to maintain."

Kälin sat back, a bland expression not quite disguising the sharpness in his eyes.

"I was thinking more of the modern Swiss railway system and its worldwide reputation for efficiency. As the slogan goes, you can count on us."

"I'm so pleased to hear it. So all of us who keep the economy ticking over, paying taxes to cover your salaries, can sleep safely in our beds. Please return your security passes as you leave."

She left the door open and disappeared down the corridor. As Chris turned to his colleague, he got quite a shock. He'd never seen Kälin smile before.

Chapter 12

St Germain du Bois 2010

Carp.

Ironically appropriate.

He slammed the door and trudged around to the boot. Just preparing his gear made him feel calmer. He would spend the day at his favourite swim and forget all about it. Push it all behind him. Unbelievable. She was perfectly happy to spend it before she got a crisis of conscience. It was a storm in a bloody teacup and would blow over in a couple of weeks. All they needed to do was to keep their heads down and let the lawyers deal with it. That, and avoid the press. The French retreat would have been perfect, but for her checking the news websites every day and relaying every hysterical accusation to him over dinner.

Forget about it. Unbelievable, really. The perfect loyal wife through the good times; well dressed, expensively groomed and a practised hostess. Now, at the first sign of trouble, she wants to leave. His retort this morning should shut her up. Tears, of course, and she'd threatened to go home. Well, up to her. One way or another he'd get some peace.

Rods, bait, landing net, waders, picnic, stool and blanket. He locked the car and headed toward the lake. A breeze blew through the forest, shaking free some leaves. Despite the reminder of autumn, the sun's warmth could be felt through his jacket and the sky was bright and clear. He was glad he had his sunglasses.

As he approached the swim, he focused his mind. Today, he wanted a big one. After all, he deserved it, the bullshit he'd had to take these last few weeks. Landing a thirty-kilo-plus carp would be just the thing to put a spring in his step.

He stepped onto the jetty and took the left arm of the T, setting himself up for maximum comfort. Bait, hooks and rod holder to the left. Book, flask and picnic to the right. He prepared his line, allowing his mood to settle in the peace of lake, forest and silence. No one around. Naturally. He'd paid his fees and this was his swim for the week. The heat was pleasant, and he took off his jacket, arranging it neatly under his stool.

He settled back on his chair and cast a line, taking a deep breath. Everybody has a chance. He has. The carp have. The odds might be stacked against the fish, but that is the nature of the game. You are in a pool, you take risks, you should be prepared to lose. You can't blame the winner. Some fish grow bigger than others and the British media were bewailing the one that got away.

A flash of white between the trees caught the corner of his eye. Someone making directly for him. No way was anyone sharing this location. All bought and paid for. Whoever this bloody chancer thought he was, he'd chosen the wrong bloke on the wrong day.

He waited till he heard footfalls on the wood and snapped round. "What do you want?"

The figure jumped and Brian realised his mistake. It was the artist, weighed down as usual with a heavy bag, sketch pad and collapsible stool. His attack had stopped her in her tracks. She wore a white shirt, jeans and a startled expression.

He apologised immediately. "Oh hello. Sorry, I didn't realise …"

She gave a relieved smile. "Hello again. You gave me quite a fright! Am I intruding?"

"No, no, not at all. I just thought you were another angler, trying to muscle in. I paid for this pitch, you see, for the week."

"I see. Well, I only came round to say hello before I set up my own pitch. I'm definitely not after your fish." She smiled again, teasing.

"Hey, look, it's OK. You can stay, if you like. There's plenty of room."

"No, no. Thank you, but no. When I paint, I must have silence. I really need to be alone. This is a big lake, there are many other places. I wish you a successful …" Shifting her load, she lost her grip on her pad and roll of brushes. The pad slipped onto the jetty, and the roll unfolded, spilling brushes at his feet. Two bounced into the water.

"Oh no, how clumsy of me!" She knelt, trying to collect all her equipment. He bent to help her, as a gentleman should. She looked at the brushes, floating below their feet.

"They were quite expensive. I need to get them back." She placed her bag down and started unbuckling her shoes.

"There's no need for that. Look!" He reached for his landing net and leant forward to scoop the two brushes out of the water. He could feel her eyes on his back. He was glad he'd removed his jacket, so she could see the muscle movement beneath his shirt. He drew the net closer and fished out the brushes.

Her face was flushed. "You see? You really don't need someone like me around to frighten your fish. Thanks so much for helping me. Have a good day. I hope they bite. Goodbye."

"Goodbye."

He debated asking her to meet for coffee later, but she'd already gone into the trees. Shame.

The Artist. He'd seen her around the lakes several times, and a couple of days ago, she'd joined him at an outside table of the *Café du Chat Noir*. They had a brief conversation about the weather. The Artist. From Alsace, quite bashful about her work, but she teased him lightly about his British tea-drinking. She drank an espresso. Her accent was sensual, throaty French and she was very easy on the eye. Fine features, milky-white skin and a ready smile topped by messy blonde curls falling out of a hairclip. He watched for occasional glimpses of white as she moved along the lake path, and shrugged. Women rarely enjoyed fishing, nearly always getting upset at the most exciting bit.

They didn't bite. All morning, nothing. He changed bait, from maize to halibut pellets. His mood grew murky along with the sky. The breeze was sharp without the benefit of the sun. He replaced his jacket and poured himself a cup of tea from the flask. At midday, he drank another. By one o'clock, he had no doubts. It was going to rain, he was going to catch nothing and he felt enormously tired. As the first fat drops spattered the wood, he began to pack up. Maybe he'd go to the café in the centre, drink a Ricard, and wait for the weather to clear. He would *not* go home. He couldn't face all that again. The rain fell hard and fast, so he donned his wide-brimmed hat. Heaving his gear up the path, the rain was unrelenting, flecking and splashing his glasses. He chose not to stop and wipe them, as he was almost at the car. A movement caught his eye and he saw the artist coming up the fork in the path. She was soaked, her shirt clinging to her like tissue paper. Her hair fell limply around her face, and she still carried her painting materials.

He shouted and beckoned to her. "This way! My car's just here. Let's get dry."

She hurried towards him, no coat, wet through. God knows what she would think of his ancient Volvo. But it would give him a close-up of that shirt.

"*Merde!*" She threw up her hands in a gesture of resignation as she placed the dripping sketch pad in the boot. There would be little worth saving in there, it was sodden.

He dumped his bag in the back seat and fishing gear in the boot, dragging off his jacket and retrieving the towels. She sheltered underneath the Volvo's hatch door, until he gestured for her to get into the passenger seat. She did so, placing her heavy bag in the foot well. He handed her a towel and as she patted the fabric to her face, he saw her small breasts press together. The blouse was totally transparent, and the bra she wore did not disguise her dark nipples. He shifted in his seat and after a brief rub of his hair, dropped his towel into his lap. She released her hairclip and patted herself dry, before arranging her towel around her shoulders.

"I'm sorry, already I made a mess of your car."

"Please, don't worry about it. This is what I call my 'fishing car'. Over twenty years old and purely functional. I keep it in France, because I can't bear to get rid of it. However, it does have a decent heater." He switched on the ignition, and twisted the dial. While his head was still fuzzy, his mood had improved no end.

"Oh! I can feel it already. Mmm, that's wonderful."

He swallowed, conscious of something he hadn't felt for some time. Desire, and opportunity. God, that accent was sexy.

"Now that we warm our outsides, I think we should do the same for our insides." She gave him a mischievous look from under her brows and reaching into her bag, pulled out a little hip flask.

"Irish whiskey. For emergencies like this."

She unscrewed the cap and poured a tiny shot. His eyes blinked, slowly. If he drank anything now, he'd fall asleep in seconds. He needed to keep his concentration.

"That's a clever idea. But I'm afraid I can't join you. Driving, you see. I'd better stick to tea." He reached behind him for his picnic bag, and his flask. Her eyes seemed to darken as he poured the steaming liquid. Surely she was not taking his rejection personally?

"OK, you know best." She raised the tiny cup. "Cheers! And thank you for rescuing me."

"Cheers. It was my pleasure."

She sipped and closed her eyes momentarily as she swallowed. He took a gulp of tea. Still hot, and sweet. Restorative.

"Did you land a good catch today?" she asked, her face open and pure as a daisy.

"Today was not a lucky day for me. I haven't hooked a single thing."

She gazed out at the lessening rain. "Well, you haven't hooked any fish." Facing forward, he couldn't confirm if that statement meant what he hoped. He drained his tea and agreed.

"As you say, a lucky day for the fish."

She turned to him, her pupils wide. She did not smile. The depth of her gaze embarrassed him.

"And you? Was your day more successful?" he asked, disliking the sound of his flat British voice.

"My day is going very well. Not the way I had imagined, but if one is prepared to be flexible, one can still achieve one's objectives." Her voice had dropped and even a gauche old fool like himself could see this woman had an agenda. It was hard enough to manage a flirtation after years of inactivity, without the fact that his mind seemed to be a complete muddle. She leant towards him and looked deeply into his eyes.

"Are you feeling well? You look sick."

She rested a cool, damp hand on his brow and his eyes closed. It was damned rude of him, but he didn't seem to be able to stop himself. She stretched across him and put his seatbelt on. That was kind of her. Feeling her presence over him, he forced his eyes open to apologise. She nodded.

"The best thing for you would be some more tea."

She picked up the cup and tilted the flask towards her. There was a price tag on the bottom. She placed it between her knees, and offered him the cup. Something bothered him. He swallowed obediently until it was finished, and she replaced the cup. The price tag. That was not possible. She stroked his forehead, and his lids fell. He'd had that flask for years. It was a little battered and scratched, and had been washed thousands of times. Someone turned the car off. The sound of rain on the roof had stopped. He'd rest his eyes for a few minutes and then drive back to the gîte. No arguments, just upstairs for a nap. And they could get chicken breasts out of the freezer. The Artist would have to wait. He felt a breeze. Doors slammed and he wondered where the fish were. Maybe they'd gone home. They said they might, if he carried on ignoring their feelings. That was not his flask. So why was she in his bag? The car started up again. Lovely breasts. He had to think, it was important. What was her name? God, he hoped she could drive, because he was in no fit state … warm, comfortable and so incredibly tired. Windows down, windows up. Who was doing that? Very nice. Chicken windows for dinner. Truth was, he was sick and tired of fish.

Chapter 13

Zürich 2012

The locker room in the Zürich Main Station was situated on the mezzanine level, which was huge, busy and perfect for the purpose. A figure left the escalator, took a key from a pocket and inserted it into locker 4149. The Jiffy bag was there, as promised, containing a phone. Seven minutes passed before it rang. The figure began walking, alert for eavesdroppers.

"Hello?"

The voice at the other end dispensed with pleasantries. *"Do you need anything else from me?"*

"No, everything's covered. All I need to decide is when. Circumstances should be perfect in the next two to three weeks."

"Complete this one as soon as possible. Because I have something else I want you to do."

The figure stopped. "Just a minute. You chose this one. And I want to hit the drugs trade next time. I already have a shortlist."

The voice did not reply.

"Not only that, but I don't want to do another short notice thing again. It's dangerous to be under-prepared. For all of us."

"You won't be under-prepared. I've already got plenty of background. I'll do the research now and you take care of the implementation. You don't have to travel far, either. It's right here."

"In Switzerland?"

"In Zürich."

The figure began pacing along the line of lockers. "I'm not sure. We've been far too close to home recently. The risks are beginning to ..."

"Yes. Which brings me to our second point. Once these two are complete, we'll stop."

"Stop? What do you mean? For how long?"

"For good. You can go back to Mozambique or whichever desperate region needs you most, and I will find myself another hobby."

"No. We can't stop now. There's so much left to do. What about my list?"

"There are other ways of administering punishment to those on your list. Look, it couldn't last forever and the risks now outweigh the satisfaction. We've reached the end of the line. I want to deal with these last two cases, that's all."

The pause lasted for over a minute as the figure stared, unseeing, at the people borne upwards by the escalators.

"Who is the second one? Someone connected to the airline management?"

"No, not the airline. A different branch of corrupt industry. The police. This is a detective. They're investigating some unusual suicides and think they've found a link."

"The police? But surely if they already think there might be a connection, acting against them would be almost ..."

"... suicidal?" The voice laughed, apparently amused. "It would be if I didn't have our alibis all prepared. Plus, if you do this right, it will be impossible to prove it wasn't self-inflicted."

"How does a police detective fit with what we're trying to do? Or is this just a case of self-preservation?"

"The role of the police is to fight crime and punish criminals. Not judge and condemn those who are doing good works while corruption and greed remain above the law. It will be our final statement."

"But ..."

"But what?"

"Nothing. Which way round do you want it done?"

"The lawyer goes first. Then immediately afterwards, the police detective ends it all, unable to bear the public humiliation and failure. It's practically poetic. I've already started the ball rolling."

The figure leant over the barrier and gazed down on the shoppers below. "How do you want it done?"

"I haven't made up my mind yet. Let me think about that. It must *definitely be spectacular. It's our swansong, after all. But I've found enough detail for you to start work and left it in the usual place. The other material you need will be sent to your home address, under the guise of a perfume sample. Keep your eyes open for a silver envelope advertising Homme Fatale."*

"Right. I'll get started."

"Good luck. And ... this really must be the last time."

The figure didn't respond.

"I'm serious."

"I know."

Ending the call, the figure placed the phone in the Jiffy bag and went in search of a post-box to send it back.

Chapter 14

Zürich 2012

Reception at Zeughausstrasse Police Station was ridiculously busy for ten to eight in the morning. Beatrice stood in the open doorway, her route blocked by a shifting crowd of people carrying microphones and cameras.

A young man spotted her and addressed her in English.

"Are you Detective Stubbs, from London, working on the serial killer case?"

Attention switched to her and a sudden panic surged as the questions began.

"Sorry, no comment."

"*Entschuldigen Sie, bitte*! Excuse me! Frau Stubbs, this way." Xavier cleared a path through the group of journalists. She put her head down and bulldozed her way forward, a little surprised at the lack of resistance as she squeezed past. They continued to ask questions, she continued to say, 'No comment', but they didn't thrust their equipment in her face or block her path, even stepping back to give her room. It wouldn't happen like that in London.

She reached Xavier, who appeared redder than normal, but rapidly swiped them both through the security doors.

"How do they know?" she asked.

"Front page of the *Neue Zürcher Zeitung*. The phones are ringing all the time and Kälin's not happy."

"For once, I feel the same way."

Everyone in the workroom seemed to be talking at once. Xavier immediately joined in. Beatrice stashed her bag in her office, collected a cup of water and stood at the briefing table, listening. She hoped her actions would convey the message she wasn't harassed. It also gave her chance to get her breath back. The room gradually quietened and Kälin spoke.

"We have a leak, Frau Stubbs."

The noise began again and Beatrice waited for some order before offering her opinion.

"Do we? Is that the only way the information could get out there? I haven't read the article, but I'd like to be sure before jumping to conclusions."

Sabine managed to make her voice heard over the wealth of opinions. "I've read it, Beatrice. And I believe Herr Kälin is right. The amount of detail in the report – the names of the men, the DNA connection, the fact that you're leading the investigation, the names of most of the team, except Conceição and me, although it mentions psychological profiling – this seems like an inside job. And to be honest, the article makes us look like a bunch of idiots."

Beatrice considered. Why would any member of her team leak confidential information? The potential damage could be fatal, stalling the investigation in its tracks, not to mention warning their target. Why would anyone in this room scupper the case? Her eyes rested on Kälin, who took it as his cue to speak.

"The most likely explanation is that this is not deliberate. Someone here has been talking to the wrong person. Think back over the past two weeks. Who have you talked to about this case? Did you share details with anyone? Journalists are experts at befriending people they think have a story. Think carefully."

Puzzled faces considered, eyes roamed the room and silence settled like dust. But the only result was a series of shaking heads. Beatrice examined her own conduct. She never shared details with anyone she didn't wholly trust and generally kept her profession quiet. Of course, she always discussed latest developments with Matthew, but he was as likely to blab to the Swiss press as he was to abseil through the window.

Kälin lifted his brows. "Frau Stubbs, I suggest you and I prepare a press statement for later this morning. The rest of you, I recommend you say nothing to anyone, not even to your families. Then, perhaps, we can work this investigation in peace."

"Herr Kälin?" Chris spoke. "It could have been you."

Kälin's head joined all the others swivelling to stare at Chris.

"I don't mean you spilled to some bloke in the pub. But you did give a lot of information to Antonella D'Arcy, about Beatrice leading the team, about using a profiler and she already knew the names of the victims from your first interview."

No one spoke.

Kälin looked out of the window, his frown dark. "That is possible. D'Arcy had enough information to trigger a news story and the journalists could dig up the rest. It would work in her interests to sabotage our investigation and to direct attention away from D'Arcy Roth, no matter whether she is involved or not. And she would enjoy making us look stupid. It's possible the fault was mine, sharing too much with a suspect. I apologise, everyone. I should also remember to keep my mouth shut."

In the shocked speechlessness that followed, Beatrice decided something was definitely up. Kälin never accepted criticism, never admitted a mistake and certainly never apologised. He was right. If this investigation appeared clumsy and ineffective, it would certainly suit Antonella D'Arcy. But she wasn't the only one.

The press briefing was short and bland, as they accepted no questions. Beatrice found it relatively painless. Unlike London, not only were the press polite, but senior police officers weren't breathing down her neck. She decided to get a sandwich and go for a walk over lunch, to allow herself some thinking time. The leak was one issue, but her concerns regarding Kälin quite another. Or was it? Both boiled down to the same thing – could she trust her team? Up until now, she'd had no doubts. Surely even Kälin wouldn't cut off his nose to spite this case? On her return to the office, her mind was no clearer and her thoughts muddled. The news she received from the receptionist made things worse.

"Frau Stubbs? You have some visitors. Herr Fisher from Lyon and Herr Hamilton from London wait in your office."

Hell's bells. Not only an Interpol executive, but Scotland Yard yanking her choke chain. Just when the day was going so well.

Rounding the corner to her office, she came face to face with Hamilton's familiar craggy features. He jerked his head, unsmiling.

"Stubbs."

She jerked hers back. "Sir." She looked past him to Fisher.

"Beatrice! Terrific to see you again. Hope we haven't put you out too much, dropping in like this? Only we thought we'd pop by and get up to speed. See if you needed anything."

Fisher shook her hand with enthusiasm before gesturing to a chair. Interesting. Her office, her desk, her chair, and yet he invited her to sit. "Have you had lunch yet? We could take you out and treat you to something stodgy with cheese."

Absolutely charming man; solicitous, informative and helpful. She could not fault Fisher's behaviour. Therefore she really ought to consider why she found him so utterly odious. He laughed at his own brand of xenophobic humour and Beatrice stretched her lips to be polite. His mud-brown hair was slicked back with gel, so that each individual tooth of the comb had left its mark. Something about him rubbed her up the wrong way; the high forehead, sharp nose and peculiarly British mouth, while his eyes had all the colour and animation of a dishcloth. It looked as if he was having a similar effect on Hamilton.

"Good afternoon, gentlemen. I had no idea we were due a visit from Head Office. Perhaps I missed the email. Forgive me if I am a little unprepared. I've already eaten, thank you, but I can arrange some tea."

"Have you? Gosh, that's early. Very well, tea must suffice. And it's not exactly a visit from HQ, which is why we didn't email. It's just that two weeks into the project, we thought it might be time to see if we can offer any further support. Particularly now the media have got wind of this."

"How kind. To be truthful, I cannot think of anything further Interpol could offer, unless it were another pair of hands. We're at the dull, workaday stage, just making painstaking enquiries."

"Oh, I think any more hands on deck would raise a few questions in Lyon. There are already six full-time experts provided, not to mention a range of professionals at your disposal. It's rather an expensive exercise, Beatrice. And given the calibre of personnel you have, we're wondering when you might be likely to progress beyond enquiries."

"I'd be happy to update you, Mr Fisher. But I'd quite like a cup of tea while I do so." She picked up the phone, trying not to grind her teeth. "Frau Stettler? This is Frau Stubbs. Would you mind bringing three black teas? And milk and sugar? Thank you." Replacing the receiver, she turned to the immaculately dressed irritant and his brooding counterpart.

"I have, in point of fact, emailed Lyon on a regular basis, just so that you know what we're doing."

"Yes. We all read your updates, Beatrice. However, there is a growing concern in respect of progress. If I can summarise, you have revisited some of the scenes, checked the DNA and produced what we call a Picture of a Serial Killer." His laughter reminded Beatrice of someone clearing their nose.

Portrait, not picture, you Philistine. She dragged the corners of her mouth upwards.

A knock at the door heralded tea and Frau Stettler placed the tray on the desk with a polite, "Good afternoon, together".

Fisher beamed. "Thank you so much. Oh, and biscuits as well? We don't get this kind of service in Lyon. Thank you very much indeed and have a good day."

Nice to the point of patronising to staff, observed Beatrice. Well-mannered, popular, and thoroughly unbearable.

"Let me recap," Beatrice began, as she distributed tea. "My brief, as I understand it, is to ascertain whether we have a case to investigate. I and my team have done exactly that. We have double-checked the DNA samples for accurate gathering. We have revisited the scenes of each 'incident', to see if there is any information to be gleaned. We have cross-checked for connections between the deceased and Sabine Tikkenen has put forward an astute profile of the man who may be responsible. There is a case. And we are taking the first steps in trying to resolve it."

"Mmm, yes. Good work. The concern, Beatrice, is not how hard you are working. I'm sure you're all beavering away. It is just we had hoped to see some concrete results by now. Just thought we'd check if we've got the balance right in terms of personnel."

Beatrice decoded and bristled. "By which you mean you want to change some members of my team?" She began to feel some sympathy for Kälin.

"Oh, good gracious! I couldn't possibly say, not at this phase of the proceedings. The point is merely that we'd like to be certain that the mix is working. Are you with me?"

"Personnel modifications at this stage would be counter-productive. The case covers four different countries, and stretches back five years. We have taken some time to get up to speed, but now we're working on several leads simultaneously. I am confident of making a breakthrough in the next month."

Fisher nodded, his angled head and plastic expression all designed to convey understanding. Hamilton glared out of the window as if displeased with the scenery.

"No doubt that it's complex, Beatrice. Bigger than we initially thought, in fact. That's why we want to check that we have tasked the appropriate people. One month. That *is* a concern. You really think it could take another month to bring this to heel?"

"I have no idea what that expression is supposed to mean. But to clarify, I said I expected to be able to show significant progress within the next four weeks."

"The powers-that-be would like to see something a touch earlier. Let's say that in a fortnight's time, we re-evaluate this project in the light of advancements made between now and then. How does that sound?"

Like management bullshit.

"In that case, Mr Fisher, I will deliver a full report to the General Secretariat by next Friday, with a copy to London. I am sure you appreciate investigating such a case does involve making diligent enquiries that would apply to any normal police procedure. We can only start running with the ball when we are convinced we have possession."

He gave his laugh once more.

"Rugby analogies, Beatrice? Had you down for more of a cricket widow. No, no one is accusing you of running with the ball. Particularly not at the pace you are progressing. You feel able to deliver a viability report by the end of next week? That will go down very well in Lyon. We shall look forward to reading it. Now, I really should meet the team, I think. Would you be so kind as to make the introductions? Thanks for the tea, it was jolly good, I have to say. And perhaps later this afternoon we might have a little chat about how the press got hold of such sensitive information. Rather awkward, that. Shall we?"

Hamilton cleared his throat. "While you explore, Fisher, I'll stay here. Want a word with Stubbs when she gets back."

Beatrice bit back a groan and opened her palm towards the doorway.

Fisher leapt to his feet, bestowing a full beam on her as he led the way out of the office. His odd behaviour reminded her of that magician fellow, David Whatzisname, who kept locking himself in peculiar places. She watched him depart, slick and sickly as molasses, discomfited by the fact that this bug-eyed buffoon probably knew more about her than most of her friends.

The main room was empty, but for one gingery head bent over a keyboard. Beatrice made the introductions.

"Xavier? Can I introduce our visitor from Interpol? Herr Racine, Mr Fisher."

Xavier scrambled to his feet as Fisher held out his hand.

"Hello Herr Racine. Heard lots of good things about you. Just a friendly visit to see if we can help at all. Are you all alone today?"

"Pleasure to meet you, Mr Fisher." He pumped Fisher's hand with enthusiasm. "At the moment, yes. Sabine is at the University Hospital and Chris and Conceição are exploring Langstrasse. Herr Kälin is in his own office."

"Ah, good. I hoped to meet Herr Kälin at some stage. Langstrasse? Now would I be mistaken in thinking that's Zürich's red-light district?" asked Fisher, with disingenuity.

Xavier nodded and pointed to the pin board. "Yes, it is. It's also the 'alternative' quarter, where we might contact anti-capitalists, political activists and so on. Sabine's profile shows that our killer could have a left-wing agitation agenda. So Beatrice sent them to investigate."

"Really?" Fisher gave a fake smile and slow nod, as if Xavier were a small child enthusing about Lego. "I have to say, it's so cosy the way you call your senior officer by her Christian name."

Beatrice took over. "Each team finds an appropriate way of operating, as you know. And Xavier's point is that we're trying to find out as much as we can about militant left-wing ..."

"Aaa-chi!" Xavier released an explosive sneeze, turning his head away and hitting his forehead against the felt board as he did so.

"Bless you!" offered Beatrice, finishing her explanation while leading Fisher away.

As the workroom door closed behind them, Fisher pulled down the corners of his mouth in sympathy.

"Is he the best Swiss police could do? Looks like a work experience boy."

A flash of petty temper provoked Beatrice but she kept her mouth shut, instead indicating the stairwell.

"So Mr Fisher, as you can see, most of the team are out on fieldwork. But you mentioned wanting to meet Herr Kälin. You'll find his office on the first floor, second door on the right. You might want to ask him for his view on the press leak. I must get back, my superior awaits. Lovely seeing you."

She strode back to her cubicle with an odd mixture of infuriation and curiosity. *Oh, to be a fly on the wall in that room.*

Hamilton stood at the window, arms folded, evidently still dissatisfied with the view.

"More tea, sir?"

"Stubbs, a frank answer, if you will. Exactly how much progress have you made?"

Beatrice sat in the 'visitor's chair'. Once again, Hamilton used his status to minimise hers.

"In my view, a great deal. I have faith in this team; we work well together. Now we're sifting evidence, tooth-combing, narrowing the net and building a solid case to prove this was a systematic series of pre-meditated murders."

Hamilton flared his nostrils and raised his eyes to the ceiling, affording Beatrice an unimpeded perspective up his nose.

"So there is a bloody case, after all?"

Beatrice grew irritable. "Yes sir, there is. You would have preferred us to chase our tails?"

With a glare at her and at the door, Hamilton picked up his briefcase.

"Come along, Stubbs. Show me the city and let's talk some sense."

Instinct guided Beatrice away from the shopping areas in the direction of Stockerstrasse; a street of merchant banks, insurance companies, art galleries and the Swiss Stock Exchange. The calm tone and sober environment worked its charm on Hamilton, his posture relaxing to merely stiff.

Taking a left towards the river tributary, they crossed the little pedestrian bridge of Bärenbrüggli. Office workers sat on benches beside the water, eating sandwiches, feeding swans and chatting in Swiss German. Hamilton stopped, peering over at the water rushing silently beneath.

"Fact is, Stubbs, they don't think you're up to it. The only personnel change they want to make is you. Seems you're not Interpol material."

A surge of heat inflamed her entire head, burning the tips of her ears and scalding her scalp. Grateful that Hamilton's focus remained on water birds, she thought his comment through.

"Can I ask why now, sir? Actually, I think I can answer that for myself. When it was a political exercise to tick paper boxes for European collaboration, any old fool would do. Now it appears a series of politically motivated murders exist, they want someone ... well, someone else."

The ducks gave up on them and bobbed back to the banks, where crumbs were more plentiful.

"Look here, Stubbs. Interpol asked for an experienced detective to lead an international investigation, which is precisely what I provided. Had I known this might degenerate into a facile game of draughts with greasy pole-climbers such as Fisher, I may just have kept out of the whole festering shebang. I've loaned them one of the best in my entire force and if they don't appreciate that, they can go service themselves."

Warmth crept over Beatrice again in recognition of Hamilton's bluff loyalty.

"Why drag you here in person, sir? To take me home on a lead? To break the news to me yourself?"

He exhaled sharply. "Buggered if I know. As yet, no news to break. You've got another two weeks, Stubbs. So for all our sakes, pull your bloody finger out."

At the end of a thoroughly disheartening day, Beatrice headed back to her apartment. As always, she made a detour to Talacker and *Big Ben*, the English tea shop. In addition to teas, cakes and groceries, they sold a range of British newspapers and magazines. It had become Beatrice's daily treat to stop in, drink a pot of Earl Grey and read *The Times*. And it seemed churlish not to have a hot buttered crumpet, or a scone with jam and cream at the same time. The sustenance was welcome, but her real attraction to the place was provided by Ken.

"Wotcha, Beatrice! Ooh, dear, don't like the look of your boat. Bad day? Let's get you a cuppa."

Ken. Born in Yugoslavia and carted off to London at the age of five, he spent his formative years in the East End. The family relocated again, leaving Britain when Ken was just shy of eighteen and he had lived the intervening forty plus years in Switzerland. His career: army officer, fitness instructor, private investigator and security guard proved him to be a fully paid-up member of Swiss society. But he had made a clear choice of identity. His heart remained in 1960s' London, a place that no longer existed. His cherished memories were of red Routemasters, mini-skirts and Minis, bobbies in Dixon of Dock Green helmets, and a feeling of being in the right place at the right time. He'd never been back.

Beatrice hoped for his own sake that he never would. She sat at a rear table, grateful for the lack of clientele.

"One pot of Earl Grey, pot warmed, of course. Noemi's made a Victoria Sponge, if you're peckish, or there's some McVitie's Jamaica Ginger Cake, very moist."

"I won't today, thanks Ken. But I will take a copy of *The Times*."

"Up to you." He reached for the paper and looked at her. "Bad day at the office, dear?"

"Not good," she admitted.

"Right, I'll leave you in peace, but when you're ready, I'm having awful bother with 17 down."

She smiled, their routine all the more precious for the illusion of familiarity it provoked. Ken collected some cups and stopped to chat to the other customers, all of whom sat outside, enjoying the early spring sunshine. His Cockney tones drifted back to her as she tried to focus on the paper. *Vote of no confidence likely for new Treasury Minister.* She poured the tea and pushed away the vision of Jamaica Ginger Cake, very moist. The viability report. If they got no further in the next fortnight, in all likelihood, she'd be sent home. They'd bring in someone younger, more dynamic to lead the investigation and she would have failed in her first worthwhile job in almost two years.

What a stupid, unprofessional train of thought. This situation was not about her. She was leading this investigation the best way she knew how. It was far from spectacular, but it was thorough. A method that had always worked for her before now. She would spend the weekend going over the whole case again, just to be sure she had overlooked nothing. And anyway, why would she not want to be sent home? Back to Shoreditch, to Scotland Yard, to Matthew. She'd recently considered running away for a weekend. And now?

If she were honest, she had to make a good job of this. She wouldn't get another chance. Hamilton had taken a gamble on her, and if she failed, she would be letting him down. This circular misery wouldn't help; she couldn't allow herself one of the troughs. Not now.

A youngish blonde with Jackie O sunglasses settled herself two tables away, ordered tea and opened a copy of Tatler. Her clothes, her hair or maybe her teeth led Beatrice to assume she was American. It was a local species she recognised, flitting in and out of designer shops, occupying café tables, promenading up and down Bahnhof-strasse. How did they always manage to look so groomed? It would take her all day to present such a polished facade. She watched idly as Ken pottered behind the counter, humming something which sounded ominously like *Jerusalem*.

This situation was very much about her. Was she seriously up to this? Confidence was key, but if it was not backed up by abil-ity, she was deceiving her highly professional team, and therefore a hindrance to their success. Unless one of them was deliberately hindering this investigation. The newspaper story could have been an attempt to destabilise her.

"Any joy?" Ken called over, as he laid the tables for dinner.

"Haven't looked yet, sorry. I was miles away." She turned the pages until she found the crossword. "Which one was it again?"

"17 down. *A sign post victory proves me right*. What you reckon?"

Beatrice read the clue but her mind drifted.

"Have you got an event tonight, Ken?"

"S'right. Skool Dinners. Bunch of geezers from one of the banks come down, eat sausage and mash with boiled cabbage, spotted dick for afters, drink a good hundredweight of Chablis and chuck bread rolls about. Messy, but we make a fortune."

"I feel for your poor waiting staff."

"You want to see 'em. We use the girls what work the *Oktoberfest*. Mess with one of them, they'll break your arm. I keep out of it, get down the Oscar Wilde for a pint till it's all over. You off already?"

"No rest for the wicked. How much do I owe you?"

"Call it fifteen. No luck with 17 down, then?"

She counted three coins. "'Fraid not. My brain is elsewhere today."

The American's blonde head rose from the magazine. "Vindica-tion?"

Beatrice and Ken turned to her.

"A *sign post victory proves me right*. Vindication. Does it fit?"

Beatrice checked. "It does. Perfectly. Thank you."

The woman smiled and returned her attention to glossy photographs.

Ken picked up the paper, filled in the letters in and gave a satisfied sigh. "God bless you both, ladies."

Beatrice said her goodbyes and made her way back to her apartment.

Two weeks to make some kind of breakthrough. You can't even grow cress that fast.

Chapter 15

St Germain du Bois 2012

Hearing Conceição speak French was such a turn-on. Her throaty pitch seemed designed for the musical cadences of the language and several sounds required her to purse her lips. Chris couldn't concentrate. The manager of the carp lakes seemed equally hypnotised and his desperation was obvious as he scrabbled to think of something helpful to say. But the facts were that Edwards paid his fees, bought some bait, and departed. The manager heard no more until the police arrived to inform him that a body had been found at Etang Gallet. With some eagerness, he volunteered to show them the spot. Conceição expressed their thanks and politely but firmly refused the man's offer.

As they returned to the car, Chris looked at her sideways. "Did I understand that right? You told him we'd seen the site."

She put the car into gear and drove off, with a small wave at the manager. "Yes. I didn't want him there while we look around. It will interfere with my thinking."

"You could have told him that."

"Sometimes a little white lie spares someone's feelings. Do you want to eat first, or shall we go to the lake now?"

"Let's do the lake. And hope we don't bump into the manager."

Parking on the road, they followed the photocopied map, walking up the track to where the police had discovered the Volvo.

Chris stopped. "Here. Good location. Can't be seen from the road or the lake and few people would pass this way."

"And even if you did pass, you would assume the person was sleeping. He could have been here a lot longer if his wife had not raised the alarm."

"The killer must have drugged him before fixing up the exhaust. How did he do that?"

Conceição flicked over a page. "The report says there was a full flask of tea in Edwards's bag. It hadn't been touched. How do you get a total stranger to ingest debilitating drugs?"

Chris inclined his head. "Assuming the guy was a total stranger to Edwards. As I said, I think this individual was known to the dead men."

They walked down to the swim and stared out at the lake. Olive-coloured water reflected the tree tops opposite and steady ripples oscillated across the surface. While Chris had no interest in fishing, he could see the appeal of sitting here, at peace.

Conceição thought aloud. "He came here to spend the day fishing. It was raining. Did he even get out of the car? He was still wearing his seatbelt."

"Perhaps he stopped for lunch and someone slipped him something then. Talking of lunch, we're not going to find much here. Want to try that restaurant on the square?"

St Germain du Bois was quiet, giving Chris the strange feeling that everyone was somewhere else. They parked on the market square and entered the restaurant. The sun was warm enough for them to sit on the terrace, and enjoy the view of the tree-lined main street. After ordering, Conceição asked to speak to the owner. The square remained empty, dominated by the shadow of the church, until a man walked past with a small dog, which stopped every ten paces to urinate against a tree. Its owner seemed glad of the frequent stops.

"Geraldine Lefèvre. You wanted a word?"

The woman's English was perfect and unaccented. She wore a white kitchen coat over jeans. Her silvery blonde hair was held back in a clip, and her expression suggested curiosity, revealing their interruption was a break from routine. The upside was they could speak to her in English, giving Chris a better chance of understanding. The downside? He wouldn't see Conceição do her pout *à la française*. He withdrew his ID.

"Yes please, Ms Lefèvre. Would you like a seat? We won't take long. My name is Chris Keese of Europol, and this is my colleague, Conceição Pereira da Silva of Interpol. We're just doing a routine follow-up of the death of Brian Edwards, who was found near here in 2010. Do you recall the event?"

"I certainly do. I knew Brian and Sheila vaguely, through the expat network. They'd been coming here for over a decade. To St Germain, I mean. And they generally ate here at least once or twice each holiday. When he did away with himself, I was shocked. Firstly, I had no idea he was the boss of that water-poisoning company. Secondly, how could he go and leave his wife and kids like that? A disgusting way to behave."

"During that particular holiday, did you see them at all?" asked Conceição.

"No. They kept their heads down. A wise decision after all the fuss in the papers. As far as I know, they avoided all their usual haunts. Natalie, who runs the hotel here, saw them in the pizzeria in Bletterans. Over there, no one would know who they were, you see. And I once I saw him at the café on the Louhans road. But he wasn't with his wife." She dropped her chin and gave them a meaningful look.

Chris picked up his cue. "Did you recognise the person he was with?"

"No. A tourist, I think. Young, blonde, pretty. I must say, Brian Edwards's true colours surprised us all. He was not the man he seemed."

"Thank you, Ms Lefèvre. You've been most helpful. Sorry to have dragged you away from work," Chris smiled.

"Oh, I was glad of the break. End of the session now, so all that's left is the washing-up. What did you order?"

"*Poulet de Bresse*. The regional speciality."

"Not just the region's, it's mine too. Hope you enjoy it. Good luck with your follow-up. All the best."

Despite finding nothing of interest in Burgundy, Chris had enjoyed his day. Even the journey provided some attractive scenery. He stretched out his legs and looked at his companion. Conceição drove along the A36 at exactly three kilometres over the speed limit. Her gaze focused on the road, while he admired her profile, knowing she was aware of it.

"What?" she demanded, eventually.

"Just wondering what you're doing tonight."

"You are unlikely to find out by studying my right ear. I arranged to have a drink with Sabine if we get back early enough."

"What's early enough? We won't be back in Zürich till about eight. Why don't you have girls' night tomorrow, then you and I can stop for dinner somewhere en route?"

She remained silent.

"It would be the sensible thing to do. You've been driving for two hours," he added.

"Somewhere en route? Where?"

"I'm sure we can find a charming little bistro somewhere near the border. What do you think?"

"Yeah, OK. I could do with a break. Although I'm not that hungry," she added.

He grinned and picked up his phone. "I'll find a nice romantic little salad bar, then."

"It doesn't need to be romantic. This is not a date." She took her eyes from the road to give him a stern look.

"Course not," he agreed, still grinning.

Not perfect. A shabby roadside Imbiss, for a cervelat and a beer. But he made her laugh, offered to drive, encouraged her to have another drink and slipped in some compliments. Everything was going according to plan as they returned to the car, discussing theories on contract killers and which countries made the best sausages.

He took the wheel and she chose the music. A little more light flirtation and laughter as they approached the city and Chris's confidence grew. He needed to make a plan. He wouldn't ask her to come back to his place, not tonight. But he would plant a seed.

Make it look as if he was wrestling with himself, forcing himself to leave her alone. That always rang two bells with women. His passion for her and his noble nature. Just a polite, but longing kiss before saying goodnight. Pretty much guaranteed she'd be in his bed by the weekend.

So she surprised him outside her apartment, by inviting him in. He accepted, but went over his plans again while she fetched beers from the kitchen. OK, he definitely had to refuse sex. Otherwise the noble nature bit goes to shit. The difficulty being, how far to go? He'd play the 'we can't, but I want to, no, it's so unprofessional, you drive me crazy, I'd better leave,' card, with a long, lingering, more-where-that-came-from kiss at the door.

She came back, handed him a beer and flopped into the armchair opposite. Not beside him on the sofa. Was she making a point?

"So what's your story, Chris? Got a girl pining for you beside a canal somewhere? *Prost!*"

He laughed and raised the bottle. "*Prost!* No, no one's pining for me. I'm getting to the stage where I'd like a regular relationship, but in this job? You know what it's like."

Conceição acknowledged the problem with a tilt of her head. "Yeah. Difficult. But not impossible. I find it easier to date people in the same line of work. Fewer explanations."

That was a come-on. All evening, little candles lit up as they chatted, laughed and found common ground. But this was a colossal flare, lighting up the room.

Tread carefully and you could be under the sheets in less than five minutes. Noble nature has a time and a place.

He sipped some beer. "Sure. Perfect solution. If you can find someone in your line of work who makes you laugh, who's intelligent, who's beautiful, who makes you ..."

The shrill blast of the telephone made Chris clench his fist as Conceição reached across for the handset.

"Hello?" Her forehead wrinkled in concern. "Sabine, are you OK? What's wrong?"

Chris faked an intensely concerned expression. Intensely concerned wasn't too far from pretty pissed-off so it was no effort.

"Of course you can. Chris is here, but he's just leaving. Come over. You shouldn't be alone if you're feeling upset. No, Sabine, it's fine. We were just having a beer! Sabine, listen ..."

She shook her head at Chris and shrugged an apology.

He picked up his laptop case. "Don't worry. I'll go. See you tomorrow."

She nodded, distracted, but waggled her fingers to say good bye. He blew a silent kiss as he left the room. She smiled.

OK. That would have to do.

As he started the car, he glanced back at the window. He could see her silhouette. He waved but she was shaking her head.

Chapter 16

Zürich 2012

The worst thing about getting up at 06.30 and leaving the apartment at 07.00 was missing the *Today Programme* with John Humphrys. That one-hour time difference could really upset a person's routine. Beatrice ate her porridge sprinkled with raspberries and scowled at the BBC website. She could listen to the recorded version later, of course, but cold news was as appetising as cold porridge. She snorted and closed down the machine. Her temper had not improved since her shower. Another restless night, caused by the prospect of a fractious day ahead.

Interpol's blunt, unflattering assessment of their progress two days ago had put the whole team out of sorts. Yesterday, Sabine sulked. Xavier worked at double speed and consequently achieved about half his usual output. And Kälin disappeared completely. Not in his office, not answering his mobile, just gone. Chris and Conceição escaped the atmosphere, driving to Burgundy to visit the scene of Edwards' death. Two weeks, and already the General Secretariat were stamping their feet. Journalists popped up everywhere they went, demanding results on behalf of the public. On top of everything, the Swiss government suddenly chose to question the validity of having a specialised Federal Task Force to deal with international crime. Beatrice had every expectation of being home by the end of May. It seemed the whole exercise had been a waste of time and resources.

She packed her computer, brushed her teeth and set off for the office in a foul mood.

The walk to Zeughausstrasse cheered her somewhat. Joggers along the river greeted her with a friendly *Grüezi*, she stopped to pat a St Bernard, and the daffodils and irises on the verges raised their heads to the sun. As she trudged up the stairs of the police building, Beatrice realised she was not gasping for breath for a change. Usually, she had to take a moment to regain her wind before entering the investigation room. A pleasant notion crossed her mind. Could she be getting fitter? Her smile dissolved as she heard angry voices behind the door. She grabbed the handle with a sinking feeling.

The guilty silence restored Beatrice's foul mood. Xavier, Conceição, Sabine and Chris stood in a confrontational circle. She dumped her bag on the nearest desk and resisted the temptation to fold her arms.

Sabine gestured to Chris and Conceição. "It seems that these two have other priorities than investigating this case. They spend the day in France and come back with nothing apart from a big smile. Now he thinks there's nothing to investigate! Am I wasting my time here?"

Chris gave an exasperated sigh. "Beatrice, I didn't say there was nothing to investigate. What I said was …"

"That my theory …"

"That your theory is not the only one! If you will stop shrieking for one minute, we can clear this up."

Sabine's face flushed raspberry-red. "I am not shrieking. I am trying to make myself heard. Why am I the only one who can see what's going on here? Xavier has spent days researching similar kinds of crime. I have explored hospital and pharmacy records for links. And you two, you two proceed with your theory that this is a professional hit man that we'll never catch. Ask yourself why this hit man leaves his DNA behind, if he's so professional. But you're clearly far too busy with each other to think this through."

Beatrice intervened. "Sabine, that is enough. Can you all please take a seat, and we can discuss this civilly. Now, I am aware that the news we received from Lyon and London was not good. But as professionals, that should not distract us from the job we are trying to do. I think it might be a good time to reassess our progress, or lack of, and consider altering our approach."

Xavier seemed uncomfortable, looking towards the door. "Beatrice, if we are thinking of changing our strategy, should we wait for Herr Kälin?"

"No Xavier, I don't see that as necessary. Herr Kälin, as he often reminds us, is a consultant to the team, not a part of it. I decide how we operate. Chris. You wanted to make a point."

"Yes, I did. The trip to France was pretty fruitless. It was two years ago, and most people have forgotten about it. The police records we already have, the locals recall seeing Edwards fishing, and that's about it. I'm not sure these visits to the scene of the crime are getting us anywhere. Especially as this character operates so efficiently. We discussed the possibility of this being a professional job, but that's the one theory we haven't followed up. We are all chasing this 'profile' Sabine created, but to tell the truth, I'm not sure that it's leading anywhere."

Beatrice held up her hand to forestall Sabine's outrage.

"Thank you for being honest. How would you like us to progress?"

"Do you mind if I jump in, Chris?" Conceição waited for his nod. "Beatrice, Chris and I have talked about this a lot." She ignored the snort from Sabine. "We think we should provide the General Secretariat with a report that states we believe different people or organisations employed a professional to get rid of these men. And then Interpol or Europol can make use of their databases to check suspected hired killers. It really does seem that we are chasing down cold leads and wasting a lot of time."

Beatrice bristled at the criticism, but nodded her understanding. Her mind raced through the conflict mediation training she had received and she played for time.

"I see. Well, that's one perspective. I think Sabine sees things differently."

The blonde head gave a sharp nod. "I see things very differently. This profile is not some fantasy I made up. It is based on serious research and tested methodology. Of course, we can write a report based on vague assumptions and go home. But I for one do not consider that to be a professional job. We have identified a series of markers which can help us locate this person. But as Beatrice said at the start, it involves a lot of boring, dull paperwork. However, it seems that only part of the team take responsibility for that. Others are enjoying themselves on their European Tour."

"Sabine." Beatrice had to act. "I take your point, but I must ask you not to make this personal. If you feel duties have been unfairly allocated, we can look at the situation. But what people choose to do in their private time is no concern of ours. Xavier, I'd like to hear from you."

Xavier hesitated and darted a glance at Chris. "In my opinion, to write a report saying we think it was probably a professional and leave it there would not be satisfactory. The traces of DNA, and nothing else, at each scene makes me think it could be deliberate, to confuse us. It is possible to fabricate DNA, and make us hunt someone who is not existing. Beatrice, this is the first international project I'm working on. I learn a lot. But I would be interested to stretch myself further. For me, visiting a scene of crime could be an education."

"Am I allowed an opinion?" Kälin spoke from the doorway, making everyone jump.

"Herr Kälin. Good morning. Please, come in. We'd be most interested to hear what you have to say. I'm not sure how much you heard while hiding outside. Would you like us to recap?" Beatrice wrestled with her temper.

"Two things before I begin. The morning briefing happens at 08.00. It is now 07.53. If you expect your team to participate fully, I suggest you stick to the agreed time. I think I may have said that before. Secondly, this team is intended to be a covert, discreet operation. Having an internal argument with the door wide open is, in this regard, counter-productive. I heard quite enough while ascending the stairs to form an accurate picture of what you are doing. I agree with Frau Stubbs, personal feelings should be kept out of this, which prevents me from agreeing with Frau Pereira da Silva. I think we should exhaust all the leads we have before giving up and going home. It might be a good idea to change duties, and I suggest Frau Tikkenen accompanies Herr Keese to St Moritz."

Beatrice inhaled. "Thank you everyone. I appreciate your candid responses. And as Herr Kälin mentioned, it will shortly be time for morning briefing. I suggest you get yourselves a coffee etcetera before we begin. And he is absolutely right. Leaving the door open was a foolish mistake. Entirely mine. I apologise, everyone. Finally, I have decided to rearrange duties in order to maximise efficiency and learning capacity. Sabine and Xavier, you will take the next scene of crime investigation. Right, five minutes, everyone."

She didn't even look at Kälin. Why bother? She could mimic that expression of utter loathing by now.

Twenty minutes later, the depressing lack of progress was evident. Sabine had turned up no one in her search for pharmacological employees, despite an impressive search system in three countries. Chris and Conceição learned nothing of obvious value from Burgundy. The local villagers mentioned that Edwards had rarely eaten in local restaurants during that visit, only seen once in a pizzeria with his wife, and once in a café with an unidentified blonde. Beatrice confirmed that Interpol were prepared to give them another two weeks to produce some concrete results, or their status would undergo review. The atmosphere was despondent.

Xavier cleared his throat. "I may have something. It's not definite, but looks possible. Sabine suggested this person commits one of these offences per year. February 2007. March 2008. September 2010. April 2011. I did a search for unusual deaths across Europe in 2009, with a filter for high-profile businessmen. Several incidents showed up. One of them in particular could be worth investigating. It was not reported as a suicide, as the Czech police suspected a gang execution. The man was an arms dealer from the Ukraine, and killed near Brno, in the Czech Republic. Shot in the mouth. The site was completely clean, apart from some DNA, on a vodka glass. I cannot say if the sample is good, but I have asked to see the results of their tests."

A fizz of excitement surged through Beatrice. "In that case, it seems like your first scene-of-crime visit is on the agenda, Xavier. But first I want you to thoroughly brief Chris, who'll do the legwork while you're away. Chris, make sure you check for any connection with D'Arcy Roth. Sabine, I hope you'll forgive me. If we need to verify DNA, it will have to be Conceição who accompanies Xavier."

The girl received the news with such equanimity Beatrice wondered if the objections to task allocation were simply a ruse to get closer to the Dutchman. Judging by Conceição's expression, it seemed Chris had provoked some rivalry. Sometimes, it was such a relief to be beyond all that. Xavier's expression glowed like a chestnut-vendor's brazier, triggering a concern in Beatrice.

"Ja?"

Kälin's office was dark, his expression lit solely by the computer screen. His moustache, eyebrows and frown cast shadows, making him look impossibly grim. Despite her unease, the urge to laugh bubbled up inside Beatrice's throat.

"Apologies for the disturbance, Herr Kälin, but I have a question which I'd rather ask discreetly."

"You can sit, Frau Stubbs."

"Thank you. My question concerns Herr Racine. I've chosen him for the Brno investigation because although he's young and lacks expertise, I believe in giving him the benefit of the doubt. He's shown real aptitude in his work so far and I feel he deserves a chance."

Kälin leant back and folded his arms. "You said you had a question. This sounds like a justification of your decision."

Beatrice refused to rise to the bait. "I can't help noticing that Xavier is a little clumsy, in terms of physical coordination. Obviously he'll need to be armed for this trip. Going on my existing knowledge, I'd take the risk and send him to Moravia, particularly as he was the one who discovered the Brno incident. But as one of his superior officers, you know him better. Would it be safer to send a more experienced officer now that firearms are concerned?"

Kälin smoothed two fingers over his moustache in a thoughtful gesture while watching the fingers of his other hand drum a pattern on the table.

Beatrice had just begun to suspect him of playing status games when he answered.

"Your question is intelligent. Racine has not yet learned to control his mouth, his enthusiasm or his gestures. There is only one area in which we can trust his abilities."

Kälin stood and pressed the button to lift the blinds. Light flooded the room, prompting an odd feeling of exposure in Beatrice. She quite liked talking to Kälin in the dark. Now his ice-blue eyes settled on her like a glacial lake.

"I'm not sure how deeply you researched this country before coming here, Frau Stubbs, but I suppose you know that all Swiss men do military service, including weaponry training. Those who excel are encouraged to rise in the ranks, to constantly improve their skills. When Herr Racine took his first firearms assessment with the Stapo, or Stadtspolizei, he scored higher than any previous trainee. Xavier Racine ranks as the top ... what would you say ... sharpshooter?"

Beatrice pondered. "I'm not sure. It's not terminology I'm familiar with. Crack shot? Sniper? Ace gunman?"

"Hmm. So I can tell you that he is one of the top ten sharpshooters of the Swiss Army and top five in the police force. Unbeaten in many cantons. I hope he will soon learn to apply such precision and care to the rest of his behaviour."

"Thank you, Herr Kälin. I'm very grateful to you. Not only do I feel my decision was valid, but you've put my mind at rest. I'm sorry for disturbing you."

Kälin watched her leave. "It's always better to ask when you aren't sure. Have a nice evening, Frau Stubbs."

The computer clock showed 18.15. Time to go. Tonight, the opera. Beatrice's spirits lifted as she closed down her machine. A casual chat with Xavier last week resulted in his telling her about his sister, the Box Office Manager at the Opera House, the number of unclaimed tickets left for most performances and the fact that *Die Zauberflöte*, or *The Magic Flute*, was scheduled that week. She planned to change, walk down to the lake and have a snack, before making her way over the river to the Opernhaus. She had practised her speech in German and all she needed to do was wait till the five minute call. Apparently, unclaimed tickets were then released. A free performance. And there was no better way of taking her mind off work, or herself, than a large dose of Mozart.

"Beatrice?"

"Hello, Chris. Shouldn't you have left by now?"

"Just about to. Sabine and I were just finishing off. I wondered if I could persuade you to come for a drink with me."

"Me? Well, I'd like to, Chris, but …"

"You're washing your hair?"

"No, no. I'd planned to … never mind. Mozart can wait."

"You sure? I don't want to mess up your arrangements."

"I know. But with Conceição out of town, someone must keep an eye on you."

He looked shocked.

"I'm joking, Chris. I've heard there's a rather good place called Oscar Wilde's. Shall we try that?"

"Sounds perfect."

She smiled. There's never any need to chase gossip. If you're not interested, gossip comes to you.

"*Ein Gespritzer und ein Grosses.*" The waitress placed the drinks on small paper coasters and a bowl of nuts between them. "*Möchten Sie etwas essen?*"

Chris looked at Beatrice. "You hungry?"

"Not just now."

"*Nein danke. Es ist gut.*"

Beatrice lifted her drink. "What do you suppose this is?"

"A spritzer. That's what you asked for."

"With lemon? A slice of lemon in wine?" She fished it out with a cocktail stick.

Chris laughed. "I'll tell her to skip it when we order the next one. So, cheers!"

He raised his pint glass and Beatrice remembered to meet Chris's eyes over the toast, before looking around the room. Deep purple banquettes, a long wooden bar, Art Nouveau murals on the wall and pale floor tiles matched more her idea of a gentleman's club than an Irish pub. There was even a glassed-in cigar area, with two serious besuited chaps sampling something from the humidor. Everything was muted, subtle and discreet, even the small stage area. Changing colours lit a single microphone. Beatrice liked it enormously. She helped herself to nuts.

"Without sounding patronising, I have to admire your facility with languages. I can just about order a coffee in French. How did you get to be so fluent in English?" she asked.

"Lived there. I trained at the NHTCTC in Wyboston."

"In Bedfordshire? National something Centre ... what's the rest?"

"High Tech Crime Training Centre. I learned a lot, mostly British slang and the strengths of real ale. Oh, and some computer forensics."

"And where did you pick up your German?"

"It's not so different to Dutch. I almost feel at home, apart from the culture. It must be harder for you, I think."

"The language or the culture?"

"The situation."

Chris lifted his glass and drank without taking his eyes from Beatrice's.

She acknowledged the kindness in his comment. "It's been quite a week, hasn't it?"

He gave her a smile. "We were ripe for that, in terms of a team. We'd done forming, and now we've got to get through storming. It gets easier from here though. Norming and performing come next."

"Hmm. You sound like someone I know. A concept for everything."

"I work for Europol. It's all very well in practice, but will it work in theory?"

Beatrice chuckled. "So what is the theory behind this case?"

"This is an administrative exercise, in my view. A non-case, but a signal of 'close co-operation between member states'. I believe they're getting us to go through the motions, turn up nothing at all, but ticking the box that says all irregularities must be eliminated."

"You're very cynical, Chris. I imagined you had more idealism."

"I work for a European governmental organisation. Idealism

smothered by bureaucracy. Are you telling me you think there's really something to this?"

Beatrice checked herself. Her method was to exhaust all possibilities, follow every lead and never to act on that most ridiculous of fictional detective accessories, the hunch.

But she had a hunch.

"I actually think there is. And I have a strong feeling there is a connection through more than just money to that D'Arcy woman. Even if I'm wrong, I want to take this case, turn out its pockets, hold it by the ankles and shake it upside down. If there's nothing here, I want to know that for certain."

"No stone unturned?"

"Precisely. Now, if I may go off on a tandem, tell me what's going on in terms of relations between Interpol and Europol."

"Oh hell." He took a long draught of his beer. "I don't know exactly, but somehow, we get on. I like her, she's very attractive and it seems she likes me. I'm trying to be discreet, but it looks like Sabine caught on and doesn't like it. Does it bother you?"

"Not unless it is likely to bother the case. In my experience, these things can be a force for the good. The destructive element comes when it ends."

The animation left the Dutchman's face. "It hasn't even started yet."

"Sorry, *if* it ends. I'm not concerned, as I trust you both to be wholly professional."

"Thanks, B."

"I beg your pardon? What did you just call me?"

"B. What? You don't like it? I'd better prepare a team email, then. We all refer to you as B."

"What do you mean, you *all* call me B? Even Kälin?"

Chris grinned. "Not quite. He calls you *Frau* B."

Several groups of people entered the bar. The place grew lively, with an air of anticipation. When the stage lights brightened, and those of the bar dimmed, Beatrice realised why. At eight o'clock precisely, applause pattered around the room and a door opened beside the stage. Receiving her welcome as a cat receives the sun, the performer lifted her face to the light. A work of art. One could only guess at her real appearance under the layers of exquisite camouflage. Her turquoise dress sparkled and a blue velvet wrap was draped across her throat before cascading down her shoulders. A torch singer! Chris ordered more drinks and Beatrice beamed at him.

"This is marvellous, I have to say. Our seat is in the perfect spot, we have fresh drinks, without lemon, and a chanteuse is about to perform. I am glad you dragged me away from Mozart."

"You like these guys?" he asked, with amusement.

"What do you mean?"

"I would have thought you'd be more into *Il Divo* than drag queens."

Beatrice frowned at him, before turning her attention to the stage. That was a man? Was Chris pulling her leg? A glance around the bar confirmed that the majority of the audience were male couples, so he might be right.

"How can you tell it's a man?" she whispered.

"Scarf around the neck. Dead giveaway. They can't hide the Adam's apple, you see. So they cover it up."

The singer opened with '*My Funny Valentine*', and whatever the gender, that voice was rich, sweet and glorious, like a chocolate fondue.

Beatrice crossed Sihlbrücke in a distinctly positive mood. Chris had made her laugh with his indiscreet observations on the team, on their assignment and on the Oscar Wilde. She'd enjoyed herself and relaxed. Tomorrow, she would try the opera, and try to extract herself from the case in the evenings. All work and no play ... Beatrice smiled. It was almost eleven and time for two of her favourite chaps; Earl Grey and John Humphrys.

Chapter 17

Zürich 2012

Detective Karl Kälin left his office a little after seven. As his BMW pulled into the traffic, a black Ford Mondeo followed at a respectful distance. Kälin drove directly to Adliswil, always observing the speed limit, and parked outside the shopping centre. He took the lift to the supermarket, where he selected some broccoli, cauliflower and a packet of freshwater fish, which was on special offer. Afterwards, he visited the off-licence, buying a bottle of Swiss white and some sparkling water. All this was covertly recorded on a digital camera.

In Austrasse, Kälin reversed his car into one of the blue bays, placed the residents' parking permit on the dashboard and hauled his laptop case from the back seat. The black Ford Mondeo drove past and pulled in further up the street. Its lights went out.

Kälin locked his car, took his mail from the post-box and crunched up the gravel path. His apartment block was the last of the four in this development and therefore furthest from the road. Lights shone from various rooms on the first and second floors, but in the bottom apartment, all remained in darkness. He entered the building and several minutes later, lights flickered into life on the ground floor. The driver of the Mondeo didn't move.

A pair of teenagers sped down the street on rollerblades. Several cars went by, some descending to underground garages, some continuing towards Soodring. A cat shot across the road and under some bushes. It had something in its mouth.

Five minutes passed before the internal light glowed in the Mondeo. The driver's door opened and a figure slipped out, following in Kälin's footsteps, but making considerably less noise. At the entrance, the figure stopped, waited and bent to check the name plates beside the buzzers. The black-clad shape then padded around the corner of the building, turning back sharply when voices drifted down from one of the balconies above.

A set of concrete steps led to some terraced gardens, with shrubs, ornamental trees and a communal barbecue area. The figure checked for observers before finding a vantage point behind some shrubbery which allowed a view into the uncurtained rooms of the ground floor. Using the camera's zoom function, the figure located the detective. The apartment was open-plan, with a wide work surface separating the kitchen area from the lounge. Kälin was cooking, although most of his attention was diverted to the TV screen and *Tagesschau*, the daily evening news programme. The figure took several more shots, returned to the vehicle, and with a last glance at the apartment block, drove away with a smile. This job was going to be easy.

Chapter 18

Rome 2011

Seven missed calls. Oh, Giuliana, please. This has to stop. He slid onto the back seat of the car, and took out his handkerchief to mop his lip. The air-con and silence, usually so soothing, could not compete with the heat and noise in his head. What a total waste of a day.

"Via Veneto."

The driver nodded and pulled away.

He dialled the number, but did not press the call button. *Give me an hour, and I'll deal with it.* With a few swift thumb movements, he turned his phone to silent. The driver swung across two lanes, into Via Napoleone III, leaning on the horn. The Vittorio Emanuele monument blazed white across the piazza, a wedding cake crawling with brightly coloured parasites. One more thing he hated about *Roma*. Tourists. Another reason, apart from the obvious, why he could never live here. The Infernal City. Not that *Milano* didn't have plenty of badly dressed gawpers, it most certainly did. But like *Venezia* or *Firenze*, the sheer numbers here spoiled its appearance, like blighted fruit.

At least he'd changed hotels. Why his assistant had booked that horrible place at the top of the Scalinata, the most crowded tourist spot in the whole city, was beyond him. The last thing he needed was to be forced into finding a new room, using his own credit card and organising his own taxi. He intended to have harsh words with her when he got back. Then to make matters worse, his room in the second hotel was too close to the ventilators, so he'd insisted on being relocated. One's hotel room played a major role on trips like these, whilst trying to persuade lazy, useless bureaucrats to recognise the exception and grant the exemption.

God, he hated politics. Worst thing this country had ever done, joining the EU. And now look at the situation. Italy in the same leaking boat as Greece, Ireland and Portugal? Too late now to reverse the damage done by that buffoon while Prime Minister. Impossible. The country's situation made his position untenable. Sweat returned to his forehead. Downgrading *Ristorex* to a safety level C would cause a firestorm in the media, wrecking their reputation and crippling their sales forecasts. It was impossible to contemplate. Impossible. He replayed his passionate arguments. The government had a responsibility to recognise the company's reports, and acknowledge that the anti-depressant could not be proved to be teratogenic. Of course it could not be disproved either, but in their study of over one hundred women who had taken *Ristorex* while pregnant, not one delivered an imperfect child. It was irresponsible and controlling to deny this medication to depressed women. Without it, these unbalanced females might drink, smoke, take drugs and self harm. How dangerous would that be for a foetus? He snorted, expelling the dusty air of bureaucracy from his Milanese nose.

Eyes closed against the hordes on Repubblica, he visualised the next two hours. The hotel. Cool room, silence, shower and change. A beer, perhaps, while researching FC Roma in preparation for tonight's dinner. A knowledgeable comment on the team's performance would earn him far more status than any research statistics. The hotel. A safe haven. But Giuliana knew where he was. He envisaged his arrival.

Signor Boldoni? We have some messages for you. Thirty-two urgent faxes – all from your wife.

His eyes opened and his idyll soured. An hour. Just one hour of peace. Not the hotel. Not now.

"*Eccoci arrivati ...*"

Cesare waited for the driver to open his door, exited and gave him instructions.

"*Grazie. Venga a prendermi alle otto in punto, per favore.*"

"Certamente, a più tardi."

Eight o'clock. He had three hours. One hundred and eighty minutes of freedom. He could steal an hour, not doing, not thinking, not dealing. Just being. He turned from the hotel's portico and strode down the street, ignoring the endless tourist bars, glancing up alleys for something small, cheap, Roman. *Café Don Pomeranus* had two tables outside and an awning striped in red, white and green. One table was free. At the other, two old men looped through an argument about coffee houses. *Sant Eustachio* versus *Frontoni dal 1921*. They both supported their views with passion and dismissed each other with aggression.

He ordered a *Peroni* and sat still. He watched the paint flake from the building opposite. The waiter poured his drink. He thanked him and observed bubbles crawl up the glass. A dark blue Vespa sped by. The rider wore no helmet. And back again, this time with a passenger. Long dark hair rippled behind her, as she grasped the driver's waist with one arm and punctuated her speech with the other. An ancient Fiat 125 filled with three large women and their shopping trundled past, barely missing his table. He watched. He breathed. It couldn't last.

His hand reached for his phone and he scrolled through the missed calls. Nine, now. He listened to Giuliana's increasing hysteria with a sense of mild numbness. It's an emergency, Cesare, the baby is crying, I can't stop him, something is wrong, Cesare, I've sent the nanny home, your mother is unavailable, I am taking him to hospital, Cesare, it was a fit of some sort, I am desperate, Cesare, this is unfair on me, I can't go on like this, where are you for the love of God, have you any idea of how exhausted I am, Cesare, the doctors told me not to get so stressed, there's nothing wrong, I want a second opinion, these people are a disgrace, Cesare, uncivilised, it wouldn't happen in *Roma*, people care there, this city is so cold and its people are hateful, Cesare, you don't care, I'm so alone, and our son, your son, Cesare, how can you be so cold, so remote, I wish I'd never moved north, Cesare, it's destroying my sunny nature, my lust for life, I can't bear it, Cesare, Cesare, Cesare.

He hung up and considered another beer. After all, he deserved it.

A voice interrupted his internal monologue. "Do you mind if I sit here?"

Tourist. No attempt at Italian. American, probably. Nasty bright clothes.

"*Prego.*" He gestured for her to sit opposite him. His expression was cool. She smiled gratefully, sat and took off her shoes. How ill-mannered. Two angry red blisters on each foot. Are these people not used to walking? The waiter's sneer was visible as she massaged her foot and asked for a sparkling water and coffee in a poor accent.

Cesare pulled his sunglasses down from his forehead over his eyes to observe her while still appearing uninterested. His mobile phone vibrated in his pocket. He ignored it. Giuliana's voice now bored him.

The tourist had the minimum of accessories; no camera, no sunglasses, a small handbag, a map and bad clothes. Her hair was frizzy and she had caught too much sun. How stupid were these people? He should keep his mouth shut. Yet the habits of finding a way into a person prevailed.

"First day in Rome?" he asked, in English.

A flicker of mistrust. "Yeah, first day. I guess that's obvious, right?"

"You are American?"

"Canadian. Close."

"Close but yet so far."

She looked at him properly for the first time. "Right. It doesn't usually matter to Europeans. We're all the same to you guys."

"Fair point. But isn't it also true vice versa?"

"No, I don't think so. For us, Europe has many strong identities. OK, we may get confused between Norway and Denmark, but I know a lot about Italy. And Spain. And France. I'm touring, trying to learn more, you know what I mean?"

"*Bene.* How did you find the Eternal City?"

"No fair. I landed this morning, but my luggage went to Germany. I started my tour in borrowed clothes and none of my cosmetics. Believe me, for a woman, that's not good."

"Bad luck. So your first day in Italy was not a success?"

"It's not my first day in Italy. I spent a few days in Florence and Milan before coming here. That was so great."

"You like the north?"

She sat back and tilted her head to look at him. "You're a Roman, right?"

"Wrong. But that's all I'm going to say."

"OK, whatever. To be honest, I totally loved the north. Maybe I'm a little culture-shocked, I don't know, but I find Rome kinda hard work."

Cesare pushed his sunglasses up onto his head to allow her a view of his eyes. He gave her a smile. "I would say you have excellent taste."

"Phew! Looks like my gamble paid off." Her laugh softened her face and her blue eyes crinkled.

"Signora." The waiter shoved a bottle and a glass on the table, tucking the bill under the bottle.

"Excuse me? The coffee?"

The man blanked her and returned to the interior.

"Shoot." Her face burned with something more than an excess of sun.

He leaned towards her. "Can I help?"

"No, thanks. I wanted cold sparkling water and a coffee. But I got warm still water and a whole bunch of attitude. You know what, I think I'll skip it and get back to the hotel."

"Wait a moment."

He swung out of his chair, grabbed her water and strode into the café.

"The woman outside. She ordered cold water, *frizzante*. And a coffee. Is that too complicated an order? Or do you always treat tourists like this? No wonder Rome has the worst reputation in Italy. You are all arrogant, lazy and stupid as pigs." He threw ten Euros on the counter along with the warm water and stormed out.

"Come. Let's find a place with better service."

She slipped on her shoes and joined him, limping slightly.

"This is ridiculous. You need to bathe your feet. Where is your hotel?"

She gave him a grateful smile. "Right up the street. Regina Baglioni. Listen, thanks for the knight in shining armour stuff. Good to know there are some nice guys out there."

"I too stay at the Baglioni. I will walk with you and arrange a cold drink."

"Can you please ensure room service deliver a bottle of cold *San Pellegrino* and a cappuccino to this lady's room as soon as possible. Have her luggage taken up as soon as it arrives, please." He slipped the clerk five Euros, disguising it as a firm slap on the reception desk, before guiding her to the elevator.

"Which floor?"

"Five, please."

The doors closed and he pressed levels three and five.

She turned to him. "You are so kind, I'm totally overawed by this. Thank you so much."

"I am simply trying to reinforce your prejudice. North good, south bad. Your baggages should be here soon, and maybe tomorrow, you can see the clean face of Rome. Wearing comfortable shoes."

"Right. Oh, is this your floor already? Ok, well, thanks again. Hey, could I get you a drink at all, maybe later? Just to show my appreciation?"

"I have an engagement, unfortunately. But perhaps we could enjoy an aperitif before I go. I imagine you and your feet would prefer not to go too far this evening. How about the bar at seven?"

"Excellent. Or, even better, could I just swing by your room? That way I can keep my slippers on."

"Of course. I'm in room 302. See you later."

Not his place, really, but he would have to tell her. These women, alone, in strange cities, no grasp of the language. You cannot just invite yourself to a strange man's hotel room. Naturally she was safe with him; he was a man of honour, *Il Cavaliere* in more than just a title. But any *figlio di puttana* could play the gentleman and she would trust him. Far too risky. The phone rang. Maybe she just had the same thought.

"*Pronto?*"

"*Cesare!*"

Giuliana was sobbing with relief. His mother, the doctors, his son, their son, this city, these people and the knowledge that he was in her beloved Rome. It was too much for her, her heart was beating strangely, she needed him, she felt so bad, she couldn't cope with this, she needed him. Cesare!

Cesare put his head in his hands. His wife needed him. He had a dinner engagement and more meetings tomorrow. Giuliana sounded terrible. It was a self-induced panic attack. She couldn't work herself into such a state every time he was away from home for a few days. He had to work, had to keep the business healthy. A sedative would buy him time, but he would never permit his wife to take any medication while still breastfeeding. Cancelling tonight's dinner would lose him anything he had already gained from the *Guardia di Finanza*. Not forgetting that drink with the grateful tourist.

From nowhere, his mother's voice arose. 'Cesare, what are you thinking? Putting a stranger before your wife's pain? What kind of man are you? You should be ashamed!'

He made a decision.

"OK, Giuliana, I'm coming home. I'll be with you in a few hours. Please rest, my love. I will be there tonight."

As the car drove away from Malpensa, he regretted not informing the Canadian woman that he couldn't make it. But finding a flight, calling his contacts to cancel and packing had eaten away all his time. And without knowing her name, he had no way of leaving her a message. Still, he hated to be impolite and really should have warned her about trusting strangers.

Chapter 19

Zürich 2012

Sabine's contact arrived at the Rote Fabrik on her bike. Chris assessed her in seconds. A beach bum without a beach. And not much of a bum to speak of, either. A camouflage vest and denim shorts covered a limited amount of her wiry, deeply tanned body, accompanied by ancient Converse trainers, vaguely Celtic tattoos and dangling things from her wrists, neck and plaited rat's tail in her hair. He wondered why these independent alternative types all bought into exactly the same uniform. Look how different I am. She joined them at the wooden table.

"Ursula, this is Chris, my colleague. Chris, Ursula may have helpful information."

After greeting Sabine with a handshake and a smile, Ursula turned to him with a hostile look. She cocked her head in an affected enquiry at Sabine.

Sabine seemed unruffled. "Chris is part of my team, Ursi. Did you find anything for us?"

"Yes and no. I'd like a beer."

Sabine went inside to order and Ursi fiddled with her mobile, paying Chris no attention. Each blunt finger was stained yellow and burn marks crossed her inner arms like the rungs of a ladder. He'd seen marks like that before, on a tandoori-oven cook at an Indian restaurant. Ursi either had an addiction he'd not heard of, or more likely, she worked in a pizzeria. Absorbing the many shades of colourful and alternative passing by on the lake path, he realised he may as well have a blue flashing light on his forehead. Everyone looked at him and saw *Polizei*. He looked past them at the lake, watching the early evening light play across the opposite shore.

Sabine returned with three bottles of *Vollmond*. Ursi drank a good third without waiting for a toast.

Chris knocked his bottle against Sabine's, met eyes and drank.

"So, let's hear the good news first," said Sabine, wiping her lips with the back of her hand.

"Good news is I fixed a meeting. Bad news is, I don't know if they'll talk. Look Sabine, I'm pretty sure that if *he's* there, they won't say anything at all." She flashed a contemptuous look at Chris, her dark eyes reminding him of a rodent as she swigged at the bottle.

He smiled and prepared to reply but Sabine got in first.

"I'm going nowhere without him. We come as a pair. Otherwise, forget it." She took a sip of beer and shrugged, as if unconcerned by Ursula's opinion.

An awkward silence settled, but Chris's instinct held him back. He'd leave it to Sabine. Let the ferret deal with the rat.

Ursula dug into her tatty fringed bag, pulled out a book and retrieved a piece of paper from between the pages. "Up to you. I've done my bit. Here's the address, mention me and don't be late. I said you'd get there by eight."

Springing up, she drained the beer and pointed at Sabine.

"Call me." She turned her back on Chris and headed for her bike.

Navigating Stauffacher as dusk leached the colour from the city took all Chris's concentration, so he barely registered Sabine's call, informing Xavier of their location and intention. Driving onto Ankerstrasse, he found to his frustration he couldn't turn left. Sabine spotted a space.

"Park it here, we'll walk."

He locked the car, conscious of wary stares from doorways, windows and the benches on Helvetiaplatz, and positioned himself on the inside of the pavement. A gentleman would usually do the opposite, but Chris had the feeling that on Langstrasse, the traffic was less dangerous than the street. The building they were looking for had a series of pink-lit windows and a sign: '*Nightclub*', depicting a naked woman in heels reclining on a crescent moon. Without hesitating, Sabine pushed open the door.

Just inside, a heavy velvet curtain screened the room from prurient eyes. Chris pulled it back, allowing Sabine through first. The room was tiny, with a bar, a stage, which was closer to an Olympic medal-winner's podium, and a few poorly lit tables. No more than ten people populated the room and every one of them gawped at the new arrivals. Chris had to admire Sabine's relaxed manner as she bid the punters good evening and settled herself at an empty table. Chris sat beside her, rather than opposite, giving him a chance to survey the room.

His eyes got no further than the barmaid. The woman hypnotised him; long black curls, black sooty eyes and skin that seemed to soak up light. Laughing with one of the customers, she showed a wide, gap-toothed smile, reminding him of Beatrice Dalle. Everything about her suggested sex; scary sex, sex without boundaries, sex limited only by imagination, and he'd bet she had plenty of ideas. Nothing about her clothes was overtly revealing, but low-slung jeans hinted at a tight belly and her scoop-necked T-shirt clung to her contours as she moved. As if she sensed his stare, she looked right at him. He ordered two Cokes, relieved the dim lighting spared his blushes. Her eyes lingered for a few seconds, weighing him up, before she gave an understanding nod.

Most people sat alone, apparently waiting for something. A small, balding man perched at the end of the bar, chain-smoking, where more burgundy velvet screened another door. As Chris watched, he ducked through, spoke to someone, came back and summoned a man at a table near the door. The john downed his drink and slipped through the curtains with a nod to the doorkeeper.

"Looks like our contact is yet to arrive. Still, it's only just eight," said Sabine.

"Yeah. I'd be surprised if he was one of this lot. Aren't all left-wing anarchists a bit younger than this crowd?"

"Of course he's not one of them. These men are all sad

middle-aged perverts taking advantage of the economic circumstances of exploited women."

"Sabine, keep it down. If we get asked to leave before our guy arrives ..."

A tobacco-roughened voice interrupted. "She's right. The women *are* exploited and these losers *are* middle-aged perverts." Betty Blue stood at their table with three Cokes. She placed one in front of Sabine, gave one to Chris with a half-lidded look and sat down opposite. "This one's for me. It has vodka in it and officers shouldn't drink on duty." Her accent sounded Spanish. She grinned at them with that incredible mouth. Chris wanted to grab her, throw her over his shoulder and run through the velvet curtains.

Slipping a small leather pouch from her back pocket, she commenced rolling a joint. "I hear you want to talk to someone in the socialist action movement. Maybe I can help. No names, no inside information, but I'll answer a couple of questions."

Sabine seemed similarly struck by this goddess. "OK. You're not what we expected but ... thank you for meeting us. I understand you don't want to give us your name, but I'm Sabine and this is Chris."

The balding man sloped off his stool and moved behind the bar to serve a customer. He looked over at their table and whined.

"Yolanda?"

Without turning, she lifted her hand, middle finger to him and returned to crumbling resin onto tobacco strands. The guy sighed and filled a glass with lager.

"And you can call me Yolanda. So, what do you want?"

Chris spoke. "We're investigating a series of deaths. Several men, whom you might call corporate fat cats, died in suspicious circumstances. Looked like suicide, but we have evidence the same person was with them when they died." He was pleased at the professional tone of his voice, as he suspected he might be drooling.

Sabine took over. "I'm a psychological profiler, Yolanda, and my research leads me to think this person is performing what he believes to be social justice. A diamond dealer from South Africa, an American vulture fund boss, a media magnate with fingers everywhere, a British CEO of a polluting water company ... you can see what Chris means about *fat cats*."

"Yes." Yolanda lit the joint and the sweet distinctive scent crept up Chris's nose. "So you think this is direct action from a left-wing activist? An anarchist on a crusade? And you want me to tell you his name and where he lives?" Her laughing eyes reflected the pink lights in the opaque windows.

Chris smiled back. "That would be great, thanks."

Sabine shot him a look. Fair enough, he was flirting with a potential informant. But who wouldn't?

At least Sabine kept focused. "We were really looking for more of an insight into how these things work. As far as I understand, most direct action groups target material things such as buildings. But I've yet to find a group which advocates physical harm to individuals."

Yolanda blew smoke into the air above them. "Ursi was right about you, Sabine. You *are* smart. And what you say is true. We don't believe in violence against people. We believe property is theft. We believe information should be public. We believe in righting capitalist wrongs and redistribution of wealth. Needs not profits. But we don't do murder."

Chris's ardour cooled. Sex, yes. Slogans? Such a turn-off.

Keeping his smile in place, he asked, "Property is theft? So where do you live?"

She took a long draught of her vodka and Coke, her eyes not leaving his. "In a disused railway terminal. Me and seven other squatters. You should come round sometime; I think you'd like it."

Chris broke eye contact, knowing he was being played with. And enjoying it.

Sabine had her teeth in and was unlikely to let go. "So if your group, and those similar, don't believe in violence to the individual, might there be someone who feels you don't go far enough? Can you think of someone who was frustrated by such policies and wanted to go further? Maybe someone who left your group because you weren't as radical as he hoped?"

Yolanda's smile faded as she listened to Sabine. "Yes, such people exist. But the one thing that doesn't make sense here is the range. People I know tend to have one cause. Anti-war. Animal rights. The diamond racket. Corruption in the pharmaceutical trade. Shit, there's even an action group against FIFA. But not all together. Yes, a lot of people feel very aggressive towards bankers and their obscene activities and I think that's probably the closest we've come to a desire for physical retaliation. What you need to understand is we're attacking the system. We want governments to take control of the banks and use the profits for social projects. We want to massively increase taxes on the rich. We want to fundamentally change the system to serve the people and the planet, not exploit them and plunder its resources. And much as it might serve some short-term satisfaction to punch a banker in the face or drag a key along an ugly great SUV, it will not achieve change. Thought and action must work together as part of the struggle."

Chris blinked, mesmerised by that supple, articulate mouth, those flashing, passionate eyes and the fact that some of what she said made sense to him. Sabine, on the other hand, retained her laser precision and sharp teeth.

"So you think it unlikely that a renegade activist would take it upon themselves to serially kill high-profile capitalists as a symbolic anti-establishment action?"

Yolanda re-lit her joint and nodded. "If the dead guys were all part of some kind of chain, like fur farmers, importers, fashion designers, owners of fur shops, that would make some sense. It's just these different random men ... to me, it feels personal."

Sabine sighed. "I agree. Thanks for your time Yolanda. I appreciate your talking to us. How much do we owe you for the Cokes?"

"Any donation you'd like to make to the cause is always gratefully received." The laughing eyes were back.

Chris withdrew a fifty and slid it across the table. She placed a hand over his, stroked it down and withdrew the money. Her hand felt cool and soft. Chris felt precisely the opposite.

Sabine stood up and thanked her again while he mumbled a goodbye, ignoring the invitation in her expression. Thrusting his way out through the red curtains, Chris appreciated the chill evening air restoring some of his perspective.

"I have to say, Sabine, you do play the left-wing sympathiser very well. Very convincing."

She zipped her jacket and looked up at him. "That's because it's not an act. As for her, useful, do you think?" she asked.

"Yes. I think she was. It sounded pretty rational to me."

Sabine's eyes narrowed. "I agree. Intelligent analysis. I'm going to add this to my profile tomorrow. But right now, I want to go home and have a bath. Listen, I can take a tram home, if that's more convenient?"

Chris looked at her, puzzled. "Why would you do that? I'll drive you."

Her sharp little face softened into a sly smile as she glanced sideways towards the pink windows. "I thought you might want to go back in, now you're off duty."

He grinned. "Was it that obvious?"

"Frankly, any minute I expected you to start humping her leg."

Chapter 20

Zürich 2012

"Kälin?"

"Hello, Herr Kälin, Frau Stubbs here. Would you be able to join us upstairs? It seems the trip to Brno has turned something up."

"Now?"

"Yes. Now."

He hung up.

His behaviour did not affect Beatrice in the slightest. An almost-forgotten buzz hummed through her system; this was a step forward. Her innate caution warned her not to get too enthusiastic, yet the news was a boost to the team's confidence. She began drafting an email to Lyon in her head, while observing Xavier's animated conversation with Chris.

Kälin arrived, his traditional scowl lightened by curiosity. Beatrice clapped her hands for silence.

"OK, Conceição and Xavier have some news. Over to you."

Conceição began. "The DNA found at the scene is a match. A thirteen-point match, which means the chances of it coming from two different individuals is effectively nil. The same person was with Belanov before he died. But as to who that person is? Xavier?"

"Thank you. The Czech police had some background on Belanov. Officially a used-car dealer, he actually traded in small to medium-calibre weapons; handguns, rifles, and so on. However, the police strongly suspected his involvement with the East European grey market arms trade. They know he supplied rocket launchers, mortars and cannons to Georgia, for example. So I got the name of Belanov's associate in Brno, Ivan Sykora, and met him at his office. He would tell me nothing about Belanov's business, but he explained a little about the methods. According to Sykora, Belanov rented a cabin in the Brno region every year, for the duration of the arms fair. He took clients and colleagues there 'to enjoy themselves without inhibition', as he put it. Belanov usually did a good trade at the event and was generous with his hospitality. Sykora knew of no problem or dispute which may have caused his death. He attended the fair on the day Belanov was killed and spoke to him several times. He noticed Belanov leaving mid-afternoon. He remembered because he was with a woman he didn't recognise. All he can recall about her is that she was good-looking and had red hair."

Kälin's eyes fixed on Xavier. "Anything else?"

"No fresh evidence. The police analysed the vodka bottle. Just vodka. They also checked the glasses. Clean. And I mean clean. Freshly washed and polished, but with saliva on one. Our DNA. We checked the cabin, of course, it is very remote. Belanov's Porsche was spotless."

"Why did they assume it was a gangland killing and not see it as suicide?" asked Sabine.

"Good question." Conceição flicked through her notes. "It looked like suicide at first. The only factor which made them suspicious was the initial report of the forensic team. The body was found by the cleaning company the following morning, so there was plenty of blood, but the police did pick up one strange detail. Most of the skull and brain matter was spread across the floor behind him. But there was a significant amount of it down his upper arms. As if his hands had been above his head. If he'd pulled the trigger himself, his arms would have been out of the way. They think he was tied up, shot and later his body arranged to look like he'd done it himself."

"How do you see this as fitting into what we already think?" Beatrice asked.

Conceição answered without hesitation. "It fits in several ways. Another morally suspect line of work…"

"Although not as high profile as the other men," added Xavier. "Which helped us."

"Yes, because there is one vital point we uncovered which we haven't even mentioned yet." Anticipation brightened Conceição's eyes.

"Please tell us, Frau Pereira, I cannot stand the suspense," Kälin drawled.

Conceição gestured to Xavier. "Go ahead. You found it."

"Well, actually, Chris was the one who made the connection. I just did the digging."

Kälin sighed. "This politeness is charming, but not particularly time-efficient. Will someone explain what has been found?"

Xavier responded quickly, despite his high colour. "Belanov had several expensive hobbies. One of which was playing polo. He wasn't very good, from what I heard, so sponsored teams in order to be able to play. For the 2008 season, he sponsored the team of Antonella D'Arcy."

No one spoke.

Beatrice cleared her throat. "All the same elements again. A suspicious death of a morally suspect businessman, the apparent welcome from the victim, the same DNA, and now D'Arcy again. She is the strongest link here and I want to talk to her again." She met Kälin's eyes. He remained expressionless.

"Not forgetting Sabine's identification of each method of killing as 'just'. How else would you kill a gun-runner?" Conceição shook her head, apparently amused by the cause of death.

Chris nodded. "And the super clean glasses, with his saliva on one, support Sabine's and Xavier's theory. He drugs them, kills them, cleans up and the DNA is a red herring."

"A what?" Sabine's frown was as severe as Kälin's.

"*Eine Finte*. A false trail," Chris replied.

The team stayed silent, absorbing the implications, when Kälin spoke.

"So, as Herr Racine enquired some time ago, our fundamental assumption – that we are hunting a man – could be completely wrong. Where does that leave your psychological profile, Ms Tikkenen? Or can we simply change the pronouns?"

Beatrice opened her mouth to dilute the acidity in Kälin's voice, but stopped short.

"Good Lord."

Chris watched her intently. "What is it, Beatrice?"

"Xavier could be right. It could be a woman. Think about it." She looked from face to face. "Belanov left with a woman, according to Xavier's source. And the uniform, in Utrecht. A staff member's uniform went missing, a female receptionist. Didn't you say that Edwards was seen with an unidentified female, in a restaurant or something? And Thompson, halfway down a dangerous ski run, was carrying condoms. Hence the access. Men would open the door much more easily to an attractive woman. And the chemical element. She can't do the physical stuff, so has to drug them first. It makes perfect sense to me."

"That has something." Kälin focused out of the window. "And if it's a woman, leaving male DNA behind in saliva is quite a clever strategy."

Xavier shook his head. "But it wasn't just saliva. She left a hair in Burgundy."

"So where does she get it from?" asked Conceição.

Sabine perked up. "I mentioned that many serial killers live with someone older, or who depends on them. If our killer has an elderly or disabled male relative at home, there would be an inexhaustible supply."

Beatrice shook some unpleasant images from her mind. "So, we may have been barking down the wrong hole. We need to retrace our steps. Chris, the case files. Go through them all and see if we missed anything because our focus was too narrow. Sabine, as regards the medical connection ..."

She groaned. "I need to do it all again. I only looked for men."

Xavier spoke. "I'll help you. I am very quick with database searches. Unless Beatrice has another job for me?"

"I do, Xavier, I'm afraid. I need you to check D'Arcy's alibis again and also to do a flight search from Zürich to Utrecht and Brno on and around the dates in question. See if there are any names that were in both places at the right times. Both genders.

"Conceição, find out if there is some kind of care-at-home support agency here. Possibly there is a register of carers who have live-in dependants. Cross check with Sabine constantly, to see if we can use her profile to narrow the net. I am going to inform Lyon about our progress and then Herr Kälin and I are going to visit Antonella D'Arcy. And this time, on our terms."

Kälin raised his eyebrows and to Beatrice's disbelief, gave her a genuine smile. She was appalled at herself. Good God, she hadn't blushed like that in twenty years.

Chapter 21

Zürich 2012

Beatrice was underdressed and it was all Kälin's fault.

The plan was to arrive unannounced at the D'Arcy Roth offices once again, so Kälin made a reconnaissance call to ensure the woman herself would be present. On discovering she had taken a long weekend to prepare herself for the first polo match of the season, he suggested the embarrassment factor would be heightened by their turning up to interview her in front of clients, colleagues and competitors at Polo Park Zürich. Beatrice could see the logic, but felt some trepidation. She had never attended a polo match before. Kälin advised her to dress '*as if for an English wedding. Or Ascot*'. She was horrified. English weddings and Ascot meant one thing.

Hats.

She called Matthew.

"Don't have to take it literally. And anyway, hats are awfully last generation. What you need now is a fascinator." Matthew spoke with conviction.

"Sounds like something you dangle in front of a child."

"It wouldn't last long. No, this is more feathers and frippery, normally stuck on one side of your head. Tanya wore one for Luke's christening, if you remember. Trouble is, in all the photos it looks like someone's doing bunny ears behind her." He laughed at the recollection.

"Well, I have no time to buy a fascinator, or even bunny ears for that matter. I have to leave early tomorrow morning; it's halfway to Germany, so I need to cobble something together tonight."

"Co-ordinate, then. A dress of one colour, with matching bag, earrings and lipstick."

"How did it come to pass that I need fashion advice from a Classics lecturer?"

"A Classics lecturer with two fashion-forward daughters. Which reminds me, Marianne wants you to bring her back a cuckoo clock."

"She can whistle. Do you have any idea how much they cost? I'm thinking about that grey two-piece, with my good handbag and some black pearl earrings."

"So you'll be wearing grey, grey and greyish. That's one way to stand out in a crowd."

"I don't want to stand out, Matthew. I want to be serious, intimidating and cast a threatening shadow over her day."

"Perhaps you should go as Darth Vader."

"Perhaps you should be less facetious. The sooner I find out how she's involved in all this, the sooner I can come home. And I want to come home. I miss you. I even miss bloody Hamilton."

"Not in the same way, I hope. I miss you, actually. Odd how a spring weekend can look so drear when there's no one to appreciate my fish stew."

"Let's see how this week goes, and if all looks good, I may fly over next weekend."

"May the force be with you. And I want to see the *gris et gris* ensemble for myself. Get Happy Bear to take a picture."

Polo Park Zürich lay just outside Winterthur. Verdant forests of pine created the backdrop for the crisp green field ringed by white. Like a cricket pitch, Beatrice thought, wondering if she and Matthew would be able to attend some village matches this summer. It seemed rather important that they should. Kälin spoke to an official, who waved them through. The lad was awfully young. Of course, it was traditional to exclaim at the youth of police officers and dentists as one aged, but this boy really could be no older than twelve. Her imagination danced away as she envisaged the youth of Mile End left in charge of traffic.

As she and Kälin approached the field, the deceptive familiarity of faded green and shabby white disappeared. The brilliant white of the pavilion was almost painful and the grass looked as if it had been combed. Close to the field stood a series of tables, covered with stiff, white tablecloths. Some high for those who wished to stand, and some lower with chairs which did not look at all comfy. Umbrellas created pools of shade, in which the glamorous gathered; chattering, laughing and tinkling. Everyone wore pastel; duck-egg blue, beige, powder pink, taupe, pale yellow, cream, lilac and ecru. It could have been the set of *Steel Magnolias*, but for the men.

"What now? Shall we wander about, flashing ID and asking where she is?"

Kälin shook his head. "We'll find someone with a badge, and ask him. Or her. And let's get a drink. It's warm. For now, we just wait."

Beatrice's eyes followed him as he threaded his way through the sea of Easter egg colours inside the pavilion. Spectacular flower arrangements stood between the tables, and the place settings themselves were a work of art. Pity they weren't invited to dinner. Children darted around the legs of tables and adults; elsewhere several small dogs sized one another up. The sparkle from champagne, sunglasses and jewellery did not distract Beatrice from noting how many heads turned her way. Matthew, infuriatingly, was right. The grey suit made her look like a thundercloud over a spring meadow. She pulled a face to match. Kälin handed her a glass.

"She's playing in the first match, for the Royal Blues. We won't have the possibility of talking to her for a while. However, we will have a chance to watch her play. Should we sit?"

Beatrice led the way to a table near the picket fence, marvelling at the snowy starched cloths, the effortless small talk and delicate colour coordination of the crowd. The scent of wealth and perfume of power was overpowering. She sipped at her drink.

"Herr Kälin, this is champagne."

"Correct, Frau Stubbs. Let us toast your skills of observation."

"We are on duty, you know. I prefer to keep a clear head when trying to needle someone. For an interview, I mean. I hardly think alcohol is appropriate."

"The police line is, '*Ein Glas ist OK*', so I plan to stick to that. And it is a quality brand, don't you think?"

Beatrice took another sip. It was rather good.

"And it is polite in Swiss society, as in most civilised countries in the world, to toast one another before drinking. Cheers, Frau Stubbs."

"Cheers, Herr Kälin. Thank you for the tip. Here's one for you. In Britain, we tend not to advise other people on how to behave."

"True. You give no advice and then despise foreigners for not knowing the rules. It is a mystery to me why the British have no word for *Schadenfreude*."

Beatrice stared at him, unsettled by the turn the conversation had taken. He looked like his old adversarial self, but the amusement in his voice and the light in his eyes reminded her of the photo she had seen. The one in which he looked like fun. She surveyed the polo field and sipped her champagne.

The tannoy, after a lengthy welcoming speech in three languages, announced the first chukka. Ten horses came onto the field and the excitement became tangible. Beatrice, having one of her more observant days, registered the players wearing royal blue were all on the same team. One of whom was Antonella D'Arcy. Impossible to tell which player at this distance. The other team wore white, and the two black-clad individuals were evidently referees.

Tension built, the horses snorting and skipping with excitement, the audience arranging themselves into optimum viewing positions, and the players faking confident laughter. When the action began, Beatrice was entranced. Hooves drummed into the hard earth, players charged one another like jousting knights and all the while, mallets swung with horrifying force. The speed, the confusion, the danger from these large sweaty beasts, violent mallets and whizzing ball absorbed her completely, although she had no clue what was happening.

The crowd gasped and sighed and applauded, at what Beatrice

knew not. But even she recognised when a goal was scored. D'Arcy's team celebrated, and without warning, after barely ten minutes, it was over. She turned to Kälin.

"Talk about fast and furious. Is that it?"

"For the first chukka, yes. The Royal Blues lead. They have a short break, change horses and play another. There will be four in total."

"How do you know so much about polo?"

"Like a good police officer, I do my research."

Beatrice chose not to respond. She too had done her research, into the dress code. And look where that had got her. During the changeover, she took the opportunity to observe the crowd. Standing at one of the higher tables behind them was a slight figure Beatrice recognised.

"Isn't that D'Arcy's secretary, the shy girl? The table at one o'clock. She's wearing peach."

Kälin let his gaze roam over the crowd, past the girl in question, and on to the pavilion. His attention returned to Beatrice. "Daughter *and* secretary. It looks like the same person, yes."

"Does the poor creature have to attend all D'Arcy's sporting events and cheer her on?"

Kälin watched the field, but Beatrice found the girl more interesting. She sat alone, hunched over her handbag as if she were trying to remain unseen. An older woman with a sour face to match her lemon ensemble approached the table and offered pleasantries. Beatrice could see the girl's awkward discomfort at answering questions and evident relief when the yellow lady left. As she continued to watch, two men greeted the girl in passing and she dropped her head.

"Typical of such a bully. Drags that poor child here, leaves her alone and embarrassed while she prances about on her pony, then insists on hearing fawning praise all the way back to Zürich."

"Frau Stubbs. You are making assumptions."

"Perhaps. But look at her, she can't even meet people's eyes, she so shy."

Kälin glanced up at the girl. "Low status body language, I've seen it before. Either that or she may have noticed you staring."

The Royal Blues won the match, and crowd reaction showed it was either well deserved or a popular result. The applause swelled again as the players emerged in small groups from their paddock. Beatrice watched Kälin's sharp eyes follow the pastel tide flowing around the blue shirts. He chose his moment with deliberation, nodded to Beatrice and stood.

D'Arcy laughed with her acolytes and shook her head modestly, every bit the gracious winner. As Kälin moved into her sightline, her face stiffened. She took in Beatrice, excused herself with great charm and moved towards them. Her smile was restrained, lacking any kind of warmth. Clocking the heads turning to watch D'Arcy's progress, Beatrice was suddenly glad she had worn grey. She could be mistaken for nothing other than a police officer. Exactly what she'd hoped. She must remember to tell Matthew.

"Good morning, Frau Stubbs, Herr Kälin. Did you enjoy the match?"

"I'm sorry to say we are not here for the entertainment, Ms D'Arcy," Beatrice replied. "We need to ask you some more questions. We tried to reach you at your office."

"And this must be done now?" Her eyebrows lifted.

"It has to be now, but not necessarily here. We can return to the police station in Zürich if you prefer?" Kälin offered.

D'Arcy's jaw was taut and she turned her blue eyes to Beatrice.

"Follow me. If you insist on disrupting my day, I insist on some degree of privacy."

She turned back the way she had come and into the players' enclosure, with a brisk word to the attendant. Weaving a path through the horse-boxes, she led them into a large tent. Clothes rails lined the walls and a sizeable table surrounded by camping chairs took up the middle. D'Arcy perched on the edge of one of the chairs.

"I'd appreciate it if we could make this as quick as possible."

Beatrice seated herself and took her notebook from her bag.

"What can you tell us about Symon Belanov?"

The beautiful face didn't flicker. She appeared to think for a moment.

"Belanov. Very poor player. Almost dangerous, I would say. But he paid his way onto teams, one of which was ours. 2008. Not a good year for us. That was the end of our association. I recall hearing he'd been involved with some sort of arms dealing and fell foul of a rival gang. If you lie with dogs, you get fleas."

"A maxim that could be D'Arcy Roth's motto. What else did you know about Belanov?"

"You know very little about me or my company if that is your impression, Ms Stubbs. As for Symon Belanov? Independently wealthy, but always looking for the next opportunity. He dealt in small weapons, although the shop window was cars. A social climber, rather ill-mannered. Reasonably attractive and made the most of it, so naturally popular with women."

"Not you, by the sounds of it," Beatrice commented.

"No. Not with me. I'm hardly his type but he still made a pass. Probably more of a reflex than anything else. But he took offence at my refusal and made life extremely uncomfortable that season. I was relieved to see the back of him."

Kälin pointed his pen at D'Arcy. "Why aren't you his type?"

"The man had rather clichéd preferences. His ideal woman would have large breasts and ginger hair, usually accompanied by a loud laugh and the manners of a peasant."

Beatrice noted real spite in D'Arcy's tone and wondered at the truth behind the rejection story.

"After that season, did you have any further contact?"

"Not much. We met once more in Argentina, for a tournament, but his team were knocked out in the first round. He deserved it."

"Don't you find it puzzling, Ms D'Arcy, that the only connection between these high-profile men is you, or your company?"

"No. As I explained before, I make contact with a lot of people, the vast majority of whom are still alive."

Kälin spoke. "The dead men. Do you know of anyone else who knew them all? Any mutual friends?"

She leaned her head back and looked at the roof of the tent, silent for several moments. Beatrice had to admire how the polo kit suited her. The dark blue matched her eyes, the white jodhpurs clung to her fit, shapely legs, and her hair, escaping in damp curls from her ponytail, gave her a touch of vulnerability.

"I believe some people are acquainted with two, even three, of the men you mentioned. I'm not aware of anyone who knew them all. Yet many such individuals must exist and some solid detective work will undoubtedly bring them to light. Perhaps when you find them, you might stop hounding me."

Kälin ignored her jibe. "I'd like you to provide us with an alibi for the third of May 2009. Here is my card; you can call me anytime on Monday."

Beatrice stood and put away her notes. "You are quite likely to see more of us, Ms D'Arcy. A fact I dislike just as much as you. Best of luck with the tournament today. We'll be off now."

D'Arcy didn't move. "I'm sure you can find your own way out. Goodbye, officers."

Kälin led the way back into the sunshine. Maybe it was watching sport, or sparring with that woman, but Beatrice had worked up quite an appetite.

"Herr Kälin, I know it's Saturday and you have already given up a large chunk of your free time. But I wonder whether I can persuade you to have lunch with me? We could throw a few ideas around; see if we can make some progress. What do you think?"

Kälin looked suspicious. "Only if I can choose the restaurant."

Chapter 22

Kälin seemed on friendly terms with the staff of Restaurant Rössli and offered to choose for Beatrice. He ordered the same dish and when their meals arrived, Beatrice was glad she'd placed her trust in him. At least where food was concerned. A pat of herby butter melted into rivulets down a startlingly large steak, surrounded by golden chips. Substantial, greasy and just what she fancied. And it smelt divine.

"*En guete.*"

"*En guete.* This looks delicious." Beatrice tucked in and chewed on a rich and juicy chunk of meat.

"If you don't like it, we can change ...?"

Beatrice shook her head. "No, not at all. I was just thinking about today." She tailed off, trying to grasp that elusive thought which kept returning, bouncing and vanishing again. She ate her food and, although deep in thought, relished every mouthful.

Kälin eyed her. "You wanted to discuss ideas?"

"Mmm. It's about that woman. I can't quite pin my finger on it, but there's something peculiar about Antonella D'Arcy."

"You don't like her."

She took a sip of red wine. "No, I don't. And the strange thing is, it bothers her. Now why on earth would that be?"

"You judged her." Kälin added salt to his chips.

"Yes, I did rather, didn't I? But why ever should she care?"

"I don't know. But your comment on her lack of conscience, at her villa, touched her. And again today, what you said about her company ..."

"Yes, I definitely seem to rub her up the wrong way. Not that she harbours a soft spot for you either. I must say, your idea to catch her off guard at the polo match was inspired."

"As was your threat that she will see us again." He stopped and Beatrice realised they had just exchanged compliments.

They ate in silence for several minutes.

"Would you mind ordering me another glass of red, Herr Kälin? I find it goes down very well with this steak."

He raised his eyebrows, but did not comment and communicated her request to the waitress.

Beatrice continued. "You know, Sabine used the word 'chameleon' to describe our killer. It's rather appropriate for D'Arcy, too."

"True. She is skilled at adapting to her environment, blending into her surroundings."

"Precisely." The waitress brought the wine. "*Danke*. And what happens to a chameleon when it has camouflaged itself blue and another environment intrudes, say, orange."

"Blue and orange? In which country is this chameleon?"

Beatrice gave him an unamused look. "What I mean is that the woman seems at odds with herself. She wanted to meet us at her home, so we would see a particular side of her. The mother, a charming woman with a weakness for macaroons. Today, she was the hard-nosed ball-breaker, out to win. It is a role, just like any other. I don't think we've met the real D'Arcy yet."

Kälin replaced his cutlery. "This is why you dislike her? Because she has two faces?"

"Partly. But I think there's something suspicious about her performance. Two of her comments stick in my mind."

"The dogs and fleas remark?"

Beatrice was surprised at his insight. "Yes. How can she judge Belanov's business operations while she profits from all manner of dirty dealings? And the second was her attitude to the dead men. She asked if they might have developed a conscience. The implication being that their actions were sufficiently reprehensible to justify their sudden deaths."

"But where does this take us? D'Arcy didn't kill them; her alibis are solid."

"I don't think for a second that she did. But she most certainly runs with the horse and the hounds."

"And this expression means what exactly?"

"She gets the best of both worlds. I think she plays the corporate cynic, but her heart is not in it. I think she genuinely despised these men and feels no sorrow at their passing. If anything, there's a sense of righteousness. Whether she was involved or not, I don't know. At least not yet."

Kälin angled his head in a half-shrug, half-nod. "What are your thoughts on our press leak? Do you think it was just D'Arcy's opportunism after my interview?"

"No, I don't. Unless you gave her substantially more information during your second encounter, she didn't know about the DNA. Which could still mean she leaked the information, revealing she knows far more about these deaths than any old innocent witness."

"I gave her some extra information about the strength of our team but nothing about the reason we linked the killings. So, you're right, she may have shown her hand. But we still should be aware the leak may have come from within."

She met his eyes with a challenge. Deflecting attention from oneself by suspecting others was an old trick. "Yes, that thought had occurred to me."

He stared right back, giving nothing away. "It might be worth squeezing the journalist, to get him to reveal his sources."

"We can but try. Let's get a bit of background and identify his weak spots." She patted her mouth with her napkin. "Herr Kälin, your recommendation was excellent. I thoroughly enjoyed that meal."

"Good. Would you like coffee, or shall I get the bill?"

"I've taken up enough of your time. Let's pay up and head for home." Beatrice finished her wine.

Kälin hailed the waitress. "I wasn't sure you'd like this kind of farmer's food."

"Farmer's food is my favourite sort. Solid and unpretentious. Not the sort of fare they would serve in those crisp white tents at the polo park."

Kälin let out a short laugh. Beatrice cocked her head in enquiry.

"It would definitely be inappropriate at the polo park, Frau Stubbs. We've just eaten *Pferdefleisch*. Horse steak."

Chapter 23

His secretary waited, as he flipped through the stack of message slips and made frequent notes. He'd noticed an air about her recently. Mouth permanently upside-down, constant worried frown and her shoulders slumped in defeat. Not the kind of attitude which added value. Ryman needed positivity, dynamism and energy. And, it had to be said, youth. Sibylle's competence was unquestionable, but she was over forty and it showed. Ryman filed the issue as something to consider over the weekend and to act upon next week. Maybe bring in an assistant, so Sibylle could train her the way he liked, then 'promote' Sibylle to a position where her skills would be better used. Out of his sight.

"Right. These have gotta be done today, the rest can wait till Monday. Is there anything else, because I'd like to hit the road pretty soon."

"No, not from my side. Your suit is ready, hanging in your closet. And I booked *Restaurant Adler* for your lunch meeting."

"Sorry? What lunch meeting?"

"That journalist, Jack. You asked me to slot her in for lunch today, as you have already cancelled on her twice."

"Hell, I don't have time to talk to a journo today. Cancel. Tell her to put some questions in an email and if I get time, I'll answer them."

"No problem. I'll cancel the reservation at the same time." She gave a sad shrug and left the room. His mind was made up. Sibylle had to go. She should know him better than that. The last thing he'd want to do before heading off for the weekend would be a chat to a hack. Let's face it, Sibylle wasn't happy here and he sure as hell wasn't happy with her. He removed his files from the drawer and laid them in his briefcase. His desk was as clear as his conscience. After a quick glance around the huge office with its view of the Kunstmuseum and the distant castle, he picked up his jacket and left the room.

Voices reached him as he locked the door, speaking that weird German he disliked. Sibylle seemed to be giving someone a hard time, judging by the tone of her voice. He rounded the corner, his expression deliberately mean and impatient. He would not be delayed. A svelte blonde in a gray suit was arguing with Sibylle, whose face registered exasperation.

"Problem, Sibylle?"

"Yes, Jack. This is the journalist who had an appointment today. She wants to reschedule your interview. I'm trying to explain to her it's not convenient."

The girl swivelled round and blushed. Cute. A natural blonde with a tiny nose and blow-job lips. His eyes flicked downward as he held out his hand. Slight figure, not all that much up top, but a killer pair of pins.

"Hi, I'm Jack Ryman. Listen, sorry for the inconvenience. You caught me at a busy time."

"Melanie Roche. Pleased to meet you, Mr Ryman. I understand that today is difficult. It's just your secretary mentioned you were leaving for Zürich this afternoon. That's where I'm based. I was wondering if there would be a window while you're there?"

"Not this weekend, Ms Roche. I'm playing in a polo match on Saturday and meeting friends on Sunday. I'm kinda all work or all play, know what I mean?"

"I see. Never mind. Perhaps I could return to Vaduz next week?"

"Nope. I'm leaving Zürich Sunday and flying to New York. I can't say when I'll be back in this office. It's only one base of many."

Sibylle folded her arms. "So, you see, Frau Roche, as I already explained, we'll call you."

A surge of irritation at Sibylle's smug manner caused him to clench his teeth. "One second. Which paper is this for?"

"I'm freelance, Mr Ryman. But this article has been commissioned by *Time* magazine. They want to give the banking world a chance to voice their side. A response from the 1% to the other 99? Here's my press pass."

He glanced at it, his mind elsewhere. "I can give you a half hour. Let's grab a sandwich. But I want to be out of here by one thirty. That do you?"

Her smile lifted her face from pretty to beautiful. The girl was a fox. "That would be great, Mr Ryman! Thank you so much."

He gestured to the lift. "Talk to you Monday, Sibylle. Have yourself a fine weekend."

Because next week, you're gonna get one hell of a shock.

"We'll take my car, as I need to dump these bags. Where are you parked?" he asked, as the doors opened into the basement parking lot.

"I came by train today, so I don't have a vehicle."

"By train? You serious? Yeah, well, I guess that's a whole lot easier here. So how are you getting back to Zürich?"

"Same way. It's not bad. I have my laptop so I can work, you know."

"You got any other business in Liechtenstein, Ms Roche?"

"No, none. I only came here to interview you."

"What say I give you a ride back to Zürich? You get to ask your questions and I get some company on the journey? That suit?"

"Really? Mr Ryman, that is so kind of you. So much more than I could have expected. I really appreciate it."

"Not a problem."

Placing his case on the back seat and hanging his jacket on the hook, Ryman made some rapid calculations based on optimistic forecasts. Taking the freeway would give him just over an hour. The scenic route could double the time they spent together, giving him chance to get past the interview and into the personal. Good thing he'd kept plans fluid. He opened the passenger door of the Audi S5 and she tucked herself in butt first, swinging her legs after her. Classy, very finishing school. She gave a quick, nervous smile up at him as he closed the door. She was intimidated. He liked that. Lucky girl. She was gonna get a whole lot more than she expected.

"I kinda like to avoid the freeway, Melanie. I figured we'd go up the other side of the lake. Takes a little longer, but gives you more time for questions."

"Whatever you like, Mr Ryman. I'm just grateful for this opportunity to talk to you."

He flashed her a benevolent smile as they emerged from the underground parking lot into the rain.

"Hell, the view's gonna be lousy if it's raining." The climate irritated him. Europe always had such shitty weather.

"It might be sunny again by the time we get there. *April, April, macht was er will*. Do you speak German, Mr Ryman?"

"Nope. Not really necessary." He waited for the inevitable. Just one snippy comment, lady, and you can walk. He stopped at lights in Schaan, his knee jumping impatiently.

"Oh. Well, it's just a saying. Basically, April does whatever it wants. I suppose the language of banking is English, so there's no need to learn anything else. You're lucky."

"Damn right. I'm an American. You're a German Swiss, right?"

"I was born in Fribourg, to a French mother and a Swiss German father. So I'm half-and-half. Where were you born?"

"You know what? You can Google all that bullshit. Let's cut to the chase here. *Time* magazine want you to get the bankers' side of the story? Well, you got a banker right here, so make the most of it. I'll tell you the truth. Because, more than most people, I can."

They crossed the border into Switzerland and he accelerated, feeling better. Open road, a weekend of fun ahead, and on Monday, he'd be back home. The journo took a notepad from her huge handbag. Why the hell did women need such epic bags? And carrying them around on one shoulder all day; in the long-term, that's gotta hurt.

"OK, Mr Ryman. Let's begin. The newspapers blame ..."

"Call me Jack. And the newspapers don't have a goddam clue who's to blame. Here's the thing. Everybody is a party to what goes on. No one is blameless. The banks have to take some responsibility, but not as much as the mortgage brokers, who set up the home buyers with real estate they couldn't afford. Add that to the central banks, reducing interest rates to stimulate liquidity. Don't forget the credit rating agencies, who gave triple-A ratings to the collaterized debt obligations, making them very attractive to those who didn't understand them. Governments? Forget it. Their aim is to keep the big boys sweet and the people passive. So everybody's got dirty hands. Sticking it to the banks is ill-informed, but typical."

She took several seconds to scribble down his words, as he turned onto St Gallerstrasse. "You see these parties as equally guilty? Although the central banks' choice to lower rates was intended to kick-start the economy, no?"

Ryman gave a tsk of exasperation. "They had to. After the dotcom collapse and 9/11, the market needed to keep cash flowing. But with lower rates, investors are forced to take bigger risks to get decent return on investment. The CDOs looked like a damn good bet. Mortgages and house prices were rising, and everyone believed they would continue to do so. You know, between 2001 and 2005, US subprime mortgages increased by 300%."

"But that kind of growth can't be sustainable."

"We're all wise after the event, right? Demand for housing was high. The economy was doing fine, people were paying their instalments, the debt obligations had guaranteed collateral. What's not to like?"

"So what went wrong?"

Ryman was enjoying this. She had him on home ground, where he was at his best.

"The real estate bubble burst. It had to happen sometime. Prices dropped, mortgages were reset, buyers couldn't pay, lenders foreclosed. Supply starts to outstrip demand. And now the collateral underpinning your debt risk is just part of that excess of supply."

Approaching Gams, their upward route remained in shadow and mist, while the sun threw an enticing light on the mountains ahead as they climbed. He drove faster.

She looked up from her notepad. "So the CDOs weren't, after all, a 'damn good bet'. Yet the investment banks were pushing them well into 2006, after the property crisis had already hit. My research tells me that around the world, CDOs issued leapt from 120 billion dollars worth in 2005 to 475 billion in 2006."

"You walk into MacDonald's and order a Big Mac with fries. You're hungry as hell and that's gonna hit the spot. You been thinking about it for the last 50 miles and now you're at the counter. Your mouth is watering; your nose is full of the smell of prime beef. Gimme a Big Mac with large fries. The kid behind the till says, No Ma'am, I can't serve you one of those. I have it on good authority that in a few years time, you'll have high cholesterol and hardened arteries. So for your own good, I'm gonna have to refuse."

"So if demand for toxic products is there, someone has to sell them. Is that what you're saying?"

"You know anything at all about economics, Melanie?"

"Can we turn to another area which has upset people? You had one of the highest severance packages of last year. People ask how this is possible, when your company went bankrupt, losing millions of dollars of shareholders' money."

"A contract is a contract. I negotiated hard before I joined Mendoza, and made sure that whatever happened, I would be remunerated for my work."

"Well done. And yet, you were the strongest advocate of performance-related pay for your top executives."

"Like I said, I fought for what I got."

"Do you think the performance-related elements contributed to these executives taking bigger and bigger risks, in order to guarantee their bonuses?"

"I guess you'd have to ask them, Melanie."

She took a couple seconds. Out of her depth and drowning. She scribbled away but you could see she knew; she'd grabbed a fully grown tiger by the tail and had nowhere to go.

Still one more try. He had to hand it to her, she didn't give in easy.

"Can I ask you about RAM's policy of buying poverty-stricken countries' debts and prosecuting them through legal loopholes? Many of our readers ask how you can demand repayment from a country which has no functioning hospitals."

"Kid, if you buy anything on credit, time's gonna come you have to pay it back. Hell, even a child can understand that. It's a matter of principle. Borrow from me, I'll want it back."

"But they didn't borrow from you. You bought their debts from someone else. How are these countries supposed to recover from civil war, drought, pandemics and so on when everything they generate goes to paying you and your investors?"

"Hey, so the system's unfair. I didn't make the system, I'm just the repo-man. Just doing my job and getting back what's owed."

"Fair point. Um, Jack, do you think we could stop quickly at a garage? I need to use the bathroom."

Her face was a little pale. Maybe the speed upset her, not just the car but the conversation. "Sure. There'll be something in this next village. You okay?"

"I'm a little dizzy. Trying to write shorthand, keep up with you and watch the road is a bit too much for me."

He shot her a wink as he pulled into the gas station. She hurried towards the rest rooms. He thought back over their conversation. Was she trying to trap him? The minute she got back in the car, he was going to ask her about her angle. If she planned to stitch him up, he would oblige, and give her totally uncensored material. A few decent sound bites would show he was unrepentant, and whining is for losers. She was back.

"Jack, I'm just going to get a bottle of water, can I get one for you?"

"I'll take a Coke. Thanks, Melanie."

Watching her walk to the shop, he knew she was watching him watching her, reflected in the glass doors. Good. Women love it when they're being admired. Fastest way to make any woman fall at your feet? Let her see you watching. Pretend to hide it. Every Jane Doe wants to be wanted. Look away that second too late. Tell Jane's best friend you're crazy about Jane, but ssh, okay? Let her think she's caught you, when she's the one who's trapped. The female ego can be used to your advantage, just like everything else. His eyes flicked to the clock. She was taking her time. How long does it take to get a water and a Coke? He looked back to the shop and saw her emerging from the restrooms once more, carrying a plastic bag.

"Sorry. Looks like I inherited my mother's Gallic stomach. I can eat anything, including snails, but movement makes me sick."

"Yeah, these roads are a little crazy. I guess the freeway woulda suited you better, right? What say we put the roof down?"

The sun had emerged with conviction, drying the roads and illuminating the landscape.

She shook her head. "As I said, April's unreliable. Maybe we're safer with the roof on."

He accelerated onto the main road with a flamboyant screech. It felt fantastic. Shit, he didn't want to talk about work anymore.

"My turn to ask some questions, Melanie." The tone of his voice told her who was boss. His car, his company, his time, his choices. She pulled the Coke from the bag, unscrewed it and handed it to him. He took a long swig.

She drank several gulps of her water and licked her lips. "We're taking turns? So what do you want to know?"

"What's your angle? Are you really telling the other side of the story? Or are you gonna do a hatchet job?"

"That depends on what you say, Jack. We're interested in what drives the bankers, what part they played in this mess and what lessons have been learned."

Ryman didn't know this route all that well, but the sun, the car, this babe beside him and the awesome scenery encouraged him to put his foot down. The car roared along the road to Wildhaus. Life didn't get much better. Whirling up a Swiss mountain in a fine automobile, with a beautiful foreign girl at his side, a weekend of fun ahead of him and a first-class flight to New York, where they were all waiting to welcome him home. How in hell could he feel guilty?

"Jack?"

"To tell you the God's honest truth, Melanie, I don't know. As for the role we played, I'm pretty sure I answered that. We were a part of the problem, but it's not like we had an alternative. So as for lessons learned, ask around. Are humans ever gonna stop wanting more than they deserve? How can you blame people for making the most of an opportunity. You know what? If you had the chance, you'd do the same. But I'll be honest about what drives me; moments like this. I feel better than ... hey, what's up? You look terrible."

The girl's skin looked pale to start with, but now she was green. Her notebook fell into her lap and her hand lay limp, pen wedged between her fine fingers.

"Sorry, I'm so sorry. I think I need to get out. Could you pull over?" She pointed to a small lane into the forest. Sweat broke out on her forehead. She looked sick as a poisoned rat. He pulled over, driving a little way into the trees, so she'd have somewhere to hide. He was such a goddamed gent. She opened the door and lurched toward the forest, but he made no move to follow. First off, she wouldn't want a man like him to watch her puke. Second of all, he was tired. His whole body weighed him down like it was made of wet sand. He had to shape up. He fumbled for the Coke bottle and struggled to get the top off. Caffeine. He needed to sharpen his mind. She'd be back soon and most of the journey was ahead of them. Not to mention the evening. He hoped she'd stop puking by then. Wouldn't it be great if he could just throw a switch and they'd be there? In his Zürich hotel, on his king size bed, with soft pillows, white linen, and nothing to worry about. He lifted his head and looked into the brush. Nowhere, goddammit. This was the last time he gave anyone a ride.

The skirt suit rolled up in the bottom of her bag, her bag folded into her rucksack, the figure emerged in hiking hues of grey, brown and green. Her hair was stuffed under a woollen hat, and she wore hygienist's gloves. His head rested against the door, mouth open, snoring deeply. She sat still for a full five minutes, checking for any signs of movement through the trees. Satisfied, she hauled him sideways and took his place, driving the car off the track, through the forest and as far into the foliage as she could go. She altered both seats to a full recline and pulled a clear plastic bag from the pocket of her rucksack. She broke two small capsules into it and pulled it over his head, tying it tightly around his fleshy neck. She watched and waited, listening to the movements of the plastic.

In, out. In, out.

In.

Out.

She waited until the sounds ceased completely before clearing up after herself. The sun broke through the tree canopy and an idea occurred to her. It took her a few seconds to find the right switch, but she finally pressed the roof retraction button and watched the mechanics open them up like a sardine can. She got out, slammed the door and walked around to the other side.

"How's that for a hatchet job, Jack?"

Chapter 24

Zürich 2012

First chance he got, Chris intended to shake Xavier by the hand. The man was inspired, though he didn't realise it. His suggestion of a picnic on the lake was prompted by his kind nature, a sense of being the host. It would never cross Xavier's mind it meant they'd get to see Sabine and Conceição in bikinis.

But Chris spotted the whiff of opportunity instantly and had to play down his enthusiasm in case he gave himself away. Sabine was all for it, persuading a curiously reluctant Conceição. She caved finally and even got excited as they planned the route. The only drawback being that Chris couldn't ask her for a date on Friday night as well as spending all Saturday in her company. That would look over-eager. Instead, he would see if the picnic might be extended into the evening, possibly as a foursome, but at some stage ditching the other two. Play it by ear and who knows how Sunday might look.

Anticipation filled the air on Saturday morning. As Chris took the tram along the lake to the jetty, everyone seemed to be going somewhere. Twenty-seven degrees forecast for the day. Plenty hot enough to swim or sunbathe. The sun flashed off the water, reflected from car windscreens and lit hopeful faces as they set off for their weekends. Chris's grin was a match for any one of them.

"Chris! Over here!"

Conceição waved from the boat. She was wearing a wraparound sundress in bright blues and purples and wearing a headscarf. She looked stunning. Xavier, in shorts and a baseball cap, messed around with the ropes holding the boat to its moorings. He spotted Chris and motioned for him to get aboard. Chris obeyed, throwing his backpack in before clambering onto the deck. Not a luxurious vessel, but in good condition, comfortable and with a sun deck. Sabine smiled up at him from the leather banquette, shading her eyes, despite her oversized sunglasses. She wore white cut-off trousers, a white halterneck top which showed off her pale shoulders, white deck shoes and her platinum hair up in a silver clip. Chris felt he should be the one shielding his eyes.

"Am I late, or are you early?" he asked.

"Bit of both, I think. Conceição and I brought the picnic." She tapped a cool box with her foot.

Xavier threw the ropes up to Conceição and leapt on board with surprising grace. He shook Chris's hand. "We have good weather so the lake will be busy. We'll go further down, direction Rapperswil, to escape the crowds. Is everyone ready?"

Chris chose to stand next to Xavier, watching him steer a course southwards, using the shore as a guide. The speed and spray created a buzz of enjoyment in Chris and he looked round to see the girls lifting smiles into the wind.

"Is it expensive to rent a boat, Xav?" he shouted above the noise.

Xavier shook his head, maintaining his constant scan of the water. "The expensive part is taking the Captain's licence. It costs a lot of time and money and even then many people fail the test."

"You can't take a boat out without a licence?"

Xavier grinned. "Welcome to Switzerland."

Sabine sighed, shoving around the potato skins on her plate. "That was a perfect meal. You know, this has been a lovely afternoon. I hope B enjoyed herself as much at the polo match yesterday. I wouldn't want to spend a day in the company of Kälin."

Xavier helped himself to more salad. "Herr Kälin is ... special. To understand him, well, it takes a while. Anyway, I'd be very surprised if they found out anything more from D'Arcy. She's tough. I don't think she'll give much away."

"No, she'll be very cagey," Conceição agreed. "I think waiting for D'Arcy to slip up is a waste of time. In fact, I wonder if we should suggest pursuing a more dynamic approach."

Conceição poured more wine for the three of them. Xavier stuck to Ice Tea.

"What I mean is research. I think we could predict where D'Arcy is likely to strike next. Or arrange for someone else to strike. With some intelligent analysis of high-profile corporate scandals, we could pinpoint who she's likely to hit and why. Then cross-reference that data with her personal or professional contacts. I think we'd probably end up with a shortlist of around five or six men, all of whom could be tailed and the killer trapped."

Sabine pursed her lips. "It's a good idea, but Interpol would never agree to the extra expense. We couldn't tail six men for however many months ..."

Conceição shook her head. "We wouldn't have to. If we alerted the personal security these men employ, and they *all* have bodyguards, they would have the profile, know what to look for. If they suspect something, they call a professional squad and catch her or him in the act."

"It could work as a parallel approach to what we do now," agreed Xavier. "We could share these thoughts with B when she gets back."

"Yes. Why not use some time this week to prepare a presentation? B and Kälin are visiting Vaduz and St Moritz, so we have a few days. Good idea, Conceição!" Sabine's face shone pink. With her colouring, she should really keep out of the sun. Xavier too. So that left him and Conceição.

Sabine turned to him. "Chris, what do you think?"

"I need to rest and digest. I'm going to lie in the sun and think this idea over. Anyone else feel like sunbathing?"

Predictably, Xavier and Sabine shook their heads.

"I'll come with you." Conceição stood up. "I want to explain exactly what I mean."

Xavier, once again, set up the perfect circumstances, suggesting a drink to round off the day. Sabine seemed reluctant, glancing at her watch. Chris willed her to refuse, especially because Conceição agreed easily. But she gave another of her disappointed sighs and said yes.

Wandering up the Niederdorf, Chris just followed Xavier. The choice of bars, restaurants, cafés and beer gardens was overwhelming. Xavier, whose nose was sunburnt, guided them up a side street to Bar Corazon and recommended the *Weissbier*. Conceição and Chris took up the challenge, but Sabine ordered a mineral water, claiming dehydration.

"This is a great area," enthused Conceição. "I've never come this far off the main streets. Good tip, thanks, Xavier."

"You're welcome. Yes, it's always lively at the weekends. And there are several art cinemas around here, where you can see films which are not so commercial."

Conceição looked up. "I noticed. *Gainsbourg* is playing this weekend. I'd love to see that film."

Chris seized his moment. "Me too. I've heard such great things about it. How about checking it out later?" He remembered his manners. "What do you say, Sabine, Xav?"

To his delight, Xavier pulled an apologetic face. "I'm sorry, Chris, I can't. I have an appointment this evening."

Sabine's nose wrinkled. "No. I've had enough for today. I prefer to go back to my apartment."

Chris shrugged. "Looks like it's just you and me, Conceição."

She hesitated and glanced at Sabine. "Could we see it another evening? Sabine and I already arranged to have dinner and watch a video tonight."

"No problem. Hey, here comes the beer. *Prost*, everyone, and thanks to Xavier for a great day out."

They raised their glasses and Chris drank deeply. Choosing to spend both weekend evenings in the company of that sour-faced little ferret instead of him? It didn't give him much confidence in Conceição's taste. As he met each pair of eyes for the toast, he saw Sabine's smug expression reflecting off every surface.

Chapter 25

Zürich 2012

She should have called James. Just because there had been no real signs, and she was preoccupied with the case, she hadn't. She'd cancelled their session, choosing to send him a jaunty text message instead. She regretted it now. She lay under the duvet, staring at the ceiling. Foolhardy and irresponsible. The only way to cope with the dogs is to consciously, constantly manage them. And she'd done extremely well. Weekends were a danger zone, so Beatrice prepared herself with care. As other people's anticipation built on Friday afternoons, Beatrice's dread of forty-eight hours of nothing grew in inverse proportion.

She'd taken to arranging a cultural event on Fridays; the opera, a concert in one of the churches, a play by the English-speaking theatre group, giving her something else to think about. Saturdays she did some shopping, had lunch at Ken's and spent the afternoon writing a report on the week's activities for Lyon. Saturday night was her television programme evening, for which she would cook something special. And on Sundays, she explored. A long hike up Uetliberg, a trip to Schaffhausen's waterfalls, a wander around the animal park; anything that tired her out before returning to her apartment and making her Sunday phone calls home. But this week, she had slipped up, due to the polo match yesterday. And found herself with a long empty Sunday ahead of her, when the dogs were pacing.

This time tomorrow, she would be preparing for work, with a routine to follow. All she had to do was weather the next twenty-four hours. Whether she liked it or not.

Whether the weather be mild or whether the weather be not,
Whether the weather be cold or whether the weather be hot,
We'll weather the weather whatever the weather,
Whether we like it or not.

Tears leaked into her hair as she recalled her mother reciting the verse. It would not do. She sat up. Find something to engage your mind. Force yourself. Shower, breakfast, read the news. But even as she threw back the duvet and headed for the bathroom, she felt defeated and tearful, in the knowledge that whatever images were dominant on the news website would drag her down, with their litany of cruelty, hunger, disease and abuse. So leave the news alone. She would not spend a day weeping over the death of a maltreated child, or the struggle to survive in a war-ravaged African state. When she had one of these days, even feel-good stories gave rise to agonies. Sweet that a little kitten had been rescued from a chimney breast, but what about all those poor wretched animals kept in cages and beaten so their meat is tender when eaten?

She'd taken her pills without fail so it did seem odd to find herself dragged into such depths without warning. Yesterday, she'd felt quite energised and chirpy, only to wake with this black shroud. Beatrice realised she was standing in front of the sink, staring at the bath mat. It would not do. With a shake, she got into the shower.

At quarter to ten, she put a bottle of water and mini-pack of After Eights into her handbag with her guidebook and walked with determination to the Hauptbahnhof. She would decide where to go when she got there. *Think positive.* One of the wonderful things about Switzerland was you could go anywhere by train. All those magical sounding names; Prague, Dijon, Lugano, Geneva, Bellinzona ... but not one of them held the attraction of Brampford Speke. International adventures at her fingertips when all she wanted to do was potter around Tesco's with Matthew. She shook herself. This was going to be a bad one. Staring up at the departures board in the huge hall of the main station, her vision was blurred with tears. It just wouldn't do. Perhaps she should just go back to bed. *Make your mind up, for heaven's sake.*

A blonde woman in a Grace Kelly dress and white neckerchief stood beside her, looking up at the board. She glanced at Beatrice and gave a polite smile. It took a considerable effort for Beatrice to do the same. Then the woman did a double take.

"Oh, hello again. I recognise you from Big Ben. The tea shop? You're the crossword expert, right?"

Beatrice gawped at the woman for a moment before her memory recovered itself. Glossy blonde hair, a perfectly made-up face and astonishingly white teeth; the Tatler woman.

"Yes, well. I can hardly be called an expert. I seem to recall you were the one who assisted Ken."

"That was a one-off. I'm normally useless with those things. So when I figured it out, I just couldn't keep it to myself. I'm Madeleine Lassiter."

"Beatrice Stubbs." She shook the proffered hand, observing that Madeleine was married and wore false nails. "Nice to meet you."

"Same here. So, where are you headed today, Beatrice?"

A panicky sense of incompetence swelled in Beatrice's throat. She looked back at the board and grabbed a name at random. "Interlaken. I've heard it's beautiful. And you?"

"Oh, I'm not actually travelling. But some Sundays, when my husband has to work, I just like to come down here and enjoy the bustle. There's not a whole lot else to do with all the stores closed and I get bored of my own company."

The woman's truthful reply touched Beatrice. "I know what you mean. I usually organise trips for myself at the weekends. Keeps me occupied."

"I hear you. Say, you're a little early, aren't you?"

Beatrice checked the departure time and saw she had picked a train due to depart in forty minutes. Small talk with a stranger would be an excellent distraction.

"Yes, I have a pathological horror of being late. But I was planning to have a cup of coffee first. I wonder if you'd like to join me?"

"Sure, I'd like that. How about that place?" Madeleine indicated some incongruously rustic benches in the main hall. "We could sit outside and people-watch. And that way I can smoke, too."

She pulled open her bag and dug out some cigarettes, offering the pack to Beatrice.

"I don't, thank you."

"Good for you. I'd given up until I got here. Seven years as a non-smoker. But you're never really free of the weed."

"No, I suppose not. I never tried, so I think I'll keep it that way."

At least Madeleine was considerate, fanning the smoke away, as they settled at a table outside *Brasserie Federal*. Beatrice noted the Chopard watch, studded with diamonds. Up close, the immaculate grooming was no less impressive, although she did look unhealthily thin. Beatrice suspected diet pills. Madeleine seemed to be assessing her in a similar way, but was unlikely to come to the same conclusion.

Beatrice did her duty. "I'm guessing from your accent that you're not Swiss."

"Nope. I'm from Michigan. But you come from Great Britain, right?"

The waiter appeared.

"Hi there. We'd like two coffees, please. Cafe latte okay for you, Beatrice?"

Although Beatrice generally disliked the common assumption everyone should speak English, Madeleine's manner towards the young man was friendly and pleasant. He gave her a smile as he took their order and returned back through the glass doors.

Beatrice looked up at the gigantic blue angel hanging from the roof of the Haupthalle. "Yes, I'm British. A Londoner. Lived there all my life."

"London's so cool. A great city. So why are you in Zürich?"

"Same as most expatriates in Switzerland. I'm here to work."

"Right. Banking?"

Beatrice deflected the question. "More advisory. What about you?"

"I represent the other expat trend. The spouses and significant others. My husband works in finance, so we're here on a two-year contract before heading back to New York." Her introduction was rehearsed, probably through repetition, yet a wistful note could be heard in her sigh.

"I see. And does he often have to work at the weekend?"

"He does at the moment. So I'm left to shop, or read, or explore the galleries on my own. It works out pretty well. When Michael is free, he always wants to do something active. Ski, hike, cycle, you name it. The cultural stuff doesn't interest him, whereas I love it."

"So do I. Much more stimulating than hurtling down a mountain. I'm the antithesis of active, I'm afraid."

Madeleine's smile bloomed and faded, like a distant firework. "I like both. But whether it's snowboarding or a jazz concert, I prefer to have someone to share it with. You know what? During my first couple weeks here, I got so lonely that if I heard someone speaking English, I'd deliberately bump into them so I could start a conversation. That's why I hang out at places like Big Ben. Just for someone to talk to."

The woman's honest need for companionship shamed Beatrice. There was such a thing as trying to be too independent. The coffees arrived, with the bill rolled up in a shot glass.

Beatrice picked it up, making a decision. "I'll get this, Madeleine. You can buy next time. Now listen, I think I'll give Interlaken a miss today. Have you been to the Kunsthaus at all? They're open on Sundays and have the most fabulous collection."

Madeleine's smile lasted much longer that time.

The dogs were quiet. Temporarily.

Chapter 26

Zürich 2012

The package in locker 939 at Baden Station contained no surprises. Just a Pay-As-You-Go mobile. The figure, aware of curious glances from the teenagers loitering on the concourse, moved outside to the sunshine. Noisier, certainly, but far better cover. Taxi drivers looked up enquiringly, so the figure walked away in search of some privacy, phone in hand.

Eight minutes later, it rang.

"This week. Do it as soon as you can."

"Tuesday's a good day. Fewer tourists. Latest, Wednesday. I want to be back in Zürich for Thursday evening. "

"Excellent. So you're ready with the other one?"

"Almost. It's not going to be difficult. Just a question of timing. And timing is one of my strong points."

"I can't argue with that. I'd like this finished by the weekend. Then I'll take the heat while both of you get away for a holiday."

"No problem. Get away where?"

"Wherever you want to go. Maldives, Seychelles, Acapulco? Take a break until you feel ready to go back to work."

"Back to work? So you've changed your mind about it being the last one?"

The voice contained a smile. *"No, no. It's definitely the last one. I was talking about your* real *work. Complete by Saturday, take her on holiday somewhere and you can go back to tending the Third World when you feel the time is right. I'll arrange everything. Now, do you foresee any problems?"*

"Not in Ticino. It's all scoped and everything's in position. You're going to love my artistic flair with this one. Inspired, even if I say so myself. Rosaria will approve." The figure laughed. "As for here, at such short notice, I think I can organise something prosaic but effective. Unless you want something more fitting."

"I'd rather it wasn't prosaic. In fact, if you don't mind, I've chosen the method I find most appropriate. And the ideal location, too. It's achingly apt. One might even say this is poetic justice. The details are on their way via our friend. Just make sure the evidence is planted somewhere other than the scene."

"Why?"

"Because I want to be sure they find it. Shouldn't be complicated, so I'm sure you'll find an opportunity. I'm leaving tomorrow but I'll be back on Saturday morning. If anything remains unfinished, it puts me in an awkward position."

"I know. I'll contact you as soon as the job's complete."

"If anything goes wrong, I can always delay my flight. Just let me know."

"Relax. Nothing will go wrong."

After the call was over, the figure put the phone in the padded envelope, posted it and headed back to the car, all the while softly singing their song.

" ... *And I can take or leave it if I please.*"

Chapter 27

Liechtenstein, St Moritz 2012

"Sibylle Keller, Jack Ryman's PA. It is a pleasure to meet you. We can speak in here. Can I get you some refreshments?"

Beatrice and Kälin both accepted a coffee, and Frau Keller disappeared into a side room. The immense office had glass walls, offering a view right up to the castle. Liechtenstein fascinated Beatrice. What appeared to be a simple turn off the motorway was the gateway to a tiny principality, with its own monarchy, number plates and tax laws.

The woman returned and joined them at the conference table, placing a tray with two tiny cups, two small glasses of water, and a bowlful of chocolates in front of them.

She smiled. "So how can I help you?"

Kälin ripped open his colourful paper tube of sugar and poured it into his cup. Without thinking, Beatrice handed over hers. He took it with a nod and repeated the procedure.

"Thank you for talking to us, Frau Keller. We are attempting to clarify the details surrounding the death of Jack Ryman. I know you have spoken to the local police on more than one occasion, but we would like to try your patience once again."

The woman gave a genuine smile. Pepper and salt hair formed a curly frame around her face; the onset of laughter lines around her hazel eyes. Her navy suit was smart yet subtle, and she projected an air of effortless efficiency. A young Joan Plowright came to mind. Beatrice had a feeling they might get along.

"I would like to help in any way I can. My opinion, like that of everyone else who knew him, is simple. Jack did not take his own life."

"Thank you. In the police report, you state when he left the office, he was accompanied by a journalist. They planned to have lunch together," Beatrice prompted.

"Correct. Melanie Roche had made three appointments and on both previous occasions, Jack cancelled at the last minute. But that day, he gave her half an hour."

"That's not long for lunch," observed Kälin.

"No. That was typical of Jack. Everything done in a hurry. In fact, he asked me to cancel Ms Roche again that day. But he met her as he came out of his office and decided to give her a brief interview."

"Why did he change his mind?" asked Beatrice, unwrapping a chocolate.

Frau Keller glanced from her to Kälin, apparently searching for the right words.

"Was Ms Roche attractive, Frau Keller?" Kälin helped her.

"Yes. Young, blonde and very pretty. Just Jack's type. I wasn't surprised when he changed his mind. Although I know they didn't have lunch at *Restaurant Adler*, where I made the reservation, because the owner called me to complain. I don't know where they went."

Beatrice made a note. "Do you remember anything else about this woman, Frau Keller?"

Judging by her stillness and her frown, she was concentrating hard on recalling every detail. A detective's favourite kind of witness.

"Very pretty, early thirties, I would guess. Pale complexion, light-blue eyes. Minimal make-up. She wore a dove-grey skirt suit, which could have been Jaeger. Rather than a blouse underneath, she wore a scoop-necked T-shirt, which was powder blue. She had a silver chain around her neck, with no pendant. I seem to have crystal earrings in mind, Swarovski, but that could be because she told me she was from Zürich. Her press pass looked authentic, and she said she'd been commissioned by *Time* magazine. Her Swiss German was more Luzern than Zürich, and she wore low heels. Black, if I remember well."

Beatrice raised her eyebrows. "If only everyone remembered in such detail, our job would be so much easier. Thank you, Frau Keller. So Jack Ryman left with Ms Roche at 12.45?"

"Closer to one."

Kälin replaced his cup. "Can you think of anyone else who might have wanted to harm him?"

Frau Keller's face creased with amusement. "I'm sorry, Herr Kälin, but it might be easier for me to give you a list of the people who didn't despise Jack Ryman. Not one person who worked for the man had any respect for the way he did business. I don't approve of people acting as judge, jury and executioner, which is why I want to help find the person who killed him. But if I can be completely honest with you, the world is a better place now he's gone."

Beatrice nodded. "And one last thing: Ryman's car: automatic or manual?"

"Automatic, Frau Stubbs. Can I get you more coffee?"

The safety bar locked into place, the machinery hummed and the ground dropped away from them. Tugged into the air, Beatrice's stomach took a second to catch up. A rush of childish excitement filled her and it was all she could do not to shout 'Wheee!' in a high-pitched voice. Given the circumstances, however, that would have been quite inappropriate. Kälin sat grimly beside her, while Herr Müller and Herr Franchi of the Kantonspolizei occupied the chair behind. The two officers probably spent much of their time scampering up and down mountains and Kälin must have grown up on skis. Her frivolity would stand out like a sore thing, so she chose to stay quiet as if visiting a crime scene via a chair lift was a totally commonplace occurence. Keeping a check on her exhilaration, she looked down at the receding car park, the people becoming as featureless as Lowry's matchstick men. She gazed around at the vibrant shades of late spring, relishing the rush of air round her ears, watching the everyday details diminish. Tops of trees skimmed past, almost close enough to touch. She lifted her head to watch the absurdly slight cable winching them to the top, before focusing on their destination. Even as summer approached, the peak remained white and crisply delineated against the blue sky. A sigh of admiration at such pure, powerful beauty escaped her and she turned to Kälin to share the moment. He faced forward, his expression pale and set.

"Herr Kälin?"

"I'm fine, Frau Stubbs. Just a small problem with heights."

Beatrice hid her amusement at finding a chink in Karl Kälin's defences and patted his arm.

"Nearly there now."

After they dismounted from the lift, she watched him taking conscious deep breaths. Herr Franchi leapt onto the platform and indicated two snowmobiles parked beside the station. He handed Beatrice a helmet. Relieved that she had plumped for the trouser suit that morning, she straddled the machine and clutched the officer's jacket. He accelerated and sped off toward the piste. Her attempts to stop grinning were unsuccessful, so she relaxed and beamed her way down the mountain. Why had she never done this before? It was terrific fun. Snow flew up as they skimmed the surface, her cold nose inhaled Alpine air and the speed at which her driver attacked the slopes made Beatrice want to throw back her head and whoop. This is not a holiday, she reminded herself.

The Kantonspolizei Graubünden had been enormously helpful. Their records were well organised, enabling the detectives to respond to all their questions efficiently. Dougie Thompson. Booked two weeks in St Moritz, only lived till the end of the first. He skied daily, taking difficult, off-piste runs, while his wife spent her days in the wellness centre. The two children attended *Skischule*, group lessons in the morning, individual tuition in the afternoon. Thompson left on Sunday afternoon to tackle terrain near Morteratsch, one of the less accessible off-piste routes. His wife raised the alarm at 12.10 on Monday.

"According to your report, she received an SMS from her husband on Sunday afternoon?" asked Kälin.

Herr Müller checked his notes. "Exactly. A message was sent from his phone on Sunday at 16.55, saying the weather was bad. It said he planned to stay at a lodge on the mountain overnight and try the run the following day. So his wife did not become concerned until Monday lunchtime."

"Excuse my ignorance, Herr Müller; I'm not familiar with this region. He was reported missing at midday on Monday. His body was located on Tuesday morning. So why did it take so long to find him?" enquired Beatrice.

"That's a good question, Frau Stubbs. Normally, a lost skier would be found much faster."

Officer Franchi chimed in. "However, bad weather from Sunday to Monday meant that search teams could not achieve much. Rescuers located him on Tuesday morning, and he was not registered at any lodge on Sunday night."

"Time of death was established as 36 to 48 hours earlier," added Müller.

Franchi carried on. "It was clear his death was no accident. The Stapo found his clothes and his drinking flask beside him."

"Suicide." said Müller. "We see this frequently. It is not an unpleasant way to die. Alcohol makes you sleep; your body temperature drops and your vital organs cannot survive hypothermia. These alcohol-related winter deaths look like accidents, but the truth is that many are deliberate."

Franchi's expression revealed some irritation with his gloomy partner. "His wife was convinced there was something wrong. She insisted that Stadtpolizei called us and that we contacted Interpol."

Beatrice sympathised with the police, but had it not been for the family's insistence that something wasn't right, they would not have checked the body for DNA.

"Did you run a toxicology report, Herr Franchi?"

"Yes, this was performed on Wednesday afternoon. After we found the saliva on his flask. And the condoms in his pocket."

The roar of the snowmobile dropped and after far too short a ride in Beatrice's opinion, the officer pulled over towards the trees. He cut the engine and turned to assist Beatrice. Aware she looked suspiciously as if she was enjoying herself, she forced some sobriety into her expression as she turned to greet Kälin and Müller.

"Here is the site. The body was found like this." Officer Müller arranged himself in the snow to give them the picture, for a second, before pushing himself to his feet. "Easy to imagine that he drank the alcohol, undressed and went to sleep."

Franchi chipped in. "But he sent a message on his mobile to his wife, knowing no one would be concerned until after the storm."

Beatrice thought aloud. "So if this was not suicide, or an accident, someone else wrote that message."

Kälin frowned. "I find that hard to believe. Possibly Thompson was forced to write it himself. How could this person plausibly write a message from husband to wife? Even with a certain amount of familiarity, can a stranger reproduce the tone, the terms of affection used between a couple, without in-depth knowledge of their relationship?"

Beatrice wondered for an instant what terms of affection Kälin would use for his significant other, if he had one.

Franchi nodded. "That's an interesting point, Herr Kälin. Because the wife had no doubt it was from him. He referred to her as *Hon*. Our unit assumed Hon was the short form of Honorable. But it seems that is a foreshortened version of Honey, an endearment like *Schätzli* in Swiss German, or *Darling* in English."

"What I don't understand, Herr Müller, is how someone could know that he would be here, at this precise time?" Beatrice asked.

Müller and Franchi exchanged a look. Franchi spoke. "Nor do we, to be honest, Frau Stubbs. The only lead we have is the children's ski instructor. Thompson told his wife that he was going to do a run recommended by one of the staff at the *Skischule*. After questioning the boy, it seems Thompson spent a lot of time talking to this particular woman, and had asked her to go with him on more than one occasion. It seems that on Sunday afternoon, she agreed. The son only knew her as Anni, but he mentioned that she understood Portuguese. Julia Thompson comes from Brazil and both children speak Portuguese as easily as English."

Müller agreed. "And when we uncovered this link, we checked with the *Skischule* on Thursday. Ana-Maria Lima, a Brazilian, had left their employment on the previous Friday. She only worked there a month. Seasonal workers, it happens a lot here. We weren't able to trace her."

"And why do you think he was he carrying condoms?" asked Beatrice.

The three men looked at the ground.

Beatrice clapped her gloves together. "I see. So if someone set a honey-trap and lay in wait to kill him, how would that person escape?"

Franchi's slight smile indicated admiration. "Down the run. You can't go back up. And this one is a real challenge, so whoever it was must have been an expert. Not only that, but the conditions on Sunday evening and Monday were horrible. I am skiing since two years old, and have done this run on many occasions. But I would never attempt it in bad weather."

Beatrice shivered as a breeze lifted her hair. Müller noticed. "Should we go down? Or is there anything else you would like to see?"

"How are we getting down?" asked Kälin, with some concern.

Frost decorated the ends of Müller's moustache. "As I said, Herr Kälin, you can't go back. The lifts are not insured for return journeys. We'll take the snowmobiles across to the cable car."

Kälin blanched and Beatrice replaced her helmet. "Herr Franchi, I do envy you working in such a spectacular location."

"Thank you, Frau Stubbs, but like everything else, after a while, you get used to it."

He started up the machine and Beatrice looked back. No matter how many mountains she climbed, she doubted she'd ever get used to it. And, she smiled to herself, neither would Kälin.

As the BMW rolled along Route 3 towards Chur, Beatrice sifted through the facts. A Portuguese speaker and an expert skier. Must also speak English to access Ryman and Edwards. Maybe van der Veld, too. Knowledge of pharmaceuticals and time to embed herself into the situation ahead of the event. Not to mention the detailed background information on each of these men. The woman had just too many advantages.

Kälin's growl drew her back to the present. "Frau Stubbs? Does anything strike you?"

Beatrice spoke without hesitation. "She's not alone. She has an accomplice who possibly performs the heavy stuff. Maybe she acts as a lure; she is most likely very attractive. Or one is the researcher and one the actor. The amount of information she has allows for intricate preparation. She knows so much, not just what these men did, but she is aware of their weaknesses. Remember what D'Arcy said about Belanov? A penchant for women with ginger hair. According to Xavier, he left the Brno arms fair with a redhead the day he died. One person to house all these skills? It's too much for me."

"I agree. I support your theory the killer has been carefully briefed. She has enough time to gather a sample of DNA to leave at each scene. And a varied source of it. Saliva, hair. The preparation must be immense, so this is a full-time job. There must be some kind of back-up."

Beatrice looked across at his profile. "You can understand why Chris and Conceição lean towards a professional hit."

"They overlook the other link. D'Arcy Roth. The person who caused these deaths had a great deal of information on all these men, both personal and ..."

The theme from *The Godfather* rose tinnily from Kälin's jacket. He pulled over to the kerb before answering the call. His gruff tones indicated it was work related, so Beatrice studied his severe expression as he listened.

"*Scheisse!*" He closed the phone, glanced in the mirror and wrenched the car around, facing the direction they had come. He accelerated, shaking his head.

"This is getting ridiculous. That was Xavier Racine. The Ticinese police have found the body of Giuseppe Esposito on the Valle Verzasca dam."

"Esposito? He was the lawyer who defended that airline ..."

"Hermair. Yes. He killed himself today. The police think his suicide looks suspicious. They found some skin underneath his fingernails. Not his."

Beatrice tucked her hands under her armpits, feeling unsettled and cold.

"You think this is another one of hers? How did it happen?"

"The man was infamous for defending a negligent airline. It seems he went bungee-jumping from the top of the dam, but rather than the rope being around his feet, it was around his neck."

Beatrice tensed. "How high is this dam?"

"Two hundred and twenty metres. This is not going to be easy, Frau Stubbs. A bungee rope contains elastic, to ensure the impact is not too great. Esposito, or our vengeful friend, used normal rope. As a result, his head came off."

Beatrice pressed her palms to her eyes and swallowed.

Chapter 28

First sun hit the slopes above as he descended. The thrust and push of muscle thrilled less now, and weariness encouraged him to use his poles more as support than motivation. Yet a feeling of achievement transcended his fatigue. Seventeen days had transformed him. Taut buttocks, powerful thighs, cyclist's calves; he had a body to admire. His breathing was calm and he felt a relaxation, the kind only physical exertion could deliver. He would sleep tonight, deep and dreamless. Lean body, clean mind. Lean. He loved that word. Fat dropping away, baggage left behind, and a cleaner, leaner Sepp emerged. Who could have known that divorce was a man's best friend?

The sun rose higher, turning the sky a fishmonger's palette of red, silver and gold, and he watched an aircraft begin its descent to Locarno. He picked up his pace; experience had taught him when the sun hit the valley, it got hot and uncomfortable. Onto the straight now and he could move as fast as he liked. Freedom made him lean. While married, he was flabby, weighted down, hindered by responsibility and care for others. Divorcing Rosaria propelled him out into the world and he flew. Focused and free, he soared. He was a winner. The victor. Not only was his name recognised in Europe, but now the wider world had heard of Giuseppe Esposito. And his critics could go fuck themselves; he played the hard game and he won.

He caught his first sight of the dam as he emerged from the trees. In this light, if he didn't look directly, he could imagine the thousands of tonnes of concrete as water, tumbling, rushing and roaring to the bottom. But he did look directly. His eyes were drawn to it, just as they always were. The scale of this edifice would always impress him. A shocking smooth expanse of white between the beard of the cliffs, a dramatic V to draw the eye down, the elegant man-made arch which stood in the way of nature. Not the time to stop and marvel at the engineering, he'd be back tomorrow. Yet he interrupted his rhythm to pull off his fleece and sip some water. It was getting warm.

Pushing the car door shut, Beatrice caught Kälin's impatient look. It wasn't closed. She tried again. This time, the mechanics shut audibly and he walked away. She followed, her mood darkening as she spotted the thin crowd of ghouls standing behind the police tape. The late afternoon sun shone into her eyes, so that the individual moving down the slope towards them was a mere silhouette in uniform.

"Herr Kälin! *Es freut mich sehr Sie zu sehen.*" The men shook hands.

"*Grüezi,* Herr Valletta. Nice to see you too. This is Frau Stubbs, from Scotland Yard, London."

Herr Valletta turned sideways and she saw a genial pair of dark eyes light up. "Scotland Yard? It is me a pleasure, Frau Stubbs. Come please."

They threaded a path through police vehicles, TV crews and of particular interest to Beatrice, a catering van, before emerging next to the dam itself. She took a breath, amazed by the immense amount of concrete spanning the valley, and another as she looked down. The dam shot downwards, like the point of a colossal arrow, to a rocky riverbed below. As the light diminished, Beatrice looked up and watched the sun sinking slowly toward the mountain. She realised the urgency of making the most of the light. So did Kälin.

"The body?"

"In the morgue. We can go there later. But the site is more interesting. The bungee operators arrived just before nine today and noticed something wrong. We got a team down there by eleven hours.

Freshly dead. The torso was found 420 metres from the head. Much damage. The coroner suggested to escalate this case. We searched the platform and found his poles. After testing, the team discovered this DNA. So we called you. Do you want to see the site?"

Despite her unease, Beatrice nodded. The officer marched with confident familiarity down the path to the dam. Beatrice had an urge to hold Kälin's hand. For his sake, naturally, not hers.

Sepp thanked his mental discipline for getting him out of bed while it was still dark, so that he could arrive at Vogorno at this time in the morning. The sun lit the forest behind him, transforming it into a kaleidoscope of shivering jade, teal, emerald, lime, bottle and leaf. Across the valley, a blank dark-green mass promised shade and coolness, enticing him across, luring him in. He replaced his water bottle in the pocket of his rucksack, picked up his poles and headed down towards the dam. At the rate he was moving, he would escape the strengthening rays around halfway across, a moment of natural beauty.

One could feel part of the planet here, sensing the history of earth, the dynamics of geography, the joy of rock formations, water reflecting sky. Yet the human influence stood out. Mastery of nature and its forces was one of the most striking things about the valley. The dam – its magnificence, its power, its strength against millions of tons of water – was a testament to the will of man. And he was part of it. Alone on this enormous edifice, staring into the abyss below, he felt a pride and nobility in his homeland, his people, himself. Emotion rose in him as he stared down the valley. There were people in this world who shot for the stars, who could achieve greatness. How many people had told Dr Lombardi that his beautiful concrete arch, holding back the whole of Lago di Vogorno, was an impossible dream? Yet, here it was. Lombardi ignored the disbelievers, and built something both fundamentally practical and aesthetically magnificent.

Rosaria would always be a chicken, scratching at the ground, head down, pecking at scraps. She'd always dragged him down. He might remarry, it was imaginable, but this time he would choose a genuine partner. Someone who complemented his lifestyle and was as free with her admiration as his ex had been with her criticism. He wanted a woman who had vision, who could see his potential and help him reach the stars. At the centre point of the dam, he left the light, stepping into the shadow of the mountain.

Kälin crossed the dam on Beatrice's right, looking out at the lake, allowing her the dramatic view of the valley below. Had she not known about his vertigo, she would have presumed it a chivalrous gesture. Ahead there was some sort of structure, with a platform protruding over the edge. Something about it made Beatrice hesitate. Dusk bled colour from the scene.

"The bungee-jumping station is the centre point of the dam. It is very popular; everyone wants to be James Bond. This is where Esposito jumped, or was pushed. Come, I show you." Herr Valletta offered his hand to guide Beatrice beneath the various supports and up onto the platform.

Kälin shook his head. "I wait here. I will be of no use up there."

Valletta shrugged. "You see, Frau Stubbs, the jumpers put on a harness, climb up here, and throw themselves off the edge. It is thrilling, but totally safe. The operation is run by professionals with the highest safety standards. The elastic rope drops you 220 metres, you bounce a few times, and they winch you back up. Now, Signor Esposito had no harness, simply a noose around his neck. The rope was only 80 metres long, and attached to the grid above us. For a suicide, it was not a quiet way to go."

Four small steps took Beatrice closer to the edge. She gripped the barrier and leant forward. To leap off here would be a horrifying prospect, attached to elastic or not. The floor of valley below looked many miles away and full of unreceptive materials. Bungee-jumping would not be on her list of things to do once retired. She gave a shiver and turned back to Valletta. The sight was no more appealing. He held a noose in gloved hands.

"The rope, tied with great security to the main structure, which was around his neck. We have not moved it."

"There's not much blood, considering ..." Beatrice could not quite say the words.

Valletta shook his head. "No, you're right. But the impact was so great that his head came off quite cleanly, leaving the body to continue to the ground. There is much blood on the dam below, if you want to see."

"Perhaps not tonight. The rope has been tested?"

"The rope, the bungee station, everything. There's nothing here but Esposito's prints. But not many. None on the metal to which this rope was attached, for example. And the rope is standard marine use, you can buy it anywhere."

Beatrice edged back to the small steps, away from the edge. Kälin was looking the other way. "Herr Valletta, if someone did this to him, how could they manage it?"

"The laboratory can help us there. They discovered traces of a sedative around his mouth, similar to chloroform, but nothing in his blood or urine. It is possible that someone disabled him, then dragged him up here, put the rope around his neck, and ..."

"How many kilos did he weigh?" interrupted Kälin as they descended.

"Eighty-two."

"Not possible. To lift eighty kilos up these steps? No, someone could not do that alone." Kälin dismissed the idea.

Valletta thought about it. "If he was strong enough, he could. I have seen labourers lift two sacks of cement, each weighing fifty kilos."

The sun dipped below the mountain, leaving them in rapidly cooling shadow. Beatrice took Kälin's point on board. "As you say, Herr Valletta, if he were strong enough. Perhaps we should head to the morgue? This skin under his fingernails ..."

"Yes, this is how we found the DNA. He had damages to his hands, of course, but our coroner is a careful man. On Esposito's right hand, someone else's skin was under two of his nails. He also had a rosary tied to his wrist."

The lake glinted and flashed in the early sunshine, trying to attract Sepp's attention, to pull his gaze from the other side, the valley below. Yet, the natural beauty of the lake could not compare to the elegant intervention of man. He had performed this hike eleven times already, each time getting off one stop earlier from Contra to improve his fitness, and each time, he was no less awed by the Verzasca dam.

As his eyes adjusted to the shade, he saw a figure on the platform of the bungee jump. That was early; they were never normally around at this time. It could be a special event; they might be doing a film, or a photo shoot. Although he couldn't see a crew. He kept up his pace, eyes fixed on the figure at the edge. It seemed to be praying. Sepp looked behind him, and ahead, straining his eyes to see if there was anyone else around. The dark shape took on more detail as he strode closer and he saw it was a woman. No harness, no elastic, and she seemed to be holding something to her face. A rosary. His body temperature dropped and his stride faltered.

She was kissing a rosary. He stopped, resting his poles silently against the rope barrier which marked the jumpers' area. Her words were inaudible, but the tone of impassioned prayer was recognisable and he understood. Standing in such a place, wearing black, and at this hour, there could be only one reason. He slipped off his rucksack and reached for his mobile phone. Keeping his eye on her, he dialled the emergency number of *la polizia*. At that moment, an idea dawned, and he locked his handset. If a reputation could be reclaimed, if individual heroism and courage could dilute cynical business decisions and public scandal, here was a golden opportunity. This was a challenge and a potential gift. Sepp took his chance.

Walking boots and metal steps up to the platform did not make it easy to be stealthy, but he reached halfway up the steps before he could hear her words.

"*Salve, Regina, madre di misericordia, vita, dolcezza e speranza nostra, salve. A te ricorriamo, esuli figli di Eva; a te sospiriamo, gementi e piangenti in questa valle di lacrime.*"

His instinct advised him to go no further. In trying to save her, the ultimate stupidity would be in frightening her and making her fall. She continued and he joined in.

"*O clemente, o pia, o dolce Vergine Maria.*"

She stopped, but did not turn. "Get back! Get away from me."

"I won't move. I'm here, on these steps. Do you want to check?"

She stiffened, but flung a rapid look backwards, before facing forward once more. "Please go from here. I need solitude."

Younger than he thought. Wild eyes, thin trembling body.

"Of course. I will be happy to give you what you want. But I see you are a Catholic, signora, like me, and I have the most terrible feeling that you want to commit a cardinal sin. My faith allows me no choice but to try to prevent you from throwing yourself into Eternal Hell."

"I am NOT a Catholic! I no longer believe. And my choice is already made. You cannot stop me. Please, I beg you, just go."

"*Va bene.* Fine, I'll go. A non-Catholic who does the rosary. Before I go, will you just tell me your name?"

Her back did not move, apart from the occasional shiver. "Why?"

"So when you've gone, I can find out all about you and shake my head, and say 'Oh Luisa/Ana/Grazia, it didn't have to end that way. It will happen, I guarantee it."

"My name is Mara. But it does have to end this way. This is my will. And no one can change this. I deserve eternal damnation."

"Funny, my ex-wife says the same thing about me. But I'm not standing over a 200-metre drop; I'm planning to hike to Brione. What's the difference?"

"You haven't killed someone."

His mind whirled through possibilities. She wasn't a teenager; she couldn't be talking about abortion. A rival in love? A faithless husband? And now she planned to end it all off the dam. Just keep her talking.

"Not exactly, no." His tone was casual. "But many people see me indirectly guilty of many deaths. Yet I still plan to eat lunch in a grotto today."

"Indirectly or directly, one must take the consequences." She stared out at the vast space. Sepp's instincts provoked him to speak, to keep her with him. But she began again.

"I am, or I should say I was, a nurse. Geriatrics. I care for ageing women, and some men, every day. But my own mother ... my own mother died in a pile of her own waste, because I was too occupied with my own life. I cannot forgive and do not deserve absolution, no matter what penitence. Now you know and if you have any mercy, you will leave me." Her voice gave no sense of emotion, as if already dead.

He'd reached the top step by now and crouched on the platform. "I've listened to your story, heard your confession. I offer you a deal. You listen to mine and I will leave this place. I will give you your privacy if you allow me my honesty."

She was silent. Her body swayed as the light and heat grew. He added one point more. He was a lawyer, after all.

"And your last act will have been one of compassion, a Samaritan, giving time to a stranger."

She turned, her eyes streaming. "I will listen." She moved slowly towards him, black leather gloves tucking her rosary into the folds of her widow's weeds. She was attractive, if a little haggard. The news conference would look even better. So fragile, next to her muscular, modest rescuer. She came closer, eyeing him with tearful concern. Her pupils were dilated with fear. He opened his palms, his arms and his face to show his trust. The Hollywood moment; she's back from the brink. She smiled and rushed into his embrace, forcing a cloth over his mouth and knocking him to the ground. He lay back, winded and disorientated, before attempting to throw her off. Her hand remained clamped over his nose and mouth, her knees on his upper arms. He writhed with enormous force, intending to buck her off. His body responded with an ineffectual twitch. His mind threw a punch, but still she sat, a Gothic demon crouching over him. His body was not responding. As if it was separated from his head.

Chapter 29

Zürich 2012

Sometimes, sometimes. Words, a phrase, or an expression just stuck. In the small hours, Beatrice would wake in the knowledge that if only she could go back to sleep, tomorrow would be perfectly fine. Yet a phrase kept popping into her head. Round and round. Sometimes it was music – Leonard Cohen made frequent appearances – but it could just as easily be a sentence in German, or a half-remembered exchange from the day.

"Man may escape from rope or gun ..."

"Das weiss ich auch nicht!"

"Maybe we could pre-act as opposed to post?"'

If this were a dramatisation of her life, one of these phrases would be relevant and her recognition of its hidden meaning would solve her problems. But it wasn't, they weren't and it wouldn't. They were merely thought-mosquitoes, buzzing around her brain, sapping her energy. She looked at the clock; twenty past four. So, what was left of the night was mapped out. Restless shifting position for an hour, maybe two, before falling into a profound sleep sometime before six. Then hauling herself to the surface mere minutes later at the shrill insistence of the alarm.

Silence, blackness and a comfortable sense of peace. Perfect kipping conditions. Arriving back from Ticino past one, Beatrice had hit the pillow like a stone. Banshees would have wasted their breath. Yet now, in the pre-dawn anticipation of the day, she had a refrain from a song in her head. And a myriad of concerns.

"Man may escape from rope and gun

Nay some have outlived the doctor's pill
Who takes a woman must be undone
That basilisk is sure to kill."

What did she need? Her mind roamed over her world. Matthew in Exeter. Her job in London and the respect of her colleagues in Zürich. Control over the dogs, everywhere. A resolution to this case. Peace. And as a consequence, sleep.

Fat chance.

"Man may escape ..."

Oh do shut up.

"Morning B. Are you all right? You look awful."

"Thank you for the welcome, Chris. I am full of life, and tact. Yourself?"

"Not bad. We've had some thoughts while you were on your Helvetian tour. I think you might like what we've got to say."

Beatrice's tired eyes widened. "You found something?"

Chris lifted his shoulders and wagged his head in irritating ambiguity. Quelling an impulse to grab his tie and pull, Beatrice turned to get a coffee. Xavier burst through the door, as bright-eyed and gleeful as a squirrel remembering where he'd put his nuts.

"Xavier. Good morning. How are you?"

"Thank you, fine. Are you well, Beatrice? You are looking, what is the expression?"

Chris opened his mouth to reply, but Beatrice cut him off. "Perfectly well, thank you. A few more hours rest would have been helpful, but we have a case to solve and the pressure has just increased fivefold."

"Yes, exactly. Conceição and Sabine are finishing some slides. They come directly."

"No hurry, Xavier. It's ten to eight. And Kälin never bothers to show his ... Good morning, Herr Kälin. You are unusually early."

Kälin carried a cup of peppermint tea, the scent accompanying his freshly showered smell. He looked clean as a cucumber. "Good morning Frau Stubbs, Herr Keese, Herr Racine. Are you feeling well, Frau Stubbs? I am afraid yesterday's scene was too much for you."

Bloody cheek! Who was it that stood on that platform and looked down into the void? Who held still as the mortuary staff pulled back that blanket? And who had no difficulty polishing off a sausage and mustard roll afterwards?

"I am stronger than I look, Herr Kälin. Hello, Sabine, Conceição. I hear you have some thoughts."

At least harmony seemed to reign in the love triangle. Sabine greeted everyone with a smile, as her colleague set up the laptop. Beatrice, disconcerted by the change in dynamic, watched and waited as Conceição took charge.

"Good morning everyone. As you know, Giuseppe Esposito's death seems to have been orchestrated by the same person. We find ourselves with a problem. Lyon is screaming for results, our approach so far has produced none. Beatrice, we talked about this while you and Herr Kälin were away yesterday and we think there might be another way to tackle this. I hope you don't mind but we have done some work on a proactive approach."

Beatrice said nothing, but lifted up her head in enquiry. The team's choice to follow a different tactic had better not be at the expense of the detailed duties she'd allotted before leaving. Her smile was tight.

Chris took over. "Beatrice, Herr Kälin, we think the procedure we have followed so far has merit, of course. But we all agreed that it is not producing results. If we know enough about the killer's MO, then we could overtake her or him and jump one step ahead. We researched the press during the six to twelve months before the deaths of the victims so far. Each one had the most negative press of the year, with the exception of Belanov. We think we can look at this from the opposite angle. Rather than chasing this person, we believe we can predict with reasonable accuracy where he or she might strike next. Sabine?"

The presentation was slick and well prepared. Beatrice's jaw clenched. All this had taken some time. Her team had indeed ignored her orders and followed their own course. What the hell did they think they were playing at? She flicked her eyes toward Kälin, whose eyebrows had knitted.

"Thanks, Chris." Sabine flashed him a smile as she stood up to speak. "Beatrice, Herr Kälin, listen. We don't want to take over, just simply to propose another way of looking at this. Presuming D'Arcy is involved in the orchestration of these killings, we can look at how she picked her targets. In each year, the dead man had the most negative newspaper inches in the business press. She, or 'the killer', selected the most unpopular man of the year. Only Belanov was different, and we know from your investigations that he was personal for D'Arcy. Going on these assumptions, we have identified three men who could be the potential victims for 2013, or even 2014."

She clicked the remote and three faces emerged on the screen.

"Based on a search of bad press on business figures linked to D'Arcy, we have reduced our net to these three men. If we act now, we can place someone close to each man, and lay a trap. For example, the first ..."

Beatrice had heard enough. "Sabine? I'm sorry to interrupt. You have all clearly done an impressive amount of work on this. However, as you rightly point out, all of this is based on an assumption. Or, if my guess is correct, a presumption. Am I right in thinking that you collectively chose to abandon the tasks I allocated in favour of developing an alternative approach to the case?"

The enthusiastic warmth in the team's faces disappeared as if doused with cold water. Xavier, unusually pale, stood up. "Our intention was not to try to change the investigation, Beatrice. We simply wanted to provide a parallel track. So we can attack on two sides, you see."

Tired, irritable and frustrated, Beatrice was in no mood to conciliate. "I am very happy to hear that. So *my* assumption is that you achieved all I asked; Sabine has rechecked all medical records, Xavier has a detailed breakdown of D'Arcy's activities and flight records on the relevant dates, Conceição is fully conversant with the Swiss home-care system and Chris has identified any gender markers previously missed in the police reports. Is that correct?"

Chris shook his head. "No, it isn't. We devoted a lot of time to preparing this angle. I think you could at least listen to our ideas. This could save us all a lot of bullshit."

Beatrice placed her coffee on the desk, stood up and switched off the screen, before turning to face the team.

189

"A reminder, if you will. This is a team, a group of people working together for a common goal. I have been given the role of team leader and thus it is my judgement which guides our strategy. I have no objection to being presented with alternative ideas or techniques, unless my team drop my instructions to follow such an alternative without permission. And much as your glamorous idea of lying in wait for the next attack and catching our killer in the act may appeal, it is the stuff of television dramas, not reality. Bullshit, as you term it, the daily slog of checking under every stone, is the foundation of solid police work. And performed with diligence, will eventually yield results. I would like the information I asked for on my desk by the end of the day. Chris, you can present this concept to me at one pm, presuming you have completed all the tasks detailed. Have a good day, everyone."

She picked up her coffee and headed for her office. The team dispersed in silence, resentment and negativity charging the air like a thunderstorm. It was foolhardy to expect support from Kälin, but Beatrice wondered if he found the team's actions as offensive as she did. After all, this had all come to pass while she and Kälin were away from the office.

She wrote a quick email.
Subject: Daily briefing
Herr Kälin
When I hear these proposals from Herr Keese, would you like to be present?
Frau Stubbs
He replied instantly.
Subject: re Daily briefing
Frau Stubbs
No. I could have heard them this morning.
Herr Kälin
Beatrice decided she would go out for lunch for a change. Nordsee did excellent fish and chips.

"Shut the door, Chris. Do you want to set up your laptop?"

"In a minute. First, I want to apologise. You're right, we did get carried away with our idea and made an error of judgement in neglecting our duties. But I want to stress that we can do both. I think a combination of the two strategies is most likely to yield results. And I'm sorry I was blunt this morning. Tact, as you know, is not one of my strong points."

Beatrice smiled. "Apology accepted. I know I came down hard on you all, but to be presented with such a vote of no confidence after yesterday felt like a slap in the teeth. I am prepared to listen to your ideas and to give them the credit they deserve, as long as we maintain our daily duties conscientiously."

"Fair enough. Shall I set up now and take you through what we think? Or should we wait for Kälin?"

"He won't be joining us. Can I ask if you have uncovered anything from the file reviews at all?"

"Nothing concrete, although certain elements do support our theory. Sabine may have got something. She skipped lunch to travel to Luzern. I'm not sure what she found, but she was pretty excited. OK, I'm ready. What about you?"

"Fire away." Beatrice sat back with her bottle of water and trained her attention on the screen.

"The theory behind this you know. We can make a pretty intelligent estimate as to how D'Arcy, or whoever, selects the victims. And as Sabine explained, there seem to be three candidates for the next hit."

"Yet if Esposito was the latest in line, won't we be waiting another year for our next one? I'm not raining on your fireworks, Chris, but how can you be sure that between now and then some corrupt government official, or avaricious trader will not come to prominence and unseat your trio?"

"We can't. But the killer leaves a cooling-off period, we believe. It was over a year in Belanov's case. It may be that the victim is marked up to twelve months before he's taken out. If another possible target arises, we just have to add him to the list. If they have any connection with D'Arcy Roth, if they attract negative media attention, or if they piss off Antonella herself, these are the guys we need to watch."

"It's a smart strategy. My concern is mostly to do with timescale. How do you propose that we ..."

A knock at the door caused both of them to frown. Xavier's head popped round, his face animated.

"Sorry for the interruption, Beatrice. I thought I should tell you, I am going to join Sabine in Luzern. She has found something, I think. May I?"

Beatrice nodded and gestured to a chair, but Xavier was too fidgety to sit. He closed the door and shifted from foot to foot. "Kantonsspital Luzern has a record of an anaesthetist who was … how do you call it, when you stop someone from working in medicine?"

"Struck off. This person was struck off?"

"Exactly. Helene Richter was struck off after a case in 1993. Found guilty of assisted suicide. She administered a fatal dose of pain-killing drugs to a patient with terminal leukaemia. His name was Jean-Baptiste D'Arcy. Antonella's stepfather."

The pace of the afternoon's activity kept Beatrice entirely occupied and filled with adrenalin. At 16.00, the team gathered for an update. In Luzern, Xavier and Sabine found a current address for Helene Richter and asked for permission to question her and search the apartment. Kälin spoke to D'Arcy's secretary and discovered that she would be returning from Buenos Aires early Saturday morning. Beatrice requested the search warrant and authorisation for D'Arcy's arrest. Conceição would accompany Kälin to the offices of D'Arcy Roth the following morning to test every male staff member's DNA, while Beatrice and Sabine did the same at D'Arcy's home. With considerable satisfaction, Beatrice updated Lyon, spoke to a GEOF representative of the Argentine Federal Police and forced everyone to go home at five. Not only did she want them fresh for the following day, but she also had an appointment. One she was dreading.

Chapter 30

Zürich 2012

"Come on, Beatrice, you won't regret it," Madeleine promised, when coercing her into this.

Beatrice already regretted it deeply and she hadn't even arrived yet.

Dragging her heels up Gessnerallee, her attention was drawn back to the Sihl, where a group of teenagers sat on a blanket, laughing and dangling their feet into the coolness of the river. The sun glinted off the water, the greenery of the bank provided a peaceful backdrop to the colourful party and an Appenzeller dog bounded in and out of the water after a stick. A Seurat come to life. A sudden swell of joy coursed through her, driven by optimism and vindication that her determined methodology had finally produced results. They had a suspect. This case could be closed by the weekend. She lifted her chin and picked up speed. After all, how painful could a haircut be?

"Hey Beatrice! Am I happy to see you! I thought you were gonna bail on me."

Dressed in a suit even Beatrice recognised as Chanel, Madeleine's glamour was such that a beautician seemed redundant. Her make-up seemed air-brushed, her jewellery co-ordinated exactly with the pinks in the suit and the silk scarf at her throat reminded Beatrice of Lauren Hutton.

"Hello, Madeleine. I did think about it. I already wish I hadn't agreed to this."

"Too late to back out now. This is Susana, who's doing our treatments today."

"Treatments? I thought I was just getting a trim."

Susana, a generously proportioned woman with a permanent smile, exchanged a look with Madeleine, before extending her hand.

"Pleased to meet you, Beatrice. Today, I'm going to cut and colour your hair while my colleague threads Madeleine's brows. Then our manicurist will take care of your nails while I deal with Madeleine's roots. Now, I'm going to put you side by side so you can chat. What can I get you to drink?"

"Beatrice, don't pull that face." Madeleine laughed. "It doesn't hurt, it won't take long and you'll feel a new woman when we're done. And this is my treat. You bought the tickets to the gallery on Sunday."

Beatrice succumbed to the pressure and allowed herself to be led to a leather chair in front of a mirror. She accepted a cup of tea and looked across at her companion.

"It's you I feel sorry for. Threading your brows sounds agonising."

Madeleine dropped her voice. "It's not so bad. Nowhere near as painful as sugaring your pits."

Beatrice shuddered.

The stylists went about their work in silence, gently adjusting heads and faces as necessary.

"So, how was your day?" asked Madeleine.

"Well, all things considered, not too bad. But I'm afraid the trip to Hiltl tonight must be postponed. I have to turn in early. I've got a big day tomorrow and I had a rotten night's sleep last night."

"Oh, that's a shame. Nothing wrong, I hope?"

"No, not particularly. Work problems, my own mind and some interference from John Gay. How are you?"

"Oh, I'm fine. Well, kinda. Michael just told me he has to attend a conference in Brussels this weekend, so I guess I'm a little bummed. But I was so looking forward to this girls' night, I almost forgave him."

"That makes me feel worse about pulling out of our restaurant arrangement."

"Forget about it. We can do that anytime. I just wanted to go somewhere after the salon so we could show off your new look."

Beatrice lifted her eyes to the mirror and immediately returned them to the magazine in her lap. She didn't want to know. And if the results were preposterous, there was always a hat.

Madeleine, her head stretched back as some girl performed God knows what atrocities on her eyebrows, asked a difficult question.

"So what's the deal at work? Anything I can help with? I may be only a *Hausfrau* right now, but there was a time when I ran my own company."

"It's kind of you to offer, but it's just the usual frenzy when a project comes to an end."

"Your project's ending? No way! Does that mean I'm gonna lose my new best friend?"

Beatrice smiled. "Not yet. But one way or another, I expect to be home by next weekend."

"Shoot. Bad news for me but great for you, I guess."

Susana finished snipping and a discussion began as to the most suitable colour. Beatrice's own opinion, that brown and grey worked perfectly well with her wardrobe, seemed the least influential. Madeleine thought honey and caramel lowlights; the eyebrow expert said dark chocolate with a hint of macchiato at the temples; while Susana put forward a forceful case for champagne and cinnamon as not requiring frequent touch-ups. Beatrice lost interest and began to feel peckish.

The manicurist arrived and added her view in German, '*wie ein Dachs*', before settling down with a sweet smile to massage rich lotion into Beatrice's hands. Beatrice smiled back before recalling that *Dachshund* translated as 'badger hound'. She gave the skinny little teenager a frosty frown.

Madeleine interrupted her thoughts. "OK, so if you're taking a rain check tonight, how about tomorrow?"

Beatrice hesitated. Plans were likely to be disrupted if an arrest could be made. "That depends. We may be working late and over the weekend. Things have rather come to a head, you see."

"Wow, it sounds so exciting. Or isn't it?"

"At the moment, I'm not sure. But it certainly involves a lot of hard work. What did you have in mind for tomorrow?" The hair dye, whatever colour it was, began to sting Beatrice's scalp.

"Well, it's nothing important. But I've been getting about a bit, checking Zürich out. And I got a hold of a couple tickets to see a yodel choir, in Hotel Widder. It's one of the guilds of the city and it's so totally Swiss. Could be fun?"

"Yodelling? How absolutely marvellous! I would love to come with you, but as I say, it's crunch time at work. Could I call you tomorrow to confirm?"

"Sure. Don't sweat it if you can't make it. I know you're busy. Wish I was."

"It may come to nothing. These things often raise hopes then fall flat."

Madeleine paused. "OK, I'll wish you luck. And if you can come along, what say we check out the Fraumünster on the way? They have some stained glass windows by Chagall and Giacometti which I hear are quite something."

"Really? I am a devoted fan of Chagall, as you probably remember. Don't know all that much about Giacometti but I'm very keen on stained glass. I had a bash myself once. The tutor told me my work was 'energetic' and I felt about five years old. You've really been bitten with the tourist bug, haven't you?"

Madeleine looked into the mirror at Beatrice's reflection. "I figured I may as well. What else have I got to do? Hey, how do my eyebrows look?"

Three hours later, no longer feeling sore, irritable or bullied, Beatrice was still gazing at the mirror in the bathroom. She couldn't stop. For the first time in her life, she was proud of her hair. She'd looked at her reflection in the microwave, in the TV and every shop window on the way home from the salon. Every half hour, she wandered into the bathroom to stare at the sleek, polished individual who waggled shiny fingernails back at her. She should take a photo because it would never last.

The phone rang.

"Beatrice, it's Madeleine again. I hope I'm not disturbing."

"Not at all. I was just ... actually, I was still admiring my hair. It's lovely. I can't get over it. Thank you so much."

Madeleine's satisfaction could be heard in her smile. "Isn't it? Thank Susana. She did a brilliant job and you look amazing. Listen, I was just calling to let you know the concert tomorrow starts at eight, but we can drop in anytime we like. Kinda takes the pressure off, huh?"

"Oh, eight should be manageable. I'll call you in the afternoon and hopefully we can do both the windows and the yodellers."

"Great! Let's talk then. You get some rest, OK?"

"I shall do my level best. And thanks again. Goodnight."

"Goodnight Beatrice. Best of luck tomorrow. Sweet dreams."

Fluffing up the pillow, Beatrice found she was smiling. She might be long in the hoof but was still capable of making new friends. Yodelling and stained-glass Chagall with Madeleine, the ideal antidote to work. Her eyes closed and her mind replayed the image of Madeleine's perfect make-up, beautiful jewellery and sensual scarf at her throat. Her mind wandered. Perhaps a classy scarf would bring her own image up to date. A natty knot at the side? No. Rather than displaying Grace Kelly elegance, Beatrice would look more like a drag queen.

Her eyes opened again. Throwing back the duvet, she padded into the living area and found her mobile phone.

"Conceição, I'm sorry to disturb you so late."

"It's fine, Beatrice. It's only ten past nine. Is something wrong?"

"Just a quick question. If someone has a sex change; you know, hormones, operations, the works ... it wouldn't change the structure of their DNA, would it?"

"No. There are some factors which may cause minuscule alterations in a few DNA cells, but nothing alters the building blocks. If you're born a woman, no matter how many external changes you make, female DNA runs through you for life."

"Like a stick of rock. Thank you, Conceição. That's given me food for thought. See you in the morning. Good night."

"Good night, Beatrice. Sleep well."
The chances of that were negligible.

Chapter 31

Zürich 2012

Trotting up the stairs to their workroom at five past seven, Beatrice was joined by Xavier, carrying a bakery bag.

"Good morning, Beatrice." He stopped short when he saw her hair.

"Your coiffure! You look so different. But it suits you. I brought croissants."

"Thank you, Xavier. They smell wonderful."

"My mother says that a good breakfast is the best way to begin the day. Did you sleep any better?"

"Not really. There's an awful lot to think about."

"You should try to do something else before bed. Watch TV, go out to a restaurant, take your mind off the case. When I need to clear my mind, I play football."

"Tonight, I plan to do just that."

"Football?" His eyebrows leapt upwards.

"Xavier, look at me. Can you seriously see me running around after a ball?"

He struggled to find an appropriate response so Beatrice saved him the trouble. "No, not football. However, I certainly intend to clear my mind. I wanted to ask you, is Fraumünster the one with the two towers?"

"No, that's Grossmünster. Fraumünster is on Münsterhof, this side of the Limmat. Just before you go over the bridge. Please, let me."

Xavier opened the door for her. All the team, with the exception of Kälin, were present, bristling with anticipation like foxhounds on Boxing Day. Everyone did a double take.

"Beatrice! You had a haircut!"

"B, you look fantastic. I love the colour."

"Takes ten years off you, B! You look no older than f..."

"Shut up, Chris. Good morning, everyone. Xavier has brought us all breakfast."

Before Beatrice had even deposited her handbag, Chris was at her side.

"The search warrant is here. I think it would make sense if Xavier and I went to Luzern, to question Richter and search her apartment. Firstly, sending two men makes sense if she's potentially dangerous. Secondly, I can be useful if there's an opportunity for digital forensics. And Xavier's Swiss German will be essential for interviewing her or anyone else."

"All sound arguments, Chris. But before we plan our day, can I hear the latest and get a coffee?"

Xavier lifted his paper bag. "And a croissant."

"I just think it is important to get started because if we ..."

"Chris. It's seven am. We'll all be more effective if we know exactly what everyone is doing and why. Can you wait half an hour, do you think? We'll start as soon as Kälin gets here."

"And here is Herr Kälin, so now we can start." Xavier's bouncy eagerness reminded Beatrice of a Red Setter puppy.

She poured a coffee and turned to the team. "Under the circumstances, I think we could start. Chris tells me the search warrant for Richter's apartment is here. What else is new? Good morning, Herr Kälin."

Kälin opened a file and withdrew a slip of paper. "Good morning everyone, I received permission ..."

Kälin's eyes flicked over Beatrice and he appeared to lose his thread. He raised the paper as if to remind himself.

"... permission to test employees of D'Arcy Roth, and of Antonella D'Arcy. Arrest warrant for D'Arcy granted."

Beatrice sipped her coffee. "Sounds good. Does the permission state we can request DNA samples only from men, Herr Kälin?"

He looked at her, frowned and checked the permit. "Yes, of course it says men. Where else would you find male DNA?"

"It occurred to me last night that our quarry may have had a sex change. Outward appearances indicate a woman, but the DNA remains that of a man. I checked this with our expert."

Conceição gave a confirmatory nod.

"So I want to test everyone who works for D'Arcy. I know it's unlikely and I am adding a lot of extra work for the lab, but I want to look into every possibility."

"Beatrice, you have to be joking!" Conceição shook her head. "That would be a huge waste of time and money. And it means the lab will take twice as long to process anything relevant. I really can't agree to this."

Chris arched his eyebrows. "You really want to tell Lyon that we've invested so many resources in testing women for male DNA? Rather you then me."

Beatrice raised her chin. "It was not a request for permission, in fact. It was an instruction. I will submit another official form and explain why. We have to test everyone and turn every stone. I accept the consequences.

"Chris and Xavier can go to Luzern to search for this Richter woman, Herr Kälin and Conceição can begin testing at the D'Arcy Roth office, while Sabine comes with me to D'Arcy's villa. I'd like to talk to her staff, anyway, and look around the property."

"Be careful, Frau Stubbs. We don't have a warrant to search her home, and I would prefer it if you take some uniformed officers in case of difficulties," Kälin warned.

His words contained no criticism of her decision, thus acting as a balm.

"That's a fair point. I'll do that. Does anyone want to raise anything else before we head off? Yes, Sabine?"

"Conceição and I were talking about Helene Richter. From what the hospital told me, she was a rising star. To deliberately perform euthanasia on a patient would send her career crashing. And she must have known that. So why would she administer an overdose to Antonella D'Arcy's stepfather? We think D'Arcy paid her to do it. After the doctor was dismissed, she managed to retain her somehow and they worked together to 'arrange' these suicides."

Chris frowned. "If so, that was a long time in the planning phase.

Richter was struck off in 1993. Van der Veld, the first death that we know of, was in 2007. And why did D'Arcy want her stepfather dead?"

"That's what we must find out," answered Beatrice. "Sabine and I will dig up as much as we can on D'Arcy's background and look into what happened to Richter after 1993. I want everyone to be thorough, check every story and make no assumptions. Take nothing at face value. We are extremely close, so we are going to get this right. Obviously, any major breakthroughs, I want to hear about it. Otherwise, I would like an update at lunchtime. In person or by telephone, let's speak at midday. Have a productive day, everyone."

Richter was not at home. The *Hauswart*, or caretaker of Richter's apartment building, took her job seriously. Refusing to believe the warrant, she insisted on calling the Kantonspolizei to confirm. Chris raised his eyes to heaven, but followed Xavier's example and gave her an understanding smile. As she closed her apartment door to telephone Zürich, Xavier reassured him.

"We'll get a lot more help out of her if we show her respect for doing her job. These people know a huge amount about the other tenants. I can guarantee she knows all their movements, right down to who had a shower this morning."

"Yeah, you're right. I just wish everything didn't take so long, you know." He leaned back against the wall and tried to remember his Tai Chi.

The door opened and Frau Pfenniger looked from one to the other. She frowned at Xavier and asked for their IDs again. Suppressing a sigh, Chris handed his over once more and the woman nodded. She led the way upstairs and after each reply to Xavier's enquiries, threw back questions of her own. Xavier's responses were brief, polite and guarded. Her accent and use of Swiss German made it hard for Chris to follow, but it was obvious she was trying to find out the reason behind their visit. After she unlocked the door, Xavier thanked her and with great diplomacy, persuaded her to leave them to it.

The slight figure disappeared down the stairwell, casting one last look back and returning their wave. Chris grinned at Xavier.

"Well done on getting rid of her. You refused her offer of tea, right?"

"Yes, I did. Otherwise, she would be up and down with all kinds of excuses. And we have work to do. But she did give me some useful information.

"She told me that Richter is a doctor and works away most of the time, as a volunteer in developing countries. Apparently, she was last here on Monday. Very quiet, been a tenant since 2005. Doesn't smoke, very few visitors, but likes Chinese food and classical music. I told you, they know everything."

Entering the flat, Chris was immediately impressed by the space and light. Floor-length windows allowed sunlight to warm the large living area and the kitchenette, back against the far wall, had a wall of glass bricks. Drawn to the windows, Chris pulled back the white gauze curtains and studied the view. The street dropped away below to a river rushing past on its way to the lake. No one's apartment overlooked the building, so she could sit out here and enjoy the sun in privacy. He turned back to Xavier, who had donned gloves and already begun searching the desk. Richter obviously went for the Zen approach to interior design. An L-shaped corduroy sofa faced the windows, the glass coffee table before it bearing nothing more than a remote control, and a vase with three artistic silver branches. The kitchen to Chris's left was all pale wood with dark marble worktops. So clean it looked like a kitchen in a showroom. Pausing to pull on his gloves, he opened the fridge. A half-drunk bottle of rosé, a butter packet and a variety of jars: pesto sauce, quince jelly, sauce bourguignonne and horseradish. The cupboards were equally Spartan: plastic containers with pasta, muesli, and packets of noodle soup. Removing everything methodically, Chris checked the cupboards, the dishwasher, the freezer compartment and the cutlery drawer. Nothing of any interest.

Xavier sat at the table, looking through papers, the picture of concentration. Chris decided to explore the two doors at the opposite end of the room. The bedroom, with large bed, fitted wardrobes and dressing-table was decorated in deep blue and white, giving a restful, expensive feel. Judging by the number of labels he recognised, she owned some quality clothes. A Donna Karan wool dress, two jackets by Dior, a long cardigan by Nicole Fahri, Gucci boots ... the wardrobe of a volunteer doctor? Next door was the bathroom, revealing a cabinet full of expensive products, thick towels and a power shower. Chris pulled several strands of blonde hair from the brush, and slipped them into a plastic bag. It wasn't much. He hoped Xavier was having more luck.

If Beatrice had never met D'Arcy, she would have felt some sympathy for her. Her history, baldly stated in black and white, was rather sad. No matter how spectacular her trajectory, the loss of both parents and a stepfather at a young age must have been terrible blows. Sabine lifted her head at Beatrice's sigh.

"Something wrong, B?"

"No, just feeling a bit sorry for the woman. Her father died of a stroke when she was nine years old. Then she lost her mother at seventeen. That's very tough."

"Hmm. I find it hard to feel sorry for someone who can take other people's lives."

"Sabine, we have no proof that D'Arcy has taken anyone's life yet."

"We will. You know that before she became partner at Hoffmann Roth, they had a reputation for honour? They would refuse any business not aligned with their principles of fairness, humanity and justice."

"How did it move from those ethics to its cut-throat reputation of today?"

Sabine read aloud. "From the annual report of 1999/2000. I'm sure you can translate this bullshit: 'Strategically, the company has embraced broader views, driven by our new Senior Partner, Antonella D'Arcy. As part of our ongoing mission to add value for shareholders and stakeholders alike, we will strive to explore new areas of business opportunity.' In other words, Hoffmann's moral code is thrown out of the window and we just want to make cash. Lots of it. And we don't care where it comes from."

Beatrice couldn't help but laugh at the fiercely cynical expression on Sabine's face.

"I would hate to get on your wrong side. It should have been you who accompanied me to that first interview. Bad cop and worse cop. Did you find anything in your material about relationships? From everything I have read, she has been linked with several men, but I can find no one special in her life. No indication of who fathered her daughter, for example."

"You won't find a father. The child was adopted from South America."

"Adopted? I didn't know that. But it fits, I suppose. I couldn't imagine D'Arcy pregnant. Do you have a date of birth there?"

Sabine shuffled through the papers from the local government office. "No birth certificate, apparently lost. But D'Arcy adopted her from a Brazilian hospital on 12 October 1994. And ... I don't believe it! The adoption certificate was signed by Dr H. Richter."

Beatrice stared. "So. Struck off in Switzerland, Richter went to Brazil. Which is why she speaks Portuguese. In the right place at the right time to organise an adoption for Antonella D'Arcy. How convenient. Or perhaps D'Arcy sent her?"

"We should try to talk to the girl this afternoon, see if she lets anything slip."

"Good idea. Right, call that Brazilian hospital and find out what you can on Richter. Then it's catch-up time and lunch. My stomach is grumbling. I tell you, I could eat a scabby cat. Oh Lord, don't look like that, Sabine, it's only an expression."

Kälin had cream sauce in his moustache. As Conceição updated them on the lack of progress at D'Arcy Roth, Sabine made short work of *Fischknusperli* with salad, Beatrice enjoyed the police canteen *Schnitzel* with noodles and Conceição managed the occasional forkful of the fitness menu; or raw strips of vegetable. Throughout the conversation, Kälin stabbed at the slices of meat in his plate of *Zürcher Geschnetzeltes* as if he were spearing each awkward, obstreperous D'Arcy Roth employee who had caused them such problems.

Conceição explained. "And that means we're not as far forward as we'd hoped. But the first two batches are already in the lab, so they can get started. We should be done by mid afternoon. Unless we have any further 'I know my rights' big-mouths this afternoon." She shrugged as if it were inevitable.

Sabine patted her mouth with a napkin. "B and I have been going through all the documentation available on D'Arcy, her family, and her company. The only thing of interest so far is the fact that Dina is not D'Arcy's biological daughter. She adopted her in Brazil about eighteen years ago. And Helene Richter signed the adoption certificate."

Kälin glanced at Sabine in surprise. "Here, or in Brazil?"

"São Paulo, 1994. I called the hospital, they have no records of a Dr Richter employed there in the early 90s."

Conceição turned to Beatrice. "And news from Luzern?"

"Still waiting. I did tell Chris to call at twelve, and it's now twenty five past. But I know he will phone in as soon as it's convenient."

Sabine sighed. "If I only wait two minutes, this desire for a dessert will pass. I must be strong."

"No matter how long I wait, my mind will never forget that they have vermicelli, chocolate mousse and éclairs," Conceição added, mischief in her smile.

"You, Conceição Pereira da Silva, are a bad influence on me." Sabine picked up her tray and headed to the buffet once more, followed by Conceição.

"Any dessert for you, Herr Kälin?"

Fortunately, Kälin chose to wipe his mouth before replying, as Beatrice was perilously close to getting the giggles.

"Thank you, no. I think we both see this link to Richter as our way in." It was not a question.

Beatrice placed her knife and fork together. "Certainly. We can threaten charges of illegal child-trafficking and all sorts. All or any of this information about her could be useful."

He leaned his forearms on the table. "So tell me more about Ms D'Arcy."

Beatrice did so. He listened without interrupting. After she finished, he asked a question.

"Does anything here seem significant to you?"

"Apart from Richter, not especially. I was struck by how the steely female we see today experienced some dreadful losses in her youth. Yes, her upbringing was privileged in the monetary sense, but in terms of loved ones, everything was taken from her. Perhaps this is one reason why she needs to control her environment."

Kälin thought it over as he gazed at his empty plate. "Possibly. Can you see a way of using this information?"

"Not yet. We just need to keep doing the groundwork, covering all angles and see what happens when we arrest her tomorrow morning. Do you have flight details?"

He nodded. "Yes. I'll pick you up at six thirty. We'll take some back-up and be ready for when she touches down. You should warn the team that we'll probably be working all weekend. I hope you had no plans?"

"No. Well, I did for this evening, but nothing that can't be cancelled, if needs be."

"This evening shouldn't be a problem. We will all need some rest and relaxation."

"That's what I thought. And it's an opportunity to sample some Swiss culture."

Kälin frowned. "Please don't tell me you're going to have a fondue. Not in May."

A low buzz of electricity hummed through Beatrice. Tricky to tell the difference, but she was beginning to distinguish Kälin attacks from Kälin banter.

"No, I'm going to see some religious art and then I've been invited to a yodelling concert. And why, in the name of Emmental, can't I have a fondue in May?"

Before he could answer, her mobile rang.

"Chris! We were wondering where you'd got to. Is everything alright?"

"It's fine. But the caretaker person was hanging around just now, so I couldn't call. Richter's not here and we found nothing much in her apartment. But apparently each flat has a share of the cellar space. Xavier's gone down there with Frau Fish-Face to take a look."

"And you don't know where the Richter woman is?"

"Nope, but she's been here recently, after an absence of six weeks.

We have her home computer, so as soon as we start unpacking that, we'll get more idea."

"Chris, listen to me. I want you to bring the computer back to Zürich. Any use of computer data has to be done with the utmost care."

"I know that, B, I am your digital forensics expert. Why do you …"

"Yes, and I am the case officer in terms of law. I am responsible for making sure all data has been handled correctly. We also need an independent party to vouch for all our processes. Bring it back and let's tick all our crosses. If there's anything there, Chris, we have to be able to prove we haven't fiddled with it. And let's not forget, if you do the analysis here rather than there, you get to spend the weekend in Zürich with us, your loved ones."

She heard his indignation deflate into a laugh. "OK. You're right. I'll pack up now and we'll head back. The machine will remain untouched until we can decide the best process and legal compliance. B, are you eating?"

"Yes. *Schnitzel* in the police canteen. It's excellent."

"I don't believe it. You're eating *Schnitzel* and Xavier and I can't even have a cup of tea. My stomach is … what? Hang on a minute."

Chris's voice was muffled and Beatrice could hear the urgent tones of Xavier in the background, but could make out no words.

"B, I've gotta go. Seems Xav has found something in the cellar. We'll check it out and get back to you. Save me some *Schnitzel*." He rang off.

"Wigs." Xavier threw the various hairpieces onto the table with a flourish.

"And suits, bags, padded bras, accessories, jewellery and outdoor gear," added Chris.

"This gives us precisely nothing. What else do people keep in their winter wardrobes? This discovery is hardly the body in the basement." Kälin's tone was scathing.

Chris lashed back. "You're wrong. I will go back through these case files and show you that this stuff is not just a dressing-up wardrobe of your girl-next-door. What we found, what Xav found, were the disguises this female used."

"Good luck." Kälin left the room, a chill wind behind him.

Time for Beatrice to step in. "Chris, Xavier, I'm sure you're right. But can we prove it? None of it is anything more than circumstantial unless any trace of her DNA turns up at these scenes. Which, given the time lapses, is unlikely. It's much more feasible we can prove this woman had regular contact with D'Arcy. Then we might have a case. Our only hope is to get something from her home computer. Even there, I fear we may hit a dead end. If she has anything to hide, she will have taken it with her."

"Look, don't waste your time on case files. Get onto that machine and find out what skeletons are under the floorboards. Xavier will support you, and the rest of us can go through the files once more. We may as well face the fact we'll be working all weekend."

Chris shrugged. "I can live with that. Xav and I will go through the PC, and if there's anything to find, we'll drag it out. And you take the files and check details against this bag of tricks?"

"Relax, Chris. We got it. Now, we were wondering if you two might be hungry?" Conceição's voice drew a smile from both men.

Sabine held up two brown paper bags. "So we brought you a picnic each from the canteen. A sandwich, an apple and a yoghurt. Healthy and light enough to keep your brains alert."

Chris drew his eyes to slits. "A yoghurt? Are you serious? We've been working since 7am with nothing but coffee to keep us going. Haven't we, Xav?"

"Yes, that's true. Apart from the burgers and fries we ate on the way back."

Chris dropped his head onto the desk and as Kälin was absent, Beatrice allowed herself to join in the laughter with a sense of abandonment.

A security guard opened the gates as the police car approached, watching with a look of extreme suspicion as they rolled up the drive to D'Arcy's villa. Sabine's slow scan revealed her awe at the extent of the grounds, the view of the lake and the beautifully tended gardens. Unlike Beatrice's last visit, the front door remained closed as they exited the car. Beatrice spoke to the uniformed officers, reiterating her request they stay put unless needed and ascended the semi-circular steps with Sabine, who rang the bell. Several moments later, a heavy-set woman appeared at the side of the house, with her hands on her hips. She wore a cleaner's blue-checked smock and her hair was drawn back in a loose knot. Her face was unwelcoming.

"Good afternoon, Frau ...?" opened Beatrice. She received a blank stare.

Sabine tried in German. "*Können Sie Deutsch?*"

Transferring her suspicious glare to Sabine, the woman responded. "*Frau D'Arcy ist im moment nicht hier. Sie kommt morgen früh zurück.* She comes tomorrow."

Sabine smiled. "Yes, we know. But we would like to talk to you, and any other staff members available." She gestured in the direction of the gardener.

"This is not possible. *Ich darf keine Gespräche führen ohne Frau D'Arcy.*"

Sabine nodded her understanding and relayed her words to Beatrice. "She can't talk to us without her employer."

"Fair enough. But let her know that we have authorisation to test all D'Arcy's male employees for DNA. They may not want to talk to us, but they must give us a swab. You needn't tell her that we'll be back for hers tomorrow. I think we could use the officers now."

Sabine explained the reason for their visit to the housekeeper, while Beatrice asked the officers for their help in gathering all the household staff to the hall for the testing procedure. Five minutes later, the embarrassed officers returned with the grand total of the gardener and the security guard, both sulky and recalcitrant.

Indicating they should sit on the chaise longue, a gloved Sabine prepared her kit. The uniformed police retreated to stand by the front door and the housekeeper to the kitchen, while the gardener and security guard sat stiffly, listening to Sabine address them in German. Beatrice watched the preparations, feeling a little extraneous. The sense of the empty house resonated with all of them, including the awkward officers by the entrance. An air of being watched, being judged filled the hallway, making them all into performers, demonstrably doing their duty. D'Arcy's absence was the strongest presence in the room.

Sunlight from the cupola illuminated the space, highlighting the greenery of the indoor foliage and the inlaid colours of the floor mosaic. Golds, creams, purples and plums and more green. A hand, a vessel, some folds of cloth? With a glance at Sabine, who was evidently in control of the situation, Beatrice wandered up the stairs for a better look. Her curiosity piqued, this was her chance to see what the image was all about. All eyes observed her departure, but she had no intention of going far. On reaching the landing, she looked down. Directly beneath her sat the two unhappy staff members of D'Arcy's household. In front of them, Sabine sat beside an occasional table, reaching towards the gardener with a cotton swab. The officers stood against the main door, allowing Beatrice a clear view of the mosaic tiles.

Three women poured large golden jars of water into a central vessel, also made of gold, or brass. They wore draped garments of plum, rose and faded green, their limbs pale, their faces resigned. The water shone silvery as it flowed from the jars into the cauldron, and out again. At the base of the vessel was the mouth of a gargoyle, with two holes either side, allowing the water to flow away. The palette of colour was astounding, sitting perfectly in the generous hallway, light catching the auburn hair, the curve of the gilded jars, the blush of a bare breast. Whatever Beatrice might suspect of Antonella D'Arcy, the woman had fine taste.

"Beatrice? I'm finished here. Is there anything else you want?"

Hurrying down the stairs, Beatrice faced two reproachful faces; three if you counted Sabine's.

"No thanks, Sabine. If you have everyone's details, I think we can let these people get back to work."

She tried to offer grateful smiles to the staff, but none returned the gesture. The guard closed the door behind them with a face so lugubrious Beatrice was tempted to laugh. As they loaded the car, Sabine seemed uncharacteristically quiet. They fastened their belts and the driver checked they were heading back to base. No one spoke as they drove back into the centre.

"I hope that wasn't too unpleasant an experience?" Beatrice enquired.

"Not at all. Only two people, all passive and silent. I'll bet Conceição is having a much harder time. You can see these people are used to observing orders."

"Yes. I have the feeling that D'Arcy rules that place like a dictator. One crack of the rod, everyone jumps. They're probably afraid to go to the toilet without permission."

"You know not one of them is Swiss? The housekeeper is Croatian, the gardener comes from Greece and the security guard, who's also her driver, is Lebanese. Which reminds me, she took two other members of staff with her. Her bodyguard and her daughter, or secretary. We should test them tomorrow morning."

"We will. What a life that woman leads. Private jet, staff of five, fabulous villa. Seems dirty money is rather profitable."

"Hmm. What were you looking at up there?"

"The floor. It's a mosaic, a beautiful piece."

"Modern art?" Sabine asked, as she watched shoppers along Löwenstrasse.

"Classical. Women with water jugs. Put me in mind of Rossetti."

Sabine gave her an indulgent smile. "Not a name I know, Beatrice. My kind of artist is more Warhol or Lichtenstein. Have you been to the Kunsthaus yet?"

"Yes, very enjoyable it was too. I loved those dark Nordic Expressionists. And the Chagall room was a joy. In fact, tonight I'm off to see some more."

"Yes, I like Chagall, too, although I prefer Matisse. Less ambiguous. Cleaner."

At a loss as to how to respond to that, Beatrice checked her watch.

"So, it's four thirty. Let's go and see how the boys got on with the toys."

Chapter 32

"You sure you wouldn't like an apple, Herr Kälin? We have plenty of our healthy picnic left."

Kälin smiled. "I will have dinner later, thank you Herr Keese. *En guete.* Enjoy your meal. I am only here to ..."

"Ensure there are no mistakes?"

"No, not really. True, I have some authority reasons for being here. But my main purpose in observing is to learn. At my age, Herr Keese, I need to keep learning."

The detective's sudden humility and politeness took Chris aback and he instantly dropped the macho stuff. The problem with Kälin was you never knew when to hold up your hands, or come out fighting. That feeling of handling explosive material reminded Chris of his ex-girlfriend.

The basement area was smaller than their workroom and proximity unavoidable. Kälin, if he wanted to stay, would be up close. There was no room for hostility.

"OK, Herr Kälin. I'm happy to share what I know. So far, we've imaged the hard drive. Everything on Richter's machine, and I mean everything, is now on these little dynamos." He patted the laptops in front of him.

"So, after you copy the hard drive, what next?" Kälin asked.

Xavier, illuminated by the semi-circle of blue screens around them, corrected his superior. "It's not a copy, it's an image. While we make an image, we write-protect it. So no one can alter data during the process. That ensures our image is an exact replica of the original."

Chris shot Xavier an impressed look. "He picks up pretty fast. Right, so the original hard drive goes under lock and key. That's one of the reasons you're here. Chain of custody. And we continue our work on these. But we'll need to hash again sometime tomorrow."

Xavier nodded, frowning and watching the movements on the screens. Kälin stood in silence and asked no questions. Chris took another mouthful of water, waiting. It didn't take long.

"Once I take charge of the original machine, what will you do with the image?" Kälin's curiosity was as wild as Xavier's, but the old sod held back, as if uninterested. Chris swallowed and began his explanation, trying not to sound too excited.

"When we're sure the source data has not been corrupted and made sure it is safe for later reference, we start exploring. I want to know everything that's on here; obvious, hidden, deleted, encrypted, protected, and temporary files. I want to know what all the gaps are, why there's unallocated space and where there's slack. Finally, I want to produce a map of this machine. When we can see, as a geographer can, the valleys, tunnels and caves, we know where to dig for the hidden treasure. The only thing I cannot know is how long this will take. Sometimes, you get lucky and your first strike turns up gold. But those times are rare. We'll probably be here all night and we may have to call for more refreshments."

Xavier beamed. Kälin's eyebrows joined.

Chris reached for the mouse and continued. "Armed with our map, we'll split up. I intend to go for the areas which ... Beatrice! Hello ladies!"

Conceição and Sabine followed Beatrice into the room, bright with curiosity.

"How are you getting on?" Beatrice enquired.

Chris leant back with a smile. "Well so far, we've satisfied the compliance requirements. Now we can get to work."

"I see. I just wanted to tell you that it's approaching five o'clock and we have already done ten hours today. How much longer do you intend to keep going? And is there any way we can help?"

Chris let his eyes fall in stages from Beatrice to the floor. No one spoke, afraid to disturb his concentration.

"When does D'Arcy get in?" he asked.

Kälin answered. "At seven-twenty tomorrow, her private jet arrives at Kloten. We'll be there as her welcome party. And we intend to bring her here, to ask her some questions."

"Right. In that case, why don't you leave me and Xavier to get on with this? You have a busy, difficult day tomorrow. I'd like to get something decent to eat and then start some serious work, without distraction. I'm happy to keep at it until I feel I need a break."

Xavier's head bobbed agreement before Beatrice could formulate the question. Kälin's shoulders lifted a centimetre as he met Beatrice's eyes, while Conceição and Sabine looked relieved.

Beatrice sighed. "Yes, Chris is right. Much as I feel guilty about leaving you two on the night shift, it does make sense for the rest of us to take a break now. But the least I can do is order something for you both. What would you like for dinner?"

The two men spoke as one. "Pizza."

"Naturally. That well-known brain food."

"Beatrice? Sabine and I were also thinking of getting a take-away and going back to her apartment. We thought we could discuss the developments over a glass of wine and share any thoughts. Would you like to join us?" Only Conceição's head was visible, as she leant back around the office door.

"How kind of you to include me. And how dedicated you are to continue working. You give me a twinge of guilt, off out to enjoy myself. I'll decline, Conceição, but only because I have a prior arrangement. Thank you for asking me, though."

"No problem. Are you going somewhere nice? It's not a hot date with Kälin, is it?"

Beatrice's head snapped round. "You are getting as lippy as your boyfriend! No, once I have completed all the paperwork here, I am joining an acquaintance for an evening of culture, as a matter of fact."

Conceição appeared to be suppressing a smile. "Well, don't stay in the office too long, you deserve a break. Enjoy your culture and we'll be in for seven in the morning, just in case you need us. Have a nice evening, B."

"You too." The door closed before Conceição's over-familiar address registered. The lack of respect in this team was a disgrace, she thought, picking up her mobile to dial Madeleine. She was still smiling when she left the office.

The handover of Helene Richter's original machine was a solemn occasion. A trolley was delivered by two uniformed officers, the computer loaded onto it and the entire ensemble escorted to the evidence safety vault, under the supervision of Herr Karl Kälin.

"*Schöne Abig mitenand*," called Xavier, folding up the empty pizza boxes into the bin.

With their return wishes dying in the clunk of the closing door, Chris turned to Xavier with a huge sigh.

"We'd better get to work. Another Friday night and I still haven't managed a date with Conceição."

Xavier laughed, settled himself in front of his screen and shook his head. "Perhaps you've missed your chance already."

"No way. It's just a matter of picking the right moment. But I don't have too many moments left. How is it possible that we're closer to cracking the case than I am to cracking that woman?"

Xavier twisted round to look at him. "Probably because you're not her type."

"What do you mean? I'm everyone's type. Tall, good-looking, modest ... Don't tell me you think you're in with a chance?" Chris faked outrage.

"No, not at all. But that's the difference between us; I know when a case is hopeless. Now the clock is ticking, so where should I start?"

"You're right, let's attack. I'm going underground, you're patrolling the surface. I'll check everything that looks suspicious; deleted, encrypted, odd blanks. You search her 'open' files; documents, emails, website history and build me a picture. And Xav, if anything looks funny to you, it is. Tell me as soon as something doesn't feel right."

Chris had no truck with auras, but right at that moment, Xavier was glowing like a hot coal.

Bullshit. So much bullshit. The clock read 18.27. Chris was already bored and the pizza had made him sleepy. Yawning, stretching and occasional deep breaths were no longer effective. He looked over at his colleague; intense, keen and extremely annoying.

"Pssst."

No response.

"Pssst!"

Xav pressed his fingers to his ears. Chris couldn't believe it. He stood and went over to administer some gentle violence. But before he got close enough to yank on Xavier's ear, he saw what was on the screen.

Art. A depiction of a figure in a chair, maybe an electric chair, with updraughts of air or light or electricity, and a man in purple screaming his head off. Hideous, raw picture of pain. Not nice. Who would ever want to look at that? Using his knee, he nudged Xavier, who lifted his upper arms, threaded his hands behind his head and stretched.

"You already want to take a break, or ...?" Xavier's face bore no traces of weariness.

"Yeah, I'm flagging."

"Did you find anything?"

"Nope, not yet. But I'll be more effective after some coffee. What is that you're looking at? I think it will give me nightmares." Chris couldn't tear his eyes from the screen.

"Images she downloaded from the *may-not-know-much-about-art* forum. She was a busy member on there, but only at specific times. I looked at her web history, you see, and focused on the six months before these deaths. This is what I found. I cannot really see a pattern, but she is active for weeks, sometimes months before one of our guys' deaths, but completely silent in the weeks just after. It feels funny, Chris."

Coffee could wait. "Say that again. She looks at these images from a public forum for months before the guys go down, then doesn't touch it in the weeks just after a death? In all cases?"

"No, there's a strange slip in 2011. She's consistent until early January and then goes quiet. After that, early March to April, which was when Ryman died, she's almost constantly online. I just wondered if this site could be a way of passing information. Encrypted, or coded, or ..."

Chris's mind cleared and a possibility smacked his forehead.

"This activity you describe – is she just posting, or uploading, downloading, what?"

Xavier looked at a printout. "Mostly downloading, but a lot of commenting too. Endless thank-yous. Very few uploads."

"Uh-huh. It could be. What's she downloading? Art images, digital photos, JPEGs, documents, what is it, Xav?"

"The site is for amateur art lovers. Pretty small. Around 60 members and they seem to work like a book club. Discuss an artist, share your images, have a chat. It doesn't seem to be anything exciting, just people talking art. I only noticed the activity records and matched them to the dates."

"She chats and what else? What else does she do on this site?"

"As I said, she downloads. She and another user are fans of this artist," Xavier spread a palm toward the screen. "And they share pictures, talk about them, and that's about it."

Chris kept his voice cool. "Richter downloaded what exactly?"

"JPEGs of fine art... I am still counting how many painting files she has from the same artist. But she uploads very little. An article on him, a story she heard, but no images."

"Articles and paintings of which artist?"

"Francis Bacon. British. He died in 1992. He did a lot of triptychs. Like this one. The first thing she downloaded."

Xavier clicked on the icon and Chris craned in to study the three rectangles. The title below the image read, *Three Portraits: Posthumous Portrait of George Dyer, Self Portrait, Portrait of Lucien Freud*. The figures were strangely twisted and deformed, features like gargoyles, and pools of black seeped from them, like oil-slick shadows. The space in which each figure sat had a marbled floor, and yellow and blue walls, empty but for the photographs in the background of the left and right panels. A photograph within a painting; it made for an odd contrast.

Chris's mind whirred up like a drill. Images within images. Hiding something by not hiding. Something else, there was something else. Receiving large amounts of coded information. He looked again at the smudged faces.

"Xavier, you ever heard of steganography?"

Chapter 33

Zürich 2012

Kälin's BMW pulled onto Kasernenstrasse, nosing its familiar route towards Adliswil. The Mondeo swung out soon afterwards, remaining a good distance behind, as if it knew its destination. Friday evening traffic made for heavy going until they hit Manesse, when the motorway opened up the flow.

As usual, Kälin took Route 4, heading south. The figure at the wheel of the Mondeo relaxed. *Alles in Ordnung.* All going like clockwork. Kälin's dull routine was unchanged. No supermarket stop tonight; it appeared he was going straight home. Which was exactly as it should be.

While Kälin remained inside his apartment, the figure remained in the car, checking the paperwork, memorising every detail so that nothing would be unexpected. Sure enough, the detective, wearing jeans and a casual jacket, left home at six-thirty and turned left along Austrasse. The figure gave it a few moments before following on foot. Kälin turned right onto Bahnweg, checked for oncoming trains and crossed the railway tracks.

There was no need to check. Trains ran this line at ten minute intervals during rush hour, and the last one had gone through five minutes ago. The figure knew the timetable by heart. As they progressed further into the industrial estate, it became increasingly difficult to keep the target in sight without being seen. But there was no need for concern. Kälin never deviated from his routine.

He made for the working man's bar tucked away behind the paint factory. As the figure passed and glanced in, Kälin was shaking hands with three men at the back. Sitting at the bar to observe was not an option. So the figure sat at an outside table, ordered a coffee, engaged the waitress in conversation regarding the menu and watched. None of Kälin's companions looked familiar. One older man began dealing cards. It was *Jassen* night, which could take several hours.

Perfect timing. Some other chores needed completing. The figure paid for the coffee and headed back to Austrasse. Nothing to worry about. The routine was always the same. Kälin would drink three beers, eat two sausages, play a few hands and walk home alone.

Across the railway tracks.

Chapter 34

Zürich 2012

Heat rose from the street, people slung jackets over their shoulders and pavement cafes filled with sunlit smiles. Beatrice found herself approving of the world in general, spreading the late afternoon warmth. She trotted along the river side of the street, water sparkling in her peripheral vision. One of Ken's crumpets would have gone down a treat, but there simply was no time. She would have to call him in the morning.

Madeleine was due at seven. Culture and companionship tonight, coupled with the prospect of unearthing the truth tomorrow made Beatrice almost giddy. Her pinkish blouse would do, with a pair of navy slacks. She stopped, realising she had left her jacket in the office. Never mind, the blue pashmina, her birthday present from Tanya, would suffice instead. Rather a colourful ensemble for a change.

Approaching the turn-off to her street, she saw Madeleine crossing the road, looking for all the world like Lee Miller. Her blonde waves bounced off her white shirt, her khaki trousers were fastened with a leather belt and she carried an enormous designer bag. She noticed Beatrice, waved and hurried to meet her.

"I'm so happy you could make it. Your evil employers released you for the evening?"

Beatrice grinned. "Just. You look wonderful! Can I have five minutes to change?"

"Sure, go ahead. I'm way early but I thought we could have an aperitif before we go. I just need to hit a store to get a couple ingredients. We got plenty of time. The concert starts at eight, so we can wander up and peek at the church windows with a half hour to spare. Shall I come up in about ten minutes?"

"Ideal. See you then. Just tap on the door, room 305 and come on in."

Dumping her bag on the sofa, Beatrice picked up her mobile and dialled as she began to disrobe.

"Matthew, it's me."

"Hello, Old Thing. You're early tonight. I've just come through the door. You checking up on me?"

"Yes. And it seems with good reason. I hear voices."

"You should see someone about that."

"There, I mean. In the background. You have someone with you. No, there's more than one and they're both female. A pair of Swedish masseuses?"

"Tarnation. I've been rumbled. Ingrid, Greta, I'm afraid you'll have to pack up the birch twigs. My other half disapproves."

Beatrice heard Tanya and Marianne laughing and calling their greetings.

"Hello Beatrice!" Both added a comment, but Beatrice only caught '... eye on him', and 'cuckoo clock', amid some strangely simian grunts, which may have been Luke.

"Hello back and give them all a hug from me. You have your hands full this evening, then?"

"Rather. Luke's teething, Marianne is furious with someone at work, and Tanya's computer has a virus. Or maybe Marianne has a virus and Tanya is furious with her computer at work?"

"Good luck, Pops. Now listen, I won't add to your burdens. My day has been most successful and I think tomorrow will be our breakthrough."

"Tally-ho! So we might have you home soon?"

"It certainly looks that way. I'm so glad the girls are there with you. I feel less guilty now. I was only calling to say I couldn't call this evening. I'm going out with my friend – I told you about Madeleine – to see some stained glass and hear some yodelling."

His amusement was audible. "Yodelling?"

"Yes, yodelling. As a matter of fact, I'm thinking of taking it up. James said I could do with a hobby."

His smile became a laugh. "How charming! I'm all for it. It will certainly enliven a Sunday morning in Brampford Speke."

"I have to go. Call you tomorrow."

"Until then. Have fun."

As she replaced the receiver, she thought she heard him singing '*High on a hill stood a lonely goatherd ...*' Chuckling, she headed for the bathroom.

She might even attempt to style her hair. It wasn't every night that she had fun.

"Are you decent?"

"I'm never anything else. Come in, Madeleine, take a seat. I'll be two minutes." Beatrice gestured to the sofa and returned to the bathroom. Her hair refused point blank to return its previous sleek and shiny incarnation. Tonight, it was especially troublesome.

Madeleine's voice wafted through the door. "No hurry at all. I'll pour us a drink. We should celebrate."

"Good idea. Oh!" She came back to the living-room to face her guest. "Have you had some good news?"

Madeleine's blue eyes scrunched up and a huge smile lit up her wan cheeks. "You got it! Michael got promoted and we're going back to New York! Permission to leave – as of next month!"

"Oh Madeleine, that is wonderful news. I am so pleased for you. I know you found life in Zürich awfully tough. Have you booked a flight yet?"

"Hey, I'll get one tomorrow. But finally I can go home and start rebuilding my career, you know? So let's drink to our successes, eh? These are Kir Royales – I think we deserve it. To us!"

The glass of blush bubbles looked elegant, appropriate and even matched Beatrice's blouse. She tinked her glass against Madeleine's and smiled. "To us!"

As she sipped, a flush of warmth filled her. Even a dispassionate observer could see the change in Madeleine's demeanour. The woman vibrated with energy and good cheer.

Madeleine waved her glass. "Don't let me hold up your preparations. Take your glass with you, and I'll tell all when you're ready."

"Right. I'll just finish my hair. And tell me anyway, I can hear you from the bathroom. When did you get the news?"

Madeleine raised her voice over the hairdryer. "Just after lunch. Which was so annoying, I can't tell you. I had a pretzel and a Coke on the run, then found out I could have been at Brasserie Lipp, popping champagne corks and shucking oysters. Ah well, it's almost over now."

"You must be so relieved. Mmm, this Kir Royale is hitting the spot."

"My own recipe. Say, how was your day?"

Beatrice despaired of trying to recreate her salon hair, gave it a pat and returned to the living room.

"My day was very pleasing. I have high hopes of soon being able to return home too. So, let's have a toast."

Madeleine stood and lifted her glass. "So let's toast. To my ticket out of here, your breakthrough and future happiness for both of us! To going home!"

"To going home!"

The sweet blackcurrant and dry champagne was most appealing. One of those drinks that tasted dangerously innocent.

Beatrice smacked her lips. "But before we leave, we're going to sample some genuine Swiss culture. I'm very excited about this."

"Me too. To be honest, it's not likely that I'll ever be back, so I should see as much as I can before I ship out." Madeleine drained the last of her cocktail. "So! Shall we go local?" She picked up her oversized handbag.

"Let's." Beatrice gathered her accoutrements from the coffee table. "Key card, mobile, handbag and my shawl. It's a lovely evening, but might be chilly later. Right, I'm ready to go."

As she pulled the apartment door closed behind them, Madeleine started to sing.

"I love Zürich in the springtime, I love Zürich in the fall ..."

"Hush, now!" Beatrice assumed her schoolmarm voice, summoning the lift with a grin. "One Kir Royale and she's anybody's."

But the truth was that she was twice as high-spirited and gigglesome as her companion. Must have been the champagne.

Keep calm. There could be nothing in it.

Chris tried to ignore the adrenalin rush that charged his body.

"Steganography is a way of hiding data within data," he began, before drawing a long breath and trying to focus his thoughts. Xavier waited, full of concentration.

"It's been around since, oh I don't know, the Greeks? It's an old art. But now you can apply the ancient principle to technology. To the casual observer, the piece of music, the photo, the video file looks completely innocent. But it has been altered to include information. Text, visuals, you name it. And the resulting image looks almost exactly the same as the original. Only with the right key; like change every third pixel to 25% darker and so on, can you uncover what's really in there."

"I know a little about that. It is the method of data transmission used by terrorists and military spies, that sort of thing? But even if we have the images, or think we do, we can achieve nothing without the key. Can we?" Xavier's voice sounded hopeful.

"There are two ways of going about this. We can try a universal application, taking this image and analysing it for embedded material. Depends on what's in there, if anything. If the payload is small, we may find nothing. But if there's significant data hidden behind this picture, there are lots of ways of slicing it up to see what's inside. That should give us enough information to see if the image needs investigating. We have the tools to find out where to dig; but unearthing whatever is hidden could be more of a challenge."

"And the other approach?"

"We find the key. This is not a simple 'two steps left, one back' code. This is a complex instruction for this algorithm which she must have recorded somewhere. Maybe it's encrypted, coded ... goddam it to hell!" He slammed his palm onto the table.

"Chris? Is everything fine?"

"Sorry, Xav. Really. It's just that there's something ... I don't know. An idea, a hint of something keeps bubbling just under the surface. But every time I try to grab it, it's gone. There's a clue here, I just know I haven't picked up on a vital point. Maybe coffee would help. You want some?"

"Yes. Would it be intelligent for me to look for the key? While you try the applications to open these pictures, and maybe with luck, one of us will find out what is interred there?"

"Coffee. Come. Give your eyes a break."

Xavier followed Chris to the rest area. Two brains whirred, clunked, hissed and fizzed in an echo of the coffee machine.

"Xav, are we wasting our time? Should we keep analysing the rest of this data and not run off after a wild card?"

Xavier stirred his coffee thoroughly, despite the fact he'd added no sugar.

"If you really feel we are gambling on a wild card, let's call Sabine and Conceição back. They can make sure there's nothing significant somewhere else on the hard drive. My gut tells me we have something, but you're right. We shouldn't run in only one direction and forget the rest. Shall I call them?"

Chris felt a buzzing between the joints of his fingers. He threw back his espresso and tossed the cup into the recycling bin.

"My gut is with your gut. We've found our way in and now we have to crack it. You explore anywhere she might have hidden the key, while I'll apply every steganalysis technique I can access. We'll pull this bastard out of there and present B with a *fait accompli* by the morning. Come on, this has just started to get interesting."

Xavier threw his cup after Chris's and dabbed his mouth with a napkin. Chris filled a paper cup with water and looked at the younger man.

"It's a lot to ask of you, working through like this. Do you need anything?"

Xavier shook his head and met Chris's eyes. "It is nothing to ask of a member of the team. And no, I want no more food. The only hunger I feel is for knowledge."

Chris burst into laughter and wrapped his arm around his colleague's shoulders. "Sometimes, Xav, you are so bloody French."

Bahnhofstrasse was busy. Couples strolled along the wide pavements, groups of businessmen left their offices to continue talking shop in one of the many discreet bars, and a gaggle of shrieking teenagers ran for the No. 7 tram. Crossing the street, Madeleine led the way up Rennweg. No trams, no vehicles of any sort, just cobblestones and wandering pedestrians.

"That's the hotel we're going to later," Madeleine indicated to their right. The white building sported blue shutters and the image of a mountain goat. Beatrice nodded. Hard to imagine yodelling in such an enclosed space. But she supposed yodellers must practise somewhere. As the street narrowed and descended toward the River Limmat, both women were absorbed by the variety of shop windows, intriguing alleyways, courtyards with murals and, the first time for Beatrice, a display of cuckoo clocks.

"Madeleine, look! I haven't seen a single one since arriving in Switzerland. But here they all are. There is something so kitsch and charming about them. Someone wants me to bring one back."

Madeleine wrinkled her nose. "Not my sort of thing. I love the Swiss railway clock. Clean, functional and precise. These things are for tourists."

"True. For people like us." She peered closer. "But as I told her, not at those prices. I'll buy her some chocolate and be done with it."

Before entering the church, Madeleine suggested walking to the Stadthausquai to see the famous windows from the outside. Turning their backs to the river and the sound of swans quarrelling over scraps, they looked up. Passers-by paid them no attention. Madeleine leaned toward Beatrice.

"I thought about buying a camera. But you know what? I am going away with all these pictures in my mind. My skills in photography couldn't do justice to this, anyhow. You wait there a second and I'll just check it's still open."

Beatrice wasn't really listening. The windows must have been 30 foot tall, such fabulously dense works of art. She stepped back to the riverbank railing, leaning back to take in the whole wall. She had no idea what the pictures signified, but they were undoubtedly uplifting.

Madeleine came back and tweaked her sleeve. "Yes, we have another hour before they close. Shall we go in?"

"This is where the bodies are buried, I'm sure of it." Chris called over his shoulder. "The only compressed files which seem to have a data irregularity are those posted by 'Mother-of-Pearl'."

Xavier tapped at his keyboard. "I'll look back at the conversations between the two of them, and see if anything comes up. 'Mother-of-Pearl' is definitely her favourite poster; they have a whole series of private messages to each another."

"Print them out, and let's take a look. Do they discuss any other artists?"

"A little. There are some comments on Paula Rego and on Freud."

"Freud?"

"Yes, Lucien Freud. He was in that Portrait triptych. Oh, you were thinking of *that* Freud. No, it's the other one."

Chris's head jerked up and he stared at Xavier. "The other one."

He clasped both hands to his forehead and leant back as the realisation hit him. "Xavier, that's it. That's what I was trying to grasp. The other Bacon. There was another Francis Bacon, a scientist, philosopher and so on. Some people think he wrote Shakespeare's stuff. But what's important is he was one of the earlier print steganographers and he came up with a cipher. Shit! I think we've found the way to decode it."

"Have we? Even if we have, what is it that we decode?"

"It has to be in the early communication between Richter and this 'Mother-of-Pearl'. Did you print those personal messages? Give them to me. We're looking for anything that looks like strange English. Or just strange."

All of it was bloody strange. Chris scanned the bland exchanges with increasing irritation. Then something caught his eye.

Yes, the skin quality was the first thing that drew me. It's like meat.
Is that where you got your name? Mother-of-Pearl?
Yes! I find an agony in his work. Such pain, such tragedy.
He had such pain and tragedy in his life.
Everything about him breaks my heart.

You're right. Bacon seems so sad. There is a sadness about him, poor boy.

I understand his work. It makes sense to me.

I'm happy to hear that. Me too.

"What do you see, Chris?"

"What do *you* see, Xav?"

"The only thing that made me wonder was this bit. *I understand, it makes sense.* I'm probably naïve, but does this communication mean 'message received', do you think?"

"In which case, the previous sentence, or conversation above is our payload. What do you see there?"

"Nothing. I tried everything. First letters, take out vowels, I think I may need some time to work the code."

"We already have the code. It's Bacon's cipher. We need to find some communication which uses a binary combination. For example, a combination of two different size fonts?"

There was a moment's silence. "Yes! It's there! *'You're right. Bacon seems so sad. There is a sadness about him, poor boy.'* That's got two different sizes."

"It has, but they're pretty close. You wouldn't notice unless you were looking for it. Now what we need to do is decode. Let me drag up Bacon's cipher. Shit, it's so true. Keeping it simple always works best. Right, Xavier, copy this into a WORD document, then denote each use of a font with *a* or *b*, starting with *a*. And group them into five."

Xavier nodded, and like a trouper, got down to work. "Twelve, twelve, eleven, twelve ..."

Chris did exactly the same in his head, and reached his conclusion minutes before his colleague. While waiting, he proceeded to do the decryption the other way. Belt and braces.

Xavier's head snapped up. "Finished. You want to hear? I've got aabab, abbab, baaaa ..."

"Hang on. What you have is a series of a/b combinations. Here, look. Each combination of a/b delivers a letter. So now we apply Bacon's cipher. For example, aabab in Bacon's chart represents the letter F. Now we need to decode the rest. God, I hope we got this right. Go, take your text and work it out."

Xavier's eyes flicked from Chris's print-out to his own handwriting, making notes and noises of satisfaction. Chris checked both his versions mentally and forced himself not to crow as he saw it.

Xavier got to the end. "It says 'forty two LSB'. Least Significant Bit! That's pixels, that's the instruction for how to explore it. I think we found it, Chris!"

Chris kept the lid on his elation.

"Well, we found part of it. There must be a whole lot more, but we can get started. Keep looking for more phrases like that in their conversations, and transcribe it the same way. I'm going to begin unpacking some of these images."

Reseated at his workstation, Xavier turned. "Are you going to look at the most recent stuff, in 2012?"

"I think I'll start with 2007. Let's build up a chronological picture. There's no hurry. As B said, she's already got her victim for this year."

The heavy handle banged an echo to announce their entrance, but no other tourists were in sight. Stopping just inside the doorway, Madeleine carefully closed the door, while Beatrice took in the huge vaulted transept. A change in atmosphere drained her frivolity. This was obviously a perfect time to come sight-seeing – not a soul around. Jewel-bright colours up to her right caught her attention. The Giacometti window. Row upon row of men and angels robed in rich shades looked down on her. Feeling under-informed, she picked up a brochure bearing a Union Jack and began to read.

Madeleine bumped her hip up against her. "Beatrice! Come on, we can do the research later. Let's just take a look at the real thing."

Turning the corner, they entered the choir area and stopped in their tracks. Five Chagall windows; one right, one left, and the three they had seen from outside. The late afternoon light, contrasting with the darker interior, enriched the vivid pictures and threw reflections at their feet. Like a patchwork quilt of glass, leaded seams joining squares, triangles and parallelograms of cobalt, daffodil, cyan and turquoise. A raw joy pulsed through Beatrice, elation at experiencing such beauty. Twin impulses rose: to cry and to laugh.

She did neither but soaked up the scale of the vision. Such grandeur, such majesty; unsurprising that one should feel a sense of religious awe. Stars adorned the ceiling and the clean, palest grey stone bore engravings of angels' wings. The collusion between Nature and Man achieved its objective – she felt small in the presence of grace.

"What's the time?" asked Chris, returning from the bathroom.

"Twenty past seven." Xavier stood behind Chris's chair, reading the data extracted from *Fragment of a Crucifixion*. Photographs, bank details, company description, financial statements, news reports and medical history, along with a detailed record of the movements and sexual preferences of Jens van der Veld. "It's unbelievable. So much information hidden in one picture."

Chris scanned the bottom of the screen, packed with tiny icons indicating the various documents he had found in the file. "Like the Tardis."

Xavier looked up in enquiry.

"Never mind. OK, so it's taken me over an hour to reveal this. Presuming the steganalysis tool is accurate, we have eight more files to unpack. We can do two at a time. Now, if the key were different for each image, we could be here a long time. However, it seems that the same key is valid for each of these JPEGs, with some slight adjustments. All of which she has communicated through the same channels. So we could, in theory, expose the lot by midnight."

Xavier's expression was puzzled. "Why are there eight, Chris? There's a pattern up to a point. This *Crucifixion* stuff was communicated in 2007, and obviously correlates with the Utrecht killing. There's one image per year, so presumably we'll find Thompson behind *Three Studies from the Human Body*, and *Man in Blue I* contains everything on Belanov, and so on."

"Yeah. And so the only oddity is the number of images for 2011 and 2012. There are two for each. In 2011, *Untitled (Marching Figures)* was downloaded in January, and *Blood on the Floor* in April. So the latter must contain data on Ryman. Who's behind *Untitled*, then? Did we miss someone?"

Xavier shrugged. "Maybe we did. Two deaths in 2011? But I'm

more worried about the extra file for this year. One of them must be Esposito, of course. Probably *Head IV*, downloaded April 2012."

"That was the one you were looking at, right? The purple agony? Oh God."

"Yes, why?"

"Xavier, you do remember how he was killed?"

"Oh." Xavier's expression of disgust seemed less repulsion at the man's demise and more disapproval of the killer's poor taste. "So why is there another image for May 2012?"

Chris shook his head. "I guess it's possible they have a secondary target in mind in case they fail for some reason with the guy in pole position. Maybe Esposito and Ryman were second choices? What do you think?"

"That's possible for Ryman. But this year, the first choice has already been executed. In which case, whoever is in the second picture is probably still alive. Would they try to kill two people so close together?"

"Maybe. Or if there were targets she missed, she may come back for a second try. Let's work on the living first, before digging up the dead."

"Right." Xavier's leg bounced with nervous energy. "Which one do you want?"

"I'll take the *Marching Figures*. Which leaves you with the *Nurse from Battleship Potemkin*. Rather you than me."

Xavier was already back in his seat.

Chris's mind ranged over the possibilities as he applied the codes to the picture on his screen. He was missing something, he could feel it. He shook his head to clear his thoughts and scanned the details below. Cesare Boldoni. Nice-looking guy. Chairman of Aceso, the Lombardy pharma giant. Lots of accusations against the company centred on one particular drug: *Ristorex*, the anti-depressant. Wealthy guy, married with a kid. Some powerful allies in Milan, but few in Rome. Apparently faithful, Catholic and hard-working. What happened, Helene, did you change your mind? Why did you let Boldoni go? Or did D'Arcy make that decision?

Pressing his palms against his eyelids, he ran through it. If Antonella D'Arcy is on the other end of Richter's leash, then why these men? An avenger in the form of struck-off doctor he could understand. But a woman whose lifestyle is funded by working hand-in-glove with these profiteers?

"Chris."

He lifted his head from his hands, the soft sound of skin parting. His eyes refocused on Xavier's stricken face and all the hairs on his arms rose. In one stride, he was at Xavier's screen.

"The other target for this year."

With her typical preoccupied expression, wayward hair and familiar grey suit, the image Xavier had extracted from behind the screaming *Nurse in Battleship Potemkin* was unmistakeable.

"Beatrice. Oh Christ."

"Giacometti has something special. But then I always tend to favour the underdog."

Beatrice agreed. "Poor devil is rather overshadowed here, but I agree, he certainly has something."

Madeleine glanced at her watch. "We should get out of here pretty soon, but I so want to take a look at the crypt. Wouldn't it be the coolest place for a Halloween party?"

Madeleine's laughter jarred in the wood and stone, stained-glass peace.

"I can't imagine the crypt would be open to the public."

"Sure it is. There used to be a convent on this site, which is why it's called Fraumünster. The original abbesses built the crypt to house the relics of the martyred saints. And we should take a peek before we leave, we owe it to the girls. But we need to be quick; the concert starts in a half hour."

"Very well, let's have a look. Always best to get in a martyred saint before a batch of yodelling. Come along then, you ghoul."

Madeleine laughed again and made a sweeping gesture. "After you."

Beatrice led the way down the steps. "Take care, Madeleine. There's not much light down here."

As she descended, a stone chill wound around her like a musty hound. Spores of chalky damp clung to her hair, her clothes, her skin. She was turning into a mushroom. She stopped at the bottom of the steps, with no inclination to go further. Madeleine slipped past her and into the murky interior. Candle-shaped bulbs in brass sconces reflected a weak glow up the stone walls, so that the central area, containing the tombs, remained in half shadow.

"I am surprised they let the public in here. It doesn't feel at all healthy."

"Don't worry. I just want a quick look at these, and we're gone." Madeleine studied the ancient remnants of an altar. Beatrice moved a few paces into the room, which had none of the spruce of upstairs. A damp dust lay on the floor and the graven images of the stone centrepiece, settling in the corners on some spiders' webs, giving them an appearance of old frayed cloth.

"What an eerie place." The final, funereal atmosphere punctured Beatrice's mood. Optimism here was unimaginable.

"Damn right. But you know what's weird? Like I say, I have no plans to return here, but this cathedral will always stay with me."

"I'm pleased to hear that. At least, you'll walk away with some happy memories of Zürich." Beatrice joined Madeleine and they looked down at the faded representations of the long-deceased.

"Yeah. I saw some fun sights, I learned a bit about Switzerland and I met you. Those things are all mine. Thanks to you, not all my memories of Zürich are shopping, surfing and the absence of Matthew."

"Michael."

"Michael, yes. That's what I meant."

An icy wave broke over Beatrice and her scalp contracted. Frozen, she stared down at the stone, as a series of images blew through her mind like playing cards on the wind.

Matthew.

"My day has been most successful, and I think tomorrow could be our breakthrough."

"Tally-ho! So we might have you home soon?"

She'd told Matthew it was a breakthrough. No one else.

"My day was very pleasing. I have high hopes of soon being able to return home soon."

"Kir Royales. Let's toast your breakthrough."

Matthew. Michael.

"Be careful of anyone with an interest in this case."

The empty church.

"I'll just see if it's still open."

Good God, she'd fallen into the most obvious of traps. Her quarry was standing beside her. And both of them knew the veil had dropped. Beatrice raised her head. Madeleine lifted her gaze.

"Beatrice ..." she reached out a placatory hand to catch Beatrice's arm. Beatrice recoiled, her forearm pulling through Madeleine's palm. The syringe caught her wrist, a needle slipped through cherry silk and a piercing pain arrived simultaneously in her arm and the pit of her stomach. She wrenched her arm away, tearing open a wound, and backed toward the steps. The syringe fell to the floor.

Madeleine watched her with a resigned expression. Her voice changed, the accent flatter, and the permanent expressive sparkle in her eyes turned dull and cold.

"Beatrice, I'm actually sorry about this. You have many fine qualities I admire. But fundamentally, you're on the wrong side. You know, we could have been friends, in another life."

Shot through with fear and adrenalin, Beatrice lunged up the stone stairs, ears straining for the sounds of pursuit. None came and she knew before she pushed at the door that it would be locked.

After you.

Madeleine had not moved, obviously trusting the drugs to disable her. Whatever it was would probably take effect in seconds. If she was quick, she could call for help. Scrabbling for her mobile, she sensed a shadow blocking the light.

"Come down, Beatrice. I don't want you to fall and hurt yourself. I doubt you'll get a signal down here, but just in case, I removed the SIM card from your phone while we were having our Kir Royales. It's now floating somewhere in the Limmat. Come down, please, we're going to have another little cocktail."

Beatrice's descended on unsteady legs. This was not over. She would fight this bitch, this vigilante, this dispenser-of-misguided-justice till her last breath. Madeleine smiled at her, before glancing back at the altar, bearing her huge handbag. Two things occurred to Beatrice. Whatever Madeleine's chosen method of disposal might be, it was in that bag. And albeit smaller, but still carrying substantial weight, her own handbag rested in her left hand.

With enormous effort, she swung it at Madeleine's head. It connected with a weak clout.

"*Gott verdammt*!" Madeleine's voice seemed to come from the other end of a long corridor. Beatrice's legs gave way and she collapsed onto her knees. As Madeleine eased her onto her side, Beatrice's eyes closed against her will and her last conscious thought was what a shame they were going to miss the yodelling.

Chapter 35

Zürich 2012

Chris snatched up the desk phone before realising he didn't know her number. Xavier was a step ahead and had already dialled on his mobile. Chris listened as he reached for his own handset to call Kälin.

"Her mobile is unobtainable."

"Shit! Call the hotel. And Xav, let's get round there. Find the address while I call Kälin."

His fingers clumsy, he found Kälin's number. His hands shook as he listened to the spaces between long ringing tones.

"*Kälin?*"

"Herr Kälin, it's Chris Keese. We found data on Richter's computer on all of the victims, one every year, downloaded shortly before the murders. She's recently downloaded two more. Giuseppe Esposito and Beatrice Stubbs."

Kälin drew a breath. "*Where is Frau Stubbs now?*"

"We don't know. We called her mobile and her hotel room ..." he took in the shake of Xavier's head, "but there's no answer. We're going there now."

"*Call me if you find anything. I'll meet you back at Zeughausstrasse in twenty minutes. And get the others.*"

Chris dialled the girls as he ran down the stairs after Xavier, the long lens photograph of DI Stubbs burned onto his retina.

Kälin's black hair and thick moustache sharpened the contrast with his white face, as he entered the fluorescent-lit workroom.

Chris walked to meet him, leaving Sabine and Xavier to continue their calls. He dispensed with greetings.

"Not at the hotel. The staff didn't see her leave. Her room is clean and tidy with no sign of any problems. They have no CCTV. Conceição is still there, looking around."

Sabine and Xavier joined them. Kälin acknowledged them with a nod.

"What do we know?"

Sabine appeared pale and tired without her make-up. But her energy was undimmed. "The receptionist has no idea where she might be. But tonight she had a visitor. An American, blonde hair. They left together, apparently happy and laughing."

"And we have no trace on Frau Stubbs' mobile phone?"

Chris shook his head. "Nothing."

The door opened, and for an instant, Chris expected Beatrice to walk in, with a look of surprise and irritation to find them all there.

For the first time since they'd met, he was disappointed to see Conceição.

"Good evening, everyone. Forensic officers have examined B's room. Her stuff is still there, but there's no sign of anything untoward. Apart from two glasses on the draining board. One clean, one dirty. It's already gone to the lab, but we've seen this before."

The skin of Chris's buttocks and thighs chilled into gooseflesh.

Kälin clasped his hands together and looked from one face to the next. Chris observed the thin line of his lips before he spat out his words.

"So Richter has attached herself to Frau Stubbs and the murder of Esposito threw us off the track. Frau Tikkenen, with your knowledge of this woman's mode of operation, what is her plan? As quickly as you can, please."

Sabine's complexion was startling. Chris had never seen such a bluish pallor on something living.

Her voice was quiet. "It makes no sense. The deaths have always been merited, in the killer's eyes. So why Beatrice? And in orchestrating their end, she uses something that she sees as just in her method. I don't see what 'sin' Beatrice has committed and therefore I can't imagine how she plans to kill her. But one thing we do know is that Richter always has sufficient information to find a way in."

Conceição drew in a breath. "Well, we now have the same information. It's all on that computer. We don't have the luxury of time, but we could know as much about Beatrice as Richter does. Let's look at those details and see if there's something which can help us."

"Chris and I have already looked. It wasn't only her photograph hidden in there. She even had Beatrice's bank details, transcripts of telephone conversations and her police personnel file." Xavier seemed despondent, and with an inclination of his head, handed the baton to his colleague.

Chris hated this. It was like rooting through her diary. But he had no choice.

"Beatrice suffers from bipolar disorder. According to this information, she has done since her early twenties. She's been managing it with a combination of mood stabilisers and anti-depressants for a long time. But it seems she had a pretty serious episode about a year ago and is just getting back on track. This is her first major case since."

"Can you elaborate on 'a pretty serious episode', Herr Keese?" By the look on his face, Kälin had guessed. Or already knew.

Chris rested his mouth on his fist and took a deep breath, unable to look at the misery on Xavier's face. He straightened.

"She tried to kill herself, Herr Kälin. She took an overdose."

Conceição's hand rose to her throat. "And Richter knows."

Kälin broke the silence. "Think! Richter has somehow got Frau Stubbs's confidence and has taken her somewhere to stage a suicide. They are not at her hotel, so where are they? Where did they go?"

Conceição spoke. "She had plans for tonight. Sabine and I invited her for dinner, but she had plans. She said she was going out with an acquaintance to get some culture."

"Culture? That narrows it down," observed Chris.

Kälin looked up. "Swiss culture. That's also what she told me. Religious art and yodelling."

"You could kill someone at a yodelling concert, I suppose. But faking a suicide? I don't think so." Conceição shook her head.

Silence can take many forms, thought Chris. Calm, comfortable and soothing. Or charged with the electricity of five frantic minds.

Sabine took a sharp breath. "The Kunsthaus! She was going to see some art tonight! We were talking about the Kunsthaus, and she was going to see some more."

"That's a possibility," said Kälin, reaching for his mobile. "Was there a particular exhibition, Frau Tikkenen, involving religious art?"

"She mentioned the Expressionists, and Matisse, and Chagall. She liked Chagall and said she was going to see some more tonight."

Xavier grimaced as if he were in pain. "How can I be so stupid? She asked me this morning which church was which. Herr Kälin – religious art, Chagall, it must be Fraumünster!"

Chris saw Kälin's face change, each taut muscle relaxing. "*Genau!* Exactly! The Chagall windows. The perfect place, it's closed at night. Herr Racine, find a number for the church management. The rest of us will go there. Come!"

On such occasions, Chris's long legs gave him an advantage. Running down the steps as fast as he could safely manage, he left his colleagues behind. Except for Kälin, who was right on his heels. As they reached the door to the car park, Kälin turned and shouted something back to Xavier in German. Shoving open the door, Chris couldn't be sure, but it sounded like '... *die Hunde.*'

The dogs?

The church sexton, despite radiating disapproval, was punctual. Kälin's brief explanation received no queries and the man opened the door. He led the way, turning on the lights, Kälin at his shoulder, Chris, Sabine and Conceição close behind. The church was huge. Chris grew despondent at the plethora of nooks and crannies, chapels, alcoves and tombs. Kälin instructed them to search a section each and proceeded towards the other end of the building.

Some sense of place held Chris back from calling out Beatrice's name. Instead, he investigated the nave, checked behind curtains and explored the pulpit. He lifted his head occasionally to check with his colleagues. Nothing. What if Richter had taken Beatrice some other place? That maniac could be slitting B's wrists else-where while he knelt on the floor, looking under pews. Frustration and impotence built into anger. Kälin was wrong, she wasn't here. It couldn't happen here. Tourists would be swarming through the very next day. There must be a vestry, or a separate chamber you could use for storage. There had to be a hiding place. Just like a computer; some data visible, some encrypted. But how do you hide a human being? A door banged open and Chris's hair stood on end as he heard panting.

Xavier led the way down the aisle, followed by two armed of-ficers with police dogs and caught Chris's eye with a hopeful look. Chris shook his head. Kälin marched towards them, but said noth-ing and watched as Xavier knelt to offer the dogs a piece of cloth. Only then did Chris notice the traditional Alsatian was accompa-nied by a bloodhound. Without lifting his head, Xavier explained. "Her jacket."

The handlers spoke gentle motivating words and the dogs responded, tails wagging as they inhaled essence of Stubbs. Along with the team, the sexton was fascinated and on request, gave his permission with enthusiasm. Unleashed, the dogs went to work. Beginning in small circles, like metal detectors, they sniffed, stopped and started; sudden runs interrupted by a slow study of a particular spot. The handlers followed, muttering encouragement.

Sabine descended from the balcony to watch, standing close to Conceição. The quiet tension built as they all watched. A bark made everyone jump.

The bloodhound took off, followed by its colleague. Without lifting its snout from the ground, it ran in a direct line to the door in the south transept, where it stopped, barking, scraping and wag-ging.

Kälin turned to the sexton. *"Was ist dahinter?"*

"Die Gruft."

Conceição looked to Chris for a translation.

Why had he not listened to his subconscious? *Just like a com-puter; some data visible, some encrypted.*

"The crypt."

The police team formed a reception line, as if they were at a wedding, allowing the sexton to come forward with the keys. The poor old guy shook, a combination of nerves and the spotlight of attention.

Door opened, the two dogs hared down the stairs, stopped and began a relay of barking. As Chris stumbled down, he recognised there was no aggression in that sound. It simply said, 'We found it.'

And they had.

Chapter 36

Fluorescent lighting at Kloten Airport's Jet Aviation terminal did Kälin's grim features no favours. Catching his own reflection in the tiny arrivals area, Chris realised he looked even worse. Each absorbed in his own thoughts, neither man spoke, but occasionally checked his watch or mobile phone. D'Arcy Roth's Gulfstream G550 touched down twenty minutes late. Two police cars were already stationed on the tarmac and airport security escorted Chris and Kälin to the aircraft.

Chris couldn't help but be impressed by the performance as she descended the steps. Hair swept up, she wore crisp white trousers, brown loafers, a gold silk shirt and over her shoulders, a suede jacket. She carried a brown leather briefcase and her gold jewellery caught the morning sunlight. Her make-up was light and she looked fresh, as if she were leaving her apartment for work, rather than coming off a sixteen-hour flight. With an artificial smile, she walked up to them. Her bodyguard and her daughter stopped at the bottom of the steps.

"Hello again, Herr Kälin. It seems I just can't get rid of you. And Frau Stubbs?"

Kälin held her gaze. Neither blinked.

"We have a few more questions, Frau D'Arcy. Will you come with us, please?"

"Oh God. This has gone beyond a joke. I have work to do. I cannot sit around waiting while you people try to find some way of making me your scapegoat." She shook her head in exasperation. "Wait, I must instruct my staff."

"Frau D'Arcy? You may not remember me, but I'm Chris Keese, a member of Frau Stubbs's team. Your staff will need to accompany us to the police station. You can take the first car. Would you like your daughter to travel with you?"

Without even registering his question, she barked over her shoulder.

"Dina!"

The girl jumped and hurried towards them. D'Arcy stalked straight to the waiting police vehicle and stopped. As he suspected, a first-class bitch who can't even open a door. Chris yanked the handle and swung the door open as if it were a limousine. D'Arcy slid into the back seat without acknowledging Chris. Again. The girl dropped her head and ducked into the car as if she hoped she'd gone unnoticed.

Seemed like Kälin had no intention of helping out, so turning to the bodyguard, Chris indicated the second patrol car. The man obeyed with a worried frown. Closing the door behind him, Chris instructed the officers to take them back to Zeughausstrasse. Kälin stood watching the cars pull away as Chris joined him.

"Shouldn't we head back to the station?"

Kälin did not reply. Chris saw the tiredness in the detective's expression had been replaced by something else. A commercial jet took off from the main airfield, the roar of engines making speech impossible for a moment.

"Herr Keese. Please tell me exactly what you saw just then. In detail."

Chris needed coffee. And sleep. Not mind games with Kälin.

"A very glamorous, very fresh 24-carat bitch just got off the plane, got mad with us for taking her into custody and showed her true colours by treating me and her daughter like non-humans. Did I miss something?"

"I did. Surprise. Her reaction was rehearsed. She was expecting us. This whole scene was prepared." He began walking back to the tiny terminal.

"And?"

"And I don't know. But for some reason, she thinks she's invincible."

"D'Arcy refuses to talk without legal representation. The company's lawyer is coming. Should we get coffee?" Chris rubbed his eyes.

Kälin lifted his chin abruptly in acknowledgement. "Get that warrant. We'll need it."

"Warrant?"

"Herr Keese, we need permission to take samples from all D'Arcy's female employees."

"Why do you want to do that now? We can't take samples until Monday. The only females we could test today would be D'Arcy's daughter and her cleaner. One of whom is too young and the other too old."

"We leave no stone unturned. Get the warrant and test them, please. Out of respect to Frau Stubbs. Call me when that lawyer arrives, I'll be in my office."

Chris chose not to be offended; the man's stress hummed like a piano wire. He delivered the warrant to Conceição, insisted she took samples from the daughter and the housekeeper, before excusing himself and returning to the computer room. He switched off the light and his mind, rolled up his jacket and lay on the floor.

"I repeat, Herr Kälin, I have no idea what happened to the doctor who made that mistake. That was the last I heard of her. I decided to take the matter no further as the hospital had already begun an investigation." D'Arcy voice was controlled and patient, as if talking to a child.

"You had no contact with her at all after she was struck off?" Chris demanded.

The deep blue eyes flicked in his direction, but she addressed her question back to Kälin. "Are all policemen this slow?"

Chris was used to this; her hostility was a good sign. Her lawyer – grey hair, navy suit, forgettable face – barely looked up from his note-taking.

Chris pressed on. "I repeat. You had no contact with her at all after she was struck off? This question is not restricted to Switzerland. Did you have any further contact with this woman – real or virtual?"

Her focus remained on the wall. "I repeat. No. I had no contact with her. Real or virtual, whatever that means."

"You never communicated with her via the Internet, for example?"

"Why would I do that? What on earth would we have to discuss?"

"Modern art, perhaps? Did you ever participate in an art forum?"

Her full focus returned to him. "Modern art? I am the CEO of a major financial services provider. We have a turnover of 16 billion Swiss francs, and we employ 50,000 people worldwide. In my free time, I am a highly regarded polo player, which demands several training hours a week. I have an active social calendar and spend 90 minutes every day in the gym. I have better things to do with my time than an art forum."

Kälin sighed. "Repeating your position in society will not work as a smokescreen here. Until you can prove you did not orchestrate these killings through Helene Richter, we will continue to believe you are involved."

D'Arcy gave a patient, pitying smile. "I am not one to teach a man his job, Herr Kälin, but I think you'll find that the burden of proof lies with you."

Chris spoke. "Don't worry about that, Frau D'Arcy, we are very confident we have the right woman."

"I do hope so, Herr Keese. Because from here, it looks like you are wasting both my time and yours."

So she had taken note of his name. Chris could feel the balance of power tilting. And he wasn't the only one. He saw her direct a cold glare at her brief.

"Ahem." The lawyer, Herr Wortmann, prepared to speak, but a knock at the door prevented his response.

Xavier entered the room and bent down to whisper in Kälin's ear. The older man's brow creased into incredulity and he turned to face Xavier, with a shake of his head.

Xavier nodded. Kälin, expressionless, looked at Chris, and with a minute eyebrow movement, indicated the door.

Once outside the interrogation room, Kälin voiced his question. "Are you sure?"

Xavier's head bobbed up and down again. "The laboratory says 100%. The DNA is the same and Conceição agrees. A complete match on all points."

Chris looked from one to the other. "Who?"

Xavier jerked his head towards the cells. "The daughter. I put her under arrest."

"And does her DNA match what we found in Frau Stubbs's hotel room?" asked Kälin.

Xavier nodded again.

Chris shook his head. "How is that possible? Not only is she clearly a woman, but she can only have been a kid in 2007. And she was in Argentina last night. It makes no sense. What does she say?"

Xavier shrugged. "Nothing. She won't talk."

The three men stood in silence, until Kälin exhaled a sharp breath.

"I've had enough of this. That smart-mouthed female is going to tell us what's going on. Herr Keese, where are her weak spots, from your observation?"

Chris forced himself to think. "She thinks she's cleverer than she is. She overestimates her own intelligence. And underestimates ours."

"Good idea. Herr Racine?"

The request clearly came as a surprise and Xavier's face went blank, before his eyes sharpened. "Her principles. We know she's behind this, so we have to get at what drives her."

"Thank you. Let's go."

"Herr Wortmann, more water? Frau D'Arcy? So, perhaps we can go back to my point. The connection with Frau Richter."

"It does not exist."

Kälin's voice changed from amenable to icy. "Here's the theory, Frau D'Arcy. We know you lost your father, Robert Wolf from Seattle, in 1976, and your mother remarried, rather quickly, in '78. You were eleven, correct?"

Satisfaction warmed Chris as D'Arcy sat frozen, unresponsive. They were getting to her, without a doubt. He used the side of his foot to nudge Kälin's, whose face twitched in acknowledgement.

"Jean-Baptiste D'Arcy. Your stepfather. A large personality, by all accounts. He must have entirely eclipsed your father; being so successful, genial, popular and rich. Your mother finally hit the jackpot. The American was a bit of a dud, wasn't he? Still, she struck gold with D'Arcy. The provenance of his wealth is shadowy, true, but on the surface, he was the perfect humanitarian. Sadly, your mother had only a short time to enjoy such good fortune. Six years of living the high life and she succumbed to cancer. That must have been very hard on you. Your stepfather, on his death, was worth some seventeen million Swiss francs, is that right?"

D'Arcy rested her chin on her hands. "And this is your theory? Despite the fact I was his only heir, I killed him for the money. You are of course aware, thanks to your impeccable research, that I had already inherited my mother's property, been headhunted by Hoffmann-Roth, and earned an impressively high salary. At the age of twenty-two. I had no need of his money."

"Need and want are two different things. After your mother died, you lived with D'Arcy for another five years. You were a high-flying businesswoman. You had more than enough money for a place of your own. A palace of your own. What possible reason would a young, successful woman like yourself have to spend five years in the same house as an older man, with whom you had no blood ties whatsoever? You say you had no need of his money. Maybe you stayed because of *his* needs."

Chris forced his expression to remain cool. Kälin's tactics surprised him, but he delighted in the result. The lawyer seemed to wake up. "Herr Kälin, that is unacceptable! I cannot allow my client …"

D'Arcy snapped her head toward Wortmann and he petered out. She took a breath and returned her eyes to Kälin's.

"You are a small-minded little pervert. My stepfather was the most wonderful man I have ever known. My father taught me ethics, but when it came to practical applications, he was weak. Jean-Baptiste showed me that ethics and business are not divorced.

Not even separated. It's a question of perspective. After you make difficult decisions, you have to compensate by being a force for the good. A lesson I learned well and have applied ever since. Jean-Baptiste was one of the greatest men I have ever known."

"So why did you have him killed?"

She locked onto Kälin's eyes. "I did not 'have him killed', as you put it. I gave him the one gift I could. I had already buried two parents and faced the loss of the single most influential person in my life. He was my guiding light, my star. I loved him more than anything. I would have taken his place if I could. When my parents died, I was too young to influence their suffering. But Jean-Baptiste knew he was dying. The only question was how long it would take. For the first time in my life, I was able to act. I talked to the anaesthetist and found a sympathetic mind."

She stopped, aware she had been provoked. Her brief leaned in to speak to her, but she ignored him. "An act of supreme humanity on that doctor's part, not to mention her bravery, for which she was richly rewarded. End of story."

"But that was only the beginning for Helene Richter. Seems she had a taste for wiping out influential men and your stepfather was only the first. Or were they also 'mercy killings'?"

"Jean-Baptiste's death has nothing to do with this. And why would you suspect Richter? You're making ridiculous assumptions."

D'Arcy fixed her eyes on Kälin and blinked. But Chris knew the calm gaze obscured a maelstrom of thought. He tapped his foot to Kälin's. The response was immediate.

"So you're telling me Helene Richter had nothing to with the deaths in question?"

"I cannot imagine why you think she would."

"You're sure?"

She lifted her chin with an expression of boredom.

Kälin inhaled. "In which case, the prime suspect is clear. We have evidence that indicates the involvement of a woman, despite the DNA discovered. I am sorry to inform you that we have arrested your daughter, Frau Dina D'Arcy. She is now in police custody."

Chris didn't need to nudge Kälin for this one.

The pale face lost all colour. In the harsh light of the police interview room, she looked sickly, although her dark pupils shone.

"That is impossible. You have made yet another huge mistake."

"No. The male DNA planted at the site of each murder is a perfect match for that of your daughter."

The tension dropped from her jaw. "You took a sample of her DNA? Surreptitious gathering of samples can be challenged in law." With a slow turn of her head, she faced her lawyer.

"That is correct. We would certainly question the validity of ..."

Kälin interrupted. "There would be no question about the authorisation and technical accuracy of these samples."

D'Arcy shook her head. "You only tested the men yesterday."

"That is true, we did. But Frau Stubbs decided that we should also test your female employees. A wise move."

D'Arcy stared at Kälin for so long that Chris began to shift in his seat. She suddenly switched her attention to her brief and dismissed him. He hesitated, but not for long. As the door closed behind him, she exhaled a long, controlled breath.

"How ironic. When this was to be the last one." Closing her eyes, she took several slow breaths, before returning her gaze to Kälin.

"If you can assure me that you will not question Dina, or treat her as a suspect in any way, I will tell you what you need to know. You must be careful with my daughter. She is very fragile; her life has always been sheltered. She doesn't really understand the outside world. She is special."

"So her DNA seems to show." Kälin observed. "I give you my word we will proceed no further with Frau Dina D'Arcy until we have heard what you have to say."

Chris watched D'Arcy compose herself. His fatigue gave way to fascination; she was going to spill.

"Everything I said about Jean-Baptiste is true. I loved him. I persuaded Helene to help me end his suffering, because I could not bear to see his pain. It was an act of kindness. He never hurt me, or treated me as anything other than an adored child."

"What happened to Richter?" asked Kälin.

"Helene continued her studies. First in Brazil, and later in

Canada. I had to pull more strings to get her a place there than I did to adopt my daughter. But she performed very well and exceeded expectations. I'd say my investment was repaid."

"Why did you pay for her education?" asked Chris.

"Because she should never have lost her place in Switzerland. Our plan, at the time of Jean-Baptiste's death, was for Helene to study anaesthesia and euthanasia, and for us to open a clinic where people could choose to end their lives, without pain and with dignity. We both agreed on that as a basic human right."

"A noble concept. I am curious as to how you made the leap from assisted suicide to serial murder." Kälin's tone sounded calm, but Chris sensed a seismic anger building.

D'Arcy frowned. "There was no leap. In fact, we saw our work as exactly that. Assisted suicides, where the individuals concerned required some help."

Chris paused to take that in. "Where does Dina fit into your 'work'?"

"She doesn't. She had nothing to do with it."

"So how do you explain ..."

"Herr Keese, your interrogation techniques appear to come from American television programmes. Please, let me speak."

Chris did not react, but watched her take a sip of water. There was not one sign that she was feeling the pressure. He admired her, in the same way he would admire a scorpion.

"After Jean-Baptiste died and Helene left for Brazil, I felt more alone than ever in my life. I had no one, nothing apart from my work. I wanted to be with someone, to have someone of my own. I considered an adoption and discussed the idea with Helene. She was a good friend to me. Then she had a stroke of luck. A small boy from one of the favelas got badly burned and Helene treated him. The family could not pay her; they had more children than they could afford and the woman was pregnant again. So Helene arranged a payment in kind. I paid her a large amount for her unborn child and prepared to embrace a baby into my life. In September 1994, she had a boy, Nino. I was desperately disappointed. I wanted a little girl."

"Did you sue her?" asked Chris, with heavy sarcasm.

D'Arcy gave a dismissive shake of the head. "No. Everything was arranged, and I intended to adopt a baby. A baby girl. Helene signed the certificate, confirming the age and gender as I instructed, and I took Nino back to Switzerland. I bought him dresses, I plaited his hair, I gave him dolls, and told him how beautiful she was. Nino became Nina."

Chris gaped, unable to think of a thing to say. Kälin seemed equally stunned for a moment, before recovering himself.

"What about when he went to school?"

"There is no 'he' anymore. We began gender reassignment operations before puberty. As for school, Nina was home educated until the age of fourteen, and very successfully, in fact. She has an impressive IQ, despite her parentage and may take up a place at a major university. This is why I insist you must be careful with her. She rarely leaves our house alone. Talking to strangers is hard for her."

Chris shook his head, his belief stretched. "Did Nino want to become a girl?"

"There was no question. To all intents and purposes, she was a girl. A sweet girl who has grown up into a lovely young woman. I am very proud of her." Her taut jaw indicated genuine emotion.

Kälin nodded. "It's no surprise the girl is so shy. You control her whole life. Most people would prefer their child to grow up with a little more worldly wisdom."

"Oh she *is* worldly wise. These days you don't have to go out there, Herr Kälin, the world can come to you. Her knowledge of the Internet allows her a whole online life. You know, sometimes even I don't know what she does out there. Her own mother!"

Her light laugh, with the confidential tone of parents at the school gate, caused Chris to hunch his shoulders against a sudden creeping thought.

He asked the question. "Did you change the child's gender in order to help you effect these fake suicides?"

D'Arcy glanced away and back in irritation. "Please try and keep up, Herr Keese. I explained that I wanted a daughter and that is what I achieved. Yes, there were barriers to reaching that goal, but I overcame. My choice to take some action against malevolent elements of society came much later."

Kälin's brows formed one continuous shadow over his eyes. "Yes, let's talk about that choice."

She sat back in her chair, as if being interviewed on a popular chat show. Chris had to admit, the woman had balls.

"By 2006, the strategy I learned from my brilliant stepfather had turned Hoffmann-Roth into one of the Big Five. I was made Senior Partner and when Hoffmann retired, the company became D'Arcy Roth. My personal wealth exceeded the one billion mark. It was time, as Jean-Baptiste had always taught me, to give something back. The difficulty was that I was surrounded by 'takers' who never paid their dues. True, it was entirely my idea to drop Hoffmann's ethical standpoint and the decision proved profitable for the company. But the downside was that I spent years of my life smiling and shaking the hands with the foulest beings on the planet."

"So the next logical step was to get rid of them?" asked Kälin, head tilted.

"It had occurred to me. Planning the demises of certain individuals occupied much of my thoughts. Nevertheless, I believed they should do the honourable thing and make the world a better place by leaving it voluntarily. Only when Helene returned from Sault Sainte Marie did I realise the two things could be combined. We talked about it for almost two years, solving practical problems theoretically. The idea of leaving DNA to muddy the waters arose long before we realised we had the perfect source." She laughed, as if recalling a happy memory. "So that's when we changed Nina's name. It was our little joke."

Chris stared at her, aghast. Kälin looked down at the table, pressing his fingers to his forehead. When he looked up again, there were four white pressure points above his eyebrows.

"I think a break would be beneficial. I will send someone to see you have everything you need." His chair scraped back and he reached for the recorder. Chris stood and made for the door. D'Arcy's voice halted them.

"Herr Kälin. Dina submitted to the DNA sampling as she had done the operations. She thought it was part of her life and never asked questions. She had no idea what we used it for. She's entirely innocent."

Kälin turned, his eyes dangerously dark.

"All the men you targeted … you believed that killing them was for the greater good. So why Frau Stubbs?"

D'Arcy leant back in her chair. "A combination of reasons. I dislike people passing judgement on me. I take it personally. We were, in fact, on the same side, if only she could have seen it. We both wanted to take out the bad guys. But her perspective was so narrow, bound by petty legal constraints. I shouldn't speak ill of the dead, but it's no wonder she was an unhappy woman. She fought a constant battle against bureaucracy. In another life, she might have joined us in making the world a better place."

Kälin's growled. "You think the world is a better place without Frau Stubbs?"

D'Arcy thought for a second, before offering them a smile.

"My world is."

Seconds ticked by and no one moved. Kälin froze, his finger poised above the recorder. Chris trained his eyes on D'Arcy, mentally hurling every curse he knew in her direction. Finally, Kälin spoke, directly into the recorder, without looking at either D'Arcy or Chris.

"So, you hunted down men who broke the law for their own selfish needs. You removed individuals who profited from the misery of the poor and disadvantaged. You took out those people who treated others like puppets for their own ends. You decided you were above all the systems and moral codes others adhere to and nominated yourself as judge, jury and executioner. And finally, you chose to kill someone who quite simply disagreed with you. In short, Frau D'Arcy, you became one of *them*. For your information, Frau Stubbs is recovering in hospital and quite determined to be fully fit to testify at your trial. Interview terminated, twelve forty-three."

Chapter 37

Zürich 2012

Klinik im Park was much quieter than the University Hospital. Out of the window, there was a glorious, blossom-filled park, and beyond, the Lake of Zürich. Nordic walkers, cyclists, joggers and a varied group of bathers revelled in the sunshine. A light knock sounded and the door opened. About time; she was starving.

"Beatrice! You're up!"

The sight of Sabine and Conceição's familiar, bright faces brought tears to her eyes.

"Beatrice?" They rushed to her side.

"No, no, it's silly, I'm fine. I'm just awfully pleased to see you."

Sabine leant down to give her a hug. Conceição's hand squeezed her shoulder. These wonderful girls.

Dabbing at her nose, Beatrice turned her attention to their bags. "I hope you've brought me something to eat. I don't think I've ever been so hungry in my life."

Smiling, the two women sat on the bed. Sabine unwrapped flowers and Conceição unpacked the contents of her paper bag.

"Food, yes, but the nurse says you must take it slowly. We also brought flowers, some books and magazines, all best wishes and the latest news. Number one topic? Your doctor says you can go home tomorrow, if all is well with the tests," Conceição announced.

Beatrice's heart leapt. Hospital was not all that dissimilar to prison, in her view, so when a reprieve was in sight, her hopes soared.

"Really? Oh, that's wonderful."

Sabine arranged the yellow bouquet in a water jug. "You don't really need to stay in hospital another night. The main reason they moved you here was to avoid the Apart'hotel. Kälin thought it would be best."

"That's very kind of him. But I'll have to go back there to pack, anyway."

Conceição shook her head. "It's all done. Your cases are at Sabine's, ready to go when you are. We did it this morning."

"Oh you are marvellous. Right, I need food, immediately followed by an update. Sabine, those flowers are delightful."

"Courtesy of the boys. They're coming in later."

"Potato salad, pasta with pesto and tomatoes, or a blueberry yoghurt?" Conceição held up three plastic tubs.

"All of them and in that order."

Sabine brought Beatrice's tray from the bed to the window chair, and Conceição opened the lids for her.

"The nurse did say that you had already eaten lunch," Sabine said, with an air of innocence.

Beatrice put down her fork. "I was given some thin soup, around elevenses time, for your information. And the doctor at University Hospital emphasised the importance of keeping my strength up. So allow me a light snack, while you bring me up to speed with the case. News, please."

Conceição kicked off her shoes with a laugh and tucked one long leg underneath her.

"*Bon appétit.* D'Arcy has confessed to organising all the murders, including one that didn't happen. A pharmaceutical boss slipped the noose, after having met Richter. They couldn't risk his recognising her on her second attempt, so they chose Ryman as the substitute ..."

Sabine interrupted. "So we've got D'Arcy, but still no sign of Richter. All border police have been alerted."

Beatrice shook her head. "She's long gone. After thirty-six hours? We've lost her, I'm afraid. What about the girl, Dina?"

"Under psychiatric observation." Sabine responded with enthusiasm. "She's a fascinating mix. I observed a few interviews. One minute, brilliantly intelligent; the next, you would think she had some significant learning disability. She was the person who kept the art forum active, logging in as all the different members, raising discussions, having arguments, and creating an entire imaginary world for Richter and D'Arcy to use for their own purposes. I have asked Dr Thiel, the psychologist in charge, if I can follow this case. I want to know what happens to this girl."

Beatrice nodded. "So do I. I feel for that poor child. Did D'Arcy confess to the press leak?"

Adding sliced gherkin to a potato salad was a sublime idea. A top tip she intended to use to impress Matthew. Beatrice tore the lid off the green and red pasta fracas and tucked in.

Sabine bit her lip. "B, the police team checked your room and belongings for any forensic evidence. They found a bug in your mobile phone."

Beatrice closed her mouth. "No. So *I* was the leak? Oh how awful!"

"We think D'Arcy probably organised that after the first time you locked horns."

An uncomfortable heat crawled up Beatrice's neck, making it harder to swallow.

"How's your throat, B?" Conceição asked.

Beatrice waved her fork in an indiscriminate gesture to communicate the fact that she was fine and they were to get on with it.

"So the case is finished. We have the woman behind these killings, and you led your team to a successful conclusion. Everyone's happy and tomorrow we go home!"

Sabine's comforting words stuck in Beatrice's throat and tears tickled her nose. Conceição knelt beside her, offering a tissue.

Beatrice grimaced. "I'm sorry. I seem to cry at the daftest things. Please ignore me. There's really nothing wrong with this pasta."

Conceição gave her shoulder another squeeze. "B, you're bound to be a bit raw. We've been just the same, haven't we?" She glanced at Sabine.

"Yes, and none of us went through what you did."

"Thank you, girls. You've both been wonderful to me. Visiting with food, news, a super pair of pyjamas, and more food. Worth your weight in coal. I shall miss you, you know. And I suppose I'll miss the boys, too. Are things still running smoothly with you and Chris, Conceição?"

Scooping up a cherry tomato, it took Beatrice a second to catch up. But the look between the pair was unmistakeable. She stared for a second, her mind processing what she saw.

"Oh, I see."

She really should get her radar re-tuned; she'd made the classic sexual jealousy assumption. "Well, congratulations! Oh dear, how did Chris take it?"

Conceição gave a resigned smile. "He's a cool guy, actually. He took it in his stride. Look, B, it's not common knowledge, okay?"

"I am the soul of discretion. Can I have my yoghurt now?"

Halfway through a BBC Prime episode of Doctor Who, Beatrice was lying on the bed when three light raps announced the arrival of Xavier and Chris. She felt a slight blush, hopefully imperceptible in the light of the television screen. The last time she'd seen these two was just after her stomach pump. But a civilised veil should be drawn over that.

"B! You look so much better than the last time we saw you! After they pumped you out at *Universitätspital*, you were grey. Like more dead than alive?"

"Chris, you are always such a joy. Xavier, I am thrilled to see you again. Have you brought cakes?"

Xavier beamed. "Sabine mentioned you are hungry, but all food must be soft. I brought you a *Birchermuesli*. How are you feeling?"

"Better. Hungry. Emotional. Sore. Curious."

Chris laughed and stretched out on the window chair. "We can satisfy the 'hungry' and 'curious'. I got you a tiramisu. Where do you want to start?"

"With the tiramisu, please. Oh, I see what you mean. What happens to D'Arcy now? And how's Dina coping?"

"D'Arcy will be charged tomorrow, but Dina will spend at least two weeks under observation before a decision is made. We have written up all our reports, Lyon's handing out gold stars, and tomorrow we can leave. Although I was thinking of staying on for a couple of days." Chris had a certain light in his eye.

"For work or pleasure?" Beatrice swallowed a large mouthful of coffee cream to disguise her curiosity.

"Could be both. I've got an opportunity to see how the extreme left works. I'm hoping to achieve some undercover anarchist penetration."

Xavier's face was a mixture of embarrassment, amusement and concern. "Can you also go home, B?"

"Pending the test results on my liver, yes. As you obviously know, this isn't the first time I've taken an overdose. My liver can't tell the difference between voluntary and not. So the damage is likely to be similar."

Meeting two pairs of sympathetic eyes was unbearable. "What about you two? I hope you received a glowing report from Kälin at the end of this."

"He's not writing our reports. He says it's your job," Chris replied.

Xavier hurried to add his comment. "But this time, B, he means it in a good way."

After taking note of her flight wish-list for the next day, the two men said their goodbyes. Beatrice remained professional throughout, only admitting gloom after the door closed. Switching off the light to allow her to watch them unseen, she stood at the window until their dear familiar forms crossed the road and got into their vehicle. With a sad smile, she gazed out at the lights across the lake on the Gold Coast. That beautiful empty villa. What would happen to that mosaic floor? What would happen to that mixed-up young girl? The tail-lights of Xavier's car disappeared around the bend. Goodbye, Chris, goodbye Xavier. What were the chances she would ever see them again? And since when had she started talking like Ingrid Bergman? An age-old ache cracked her chest, and a chasm began to open. Then a movement below drew her eyes. A few spaces back from Xavier's slot, a car's interior light glowed as the driver's door opened. It looked like a Ford Mondeo. A figure exited and made its way across the road to the clinic. Beatrice was ready.

"Ken! I am so pleased to see you."

"Thank Gawd you're still in one piece. Me and Noemi have been worried sick. What the hell was all that about? Kälin didn't have nothing to do with it, I'm sure of that. I was watching him all evening. I don't think he's your man."

"I know, I know. Rather embarrassingly, it seems I was the leak. I found out this afternoon my phone was bugged. Probably by the same person who tried to do away with me."

Ken folded his arms. "Well, I'll be blowed. And old Kälin was clean as a choirboy all along."

Beatrice agreed. "He was. He is. I was being over-cautious. I'm so sorry to have sent you off after a dead herring when it was my own indiscretions that let us all down."

"But you are all right, eh?"

"Right as rain. Now you're here, you may as well deliver your report."

"If you like. But that's not all I'm delivering. I got you some grapes. I wanted to bring you a Bakewell tart, but Noemi said it might be too much for you."

For once, Beatrice wasn't interested in food. "Thank you, that's most considerate. So, Karl Kälin? What did you find?"

"Here you go. Typed and everything. But there's nothing much there. I followed him for over a fortnight and found sweet Fanny Adams. Never seen him with any journos, apart from the official stuff. Divorced, lives alone, creature of habit, never breaks the law, a few close friends and he plays cards on a Friday. I could get to like this geezer."

"Thank you, Ken. And I'm sorry for dragging you out of retirement."

"None of that, mate. I had a right laugh getting back in the saddle. Tell you what, B, I wish you was staying longer."

The strangest thing was, so did she.

The sun sank, leaving both coasts illuminated by the thousand individual twinkles from streets, homes and cars. Beatrice had tucked herself in for the night and found Bergerac on TV when the knock came at the door.

Kälin's bear-like shape filled the doorway.

"Good evening, Frau Stubbs. I hear you are recovering."

Beatrice killed John Nettles with the remote. "What a nice surprise, Herr Kälin. Please come in, take a seat."

He sat on the window chair, his expression uncomfortable. His empty hands showed he had brought her nothing to eat.

"Does the Clinic suit you?"

"Apart from their appallingly tiny rations, yes. It's comfortable, private and most attentive."

"And professional. They check everything your guests bring and adjust your diet accordingly. They know what they are doing."

"I am going home tomorrow," she blurted.

"Congratulations. I know that makes you very happy."

Beatrice opened her mouth to correct him, but had no idea what to say.

Kälin cleared his throat. "Frau Stubbs, I came to say I am glad we had an opportunity to work together. I learned from you and that is my definition of a good collaboration. I leave you now, and wish you every success in your future career and the very best of health." He stood up to shake her hand.

Beatrice swallowed down her unreliable emotions, shook his hand and forced a professional, chirpy smile.

"Thank you, Herr Kälin. It was an experience I shall never forget, especially as it is likely to be my last case. But I will take many happy memories away. I wish you all the best for your future and I have one small request. I see a great deal of potential in Xavier Racine. Should you ever find yourself in a position to help his career, I would consider it a personal favour if you did so."

"You have a good eye."

"I used to have. None of us escapes time, Herr Kälin."

Kälin stepped back. "As you told me once before, you are stronger than you look. You led this investigation to its conclusion through sound leadership and good judgement. Perhaps your dreams of retirement are premature."

"Lyon may take an alternative view of what constitutes good judgement."

Kälin walked to the door, the corridor illumination silhouetting his form and hiding his expression. "It was a tough task. Under the circumstances, your performance was not too bad. All the best, Frau B."

The door closed.

Beatrice's brow creased and more infuriating tears seeped out. Sniffing and stemming the flow, she barely heard the knock. The bossy nurse.

"Frau Stubbs, you have eaten far too much today. But as this is a special request, you can have one more thing before bed. Now, after you have eaten this, you must drink a herbal tea and I will check you every hour. It is not recommended for this situation."

The smell was delicious; garlic, cheese, a hint of alcohol ... the woman placed a small plastic pot in front of her, beside a tiny plate of cubed bread. She handed Beatrice a fork.

"It is only microwaved, I'm afraid. But Herr Kälin said no one should leave Switzerland without eating a fondue. Not even in May."

Chapter 38

London 2012

As the five-note melody announced her phone restored to life, the baggage carousel in London City Airport cranked up. Intolerably excited by the knowledge that Matthew was waiting the other side of one of those bland grey panels, she fidgeted from foot to foot. Would he have thought to get milk? They could always stop on the way home. What did it matter, he was staying for the rest of the week. Such luxury. There would be time enough to do all the galleries, to loiter in Borough Market, to while away afternoons in the second-hand bookshops, to cook, to eat, to talk. Impatience swelled and she paced around to the other side. Her suitcase, naturally, was nowhere to be seen.

Vibrations from her mobile made her jump before she heard the ringtone. She checked the screen.

"Herr Kälin?"

"No, I am Herr Kälin. You are Frau Stubbs."

"I am aware of that, thank you. It was a question. What can I do for you?"

"It is really only a courtesy call. I thought you would be interested to know that Frau Dina D'Arcy managed to leave the psychiatric facility last night. As yet, she has not been located."

The bloody suitcase appeared exactly at the wrong time.

"What do you mean, 'leave the facility'? Wait a minute." Beatrice shoved forward to drag her case off the conveyor belt. "How did she get out?"

"She was not a high-risk patient, so she was permitted to go out in the grounds. This afternoon, when someone went to find her for an appointment, she had gone missing."

"She can't go far. She has no money, and no idea of how to get around. Surely she'll be picked up in a matter of hours."

"A visitor's handbag is also missing, containing cash, ID, a mobile telephone. I think she might get further than we think."

"So the case is not closed at all. Do you think I should come back?"

"That's not necessary, Frau Stubbs. The case has been assigned to another team. But they have an excellent consultant."

"You."

"No, they don't need me either. They already have an expert in the form of Herr Racine."

Beatrice beamed. "Wish him all the best from me. And Herr Kälin, if you wouldn't mind, I'd appreciate the occasional email. Just to let me know what's going on."

"From Herr Racine, or me?"

"Both."

"I'll see if I have time. I must go now. I wish you a nice afternoon."

"Same to you. Goodbye, Herr Kälin."

He rang off and Beatrice dragged her case through the automatic door and into Matthew's embrace. He looked down at her, concern showing behind his smile.

"Nice hairdo. How are you feeling, Old Thing?"

"Surprisingly full of bees. Did you get milk?"

Chapter 39

Lake Konstanz 2012

The sun sat low over Lake Konstanz; pink, purple and silver flashed in the subsiding wake of a departing ferry, like the rippling flank of a rainbow trout. The white boat churned white water, confetti after the bride, as it passed its sister ship on the opposite journey. A figure rose from the bench outside the Zeppelin Museum and walked along the lakefront to the harbour to meet it. Shadows crept across the lake as the sun faded, yet it seemed as if the boat would beat the darkness to the shore.

Passengers gathered on deck, eager to step into another country. Docking, the engines' grinding ceased and the silence filled with the lively voices of tourists. Loud colours and opinions flickered past as the figure waited. Eventually, as the final few pensioners descended, she saw a slight, nondescript shape come along the deck, scanning the shore. Helene raised her hand, as if identifying herself for roll call. Dina lifted a palm and splayed five fingers in recognition.

Helene waited where she was. With great care, the girl stepped off the boat, almost as if it were her first time, and with similar caution, walked over to greet her. Three kisses.

Always three.

But now only two.

RAW MATERIAL

JJ MARSH

Chapter 1

Twenty minutes after the alarm blasted her out of a profound sleep, Fernanda dragged on her uniform and locked the flat. Her eyes were open but yet to wake. She trudged down the path in the dark, squeezed past the wheelie bins and out onto Biggerstaff Street. The cleaning contractors' depot was a good half hour away. Thirty minutes walking in the cold would liven her up, as it did every morning. Not much movement on Fonthill Road. She gave a long, creaking yawn, before getting into a determined stride towards the Tube station. Her teacher had taught the class a new expression this week – *no rest for the wicked*. She liked that. Sounded like there was some fun involved.

Despite her fatigue, her main feeling was one of relief and optimism. Luis would sleep until she returned. His fever had broken and now came the easy part. And Rui could answer any fretful calls. He was a caring man. A fine father and such a kind husband, insisting she go to bed at midnight and taking over the watch. She was grateful; three hours' sleep was better than none.

The railway bridges loomed above and Fernanda picked up her pace. These new lights meant you could see the length of the tunnel, check there was no one waiting in the shadows – no one following some paces behind – and relax as you walked. Fernanda never relaxed. She scurried under those bridges as fast as she could without running. Denim on her inside legs brushed a regular beat, while her heels ticked in syncopation. The street lights at the other end beckoned her to safety and her breathing was short. She was awake now – eyes, ears, everything. Clearing the last of the bridges, some of her tension dissolved and she began to climb the ascent to the main street. That was when she heard the voice.

"Hello. I've been waiting for you."

She snapped around, her breath tiny, fearful puffs. There was no one behind her. The sodium light created shadows on the banks rising from the underpass, but she could be sure no human shape hid there. Electric pulses buzzed through her, even between her fingers. She turned and began hurrying away, just short of a run.

"Aren't you even going to say hello?"

She whipped back, the voice so close, so intimate. A light clicked on. Her eyes flew upwards. Balanced on the railway bridge, above the security camera, a man stood with a torch in his hand. A baseball cap kept his face in darkness, but his naked white thighs and abdomen were exposed in the torchlight. One hand provided the illumination, the other worked rhythmically at his groin. The images took their time to reach Fernanda's consciousness. He grunted, like Luis passing a stool, and something spat onto the tarmac near her feet. These random elements connected in her frightened mind and she realised what she was watching.

Her stomach contracted and bile rose. She turned to run, tears of shame filling her eyes, when she heard his satisfied voice.

"Thank you, darling. See you tomorrow?"

She finally stopped running on Seven Sisters Road and vomited at a bus stop. The birds were singing.

Chapter 2

Surf and snoring, in a perfect call and response rhythm. Soughs and sighs, breaths and breakers. Deeply soothing. The creaking of the wooden ceiling added an irregular percussion to the symphony. Nothing could be more conducive to relaxation. A long weekend by the sea, Matthew asleep by her side and an excellent forecast for the day. Beatrice looked at the clock. 05.03. She'd slept a full six hours. The sea air must be having the right effect.

She shifted onto her side and gazed at the moonlit contours of Matthew's profile. The slope of his forehead, bulb of his nose and bump of his chin were striped with pale grey; eye sockets, cheeks and mouth in shadow. She squeezed her eyes almost shut and wondered, if his profile were not so dearly familiar, what he would look like. The chiaroscuro hinted at Radcliffe's murderous monk, or Bronte's brooding Heathcliff, or a lantern-jawed swashbuckler called Cliff Hanger ... He stopped snoring. His eyes remained closed as he spoke.

"Why are you staring at me?"

"I was imagining you as the hero of a Gothic romance."

He opened his eyes, looked past her to the digits on the clock and returned his blinking gaze to her. "How did I do?"

"Marvellously. Murder, passion and swordfights, but tragically you fell off a cliff."

"Could be worse. Can't you sleep?"

"No, but you can. I'll get up and read awhile. It'll be light soon." She threw back the heavy eiderdown and dragged on her bathrobe. Cool air chilled her ankles.

Matthew heaved himself up on his elbows to look out of the

window. "It could be a glorious sunrise. Should we get down to the beach and *carpe diem quam minime credula postero*?"

"What a lovely idea! I'll go along with the seizing the day bit, but I'm afraid I insist on keeping my belief in the future."

He stretched and yawned. "As you've just fantasised about pushing me off a cliff, that sounds rather ominous."

"I didn't push you, you fell."

"That's what they all say." His martyred expression, in the half-dark, made Beatrice snort with laughter.

The expedition was precarious. Although the Pembrokeshire Coastal Path was immaculately kept, it was intended for those who walked by daylight. A bright flash in the sky made them both stop and listen for thunder, but none followed. Probably car headlights on the other side of the bay. Being caught in a storm in the dark on top of a Welsh cliff ... Beatrice could imagine the 'stupid tourist' headlines.

Birdsong anticipated the dawn, yet the sandy path and its attendant obstacles were lit by nothing more than the moon and Matthew's Maglite. Beatrice appreciated the faint glow as she navigated the metal steps leading down to the bay. The scent of surf hit her at the same time as the saline dampness in the air. Her hair would be uncontrollable. She dismissed the thought and embraced her irrational excitement at the pull of the sea. When they finally reached the sandy cove, Beatrice slipped off her shoes, wriggling the cold, damp grains between her toes. She hunched her shoulders against the wind and smiled at Matthew.

"I feel practically pagan."

He shook his head and smiled. "Don't take this the wrong way, my love, but at this moment, you look it."

Beatrice laughed and moved into his arms to watch the paling moon, its reflection in constant flux with the restless sea. The white tips of the waves, black headland, and opalescent moon gave the impression of a silver lithograph in motion. As the sky expanded, the sea began changing from black to grey, as if someone were adjusting a monitor. The density of the cliffs took on shapes, a large mass separated and became individual rocks, and clouds on the horizon basked in rosy light. Vapour trails scored the growing saffron glow from behind the cliff. The smoky swirls of clouds, the immense canvas of colour, the shades of hope and morning inevitably brought Turner to mind. Beatrice resolved to visit the Tate on her return home. As the sun hit the sea, flashes of precious metals refracted back to the beach. Coarse calls of seabirds announced the start of the day.

"Worth getting out of bed for, I'd say," Matthew murmured. "Would you pass me the camera?"

She rooted in her bag and handed him the dinky device. "You won't do it justice."

"Certainly not. But I might be able to capture the essence of pagan Stubbs. Look at me."

Beatrice did so, her smile already in place. He stood in the sand, legs apart, took a shot, fiddled with the settings and took another. His hair blew upward in a spectacular peak, tipping his appearance towards the rakish.

"My turn," she called, and caught a couple of inexpert shots on her phone. Matthew with mad hair, the sunlit beach, a boat in the distance and a seagull overhead. Perfect.

They compared results. Beatrice was unimpressed with her photogenic qualities – the face of an ancient Celtic warrior in a jumper from British Home Stores.

Matthew examined the small image of himself on the screen. "Oh dear."

Her stomach gurgled. "Yes. Photographic proof that Professor Bailey has bad hair days. Now, shall we head back? I've worked up a tremendous appetite."

"How unlike you. Would you put the torch in your handbag? I'll hang onto the camera."

"You use me like a pack horse."

"I think of you more as a kangaroo. A female with a handy pouch."

They retraced their route back up the metal steps, which was brighter, warmer and far steeper. Conversation was limited to the odd grunt as they neared the top. On their final ascent, a vehicle stopped on the lane above. Seconds later, a hooded youth appeared, making his way downwards. His face was barely visible. Hot and out of breath, Beatrice offered no more than a nod as he passed. A sudden wrench threw her sideways and she slipped down several steps. Her hip hit steel and she let out a cry. Matthew hurried back.

"Beatrice! Are you hurt? What happened, did you fall?"

"My bag! Matthew, he's got my bag!"

Beatrice lay awake, frowning.

I always like talking to drivers and people when I'm here. Very Welsh thing.

It was 03.22, pitch dark, and a line from her book looped through her mind. Beside her, Matthew slept the sleep of the just.

I always like talking to drivers and people when I'm here. Very Welsh thing.

Amis was right; she wouldn't have the time or inclination to make small talk in London, but as soon as she was on holiday – bar staff, shopkeepers, taxi drivers – she became loquacious in the extreme.

Especially with that policeman. PC Johns of the Fishguard force had stayed a good hour, drinking tea and comparing notes on their respective jobs. Someone had found her handbag in a rubbish bin and taken it to the station. PC Johns kindly returned it to its owner and with the proud air of achieving a precedent, said it was the first case of physical mugging he'd ever seen. Beatrice rifled through her bag, which looked considerably more battle-scarred than when she'd last seen it. Apart from eighty pounds in cash, nothing was missing. A friendly sort of chap, with a steady sense of procedure, PC Johns ensured the paperwork was complete before accepting Earl Grey and a Hobnob and asking fascinated questions about life with the Met.

Beatrice sighed, pondering the experience once more. A mugger, on a remote Welsh beach just after dawn. Did bad luck simply follow her around? Why them? Why then? Local hoodies preying on dopey tourists. *The first case of physical mugging I've ever seen.*

No, it made no sense at all. Assaulting someone on cliff steps was foolhardy in the extreme. A simple bag-snatching could result in serious injury to either party, or even a fall and subsequent murder charge. It was personal. That hoodie wanted her handbag and took an extreme risk to get it. What on earth for? Her eyelids drooped. Matthew's breathing had a soporific effect, so Beatrice ordered her mind onto standby and wriggled back down under the duvet. Bloody mugger wouldn't rob her of sleep as well as eighty quid.

Her eyes flew open again at a noise from the kitchen. Something breaking. Or rather, somebody breaking something.

Beatrice tensed and drew shallow breaths. She replayed the sound to find an explanation while listening for more. Broken glass, certainly, but more of a crunch than a shatter. Waves hushed and rushed outside, yet the house remained silent. It was not her imagination; she'd heard it whilst wide awake and repeating a line from *The Old Devils*. She nudged Matthew, whispering in his ear, in case he woke with one of his Lazarus-type gasps.

"Get up. Quietly. There's someone in the kitchen."

After a moment's blinking, he obeyed, easing out of bed and retrieving the Maglite from her bag. She picked up her phone and followed him to the landing. No light, no movement, no sound from below. But she knew with total certainty someone was down there. Matthew clutched the heavy torch more as a weapon than for illumination and they listened from the landing. Beatrice breathed through her mouth and waited.

Someone banged into a chair. Unmistakeable! The graunching of wooden leg on tile, followed by an intake of breath. The tiny hairs on her scalp rose in fear and anger, as Matthew charged down the stairs, wielding his torch and bellowing.

"Get out of my house, you bastards!"

As they rounded the corner to the kitchen, a figure fled out of the kitchen door, knocking over a chair. He glanced over his shoulder, revealing himself as a frightened young man, rat-faced with a weak chin and the oddest haircut. Short and dark at the front and long at the back with blonde highlights. He looked ridiculous. Like an 80s pop star.

Matthew lurched into a half-hearted pursuit, but Beatrice

grabbed his pyjama top. They stood still, panting, as the sound of running footsteps faded away. Although her hands still trembled from the rush of adrenalin, all Beatrice's fear had evaporated after that glimpse of the intruder's face.

Matthew locked the door with a wry look. She'd left the key in the lock. All a burglar needed do was break the glass and he was in. How incredibly stupid of her. She righted the chair and checked for losses as she dialled the police for the second time that day. Her handbag and laptop were safely upstairs; their keys, her Kindle, Matthew's iPod and his mobile still remained on the kitchen table. But the camera had gone.

"Dyfed-Powys Police?"

"Good morning. I'd like to report a burglary. My name is Detective Inspector Beatrice Stubbs."

Chapter 3

"Good weekend, Beatrice?"

"Not exactly. How was yours?"

Melanie's face softened. "Oh, it was lovely! We went to Bluewater on Saturday and looked at bridesmaids' dresses. On Sunday, we went to my mum's for lunch and finally worked out the guest list. So I spent Monday designing invitations. I am so excited, it feels real now."

Beatrice smiled at the team's admin assistant. Melanie was never anything but perennially delighted. A ray of continual sunshine whose whole life was filled with plans, hopes and happiness. Pollyanna of the Yard.

"I imagine it would. It's only fourteen months away. Shall we have a cup of coffee and you can tell me all about it before I make a start on my emails?"

"You haven't got time. Hamilton wants a meeting at nine." Melanie pointed a decorative nail at the whiteboard.

COOPER, RANGARAJAN, STUBBS, WHITTAKER – MTG
TUES 9AM <u>SHARP</u> – REALLOCATION OF RESOURCES

Beatrice didn't like the look of that.

Dawn Whittaker was the only person in the meeting room. Something to be grateful for. Busy composing a text message, Dawn looked up from her mobile and greeted Beatrice with a sad smile. As always, she looked like an abandoned Labrador. Only a few years younger than Beatrice, but saddled with a plethora of personal problems, Dawn's face had prematurely aged. Despite her worry lines, she had a gentle air one couldn't help but trust. Her straight grey bob and smart suit should have been intimidating, but her face radiated kindness and sympathy. Small wonder she had achieved such success in her campaign to encourage rape victims to come forward. Dawn was the closest thing on the force Beatrice had to a friend.

"Hello Beatrice. Did you have a fun weekend?"

The graze and bruises on Beatrice's hip seemed to flare up as a reminder of her 'fun' weekend. "Don't ask. How about yours?"

"Similar. Any idea what this is about?" She stuffed her phone in her bag as Beatrice sat beside her.

"No clue. I've been with Cooper and Ranga for the last few weeks. Maybe you're the extra pair of hands we need for the knife crime op?" Like every other officer involved, she refused to call it by its formal title.

The door opened and DS Cooper entered, followed by DS Rangarajan. They both raised eyebrows but said nothing – a tacit signal to indicate the presence of an authority figure. Hamilton strode in behind them, closed the door and began the meeting while walking to his seat.

"Good morning everyone, hope you're all refreshed after the Bank Holiday. Thank you for attending so promptly. Situation is, we need to rearrange personnel. Whittaker, taking you off the missing twins case. You're to join Operation Sheath."

Dawn seemed lost for words; a state of affairs Russell Cooper had clearly never experienced. He leant his arm over the back of his chair. "Good news, for a change. Thank you, sir."

Hamilton fixed Cooper with cold eyes. "You will remain a team of three. Stubbs is coming off the team and joining a special project with British Transport Police."

"But sir!" All four voices rose in protest. Cooper, the loudest and deepest, won.

"Sir, with all due respect, if a female detective is required by BTP, why not Whittaker? It makes no sense to replace Stubbs at this stage. No offence, Dawn."

"None taken. I agree with you. Is there a reason for this, sir?"

Deep creases appeared between Hamilton's brows and his voice was low and acidic. "What do you think, Whittaker?"

Dawn looked away and shot a sympathetic glance at Beatrice while Hamilton waited for further protests. Beatrice noted his brick-wall expression and accepted defeat. Any arguments would be wasted. Exactly what she needed after a bloody awful weekend.

Ranga hadn't yet given up. "Sir, although Whittaker is one of our sharpest minds, it will be time-consuming to bring her up to speed. We have made significant progress on this case and arrested three suspects already. It would be quite a blow to lose Stubbs now."

Hamilton seemed unmoved. "I'm sure you'll manage. Incidentally, three arrests in six weeks is not what I call significant progress. Now look here, Stubbs is the right person to work on this transport case for two reasons. First, she has a record of successful collaboration with other agencies. And secondly, her counterpart in this investigation will be Virginia Lowe. So, does anyone require any further explanation?"

Ranga, Dawn and Beatrice dropped their heads in an embarrassed silence. Cooper, who had only been promoted to Scotland Yard a year ago, looked from one to the other in confusion.

Bomb dropped, Hamilton rose from his seat and leant forward on his hands. "Thought not. I suggest you brief Whittaker this morning, so she can work alongside you this afternoon, and be ready to take over as of tomorrow. Stubbs, my office after lunch. Shall we say one o'clock?"

One o'clock was *after* lunch? He who pays the piper calls the tuna sandwich.

"Yes sir." She knew she sounded like a sulky schoolgirl.

Hamilton fulfilled his part by giving her a headmasterly stare. "You may as well start by updating Cooper. Good day to you." He picked up his papers and left the room.

Beatrice ached in sympathy for Dawn. How many times would this come back to haunt her?

Cooper looked across the table at the two women, while Ranga shifted awkwardly beside him. Dawn heaved a huge sigh.

"I'm sure the PBA story even reached as far as West Yorkshire."

Cooper frowned and shook his head. His puzzlement was genuine, Beatrice could see.

Dawn sighed again. "In 2008, the Police Bravery Awards were held in London, at the Dorchester. Chief Superintendent Davenport was on crutches after his knee operation. So he made use of the disabled toilet. As he opened the door, he discovered a man with his pants round his ankles and a woman with her mouth full. The woman was Virginia Lowe. And the man was Ian Whittaker. My husband."

Cooper winced. "Shit. Sorry."

Dawn shrugged with her eyebrows. Ranga and Beatrice kept their heads down.

Attempting to recover, Cooper spoke. "Look Dawn, I hadn't heard about that, but I'm glad you explained. So Hamilton thinks he's doing you a favour by giving the gig to Stubbs?"

"Doing Lowe a favour, more like. He knows I'd shove her under a Tube."

Beatrice looked up with a grin. "But you'd make it look like an accident?"

Dawn met her eyes. "Why not? I have the expertise. And so do you, for that matter. Beatrice, we've been mates a long time. I can't exactly offer you hard cash, but if you could see your way clear to pushing that predatory bitch onto some electric rails, I would consider you a true and loyal friend."

Ranga laughed and the tension eased. "Shall we get coffee and start the handover? Beatrice, you OK with this?"

"No. But what choice do I have? Hamilton's right, much as it pains me to say it. And Dawn's going to be a real asset to you. Will you keep me updated, though? I've invested a lot in this operation."

Dawn patted her shoulder. "Believe me, you're going to get so much 'updating' that you'll tell me to piss off. By the way, I think you should wear your skirt suit for this assignment."

"My skirt suit? Why's that?"

"She'll have anything in trousers. That's what they say about Virginia."

Beatrice grinned and shook her head. "Was ever a woman so unfortunately named?"

One o'clock was an absurd time for a briefing. Instead of lunching with her colleagues in the canteen, she grabbed a sandwich and returned to her desk to complete her paperwork. She hated eating at her desk. So uncivilised. And messy. At one minute to one, she knocked on his open office door. Hamilton gestured to a chair and commenced without pleasantries.

"Yes, awkward business really. Wouldn't pull you off Operation Sheath otherwise."

Beatrice knew that was as close as he was likely to get to contrition.

"Fair enough, sir. Needs must. The British Transport Police case?"

Hamilton cleared his throat and shuffled some papers. He looked most uncomfortable. Whatever was the matter with the man?

"Yes, well, it's all rather unpleasant. Have you heard anything at all in the media about the Finsbury Park Flasher?"

Beatrice gritted her teeth. He was pulling her off a major case involving serious weapons for a dirty old man? "Can't say I have, sir."

"Thing is, this chap does a bit more than just exposing himself. He seems to be targeting his victims quite carefully and sometimes threatens or even gives a repeat performance. Psychological profiler fellow says a pattern is emerging. Looks like this man is growing more confident and is highly likely to commit a sexual assault. We have agreed to collaborate with BTP on a preventative exercise. See, Stubbs, this is political. After the Reid case, not to mention that taxi driver, this one needs to be handled correctly. Whittaker would have been the obvious choice. Used to working with victims of sexual aggression, but under the circumstances ..."

"You don't think this is simply a matter of surveillance, sir?"

"You don't think this is a matter of Bloody-Stupid-Questions, Stubbs? Would I pull a senior detective off a crucial, not to mention media-friendly, case if it were? No, I do not think it is a matter of surveillance. It is a case for experienced, intelligent minds to analyse and resolve. Hence yourself. Now, please take the case file and study it well. A meeting has been arranged up the road, BTP

HQ, tomorrow at nine o'clock sharp. DI Lowe will give you the background."

"Yes, sir. Am I to be based there?"

"That will be something for you and DI Lowe to decide. This is a joint effort, so should you wish to work here, that is acceptable. Now look here, Stubbs, I hope you will not allow personal feelings to cloud this case. We all make mistakes, and DI Lowe has atoned for her transgression."

Heat rose to Beatrice's cheeks. "An official reprimand and missing out on a promotion? Sorry, but I don't see that as atonement, sir. Not only was DI Whittaker's marriage wrecked, but she has had to live with the humiliation ever since. She was forced to rehash it again today, for example."

"Dispense with the dramatics, Stubbs. Whittaker is not on this case. You are. Do you think you will be able to remain impartial?"

"Yes, sir. My professional opinion will not be influenced by my personal view of that woman."

Hamilton studied her for a moment, exhaled and shook his head. "The case file, if you would. And you're meeting *that woman* at nine am sharp tomorrow. Good day to you."

Beatrice returned the wishes, picked up the file and headed back to her desk. Bloody Hamilton. Bloody flasher. And bloody Virginia bloody Lowe.

Chapter 4

After a long weekend with Matthew, the first few evenings at home always held the lurking chance of an emotional trough. Today was no different. The flat seemed empty, work looked bleak and uninspiring, and she still felt cheated of her relaxing Bank Holiday by the bag-snatching and burglary. Life could be very unfair at times.

In an effort to prevent a self-pitying spiral, she took a trip to Marks and Spencer's, where she bought far too much food and a bottle of decent Chardonnay. After performing the minimum of household obligations, Beatrice prepared her meal and listened to *The Archers* while enjoying pasta puttanesca. She was reluctantly dragging out her paperwork when the doorbell rang. She leapt up with relief. Anything to delay the flasher file.

"Hel-lo?"

Adrian's familiar voice crackled through the intercom. "It's me. Has *The Archers* finished?"

"Hello you. Yes, it has. But I have work to do."

"Can I come up for half an hour? I've brought you some wine to replace what I tucked away last night, and also, I've had a thought."

Beatrice beamed and pressed the buzzer. Adrian was a godsend. Yesterday evening, the poor boy had happily listened to her letting off steam about her spoilt weekend, so long as she kept his glass filled. He offered sympathy and outrage as required, invariably on her side.

She opened the door as he arrived on the landing. He bent to kiss her cheek and she felt the lightest graze of stubble, accompanied by a whiff of something fresh and lemony.

"I really will only stay a half hour. I've got choir practice at eight-thirty and I need to shower before I go. Here."

He thrust an Oddbins bag at her.

"Ooh, two bottles. Thank you."

Adrian hung up his coat. "Don't just say 'two bottles' – look at the label."

"Sorry. Ooh, two bottles of Chablis Premier Cru Beauroy. Lovely."

"It *is* lovely. Very fresh, with complex layers. I want you to save at least one bottle to drink with Matthew. Accompany it with seafood, or cheese. How was work?"

"Vile. Let's not talk about it. Thank you for the wine. How was your day?"

"Good. Bank Holiday weekends are always a boost for trade. But I spent most of the day pondering your adventure." He arranged himself on the sofa and looked at her expectantly.

"What? Oh. Would you like a glass of wine, Adrian?"

"Why, that would be marvellous, Beatrice. Thank you. Don't open the Chablis. You're bound to have some supermarket tat in the fridge, so I'll suffer a glass of that."

Beatrice laughed as she poured him a Chardonnay, already anticipating his wrinkled nose and pained expression. He was awfully handy to know, not just because he ran the local Oddbins, but as a kind, entertaining neighbour. He'd moved in downstairs six years ago and they'd never had a cross word. She returned to the living-room, handed him his glass and settled in the armchair opposite.

"You said you'd had a thought," she prompted.

He sipped, but did not grimace. "Where is this from?"

"M and S. Don't start."

"I'm not. It's actually drinkable. Unlike that foul brew you plied me with last night. No wonder my head was mush until lunchtime."

"That may have been more to do with quantity than quality. Now, what did you want to tell me?"

"Yes. You see, I was thinking." He hitched up his grey trousers and leant forward. Adrian always dressed beautifully. It helped that he was tall, lean and catalogue-man handsome, but he also possessed natural style. His suit today was marl-grey and the black polo-neck beneath framed his strong jaw. He reminded Beatrice of a Crufts champion. Pleasing to the eye, yet highly impractical.

"The maniac who stole your bag. The one who broke in and half-inched the camera."

"We can't be sure it was the same man. I can recall nothing of the hoodie's face and we only caught a tiny glimpse of our intruder."

"I'm quite sure it was the same man. And I think he was looking for something. Listen, the mugging was just after dawn. What was he doing hanging around at that hour? Hmm? Let's work backwards. You and Matthew arrive on the beach, take some photographs and climb back up the cliffs. A man suddenly appears from nowhere and races off with your handbag. Why would he do that?"

The same thoughts had occurred to her, and to Matthew, and to the Dyfed Powys police force. But she played Devil's Advocate, just to see what conclusions Adrian would reach.

"You're making too much of it. I don't know what he was doing, but I'm pretty sure the mugging was opportunism."

Adrian exhaled a scornful huff. "You disappoint me, Detective Inspector Stubbs. Think about it. What were you doing before that punk assaulted you?"

Beatrice smiled at his hardboiled tone. "We were watching the sunrise. Taking photos and nothing else."

"Exactly. So you take some photographs on the beach. Then, just after the sun comes up, a car happens to drive along the top of the cliff, stopping at the end of the same path you are following. They drop off a hit-man, who steals your bag and tries to push you off the steps. He runs down to the beach with his booty, meets his accomplice in a cave and they search your handbag. But the search is fruitless." Adrian took a sip of wine and looked intently at Beatrice. His dark eyes were full of drama. "And they still haven't found what they're looking for."

"Adrian ..."

"Wait, I haven't finished. Despite almost killing an innocent woman, these people refuse to give up and they come back, in the dead of night. Ruthlessly, one of them breaks into your cottage, terrifying the poor woman inside – that's you – and snatches his prize. At last, he succeeds in obtaining the camera. The evidence."

She adopted the same cynical tone Matthew always used when she got carried away. "What on *earth* have you been reading? Firstly, I suffered nothing more than a slight graze. Secondly, I was not terrified. Thirdly, I have no reason to think the burglar was the same man. And even if he was, why would he want Matthew's camera? It's nothing special."

Adrian relaxed back on the sofa, pressing his fingertips together as if he were a prosecution lawyer about to sum up.

"The camera may be nothing special, but what of its contents? Did you take a few carefree snaps of something rather less than innocent? Sadly, we'll never know, as any incriminating images are probably swimming with the fishies." His eyes flashed, he crossed his legs and clasped his hands together in satisfaction. Beatrice gazed at him in amusement. Such a wonderful-looking man, all sharp planes and dark features, rather like Montgomery Clift. Yet his mannerisms reminded her of no one more than Ronnie Corbett.

She assumed a serious face. "You think like a detective, Adrian. I've been wondering the same thing. But all is not lost. We can test your theory. I downloaded the pictures onto my laptop before we went to bed that night."

His mouth opened, his eyes widened and he broke into a triumphant grin.

"Beatrice! I always forget your training. You are a star! Let's check them now, I have a programme downstairs for refining images and we can find exactly what it was they were trying to hide."

"I've already looked. I can't see anything. But who knows, perhaps your whizzy technology might shed some light. There might be something, I suppose. Look, let's do it tomorrow. I'll bring them down on a memory stick. However, tonight you have Gay Men's Chorus and you're going to be late. And I have to familiarise myself with a flasher."

He glanced at his watch, torn. "OK. Any other day, I'd give it a miss for something so thrilling. But *Oklahomo!* opens on Saturday and tonight is a key rehearsal for the soloists. I have to go. But tomorrow evening, we're gonna uncover the shady plot behind all this. I'm riding piggyback as your rookie, but don't worry, boss, I know when to button it."

Adrian's accent was woeful. Beatrice hoped his Midwest cowpoke was better than his Detroit dick.

"Thanks, Cagney."

His face dropped. "I was aiming more for Jimmy Stewart than Jimmy Cagney."

She picked up his coat and kissed him on the cheek. "And I was aiming more for Cagney as opposed to Lacey."

Adrian gave her a radiant smile. "That changes everything!"

"Have a great rehearsal and thank you for the wine. By the way, you smell gorgeous. Don't worry about the shower."

He shook his head with a devilish grin. "I always shower. Because, Beatrice, you never know what might happen. Night, night."

"Goodnight, Adrian." Gratified by his interest but relieved that he had been successfully deflected, she closed the door. After refilling her glass, she resigned herself to spending the evening with a dirty old man. She'd probably need a shower herself. Maybe just a quick call first.

Chapter 5

"Inspector Howells, how can I help you?"

"Good evening, Inspector. DI Beatrice Stubbs here, from the Met. We spoke at the weekend, if you remember."

"Oh yes. I remember. The bag-snatching and the break-in. Has something new come to light, Detective Inspector?"

"No, nothing new at this end. I was just calling to see if you have managed to make any headway with this case. Hear your latest report, as it were."

No response.

"Inspector Howells? Are you still there?"

"If you mean am I still at work, then no, I'm not. It's almost eight o'clock in the evening. I'm at home and about to have my tea. As I told you on Sunday, I will call you if we find anything to connect the events in question. Until then, there is no case, and there will be no reports. DI Stubbs, you were involved in two separate incidents this weekend. I have no doubt you feel a personal involvement, but I don't make a habit of calling witnesses to keep them updated with my enquiries. Regardless of their position."

Warmth flared in Beatrice's cheeks.

"I apologise for disturbing you. However, I would describe myself as a victim of two connected crimes, rather than a witness to two separate incidents. I don't think you will find anything more about the two events by treating them as unconnected petty crimes. You said yourself, the thief, or thieves, wanted the contents of that camera. Therefore, as I mentioned, regular surveillance of the beach might well throw up something more concrete. I'd strongly recommend a proactive approach in this situation, Inspector."

"Thank you for the advice. The likes of us bumpkins are eternally grateful. Now, if it's all the same to you, I'd like to eat. Goodnight, DI Stubbs. And next time, I'll call you."

Beatrice stomped into the kitchen, opened the fridge and closed it again. She walked back to the living-room, picked up the phone and put it down again. Pacing around the flat, she wrestled with her indignation.

It was grossly unfair to assume she was interfering. As the victim of two robberies in twenty-four hours, she had a right to know where the investigation was heading. Howells was out of line speaking to her like that. All she wanted was information.

She pressed her forehead to the window and fumed. The bustle of Boot Street went unnoticed as she rewound the conversation. Of course, she understood that persistence on the part of those affected by crime could be an annoyance. And she might have been wiser to call him at the station than at home. But to dismiss her as a supercilious busybody was quite intolerable. It wasn't as if she was trying to teach the man his job.

I'd recommend a proactive approach in this situation.

She picked up the phone again, dithered and finally pressed speed dial one.

"Good evening. This is Professor Bailey."

"Matthew, do you think of me as patronising? An interfering old biddy? Am I unreasonably demanding in my curiosity?"

"Well, this is merely my subjective opinion, you realise. But I'd say generally no to the first, absolutely not to the second and quite possibly to the third. However, the answers will very much depend on who you're asking. What's up, Old Thing? Have you upset someone?"

"No. Yes. I don't know. But that police inspector in Wales was very short with me this evening and said that next time, he'd call me."

"There you are then. Don't call him again and let those people do their job."

"That's all very well for you to say. What if they aren't doing it properly? They should have people watching that beach every morning. It's obvious something untoward is happening. Why won't he take it seriously?"

She could hear Matthew stretch and yawn. "If a police detective from, let's say New York, was in London for the weekend, reported a crime and then called you daily for an update, how would you feel?"

"That's not very supportive of you."

"But you see my point? Leave them alone to get on with it. You have enough on your plate with knife crime."

Beatrice's mood sank still lower. "No, knives are no longer on my plate. Instead, I'm working with British Transport Police on apprehending a flasher. And my partner on this one will be none other than the man-eating Virginia Lowe. I tell you, I'm dreading every minute of this, especially when I could be in South Wales or Lewisham, assisting with serious and worthwhile investigations."

"A flasher? I thought they'd rather fallen out of fashion. Isn't it all stalking and cyber-porn these days? And I feel sure the Welsh police have their investigation under control. From what I saw, they're keen, young and enthusiastic. You get on with your job and leave them to theirs."

"Doesn't seem like I have a choice, does it? That inspector has some sort of regional inferiority complex, in my opinion. Anyway, as far as I've gathered, the flasher is also a stalker and may well have a penchant for cyber-porn. I really ought to knuckle down to this case file. See? I called you to soothe my conscience but now feel doubly guilty."

"Marvellous! So pleased to have been of assistance. Now, I should begin chopping my stir-fry and put the rice on. And you should focus on the task in hand. Goodnight, Old Thing. I'll call you tomorrow to hear about your first day."

Beatrice said goodnight, made a herbal tea and returned to the folder, still vaguely indignant.

Keen, young and enthusiastic was all very well, but no substitute for experience.

Chapter 6

"No horror movies tonight, you said. Well, that was the most horrific thing I've ever seen. I feel a small part of my life was wasted ..."

Laure caught Ayako's eye and grinned; there was no stopping Urtza declaiming her opinions, positive or negative. Ayako hugged her knees and laughed. Small, tinkly noises came from both her mouth and her clothes. Urtza paced the two metres of the lounge, throwing an exasperated arm at the television as she ranted. Laure's flat always seemed smaller with Urtza in it.

It was four minutes past ten.

" ... a terrible waste of all that talent! That is the real shame. Cheap, and a copycat. That makes it worse! If you do such a rip-off, you choose a brilliant movie. *Love, Actually* is not a brilliant movie, it is average. And a lot of the writing is very bad. *Love, Actually* was saved by the actors. Here, the acting ..."

"Come on, Urtza," Laure interrupted. "Eric Dane was amazing. And Jessica Biel surprised me."

Urtza stopped her pacing, glared at the two on the sofa and placed her hands on her hips.

"Laure. Oh Laure. Are we going to have the same argument again? Beauty does not equal talent. There was much beauty in *Valentine's Day*, but as for talent? Ayako, don't tell me you agree with her?"

Tiny Ayako, with her asymmetric bob, abundant hair-grips and predilection for pink, nestled further into the cushions. Her knee-high socks were striped pink and purple, and white tights kept her thighs decent below the frilled micro-skirt. She leant her head onto one side and widened her eyes.

"I liked it. Fun and pretty to watch. Not every movie has to be art, Urtza. And what did you expect? It's called *Valentine's Day*, not *Valentine's Day Massacre*." She was already giggling at Urtza's outraged expression.

The pairing of these two inevitably drew attention and Laure still wondered what drove their friendship. Urtza, size 18, voluble, passionate, committed to classic black and silver jewellery. Ayako, size 6, shy, precise, almost hidden under multi-coloured Harajuku layers and childish accessories. They now shared a flat in Highbury, spending all their free time shopping in Camden Market or watching movies and disagreeing.

"Even now, after I know you for over a year, you still shock me, Ayako. 'Fun and pretty to watch?' This is the opinion of a teenager."

Ayako's piping laugh rang around the cluttered room. "I *am* a teenager! And so are you, but secretly, you want to be middle-aged."

Urtza attempted to take outrage to an operatic level, but the effect was too comic. Even she succumbed to laughter and deflated onto the sofa between them. Laure laughed and laughed and forced herself to keep laughing longer than felt natural. Laughing was good.

It was twenty past ten.

In a way, the closeness between the three would not have happened anywhere else. In London, she was free to choose, making friends on the basis of shared interests, and personality. So what if they were a quirky Japanese girl with startling dress sense, and a large, loud Spaniard with a natural theatricality. Both enjoyed cinema, food and markets, therefore they were the perfect people to be her friends. In Lille, Laure had a close circle of well-dressed, well-read and understated associates, assembled on the basis of education and family connections. Nearly all were blonde. Introducing them to Ayako and Urtza was unthinkable. Laure started laughing again.

Urtza emptied her glass and Laure reached for the wine bottle. Mouth full, Urtza placed her hand over her glass and shook her head.

Ayako heaved up her bag. So adorned with baubles and trinkets, it was practically a percussion instrument. "Yeah, we should be going, Laure. Thanks so much for the dinner. You are a fantastic cooker. And I enjoyed the movie, even if she didn't."

Panic began to rise.

"Listen, Ayako, Urtza, thank you so much for coming over. It is impossible for me to say how much ... it's wonderful for me, you know, just ... just not thinking."

Urtza opened her arms in a dramatic embrace. The scent of cigarettes, Narciso Rodriguez and sweat made Laure tearful, as her cheek pressed against Urtza's décolletage.

Ayako's childlike hand stroked her shoulder. "Laure, we will come again tomorrow. We will come every night until you are ready to go out. We are your friends." Her sweet voice was accompanied by the miniature bells on her white leather jacket.

Laure swallowed and stopped the flood. "Thank you. You two are very kind to me. OK, you should go. You need to catch the bus. See you both tomorrow. Safe journey!"

It was half past ten exactly.

She watched them down the stairs, listened to the tinkling and heard the front door close. Then she locked and bolted the door. For the fifteenth time that day, she wondered how she could find herself a flatmate, a friendship just like theirs, without exposing herself to any more psychos.

Picking up the rest of her drink, she moved to the window and watched Ayako walk away from the block of flats. Tears filled Laure's eyes. Again. If only they could stay. The doll-like figure stopped to pick something from the path. Where was Urtza? Ayako turned, showing something to the darkness. A hand came out of the black and took the object. Urtza's colouring and camouflage would make her a perfect cat burglar. Laure smiled at the thought. Ayako was laughing and Laure wished she could hear it. Six floors up and double-glazed, there was no chance of that.

Ayako stepped into the street, her colours turning acidic under the sodium light. Laure could just make out Urtza, still in the shadow of the hedge, lifting the lid of a wheelie-bin. What had they found? She would check on the way to school tomorrow.

Across the street, a shape moved. Laure recognised it, dismissed it as an overreaction and acknowledged she was right, all in under a second. In a reflex, she clenched her hands. The TK-Maxx glass shattered, pain and liquid registering somewhere, as her eyes strained to see the street.

Crossing the road with a clear purpose, he approached Ayako. Blood and wine stained the pane as Laure struggled to open the double-locked window catch. Not enough time. She began beating on the glass, screaming three syllables, blurring her view of the scene with tears and blood.

Laure watched as he said something to Ayako. Where was Urtza, where the hell was Urtza? That was when he opened his coat. Ayako recoiled from his jerking body, horribly close to her. Almost touching. Oh God, if he got off, it would hit her.

Six floors up and double-glazed, but she could hear Ayako's scream; it mingled with her own. Their harmony developed a bass tone – a roar. His jerking body sprang backwards as a black mass barrelled its way out of the gate, arms flailing. Urtza missed him and whirled to grab his coat, but he'd already begun to run. She charged after him, shouting curses in Spanish, and Laure realised he might get away.

Again.

Dialling 999 left-handed on her mobile, she unlocked the door with her bloodied right, and tore down the stairs to Ayako. Him. Outside her house. Waiting. He knew where she lived.

No horror movies tonight, she'd said.

Chapter 7

Wednesday morning, and the weather refused to chime with Beatrice's mood. Her rush hour journey on the Northern Line, including a change at Bank, compounded her sour sense of resentment at the injustices of this world. Yet as she ascended from St James's Park station, strangers smiled, glorious sunshine lit the streets and it took a real effort to hang on to her black cloud.

She was early, so sat in the window of Prêt-a-Manger and drank an excess of coffee. Her eyes absorbed the human traffic – short sleeves and summer dresses, sandals and exposed skin, sunglasses and already-sweaty shirts – but her mind was picking away at a problem like a child at a scab.

Assuming the rat-faced man with the terrible hair was either the same person as the mugger, or a close associate, he was determined to get those Pembroke beach photographs. Surely, he'd achieved his wish. His first attempt at retrieving them, with snatch and grab, had failed, so he came back at night. Having successfully taken possession of the camera, he was free to destroy anything incriminating. He couldn't possibly know she'd already downloaded the contents, so that was the end of the story. Yet a low-level discomfort came from the awareness that the thief had pictures of her and Matthew on the beach, of Matthew's family, of Matthew's work. Nothing revealing in those shots, so it shouldn't make any difference. But she couldn't shake the feeling that it did.

Five to nine. She should shift herself. Draining the coffee, she hurried towards the TfL building on Broadway, hoping it was Hamilton who'd insisted on nine a.m. sharp. She really didn't want to be late. Partly due to politeness, but mainly because she wanted to retain the moral high ground. It's hard to look down on someone when you have to start with an apology.

She waited for seventeen minutes in reception before a large fair man approached with a crew-cut and a grin. Beatrice guessed he played contact sports.

"DI Stubbs, nice to meet you. I'm Sergeant Ty Grant."

They shook hands and he gestured up the corridor. Tie? What kind of a name was that? And his hands were sweaty.

He glanced back. "Have to apologise for Virginia. Several incidents overnight added to the morning briefing. Result? Total overrun. She's down as soon as. Get you a coffee?"

Beatrice picked up her bag, her irritation at boiling point. Was he incapable of speaking in full sentences?

"Thank you, but I won't just now. I reached my caffeine limit half an hour ago. Do you have any idea how long DI Lowe might be?"

His security badge unlocked a door to an open-plan room, filled with messy desks and people staring at computers. No one looked up. Grant indicated Virginia Lowe's office at the end and lifted his substantial shoulders.

"Five? Ten? Why don't you park yourself? She'll be as quick as poss. Sure you don't want anything? Just get myself an espresso. Back in a flash."

What a well-chosen expression.

Evidently an insensitive fool who could only converse in txt-spk. One ought not to judge on appearances, but he looked just the type to suffer from foot-in-mouth.

This was altogether a very poor start. Beatrice withdrew her case notes, pulled out a pen and practised variations on a displeased expression. Her eyes scanned the display board to her right, taking in the map, featuring locations of the women who'd reported incidents, and the identikit image of this shadowy lurker which gave them precious little. He looked like 'some bloke'. Her annoyance diminished and her interest grew.

Who is he? What on earth makes these vile men expose their

genitalia to strangers? Why do that to solitary females in darkened pockets of the city? They must know how they frighten their victims, how they instil a fear of the streets in these poor women. Throwing an ugly shadow over their lives, for what? What possible satisfaction could this filthy little toe-rag get from rubbing himself in front of barely-awake cleaners, harassed teachers, foreign students and coffee-shop workers, whose lives were hard enough? Beatrice tried to imagine the sexual frustration behind the act. The man deliberately picks on the vulnerable, those whose resources are low. He knows. None of the recipients of his performance have been strong, confident women who might laugh in his face, give chase or fight back. He is an awkward individual, with a conviction that he must be seen, even if he has to force it. Weak and ignored in his everyday life, he finds another way of raising his profile.

The door burst open, making Beatrice jump. The tall woman reaching for her hand looked completely unfamiliar. Short peroxide spikes, a white shirt-dress and court shoes reminded Beatrice of the 1980s for the second time in a week.

"Beatrice! You've been waiting ages. I am so sorry!"

"Virginia Lowe?"

"Yep, that's me. We have met before. You don't remember?" she asked, in evident disbelief.

"Of course I remember. But I wouldn't have recognised you."

"Oh, the hair! Yes, I had the Veronica Lake stuff hacked off two years ago. Going grey, you see. So bleach and hair gel are back in my bathroom cabinet, after an absence of twenty years. Did no one get you a coffee?"

"Everyone offered, but I've had quite enough, thank you."

Virginia sat opposite and looked directly at Beatrice. She'd aged a little since their last meeting; her face was somewhat fuller and noticeable lines scored her forehead, yet she still made quite an impact. Her blue eyes were sincere.

"Of course. You've been waiting half an hour. Apologies. We had an extended briefing this morning. Amongst other things, it looks like our flashing friend has been at it again. Look, Beatrice, this is a shitty way to start and I'm sorry I kept you waiting. Honestly, it wasn't deliberate. So, let's waste no more time and get down to business."

Her open approach spiked Beatrice's hostile guns. "Fair enough. I know how these things are. But I admit I'm impatient to get started."

"Me too. As it stands, this is a preventative exercise. There's a serious danger of it becoming a sex offence if we don't move quickly. He took one step closer last night ..."

The door opened and the rugby player returned.

"You're here! Brought you a coffee. DI Stubbs didn't want anything. Can I do anything else for you, ladies?"

Beatrice watched the transformation in awe. Virginia's movements became languid and slow and she looked sideways at him. Her voice dropped as she held out her hand for the paper cup with a lip-parted smile. "That's very sweet of you, Ty. But I think Beatrice and I are just fine for now."

The look that passed between the beefy suit and his boss made Beatrice thoroughly uncomfortable. She recalled the same feeling in a hotel room once, when flicking through TV channels, she'd stumbled upon something involving moans, slapping flesh and pinkish close-ups.

The lump retreated with an expression just short of a leer. Beatrice's hackles rose. But after the door closed, Virginia snapped back to business like an elastic band.

"The file I gave Hamilton contains all the details on incidents so far. But last night, we think he did it again. Apparently, a student at the international school in Lennox Road was approached by a man who told her he'd been mugged. She offered to help and asked what had been stolen. His cue, naturally. 'They took all my clothes!' He opened his coat and began masturbating. The girl screamed and her friend, who was still some way behind, took off after him. She didn't even get close, but it must have given him a fright. Two real concerns result from this. One – this is the first time he's tried it with more than one person. Bad sign. Two – they were leaving a friend's place."

"And why's that another bad sign?" Beatrice asked.

The white-blonde head bent to check the files. "Their friend,

Laure Marchant, was the third person to report an incident. Last night's victims were visiting her flat – she's a student at the same school. Or at least she was. After what happened yesterday, she's decided to go back to France. He seems to be following certain women, exposing himself more than once to the same person, or their friends and relatives. He's not just a flasher, he's a stalker, and that leads us to the conclusion that sooner or later, he'll go that much further."

"Is that how it works?"

"Not always. But repeat offenders are more likely to assault or attempt to rape. This guy's following the pattern as if he's read the manual."

Beatrice turned and considered the map. "Lennox Road. A hop and a skip from Finsbury Park station, as the stone flies. He's not too adventurous, is he?"

Virginia shook her head, slugged some coffee and moved to the meeting table and display board.

"No, he's not. On the mapped area, the red dots signify incidents. Nearly all these happened on the park side of the railway tracks, but Marchant's experience, and that of her colleagues last night, took place the other side. So I need to add one."

As she bent over her desk to retrieve her stickers, Beatrice noticed that Virginia's white shirt-dress was made of linen, rendering her underwear clearly visible through the fabric. So clearly that Beatrice saw she favoured those cut-away pants which looked terribly uncomfortable. Surely she must realise that white knickers would show through her dress. Why hadn't she chosen flesh-coloured? It would be nothing short of churlish to imagine she had done it on purpose.

Virginia stuck the dot onto the map. "Just here. So this pattern tells us he probably lives somewhere between the park and the reservoirs and definitely close to the Tube."

"And not once has he appeared on CCTV?"

"Nope, he's not daft. I've got Fitch scanning the Lennox Road data as we speak, but so far this guy's thought it through and made damn sure he's not on camera."

"What about the victims? Is there any connection that might hint at how he selects them?" Beatrice asked.

"I can't see anything, but maybe two heads are better than one. Want to go through the notes together?"

"I think we should."

They sat side by side at the table and spread the files. Virginia smelt of flowery perfume, and strong coffee. Her nails were perfectly manicured, with long white tips. Beatrice wondered how she managed to type.

"The likelihood is that we know less than half of it." Virginia leant her face on her hand as she stared at the paperwork, her expression disconsolate.

"I thought that too. It stands to reason that if the number of unreported rapes is huge, those who simply dismiss a flasher must be far greater."

"And we've all dismissed a flasher, right? I know I have. We're receiving a noticeable number of reports, which means he's doing more than a noticeable amount of harassment."

With a mixture of gratitude and a small sense of exclusion, Beatrice realised she'd never been flashed. She opened the details of the first incident.

"Right, it's time we put a stop to that."

The bar was already busy with civil servants and off-duty officers as Beatrice pushed open the door of The Speaker. To her relief, Dawn had bagged a table by the window, where late afternoon sunshine spotlit two large glasses of white wine.

"A sight for sore eyes!" Beatrice said, tucking her laptop bag under the table.

Dawn smiled and handed her a glass. "Cheers."

"Cheers." Beatrice took a sip. "That hits the spot. Thank you."

"Thank you for meeting me. I told you I'd be a pain in the arse till I settle in."

Beatrice maintained the pretence that the rendezvous was work-related. "Not at all. As I said on the phone, you can pick my brains whenever you feel the need."

Dawn gave her a sheepish look. "Tell the truth, I'm more curious about how you got on, working with that predator."

"I'd never have guessed," Beatrice laughed. "Actually, it wasn't too bad. She's like a split personality. Focused, intelligent and professional, unless there's a man in the room. Is there such a condition as a pathological flirt?"

"She's always been that way, apparently. But I heard she turned forty last year, and she recently got married. That's had no effect?"

"Not so as you'd notice. Colleagues, senior officers, the chap serving pizza in the canteen, she can't seem to help herself. And they all seem to lap it up."

"I'm sure they do." Dawn tore a corner off her beer mat.

An odd need to justify her new colleague prodded Beatrice.

"Maybe it's her way of coping. We all have strategies for working in a male-dominated environment. Ice queen, one-of-the-lads, ball-breaker, girlie-girl ... Jessica Rabbit could be Virginia's work persona."

"I wouldn't mind betting she's a rabbit in her free time as well. How about the case?"

"It's a pre-empt. We have to catch him before he goes any further, which will provide some excellent marketing both for us and them. May even earn us a Tilley Award for crime prevention. "

Dawn lifted her eyes from the shredded bar mat. "Super. We all know how Virginia enjoys her award ceremonies."

"You have a grim sense of humour, DI Whittaker. Tell me what happened today on knife crime."

On her way back from the toilet, Beatrice glanced at her watch. By the time she got home, it would be almost eight and Adrian would be impatient. She ought to get her skates on. She shoved her way through the crowded bar and back to their table. Dawn was gazing out the window with a vague smile.

"What's tickled you?" Still standing, Beatrice drained her glass.

"Just feeling my age – observing the latest trend in haircuts

– what *do* they think they look like?

"Reminds me, I have a story to tell you. But right now, I must make a move. I'll buy you a drink on Thursday. Good luck with surveillance tomorrow." She hooked her handbag onto her shoulder and reached under the table for her laptop case.

"Thanks. It'll be a long, boring day, full of Cooper's bullshit and ... Beatrice? What's the matter?"

"My computer. It's not here."

It took a thorough search, an appeal to the bar staff and a check that none of their neighbours had made an innocent mistake before Beatrice faced facts. From the pub well known as the watering-hole of the Metropolitan Police, from under the feet of two senior detectives, someone had stolen her laptop.

Chapter 8

Amber was still talking. Zahra pressed the button on the pelican crossing, hitched her bag higher on her shoulder and listened. It wasn't as if she had a choice.

"... asks me if I'll miss her. So I'm like, I guess so. And she says, is that it? So I'm like, yeah, pretty much. And she goes all quiet and walks off. I mean, whatever."

"She gets like that." The beeps signalled they were safe to cross. Zahra kept an eye out for speeding cyclists. "She'll be back to normal by next week."

Crossing Green Lanes without incident, they headed for the river. Almost home, and tonight Dad was doing a barbeque. Zahra picked up her pace.

Amber was still talking. "Don't care if she is or she isn't. I mean, what is she like? Does she want me crying my eyes out and begging her not to go? As if. I mean, yeah, I'll miss her, but life goes on, and anyway, it's not like we're not linked up. We so totally are."

Turning onto the river path, they left the noise of the traffic behind. Green verges, daisies and dandelions. You could almost imagine it was the countryside. Nearly home. The only cloud on the horizon was Amber. Her friend's bitching could really ruin a good day.

Zahra switched subjects. "Aren't you getting nervous about the show? I think I'm the nervousest I've ever been about anything in my whole entire life. But it's the first time in my whole entire life I've ever had a solo."

"When you've had a few solos, you don't get nervous anymore. You know what? Miss Rice told me I shouldn't be over-confident. She said a few nerves are good for you. And I thought to myself, what would you know? I mean, if she was any good as a dancer, she'd be doing it. Not teaching it. She gets on my nerves, always going on about her performances. Like, living on past glories, know what I mean?"

The sun sank below the houses and long shadows stretched across the river. The water, sparkly and fresh in sunshine, revealed itself as dark and filthy, littered with beer cans, polystyrene and a floating nappy.

"And anyway, when you've rehearsed as much as we have?" Amber went on. "Like. Every. Single. Day? We should be confident. You know what I mean? I'm full of it, I really am. God, I hope you're not gonna get stage fright, Zahra. That would be SO embarrassing."

Her words stung. "Of course I won't. I am totally going to give my best performance ever. If I do mega well, my parents might just think about letting me go to stage school."

"Stage school! You're so funny. Whatever. I'm giving it everything I've got in case there are any casting agents in the audience. Most def. I mean, next year I'll be fourteen, and I need to make choices about my career direction."

They turned the bend in the path. Halfway along the next stretch, a man crouched, looking at the ground.

"Victoria Beckham went to stage school," Zahra replied, kicking a stone into the water.

"Victoria Beckham also did every audition going. You don't get anywhere without ambition, Zahra. What's that bloke doing?"

Zahra looked up. The man peered at the grass and made little kissy noises. He seemed searching for something, although any kind of animal he hoped to find along the canal was bound to be rank. He wore a big black coat which was well tatty; his legs were bare apart from some even tattier trainers and he had a baseball cap pulled down low. As the girls approached, he stood up.

"Hello, girls. I don't suppose you've seen a ferret along here? I've lost Ginny, my little furry friend."

Zahra didn't want to speak to the bloke. Amber obviously wasn't bothered.

"A ferret? No. What are you doing out here with a ferret anyway?"

"She comes with me when I go fishing. She normally sleeps

round my neck, but she's wandered off and I can't find her. I'm getting a bit worried. It'll be dark soon."

His words acted as a trigger for Zahra. "Hope you find her. We have to get home. Bye."

Amber didn't move.

"Am-ber!" She spoke through clenched teeth and boggled her eyes.

"Zah-ra!" Amber mimicked her. "Let's help the guy look for his ferret. We're doing a good deed."

"No. Ferrets bite. And I want to go home."

"This one's tame, love. Had her four years and not so much as a nip."

Zahra didn't look at him. "Amber, I'm going. Come on!"

"Bye then." Amber put her bag on the path and began looking along the verges. The man joined her, making the kissy noises again. Zahra's frustration built. She should just go. It would teach her a lesson. But she couldn't and it wouldn't. Leave her friend by the river, with some weirdo? No way. But she wasn't helping them look for any crappy ferret.

The smell of a barbeque wafted across from the back gardens on the opposite bank. Zahra heard voices, laughter. She was hungry. She wanted to go home. The ferret-friends moved further away from her. Amber was still talking, firing questions at him about the colour, housing arrangements and eating habits of the animal. Zahra frowned. Why did he need that long black coat? If it was warm enough to wear shorts, why did he need a massive great coat over the top? Where was his fishing stuff? He should have a rod, and bait and that. And what did he expect to catch in New River? A nappy? The man stood up.

"Well, thanks for the help, but I think she's lost." He put his hands in his pockets and burst into a laugh. "I don't believe it! Here she is! She was curled up asleep in my pocket all the time!"

Amber's face broke into a curious grin. "And you didn't notice?"

"She's so light. Put your hand in and you can feel. You can stroke her." He gestured to his coat. There was something funny about his eyes.

Zahra's whole body flooded with fear. "No! Amber, no!"

Amber glared back at her. "Zahra! Who died and made you boss of me?" She approached the man, who was smiling and holding open his pocket.

"She's all warm and furry," he said. "Come and feel. She won't bite."

Amber hesitated. Blood pounded in Zahra's chest. She rushed forward and snatched at Amber's arm. "We're going. Now!"

The man's voice changed. "I don't think so."

Shoving Zahra away, he caught Amber's wrist and tried to force her hand into his pocket.

In her family, Zahra was known as The Screamer. When she was only eighteen months old, her shrill shriek could force both her brothers to flee the room, hands over their ears. At thirteen, her voice was louder, lasted longer and could shatter glass. Landing on her backside beside the river, she let rip.

The sound stopped the man for a second, before he tore open his coat and forced Amber's hand into his groin. Underneath the coat, he wore a sweatshirt and nothing else. Zahra's pitch went up.

"Oi!"

On the opposite bank, a man's blond head appeared over a garden wall. Ferret-man jumped, released Amber and ran back in the direction of Green Lanes. The blond man climbed over the wall, shouting to people behind him. Amber collapsed, sobbing, cradling her arm, but holding her hand at a distance.

Zahra was still screaming.

Chapter 9

As she slammed the front door, Beatrice heard Adrian's voice coming from his flat.

"About time! I was beginning to think you'd forgotten. Now I hope you haven't eaten, because I've done chicken cacciatore and opened a red to die for." He appeared in the doorway, wearing a Breton-style striped top with black jeans. He rested his hands on his hips and noticed her expression. "Oh Lord. What's happened now?"

"Some bastard nicked my laptop."

Adrian clapped his palms to his cheeks and his jaw dropped. All he needed was a bit of white panstick and he could have passed for a French mime.

"Not the one with the photos on it?"

"I only have one laptop. And it's police property. The infuriating thing is that whoever stole it cannot possibly use it. It has a security lockdown and will destroy all the data before allowing unauthorised entry."

"But if all you wanted was to get rid of any images that might be on there, that fact wouldn't bother you. This cannot be coincidence, Beatrice. Someone wanted to make sure any trace of those pictures disappeared."

"Yes, I had actually realised that much."

"See, we should have looked at them last night. We've lost them now." His voice was reproachful.

"Wrong. I told you I'd put them on a memory stick to bring down with me tonight. Which I did. I'll go and fetch it. I'll be a few minutes, mind, I have to call Matthew to check he's OK."

The chicken was sublime. Rich tomato sauce with garlic and oregano, a generous splash of wine and green peppers at the crunchy stage blended perfectly with the delicate meat. Accompanied by a glass of Portuguese Dão, the meal and the company combined to make Beatrice's noxious mood recede.

"Whoever stole the laptop was determined to destroy those images, you know. Therefore you should count yourself lucky it was just taken from the pub." Adrian pointed at her with his fork.

"Yes, you're right. But it's so bloody embarrassing, on top of everything else."

"At least he's convinced that he's got the pictures now. So he'll leave you alone." He topped up her glass.

"Don't make gender assumptions. Lazy police work. But what I don't understand is how they knew those photos were on my machine. I can see how they might get my address – all the identification I possess was in my handbag. God knows, they could have taken impressions of my keys and all sorts. Copied my driving licence, noted my address. I must change the locks and use the safety chain. But how did they know I'd already downloaded the pictures?"

"The only person you've seen so far was male, so there's nothing lazy about that assumption. If he was watching the house, waiting for you to go to bed, he could have seen you. It's the countryside. You can creep up to a house and even from quite a distance, you'd see if someone was looking at a screen." Adrian shuddered.

Beatrice rolled her eyes. "And he followed me all the way to London, to work and to the pub to get those photographs?"

"Looks that way. Is Matthew all right?"

"I don't know. He wasn't home. I'll call again in a minute." She put down her cutlery, her stomach acidic. She felt a powerful urge to go upstairs, to be alone, but couldn't be so rude.

"Let's check the pictures."

As Adrian set up the program, Beatrice looked out of the window and worried. It really was time Matthew got himself a mobile. Stubborn old Luddite. It was no longer charmingly eccentric, it was a bloody nuisance. She would talk to his daughters; Tanya and Marianne could be forcefully persuasive.

"Beatrice? Most of these photos are of some child."

"That's Luke, Matthew's grandson. The beach ones will be at the end."

"Thank you, I worked that out for myself. But there are only two of you on the beach."

Beatrice felt a guilty twinge. "I deleted a few. I didn't look my best."

"Those were also on the beach?"

"Yes, exactly like the others. I didn't move, just let Matthew snap away."

"The only thing in the background is cliff."

Her mobile rang. Matthew. She sighed into the handset. "Good timing. I called you about half an hour ago and I was just starting to worry. Did you work late?"

"No. Marianne and I attended an exhibition. Queerest thing. This artist friend of hers has some sort of disease and makes pictures out of her own dead skin."

"How disturbing. Is everything else all right?"

"Absolutely. How's your hip?" His voice sounded relaxed and believable. But she knew he was practised at disguising his concerns when he didn't want to worry her.

"Fine. Itches like buggery, which is a sure sign it's healing. So no problems at your end?" Beatrice was ashamed of her unsubtle probing.

"Nothing to speak of. I just called your flat. Why aren't you at home? And how was your first day with the Man-Eater?"

"Productive. She's an interesting individual, but still a complete carnivore. I'm downstairs having dinner with Adrian. Chicken cacciatore with a spectacular Portuguese red."

"I'm furiously jealous. Mainly because of the wine. Did you thank him for that Toro Termes? What's his view on the Amarone?"

"Yes, I did. I haven't asked yet. But all is calm at home?"

"Of course. Why wouldn't it be? Are you all right, Old Thing? You sound a bit off. And you don't normally call on consecutive nights."

"No, but neither do we normally get mugged and robbed in one weekend. I'm perfectly well. Just checking up on you. Right, I'd better neglect my host no longer. I shall call you again tomorrow, whether you like it or not."

"I like it. It's unusual for you to make a fuss. I adore the attention. Give my best to Adrian and wish him luck with Saturday's Cowboy Camp. Have a good week, my love."

"You too. Bye-bye."

Adrian did not look up from the screen as she joined him.

"Matthew said to thank you for the Spanish red. We had it with marinated kebabs."

"My pleasure. And when you next speak, do thank him for the Alsace Pinot Blanc. He was right about the asparagus. I'm saving the Amarone for the right occasion."

"Whilst we're on the subject, you two can stop sending each other bottles via me. I feel like a wine mule. Have we found anything yet?"

"I'm still refining." He hesitated. "Beatrice, this is none of my business, but I'd say there was an omission in that conversation."

"You're quite right. It is absolutely none of your business."

"If someone I loved was robbed, especially for the third time in a week, I'd want to know about it."

Stress levels and insecurities unnaturally high, Beatrice was in no mood to be lectured. Her patience snapped. "Firstly, that's how *you* feel. It has no bearing here. Secondly, Matthew lives in Devon. The only thing he can do at that distance is worry. Thirdly, I will tell him next weekend, when I can look him in the eyes and reassure him. And explain to him how, thanks to my protective, concerned and slightly interfering downstairs neighbour, I feel safe as trousers."

Adrian clicked the mouse and turned to face her. "It's finished. I'm sorry. Seriously, I am. I really should keep my nose out and I apologise. I think we just had our first row. Perhaps we should have a toast?"

"Hardly a row. Yes, we probably should. Cheers. I'm very grateful to you."

"Cheers. I'm happy to help. Makes me feel useful. Shall we look?"

Nothing.

In the background: rocks, cliff, and sand.

In the foreground: Beatrice, looking every bit as grim as she remembered. She replayed the beach scene in her mind. Sunrise, seagulls, rushing waves, sandy toes, wind and wild hair. She shook her head and looked at Adrian.

"I'm being particularly dense. Of course it's not on the camera. I took a couple of pictures of him from the opposite direction, on my phone."

Adrian's eyes widened and he rubbed his hands together. "Come, detective, we have work to do."

"Yes, you're right. But do you think we could do all the refining business tomorrow? I'm awfully tired and there's really no rush."

"Up to you. At least let me download the pictures so I can make a start."

Beatrice fetched her handbag. "You see, there's no way I can deal with this while working the London Transport thing. I need to get back to the Met. What I have to do is get upstairs, boot up my old computer and write a report which will get me off this flasher. Maybe then I can concentrate on suspicious happenings on a Welsh beach. Tomorrow is going to be another difficult day."

"And tomorrow is going to be another exciting evening. I'll have everything ready for you and by bedtime we'll have hammered out a theory. I'll cook."

"No, you won't. And nor will I. But I'll pick up something suitably sophisticated for us on the way home."

Adrian raised his eyebrows. "I know your definition of sophisticated. But what the hell, it's been ages since I had fish and chips. Please may I have your mobile now?"

Beatrice sighed and handed it over. "You have all the qualities of an excellent police officer. Tenacity, enthusiasm and bloody-mindedness. Have you never thought about joining the force?"

Adrian was busy umbilically attaching the phone to the computer, but gave her a superior smile.

"I know it's a gay cliché to fancy men in uniform, but it's just not me. The outfit puts me right off, especially with all those accessories. Do you want to check there are no embarrassing shots before I download?"

"No, go ahead. When taking embarrassing shots, I prefer a camera. What do you mean by accessories?"

"Hmm? Oh, you know, handcuffs, truncheons, great ugly walkie-talkies. I couldn't be seen in public dressed like that. Imagine if someone saw me! I'd feel like a low-rent strip-o-gram and never go out again. There! All done."

Shaking her head and smiling, Beatrice took her phone, thanked him for dinner and trudged up the stairs, humming *Dedicated Follower of Fashion*. As she unlocked the front door, her mobile rang.

"Hello Virginia?"

"Hi Beatrice, sorry to disturb you so late, but I thought you'd like to know. He's done it again."

Adrian sipped at his Dão and brought the screen back to life with a touch of the mouse. Matthew's hair looked absurd. But much more importantly, the background contained more than beach, cliffs and gulls. A boat.

He zoomed in. Despite the poor definition, he could determine that the boat was dark blue, and the two figures heading up the beach were dressed in black. Both carried some sort of package. It reminded him of something. He zoomed again, but the quality was too poor to make anything out. He clicked on the second shot.

The detail behind Matthew's clownish coiffure revealed the two disembarkers heading towards a solitary figure, standing up the beach. The wind had messed with her hair too, whipping it into a streamer behind her. No features were discernible, but it was unquestionably a female. This was evidence!

Adrian clasped his hands together and glanced at the phone. Beatrice had been fidgety, stressed and tense all evening. Instinct told him she would not be pleased to have him disturb her now, while she was working and he was full of excitement. It could wait till tomorrow night.

He studied the photographs again. No doubt about it. Something was definitely going on and Beatrice had visual proof. He wondered if they would ever have noticed the backdrop to Matthew's comedy hair pictures if these shady characters hadn't been so hell-bent on getting rid of the images. He sat back with a satisfied smile. Fabulous! Detecting was so much more fun than watching *Grand Designs*.

Chapter 10

"Stubbs, you are deliberately wasting my time. This is not a football match in which I can substitute players at will." Hamilton's frown deepened to such an extent one could have played noughts and crosses on his forehead. "I cannot change personnel one day and reverse my decision the next without making either or both of us appear a total arse."

"My point, sir, is an extension of your decision. You sent a senior detective to assess the importance of the case. I delivered a report to you, indicating my view. Which is ..."

"I heard you the first time. And I've read your report. My answer remains unchanged. I thought I had made it clear at your first briefing – this case is about much more than getting a dirty old man off the streets. It's vital proactive police cooperation to promote a positive image of the force, in the face of media hostility. Following up claims of harassment is insufficient. Taking rape victims seriously is not enough. The IPCC's accusation of sustained failure regarding serial sex offenders can only be countered by an exercise such as this."

"But if someone else investigates the indecent exposures, such as Detective Sergeant Reynolds, we can achieve a double media coup with knife crime. All I am asking ..."

"We're failing women, Stubbs. And if you, as one of the party, will not stump up by putting personal concerns aside, my belief is beggared. Frankly, after yesterday's events, rather than trying to persuade me to send someone junior, you need to change up a gear with your sexual harasser."

"Sir, if I can simply explain my reasoning ..."

"I have heard more than enough. And can I remind you, this

is supposed to be a preventative exercise, *id est*, catching the man before he goes too far. As far as I am concerned, what he did to those little girls yesterday means he already has. Pull your finger out, Stubbs. Have your phone routed to BTP HQ and make sure the loss of your machine is properly reported. Data protection, and so on. Good day to you."

Kicking cabinets in the ladies' toilet at Transport for London did little to calm Beatrice's anger, and merely hurt her foot. She leant against the sink and steamed, cursing Hamilton with every malign expression she could conjure. The door opened.

"Back already? I thought we wouldn't see you till coffee break." Virginia wore a pale blue dress, modestly cut below the knee, with a matching jacket. The duck-egg shade accentuated the colour of her eyes. Her heels were low and her legs were tanned and bare. She looked lovely, which irritated Beatrice still further.

"I overestimated my reporting time back at Scotland Yard. But I'm here now. Do you want to get some coffee and discuss the latest incident?"

"We can do better than that. I've spoken to the Family Centre and got permission to observe the interviews with those two girls this morning. Facilitators are going to chat to them and elicit statements, while we watch and see if we can glean anything from their stories. If we get over there now, we can brief the facilitators first. Are you fit? Or do you want a bit more time to abuse the furniture?"

Beatrice spotted the dark smudges against the cupboard door. "Come on, let's go. But I'd better come back later. I'm not leaving that for the cleaners."

Virginia gave an understanding smile. "Believe me, it won't be the first time they've removed shoe leather from those cabinets. I once fractured a toe."

The Family Centre on Piccadilly reminded Beatrice of a doctor's surgery. Cheerful, welcoming entrance, all pastel colours, pine and glass. After announcing themselves at reception, they waited in the vestibule. Neither of them wished to join the pale faces and hollow eyes in the waiting-room. A woman strode towards them, with tumbling red hair, jeans and an outstretched hand. A face familiar with smiles.

"Hello, I'm Doctor Maggie Howard, sorry to keep you. Who's low?"

Beatrice stared. "Sorry?"

The redhead gurgled with laughter.

"That didn't come out right. I'm meeting a Detective Stubbs and a Detective Lowe. I just wondered which was which."

Virginia offered her hand. "I'm Virginia Lowe, of British Transport Police. My colleague is Beatrice Stubbs, from the Met. Pleased to meet you, Doctor Howard."

Beatrice noted Virginia's use of first names and the fact she didn't correct the doctor's omission of the word 'inspector' in their titles. She understood. In such an environment, a friendly atmosphere took precedence over protocol. The doctor shook their hands. Her grip was firm, but her skin was soft and she smelt vaguely of aniseed. "Likewise. And please call me Maggie. We have time for a chat before our interviewees arrive. Can I get you a cup of tea?"

Beatrice chose to observe the interview with Zahra Esfahani, while Virginia opted to watch Amber Clarke, who had suffered the physical assault. Sitting in the darkness, behind the one-way mirror, Beatrice had the impression she was almost in the room with Maggie and Zahra. They sat in two adjacent armchairs, as if it were a cosy lounge, thus lessening the pressure of eye contact. Magazines, toys and games were scattered over the coffee table in front of them. The girl had the typical coltish proportions of a thirteen-year-old. Skinny denim-clad legs, a purple T-shirt with a Pineapple Dance logo across the front and white leather ballet flats. She wore her hair in a high ponytail. Her bone structure would serve her well in the future, as would her large black-brown eyes, which she occasionally flicked upward from the floor.

Maggie Howard's technique was awe-inspiring. She managed to create an atmosphere of near-complicity in their first few exchanges, like a favourite aunt. Fascinated by the delicate process of gaining reliable testimony from a child, Beatrice noted the pattern.

Closed question, open question, sympathetic comment, closed question, subjective question, positive reinforcement, expression of validation.

"So you were coming home from rehearsals. Do you rehearse every evening, Zahra?"

"Yeah. For our performance."

"Yes, your performance. What's the show about?"

"It's, like, modern dance? Ensemble and solo pieces on the theme of 'The Elements'. It opens Friday night."

"I'll bet you're getting butterflies! I would be!"

A shy smile. "I am a bit."

"You and Amber live close to each other, don't you?"

"Same street. So we always walk home together."

"When you walked home yesterday, what was different to usual?"

She thought for a moment and shrugged. "Nothing. Amber was moaning, as usual. The river was dirty, as usual. The only different thing was that perve on the path." The girl's voice darkened and her fingers fiddled with the woven bracelet on her left wrist.

"OK. That's great. You're doing very well, Zahra. I have a feeling you could be a very helpful witness."

Despite her invisibility, Beatrice nodded in agreement. In the first thirty seconds, she'd already decided the teenager was bright and reliable.

As if Maggie sensed her approval, she continued. "The whole police force is so pleased that you and Amber came forward. Without people like you, we'd have a much harder job to catch him. But with your testimonies, I think we've got a better chance."

The girl looked down, but tried to smile.

Maggie got to the point. "Now, can you tell me, in your own words, exactly what happened from the moment you first saw the man? Take your time, and I'd like you to use these rag dolls to demonstrate. Just to help me understand who was where and so on."

Beatrice found herself nodding again. By using the harmless-looking dolls, Zahra could avoid using words that might embarrass her. Showing was easier than telling, and Maggie made it sound as if it were for her own benefit. Zahra's shaky but coherent description of the encounter made Beatrice thoroughly uncomfortable, building a sense of dread. Maggie asked frequent open questions on his accent and appearance, encouraging the girl to make comparisons to celebrities Beatrice had never heard of. When Zahra manipulated the dolls to show exactly what he'd done to Amber, a nauseous disgust washed over Beatrice. Followed by a swell of anger. Her toes and fists clenched, and for the first time, she really wanted this filthy bastard off the streets. Zahra put down the dolls and seemed to curl into herself.

Beatrice wanted to give the child a hug, but Maggie made no move to touch her. Of course not. Exactly the wrong thing under the circumstances. Beatrice's admiration for Maggie's professionalism rose still higher. It must be the most distressing work, dealing with these frightened victims of assault and abuse, coaxing details from damaged young people. Although Beatrice knew she could never do such a job, she was grateful for people who could. Softening her voice, Maggie began asking questions about Zahra's role and costumes for her show. Gradually, she pulled it around to a description of their assailant.

"Sounds gorgeous. I can almost see that dress. You're very good on details, Zahra, I'll say that. Something else I meant to ask: you mentioned the man's 'skanky trainers'. Can you give me any more details about the sports shoes he was wearing?"

Zahra's enthusiasm faded, but she gave a nod of comprehension. "They were just old, you know. Grey and skanky-looking. I couldn't see any logo. I *thought* it was weird, wearing a big coat and trainers with no socks."

"No socks?"

"I couldn't see any. But I didn't look at him for long, you know."

"No, of course you didn't. I always find it amazing, though, how people can take in the smallest details in a quick glance. The human mind is incredible. Younger people tend to have even better recollection, in my experience. OK, Zahra, you spotted the fact that his trainers were old and he wasn't wearing socks. What about his sweatshirt, can you picture the colour?"

The girl flushed and shook her head. No, that was natural. When he opened his coat, her eyes would be drawn down, not up.

"Fair enough, I understand. Now, last thing, you said he wore a baseball cap. I don't suppose you'd remember the colour."

The girl cocked her head to one side, thoughtful. "It was dark, maybe black or navy blue, and it had writing on the peak. Well, not writing you can read, but ..." She tailed off.

"Not writing you can read. Maybe it was in another language?"

"No, not another language, but more like symbols." She closed her eyes and thought. "Like three stripes horizontal, three vertical and so on. A bit like a floor, you know?"

"Hmm. If you saw this man again, Zahra, do you think you'd recognise him?"

"Too right. Weird eyes." Her face paled. "I won't have to, will I? You won't make us identify him in a line-up or something?"

"No. As I explained on the way in, you don't have to do anything. We asked for your help and you've given it. When we get this man under arrest, we may ask you to confirm from a photograph. That's all. Now, I think we should get something to drink and see if Amber has finished. While I pop out, would you do me a favour and see if you can draw those baseball cap symbols for me? Coke, juice, water ...?"

"Water, please."

Seconds after Maggie closed the door behind her, she entered Beatrice's observation room with a quick smile.

"She's good, isn't she? Just wanted to check before I wrap it up – anything else you need me to ask?"

"I don't think so. You've covered age, accent, physical description and clothes. I just wondered, could you ask her to go further on the 'weird eyes'?"

"No problem."

Maggie ducked out and Beatrice stood up to peer at what Zahra was drawing. She could see what the girl meant. It looked like parquet flooring; tiles of three grooves, one horizontal, the next vertical. She went on to sketch the baseball cap, thereby indicating exactly where the symbols were, and made a note on colour, before Maggie returned with two tumblers.

"That's fantastic, Zahra, thanks. Here's your water. What happens next is I'm going to write up our chat from the recording. Then I'd like you to check it, make sure I didn't get anything wrong, before we give it to the police. Now, do you have any questions you'd like to ask about all this?"

Zahra didn't drink but lifted her eyes to Maggie. "Do you think they'll catch him soon? The papers say he often comes back again."

"That's an exaggeration. You know what the papers are like. Plus we've asked your area community officers and neighbourhood watch to be particularly attentive for the next few weeks. The police will catch him, yes, and it won't be long. I can't make you any promises, but believe me when I say everyone wants to stop him as fast as possible. And you've given us a lot to go on."

The girl nodded. She didn't look entirely reassured, but it was clear she trusted Maggie to tell her the truth.

"Before we finish up, Zahra, can I ask you one more thing? You said the man on the path had 'weird eyes'. How do you mean?"

Zahra picked at her bracelet. "I don't know. Weird. Like, really black, sort of shining. Scary."

"Right. I see. You've been a great help. Thank you. I'd like to talk to your mum and dad now, so shall we go find them?"

Zé's came out top as the preferred lunch venue. By the time Beatrice paid for her soup and sandwich, Virginia had already plonked her tray outside in the sunshine, slipped off her jacket and was making eye contact with the suit sitting on the adjacent table. Beatrice joined her, with a sigh of release. The tension of the past two hours, extreme concentration and no natural light had affected her mood. She sat back and tilted her face to the sun. Tourists and office workers swarmed along the street, enjoying lunch alfresco.

"The only trouble with this place is they lay the mayo on so thick." Virginia scraped white goo from her baguette onto a napkin.

"How odd. That's one of the reasons I like it." Beatrice heard the chair behind her scrape back and watched Virginia's eyes follow the departing suit. She caught Beatrice's scrutiny and went on the offensive.

"Good. He's gone. So now we can talk. I'm not sure whether that Clarke girl was any use, to be honest. Little drama queen. Half the time I wasn't sure if she was acting or seriously distressed." Virginia took a bite of her undressed sandwich.

"Seeing as she was sexually assaulted yesterday afternoon, I'd lean to the latter," said Beatrice.

Virginia stopped chewing. "OK. That probably sounded unfair. But the facilitator agreed with me. Plenty of theatrics. I'm guessing your Esfahani was more genuine."

"Yes. What she witnessed left Zahra deeply shaken. And hearing about it did something to me, too." Beatrice stirred her soup.

"Aha. I think I can guess what." Virginia put down her sandwich and wiped her fingers. "She's the first victim you've met. This case became personal for me after interviewing the French girl. You know what I felt? Shame. I was embarrassed and ashamed that this lovely girl couldn't stay here, learn our language and quietly earn her living without some dirty deviant putting the fear of London into her. And that's why when I see a 'performance' of traumatised, compared to the real thing, it gets on my tits."

"Fair enough. I didn't meet Amber Clarke. But as a matter of fact, you're right. I was going through the motions before, if I'm honest. Now, I want to grab this ugly little bastard and put him away."

Virginia nodded with enthusiasm. "I want this fucker so badly I'm losing sleep. He's already preparing his next victim, Beatrice. If he gets that far, we've let her down. For all kinds of reasons; professional, political and just from the gender standpoint, we've got to nail him. And I reckon we'll be more efficient if we're on the same side."

Her cool blue eyes were intense. Beatrice put down her spoon and held out her hand.

"We're on the same side."

They shook, exchanged a smile and returned to their lunch.

Virginia took a sip of juice. "I thought we could prepare tomorrow's briefing when we get back. I really want to whack them with how important this is. I'm bringing in that psychological profiler."

"Good idea, but I have a medical appointment at two, so I may not be back till around four." Beatrice kept her expression open.

"Oh. Sorry to hear that. Nothing serious, I hope?"

"No, no. Just a check-up. Shall we say four o'clock and bash out a plan?"

"Fine. I'll add the data from the girls' interviews and crosscheck. Did yours give us much?"

Beatrice felt a dual pull of relief and guilt at Virginia's blithe acceptance, but pressed on. Mind on the job.

"Zahra said he had 'weird eyes; black, shining and scary'. I'm thinking drugs."

Virginia tore off a piece of baguette and considered. "Could be. But in my experience, drug users are sloppy. This guy seems meticulous. I suppose it could be poppers, to elevate the sexual high."

"Did you get anything useful from Amber at all?"

"Not exactly. She said he smelt. Bad B.O. apparently. But as for description, useless."

Beatrice tilted her head. "That's got potential. We should put that in the profile mix. I got lots of detail on appearance and a picture of a logo he had on his hat." Beatrice reached into her pocket for Zahra's drawing. Since the robbery at The Speaker, she kept things close.

Virginia pursed her lips. "Don't recognise it. But we can run some checks. How's your soup?"

"Cold," Beatrice said, taking a spoonful.

"Sorry. We should eat first and talk later."

"No, it's supposed to be."

"Cold soup?"

"Gazpacho."

"Bless you!"

Beatrice let out a belly-laugh, attracting amused attention from passers-by. Despite all her best efforts, she rather liked Virginia Lowe.

Chapter 11

"James, I'm sorry I'm late. Bloody hold-up on the Piccadilly line."

"No need for apologies. That is London transport. But we will still have to finish on time, I hope you understand?"

"Of course." Beatrice flopped into the armchair and dragged a bottle of water from her bag." I don't think we'll need the full hour today, anyway. Not much to tell."

"Well, let's wait and see. Shall we begin with practicalities, or is there a particular issue you would like to work on?"

He gave a faint smile, as James often did, lulling one into a feeling of unconditional support. His short grey hair shone blond in the sunlight and his skin had a post-holiday glow. White gauze curtains softened the view of the opposite office block, the parquet floor and cream rugs gave an impression of cleanliness and peace. The room's air-conditioned coolness and calm atmosphere began working on Beatrice instantly.

"No, there's nothing ... Well, I'm lying to Matthew." It blurted its way out before she had even formulated the thought.

James's head lifted in enquiry.

"Not lying exactly. Just being economical with the truth. My laptop got stolen and I haven't told him. The thing is ..."

It looked like they would need the full hour after all. James sat absolutely still, listening to her complex explanation.

"So I want to investigate this, without Hamilton, without Matthew and without that inverted snob Howells. I want to show them this is not hysteria, or paranoia or even a whole new dementia. There is something untoward going on in Wales and I want to prove it. Hamilton thinks it's personal, Matthew thinks I should stay home and concentrate on what I'm good at and Howells thinks I'm trying to teach him to suck eggs."

"You seem very sure of what all these people are thinking. I'm going to ask some questions and I want you to answer honestly. If you'd rather think about it before doing so, that's fine. Is it possible that you're building a wall of hostile men from a series of disconnected resentments?"

"I don't know what you mean by that."

James paused to look at his notes. "Might each man have his own agenda, unrelated to personal perceptions of you?"

"That is exactly my point. They're trying to keep me in my place, slap me down, hold me back. The little woman who belongs in the kitchen, but not in the workplace. Well, not Matthew so much, but he doesn't want me to rock the boat either. He'd rather I did découpage than detective work. They all want to chain me to my own little groove and stick to the script."

"Your tone seems unusually defensive. And, if I may observe, full of 1970's feminist rhetoric and mixed metaphors. What chance is there that your own insecurities in each case are projected onto these individuals?"

"James, you know perfectly well how hard I fight to be taken seriously in the professional sphere."

"Fight? I think I could accept 'fought', but I ask myself how that is relevant. I also wonder if you're feeling a little victimised for no reason."

Beatrice felt a flare of annoyance at James's deliberate deflation of her righteousness. Fanned by the awareness that he had a point.

"Howells may well have rubbed me up the wrong way, that's true."

"And perhaps vice versa?"

James was exactly like a dentist of the mind, invariably prodding at the painful bits.

"Fair point. But Hamilton still regards me as a loose cannon and Matthew clearly wants me to settle for an easy life, calm down and stop looking for trouble."

"Let's deal with one thing at a time. Hamilton. Entrusting a person with a vital case for the force's image is not where most people place a loose cannon."

Beatrice huffed through her nostrils, but James didn't push it. He didn't have to, the seed was planted.

"So you're saying I shouldn't feel it's a conspiracy to undermine me. That each man has belittled me and made me feel inadequate for the sake of their own egos."

"You began this session by telling me you were lying to Matthew. So in your view, which of the two of you is showing least respect for the other?"

Beatrice looked at the floor, her mind whirling back forty years to the headmaster's study, to the day she was carpeted for starting a fight in the cloakrooms.

James wasn't going to give up drilling. "Howells, you claim, is defensive and resistant to what you described as 'interference from the big boys'. Thus your depiction of a patriarchal bully rings hollow. Do you see where I'm going?"

Beatrice rested her forehead on her hands. "Yes. I think so. I've painted black hats onto the good guys." She inhaled deeply. "As a victim without a perpetrator, I feel frustrated. I'm laying blame so I can feel hard done by."

James's voice softened. "You know yourself very well, Beatrice. Now let's return to your original worry. If you intend to tell Matthew about the loss of your computer soon, what exactly is your reason for feeling guilty? Waiting for the right time to tell someone is not the same as lying. And you've stated that you're going to tell him at the weekend."

"Yes, I have. And I will." She shifted awkwardly in her seat, unable to envisage that conversation.

"Beatrice, forgive my pushing, but I wonder if there could be another reason for your feelings of guilt, or disloyalty."

"No, there's nothing more than that, really."

"When you have found someone you trust, like Matthew, that trust becomes precious. As time goes by, if you are truthful, open and believe in each other's honesty, a bond grows. A precious bond, like a gold chain. It's strong, forged from two people's love and loyalty. It can withstand immense external onslaughts. Almost nothing can break it, except for a moment of dishonesty from within. Being deceptive, in any form, has the potential to crack a link of that chain. The relationship between you and Matthew is based on truth."

"Which is ironic considering its origins."

"Its origins, if you really want to revisit that topic, can be discussed in our next session. However, they are immaterial in the context of this discussion. Look at it for what it is now. It is and always has been a relationship based on truth. You have a responsibility to that."

"I know." Beatrice's eyes stung and her voice sounded small.

"Another relationship based on truth is the one between you and me. So if I think you are not being entirely honest with me, I feel I have a responsibility to find out why."

Her nose was running. She reached for the box of tissues with such familiarity, this could have been her own bedroom.

"Yes, okay, okay. You're bloody right, as usual. I justified not telling him for all those reasons, but in fact, I want to keep this thing to myself. There's no way I can get it taken on as a case; Hamilton won't have it, so I'll have to do this in my spare time. Howells is being deliberately obstructive, so I'll just go behind his back. And I can't tell Matthew, because he will fret for me, or want to help me, or try to stop me. And I don't need any of that."

"Are you planning to do this alone?"

"Not exactly. I have a neighbour who's helping."

"A neighbour. Who presumably knows Matthew?"

"Yes. A neighbour who knows him well and who's mad keen to become Clouseau of the East End. I'm trying to rein him in, but it's like trying to rationalise with a spring lamb." She released an enormous sigh. "I have to tell Matthew, don't I?"

"I can't tell you what to do. I just want you to make decisions that are both right for now and for later. I have no doubt you know what the best thing is."

"Yes. I do. James, I'm sorry for being so bloody awkward."

James looked up from his notes with a frown.

"Beatrice Stubbs, if you break the terms of our contract one more time, you will be fined. We agreed, and you have had more verbal warnings than I care to count, that you need never apologise for yourself. Not in this room. Now look, we have five minutes left. So to practicalities."

"Practicalities, yes. The mood balancers seem to be working and I take one daily. As for the diary, well, I've been busy, so I can't say I'm up to date."

"When do you take your medication, Beatrice?"

"Last thing at night."

"The perfect time. Keep a notebook under your pill box. As you take the tablet, make a note of the day's moods. Even if you write only one line, that will help us chart your emotional movements. Will you try?"

"Fair enough, I can manage that. Look James, thank you. You have phenomenal patience. You knew we'd need the whole hour, didn't you?"

"Mostly when people announce there's nothing to say, the opposite tends to be true. Please take care of yourself, Beatrice. See you in a fortnight?"

"I'll look forward to it. Goodbye."

It was true. Whenever she left James's office, she couldn't wait to return. As so often after one of his sessions, she felt like a power hose had cleaned the inside of her skull and she wanted to skip all the way back to the office. But she knew from experience such enthusiasm would be short-lived. Two weeks later and she would resent the trip to Islington. Dreading the illumination of dark and dusty emotional corners and anticipating her embarrassment at how, in only fourteen days, she had allowed her mind to get into such an appalling mess.

Chapter 12

Only three stops and they were already south of the river. Beatrice and Adrian came out of the Tube at London Bridge and walked through Borough Market, thankfully closed, otherwise Beatrice would never have dragged him away from the food stalls. He could waste an entire morning sniffing chanterelles and tasting goat's cheese. She always insisted on taking this particular route when they had their Tate Nights. Walking along the South Bank, full of atmosphere both ancient and modern, was part of the whole soothing experience.

They dodged another cluster of guidebook-reading Nordic sorts and walked under the shadow of Southwark Cathedral. Beatrice waited till they had turned the corner before firing a question at her companion.

"How many people were in that group of tourists we just passed?"

Adrian faltered and made as if to turn but Beatrice wagged a finger.

"Just approximately. And if you can hazard a guess as to nationality, I'll give you another point."

"Six, I think. And they were all adults. As for nationality? British, possibly from Newcastle, judging by the accents."

Beatrice sighed in mock despair. "Eight. Grandparents, parents and four children. Scandinavian, certainly, but I could have been no more specific than that until I saw the Swedish flag on the teenager's backpack."

Adrian didn't seem particularly impressed. They passed The Golden Hinde and circumnavigated the queue outside The Clink before he spoke.

"I think you're cheating. If I were actively detecting, right now, I'd keep my eyes open for anything relating to my case. Not wasting brain space with lots of irrelevant detail about Swiss tourists."

"Swedish. How do you know exactly what is relevant to your case?"

"Here, probably nothing." Passing Vinopolis, they stopped for a moment to admire Banksy's artwork on the bridge. "But if I were in Wales, I'd be looking very carefully at anyone wearing boaty gear."

"Boaty gear. I see the logic. Anything else? Which other angles would you use for such enquiries?" Beatrice increased the pressure.

Adrian rose to the challenge. "Apart from checking out boat people, I'd find out when the tide comes in, so I'd know when to wait for boats arriving in the dark."

"Very astute." The laughter and chat from the crowd outside The Anchor flowed over them as Adrian's head flicked left and right, overtly taking in every detail. He expected another test, so Beatrice changed tack.

"It's natural that men are less aware of their surroundings. You have a different kind of focus. Single-minded. Whereas women, from our hunting and gathering days, developed far better peripheral vision."

"Beatrice, please don't tell me you buy into all that hard-wired gender traits crap. You are an intelligent woman. Surely you cannot believe we have evolved so little from the days of the woolly mammoth."

She laughed. "No, I don't. No more than I believe in behaviour dictated by signs of the Zodiac. But I knew it would get your shackles up."

It was Adrian's turn to laugh. "Get my shackles up? That's a Bea-line I've not heard before. As a matter of fact, I share far more typical characteristics with fellow Sagittarians than I do with cavemen. Oh, look at The Globe. I do love it when it's all lit up."

Beatrice stood beside him to admire the theatre, listening to the rush of the Thames at her back. The warm evening, the feeling of people making the most of their city, the anticipation of a couple of happy hours at the Tate Modern, followed by dinner at their favourite Thai, filled Beatrice with optimism. She bunted Adrian with a shoulder and they walked on towards the Millennium Bridge.

"So, which play was on at The Globe tonight?" asked Beatrice.

"Is that pertinent to a case involving criminal activity on a Welsh beach?"

"It's pertinent to your powers of observation. You stared at the poster for several minutes so you must remember some of the detail. I'll give you a clue. It's a play by Marlowe and the title is just one word."

Adrian's face was a study of concentration as they approached the art gallery along gravel paths. Beatrice looked up at the immense edifice, crowned by its monolithic chimney, with a sense of admiration for its functionality, past and present.

"I remember! *Cymbeline!*" Adrian's expression was triumphant.

"Tsk. That's Shakespeare. It was *Tamburlaine*, twerp. Come on."

"*Tamburlaine Twerp* is two words."

After nosing around the Turbine Hall, they made their way upstairs.

"Can we start on Level Three?" asked Adrian, leading the way to the escalator. "I want to feed my Surrealist urges."

"You're becoming fixated with weird types and I'm not at all sure it's healthy. Yes, let's start there but I do want to see some Impressionists this evening. I've had a hankering since Wales." She held onto the handrail. How refreshing to just stop and stand still on an escalator rather than barging up on the left, tutting at tourists.

"Talking of Wales, have I convinced you yet?" He looked down at her from the step above as they travelled up two floors. The olive-green shirt looked most elegant against his tan. Summer suited him.

Beatrice decided it was time to be honest.

"I am most grateful for the photographs you managed to print from my phone, don't get me wrong. And as I told you before, you have many of the right qualities I look for in a detective. Unfortunately, you lack training, experience and an understanding of protocols. So while I am happy to bend the rules by sharing information with you, I can't possibly sanction your taking on a potential crime investigation. Not on your own."

He didn't answer, turning to look forwards as they neared the top. He walked ahead to the first room without waiting for her. Beatrice sighed. After all these years of neighbourly harmony, it would be a shame to fall out over such a situation. She wandered through various rooms and found him standing in front of Paul Klee's *Walpurgisnacht*. The strange, scratched canvas of blue straw-like figures evoked bats and rituals and owls and paganism. It appealed to her in a way she couldn't explain.

"I like it. Very witchy."

Adrian smiled. "I hear the New York Times art critic said exactly the same."

They moved on to Edward Wadsworth, Yves Tanguy and David Smith. Adrian seemed drawn to these juxtaposed angles, odd assemblages and curious compositions, in the style of de Chirico.

"They like sticking things together to create bizarre representations, don't they? Sort of artistic Lego."

Adrian shot her a sly look. "Perhaps it's a male thing."

Beatrice drifted away to Franz Roh's *Total Panic II*, involving a rather well-drawn elephant scene, incorporating an apparently random bat and snail. Adrian joined her.

"Makes you want to hear the whole story, doesn't it?"

She nodded. "Yes. Funny how these things can work on our emotions, despite not having a clue as to their true meaning."

"Do you want to go stare at some pastels now?" he asked.

"When you're ready. I have no wish to exacerbate your sulk."

"I am ready, after our usual stop for *Metamorphosis of Narcissus*, and it's not a sulk. I just feel a little disappointed that you don't trust me."

Beatrice frowned at him. "I do trust you. With all my secrets. Well, most of them. But I'm not prepared to put you in harm's way. It's lovely of you to offer to help, and I'm touched. The fact of the matter is, I can't investigate, because I have to throw all my energies into catching this twisted sex offender. And if I can't, you can't either. It's too dangerous. We have no idea what we're dealing with."

They stopped and gazed at the Dalí. Disregarding her lack of enthusiasm for Surrealism, she admired the wonderful use of light, echoes and reflection, the rich colours of the sky, and the always intriguing background detail. She never minded pausing for Narcissus.

Adrian sighed. "It does seem a real shame to let these thefts go unpunished. There could be something far worse behind the pictures. And all because you can't get away from the Finsbury Park Flasher."

"Yes, but when I've got him where he can do no further harm, I'll insist on chasing any leads myself. And the evidence hasn't been abandoned. Don't forget, the Welsh police have all the facts, including your photos, and are still making enquiries."

"You said yourself you had no faith in Inspector Howells."

Beatrice acknowledged the truth of that. Perhaps she should share a little less with her nosy neighbour who forgot nothing, so long as it interested him.

"Well, never mind that now. At the moment, there's nothing you or I can do about it. Just as soon as I am free to look into things myself, I'd be happy for you to join me. Does that pacify you?"

"A bit. OK, I've had my Surreal fix. Let's go and see some Old Lady Art."

Beatrice swiped at him with the back of her hand but he was already out of reach.

Chapter 13

Trouble with these girls is they think too much.

Rick rolled up the shutter without checking the window display. No need. Sign says 'Sex Shop' in pink and blue neon. A few vids, pair of handcuffs, crotchless drawers and your punter knows what he's getting. Yeah, it looks tired, a bit sleazy, but who cares? When he finds the next shop girl, she can do a bit of dusting. Or not. Shiny shop front or shabby faded velvet, they'll come. *Heh, heh. They'll always come.* Maybe dirty makes them feel at home.

He'd not expected Caz to lose her bottle. Well disappointing. She was a cynic from the start; tats, studs and a tongue-lash he'd not heard the like of since Madam D. She understood money and sex. Or at least Rick thought she did. One of the few girls he trusted to handle herself without security. Saved him a packet. And now she'd quit. Bad news.

The door opened and the bell pinged as the first one arrived. Rick nodded at him and looked back to the computer. He never judged them. Not to their faces. These losers were his bread and butter. But how sad are you if you need wank-fodder at ten past nine? Geezer went straight in the back for the DVDs. Rick sighed as the door opened again.

Jason. Another wanker.

"Alright Rick?"

"Jase."

Jason stood beside the soft-porn mag rack as if he was comfortable, but Rick saw his eyes flickering over the opposite wall. He was staring at nurse costumes, rubber gimp suits and lubricants with a giggly compulsion.

"I said I'd call you if I needed any deliveries, didn't I?"

"Yeah, deffo. Just thought I'd pop in and see if you needed a hand, now Caz has pissed off."

Rick didn't look up from the screen. Jason was desperate to manage the shop. Desperate. And therefore the worst possible person to leave in charge. Like letting an alkie run your Ibizan beach bar.

"Nah, you're alright, Jase. I got it sorted. I'll give you a bell if I need anything."

Another bloke came in, greeted them and made straight for the back room. Obviously a regular. The shop was doing decent trade, so all Rick needed to do was find a decent manager. Jase was still hanging about.

"Jase, I got work to do."

"Yeah, sure, got it. I'm off then. Listen, why did Caz leave?"

Rick shook his head. "Dunno, mate. Maybe she's got a bloke? Just said she'd had enough, is all."

The phone started ringing and Jason finally pissed off out of it. Rick dealt with a coy query about lesbian films and a professional sales geezer trying to flog paperbacks of Mommy Porn. Could help the first, no chance with the second. Randy housewives don't go to sex shops. Try Mothercare.

By lunchtime, he'd sold sixteen DVDs, a chocolate lubricant, a gold cock ring, thirteen mags for differing tastes and two Rabbits. Busy morning. He planned to close up over lunch and go to The Blue Posts for a pie and a pint. Five to one, the bell pinged and another punter turned up. Rick looked up to acknowledge the guy but he kept his head down. Classic. Baseball cap, shifty behaviour, no eye contact, just standing there looking at restraints. Rick waited for the bloke to decide and thought about Caz.

He missed her. Simple as. Always timed it so as he was here around eleven, brought her cakes and coffee and they had a laugh. Why would she up sticks and walk? He'd always treated her right and never tried it on. Not his type, anyway. And he had a funny feeling he wasn't hers either. But she was a great laugh and a damn good manager. Shit. He knew she wouldn't come back, not even for a raise. She'd gone for good. He'd probably never see her again.

He was hungry, he needed a pint and there was a right pong

in the air. This punter was giving off a chronic stink. Rick closed down the till and picked up his keys. The bloke carried on staring at the handcuffs. Rick recalled Caz's voice. *Sometimes, you look into someone's eyes and you just know. No matter how much they spend, you don't want any part of that world.*

The stink was getting worse.

"Right then, sunshine. I'm off on my lunch break. Back about two. Unless you've already decided?"

The foul-smelling git looked over his shoulder, back at the display and slunk out the door, the bell signalling his departure. Rick shook his head. Not known for civilised small talk, your average pervert. He locked the door and bent under the counter to find the Febreze.

Chapter 14

"Classics Department, Professor Bailey?"

"Matthew, hello. This is Adrian speaking. I hope I'm not disturbing you?"

"Hello Adrian. No, not at all, it's nice to hear from you."

"I called you at home, at first. I thought one of the perks of university lecturing was a massive summer holiday. So I was surprised when your cleaner said you were in your campus office."

"Not so much of a cleaner, more of an untidier. That was Tanya, my youngest. She's using the library, hence my banishment. Er, is everything all right?"

"Oh yes. Beatrice is fine, don't worry. We had dinner the other night, as you know. No, the reason for calling was simply to thank you for that heavenly Amarone."

"Ah. The Tommaso Bussola. What did you think?"

"Dense. Both colour and nose and the palate goes on forever. Spices from entry to finish, but so well balanced."

Adrian could hear Matthew smiling. "Quite. It's powerful, impressively so, but has real elegance. Did you try it with duck?"

"No, I gave the wine centre stage. Supporting acts were some organic bresaola, parmigiano reggiano with a drop of balsamic vinegar and fresh crusty ciabatta. It was absolutely sublime. So much so that I couldn't have shared it. I can't thank you enough."

"You're more than welcome. Your appreciation is my reward. Are you well?"

"In rude health, thank you. And you?"

"Almost normal, apart from a certain frustration at a loss of research data. Beatrice told you of our mishap in Pembrokeshire, I presume? When my camera was stolen, I lost a fair few images which were important to my work. I should learn from Beatrice's example and always make a back-up."

"Yes, she did tell me. To be truthful, Matthew, that's my other reason for calling. I hope you won't mind, but I've tried talking to Beatrice about this a couple of times. She's so absorbed in chasing her flasher, she seems to have lost all interest in this case."

"Which case would that be?"

Adrian explained the photographs, taking care not to mention the stolen laptop, outlined his theory and stressed his conviction that someone, somewhere really should investigate. Matthew was silent for a long time.

"It's decent of you to be concerned, but I'm not really sure how I can help. Chasing the Welsh police is likely to be counter-productive. The local inspector has already told Beatrice to keep her beak out."

"I agree. Which is why I thought you and I might be able to lend a hand."

"Taking on the role of the Hardy Boys while Nancy Drew is occupied?" he asked.

"Well ..." Adrian didn't want to admit it, but he was thinking more along the lines of Poirot and Hastings.

"Despite the fact that Beatrice has access to all the necessary resources, possesses years of expertise and experience, and bearing in mind this may not even be in her jurisdiction, you think we should poke about and ask questions, possibly jeopardising any official investigation?"

Adrian found Matthew's tone patronising. "My angle was more as support. Matthew, Beatrice has no time to apply all her resources and etcetera. All her time and energy is dedicated to this dirty raincoat. And rightly so. But she's frustrated by the fact she hasn't got time to make enquiries. She told me she couldn't allow me to investigate alone. The way I see it, there's nothing stopping the two of us doing some helpful groundwork, asking casual questions, making enquiries in a subtle fashion and then handing over our findings when she's got time to take it seriously."

"That sounds reasonable. But I don't think she'll be keen."

"Nor do I. She'd probably issue a three-line whip. Which is why I called you, to see if we can't manage something discreet and supportive, but keep it to ourselves. A sort of gentleman's investigation."

Matthew laughed. "A gentleman's investigation. Well, that's certainly an idea. It could liven up my summer holiday no end. Why don't you tell me what you have in mind?"

"Great! It would be better to do that face to face. Who's doing the travelling this weekend? Is she coming to you?"

"No, she's staying in London and I've been given the choice. She will have to work part of the time, so if I can promise to amuse myself, I am allowed to come for a visit. That fits in rather well with our potential scheme, I'd say."

Adrian smiled. "It most certainly does. And I'm free all weekend during the day. I have a dress rehearsal on Friday and my performance is on Saturday night. Oh, I'm so pleased you're up for this. All detectives should have a sidekick, because apart from anything else, it's so boring on your own. So, see you sometime over the weekend? Do you have my mobile number?"

"I do, but I might just pop downstairs and knock on your door, when I get a chance. I wish you all the very best with the show, break a leg and all that. And yes, you're right. All the best detecting tales involve an older, wiser professional supported by a keen young pup. See you on Saturday at some point. Thanks for calling, Adrian, I appreciate your trust."

As Adrian hung up and returned to the computer, he tingled with anticipation. All the fun of detective work with none of the unattractive uniforms, paperwork or politics. He just hoped that Matthew understood the situation. Keen young pup, indeed. No one puts Adrian in the chorus.

Chapter 15

"Morning everybody and thanks for coming. As you all know, this is a special operation and let's just get one thing straight. I've heard more than one person saying, why the fuss, it's *just* a flasher. Well, that stops as of now. There is a far more serious reason for getting this man off the streets." Virginia paused, her eyes scanning the room.

Beatrice did the same, searching for any tell-tale sneers, any significant looks, any evidence of disbelief. Such officers would be either replaced or stuck on paper detail. Both women had agreed they wanted total commitment from all involved. None of the twenty-six faces; British Transport personnel, constables from the Hackney, Islington and Haringey boroughs, Safer Neighbourhood officers and Met Police Volunteers, showed anything but curious interest.

"Right, so I'll hand you over to Doctor Simon Rosenbaum, our specialist profiler."

The presence of the profiler increased attention from the assembly. Beatrice noted shifts in seats and a few slouchers straightening up. Rosenbaum's appearance was unremarkable. His fair hair was thinning, his eyes were grey and his clothes – a striped shirt with no tie, jeans and deck shoes – reminded Beatrice of Sundays in Greenwich Park.

"Good morning folks. DI Lowe has asked me to explain the reasoning behind this case, as it is largely due to my concerns that you're all here. I work with a team of psychologists and behavioural experts at University College, London. We've collaborated over the past six years with nine other European universities, all of which have strong links with their local police forces. Our research, compiled from six years of data on sex offenders, shows a pattern.

"The vast majority of those who indecently expose themselves are no cause for concern. Exhibitionism, drunkenness, a momentary misjudgement ..."

"A wardrobe malfunction," added Ty Grant, to general laughter. Virginia joined in. Beatrice, hiding her irritation at the interruption, smiled briefly. Rosenbaum handled it well.

"Precisely. That can happen too. But these are people that do it once, and with a different set of objectives. When someone exposes himself, and it is usually a male, with the intent to intimidate, frighten or shock the recipient, we class that as a sexual offence. Now, those who repeat the offence are the ones we need to watch. Point one: repeat exposers frequently demonstrate other kinds of anti-social behaviour, which is often an indication of some social maladjustment. Point two: the offences generally become more serious. In these cases, we have found that the offender is likely to assault, even rape and on some occasions, kill. We are working with forces all over Europe to try and encourage greater awareness of this phenomenon and thereby prevent serious sexual assaults."

His message provoked sober nods and thoughtful expressions.

"Our Finsbury Park man is following the behavioural sequence exactly. Just from the cases we know about, the incidents are increasing in frequency; he started off roughly once a fortnight. In the last three weeks, we've received three reports, and this week he's struck twice. Not only that, but at first it was one woman, usually in the small hours. The last two incidents: two foreign students leaving a friend's flat at around 10.30pm. The friend was an earlier victim. Any alarm bells ringing yet?

"Then he waited for two girls, aged thirteen, and encouraged one to put her hand in his pocket. When she refused, he opened his coat and pressed the girl's hand to his genitals. He was interrupted, fortunately, or it might have gone further.

"I cannot stress highly enough how urgent this is. My team and I believe he will commit a serious sexual assault in the next few days. Your job is to stop that happening."

Rosenbaum sat down, and Beatrice could see how the atmosphere was galvanised by a sense of collective responsibility. Good job, Doctor Rosenbaum.

Virginia gave it a second before she got to her feet. Her sleeveless scarlet polo-neck, paired with pedal pushers, gave her the air of Jeanne Moreau. "We're grateful to you and your team, Dr Rosenbaum. Right, this is how it's going to work. The guy's victims have nothing more in common than their gender and the fact they all use Finsbury Park Tube. He selects them, follows them, understands their habits and chooses his moment. He's very aware of cameras. He hasn't yet been recorded. We believe he learns their routine and follows them from the Underground.

"We run two parallel plans of attack. First, surveillance teams in pairs stationed in and around the Tube station. In your briefing pack, page nine, you'll find your partners and your locations on the map, specifically chosen to be in the gaps between cameras. You watch, you wait. In shifts from six till six. We're looking for a man acting suspiciously, wearing the gear described on page thirteen. Or a woman alone, especially the more vulnerable. He's picked on a train cleaner, a primary schoolteacher, a foreign student, a barista, a new immigrant, two contract cleaners, those students and now these teenage girls. That we know of. Now I'll ask DI Stubbs to describe procedure."

Heads lifted toward Beatrice. Her skirt suit and flats gave her the air of Miss Marple.

"Hello everyone. Priority number one is to get this man into custody. If you're suspicious, follow him. Do not let him know you're there. Do not attempt to apprehend unless you are sure of success. If we scare this man and lose him, he will run. He may wait a few weeks, he may change his patch, but he won't stop. We are not advertising our presence, we're not a deterrent, we want him where he cannot terrorise any more women. This activity will be called Operation Robert, and Robert will be your codeword to alert other teams that you are following a suspect."

Grant was grinning. "Operation Robert? Shouldn't it be Operation John Thomas?"

At least some of the meathead's colleagues found him distasteful, judging by the mixture of subdued sniggers and disgusted glares.

Beatrice fixed her gaze on Grant's ruddy, self-satisfied face. "The reason we decided on Operation Robert was in acknowledgement of Robert Peel, founder of the Metropolitan Police Force as we know it. As I'm sure you're aware, this is why police officers used to be described as 'Peelers.' Also, Robert is an innocuous name which is unlikely to attract attention in an awkward situation. The reason we decided against Operation John Thomas was that, unlike you, Sergeant, we find nothing amusing about sexual assault. Does anyone have any more pertinent questions?"

Grant looked at Virginia in confusion. After a second's discomfort, a female officer raised a hand. "The girls, on Wednesday. That's quite a distance from Finsbury Park Tube."

Beatrice nodded. "They go to a dance school in Arsenal. They catch the Tube and the twenty-nine bus back to Green Lanes, then walk along the riverbank. It's quite a journey. Recently they've been doing it every night, at exactly the same time."

The officer wrinkled her nose. "He followed them all that way? Stalker."

"Exactly. Which leads me to the second plan. DI Lowe?"

Virginia shot her a look. If that was intended as some kind of disapproval regarding her remark to Grant, they would have words. That man was an oaf.

Virginia took Beatrice's place in front of their team.

"Honey trap. Sergeant Grant and Sergeant de Freitas will be hovering at Finsbury Park Tube Control Centre. They'll be watching all the exits and entrances, all the in and outs."

Grant gave Virginia a sly smile.

"Meanwhile, Constable Harrison of BTP is our decoy. She'll be leaving early and returning late. We're hoping our man will spot her and make her a target. She'll have a team of three officers nearby at all times, watching her, and watching anyone who's watching her. Harrison, you want to introduce yourself?"

Harrison raised her index finger to identify her presence. With a jerk of her head, Virginia indicated she should stand. Reluctantly, the constable pushed out of her chair, and glanced around the judgemental faces. Everyone was thinking the same thing: is the lure attractive enough?

Her short blonde hair was cropped close to her head, framing a milky complexion now reddened with embarrassment. Her uniform did not flatter her skinny frame. She wore no make-up, but her eyes seemed bright and lively.

Virginia continued. "Harrison will be playing Party Girl. Well, obviously we'll dress her up a bit, pile on the slap and she'll pass. The plan is for her to act like she's spent the whole night on the alco-pops and is off her head."

"Should be a doddle for you, Karen." Grant just couldn't keep his mouth shut. This whole briefing drove Beatrice to distraction. She had never experienced such sloppy attitudes and poor discipline. Hamilton would have had a fit.

She turned with a frown to stare at Big Mouth and even Virginia adopted a warning tone, saying, "Ty."

He merely grinned back as the constable sat and lowered her head.

"Read your packs carefully, and get some sleep tomorrow, because you're all going on twelve-hour shifts. Any questions, DI Stubbs and I will be happy to answer them. Thanks all and best of luck."

On the grim march back to Virginia's office, both women strode side-by-side, breathing through their noses, keeping an ostentatious hold on their tempers. Beatrice pictured a pair of livid chickens, on their way to a hen fight.

She'd barely closed the door before Virginia began. Standing behind her chair, she slammed the heel of her hand onto the desk.

"What in the name of God do you think you're playing at? Do you want to poison this whole team against us before we start? Ty Grant is probably one of the most popular men on this op and you start by making him look an insensitive fool!"

Virginia had taken the high position, on her feet, taller, louder and demonstrably angry. Although she'd rather not, Beatrice could play status games. She pulled out the chair opposite, sat and kept her voice and expression calm.

"He didn't need my help for that. And he's not the only one. Insensitivity? How do you think Karen Harrison felt during that briefing? You exposed her and basically said, 'OK, so she looks bloody awful now, but we can sort that out'. Then you allow Grant his little pot shot at discrediting her ..."

"For fuck's sake, Beatrice, can't you take a joke? He was trying to lighten the atmosphere. He works, and has always worked, as the team glue. Keeping morale high, voicing many people's unspoken thoughts, he's solid gold."

"I see it differently. First he attempts to demean and belittle this op with his suggestion of a better name. Then he makes a slur against a colleague, albeit couched in humour. This is exactly the sort of behaviour we agreed not to tolerate. But now you seem to have changed your mind. Why is that? Is it personal, Virginia?"

In Gibraltar one year, Beatrice and Matthew spent many happy hours watching the monkeys. One could learn much from watching the interactions of a bunch of apes. Beatrice had noted one particular expression, which remained with her. When crossed, one of these primates' frowns would clear as it pulled up its scalp. The effect was to reveal the whites of the eyes, she supposed. Whatever the reason, it signalled danger. Virginia did something very similar. Her face went blank and hard, as if a line had been crossed.

"Are you calling my judgement into question, Beatrice?"

"Frankly, yes. I'm sorry to say this, but your treatment and tolerance of the men on your team is very different to the way you handle the women. As far as your department is concerned, that's your own affair. But as Operation Robert is a joint effort, I cannot allow a case like this to bear any tones of sexism. We are going to have to find a compromise."

"I knew it. Just when I thought we were making progress, you have to score petty points. I presume this is down to Dawn Whittaker? You are determined to punish me for that three-minute indiscretion and just waited for the right moment to raise sexual politics. That's bullshit, Beatrice, and you know it!"

"I am not prepared to discuss what happened between you and Ian Whittaker. That has nothing to do with this case. I assure you, had I never heard about that, my reaction today would have been the same. You treat certain team members differently and it's counter-productive. The atmosphere you created today encourages the nudge, snigger and snort attitude to a situation that apparently disturbs your sleep. I think you need to nail your colours to the flagpole. If you take this seriously, so will your team."

Virginia glared at her and then turned to the white board, apparently studying the data gathered so far. Silence echoed around the room, the change in tempo as unnerving as the shouting.

Virginia spoke. "What are you doing this afternoon?"

"Talking to victims again, with Harrison. You?"

"Calling at Finsbury Park Tube station, talking to security."

"Good. Shall we debrief tomorrow unless something major occurs?" Beatrice stood.

"Sure. Have a good afternoon."

"You too." As she left the office, Beatrice sensed something. A feeling of freshly tilled ground, of ashes and earth, of potential.

Chapter 16

Ray whacked the doors shut and banged home the deadbolts. Jules relaxed. Gorgeous sound. On his way back to the bar, Ray unplugged the fruit machine. Jules switched off the stereo and silence rushed into the space. Even more gorgeous. She loved the peace. Maybe she was getting too old for this game. Ray lined up the remaining empties on the bar and Jules set to stacking them in the glass washer. Neither of them said a word. While that cycle went through, she took the wheelie-bin of empties down the slope to the cellar, rinsing it out and trying to shake the unsettled feeling that hung on her like damp clothes. She'd made a lot of mistakes tonight. Tiredness, partly, but also that staring bloke at the bar. Made her uncomfortable, being watched like that, made her clumsy. He'd gone, eventually. But if he ever came back and did that again, she'd ask him if he wanted a photo.

Ray was restacking the machine when she got upstairs. "Want a drink, Jules? I reckon you earned it tonight."

"Cheers, Ray. But I'm dead on my feet and I got to be back here at eleven tomorrow. How about we have one tomorrow night? I don't have to get up so early on a Sunday."

"Won't say no to that. I'm knackered and all. Listen, how you getting home?"

"Same way as always. Night bus. I got another fifteen minutes, so you want me to mop behind the bar, or what?"

Ray scratched his scalp through its scanty covering of grey hair.

"Tell you what, I want to get some chips for Pam and me, so why don't I give you a lift? You go check the ladies' for me and I'll tell the missus what's going on."

"You sure? It's out of your way." Jules could have kissed his grey-stubbled cheek.

"Yeah, no bother. All the talk about that pervert round the station, you shouldn't be out at this time of night, not on your own. Go on, sort out the bogs and we'll be off."

The ladies' toilet was on the first floor, and it was quite normal for the queue to stretch right across the landing to the top of the stairs at the weekends. Only two cubicles and one was always out of order. Dragging a bin bag from the wall cupboard, Jules pulled on rubber gloves and steeled herself.

After she shoved open the door, she observed the usual shambles. Overflowing bin, wet toilet roll all over the floor, a smell of urine and vomit and a pair of tights left in the sink. Goodnight, ladies. Hauling the worst of the mess into the bag, she nudged open the cubicle doors. More soggy toilet roll and a discarded lip gloss. Not half bad for a Friday night. Some of the things she'd found in there you wouldn't believe. Used condoms, soiled knickers, a bag of courgettes and on one memorable occasion, an unconscious anorexic from Stoke Newington.

"Jules? You done, love?" Ray called up the stairs.

"Just about. It's not too bad tonight." She pulled off the gloves and closed the landing window. Focused on the stubborn catch, her eyes registered the movement on the street just a second too late. Something had retreated into the darkness of the dry cleaner's doorway. She turned off the light and peered out. It was pitch black in that recess. Nothing moved. She gave up and carried the bag downstairs.

"Listen sweetheart, Pam don't want chips, after all. But I'll walk you to the night bus. Like I say, I feel better if I know you're safe, innit?"

His face relaxed into the well-worn grooves of an easy smile.

"You don't have to do that, Ray." But she hoped he would.

"Yeah, yeah. Come on, Droopy Drawers, shake a leg. Pam's doing me a toasted sandwich."

They left through the back door and as they exited the alley onto

Adolphus Road, Jules tucked her arm into Ray's and resisted the urge to look at the dry cleaner's doorway. Ray was still enthusing about his Breville.

"And then I discovered ham, cheese and pineapple. Never looked back. Ray's Hawaiian, I call it. You got a top toastie filling, Jules?"

"I don't really eat them. Bit fatty for me."

"That's half your trouble, innit? If you was to eat a toastie now and then, there might be a bit more of you. You women, always counting the calories, you want to live a little."

As they turned onto Alexandra Grove, a shadow in Jules's peripheral vision caused her to stop. She snapped her head around and stared, convinced she'd seen the peak of a baseball cap ducking into the dark.

Ray stopped. "What?"

"Nothing. Sorry." They resumed walking.

"Jules, love, you can't let yourself get too jumpy. Just keep safe, girl, and don't take no risks. But don't go leaping at your own shadow, eh?"

"Yeah. I know. Just all this stuff makes you a bit … you know. Oh shit, there's the bus. Cheers, Ray, see you in the morning."

Her jazz pumps were useful behind the bar, but essential when running for the bus. She could never have shot across Seven Sisters Road like that in heels. Turned out she didn't need to; there was a small queue which took a while to board. She sat halfway back on the bottom deck, looking ahead at her reflection in the glass. Under the brutal lights, her image was unappealing. Tired, drawn and thin as a rake. How come size eight looked good in magazines, but haggard on her? She turned her attention out the window to see if Ray had gone. No sign of his cardigan-clad shape. The bus closed its doors, before opening them again for one final passenger. Jules almost didn't see him, still gazing down Alexandra Grove after dear old Ray, but as he approached, her skin cooled and she raised her eyes. She looked away instantly, tasting the sour metal of fear. He passed her without a glance and sat somewhere further back.

The baseball cap. She recognised it straight away. The Starer. All night, she'd felt his eyes on her. Not that you could see much of his eyes, with that cap pulled down low. He'd positioned himself on the corner of the bar, so the pillar hid him from sight. But she'd worked there for over a year so she knew where the mirrors were. Reaching up to an optic, she saw him lean so as he could see her. Handing over change for the fruit machine, he watched. Now when some bloke watches you all evening, but leaves without even saying goodnight, it's a bit peculiar. Sometimes they want to ask you out, but can't pluck up the guts. She could understand that. But when someone watches you all night and follows you from outside the pub? She could understand that too. And it frightened her to death.

He was behind her, somewhere. She didn't need to turn; she could feel that cold observation. *Just keep safe, girl.* She was safe on public transport, full of the public. Only when she got off would she be in any danger. She had to make a plan. The glass behind the driver reflected an indistinct image. She saw herself, pressed against the window. Directly behind her, a young Chinese guy, whose earphones emitted repetitive treble tones, sat in his own little world. And two seats back, staring at the back of her neck, him.

Don't get too jumpy. She wasn't. That guy was following her. No question about it. And when she got off, he would follow her home. No way. She wasn't going to show him where she lived. Leave one stop early, but get someone to come and meet her. Slipping her hand into her bag, she located her mobile. No point calling John, he'd be out cold by now. Who, then? Most people were in bed. Quick, Jules, think. You've got seven stops to work something out. Aaron? He'd still be up, but God knows where and who with. Or she could just walk up the front there and tell the driver that she was being stalked. He could take her to the police station.

Her eyes lifted to the reflection in the glass ahead. His cap was pulled down, so all she could see was his chin, and his mouth. She had no idea if he was looking at the glass or at the back of her neck. Neither was good. The Chinese guy rang the bell and stood up, ready to leave at the next stop. Her stalker stood up too. Jules's surprise switched to panic as she watched him slide into the Chinese bloke's spot. Right behind her. She could smell him. He stank. Her shoulders stiffened and her pulse picked up.

The tune to *Sex in the City* bursting into life almost made her lose her grip on the handset. Aaron. Why the hell was that little bugger calling at quarter to one?

"Aaron? Where are you?"

"All right, Mum? You aren't home."

"No shit, Sherlock. Where the hell are you?"

There was a pause. She never normally spoke to him like that, but fear made her sharp.

"Still at the Snooker Club. Thing is, Mum, I've sort of run out of cash. I thought, maybe if you were home, you could jump in the car and come up here to give me a lift."

The Snooker Club. Two stops further on, so they could get the bus back home together. Thank God. Relief and outrage combined to hone her tongue.

"Oh you did, did you? After I've been on my feet from six till twelve, earning some cash to keep us afloat, while you piss it away with your mates. Then you spend everything you've got, can't get home and expect your mother to sort it out. When are you going to learn to wipe your own arse, Aaron? I am so sick of this selfish, ignorant bloody attitude. Nineteen years on and I am still carrying you, you little shit!"

"Mum!"

"I'll be there in under ten minutes and you had better be outside, waiting. Because if I have to come in there, Aaron Michael, you are going to fucking well regret it. I am NOT in the mood for this!" Her teeth were clenched, aware that her speech was directed as much behind her as into the mouthpiece.

"All right, Mum. Jesus! I'll go and stand outside now, OK? And I'm sorry, I really am."

"Talk to the hand, Aaron." She ended the call and clenched her hands to stop them from shaking. She wasn't exactly sure what 'talk to the hand' actually meant, but the way Aaron used it was the equivalent of sticking your fingers in your ears and going, 'Ner ner ner ner'. Pretty much how she felt right now.

The bell tinged, requesting a stop. Her eyes flicked back to the glass. Stalker moved to the door. Jules held her breath, facing forward.

The doors opened, his long coat swung out into the night and he was gone. Jules watched him walk off, just in case. The bus pulled away. He'd gone. He left her alone. Thank God. Thank Aaron.

She was three stops away from her son.

Aaron. Her accidental saviour. And as soon as she saw him, she was going to kick his arse.

Chapter 17

Insomnia isn't always a bad thing, Beatrice thought. Something about the combination of Matthew's company, which inevitably involved fine dining on a Friday night, and a feeling of officially sanctioned disengagement tended to bestow a sense of release, relief and indulgence at the weekend. She always slept far better on Friday and Saturday nights. So what the hell was she doing poring over spreadsheets at five o'clock on Saturday morning?

This guy's following the pattern as if he's read the manual.
Patterns.

She skimmed the skin off her coffee with a teaspoon, took a sip and ran the program again. Dates, times and locations formed an unmistakeable link. And an ugly one at that. Even when the coffee was cool, the results were the same. Beatrice ran it again. One more time, she tried to prove herself wrong.

"Beatrice? What's wrong?"

"Hello, Virginia. I'm sorry to call so early, but I need to ask you a question. Who operates the CCTV cameras at Finsbury Park Tube?"

"The cameras? I don't know. Shit, Beatrice, it's ten to seven. On Saturday. And you want names of the camera operators right now?"

"Not names, although I suspect that will be necessary in time. What I want to know is which organisation is responsible for observing the daily footage of all the British Transport Police cameras in the Finsbury Park area."

"Well, that would be the London Underground and DLR. We share footage with the Met or City of London police when required, but everyday surveillance is carried out by our own people. Why?"

"I see. That's both good and bad news. Look, Virginia, I think I've found something rather disturbing. But I don't want to spoil your weekend lie-in. I can call back later this morning, if you like?"

"How much sleep do you think I'm likely to get after your telling me you've 'found something rather disturbing'? Come on, I'm awake now."

"Very well. I don't suppose you have the case files to hand?"

"Of course I do. They're right here, under my pillow." Virginia's voice was tetchy.

"Sorry. It is a bit early, I suppose. Well, I'm sitting here in front of my computer and I've spotted a pattern ..."

Ninety minutes later, Beatrice allowed herself a small celebration. Exotic fruit, miso soup or a salmon bagel may well do wonders for the mind, but on certain occasions, nothing in the world can beat a bacon sandwich. Large streaky rashers curling and spitting away in the pan. Two thick white slices warming in the toaster, a bottle of HP and the papers waiting on the table. *The Independent* for her, *The Times* for him. The espresso machine gurgled and hissed on the hob. The sunshine, their imminent breakfast and the thought of Matthew still crumpled under the sheets had already elevated Beatrice's mood. But the real reason for optimism was the revelation which had struck her in the wee small hours. They were closing in. She began to whistle.

"Good morning. And thank you." Matthew's hair resembled an unkempt guinea pig, and both pyjamas and slippers were candidates for the bin.

"Good morning." She kissed him lightly and returned to the coffee. "Are you thanking me for the breakfast, or my angelic dawn chorus? Do you want tomatoes?"

"Always. Tomatoes are the civilised person's brown sauce. And the cumulative effect of bacon, fresh newsprint and my loved one whistling Simon Jeffes would make any man happy to be alive." He drew the papers to him and checked the headlines. "Dare I ask why you are so chirpy?"

Beatrice ladled rashers onto bread, shaking off fat, and transferred mugs and plates to the table.

"I've had an idea. *Bon appétit.*" She gave the sauce bottle a hefty whack, dolloping a brown stain across a Warburton's Thickest Slice.

"*Bon appétit* to you too. An idea about what?" He said, cutting plump beef tomatoes onto his plate.

"The case." She placed the sauced slice atop the bacon and pressed down. "I woke up at four this morning, put together a spreadsheet and proved myself right." She took a large, satisfying bite. A superlative sandwich: classic, comforting and containing all the optimism of a Saturday morning.

Matthew poured a glass of pink grapefruit juice and rubbed a hand over his eyes. "Right about what? Spit it out, woman, I want to eat my breakfast."

Beatrice swallowed and smiled. "The women we interviewed gave us some useful information. But the most interesting was the timing. He does nothing for a week, then he attacks. It's every other week. Now in the early stages, it's just one incident. Recently, he's stepped up his activity. But still only every other week. What does that tell you?"

Matthew thought as he drank his juice. "Build-up, I'd say. The man is compulsive and has to expose himself, for whatever reason. He does so, feels temporarily satisfied, and it takes a few days for the itch to return. Also, for fear of capture, he returns to his lair."

"So why two in the same week? Why not save one for the week after?"

"Extra itchy? I'm clueless, Old Thing. Put me out of my misery."

"He can't. For some reason, he only has the freedom to serve his urges on certain weeks. Shift work."

"Oh, I see. A night worker, perhaps? Used to being awake when others are not, spending a week of boredom, possibly fantasising the time away, until finally he is released. Yet unreleased."

"Matthew, you are the most wonderful man I know. If it weren't for your snobbishness about brown sauce, you would have a fine mind. But let's go one step further. He works every other week in a job which enables him to see these women. He studies their habits, learns their routines and then, when he's free to do so, he goes after them. He's never been seen on a CCTV camera, not arriving, not leaving. Tell me, why would that be?"

He dabbed his mouth with a piece of kitchen roll. "This coffee is simply perfect. Better than anything I've ever had in Italy. Right, his habits indicate a study of his environment. You say the only link is the fact the women use public transport. And they are all working-class women, some on the poverty line. Therefore, so is he. He works shifts in a factory of some sort and thus sees these poor females on his journey to or from work. He follows them, selects the ones that he thinks will cause him the least trouble and picks his moment. Do I get a gold star?"

Beatrice popped the corner of her sandwich into her mouth. Matthew's eyes strayed to the broadsheets. She needed him to pay attention.

"How, Matthew? How does he see them? How can he follow them? Why does he avoid all the CCTV cameras?"

"Because ... because he knows where the cameras are?"

Beatrice's smile spread. "Well done. Gold star. So?"

"We're not finished yet? I thought our tradition was to breakfast silently, digesting fine food and fresh press. This morning feels like a boot camp for my brain. You'll suggest jogging next."

"He works shifts, he watches cameras, he plans his attacks. Matthew, I am in no doubt. He works for the British Transport Police. He's one of ours."

His sandwich returned to the plate. "That is a most unpleasant thought."

"Unpleasant. But correct."

"What do you intend to do about it?"

"Last week, he attacked twice. So this week, he's back at work. We have to identify him and set a trap. I spoke to Virginia about an hour ago and we're meeting at ten. I'm sorry, Matthew, but I did warn you. We have seven days to stop him, we can't afford not to."

"I understand. Please don't concern yourself about me. I thought I might say hello to Adrian, see if he fancies a trip to The Wine Academy. They have a course on perfect accompaniments for cheese today."

"Good idea. That'll give you both something to pontificate about for weeks."

Satisfied, Beatrice picked up the other half of her sandwich and opened *The Independent*. Matthew gave a theatrical sigh of relief and started on his breakfast.

Eager to get to work, Beatrice arrived at quarter to ten. Virginia was already waiting, in jodhpur-style trousers with loafers and a flimsy white shirt. She indicated a paper bag on the desk.

"Muffins and cappuccinos. I thought we deserved it. Hope you haven't had breakfast?"

Beatrice inhaled the aromas of coffee and cake. "No one could call one bacon sandwich breakfast. And as I was up with the dark, this is practically elevenses. Have you had thoughts?"

Virginia smiled as she unpacked the breakfast bag. "Yes, a few. First, we need a photo of every man on last week's day shift, to try for a positive ID."

"I agree. And when we know who it is, we have to make him believe we're looking the wrong way. He'll be on nights this week."

"Blueberry or double chocolate?"

"Do you really need to ask?"

"Here." Virginia passed over the cake and coffee. "When you say, 'looking the wrong way', you mean make him think we're following false leads?"

"Exactly. So I think we keep the surveillance pairs, and make some, if not all of them, common knowledge. He knows where they are, and will therefore avoid them. That way we can keep certain routes safe. But the Harrison honey trap stays confidential."

Virginia took a swig of coffee. "Mmm. Good thinking. And if Harrison's route is well away from the surveillance pairs, it will encourage him to ..."

"... to target her. I have a feeling we're closing in. I also have a feeling this is skimmed milk. You didn't ask for skinny cappuccinos, did you?"

"Says the woman with a mouthful of double chocolate muffin. Yes, I did. I also order a Diet Coke with my Big Mac and fries. Don't you?"

Beatrice scowled. "I'm happy to say I have never eaten any such thing. Yes, he's bound to go for Harrison. We must ensure top quality personnel are stationed at Finsbury Park Control Centre. Who's there now?"

Virginia wrapped the uneaten half of her muffin in a tissue and popped it back in the bag. "Ty Grant. I know you're not his greatest fan, but he's actually very sharp. I'd prefer to leave him in place."

"If you have faith in the man, so shall I. But our problem lies in the control room. Can we plant a presence without arousing suspicion? Can we watch the watchers?"

"I'm not sure, but I doubt it. Would you stalk while someone's watching? We need to liaise with senior officers there. This is going to be even more complicated because Finsbury Park is literally on the junction of three policing boroughs. But Hackney is the place to start. That's where most of the incidents have occurred. I'll organise a briefing for key personnel this afternoon."

"Right. And then we should head to Hackney. I'd better make some calls. Thank you for breakfast. But next time, proper milk, please."

Virginia shot her a sidelong look. "Next time, you can get it. Just remember, I cut calories wherever I can."

"Killjoy." Beatrice dialled Finsbury Park Underground Station.

With five BTP staff and one Met officer, including Beatrice and Virginia, personal space became an issue in the London Underground Surveillance Centre. Inspector Kalpana Joshi sat in front of the bank of images, a touch screen at her fingertips. The first BTP officer worked with a headset, answering calls; the other operated the replay suite, reviewing footage. Ty stood behind him, asking occasional questions. Beatrice and Virginia devoted their attention to the Inspector's brusque presentation.

"Right then, from this room, we observe the borough via a hundred and seventy cameras. As you can see, we have five control joystick panels to monitor the Petard cameras. We've also three control panels for fixed views, known as Molynx. The supervisor operates everything via this touch screen, pulling whichever image they need from any one of these forty-four monitors onto the main viewer." She demonstrated by scanning the plethora of images, selecting an angle of the underpass, and dragging it to the enormous display. The clarity startled Beatrice; the size and level of detail was impressive.

"If there's cause for concern, we've got a variety of options. In circumstances such as graffiti artists and wilful damage, reckless behaviour, smoking or mild harassment, we mostly use a 'message from God' – the customer service intercom. Alternatively, we might deploy station staff, especially for drunks or vagrants."

Beatrice asked the obvious question. "What if it's something worse?"

"If we see the incident as more serious, we can deploy officers instantly, or for something such as suspected terrorist activity, we share these images immediately with MICC."

Beatrice glanced at Virginia. "Management Information Control Centre – in our building. These places are the eyes and ears, MICC is the brain."

Beatrice nodded. "Thank you. Do you share your recordings with anyone else, Inspector Joshi?"

She twisted in her seat to face Beatrice, nut-brown eyes raised under dark lashes. "Kalpana, please. Yeah, we got two dedicated computers for communication with other agencies. For example, in an accident scenario, we can share our live footage directly with the emergency services, or traffic management. Law enforcement takes precedence, so if a camera's being used to monitor traffic transgressions, we override that to follow a suspect."

Beatrice leant her head to one side. "I'd like to go back. You mention you have moveable cameras?"

"Correct. Petards."

"Wonderful name. *Pétard* is French for 'joint', but I expect you already know that."

"As in knees and elbows?" asked Virginia.

Beatrice and Kalpana spoke simultaneously. "No, spliffs."

The inspector met Beatrice's eyes and exhaled a sharp snort of laughter. "You ever think you've been in the job too long?"

"Daily. But in my case, it's probably true. Now these Petards are presumably in and just outside the station itself?

"Yeah. Mostly on the concourse and platforms, they can pan right and left, tilt up and down, rotate three hundred and sixty degrees and, crucially, zoom in on detail, such as passing of packages."

"So you have an officer watching these, and another on the fixed cameras?"

"Depends on the time of day. During peak periods, we got one on each. But from two a.m. to six a.m., there's only one. Four people in here during rush hour. Two on these cameras, one on replay, and one on calls."

Virginia looked at the bank of monitors to their right, where Ty bent over the desk. "This replay function – checking for activity around the time of an incident?"

"Amongst other things. Sometimes we need to check footage for Data Protection reasons before releasing it. But much of it is surveillance – who was where at a certain time. We also use it to monitor patterns, especially on football Saturdays. Comes in handy."

"I can imagine," Beatrice said. "And this other chap is taking calls from where?"

"He's operating the hotline. People calling to report incidents, passengers having problems and pressing the help buttons on the platform, not to mention plenty of lazy gits asking for the next bus to Crouch End. A great deal of patience is needed for this task."

"And I bet you get lots of emergency calls which are in fact requests for help?"

Virginia's question made Kalpana smile. "Yeah, course. Dealing with the public. Drives you to tears, doesn't it?"

Beatrice laughed. "Both of desperation and admiration. But it's always bloody hard work. Do you have a quiet room somewhere so the three of us might discuss how best to proceed?"

"Sure. My office. Would your sergeant like to see how this works? Jacek, show the Met sergeant how to use it, would you?"

"Ty, you want to take over now?" Virginia asked.

He nodded and took Kalpana's place at the observation monitors, as the three women made for the door.

Ty grinned. "Mmm, you warmed the seat for me."

Kalpana replied without looking back. "Don't speak to me like that, Sergeant. I find it disrespectful."

Beatrice followed the slight figure from the room, biting her lip and memorising both line and tone.

Chapter 18

Adrian had only popped out to buy stamps, but somehow, he'd purchased a pair of African violets. As he was walking home, deliberating where best to display them, his mobile rang.

"Hello Beatrice. I'm just coming past the Co-op. Do you need something?"

"Actually, Adrian, this is Matthew. I'm calling you on your mobile phone due to the fact that I got no response when knocking at your door."

Adrian dropped his voice. "Matthew! I was wondering when you'd make contact. Has she gone to work?"

"I can barely hear you. What is all that noise?"

"Old Street on a Saturday morning. I'll be back in five minutes. Tea or coffee?"

"Tea, please. I've drunk far too much coffee and feel a little nervous."

"Tea it is. Me too, I can't wait! See you in a bitch."

Hugs seemed inappropriate, so Adrian chose the strong handshake and pat on shoulder routine. Matthew wore his own version of casual. A faded denim shirt, which had the air of real as opposed to faux-faded, paired with downmarket chinos. Fortunately, he'd opted for espadrilles. Adrian approved. Ill-kempt feet were one of summer's horrors, along with flies and cycling shorts.

"Come in! I've made tea and taken it into the office. We may as well get down to business. I thought we'd start by showing you the progress I've made."

"Sounds good to me. When you say progress ...?"

"Come this way and all will be revealed. You'll be surprised by what a knack I have for this sort of thing."

Matthew's fingers drummed on the desk as he studied the screen with a frown.

"One hesitates to jump to the obvious assumption, but does this strike you as possible drug-dealing?"

"Exactly my thoughts." Adrian pulled out a folder with print-outs of the two enlarged photographs. "Two men, I'd say, carrying bags. The first is older and you can see his face. That means he was looking in your direction. The second, with the ponytail, is side-on, looking up the beach. The person waiting to meet them is female, you can tell by her clothes. But there's no chance of seeing her face, her hair's hiding it."

Matthew left the screen with reluctance. But his eyes widened when he saw the photographs. "The ponytail man! That's the burglar, no doubt about it. His hair was unforgettable. This picture is quite startling, I have to say. Much clearer than on the computer. Well done!"

"Well, this level of magnification is down to my knowing the right people. I happen to be friendly with a graphic designer who has sophisticated technology and infinite patience. I'm lucky to have Jared." Adrian sighed. "Now look over here."

He indicated the top left of the picture. The shapes remained in shadow, with an oblique shaft of light hitting the sand in front. Lower, a small rectangle stood out as lighter than the background. Adrian willed him to see the combination for what it was.

"Ever tried the 3D picture books, Matthew? Let your eyes unfocus and then tell me what you see."

"Ah yes. The arrangement of shapes suggests some sort of vehicle. And this must be the number plate. Impossible to identify it, of course, but it's large, like an off-road vehicle, and obviously black. No wonder we can barely see it. So these two come off a boat, carrying two bags, and meet the driver. We're taking pictures, they spot us and try to get the camera back. Whatever is in those bags, they certainly didn't want it on film."

"Drugs." Adrian poured them both a refill from the pot. "What else would it be?"

"Let me see the second photograph."

Adrian handed it over, trying not to show off. All three heads had turned toward the lens and the woman's hand was raised, as if to shield her eyes, or hold back her flailing hair. Whatever the reason, her gesture made her features indistinguishable. Ponytail's rodent expression and the older man's suspicion were visible. Imperceptibly better light threw a clearer perspective on the trio, their boat and their looming vehicle.

Matthew sat back with a satisfied sigh. "Bravo! That is excellent work, Adrian. We can now connect the man who took Beatrice's bag and the camera thief to this figure on the beach."

"But we still have no proof he was the one who stole her laptop."

"Sorry? Did you say 'stole her laptop'?"

Adrian should have known. Being a double agent meant remembering exactly who knew what. And he'd already forgotten.

Matthew accepted the news without fuss. "My only challenge now is acting surprised when she tells me. One can only hope she's too distracted by her serial flasher to notice my lack of concern."

"The only reason she didn't mention it was out of worry for you. I'll vouch for that. I nagged her. Really. We almost rowed."

"Adrian, it may sound sarcastic, as we're going behind her back, but I do believe she has a genuine friend in you. As for the pictures, I'm most impressed! Congratulations on some very astute detective work."

"Thank you! Although the compliment is due more to my persistence and contacts, but what the hell. Grab glory where you can. And after all, what more is there to detective work than dogged opportunism?"

Matthew inclined his head, as if considering the truth of that statement. Adrian fidgeted. Always save the best till last. He rubbed his hands together and smiled.

"There's more?" asked Matthew.

"There is. With a combination of Jared's skill and my creativity, we have a partial ID of the number plate." Tucking his leg beneath him, Adrian passed Matthew a cropped version of the second photograph. In the centre, seven figures or letters were discernible, but rendering them comprehensible could only be guesswork.

"Now, I know it looks hopeless and I just about gave up. But as I left his studio, Jared said the only other thing he could suggest was trying out templates. Imposing letters and numbers over this image and seeing which came closest. Yesterday, I spent the entire afternoon doing just that, when I should have been doing a stock take of European beers. And through a process of trial and error, I think I have it."

He flipped open the file to reveal a sheet of A4, with one typed line in the centre.

CMG287M

Matthew examined it and shook his head. "I have to commend your persistence, but this car is relatively new. It's not possible that it would have such a plate."

"What do you mean?"

"New cars have two letters, denoting region; two numbers, denoting year; and three random letters. So ..."

"Maybe it's a personalised number plate?"

"Would you pay for a plate which read see-em-gee-two-eight-seven ... hang on."

Matthew bent forward, hands forming a triangular screen over his brow. Adrian gave him a moment and took another sip of tea.

"You may just have something here. CM, if that is correct, is the area code for Cardiff. Possible, given the location. G2, or more likely, 62, to identify its age. This car was registered after the first of September 2012. The final three elements should be letters. 87M could be BZM, or N."

Adrian's pride returned. "So I did get it, after all?"

"You did. Or at least, you've given us something to go on. I wonder how we can find out who owns it?"

"Ask Beatrice."

"Beatrice?"

"Of course. Tell her what I've got so far and see if she can trace it. Play it casual, sound a bit bored by my puppyish enthusiasm, but tell her it's worth a try. You don't need to tell her we're actively working this case."

"That's actually a rather good idea. And I have noted the stage directions. What if she finds it?"

"Perhaps, unless you have plans for next weekend, we could sneak off to Wales?"

Matthew's eyes widened and he flashed a most impressive set of teeth. "Certainly possible. I have a seminar in Rome the end of next week, so may just tell her I'm staying on a few days. She's likely to be so busy, she'll barely notice."

Matthew glanced at the photographs once more and his eyes narrowed.

"What is it?" Adrian leant forward.

Matthew jumped to his feet, looking around Adrian's tiny, but perfectly neat office.

"Something I said?" Adrian followed him into the lounge, watching him pace up and down with the pictures.

"The bags they're carrying. Why would you carry something that way? Would you happen to have a holdall? Anything with a handle?"

Adrian considered a moment and retrieved his Tod's leather sports bag from the hall. Matthew took it, with a nod.

"So here I am, leaping off a boat at dawn, with my bag." He jumped onto the cowskin rug. "Now, most folk would carry it thus, arm straight, bag hanging from their hand. However, these two," he jabbed a finger at the pictures, "have their elbows bent, holding the bags higher off the ground. Why is that?"

Recumbent, arms folded, Adrian was unimpressed. "Drugs, yo. Can't afford to get that shit wet, know what I'm saying?"

Matthew eyed him with some bemusement. "Hmm. On the beach? It could be, I suppose. It reminds me of cricketers, or tennis players. How they hold their kitbags, as if they are precious."

"Several kilos of heroin would be pretty precious. And disastrous to get it wet. It's drugs, Matthew. Stop looking for the obscure explanation when the obvious is biting you on the buttock."

"You're right. I wonder where they're coming from? A larger boat out in the bay, perhaps?"

"Bound to be. And with any luck, we'll soon have the details of their dealer. What are your plans for the day?"

"Nothing particular. Pottering over to Persephone's for a browse, organise something for dinner ..."

"Do that first. Then come back here and I'll take you to one of my favourites in old Spitalfields market for lunch. It's my treat and the wine list is an absolute joy. You won't feel like shopping afterwards, I warn you."

"That's an offer I cannot refuse. But is it wise to indulge when you have to be on optimum form for this evening's performance?"

"Believe me, Matthew, a glass or two of Chateau Plince has only ever improved my rendition of *The Surrey with the Fringe on Top*."

"I trust your judgement. Very well. Meet you back here at twelve?" Matthew made his way to the door.

"Perfect. And I'll start packing for next weekend."

Matthew turned. "Adrian, you have a full week ahead of you. Why would you start packing already?"

"The sooner the better. I need to plan the perfect capsule wardrobe, with all the appropriate accessories. Now I've done *Roman Holiday, Death in Venice* and *Leaving Las Vegas*, but I have never done Detecting Drug Dealers in Devon. So it will require some thought."

"It's Wales, not Devon."

"Even better. I'll need to buy a phrasebook and everything. See you later."

Wales. September. He would start with his panama. He rarely wore it in London, not with his linen suit, because the ensemble suggested Hannibal Lecter. But in Wales, that would hardly matter.

Chapter 19

"And she replied, 'Don't speak to me like that, Sergeant. I find it disrespectful'. Didn't even look round. Nor did I, but I'd love to have seen his face."

Dawn shook her head and picked up another piece of sashimi. "He sounds like a total baboon. He and Virginia Lowe deserve each other."

Beatrice couldn't quite agree. "The man is an utter ape, which is why I can't understand her attitude to him. She may be a lot of things, but she's not stupid. It was a glorious moment, though. That BTP Inspector, barely forty, a wisp of a little thing, slapping him down like an impertinent school boy. I could hardly contain myself."

"I can imagine. What about the case? You any closer to nobbling Jack Flash? This tuna smells a bit off, I don't think I'll eat it. Check yours before you ... Beatrice, what is it?"

Her expression had given her away. She marshalled her thoughts.

"It's hard to put into words, but the ... trivialisation of this case is at the heart of the problem. I know you mean nothing by it, but we are talking about a potential rapist, an assaulter of teenage girls. Calling him Jack Flash, or a dirty old man, or in any way diluting the threat of this individual is what allows him to get away with it for so long. Dawn, I'm sorry. I don't mean to get at you, of all people. I suppose I'm just articulating my own change in attitude."

Dawn raised her brows, but looked away. Beatrice took a slice of pickled ginger between her chopsticks and placed it down again.

She made another attempt at explaining. "The thing is, there have been so many of these casual ..."

"Beatrice, it's fine. Eat your food. I agree with you. Listen, Frances did a university project on inter-racial tensions last year. And one phrase from her dissertation leapt out at me and has kind of stuck. 'Micro-aggressions.' Those daily little put-downs, reminders of your place, flexing of superior muscle, you know what I mean? I've suffered from this myself. So have you. Obviously, Frances used it to talk about race."

"An example?"

"OK. You're at the sandwich counter. 'Where are you from?' you ask the white kid who serves you. 'Leytonstone,' he replies and you say you know it well. The next day, an Asian kid serves you. You ask him where he's from. 'Walthamstow,' he says. 'No, but where are you really from?' Subtext: I belong, you don't. It struck me as applicable to so many other situations."

Beatrice chewed over both *maki-zushi* and concept.

"What I'm saying, Beatrice, is that I agree. You can belittle a person, a fear, even a crime by the language you use. The message came across louder still when I worked with abused women. Expressions like: 'a little shake', 'only the back of my hand', and my favourite, 'an affectionate slap'. So I do get it and I'm sorry for being so tactless. I can't even blame the *sake*, as I haven't drunk it yet."

"Well, it's time you did. I apologise for getting snippy with you and I'm glad you appreciate my point. How do you say 'Cheers' in Japanese?"

"No idea. But *Sayonara* means 'goodbye' so that'll do. *Sayonara!*"

Beatrice raised her glass but was interrupted by a loud tut of disapproval. The counter worker continued his rapid chopping, but glanced up at them under his white hat.

"Sort it out, ladies. If you're saying goodbye, fair dos." His accent was pure Gravesend. "But when raising a glass, in Japanese you say, '*Kampai!*' Awright?"

Beatrice gave a respectful semi-bow. "Thank you. *Kampai*, Dawn."

"And *Kampai* to you too." They slugged the *sake*, the warmth hitting Beatrice's cheeks seconds later.

Dawn's complexion rose at the same pace as her smile.

"It works, this stuff, doesn't it?" Beatrice asked.

"No doubt. *Kampai*, I must remember that one. I have to say, this place is an unexpected find. An oasis amid the madness. You should bring Matthew here next weekend –does he like sushi?"

"Most definitely. Even makes it himself. He is a passionate Japanese fan. But next weekend would have been my turn to do Devon." An odd sense of unease slithered down Beatrice's spine, an unpleasant sensation, all the more so for being familiar. She was nurturing a microscopic resentment, prodding it, fanning it and encouraging it to fester.

"Would have been? You have to work?" Dawn asked, with her natural gentle interest.

"I probably will. But he didn't know that. I don't even know myself yet. Nevertheless, he has extended his stay in Rome after the Ostia seminar, 'just to shop and savour the atmosphere of Rome.' And frankly, that whiffs."

"Of what? Having a weekend of self-indulgence? It's his summer holiday, he's entitled. Come on, Beatrice. You must be due some time off. So when you've caught that rotten little shit from Finsbury Park, you can take a break and indulge yourselves together. What's bitten you?"

"Nothing, really. Just being a petulant brat. Tell me about your weekend."

Dawn set her chopsticks on their little china holder and rested her chin on her hand, eyes searching Beatrice's face.

"Leave me alone," muttered Beatrice, staring at her soy sauce. "I have nothing more to say. It's up to him what he does with his weekends." She picked up some sashimi. "Tuna tastes fine to me, you're just being fussy. Oh for God's sake!" She placed her chopsticks down and glared at her friend.

Dawn shrugged. "You may as well cough it up. And I'm not talking about the fish. Why have you wound yourself into a spin about Matthew having a couple of extra days in Rome?"

"Because it is just not like him. His seminar ends on Friday, but he wants to come back on Sunday. Why? He hates Rome in summer. Too hot, packed with tourists and all the restaurant prices go up. He forgets that when he agreed to present his research, he moaned to me for ages about having to go there at all. Now he wants to stay an extra day. And ... he's got a look in his eye. He's excited about something. Or someone."

Dawn rolled her eyes. "You seriously suspect Matthew of having an affair?"

"Lepers don't change their spots."

"Nor do leopards. And how can you, of all people, make such an accusation? Have you shared these thoughts with your counsellor?"

Beatrice swilled her *sake* around the glass. "Not yet. I suppose I should."

Dawn's face creased into an understanding smile. "Or better still, talk to Matthew."

"Perhaps. I'm just afraid of what I might find out. All right. I'll talk to him. It's not healthy just to hypothesise and fret; I can feel myself getting sucked into it all again. You're very good for me. And for the price of a plate of sushi, much cheaper than a session with James. I'm sorry." Beatrice smiled, before returning her attention to her food.

Dawn picked up her chopsticks with an air of satisfaction. "Actually, I'm happy you told me. Friends rarely share their fears regarding infidelity, suspected or otherwise. They must think the subject too painful for The Betrayed Wife. Ian's indiscretion has come to define me, for most people. But not you."

Beatrice studied Dawn's kind, open face. "That's the half-full perspective. It could be that I'm a self-centred, thoughtless drain, who only cares about her own problems."

"Trust you to spin yourself in a positive light. You didn't eat that tuna, did you? How far are we from the nearest A&E?"

Beatrice reached over and helped herself to Dawn's rejected fish. "If I'm having my stomach pumped, I may as well make it worth their while."

Dawn laughed and pinched an Eskimo roll between chopsticks, popping it into her mouth and turning her gaze out at the street. She shook her head in a disbelieving gesture.

"Something wrong?" Beatrice asked.

"No, nothing at all. Good food, great company. Nice little shot of liquor, and yet another amusing haircut for entertainment. Can't complain."

"Nor me. Which haircut?" Beatrice polished off her ginger slices. Somehow orchestral in its refined combination of flavours, one could almost applaud Japanese food.

"This horrible trend toward shaving above your ears, leaving a Davey-Crockett one-length hank from forehead to shoulder blades. You haven't noticed? They're everywhere; men, women and, worst of all, children."

A bell rang in Beatrice's consciousness. Picking up her *sake*, she focused on Dawn. "That night in The Speaker, when I came back from the loo, you said something about haircuts. Do you remember?"

Dawn's smile faded, replaced by a concertina of concentration.

"Oh yes. While you were in there, a guy walked past the window. He spotted me and gave me a wink so I smiled back. He mouthed some words and held his hand like this, you know?" She extended her little finger and thumb and raised her hand to her cheek.

"He wanted your phone number?" Beatrice's incredulity was unmissable.

Dawn didn't seem offended. "Apparently so. I pointed to my ring finger – he couldn't see it from there – and shook my head. He just shrugged and moved on, and I noticed his haircut. Short, dark and almost normal at the front, but at the back, he had a blond ponytail. I'm not keen on ponytailed men at the best of times, but in a different colour? Why would anyone make such a hash of their hair?"

"And do you remember, when you mentioned that, I told you I had a story to tell? More *sake*, or shall we revert to old habits?"

Dawn turned to the counter-chopper. "Do you think we could have two large glasses of dry white wine over here?"

Chapter 20

Onto camera, 7.09 p.m., Blackstock Road. Turquoise mini dress, denim jacket, white heels. Chewing gum. As she waits to cross the street, she pulls her dress further down her thighs, and pushes her hair up at the temples.

Above her, a camera tilts and zooms. Her progress through the station is slick; she's done this before. Oyster card, no hesitation, trotting down the tunnel and onto the escalator. She keeps walking and arrives on the southbound platform just as a Piccadilly line to Uxbridge thunders in. She looks pretty and fresh and expectant. And a bit nervous. Ticks all the right boxes.

In the surveillance van parked at the end of Station Place, Virginia and Beatrice watched the replay of PC Karen Harrison's movements. Current footage from Finsbury Park's Control Centre still streamed onto their system, yet their attention was on images recorded three hours ago.

Five cameras covered each stage of Harrison's route, but the main object of interest was the central screen, which reflected whatever was on the main console at BTP. When the officer in the control room dragged an image onto his main screen, the same pictures popped up in the discreet black van down the street. Watching whatever the watcher watched.

"Girl done good." The officer turned round with a grin.

"She did, Fitch. Some very nice little touches there," Virginia agreed.

"And he watched her from Blackstock Road to the platform. Got a close-up and everything." His face was lit, both by monitors and enthusiasm.

Beatrice smiled back at Fitch. She understood. There were few finer feelings than the first nibble on the bait.

Virginia seemed satisfied. "Check the record sheet for timings and find out exactly who was on the console. Double check there were no last-minute changes to the rota. And I want you to do the same after her return journey. Good work, PC Fitzgerald."

"Don't thank me, ma'am. It's Harrison wants thanking." His smile remained in place while he replaced his earphones and returned his attention to the screens.

"Should we get into position, Beatrice? It's ten to eleven. She'll be on her way back soon."

Somerfield Road, a residential street of Victorian terraces, remained quiet although it was just gone chucking-out time. Their unmarked BMW, with tinted windows, fitted in perfectly with its surroundings. Listening to the updates on the police radio, the two women sat in attentive silence, until confirmation came – Harrison had boarded a northbound train from Leicester Square. Her job was to give the impression of someone who'd spent the evening dancing and drinking an excess of Smirnoff Ice.

In reality, the girl's evening had been slightly more pedestrian. On arrival in Leicester Square, she had entered All Bar One, met a second officer in the toilets, changed her clothes and trudged down to Charing Cross Police Station, where she had spent three hours watching TV and drinking coffee. The reality of police work. Waiting. Watching and waiting and trying not to fall asleep. Dull diligence.

Virginia let her head fall backwards. "So we've got around half an hour before we're likely to get a visual. God, I wish I still smoked."

"No, you don't. Concentrate on staying alert for Harrison, picking up every detail and in about an hour, we can go home to our beds."

"Yes. Hold that thought. Bed, duvet, cat. I am exhausted. What have I done today? Push papers. But now, on the street, in the middle of the action, I'm knackered and I want to go home."

Beatrice could sympathise. This week had been stressful for all of them, and as the weekend approached, signs of strain affected the whole team. Time was ticking away. In two more days, their man would become active again. She rubbed her face; her eyes were drooping. Small wonder: she'd been awake since four. Best thing would be conversation.

"It's because you know nothing will happen tonight. He's at work, so he can't do anything. But we have to be wide awake, just in case. What's your cat's name?"

"Tallulah. A bad-tempered Burmese. You have creatures?"

"No. But the lack of four-legged, or even two-legged creatures makes my bed no less appealing. In some ways, it makes it more so."

Neither spoke, matching words with impressions.

The radio continued its chatter and Grant's voice confirmed all was calm at BTP Control Centre, everyone working their designated shift.

"From what I hear, we're in a similar position," Virginia said, folding her arms.

"In what way?"

"The men way. We both have a permanent partner, who is absent for most of the time. Or have I been misinformed?"

Beatrice considered how much she wanted to share. As a rule, she kept her private life ring-fenced and off limits.

"Yes, I suppose you're right. Although I would express it differently. My partner and I spend weeks apart, and weekends together. 'Absent' smacks of neglect. Our arrangement is very much a mutual choice."

"You're lucky. Our arrangement is very much a mutual 'no choice'. My husband works for BAE Systems and he's based in Dubai. When we married, we both assumed the other one would give up the job. I thought a London lad, with a wife and home here, would be desperate to come back. He couldn't see why I would want to continue working when I could live the luxury life of the expat housewife. He doesn't want to stop working. Nor do I. So we see each other for two weeks every quarter. Plus the odd holiday and occasional weekend."

"Hence the cat."

"Tallulah and I were together long before I met Stewart." Virginia turned to Beatrice with a laugh. "He's a dog person."

"Oh dear."

"No, it's actually fine. It's just … on paper, we shouldn't work. He's younger, by nine years. He's serious, hard-working and loves being alone. I'm frivolous, feckless and can't be without company. He likes white, I like red; I fancy beefcake, he has a concave chest; he's attracted to large breasts, I'm a 32A. But the thing is, with him, I'm totally relaxed. He makes me laugh, in person, on screen, on the phone, and I miss him all the bloody time."

"Well, that *is* a surprise," Beatrice responded. "I'd have put you at 34B easily."

Virginia snorted with laughter and gave her a sideways glance. "Well, that's me in the spotlight. Your turn."

"Would you feel terribly short-changed if I didn't volunteer my bra size?"

Virginia made a mock-disappointed face.

"My story is simple and rather dull. Matthew and I have been together over twenty years and prefer to live apart. He has two daughters from a previous marriage, and one grandson. I've never been married, have no offspring and no regrets about it. Our relationship is based on room for independence, not to mention trust. And it has always worked terrifically well."

The radio crackled, and Beatrice checked the time. Harrison should be approaching the Tube station now.

"I sense a 'so far' in that statement?"

Beatrice could go no further without a lesson in her personal history. "It's complicated. Can I ask a question?"

"On your behalf, or Dawn Whittaker's?"

Her defensive tone surprised Beatrice. Seemed like events at the award ceremony had left a bitter taste in several mouths.

"Mine. I'm curious. Where does Ty Grant fit into the picture?"

Virginia's face hardened and she looked ahead. "He doesn't."

"I see." Beatrice faced front. "Fair enough."

Virginia slid her fingers up her face, dropping her forehead into her palms.

"Look, it's the opposite of complicated. A bit of a flirtation, harmless way of passing the time. I'm not interested in Ty. I just get ... bored, you know?"

"Does Ty see it as a harmless pastime too?"

Virginia's head swivelled. "He hasn't said anything, has he?"

"To me? Good God, no. I just wondered if both sets of expectations were equally innocent."

Virginia checked her watch and sighed. "No, Ty is trying to push it further. And I really like the guy. He's exactly my type, but ..."

The radio hissed and distorted, before informing them they were about to get a visual on Harrison.

The street was silent as the poor girl maintained her persona right to the door of 'her flat'. Stopping, swaying, almost tripping over, she looked like someone whose judgement was suspect, whose coordination was clumsy and whose radar was down. An excellent performance. Once inside, she could change, rest and enjoy the weekend. Because the following week she'd be doing it all over again, with every expectation of being followed by a pervert. She made it without mishap, and staggered inside. A faint round of applause came from the watching teams over the airwaves.

Virginia turned the ignition. "I'll drop you home."

The usual stop-start journey though London became slightly smoother once on Green Lanes. Beatrice picked up the handset, announced the end of the evening's activities, wished the team a good weekend and switched the radio to its usual frequency. Virginia drove without a word. As the BMW approached Newington Green, Beatrice chose to speak.

"Virginia, I believe our earlier conversation was one-sided. I'm sorry if I offended you and I didn't mean to interfere in your private life."

"Yes, you did. But it's all right. I often think we're hard-wired to winkle out the truth. We're trained detectives, but much more significantly, women. Look, I was doing exactly the same thing, asking you if your relationship had worked well 'so far'. Your interview technique was better, that's all."

"Thank you. And you were right, in fact. I've always been wholly truthful with Matthew, about everything, good and bad. Now, for the first time in years, I find myself tempted to … how can I put it?"

"Stray?" Virginia's focus remained on the street.

"No. Not to stray. To exclude him. I want to do something, chase something, and I should tell him about it. It could be a risk, but that is precisely why I want to keep it to myself. And, well, I suppose a small part of me wants to show him that I'm not quite past it yet." The truth had a habit of sneaking up on her recently.

"I get that. A small part of me wants to prove the same thing. Although I know I'd rather be with Stu than anyone else."

Beatrice took a deep breath. "Forgive me for speaking out of turn. Let's ignore the fact that you're Ty's boss, that no police romance ever stays hidden, that you're married, that any encounter would cover him in laddish glory while seriously jeopardising your career. None of that is relevant. However, listening to you talk about your husband, I'd say you've been lucky enough to marry your best friend. The risk of losing that could never be worth a mess of porridge."

Virginia remained silent.

Along Balls Pond Road, the atmosphere relaxed. Beatrice looked out at shuttered shops, bright kebab joints, cabbies yelling and the usual flow of humanity kissing, cursing, laughing, pissing, crying, swearing, hugging and fighting. A wave of dismay crashed over her.

That's all any of us have: each other. And what a shifting, unreliable, inconstant place to bury the treasure of your hopes. Of your love. You'll probably never find it again. Some bugger will dig it up and nick it.

Virginia's voice shook her from her spiral. "And you? Chucking away twenty years of bliss for some self-determined goal? I suppose you'll go all gnomic on me if I ask you what it is. What dragon you're trying to slay, all on your own?"

Beatrice sat up. "Where are we?"

"Kingsland Road. Why, is it a long story?"

"No. But it should keep you entertained till we hit Old Street."

"Right then. I'm sitting comfortably. You may begin."

Chapter 21

Adrian met Matthew at Paddington Station with nothing more than eager anticipation and a perfectly packed Tod's holdall. It was only one day, after all. London could manage without him. Armed with Beatrice's email, they were following up a concrete lead.

Well done on the registration. You were only one letter out. DVLA confirmed it's a car hire company in Cardiff. Details below. So looks like the SUV might be a dead-end. Thanks anyway. B x

No such thing as dead ends. On the phone to Williams Car Hire, Matthew did an excellent impression of Beatrice's boss. And the rest was like taking candy from a baby. Williams Car Hire provided the name Marie Fisher as the renter of the Jeep Grand Cherokee with those plates over the Bank Holiday weekend. Fifteen minutes of research on the Internet gave them Ms Fisher's address, phone number and employer – Bevan and Gough Property Management, 56 City Road. Adrian and detective work really did seem to be a match made in Heaven.

Both men had agreed. The train was by far the most relaxing option. Matthew loathed driving anywhere more crowded than Much-Middling-in-the-Marsh, or wherever it was he lived. And Adrian, blissfully, had no licence. Not forgetting the lack of stress, the buffet car and the opportunity to discuss interrogation techniques. Matthew had treated them to First Class tickets and Adrian found himself whistling the *Poirot* theme tune as they located their seats. He stopped as soon as he realised. Apart from the lack of subtlety, whistling was second only to smoking for causing wrinkles on the upper lip. First Class proved to be an excellent choice. They enjoyed a table to themselves and the carriage was practically empty, apart from two businessy sorts absorbed in the Financial Times. Both wore suits and ties and frowns.

"Two hours. What say you to a nice read of the paper, get some breakfast and then knuckle down to making some decisions on technique?" asked Matthew.

"Very well, my friend. Can't expect the little grey cells to function on an empty stomach," Adrian replied. Matthew gave him a baffled look, but unfolded *The Times* with a nod.

On arrival at Cardiff Central Station, the two men were ready to stretch their legs, so chose to walk to their destination. Their route took them right through the city centre.

Cardiff intrigued Adrian. Gorgeous arcades, a proper castle smack in the middle, pedestrianised shopping streets, outdoor cafés and every kind of store you'd find in a half-decent London suburb. But so much more space. Wide streets and lots of sunshine. He might well consider coming back here. Two hours on the train. It was time Jared saw something more of Britain than London's East End and Old Compton Street.

Bevan and Gough's premises looked more like a car showroom than an estate agent. Double windows displaying photographs and hyped descriptions of local property obscured the interior, where presumably welcoming faces waited behind desks. The prices came as a real surprise to Adrian. Directly to his left was a beautiful Docklands flat, with a divine view, kitchen/diner and no less than two bedrooms for something approaching affordable. It wasn't beyond the realms of possibility that he could get a transfer to Wales. Downshifting. Living in a smaller city, he'd buy a bike and even get a dog. Jared could set up his own business in one of those glorious arcades, and on Saturday mornings they could shop for organic Welsh produce with their black schnauzer, called ....

"Adrian?"

Matthew gestured for him to go first and they entered the shop.

A heavily made-up blonde looked up. "Morning, gentlemen. Seen something you like?"

Adrian gawped at the Max Factor mask in front of them, while Matthew responded with his effortless grey gravitas. "Good morning. Unfortunately, we're not interested in property. We're from Williams Car Hire, Head Office. Looking for a Marie Fisher?"

Adrian caught the head to his right pop up. Dark, medium-length hair, sharp features. She might easily be the woman from the beach.

The blonde's interest waned. "Marie? Some blokes to see you from the car hire place." She returned to her computer screen. Adrian could swear he saw playing cards reflected in her glasses.

Marie approached them, hand extended, eyes suspicious. Adrian made constant mental notes on body language, hair, shoes and mannerisms. 'Every detail matters.' Beatrice had drummed that in more times than she'd cooked him hot dinners. So, Marie Fisher – thirtyish, crows' feet and hints of a growing-out dye-job. Expensive nails, good shoes, and those earrings weren't cheap. She put herself together well.

Matthew shook her hand with a reassuring smile. "Ms Fisher. My name is Michael Bryant, and this is my colleague, Andrew Ramos."

Adrian smiled, more at the thrill of hearing his new alias than social convention, and shook her hand. Matthew continued, offering his business card, which Adrian had designed and printed two nights ago.

"We work for Williams Car Hire, Head Office. Andrew and I investigate any problems resulting from our rentals, the objective being to sort it ourselves. Pembrokeshire police contacted us, regarding an incident near Porthgain a few weeks back. We generally prefer to make direct enquiries about incidents involving our vehicles and avoid adding to the police burden, if we can. Is there somewhere we could talk?"

"Oh I see. Right so, follow me. We've a staff area out back."

She'd swallowed it. He restrained a temptation to nudge Matthew.

Marie was Irish. No doubt at all. Adrian's skill with accents was legendary and this woman was watered-down Irish. Very interesting. The back yard contained two cars, half a dozen white plastic chairs and a dirty table with a pockmarked ashtray advertising Brains Bitter. Marie placed coffee cups in front of them. Adrian took one sip and held back a grimace. She dug in her bag for cigarettes, before politely offering the packet. They both refused.

"So you said this incident happened in Pembrokeshire?" she asked, lighting up.

Matthew opened his file, keeping it tilted to him. Very smart. Adrian watched Marie's eyes focus on the back of the folder.

"Correct. On the twenty-seventh of August, a couple of holiday-makers were involved in an early morning bag-snatching incident on the cliffs near Porthgain. They reported the theft to the police and gave them the possible number plate of a utility vehicle they believe was involved. The police traced the vehicle to us and asked us to confirm the identity of the renter. The couple involved were older and not sure they recalled the number plate correctly. We grabbed the chance of running our own investigation. You know, find out if there's any substance, before handing over the details. We're not keen on being involved in any criminal proceedings as you can imagine, so if we can prove it was not one of our vehicles, so much the better for all of us."

Adrian piped up. "Our files tell us you hired the black Jeep Cherokee with those plates from the twenty-seventh to the thirty-first."

Marie's eyes slid from Matthew to Adrian and back again. "I see. So you want to know where I went that weekend. It was the Bank Holiday, wasn't it? Looks like I can help you out. I did hire a car that weekend, for a trip to Snowdonia. A group of us met up on Friday and headed to the mountains for some camping, climbing and a bit of off-roading. The weather was grand and I drove us back down on the Monday evening. Returned the Jeep on Tuesday. When exactly was the accident in West Wales?"

"Saturday morning, very early. Just after sunrise."

"When I was still curled up in my sleeping-bag in Dolgellau. There has to be a mistake, Mr Bryant. Could the elderly couple have misremembered the car at all?"

Matthew nodded and turned to Adrian with a smile. "That's what we were hoping to hear. It's bad for business, our cars being used in illicit activities. So if this Jeep wasn't involved, that's good news for all of us. Do you have a name of the campsite, or anyone who can confirm that you were there, Ms Fisher?"

"Now there's a question. I can't recall the name of the site, but several people will tell you I was there. Would you like me to email you their names and contact details?"

"You couldn't just write them down for us now?" asked Adrian.

Her frown twitched. "I've already taken ten minutes away from my desk to answer your questions. Now I'll need a while to check my diary. I'm keen to help, but as you can see, I'm at work. I'll send you anything relevant, but it might be tomorrow."

Adrian squinted at her, quite deliberately. Her behaviour seemed very defensive for a person with nothing to hide. She returned his look with an enquiring twist of her head. Matthew's voice was soothing.

"That's kind of you, Ms Fisher. It would help us a great deal if you could. Now, we shall keep you no longer. Thank you for your time and the coffee. We'll make our own way out. Have a pleasant day and thank you."

As they exited the shop onto City Road, Adrian let rip.

"What crap! 'Time to check my friends' details?' Total bullshit. Time to set up some fake email accounts, more like. Does she think we were born yesterday?"

Matthew raised a finger for silence. He led the way up the street before shoving open the doors of the first pub they came across. Adrian checked over both shoulders before following him inside. You could never be too careful. While Matthew ordered two glasses of wine, Adrian sat at a quiet table by the window, disgusted by how a person could tell such a blatant lie without shame.

Matthew placed the glasses on the wobbly table. "Adrian, I agree with you. But we're powerless in this situation. We can't challenge her and she knows that. However, we can rattle her a little." He checked his watch and the blackboard above the bar. "Let's drink these and have some lunch here. After that, we'll give her a call. Now for a toast. For our first interview, we did rather well, I think. Cheers!"

Adrian lifted his glass. "Cheers. *You* did rather well. Very smooth, the way you tossed off our pseudonyms. I almost believed you. All I was good for was staring."

"Taking in all the little things, you mean. Your observations will be invaluable, I have no doubt. As Beatrice always says, the devil is in the detail. Tell me what you saw."

Adrian clasped his hands and crossed his legs, rewinding his impressions.

"Marie Fisher is Irish, in her early thirties and very well-groomed. The shoes looked Lanvin to me. The suit was Phillip Lim. No question. Jewellery, hard to pin down. Her watch, did you see? Omega, rose gold. But those earrings ... I can't be sure. Her handbag was Hermès. She takes excellent care of her nails, has quite good skin for a smoker and I'll bet she's got a hair appointment booked in the next week. Her roots need attention. She also wears a touch too much *Angel* by Thierry Mugler."

Matthew, clearly concentrating hard on Adrian's words, shook his head.

"Adrian, whilst competent in Italian and Greek, I cannot speak Fashion. Could you translate?"

Sitting there in the dusty sunlight, hair overgrown, trousers a few centimetres short, and wearing a jacket rarely seen outside a faculty office, Matthew didn't need to state his lack of street-style to Adrian. It would be such a treat to take him shopping, but he suspected Matthew would rather visit the dentist.

Adrian explained. "She's an estate agent. She earns what, twenty-five, thirty grand a year? Her handbag costs a month's salary. The watch would be more. She dresses like a woman who earns twice as much."

"Good God. You see, I'd never have picked up any of that. All I noticed was she smelt of cake." Matthew tasted the wine. "And she was a bit prickly when you asked for details right there and then."

"That's what I thought. But of course she was bound to get stroppy, because she can't prove she was in Estonia."

"Snowdonia. It's in North Wales."

Adrian shrugged. There was a limit to his enthusiasm for the provinces. A thought arose. "We could call the car hire people and see if she brought the car back all muddy! If not, she was obviously lying!"

Matthew replaced his glass with a nod. "For a standard pub, that's a reasonable Antipodean Chardonnay. Yes, we could try the Williams people again, but two things trouble me about taking that tack. Firstly, do they keep records on exterior conditions of their vehicles on return? Naturally, damage would be noted, but mud? Secondly, this firm have no idea why they keep getting calls from the 'police' regarding one of their vehicles. They may decide to be less helpful if constantly pestered."

Adrian could not help himself. Despite his annoyance at Matthew's lack of enthusiasm, he acknowledged the tactful way he rejected the idea and found himself smiling at his diplomatic associate. His wine glass was slippery with condensation as he raised it to his lips.

"Mmm, actually, you're right. Heavy on the vanilla, but it's an acceptable background wine. How exactly do you plan to rattle her?"

"I thought we might phone her, and ask her if it's convenient to pop back at five o'clock. Put her under a bit of pressure and see how she reacts. We're likely to get no real confirmation from her 'friends'. So we could prod her a little, observe her response. That might give us some idea of whether she's worth watching."

"Good plan! And I'll go and stand on the street, but the other side. No one will notice me and I can observe what she does. I'll be discreet, honestly. I'll even wear my panama."

Matthew sighed. "You're really rather enjoying this, aren't you?"

The other side of City Road was absolutely hopeless. Even without the constant inconvenience of passing traffic, Adrian couldn't see enough of the interior of Bevan & Gough to differentiate individuals. Removing his jacket and drawing down the brim of his hat, he crossed the street and examined the pictures. His eyes refocused from the details of a two-bedroomed terrace in Splott to his own reflection in the glass. His stylish appearance struck him. The white shirt and panama hinted at a youthful Pierce Brosnan, a look he could grow to like. He concentrated and casually gazed beyond the photographs, deeper into the shop, locating Marie Fisher's desk. It was empty. He scanned the room. Five other occupants: two men, the blonde, and an older woman talking to a customer. Marie must be on a break.

The blonde picked up her phone, listened for a second and shook her head. The conversation was brief. She hung up and presumably went back to playing Patience.

Adrian abandoned his post and strode back towards the pub. Matthew wandered outside, looking vague and tapping his thumb against his chin.

"She's not there, is she?"

Matthew's eyes locked onto Adrian's with an intense stare, followed by a smile.

"No, she's not. Gone out for lunch. So I announced myself as Williams Car Hire, and the young lady was positively rude and told me to stop pestering Marie. Apparently Ms Fisher has already cancelled the rental she'd booked for next weekend, as she was dissatisfied with our service. She's already arranged a vehicle from another company."

His stare bored into Adrian, as if he was trying to communicate a hidden message. Adrian thought.

"But that means ... she's ... if she was ..."

Matthew's smile broadened. "Our timing seems rather fortuitous. On the last Bank Holiday weekend, I think she drove to Pembrokeshire. I think she met some people on the beach in the early hours of Saturday morning. I think one of them used her car to try and retrieve our camera. And I have a very strong suspicion that her destination next weekend will be the same."

Hairs stood up all along Adrian's forearms. "My God! This could actually be it! We should go. Get to that beach, hide, wait, and see what happens! Oh my God!"

"My thoughts precisely. I'm glad you have such a sense of adventure, Adrian. We'll have to come up with a reason for our absence on two successive weekends, but I believe we are onto a lead. Now, what do you think? Ought we to head back to London? I had plans to visit an ex-student of mine in Chelsea this evening and arrive on Sunday as arranged. But it occurs to me that we could hire ourselves a vehicle and poke about a bit in Pembrokeshire instead. What say you?"

"Poking, no question. But you know I can't drive."

"No matter. I'll get behind the wheel, you can navigate. Where might we find a copy of the Yellow Pages, do you think?"

"You can locate the nearest car hire company on your phone."

Matthew's expression was dour. "I don't have a mobile phone. I telephoned Ms Fisher from the call box in the pub."

Adrian shook his head in disbelief. The Man That Time Forgot. He snatched an opportunity.

"Right. I'll find us a car and after that, we're going shopping. If we're planning a stakeout next weekend, we'll need the appropriate gear. Trust me, I'm good at this sort of thing."

As he turned his attention to his screen, he caught Matthew's expression of alarm. A twinge of worry nagged at him, too. Nothing to do with finding something stylish in black, but more to do with their planning a trip to a remote Welsh beach to spy on drug traffickers. For the first time since the investigation began, Adrian missed Beatrice; her presence, her good sense and her natural caution. And worse, this was his first free Saturday night in ages. What the hell was he going to tell Jared?

Chapter 22

The dread of a bleak and cheerless weekend had built up for days. Beatrice knew she would be unable to stop working herself into a state. Worried about Hamilton's scrutiny of her performance, fearful of more women suffering sexual harassment, afraid of having missed something vital in her casework, haunted by imaginings of what Matthew might be doing and with whom, and feeling generally lonely, negative and neglected. Even Adrian had plans for a weekend away with his boyfriend and she couldn't face calling James. Dismal.

Instead, she leapt out of bed at seven o'clock. She should have been exhausted. She'd stayed up till half past one, drinking red wine, batting around ideas with Virginia. It was all most out of character. But her colleague's enthusiasm, intelligent analysis and voluntary assistance last night had buoyed Beatrice enormously. To such an extent that this morning she belted out some Carole King in the shower.

At ten o'clock, Virginia would pick her up and they would drive to Wales, to investigate something which could be nothing. She had to be back by Sunday afternoon, as Matthew would return to spend the week in London. Compensation for missing the weekend. And she would find time for a conversation with him, a truthful conversation in which she voiced her fears. A little break and a change of scenery would do her good. Cardiff and Pembrokeshire on a sunny weekend. Beatrice's spirits were fairly bubbling.

Passing the exit for Chippenham, the Volvo XC60 overtook a National Express coach at 80mph, before returning to the left hand lane and slowing to the speed limit. Driving with smooth skill, Virginia made cheerful conversation, proposing theories and picking holes in them, offering opinions on music, news items and other people's driving. Far nicer than the train, it had to be said. No one could call it an attractive vehicle, but the inside was undoubtedly comfy. From her elevated position in the passenger seat, Beatrice could observe the scenery and other road users, yet her attention kept returning to the same cyclical worry loop.

If Matthew found out what she was up to, he would be hurt and disappointed. Adrian might be even worse, particularly as he was the one who had discovered the number plate. And she'd also lied to her counsellor. James asked her if she planned to tell Matthew, and with blithe confidence, she'd assured him she would. It was foolhardy, rushing off to Pembrokeshire on a whim. She should be at home, or in Finsbury Park Control Centre, protecting the public. She released a heavy sigh. Nothing was going to happen. She had Virginia with her and all they intended to do was take a look around. Their sex offender could do no harm either, as his shift would be working over the weekend. Until Monday, women of North London were safe. From him, at least. Another huge sigh escaped her.

Virginia glanced across at her. "What do you say, should we stop at Leigh Delamere? Or press on a bit?"

"I'd prefer to get over the bridge before stopping. I'm keen to get to Wales. Perhaps we could stop in Cardiff? Have some lunch and do the car hire firm today?"

"We could do, but I think it might work better the other way round. Pembrokeshire first and the car hire firm on Sunday. Everything will be open in the holiday village today, so we can ask around the shops and cafés. But everything will be shut on Sunday. Whereas the car hire people will be busy and resent our intrusion on a Saturday. If we leave it till tomorrow, it'll be staffed by a couple of bored teenagers, who'll fall over themselves to give us any information we want. What do you think?"

"Good thinking. So Pembrokeshire first. In that case, you should take a break when you're ready. You're the driver."

"Oh, I'm fine. I love driving, always have. I passed my Advanced Driver's Test before I even joined the force. That's how much I enjoy being behind the wheel."

Beatrice twisted to look directly at her. "I wondered about doing that test. Hamilton offered me ADT training, but I turned it down. Seems it's not all about car chases, so I confess it looked rather dull."

"Not at all. It increases your awareness of potential hazards, teaches you more about vehicle handling and there is a small element of managing high-speed pursuit. But you learn to be more interested in bins than flashing blue lights."

"Bins? Is that some sort of euphemism?"

Virginia laughed. "No, I mean rubbish bins. For example, you're following a suspect through Chiswick. It's a residential area, you're trying to keep your target in sight, but you need to be aware of what else is going on. Tunnel vision is your enemy. So you notice that there are wheelie bins on the pavement. And you make the connection. If there are bins, there will be a bin lorry. You are prepared to come round the corner and find a bin lorry blocking your path, or oncoming vehicles overtaking it. You heighten your sensitivity to your environment. You do drive, Beatrice?"

"Rarely. I live in London."

"What about if you move from London?"

"If that were to happen, I'd start driving again, I suppose. Or more likely leave it to Matthew. Sorry, Virginia, I know I keep reverting to the same subject and I'm even boring myself. I've just got a real bean in my bonnet about lying to him."

Virginia switched off the radio and one of Beatrice's low-level irritations ceased instantly. God, she was getting old, but really, was there anything more annoying than radio phone-ins? Wasps, perhaps.

Checking the mirror, Virginia indicated and pulled out past a horse-box. "So tell him. Play it down, you're just looking around, no cause for concern, but you've been honest."

"I think I just might. He's due back from Rome tomorrow, so I'll drop it casually into conversation while he's telling me about the seminar. No big deal."

"Good timing." Virginia nodded. "His head will be full of whatever it is Roman scholars talk about at such events. Now you and I can concentrate on digging around West Wales with a clear conscience. Blending in with the tourists and looking normal."

The chances of that were slender, as Virginia's black sleeveless dress and white blonde hair made for a dramatic image. Such a striking woman would always turn heads. All blending would be down to Beatrice.

Porthgain's tiny population was swollen with tourists, so it came as a relief to strike out on the coastal path towards the beach. Having inspected the spot where the photographs were taken, the pair made their way along the sands to the opposite end.

The beach could not have looked more innocent. Families picnicked behind striped wind-breaks, children splashed in the surf, and further up the beach, a group of teenagers posed and smoked on the rocks. Beatrice, shoes in hand, allowed ripples of surf to wash over her toes, feeling the shifting grains beneath her feet. Virginia handed over her bag and sandals, hitched up the hem of her dress and waded out to thigh level.

"There is a sudden drop a bit further out," said Virginia, splashing her way back. "Ideal for bringing a boat as close as possible to the beach. All you have to do is moor it, jump off and walk up to meet your mate with the wheels."

"How would you moor it? There's only sand here."

By way of response, Virginia pulled her dress up over her head. Underneath, she wore a black one-piece swimsuit. No gold embellishments, no halter neck fastening, no cutaway peepholes. For Virginia, it was surprisingly functional.

"That's what I was wondering." She rummaged in her canvas shopper, bringing out goggles and a towel. "I'll go and have a closer look."

She handed Beatrice the towel, adjusted her goggles and plunged without hesitation into the Welsh waves. Beatrice, dressed and dry in midday sunshine, gave a sympathetic shiver. She walked in the opposite direction and compared the overgrown access lane to the photograph in her hand. It must have been built for launching boats. Less used nowadays, but awfully convenient. She turned back to the sparkling surf, glad of her sunglasses.

Hair sleek as a peroxide seal, Virginia walked back up the beach, dripping wet. Beatrice proffered the towel and an enquiring look.

"Thanks." She rubbed her face and wound the towel around her body. "There's a concrete block out there. It's lying on the bottom, with an iron ring embedded. There's a rope, too. One end tied to the ring, the other tied to a plastic bottle, which floats on the surface, so you can find it easily. It seems our friends use this spot pretty often. Did you see anything up there?"

"Not much. There's a hard standing at the bottom of the lane, presumably for vehicles to unload boats. That's where the driver must have parked. It would be useful to walk up the lane and see where it comes out. When you've finished, Little Mermaid."

"I've finished. And The Little Mermaid has red hair and a far larger chest. Jessica Rabbit with a tail."

Beatrice suppressed her amusement at Virginia's choice of imagery. "Should we head back to the car?"

"Let's walk while I dry off. Then we should find somewhere to eat."

"Good idea. I suggest we head for The Clipper Inn. Firstly, because we can make discreet enquiries about ponytail man. And secondly, because they do excellent fish. Sea air gives me a terrific appetite, you know."

Virginia towelled her hair and picked up her shoes. She turned to scan the sea. "So it looks like they sail in here, transfer the stash in the dark and sail back to wherever they came from. What we need here is regular surveillance." Her eyes ranged over the cliff top.

Beatrice followed her gaze. "My point precisely. But can I get the local force to listen?"

"To be fair, they may not have the resources. You'd need a pair of officers on open-ended night shifts."

Beatrice remained unconvinced. "Hmm. Perhaps." They picked their way up the lane, heat shimmers suggesting tarmac at the top. Beatrice stopped. "Hang on, if that block was put there for the boat people's convenience, how can they be sure no one would find the plastic bottle and the rope?"

"Look." Virginia indicated the strand stretching away from them. Most people had congregated near the central section, where the shore dropped away gradually, where there were fewer rocks and no shade. In contrast, the shadow of the cliff loomed over their end of the beach, clusters of seaweed littered the sand and the water crashed against outcrops of stone.

"It's not the most appealing part of the beach for holidaymakers, but it's certainly convenient if you want to land some light cargo. That plastic bottle is far enough out not to attract attention from rock-poolers. And this is not what I'd call a popular beach. What was that noise?"

"Possibly my stomach rumbling. Come on. I want fish and chips. I'm starving."

Virginia slipped her feet into her sandals. "Me too. Well, fish and salad, at least."

The long, hot walk from the beach was bad enough. But the increasingly frustrating wait for a table and the delay in service due to the number of tourists put Beatrice into such a foul temper, she felt the weekend would be irrecoverable. However, after they were eventually seated, her bonhomie was restored by a large plate of battered haddock, perfectly cooked chips and fresh garden peas, accompanied by a dry German white. The crowds thinned as they ate, and by the time the waitress cleared their plates, the pub had returned to a small, friendly local. Beatrice spotted the landlord sitting at the bar, chef's tunic unbuttoned, with a newspaper and pint of ale, and seized her moment.

"Sorry to bother you, especially after such a hectic session. I just wanted to extend my compliments. The food was excellent. Does it get this crowded every weekend?"

A stained T-shirt and old jeans suggested youth. But although he could be no older than forty, his face was lined and tired. He ran a hand through ragged, greying curls, and gave her a weary smile. "Thanks. In summer, yes it does. Today was especially mad; there's some event up at the fort. Did you go?"

"No, we've been revisiting spots from our previous visit. We stayed in the Dan-y-Coed cottages over the last Bank Holiday. You were kind enough to recommend the restaurant over the road, which we plan to try this evening."

"Oh right. Dan-y-Coed cottages? You weren't the woman who had trouble with an intruder?"

"News travels fast. My name is Detective Inspector Beatrice Stubbs and I work for the Metropolitan Police."

He folded up the paper and gave her his full attention. "Gary Powell. So, whoever it was broke into a copper's cottage. What a berk. And now you're back to investigate?"

"Let's call it research. We had a couple of mishaps that Bank Holiday weekend. The thing is, I'm keen to locate a certain young man, just to eliminate him from our enquiries. I wondered if you could point me in the right direction. He's quite distinctive, you see, and this is a small enough village for him to stand out. He's mid-twenties with short brown hair but he has a blond ponytail."

The landlord scrunched up his eyes and nodded. "That rings a bell. Hang on. Lyndon? C'mere."

The young barman approached. How marvellous to be bestowed with such thick, dark curls. And glorious bones. An Eastern European perhaps?

"Lyndon, this lady's from the police. You ever seen a guy around who has brown hair but a blond ponytail? Youngish. I have a feeling he's been in here, but ..."

"Yeah, I know who you mean. Drinks lager. He's not a regular, like, but he comes in every few weeks. Very thin, with a pointy nose. He's always with another bloke, older. Miserable-looking git." No trace of Poland in that accent, but could have been Pontypool.

Beatrice cautiously withdrew one of the blown-up photos. It showed nothing of the bags, the beach and the car, but exposed the two men's faces. "This one?"

The lad nodded with definite emphasis. "Yes, exactly. That's them. They come in once in a while, on a Saturday night, have a few pints and leave at shut tap. I thought they must be fishermen; the clothes, the occasional visits, but I don't know for certain."

"I see. That's very helpful, thank you. And of course, neither of you would know his name, I suppose?"

Both pairs of eyes flicked up and right as they searched their memories. Both heads shook slowly.

"Thank you both very much. Kind of you to give me your time. Mr Powell, I'll leave my card in case anything else occurs to you. And I'd be grateful if you could keep this to yourselves."

"No worries. Best of luck with your research." Gary offered his hand.

Beatrice shook it, smiled at Lyndon and returned to her monochrome companion.

She tapped the photo. "According to the staff, those two come in here on occasion, always together on a Saturday evening. The barman said they might be fishermen, but that is mere supposition."

Virginia leant forward, chin resting on hands. "So they bring their stuff here on Saturday morning, hand it over to the contact in the SUV, come in here for a few beers, and sail back to wherever they came from on Saturday night."

"Sounds about right to me," Beatrice agreed. "But what are they bringing and where from? If we could find out when they come in here, we might uncover a pattern. And if we knew their timetable, we could ..."

"Excuse me? Could I have a word?" The barman stood at their table.

"Hello, Lyndon. This is a colleague of mine, so you can speak freely."

"Right. Well, the men in the photo, I think they're Irish. I'm not sure about the younger one, with the ponytail. But the older one told me once if ever I put a head like that on a pint in Cork, they'd throw it back at me. It's not much, I know, but I thought ..."

Beatrice smiled. "That's actually very useful, Lyndon. Can I give you my card, and ask you to let me know the next time this man comes in? This is just between us, of course."

The young man nodded and took the card. "OK. I can do that. Enjoy the rest of your holiday."

He flicked a polite glance at Virginia, who responded with a slow blink and louche smile. He turned and hurried back to the bar. Scared witless, no doubt.

Attractive and charming, with a sharp intelligence, Virginia qualified as one of Beatrice's most useful assets. If only she were a little less memorable.

Chapter 23

Who'd have thought Wales was so much like Ireland? All wild and windswept, green and sheep-covered, full of cute villages and the signs in a foreign language. All Adrian's previous impressions had been of somewhere small, inhospitable and covered in slag-heaps. He just had to bring Jared here, it was too ridiculously romantic.

Jared. Getting a Friday off work had been far less problematic than getting time away from his boyfriend. Tucking his phone back into his jacket, Adrian puzzled over the heated call. Jared's concerns about his detective neighbour were not, obviously, as a sexual threat, but more that she and her problems absorbed so much of Adrian's time. Fair point. But when he also referred to Beatrice as a bad influence, Adrian could only shrug, at a loss as to how to reply. Odd behaviour, but secretly pleasing. Jealousy, in small, non-psychotic doses, was an excellent indicator in a new relationship.

He turned to Matthew, who seemed to have finally adjusted to the gears and braking system of the rented Vauxhall Corsa. Adrian was grateful. Much longer and he suspected his neck might have suffered Repetitive Strain Injury.

"How are you feeling? Tired yet? I mean, it's not like I can take over or anything, but I can sing, tell stories or expose you to more embarrassing personal phone calls to keep you awake."

Matthew's face creased into a smile, although he didn't take his eyes off the country road and his posture remained rigid as a tin soldier.

"I'm fine. We're all but there. And I trust your new man isn't too offended."

"He'll get over it." Adrian could only hope that was the truth.

It must seem very dismissive, abandoning their evening to go off amateur detecting. Would Jared understand?

"Without trying to be intrusive, I wondered why you told him you were with Beatrice, rather than the actual facts?"

Adrian looked out at the countryside in the late afternoon. Beautiful stone houses sheltered in dips on a hillock and in the distance, the sea glittered and shone.

"Saying Beatrice just makes it easier. He knows I'm involved and totally enthusiastic about this case. He sort of understands. But if I'd told him I was with a man – despite said man being Beatrice's partner, due for retirement and so far from cutting edge that he doesn't even own a mobile – believe me, things would have been far more complicated."

"Hmm. It's always interesting what people choose to tell their close ones. And what they prefer to hide. Ah! We're very close to Porthgain, but there's a gallery I'd really like to see in the next village. Would you mind stopping for half an hour? After all, we spent over an hour traipsing round the shops."

Evidently still sulking about both the expense and the style. But he'd be grateful later, and Adrian just knew Beatrice would be overjoyed. Matthew looked stunning in black.

"Not at all. Pity we couldn't have put on our new stuff first. That gear would be perfect for posing in galleries."

"It's not that kind of gallery." Matthew's voice bordered on terse.

The whole place just got cuter and cuter. A delightful gallery filled with watercolour landscapes, the B&B with real patchwork quilts that didn't come from Habitat, a friendly landlady and the walk down the lane to the divine little harbour all combined to make Adrian feel childishly excited. After exploring the beach at sunset and finding little in the way of clues but some fabulous pebbles to decorate his bathroom back home, he followed Matthew as they made their way back to the village.

The sun sank out of sight and small lights glowed from the huddle of houses and The Clipper Inn. Stopping at the bend in the path, Adrian turned to face the sunset. Matthew, a few paces ahead, turned back to stand beside him with a satisfied smile. Pewter-col-oured sea reflected the riot of pinks, peaches, greys and deepening blue above. The insubstantial clouds scattered in mackerel patterns, ending with an almost artistic whorl. The painter whose gallery they'd visited could not complain of lacking subjects.

A long wall stretched out from the harbour, protection from the elements. A solitary figure stood facing out to sea. Too far to see the gender but whoever it was looked awfully French Lieutenant's Woman.

"It doesn't happen often, Matthew, but I am speechless. What a glorious place! I've already decided, and nothing will shake me, that this will be the location of my next mini-break." Adrian had it all planned. He would bring Jared for a weekend; they could stroll in the surf, chat to the locals and fantasise about living here, before buying some cheese and heading home. "Now, do we try the fish restaurant, or the pub?"

"I'd be keen on either, but if our friends from the beach are likely to use one or the other, I'd lean to the pub."

"Very wise. Sagacious, even. Let's go."

Chapter 24

The visit to Fishguard Police Station was surprisingly pleasant. Convinced of a hostile reception to their turning up unannounced, Beatrice was relieved to learn that Inspector Howells was making an appearance at Cardiff Crown Court. She asked to speak instead to PC Johns, who had taken her original statement. He seemed delighted to see her and positively hypnotised by Virginia. He also proved himself a bright spark by asking some perceptive questions, which they debated on the drive back to the B&B in Porthgain.

"He's right. They couldn't leave the boat out there all day on Saturday. It would attract all sorts of attention," said Virginia.

Beatrice's gaze wandered over the hedgerows. "What I don't understand is why they wait. Once they've dropped the cargo off, why not turn around and go back where they came from?"

"Ireland."

Beatrice tutted. "We don't know that. No making assumptions. All we know is that they stick around for Saturday night. So they must berth the boat somewhere. Very probably Porthgain harbour."

"And sail back to Ireland, or wherever else, overnight on Saturday to Sunday."

Two crows repeatedly attacked a buzzard, creating a graceful dogfight in the sky. Beatrice wondered if it was aggression or protection.

Virginia indicated right at Croesgoch. "But you're right. Why do they wait? Just to have cover of darkness? I don't know why that's necessary if they've got rid of whatever illicit goods they're carrying."

"Perhaps they take something back in the other direction. If only bloody Howells would put some surveillance on them, this could all be cleared up in a matter of days. And he, and his force, would be applauded all over the country for cracking a million-pound drug-smuggling operation."

Virginia glanced at her as she eased the Volvo down the country lane. "Now who's making assumptions?"

"I was exaggerating. That's different."

They fell silent as the vehicle rolled down the slope to the tiny harbour. Beatrice took in the huge sea wall, curving like a immense cradling arm around the moored fishing boats. In brilliant sunshine and calm water, the scale of the edifice seemed excessive, but she could imagine what a haven it must be when a storm hit the coast.

Virginia reversed into a parking space, turned off the engine and stuck a police permit on the dashboard.

"Right, let's find out who registers and records which boats come in and out. We might even turn up a name and address. Then I want a shower before dinner. Are we going to the fish restaurant, or back to the pub? I wouldn't mind another look at that barman."

Beatrice sighed and released her seatbelt. "We are going to the restaurant. Firstly to cover all bases, and secondly, to keep you out of trouble. And how do you expect me to get out now? You've parked right up against this Corsa."

"Not my fault. He's straddling the line whereas I have parked correctly. Come out this side. Whoever he is, that driver must be an arse."

The harbourmaster was of a similar breed to Howells. Unconvinced by Beatrice's credentials, he would only confirm that he did indeed keep records of boats coming in and out of the harbour, but unless compelled by a legal ruling, he was not prepared to share. Virginia tried sugar-coating their request, but it was clear the man's ego was fed by his own power. They gave up and Virginia ranted about little Hitlers all the way back to the B&B.

"Virginia, just forget him. I'll contact PC Johns and get him to turn up in uniform. A local lad might have more success, but it may be a little late to disturb the man now. I'll send him an email."

Beatrice, appalled by her own selfishness, felt the need for solitude. A sense of claustrophobia was exacerbated by the only remaining room available at the B&B being a twin. Her urge for space became as strong as a thirst. She chewed over how to broach the subject as they checked in. Fortunately, she had no need. Virginia let her off the hook.

"So, I'm going to shower and check in with my husband, if that's OK with you? He'll be having breakfast around now."

"Great plan. I think I might just dump my bag and walk awhile. Clear the cobwebs and see if I can see any logic behind all this." Tension lifted from Beatrice's shoulders.

"If you're sure? I'm not chucking you out; it's just that this is the one opportunity ..."

"I was wondering how to put it tactfully, but I too need some thinking time. As an anti-social old trout, this fits in perfectly for me."

Virginia's face softened. "Thank you. I just need a half an hour or so. And for an anti-social old trout, you're very good company. Here, give your bag to me. See you in a bit. Don't forget the restaurant's booked for seven."

She trotted up the stairs with such alacrity, Beatrice could not help but smile. Yet, Virginia's evident eagerness for her husband's voice threw a stark light on her own situation. In one of these moods, Beatrice could find black holes in a rainbow.

The reception room was oppressive. Prettily decorated, with lace curtains, patchwork cushions and white woodwork. Very twee. She was being unfair. But she felt like being unfair. She shook herself. She needed to walk. To think. To outpace the low growls behind her.

Once out of the low-ceilinged building, she hesitated. She'd intended to go up the cliffs but had an immediate urge to get as close as she could to the sea. The harbour wall drew her. A barrier against the elements and a path into the ocean. A safe place from which to observe the danger. She hitched her handbag over her shoulder and followed her instinct.

The inside of the harbour was all late-afternoon gentleness, slapping ripples and metallic clinks of masts and anchor chains. Oily patches of grime and detritus collected in corners. A rich smell encouraged her to fill her lungs. Half ozone, half diesel, it lifted her somehow and she picked up speed. When she reached the bend, the furthermost point of the wall, she stopped to watch the waves pounding the bricks beneath. As always, she stared in awe. *The elements have that hold over humanity; that ceaseless fascination. We believe we own earth and air, but find out soon enough the opposite is true. Yet with fire and water, we recognise our visceral urge for mastery is outclassed.* Beatrice watched the constant rhythms of the sea attack her foundations, and acknowledged its superior power.

The sea. We describe it as raging, cruel, beautiful, uncontrollable and endlessly changing, but it simply is. All we can do is strengthen our walls, be eternally prepared. It will never go away. We just have to learn to live with it.

Chapter 25

Luck had always favoured Adrian. A Sagittarian with Libra rising, he often found his heart's desires falling into his lap. Tonight was no exception. The menu offered homemade fisherman's pie, the wine list had surprising potential and the barman, with Rufus Sewell curls and cheese-grater cheekbones, was sending him certain signals. A good detective had to use every means at his disposal.

"I think I'll have the steak and ale pie," announced Matthew. "And this Australian red might be worth a punt. What do you think?"

Adrian checked the description. "Looks just the thing. And we're on holiday, sort of. We ought to indulge ourselves. I am going to try a glass of the Chenin Blanc as an accompaniment to fisherman's pie. We have to order at the bar. Now, I insist on getting this, for two reasons. First, you got the train. Secondly, I'd like to take the opportunity to chat up the barman. Purely in the interest of investigative thoroughness, of course."

"Thank you, that's very kind. He is undoubtedly a striking-looking chap. Tell him I'm your uncle or something, and I shall sit here quietly and do the crossword. Could you ask for a side order of chips? As you say, we are on holiday. And Adrian, remember to pay in cash."

On seeing Adrian approach, 'Rufus' slid past the barmaid so he happened to be ideally placed to serve him. Slick.

Adrian gave him The Look. *I'm checking you out. I'm hard to please, but so far, I like what I see.*

"Hi. Could I order some food?"

"Sure. Where are you sitting?"

As if you didn't know. You haven't taken your eyes off me since I walked in.

Adrian pointed at their table, where Matthew was peering unsubtly over the top of the paper. "Next to the fireplace. For drinks, one large glass of Stormy Bay Shiraz and one of Chenin Blanc. I'll have fisherman's pie and my uncle would like the steak and ale pie, with a side order of chips."

"What about you? You fancy anything on the side?" His head still bent over the till, he lifted his eyes to Adrian.

"Don't tempt me. I like to leave room for afters."

Eye contact, secretive smiles and deal sealed. Adrian handed over a fifty-pound note. As the barman counted out the change, he asked casually, "On holiday, is it?"

"Sort of. Doing a tour of Wales, trying to find my cousin." Adrian dropped his voice. "He got in a bit of trouble and did a midnight flit. All we know is he was heading to Wales. I agreed to help my uncle search for him."

"Wales is a big place, plenty of room to hide. Got a name?"

A name? Good point.

"Better than a name, we have a photograph." Adrian removed the picture from his bag and placed it on the bar, just as a man in kitchen whites emerged from the kitchen. While the barman studied the picture, the chef surveyed the pub.

"Lyndon, will you collect some glasses, please?"

Lyndon? Oh yes, it suits him. Just as romantic as Rufus if not more so.

"In a minute. Gary, come over by here. This man is looking for someone. He's got a photo." He turned back to Adrian. "Gary's the landlord."

Gary nodded a greeting to Adrian and picked up the photograph. He threw a sharp look at Lyndon and glanced back at Adrian immediately.

"And you are ...?"

"Andrew Ramos. This man's my cousin."

"Is your cousin in some sort of trouble?" The landlord's eyes were suspicious.

Adrian affected a laugh and indicated Matthew with an inclination of his head. "Only with his father. There was a family argument, and ... Tim flew the nest. We just want to find him and persuade him to come home."

"I see. Well, we've never seen him round here, but if he does turn up, we'll let you know. Could you leave a number?"

Odd how he spoke for both of them.

Lyndon's eyes met his, but his look contained no flirtation. More of an apology. Adrian scribbled his false name and real number on an order pad and thanked them for their help.

Matthew, annoyingly, seemed unconcerned by the landlord's behaviour, devoting all his attention to his pie. Adrian was convinced there was something suspicious behind their reactions, so explained it again.

Matthew mopped up some gravy with the last of his chips. "I think you're reading too much into it. The pub's getting busy. The boss saw a staff member dallying too long with one customer and chose to chivvy him a bit. He didn't recognise the man and wanted to get rid of you so his staff would concentrate on their jobs. Nothing sinister to it. How was your food?"

"Sublime. The thing is, Matthew, you didn't see his face when I showed him the picture. He barely glanced at it, but looked at me like a stunned mullet. I swear he's hiding something."

"And the barman?"

"Lyndon. He looked guilty, and didn't even give me a chance to ask any questions. Plus, he's been conspicuously absent all evening ..."

Matthew placed his knife and fork together. "Rushed off his feet, more like. It's only just starting to calm down now. That pie was a triumph. However, beer would have been a wiser accompaniment. The Shiraz was all but overwhelmed. Adrian, have you considered they might even know Ponytail Man? Perhaps they went to school with him, or he's the son of a local sheep farmer. And here you are, inventing a new identity and saying he's run away from home?"

That hadn't occurred to Adrian and the thought bothered him. "If that were the case, their reactions would make sense, I suppose," he admitted. "And now Lyndon thinks I'm some kind of loon, which is why he's avoiding me. How would you have done it?"

"I don't know. Pretended I was a private investigator, maybe? Which is, in effect, what we are. What do you say to a harbour stroll before we head back to the B&B? I feel the need to stretch my legs."

Adrian finished his wine with a last look at the bar. No sign of Lyndon. Shame, really. That one had potential. He hurried after Matthew.

As they stepped into the cool air of the night, Adrian's mobile rang. He didn't recognise the number.

"Hello?"

"Mr Ramos? This is Lyndon, the barman. I wanted a quick word before you leave. About the photo."

"Oh, right. I'll come back in."

"No, I'll come out. Two secs."

Matthew discreetly continued to the lane and wandered on down towards the harbour. Adrian sat on the low wall, waiting and listening to the murmurs of conversation from the outdoor tables. Lyndon appeared from behind the pub and beckoned Adrian to follow him round the back.

Amid the large refuse containers, Lyndon sat on an upturned beer crate and lit a cigarette, watching Adrian.

"I only have a few minutes for a fag break. But I wanted to catch you to explain. A police detective was here today, asking about the same bloke. There were two of them and they had exactly the same photograph. That's why Gary freaked. The detective said to keep it quiet, but now someone else turns up."

"A police detective? Did he say why he was looking for this guy? Tim, I mean?"

"It was a she. No, not that I know of. She might have said something to Gary, but she only asked me if I'd seen him before. Which I had. Like I told her, they come in about once a month, two of them and I think they're Irish. Only ever seen them on a Saturday night. You wouldn't forget a ponytail like that, would you?"

"Did the detective give you her name?"

"She gave me her card." He stood, retrieved his wallet from his back pocket and extracted the card.

Detective Inspector Beatrice Stubbs, Metropolitan Police.

Despite knowing what it would say, Adrian shivered as he read the words. He handed the card back.

"Two detectives, you said? Did you get the other one's name?"

"No. But I can give you her description. Tall, peroxide blonde and right rampant, she was. Tried to pull me. But she's not my type."

Adrian picked up his cue.

"Why are you telling me all this?"

Lyndon stubbed out his cigarette and stood up. "Because you are exactly my type. Is that bloke really your uncle?"

"No, but something very similar. Listen, we have to leave tomorrow, but I may well be back in the next couple of weeks. Can I take your number? Just in case."

"Here, I'll write it on the back of her card. Call me, OK?"

Matthew turned with a smile as he heard Adrian approach.

"I planned to give you another two minutes before beating a subtle retreat. Were you successful? I don't need details."

"Yes, but wait till you hear this. It seems we're not the only ones being devious. The police were here today, asking about the same guy, using the same photograph. The detective left her card." He held it under the street lamp.

Matthew's eyes boggled. "Good God! So much for, 'I have to work, I'll be busy all weekend'. Of all the bare-faced subterfuge! That wretched female never ceases to amaze me."

"Nor me. But if there was anything here to find, she got in first. Let's get some sleep. And I suggest we head back to London first thing in the morning. This trail is cold."

"Absolutely." Matthew shook his head as they made their way back towards their lodgings. "The most infuriating thing is ..."

Adrian finished his sentence. "... we can't complain that she lied to us. I know. But I still can't believe she did that."

"She takes the biscuit, she really does. The only advantage we hold is she has no idea we've been here. However, we know all about her duplicitous double-cross. Information is power."

Adrian's mind whirred. *Power, yes. But how to use it?*

Upstairs at The Clipper Inn, Gary Powell reached into his tunic. The copper's card was a bit greasy and smelt of onions. He picked up the phone. Half eleven on Saturday; no one was likely to answer, but he could leave her a voicemail message. He had a feeling she'd like to know.

Chapter 26

Shells tinkled a light melody along the beach and the sun sank, turning clouds rosé. Inch by inch, Matthew unzipped her wetsuit, shaking his head with regret. Her dread swelled like a jellyfish in her throat, but she did nothing to stop him. Finally, he yanked open the two edges and stared in horror at what he saw.

"How long have you had that?" he exclaimed, his expression aghast. She tried to open her mouth but her tongue had died of shame.

He shook her by her shoulders. "How long? How long!"

"Beatrice! Beatrice!"

She shot upright in bed, eyes wide and pulse pounding. There was no wetsuit. Her tartan pyjamas were warm, dry and buttoned-up. The sound of waves was coming through the B&B window and Matthew looked like Virginia Lowe. Beatrice closed her eyes and opened them again.

Virginia perched on Beatrice's bed, grey light washing her complexion to nothing. Without make-up and wearing a long white T-shirt, she could frighten a weak-hearted individual into an early grave. She placed a reassuring hand on Beatrice's shoulder.

"Beatrice? Look, I'm sorry to wake you."

"What is it? Was I snoring?"

"No, no. But we have to go. Did you not hear your phone?"

"My phone? What time is it? What's wrong?"

"It's almost half eight. We've got to get back to London now. Our man's just done another one."

Beatrice's mind accelerated and changed gear. "No! He couldn't have! He was at work, we made sure of that."

"Looks like he did this girl on his way home."

Beatrice threw back the duvet, but something in Virginia's voice made her teeth clench.

"What does 'did this girl' mean?"

"She's sixteen, doing work experience at the newsagent's in the station. She left home about an hour ago and that filthy bastard was waiting for her in the back lane. He put his penis into her mouth."

Beatrice grimaced and couldn't conceal the wobble in her voice. "Oh my God. The disgusting, vile ... is the girl all right? Stupid question." She threw back the quilt. "Right, I'll be ready in less than ten minutes. If we leave now, we can be back by lunchtime."

Virginia didn't move, but continued her glazed stare at the buttons on Beatrice's pyjamas.

"What? Virginia? What is it?" She hunched to peer at Virginia's face.

Virginia looked up, her eyes flooded and she bit her bottom lip.

"Beatrice, the girl's autistic. And that sick fucker knew."

Every muscle in Beatrice's body went limp.

Chapter 27

Their previous encounter at the Family Centre gave Beatrice the impression that Maggie Howard was in permanent control. Sensitive, thoughtful, professional and positive. So when Maggie entered the BTP office on Sunday afternoon, it shook Beatrice to see her puffy eyes and tight mouth.

A veteran weeper herself, Beatrice offered tissues and a gentle squeeze on the shoulder, as she closed the door to Virginia's office. She poured them both a glass of water.

"Thanks for coming, Maggie. I appreciate it. Virginia is still interviewing the newsagent, but will join us when she can. I'd like to hear what you managed to find out from the victim this morning. Is she ... is she all right?"

Maggie shook her head and clenched her jaw tighter. Beatrice feared something might break. She breathed deeply.

"Right, I think I'm ready to start. Look, Beatrice ..."

"Don't. If the next thing to come out of your mouth is an apology, just don't. There's no need and we're only human. I gather this morning was hellish."

Maggie's make-up was smudged and her hair disobedient. She looked like a rock star the morning after.

"I've heard some nasty stuff in this job; some really twisted thinking. This goes straight into the top five of the Shit Parade. Cherry James is sixteen and has PDD-NOS. Yeah, I know. Wait till you hear what it stands for. Pervasive Development Disorder Not Otherwise Specified. Not quite Asperger's Syndrome, not quite autism, but displays many similar behavioural patterns. All these disorders fall under the umbrella of Autism Spectrum Disorder."

"I've heard of Asperger's and autism, but confess my ignorance as to what either really means. I have some vague memories of *Rain Man*?"

"That's potentially helpful, actually. The clue's in the name. It's a neurological developmental disorder. People with this condition don't behave the way we expect them to, don't acknowledge social codes and can often be obsessive."

"About people?"

"Oddly, that's the least likely target. PDD-NOS sufferers tend to be solitary, absorbed in their own interests. And those interests often become compulsive. Dinosaurs, planets, internal combustion engines, toys, video games, anything. Cherry's into sharks. Films, toys, models, pictures and books, so many books about sharks. Which is how this despicable scumbag bastard found a way in."

"Via sharks?"

"He groomed her, Beatrice. He spotted Cherry, working her summer job at the station's newsagent, doing menial tasks but earning her own wage. It seems she loved the job, and became a favourite with some of the locals. She has some communication difficulties, but more social than verbal. She has problems reading emotions and signals, so extends a simple 'Good morning, how are you?' into a lecture on the physiology of hammerheads."

"And one of the people she lectured ..."

"... saw an opportunity. He gave her little presents, pictures he'd downloaded. Never in the shop, she says. Sometimes on her way to the shop or on her way home. Her memory is amazing on some points and entirely absent on others. She knows exactly which images he gave her but couldn't even give us a halfway coherent description of the guy. She just doesn't notice. And yes, the pictures are already being finger-printed. He chatted to her and learned her routines, her timetable. Not difficult, as it's another of her obsessions."

Maggie's voice remained steady, calm and analytical, betraying no hint of her former distress.

"When did this start?" Beatrice's skin cooled.

"We can't be sure – her time awareness is imprecise – but more than a month ago. This is classic grooming. He prepared this girl. And this morning, as she left home, he met her and offered her a deal. He must have thought it would be easy, but like many people on the autistic disorder spectrum, she hates to be touched. Even by those she clearly loves."

"In that case, how did he manage to do what he did?"

Maggie's eyes squeezed closed for a second, as if she'd rather not see. When she spoke, her voice sounded less even.

"He traded. A set of shark tattoo transfers for her, a little favour for him. She had no idea what to do, so apparently he talked her through it. First, he put one of the transfers on her skin. Clever. These kids generally hate to be touched. But she let him, for the sharks. Then he explained what he wanted in return. She's good at following explicit instructions. But that stupid fucking perverted arsehole tried to touch her head. You just can't do that with a kid like her. She reacted violently; screaming, lashing out and rocking, which frightened him off."

"Oh dear God. Did she go home or did someone find her?"

Maggie frowned and rubbed at the bridge of her nose. "No. And this is another shitty thing. He met her as she was coming out of her own back gate. They didn't go far. Just up the back lane. Her mother heard the screams." She inhaled deeply and blew out a long breath.

Beatrice attempted to empathise with Cherry's mother, but decided to close the door on that emotion. It wouldn't do for her to get distressed as well.

Maggie looked up, eyes weary, lines deeper. "Catch him. Do it soon. And when you do, let me into his cell one night. I'll show him justice."

Tired from the tense drive, overflowing with sympathy for Cherry, her mother and for Maggie, and wretched in the knowledge that she had been pursuing her own agenda, Beatrice sensed a chasm below.

She swallowed. "Fair enough. I'll hold him down."

Maggie pulled cleansing wipes from her bag and started to repair her make-up. "While I cut off his dick and make *him* eat it."

To Beatrice, that sounded reasonable.

On entering the meeting room at Finsbury Park Control Centre, Inspector Kalpana Joshi's face gave everything away. She nodded to Beatrice and Virginia, but could not even force a smile.

Virginia began. "Thanks for coming in on a Sunday, Kalpana. We've talked to most staff members, and with at least two victims making a positive ID, we think we need to make a move."

Kalpana did not react, but stared at the opposite wall.

Virginia threw a worried frown at Beatrice.

Beatrice spoke gently. "Kalpana?"

"You ever experienced something like this? Where a member of your law enforcement team uses the advantages of his position to abuse and assault?" Despite her soft pitch, Kalpana's voice sounded harsh and sore, as if she'd been shouting. Her beautiful burnished skin had an underlying redness. Beatrice wished she could give her a hug.

Instead she answered the question. "Not a member of my team, no. But someone I regarded as an ally, someone I trusted, turned out to have my worst interests at heart. It shakes your faith."

"Yeah. That's it. My faith is shaken to its foundations. So how must Cherry James's family feel?"

The three women sat in silence for a moment.

Virginia tried another tack. "Kalpana, he's out there, now. Maybe at this minute, he's on the street with his list of women. He's making plans for the next one. It could even be today. We need to dig into the backgrounds of a couple of suspects."

Kalpana's chocolate eyes turned to them and all her softness dissolved.

"A *couple* of suspects? I thought you got positive IDs from two of the victims?"

Beatrice twisted her mouth to an apologetic smile. "We did. Of two different men."

"Right, let's check their work records, personal details, track record, anything we can find." Kalpana shrugged off her jacket and unpacked her laptop. "You got people keeping an eye on them, just in case?"

"Of course," Beatrice assured her. "They're watching; we're thinking."

Virginia opened the first file. "Nathan Bennett has worked the shift patterns that fit with our man. He's the right age, build and lives in Crouch End. Practically a local."

Tapping commands onto the keyboard, Kalpana shook her head. "Can't see Bennett doing this. He's ambitious, focused on the career ladder."

Beatrice rested her chin on her hand and her gaze on Kalpana. "Can you see any one of your team doing this?"

Kalpana's fingers froze and she angled her head to Beatrice. Her eyes flicked down in thought and she shook her head. "You're right. Let's stick to facts.

"Nathan Bennett, joined the BTP in 2009, and has been raking in praise from superiors, colleagues and instructors. Came over here in May 2010. Looking for promotion. Married, no kids. Wife works as a personal trainer."

"Our profiler saw this man as single," Virginia said. "Not to say the profile is perfect, but ..."

"No, but I know what you mean. The wedding was Christmas 2011, we went to the evening party. It has to be one godawful car crash of a marriage if he's flashing strangers less than a year later. Who's the other one?" Kalpana looked at Beatrice.

"Paul Avery."

Something happened to Kalpana's face. Barely registering as an expression, her nostrils twitched and her eyes dropped to the right. She entered the details without comment, but Beatrice's curiosity was piqued.

"I asked before if you could see any one of your team doing this. Your reaction to this name makes me wonder if you are still as convinced."

Kalpana sat back, lifting her chin to Beatrice and Virginia. "I dislike Paul Avery, I admit. He lacks social skills, he can be over-zealous and his personal hygiene has earned him an informal warning. I had a feeling certain fingers might point in his direction. He's a geek, but a harmless one. I stand by what I said. I can't see any member of my team as a potential sexual offender. Not even this one."

Virginia's narrowed eyes met Beatrice's stare. Virginia asked the question.

"Personal hygiene? Does he have a problem with body odour?"

"No. Halitosis. His breath stinks."

Scotland Yard was eerily calm on a Sunday afternoon. Beatrice stood outside Hamilton's office and sighed. She was prepared to take her verbal thrashing; it was no more than she deserved and she knew it was inevitable. Although she was surprised to receive her summons so soon. Obviously Hamilton couldn't wait till Monday.

She knocked, waited for Hamilton's curt bark of permission and opened the door, expecting an incandescent Norse warrior to unleash bolts of fury.

The late afternoon sun caught his hooked nose, the grooves of his constant frown, and lit a halo behind his grey hair. Yet his eyes, as he lifted them to hers, seemed to contain no anger. His forehead motioned to the chair. She sat.

"You have a suspect."

"Yes, sir. Two, in fact, but one looks like our man."

"Plan of action?"

"A team tailing him every minute of the day. Harrison, our lure, remains in place. He will try something, without a doubt, and when he does, we'll be waiting."

"Your case is not strong enough to take to the CPS as is?"

"Sir, we need concrete evidence. As yet, everything is circumstantial. But we're onto him. He's going to step right into our trap, I'm sure of it. Really, sir, we won't fail."

"As far as I'm concerned, you already have. Cherry James."

Dark wing-beats hovered over Beatrice. She met Hamilton's eyes and waited.

"I understand you were in Wales. With DI Lowe." He forestalled any explanation with a dismissive hand. "I am not interested. Multi-tasking is a marvellous skill around the house. But you are at work. Focus, Stubbs. On your job. Should this man assault or expose himself to anyone else, I will replace you with someone more effective. Thank you for your time."

Beatrice left Scotland Yard with a heavy tread. Fatigued, miserable and dragging a weighty sense of guilt behind her, all she needed was home and bed. But she hauled herself up the road to Transport for London HQ. She owed it to Cherry James.

Ty Grant's usual expression of sardonic amusement was absent. He scrambled to his feet and snatched a file from his desk, meeting her halfway to Virginia's office.

"She's gone home. I'm pretty sure you want to do the same, but could I just have two minutes?"

"If it's relevant to nailing our pervert, you can have two hours. Let's go."

Ty spread the photographs across the table. Eight by fours, both colour and black and white, of Paul Avery. Leaving the newsagent's, smoking outside the launderette, unlocking his front door, emerging in the early evening wearing a baseball cap, boarding a bus, pulling open the door of The Coach and Horses.

"Everything we've recorded today fits the profile. He's single, lives alone, drinks alone and at the paper shop he bought fags and a porn mag. It's him."

A powerful conviction filled her and Beatrice pointed to the cap.

"Remember the logo that thirteen-year-old drew for us? This is a pretty close match. Any ideas?"

Ty shook his head. "Not yet. I'm working on it. I'll find it, if it takes me all night."

His determination surprised her. "Good. Your commitment is ... appreciated."

Ty pulled down the corners of his mouth. "Yeah, well, some things get to you. As you know. Get some rest, DI Stubbs. And don't worry. If he so much as farts, we'll hear it."

She watched him head back to his desk as if he were preparing for a scrum. Time to leave. A blinking light drew her attention to her phone. Six new messages. On a Sunday? Maybe one of them was relevant. She really should listen to them before she left. She sat still, pondering Grant's comment.

As you know. Was her breakdown that well publicised, or was she being paranoid? She shook her head and gave herself an angry reminder. Concentrate on getting this man off the streets. For Paul Avery, there must be no next time.

Messages, home, bed. She rested her head on the back of the chair and pressed *Play*.

Chapter 28

The First Class compartment of the 11.15 from Cardiff Central on Sunday morning was almost empty. Perfect for reading the papers. On his way back from the toilet, Adrian stopped at the door of the carriage to admire his styling expertise. Matthew had actually chosen to wear the black outfit they'd purchased, without any cajoling on Adrian's part. And he looked superb. Black canvas trousers and a black silk shirt. Very gentleman burglar. If only he could be persuaded to cut his hair.

Adrian was smiling as he retook his seat. Matthew cleared away some of the Sunday supplements to make space.

"Your mobile telephone just rang. I'm not sure how to use these things so didn't meddle."

Voicemail message received. Beatrice. He listened once, checked he would not disturb any other passengers, then played it again on speakerphone.

"*Hello Adrian. Beatrice here. It's midday on Sunday, and it looks like I'll be at work some time. It's all kicked off again. But Matthew is due back from Rome this afternoon, so I wonder if you'd mind lending him your key so he can get into my flat. Please call me when you get this. Bye-bye.*"

Matthew shook his head in disbelief. "And what do you suppose that means? 'It's all kicked off at work'. She must still be in Wales. Why else would she ask you to let me in? She must have found something."

Adrian nodded, with a knowing smile. "More than likely. So you'll have to pump her for information, in that Matthew way you have. As if you'd rather be reading a book about Hellenic myths, but you're showing polite interest."

Matthew's eyebrows rose and he blinked repeatedly. "Is it that obvious?"

"Sometimes. And next weekend, armed with any info you get, we go back to Pembrokeshire, catch these smugglers *in flagrante* and hand everything over to the police."

Matthew dunked his teabag in and out of his cup, gazing out at the rushing scenery.

"Might there be a point where we include Beatrice, do you think?"

Adrian scratched his chin. He needed a shave. "There have already been several. Matthew, the only reason I contacted you was because Beatrice showed no interest. I only wanted to help, to find out what was behind this series of accidents. She didn't want to know. Too busy, she said. Now, it appears she's more than interested, she's used my groundwork, but excluded both of us and gone off on her own."

"That much is true. Well, two can play at that game."

Adrian smiled at the stubborn set of Matthew's jaw. "You'll need to be careful, she won't give much away."

"She may be more forthcoming if I take the 'Come, come, dear, you're over-reacting' approach. It infuriates her and she displays proof and evidence and theories and everything."

Adrian laughed. Trust Matthew to know which buttons to press. "I knew you'd have your technique all worked out. As you should. You two have you been together forever. You know, she's never told me how you two met."

"Yes, that is one advantage of a long-term partnership. It also acts as a disadvantage on occasion, because she knows me equally well. Now, my turn to use the facilities. When I return, I may need your assistance with the crossword. Excuse me a moment."

Full of grace and tact, typically Matthew. But unmistakeably a 'No Comment'. Adrian was developing a nose for this sort of thing. And his nose told him there was a story there.

The only positive to dashing back from Wales early on a Sunday morning, having told everyone he would be unavailable, was a full afternoon to get on with his chores. *Distortion* by The Magnetic Fields on the CD, his failsafe mood-lifter, windows open and rubber gloves on, Adrian began by dusting, sweeping and cleaning the bathroom. He chose not to hoover, as Matthew would be resting upstairs. He unpacked his weekend bag, put the laundry on, ironed everything in the wicker basket, then he showered and shaved. He changed into jeans and a cheesecloth shirt, then strolled down to Old Street to buy flowers and the ingredients for Welsh rarebit, to maintain the Celtic theme. He'd buy enough for three, in case Beatrice was hungry when she got home.

At seven, Matthew knocked on the front door.

"Hello. Still no sign of her? Come in, come in." Adrian wafted his hand inwards.

"She's just called to say she's on her way home. So I popped out and bought some bits and bobs from the delicatessen. Thought you'd like to join us for a snack. Two bottles of Franciacorta chilling in the fridge, an array of Mediterranean treats and an opportunity to combine forces. What do you say?"

With a gratified thrill, Adrian noticed Matthew hadn't changed his clothes. He must have recognised how they suited him and wanted to show off. From frump to fox in just two days. Adrian had worked his magic. But he knew better than to offer a compliment.

"Wonderful. For my part, I can contribute cheese and spring onions. Have we got our story straight?"

"I feel confident. And you?"

"Let's go and face the woman. United we stand."

When the downstairs door finally slammed, Adrian jumped, spilling his drink as Matthew scrambled to his feet. Adrian called on all his performance training, leant back on the sofa and flicked through a Sunday supplement.

Beatrice looked awful. Tired, grey and pissed off. Perhaps the impromptu gathering was not such a great idea.

"Hello, Old Thing! Adrian and I got some snacks for you. We thought you might be hungry. Was your day appalling?"

Beatrice placed her bag on the chair. "Hello Matthew, and hello

Adrian. Give me a minute, would you?" She disappeared into the bathroom.

Adrian re-read the same page of an article on Corsica four times and still had no idea what it was about. Matthew picked up a bottle and was twisting the cork when they heard the sound of the shower start. He stopped and cast a worried glance at Adrian.

"She's just got back from a long drive. She's bound to be tired," Adrian reassured him in a whisper. "But if she's still crabby afterwards, I may leave you to it."

Finally Beatrice emerged, hair combed back and wearing a deep blue bathrobe with matching towelling slippers. She offered them both a smile.

"Sorry I'm late. Hellish day. Ooh, this spread looks lovely. I tell you, this is just what I needed. What are we drinking? Franciacorta? Fresh from Rome, I suppose. How was the seminar? And what about you, Adrian, did you and Jared have a lovely weekend?" She picked up a stuffed pimento and bit off the end.

Adrian's sensors twitched. Beatrice was furious. Brightly, cheerfully hiding it, but ready to blow like a mushroom cloud. It might be better to leave. But she hadn't finished.

"Let me tell you about mine. While pursuing a lead regarding the stolen camera, I received a call summoning me back to Head Office. Our sexual predator, assumed to be safely at work, attacked an autistic child. Everything has escalated and I am in danger of losing my position on this case. But the best was yet to come. Just before I left the office, I discovered my neighbour and my partner have formed an alliance against me, lied to me, and attempted delicate investigative work in great hob-nailed boots. And Matthew seems to have adopted a whole new look. Are you two about to announce your imminent engagement?"

Her voice was harsh and raw as she grabbed one of the glasses Matthew had poured.

"So, to what shall we toast?"

Matthew looked at Adrian and indicated the door with his eyes. Adrian leapt up in relief.

"Beatrice, I'm sorry you had such a horrible day. But we're on your side, both of us. I'll let Matthew explain."

He sidled out the door and returned downstairs. They couldn't have a row. Not those two. He could no more imagine them arguing than he could imagine drinking a 1987 Petrus Pomerol from a box.

And to add to his discomfort, he'd left his dinner upstairs. Ransacking the kitchen, he found a bottle of Belgian beer, a packet of kettle chips and two Portuguese Salpicão sausages. He placed the assortment on a tray and sat in front of the silent television, listening for sounds from upstairs. No screaming, no slamming of doors, no throwing of crockery. Not really their style. He picked up the remote control and looked miserably at the tray on his lap. Crisps, meat and beer. All he needed now was football and he could be a screaming great straight.

Chapter 29

Five-forty a.m. and she could tell Matthew was awake. His breathing remained deep and regular, but she knew he wasn't sleeping. Same as he must know she was faking. Both listening, both worrying. She performed a mental scan of herself.

Physical state: better. Sleep had helped.

Mood: bad. Dead weights of guilt and mistrust exerting downward pull.

Attitude toward the day ahead: uncertain, troubled.

"Matthew, look, I ... I'm sorry."

Unlike her, he spoke without hesitation, keeping his eyes closed. "So am I. It was foolish and irresponsible to lie to you. For Adrian and me, this was a bit of a game. For you, I think it's something closer to home."

"Of course it's closer to home. Investigation is my job, and your amateur attempts at helping could put the outcome at risk. Sorry. I'm not going to start on that again."

"That's a blessing. You made your point last night and I subsequently apologised. But that wasn't what I meant. I think this is personal. You are trying to protect me, somehow. You think because I suffered a loss, that of my camera, it is in some way your responsibility to make it good. You mistrust Adrian and me because we are not police officers. That is perfectly understandable. Yet you do not have to do this alone." He opened his eyes and turned to her.

In that second, looking into his dark, intelligent eyes, a surge of love surprised her. She couldn't lie.

"If only it were that noble. No, I'm not your avenging angel; I'm trying to prove myself right. I didn't tell you because I wanted to spare you the worry, in the first place. I wanted to round up enough evidence so that Hamilton would open a joint case with the Dyfed-Powys force. As I said last night, I had no plan to investigate this solo. Things just barrelled along. Hamilton refused, Adrian got involved and then I told Virginia. But by that time, yes, it had become personal. I had something to prove."

"That I can believe. You had something to prove to Hamilton. He's the one who suspects you of not being up to the job. Beatrice, Hamilton will never understand your disorder. When it comes to mental health, he's old school; *stuff and nonsense, pull yourself together*. You'll probably end your days still trying to prove yourself to that upper-class arse. On the other hand, I do understand. As much as anyone can who isn't actually bipolar. We both know your job doesn't help your condition; in fact it may even make things worse. But I supported your decision to go back to work. I told you the same thing as I drove you home from that clinic. I know you need a certain ... validation from colleagues."

Impressed and disturbed by how clearly Matthew could see her, Beatrice tried to smile as tears began an assault.

He hadn't finished. "I'm not Hamilton. I've never doubted your competence, your skill or your intelligence. I know how abysmal things must have seemed if you thought ending your life was the only solution. And it tore me into wretched pieces to think I couldn't help you. So we made a choice, as I recall. We chose to manage these black dogs. Together. You have James, you have your stabilisers, you have me, and you have your job. All working together, we can keep this under control. The point is, Old Thing, if you knock one of your supports away, you're going to have less balance."

Nodding and crying and snuffling, she could barely even see him. She sat up and groped for tissues. He was absolutely right. Why was her life one mindless loop of warnings about fire and sticking her fingers in the flames? She needed help. She had help. So why did she persist in trying to do without?

"I'm sorry. I never seem to get better at this. James will despair of me."

"As James will surely tell you, getting better is not the issue. The only lesson you need to learn is this: allowing yourself to lean on your support structure doesn't make you weak. The effect is precisely the opposite."

She slid back under the duvet, clutching her tissue, and shuffled into Matthew's embrace. He kissed her temple and rested his head on hers.

"I thought you were having an affair," she murmured.

A deep chuckle rumbled through his chest. "With Adrian? Discovering my true sexuality at sixty?"

"No. With some Roman trollop."

"Well, the same thought crossed my mind when I found you'd lied to us."

Beatrice snorted with laughter, then twisted to examine his face. "You're serious! An affair? Who on earth with?"

"I don't know. Virginia? That macho sergeant you mentioned?"

"Those are my choices? A straight woman or a gorilla?" She relaxed and shook her head. "I know when I'm well off."

Warmth, security and a sense of having had a lucky escape filled her whole body. Yet one part remained hollow and empty.

"Matthew, I know it's terribly early, but I'm hungry."

"Me too. A handful of olives is barely enough to keep body and soul together. Do you have all the ingredients for Eggs Florentine?"

"I do, if you'll accept frozen spinach."

"In that case, I'll make breakfast, on the condition that you promise me something."

"No more half-truths?"

"That, and you allow us to help. I think with your guidance, Adrian and I could prove useful in terms of legwork."

Beatrice thought for a moment. "If you give me a guarantee that you will not improvise, take chances, run risks or do anything without express permission, it's a possibility. I'll be hog-tied to London until we've got that disgusting excuse for a man off the streets, so any Welsh trips are out of the question for me. But you must faithfully promise. And mean it."

He rose and pulled on his dressing-gown. "Understood. I'll pop into Oddbins later and pass on the good news. Shall I invite Adrian to dine with us, so we can discuss how best to proceed? Or perhaps should I say, take instructions?

"Good idea, I owe him several dinners. Do apologise for my theatrics last night. I wasn't myself. Right, I'll have a quick shower. Oh, Matthew?"

"I know. You want yours fried, not poached."

"Naturally. But what I wanted to say was, I think you're wonderful."

"You're not so bad yourself."

As Beatrice stepped under the cascade of warm water, she felt lighter, almost skittish, and very, very lucky.

Chapter 30

Karen Harrison's nerves showed after the Friday morning presentation. As Beatrice brought up the lights, Karen sat on her hands. Beatrice softened, recalling her own use of the exact same technique to disguise visible trembles. None of the three women spoke for a moment.

Virginia must have also noticed the young officer's tension and began addressing the girl by her first name.

"Karen, you're doing a storming job. It's been a long, tense week for all of us. Not your fault he hasn't bitten yet. But all the signs point to this weekend, which is why we wanted to talk to you again. If there is any aspect of this operation that makes you uncomfortable, or anything that's not wholly clear, I'd like to hear about it. Your safety comes before everything. If you feel in any way vulnerable, it would be useful to let us know. Now."

"No, ma'am, I'm confident." To Beatrice, Harrison sounded anything but. Her pale skin, wide eyes and determined jaw triggered thoughts of teenage Russian gymnasts.

"Good for you," Beatrice chimed in. "All we really want is your perspective. Remember, DI Lowe and I are on the outside. We're guessing, analysing and making predictions from our standpoint. But you? You're in the victims' shoes. Help us, Karen. Are we missing anything? Do you feel there's a vulnerable side?"

"No, I don't think so. Officers ahead, behind, watching on camera, response units and several vehicles on the route. What could he possibly do?"

Virginia scrunched up her eyes and sucked air through her teeth in exasperation. "Karen, you have to be realistic about the risks. You can't just wander into this like bloody Bambi. He could pull a gun and take you hostage. Or a knife and stab you, slit your throat. It will take any one of our back-up team at least ninety seconds to get to you, and ..."

"I know." Swellings grew beneath her eyes and two blotchy triangles took over her cheeks. "He's not going to do that unless he knows I'm a plant. The thing is, he's going to make a grab at me. I'm ready for any of this, I really am. But I so hate the idea of being *touched* by him."

The clenched fists, the downward flick of her eyes and the miserable moue on Karen Harrison's face stalled Beatrice. In an instant, she understood how this girl could not escape. The police force needed him to get as close as possible, to attempt to assault her, to sexually threaten this fine-boned girl. After they caught him, she would be feted and celebrated and given an award ... but she would still be a victim of assault. *What the hell were they asking of Harrison? What sort of job was this?*

"Karen, we can't guarantee he won't lay a hand on you. But we'll give you every kind of protection we can. Might mess up your outfit, but I'll organise a Kevlar vest for you." Virginia's voice remained even. "I don't know if they do underpants, but I will make sure you're wearing the equivalent. God knows where I'll find some. DI Stubbs?"

"Yes, DI Lowe. It would be a privilege to lend PC Harrison a pair of my reinforced concrete knickers. However, we're clearly different sizes. She may need a pair of braces."

The girl's explosion of laughter was genuine and a convenient chance to release a few tears. Beatrice held onto hers.

It appeared Harrison's sense of dread had also affected Virginia. Her 16.00 team briefing was direct and brutal. Beatrice was grateful the girl herself was absent.

" ... so if any one of you takes your eye off the ball for a second, half a second, Karen Harrison could be sexually assaulted. She's a police officer, but she's also a woman. She'd have to live with that for the rest of her life. And so would we; because we let him get too close. Or she could be wounded. This guy's ready for physical contact now and could be carrying a knife, a gun, who knows. Ladies and gents, the profilers believe that non-consensual penetrative sex is where Paul Avery is heading. And the chances are high that it will be tonight or tomorrow, because he's back at work on Sunday. If we mess this up, one of our colleagues could get raped. And there's another possibility. Maybe he's already sussed us. He knows she's a trap. In which case, Karen stands a realistic chance of being killed.

"Do you understand what Police Constable Harrison is facing? Seriously? Would any one of you want to change places with her tonight? Nope, nor me. So for fuck's sake, don't let her down. We're all she's got. Good luck."

Beatrice followed the team out of the briefing room and headed for the coffee machine. She had no interest in caffeine, but when it came to casual eavesdropping, its location could not be beaten. Pouring a sparkling water and straining to hear a nearby exchange, she was irritated to see Ty Grant's large, florid bulk in front of her face.

"DI Stubbs? Look, sorry. I know you're on a break, but I'd really appreciate a word."

"I've only got about ten minutes before I go out. Can't you talk to DI Lowe?"

His voice dropped. "I'd rather deal with you."

Beatrice picked up a paper napkin to give her time to arrange her expression.

"Come on, then."

The interview room, cool and anonymous, brought Grant into unpleasantly close proximity. Unlike her, he seemed at ease with the atmosphere. After setting the comms to silent, Beatrice raised her gaze to him.

The dam broke. "DI Stubbs, I can't thank you enough for hearing me out. I did try to explain to DI Lowe, but she thought I had ulterior motives and if I'm honest, and I know I'm out of line for saying this, but some things are bigger than others and she should get over herself."

"Grant, you're not ..."

"Making any sense? I know. Sorry. I was in that briefing and I heard what DI Lowe said and it scared the living shit out of me, as it should. But I am a whole fucking shitload more scared because from what I've seen, we're following the wrong man."

Beatrice studied Ty Grant's high colour, keen eyes and nervous tics.

"Be honest with me and I'll take you seriously, Grant. Have you taken any kind of amphetamines?"

"Amphetamines? No! No, I'm totally clean. Apart from a Pro-Plus last night. Look, I know I'm acting manic. That's the point, DI Stubbs. I worked through the night to find any kind of concrete proof on Avery. There's nothing but circumstantials. So we got Karen out there, showing some tit and hoping to reel in Geek Boy. What if it's not him?"

"If not him, who?"

"Nathan Bennett. Listen, his evidence is just as damning. The logo on the baseball cap? Looks like a woodcut. It's a gym in Crouch End, called *CrossTrain*. Paul Avery's a member, we know. But so's Nathan Bennett. Both these guys work on the same BTP shift, and the thing is, we really don't know who's doing what in that control room unless we're physically there. And we're not. We know who's supposed to be doing which task, but from what I've seen, when there's no senior officer in the room, it seems they spend time on phones or screens or recorded data till they get bored and they switch. So that you can't be sure who's on that screen at any given moment." Ty's face gave away genuine concern.

"What about the positive ID? The smell?"

"We got two positive IDs, Avery and Bennett. The Avery positive came from the bridge woman, who admitted she couldn't see his face. A ditzy teen and a kid with mental problems confirmed it was the same guy. Apart from the French girl, who fingered Bennett, none of the others could be sure. The ID is far from solid.

"Smell, I don't know. But he spends a lot of time at the gym. *CrossTrain* provided all but one of his alibis. The manager, Carlos da Silva, showed me printouts to prove he'd swiped in and out. But I poked around on Facebook and found some photos of Bennett's wedding. Carlos da Silva was Bennett's best man."

Beatrice saw the logic. Her blood seemed to sink to her ankles as she considered how easily they had reached the conclusion that Avery was their target. She shook her head.

"If you're right, we need to widen the op. The security around PC Harrison remains unchanged. But we have to get officers watching Bennett."

"Now, DI Stubbs. Get people on him right now. All our guns are pointing at Avery. Nathan Bennett has the freedom of the city."

Beatrice looked into Ty Grant's eyes and saw fear and hopelessness. She recognised the expression. She'd seen it in the mirror.

Chapter 31

A deep-blue Ford Focus sat in a dip on the Pembroke coastal path. Two figures occupied the front seats. One peered into the darkness, head rotating like an owl, while the other slept, curled up under a cashmere rug.

At five am, a mobile phone emitted a gentle Japanese wind-chime effect.

"Adrian, turn it off. Quick!"

Matthew thrust the handset towards him. Adrian took it, killed the alarm and tucked the still bright screen into his jacket, all while waking up. He blinked into the darkness. It was totally pitch black. He couldn't even see Matthew.

"Sorry. Didn't mean to snap. But round here, even such a tiny light is like a beacon."

Adrian nodded, before realising the gesture was pointless. "Of course. Sorry. That didn't occur to me. But how are we going to find our way to the cliff? I can't see enough to find the door handle."

"We'll manage. Your eyes get used to it after a while."

Adrian rubbed a hand over his face. "You've been awake some time then?"

"An hour or so. Shall we go?"

Sleeping in cars was best done as a teenager. Rumpled, dry-mouthed and in need of a fully appointed bathroom, Adrian knew he probably looked like Matthew.

At least it occurred to him to turn off the interior lights before they exited the vehicle. He closed his door silently, bunted it with his hip to close it properly, slung the strap of his camera around his neck and allowed his eyes to adjust. The moon gave limited illumination through thin cloud cover and far across the fields, Adrian could see the friendly glow of a single sodium lamp. He followed Matthew through the scrubby grass, scanning each flank as if he were in *Platoon* until he tripped over a tussock. After that, he kept his eyes on the ground ahead, remaining alert for the glint of binoculars. Although, would binoculars glint if there was no light? He was still pondering this when Matthew held out his hand to stop him. Below them to the right, a vehicle bumped down the track to the beach, using only side-lights. The sight came as a shock and Adrian froze, his pulse pounding with the horrifying realisation that this was real. Actual drug dealers were down there, driving through the dark to an assignation. And he and Matthew, enthusiastic incompetents, were in the right place at the wrong time.

They should leave. Immediately.

Matthew watched the SUV till it disappeared from their sight-line and turned back with an appreciative smile. "It must be a great feeling for you," he whispered. "Being proven right."

Adrian unlocked his jaw. "Absolutely. You don't think we should call for backup or anything?"

"From whom? Come on. Sunrise is due in twenty minutes. We need to be ready."

Woefully under-equipped, they lay on their fronts in the dewy grass and gorse or whatever sharp, prickly stuff covered the cliff top. Despite the discomfort to his chest and groin and damage to his silk-mix roll-neck, Adrian appreciated the view. A generous spread of beach seemed to expand as the light swelled behind them and the scene below no longer caused him eye strain. He played with the zoom of his Pentax, bringing the Chelsea Tractor to the centre of the frame. Parked in darkness on the hard standing, the driver sat smoking. He was sure because he'd seen a cigarette lighter flash. Matthew was right about these tiny lights.

He kept scanning the bay for the smugglers' boat. Not even a speck.

"Here they come." Matthew kept his tone low, but the tension hit Adrian like a whiplash.

"Where? Could I please have the binoculars for ten seconds? Just ten?"

There was no reply. Just when it seemed his request had been ignored, Matthew sat up and looped the binoculars over his head.

"You may have a full minute. I need to attend to a call of nature." He scuttled back over the gorse ridge.

The boat was miles away. What kind of boat was that, anyway? A launch? A tug? Who knew? But it had a motor, just audible, a little hut sort of affair on the front, and was heading their way at speed. A light on the shore caught his eye. The SUV door opened and an interior lamp came on. Marie Fisher stepped out, dressed in a fleece and jeans. She lit another cigarette.

He lifted the binoculars back upwards, searching for the boat. It had come a lot closer while his attention was distracted. A figure was visible at its steering wheel. White hair? Or captain's hat? He flicked down to Marie Fisher, who was smoking and watching the boat's progress. Adrian's heart rate increased and he glanced back for Matthew. The ridge, silent and empty, offered no reassurance.

Without warning, a huge floodlight hit the cliff, illuminating the beach, the road, the steep rock face and Adrian. He ducked, pressing his face into the grass. The light flicked off the next second, but Adrian remained where he was, breathing in shallow gasps. How lucky he hadn't been using the binoculars at that moment. The reflection would have been a clear giveaway. Thank his own good judgement for the black polo neck and the fact that blond had never suited him. Rustling through the undergrowth heralded Matthew's return.

"What was that flash?" he whispered.

"Get down! They've got a massive light and they flared it at the beach. They might do it again," Adrian hissed.

"I doubt it. They were probably checking the coast was clear. Our black outfits came in handy after all. Binoculars, please."

Adrian raised his head six inches, lifting the binoculars from under his chest, relieved to get his nose off the ground. The smell concerned him, country bordering on farmyard. He reached for his camera as Matthew continued his observations.

"The boat has stopped, and I can see our friend with the ponytail. He's doing something with a rope. There's another man, older, with white hair, bringing a package onto the deck." Matthew paused. "I hope to God she's on her own."

"What do you mean? No one else was in that car." Adrian snapped some shots of the men on the boat, and of Marie, waiting on the shore.

"If she had accomplices keeping watch, where would they be, do you think?"

Adrian rolled onto his back, lifted his head from the ground and scanned the lightening horizon. He sent silent thanks to his gym instructor as the position was hell on the abs. The peach-coloured sky softened the contours of the land, revealing shrubs, scrub grass and sheep. He rolled back to Matthew.

"Can't see anything."

"Quick. Get some shots of this. The two men are on the beach now. The older one has passed the package to Marie. No, it's a bag, with handles. She's put it on the ground and is looking inside. It looks more like a basket, you know, but she's blocking my view. I can't see what's in there."

Adrian tweaked the zoom, and began clicking the shutter. He watched Marie Fisher's movements. She was not happy. From her crouching position over the goods, she jabbed her finger at both men, making short, angry gestures to the basket and back to them. If only they could hear her. The men's faces grew more distinct in the growing light and a seagull cried, as plaintive and haunting as the wail of a baby.

As if aware of her visibility, Marie picked up the basket, placed it on the passenger seat and got back behind the wheel.

"Quick!" Matthew crawled backwards, keeping his head low.

"What now?"

"Let's get back to the car, we have to follow her."

"Oh my God."

"Adrian, don't go all wet on me now. You've been a great sport so far."

"It's not that. I've been lying in sheep shit."

Adrian glanced at the speedometer. 95 miles per hour. Matthew sat rigidly, clenching the steering wheel. Adrian sighed.

"Slow down. We've lost her. Either she turned off somewhere, or picked up speed as soon as she was out of sight. She's gone."

The vehicle dropped back to the speed limit and Matthew exhaled. "My fault. You were right. I should have stayed closer. I was over-cautious about her noticing us."

Adrian shook his head. Matthew was such a thoroughly decent man. "Actually, I think you were probably nearer the mark. She'd spotted us and decided to ditch her tail at the first opportunity."

"Perhaps she thought we were the police. Her driving was impeccable, sticking just under seventy and always indicating to overtake, despite the paucity of traffic."

"So what now?" Disappointed and tired, Adrian's enthusiasm was running low.

"Well, first priority is to clean you up. I'm going to pull in at that garage, and you're going to dispose of that jumper. The stink is truly appalling."

He indicated and slowed as they approached the Esso sign. The garage was almost empty. Apart from a large black SUV.

Adrian saw it first. "Keep going! That's her. Don't pull in, Matthew. Just drive!"

Matthew's eyes flicked to the mirror. Knocking the indicator off, he picked up speed again.

"But now we're ahead of her. How will we know when she turns off?" he asked.

Matthew asking him what to do struck Adrian as absurd. Neither of them had a clue what they were playing at. They needed Beatrice.

He feigned a laid-back tone. "We know where she's going, roughly. We'll do as she does. Stick around seventy, or just over, and keep her in our sights. Then, after we get onto the motorway, nearer to Cardiff, we let her overtake and tail her again. From her perspective, it won't look suspicious because there'll be a lot more traffic as we approach the city."

Matthew spent the next ninety minutes checking all three

mirrors repeatedly, unable to uphold his end of any conversation. Adrian observed the tension in his shoulders, brow and face. He'd be exhausted by the time they reached Cardiff.

After the turn-off to somewhere completely unpronounceable, early morning road usage increased, as Adrian had predicted, and they allowed Marie's distinctive bullish vehicle to overtake. Matthew hunched towards the windscreen, gripping the wheel with taut hands. The possibility of losing her in the flow of vehicles affected Adrian's nerves too, so he squinted ahead with determination.

He saw the indicator light and yelled, "She's turning off!"

Matthew jumped and touched the brakes.

"Sorry, got over-excited," Adrian said, without taking his eyes from the SUV. Matthew didn't reply, but drew closer as they took the slip road off the motorway. He kept close on the roundabout, but fell back again as she indicated her exit. Adrian perched on the edge of his seat and picked up his camera. Lots of almost-opportunities to grab a decent shot slipped past, so he replaced it on his lap. The orange light flashed again and she turned towards a place called St Bride's-super-Ely. They were the only two vehicles on the road, so Matthew allowed her some distance and she disappeared around a bend. They had just regained a visual as she turned left, without indication.

The bright morning light enabled them to watch the huge black beast's progress over the top of the country hedges, while remaining safely out of sight. She turned off once more, into a newly built estate of six detached houses. It reminded Adrian of the set of *Brookside*. Matthew stopped the car just after the entrance, pulling in beside a farm gate. He hopped out of the car, stood on the door chassis and trained his binoculars over the hedge. Adrian got out and listened to Matthew's low commentary.

"Out of the car, and she's heading to one of the houses. She hasn't got the drugs with her. She's looking through a bunch of keys. Now she's opened the front door of number ... seven and gone inside. She's in a foul temper, you can see that from here. What an unpleasant woman she is. I tell you what, it's lovely to have some fresh ... hello, she's back. Opening the car door, picking up the package ..."

Once more, a seagull's cry soared into the air. But this time Adrian realised he'd been mistaken. That plaintive wail was no sea bird imitating a child. It was the real thing.

Marie took the basket inside, and Matthew, dropping the binoculars onto his chest, got off the car and rested his arms on the roof. Adrian stared at him, unable to articulate a single word. Just for something to do, he delicately eased off his jumper. With a glance at the houses beyond the hedge, he opened the boot, yanked out his weekend holdall and rolled up his stinking jumper in the plastic laundry bag. Unusually for him, he didn't even wonder if the silk-cashmere mix would be salvageable. He pulled on a T-shirt while still shaking his head. A baby. It made no sense.

Matthew appeared, staring with the same uncomprehending look as before, and reached into his bag for a water bottle. He sat on the edge of the open boot and swallowed several large gulps, before turning his gaze to Adrian.

"I believe the modern expression is, *What the fuck?* Is senility assuming control so soon, or did two men sail into that bay and hand over a baby?"

"I don't understand. I'm tired and confused and can't believe what we've just seen. Matthew, my instinct is to call Beatrice."

"I wholeheartedly agree. We're out of our depth. Fetch your device and let's call the boss. Hopefully she'll still be up. She's on surveillance."

As Adrian returned to the passenger seat and located his mobile, he heard a noise. An engine approached.

Matthew hissed from the boot, "A car's coming, hide!"

It was too late. The car was following the same route they had taken, and when it turned the corner, its occupants would have a clear view of them both and their vehicle. But it didn't turn the corner. The car slowed almost to a halt and pulled into the driveway of the cul-de-sac. Adrian snatched his camera, and stepped up onto the bumper of the Focus, using the wild hedge as a screen. Matthew repositioned himself in the doorway, leaning back against the roof, binoculars in hand.

The hesitant approach suggested this was the driver's first visit. Unlike Marie, who'd clearly known exactly where she was going. After parking on the drive behind the SUV, both the front doors opened. Adrian's nerves hummed and he took a second to check that no one had crept up on them while their attention was focused elsewhere. Apart from the ruckus created by birds, insects and wind, the lane was silent.

The driver, wearing jeans and a rugby shirt, came around the car to meet the passenger, a woman. Taking her hand, he leant to look into her face, as if concerned. She had blonde highlights, and was a good foot shorter than him. Adrian's lens followed them up the path, and caught Marie as she opened the door. He got shots of every single thing.

He removed the camera and looked at Matthew. "What now?"

"Did you take a photograph of the number plate?"

"Several. Let's call HQ."

Beatrice was not happy about being woken after a 'bloody wretched night'. Her terse tone persuaded Adrian to hand the phone directly to Matthew. Adrian resumed his perch on the vehicle and waited to catch someone coming out of the house, while trying to pick up the drift of what Matthew was saying. Both efforts were fruitless. Finally, Matthew returned with his phone.

"She wants to talk to you." They swapped places and Matthew trained his sights on the close.

"Adrian, listen to me. Leave now. You have photographs, a vehicle registration and plenty of evidence for us to work with. If there really is a child involved, you have no choice but to report this to the South Wales police. Leave now, please, and go to the nearest police station. If either party in that house suspects you of watching them, you are in serious danger. I don't need to tell you what the consequences could be and I'm not there to watch your neck. Adrian, are you listening?"

He was, mostly. But his attention was drawn by Matthew, who stood alert as a meercat. Adrian hopped onto the bumper beside him and raised his camera.

"Absolutely. Understood. We're going now. Call you later!"

Adrian caught a few shots of the couple placing the now-silent basket in their car and swung into his seat. Marie remained out of sight.

Matthew rushed to the driver's side, waiting till he heard the other vehicle's engine before starting the car and pulling away with minimum noise. They continued in the direction of Cardiff, both constantly checking the mirrors. After a mile or so, Adrian saw a farm track, and suggested a stop. Matthew drove in for several yards, so they couldn't be seen from the road. A few seconds digging in the glove compartment provided Adrian with a map, and thus a good reason to be there, which he unfolded across the dashboard. They returned their attention to the mirrors. Three minutes passed. Five. Seven.

"They must have gone back the way they came," Adrian suggested.

"Yes, it looks that way." Matthew made no move.

Adrian sighed. "I don't know about you but I think we should find the nearest Prêt-a-Manger and indulge in a ..."

"Hang on a sec! Here she is."

Marie's vehicle rumbled past and continued into the dappled shadows of the tree-lined lane.

"Right, come on then." Adrian folded up the map but Matthew shook his head.

"We can't follow her. Not any further. Firstly, we promised Beatrice. Secondly, if she sees the car again, she will certainly suspect observation. No, we've done our bit."

"So what now? Should we locate the nearest police station?" Despite his tiredness and discomfort, Adrian's adrenalin was still pumping.

"Hmm. You know, I wonder if it might be more diplomatic to deliver our evidence to the Pembrokeshire force. After all, it is their territory and might just redeem Beatrice in the eyes of the local inspector. We'll need to make statements and possibly accompany them to the scene."

Adrian gasped. "You know what we could do? Go to the pub!" He sat up, energised by the thought.

"It's a little early for me."

"Not now. Tonight. Those men hang about all day and go to the pub in the evening, remember? They'll be there this evening. Listen, why don't we check into a hotel? Then I can clean myself up, send these photos to Beatrice and we can both get some beauty sleep. Later, we'll drive back to Pembrokeshire and give our evidence to the local police. Tonight, we could lie in wait at the pub and identify them to the undercover officers. We could actually be present at the arrest!"

Matthew glanced at him, with a growing smile. "That's not a bad idea. It does seem a shame to miss the excitement of the final scene, after we've done all the donkey work. It would be foolish to pass up such an opportunity. Very well. There's a Travelodge a few miles back. But we ought to tell Beatrice what we're doing."

Adrian clapped his hands together. "Hell, yes. And we'll promise to be careful, not take risks, etcetera. I can shower, shave and perform other necessary ablutions, and possibly even call my friend the barman. Turn around! To the Travelodge!"

With a smile, Matthew began reversing. "I wonder if I should buy a hat?"

"Sorry?"

"A hat, to obscure my identity. The ponytailed chap has seen me before, albeit briefly, but if he were to recognise me, it could complicate matters. He might put two and two together and make a run for it."

Opportunities were falling into Adrian's lap like ripe fruit.

"You know, a half-decent haircut would probably be a better disguise. We'll see if the hotel has a proper pair of scissors."

Chapter 32

The sense of triumphant purpose and excited discussions as to the possible outcome of the evening, which accompanied the drive west, came to an abrupt halt. Fishguard police station was closed. Matthew and Adrian stood in front of the door and read the notice detailing opening hours.

Adrian was shocked. "I can't believe it actually closes! It's not even five o'clock. What happens if there's an emergency?"

"One dials 999, naturally. Emergency Services. These rural police stations don't need to be open around the clock. Crime rates hardly match London's and the expense is unjustified."

"Well, we have to call the emergency line. We can't let them get away."

"Hmm. Could we really say this is an emergency? All we'd planned to do was hand over our evidence, give statements and assist the police in identifying potential suspects. Which wouldn't even be necessary when they have photographs," said Matthew.

Adrian's Have-A-Go Hero headlines were fading fast. "But what about the arrest? If we don't grab them tonight, they'll sail out of here and we've lost them. All because the station is closed. It's ridiculous!"

"I suggest we stick to the plan. We go to the pub, keep our ears open, glean what we can and add that to our report. Then we return here in the morning, with a full dossier. The police can subsequently use our information to apprehend these men. All is not lost, Adrian."

Adrian hesitated. "Apart from us missing out on the action. Oh hell, you're right. Let's go back to the B&B. Do we have to tell

Beatrice?" He caught Matthew's expression, sighed and reached for his phone.

The two men sat on the harbour wall in Porthgain, processing their orders. DI Stubbs had laid down the law. Adrian tried every which way to maintain his indignation, but had to admit the justice of her argument. Matthew was to go nowhere near Ponytail and his associate. As far as Beatrice was concerned, the passage of time, the black polo neck, black moleskin trousers and the short back and sides, which showed off his silvery temples in contrast with the rest of his thick black hair all counted for nothing; he could still be recognised. That meant endangering themselves, or wrecking any investigation if these people chose to move their operation elsewhere.

She granted permission for Adrian to go to the pub, to observe and keep his ears open, but forced him to promise several times to do nothing risky, nothing to draw attention to himself. As if he would.

"And whether you hear anything or not, first thing tomorrow morning, you go to the local police and tell them everything. You must. I've left a message for Inspector Howells and given him your number. Adrian, I really don't have time to deal with this, so I'm relying on you two to do things properly. This is now out of your hands."

"We will. First thing. But Beatrice, you needn't worry. I've got a natural skill for covert people-watching. I do it all the time." A brighter thought crossed his mind. He could now spend the evening chatting to Lyndon without neglecting Matthew. Luck was on his side once again.

He handed the phone to Matthew to say his goodbyes and wandered along the sea wall. He spent several minutes watching a large boat pitching and swaying with the movement of the waves. Sailing didn't look all that much fun. *Strike world cruise from the To-Do list.*

Matthew approached. "She's not budging. Looks like you're on your own this evening." He handed back the mobile.

"It seems totally unfair, but I have to say she's right. You can't risk being spotted. So what will you do with yourself tonight?" asked Adrian.

"Oh, I'll be fine. I shall head over to the fish restaurant and indulge myself. I feel more concerned for you, sitting alone in a busy pub, trying to overhear any information about a pair of shady characters. Part of the fun of this is the teamwork and now I have to leave you to it." His expression gave away sincere concern.

"Matthew, you've forgotten my barman. My evening might turn out to be a tiny bit more than spying and surveillance."

"Of course! The chap with the cheekbones. In fact, that's even better, because you can sit at the bar and talk to him. You'll be able to eavesdrop on any conversations as they order their drinks. Well, this has all come out rather well!"

Adrian laughed and turned his mind to the next problem. *Your sartorial challenge, should you wish to accept it, is as follows: to dress like a nondescript tourist, while still demonstrating style and class to those who count. How to stand out while fading away?*

The clientele of The Clipper Inn on a Saturday night was a varied bunch in terms of dress and age, but all were uniformly loud. Adrian sat on a bar stool, drinking a spritzer, pretending to read the local paper and exchanging shy grins with Lyndon. They were able to have a few brief conversations at first, but as the pub filled, Lyndon had no time for anything but pouring beer, wrestling with the till and rushing to the next customer. Adrian's perch allowed him the full view of the low room. The smugglers had not made an appearance.

Just after nine, Adrian began to get bored. The paper was a typical local rag, so if you didn't know these people who'd won scholarships to Aberystwyth, or been elected to the County Council, all you could do was criticise their choice of clothes. And even that was shooting fish in a barrel. Crossword completed, even if a few answers didn't quite fit, he'd exhausted the paper and had no one to talk to.

He sighed, the door opened, and in they came. Ponytail and a truly grim-looking older guy gave the room a quick scan, then made straight for the bar. Although he stood several feet away, Adrian could hear his accent as he ordered two pints of lager. Irish, certainly, but there was something else, a guttural sound which made his voice unusual. Propping themselves against the bar, they turned inwards, their backs to the rest of the customers. This gave Adrian the perfect opportunity to note details.

Beatrice was right. That hair was utterly horrific. From the front: a sharp face with an unfortunate chin, framed by dark brown hair. Short sides, floppy fringe. All perfectly acceptable until you noticed the harshly bleached fronds splayed across his shoulders. He wore dark jeans, a faded black hooded sweatshirt and battered trainers. His accomplice looked worse. White-grey hair cut short and the dour, miserable lines on the man's face made Adrian think of a US Army drill sergeant. Some faces bear the imprint of their most frequent expressions; you can recognise a veteran smiler, just as you can spot someone used to frowning. This man's face had spent far too long showing contempt. His green Army surplus shirt and black combat trousers indicated a man inordinately fond of pockets.

Lyndon shot Adrian a significant look as he spotted them and the next chance he had, he came along the bar under the pretence of retrieving some ice.

"Have you had a word?" Lyndon asked.

"No. And I don't intend to. I just want to find out a bit about them. See if you can serve them next time, get into conversation, you know."

Lyndon shrugged. "I'll try. But I've served these two before." He indicated the stuffed pike in its glass case above the fire. "I've had more fun talking to him. By the way, what you doing later?"

The chef appeared through the kitchen door. "Lyndon!"

Lyndon took his ice bucket and scooted back into the fray.

It took another twenty-two minutes. Eventually, Adrian watched the older man signal to the barmaid and elbow his colleague. Lyndon ducked in front of the approaching girl and picked up their glasses. The guy was quick, Adrian had to admit. Ponytail leant onto his right buttock and reached around to pull his wallet from his back pocket. An idea began to form in Adrian's mind. Ponytail paid for the drinks and replaced his wallet in his jeans. The 'conversation' wasn't going well. Lyndon made another comment, but received nothing more than a blank stare. He shrugged and moved off to serve some shrill Italians.

Lyndon spoke from the corner of his mouth next time he hurried by.

"Nothing. Miserable sods. You going to have a go?"

Adrian shook his head. "No. But I'm going to lift his wallet. When you ring the bell for last orders, ask them a question or spill their drinks or something. With the rush to the bar as well, that should cover me. Can I borrow one of your little waiter's pads?"

"You serious? First time anyone's asked me to create a distraction. You be careful, right? If you get smacked in the puss, I'm not taking you home tonight. Here you go. I want it back after, mind."

Adrian grinned, masking his nerves. Would Beatrice approve of his picking the pocket of a child trafficker? The thought made him pause. But a good detective should seize every opportunity. He'd be careful. He wasn't stupid and here was a chance to prove it. Professional athletes rehearse their moves in their minds, over and over until the sequence is perfect. No reason why a wine-merchant, rich tenor and part-time detective couldn't do the same.

Lyndon directed several meaningful stares across the bar as the clock ticked closer to eleven, but Adrian refused to be distracted. He kept as still as possible, not drinking, not watching, but focusing on his inner picture of a successful lift.

"Last orders, ladies and gents, last orders." The landlord, stupid git, came out of the kitchen and rang the bell, taking both Adrian and Lyndon by surprise. Adrian slid from the stool and hurried along the bar, with the rest of the 'just one more' crowd. Lyndon shifted into position and picked up the two almost empty glasses from their targets.

"Oi! We haven't finished those!" The older man's arm shot out and grabbed Lyndon's wrist.

Adrian rushed forward, pressing himself against Ponytail and slipping out the wallet with his left hand, apologising all the while.

"Shit, I'm *so* sorry. Are you okay? Did I spill your drink? Everyone's in such a hurry tonight. That bloke shoved me off balance." He looked over his shoulder in disgust at some imaginary figure. Ponytail frowned but said nothing.

Lyndon apologised and replaced the drinks, offering to serve them fresh pints before the crowd. The two men agreed and Adrian slipped away to the bathroom, with his booty. He sat on the toilet seat, and flicked through the wallet. Cash in both Euros and sterling, a driving licence in the name of Eoin – *how on earth was he supposed to pronounce that* – Connor, and a set of business cards. Lannagh Farm, Kilmore Road, Ballyharty.

Adrian debated calling Beatrice's mobile, but if she was busy entrapping a flasher, she might not appreciate it. Instead, he sent her a text message and wrote the address on Lyndon's notepad before replacing everything in the wallet. Afterwards, he switched his phone to silent. He was thorough, just as Beatrice had taught him. While he was there, he relieved the pressure on his bladder and congratulated himself on a fine piece of work. Ponytail wouldn't miss his wallet, as it was the older guy's round, and Adrian could 'find' it for him on the way back. Lyndon certainly deserved some kind of reward for his assistance, which was unlikely to be a chore. A coup de théâtre, indeed.

The two men hadn't moved from their positions, hunched at the bar, already nearing the end of their pints.

"Whoops. There's a wallet on the floor here. Does it belong to either of you?"

They both turned. Ponytail eyed Adrian and the wallet with suspicion before taking it. "It's mine."

"Must have fallen down when I bumped into you. Listen, I am sorry about that. Can I make amends by buying you both a beer? Or how about a chaser?"

Ponytail looked to his companion, who shook his head without even acknowledging the offer.

Ponytail shrugged. "No, you're all right. It's closing time anyway. Thanks anyway." He drained his pint and climbed off the stool. "Goodnight to you."

"Oh, goodnight."

They shouldered their way towards the door. Adrian returned to his stool and scanned the room for Lyndon.

"What did you find out?"

The voice at his elbow made him jump. His nerves were a little stretched. Lyndon ducked back behind the bar, carrying a tower of empty pint glasses, face expectant.

"Name, address and occupation. Not bad for an amateur. Is it too late to get a glass of wine? I feel safe enough to dispense with the soda now. And I'd like to buy you a drink, for your help and all." He tore off the address and tucked it in his wallet, handing the pad back to Lyndon.

Lyndon took it, with an impressed nod. "Not bad at all. How about we share a bottle? I've put one in to chill, so as soon as I've finished, we can go back to my place. If you like?"

"I like." Adrian's grin spread. Naturally lucky. He couldn't help it.

"Only you'll have to wait outside for me. We need to clear the pub by quarter past. Sorry. Why don't you sit on one of the benches outside? I'll be with you in two shakes of a lamb's tail."

"Better still, why don't I wait by the harbour? Absorb the view."

The glow from the pub windows faded as Adrian traced his way down the stony track to the sounds of the sea. The cold air made him wish he'd brought a jacket. He rubbed his arms, absorbing the relaxing ebb and flow of the water, the metallic clinks and clangs of boats moving with the tide, and the black, white and grey perspective afforded by the moon. He could have been in a Truffaut film. To his left stood the quarry hoppers, massive constructions of the Industrial Age, supported by a vast brick wall. Their sheer scale, not to mention dangerous edges, depths and harsh surfaces sent another chill over his shoulders. He chose to look to the right, at the moonlit water, the spots of light coming from distant cottages and the huge black solidity of the landmass which dropped to the sea.

He heard a footstep. Quicker than he expected, but there was no doubting the guy was eager. It would be perfect if Lyndon's house had a sea view. With a smile, he turned to greet him. The shock of seeing Ponytail caused his face to fall. Before he could open his mouth, someone came up behind him and wrenched his arm painfully behind his back.

That strange accent. "Right, you're coming with us."

Chapter 33

"You must be out of your mind. Did you not hear what I said in there?" Virginia jerked her head in the direction of the briefing room.

"I don't have a choice. If there are no more officers available, we have to take some of the people off Harrison. I don't like that anymore than you do, but we can't put all our eggs in one blanket when there's just as much evidence to incriminate Bennett. I want people watching him."

"Beatrice, I'm sorry, but I can't agree. We've put Harrison into a vulnerable position. You were the one lecturing me on treating the girl with respect. You sat there with me today and we both assured her of our total support. And now you want to renege on our promise to keep her as safe as we possibly can."

Beatrice clenched her teeth. "I have a duty to all the women in this city, and no plans to renege on any of the promises I made. There's nothing specific in our case to make Avery more of a suspect than Bennett. As Grant pointed out ..."

Virginia groaned. "Grant? Oh please. See this for what it is. An attention-seeking exercise from a detective hungry for promotion. All eyes are on Harrison, and he doesn't like it. He tried talking me into this wild goose chase but I had the sense to look behind the 'I-worked-all-night-and-I-think-I-found-something-ma'am' bullshit. Basically, I've been ignoring him, and this is just another technique to put himself centre stage."

The woman's ego was astounding. Beatrice took two deep breaths, determined to remain in control of her temper.

"As a matter of fact, Virginia, this is not all about you. I believe our detective work has been shoddy, and we've leapt to conclusions.

We have two suspects and should be watching both equally hard. Karen Harrison seems to be an object of interest to either or both. Given that we are exposing her to a potential assault, I agree that the majority of our force should be with her. But in addition to a team of two on Avery, I want the same on Bennett. Which means taking two people off Harrison."

"No. We can investigate Bennett in more detail tomorrow, but tonight, all hands on deck for our set-up. Let's face it, you don't even know where Bennett is."

Beatrice had heard enough of Virginia's patronising tone. "We will. I've briefed the Surveillance Centre to inform us if he appears on camera. Grant and I plan to locate him, follow him, talk to his wife and find out everything we can."

"Leaving me to manage the Harrison operation single-handed?"

"Exactly. Totally on your own, backed up by a mere twenty-six officers. Which makes fifty-two hands."

Virginia's expression was hard and cold. "I find this extremely unprofessional, I have to say. We're supposed to operate as a team, not run off on different tangents. You're being pig-headed."

"And you're being blinkered. We have the same objective at heart. Just differing opinions of how to achieve it. I want to turn every stone to find this reptile. I'll report back as and when I find something."

Grant's gratitude for her support manifested itself in a non-stop justification of himself on the drive to Crouch End.

"... which is why I approached you, because even if I rate her as a senior officer, all the personal stuff has clouded the issue, although for some reason she's definitely keeping me at arm's length now, which is fine, plenty more fish and all that, but she should still see the difference when I'm trying to get her attention for a genuine issue, and I think part of the reason she's slapping me down is because she knows I want to transfer to the Met, but the way I see it, in situations like this, we should rise above politics ..."

Eventually, Beatrice shut him up. "I appreciate everything you've said, Grant, and your candour is reassuring. So I'll be equally honest and tell you that if another woman is assaulted in the Finsbury Park area, the Met intend to replace me on this investigation. Thus my motives for keeping an eye on Bennett are as much self-preservation as anything else. Now, what say we leave both the personal and the politics out of this and just concentrate on finding the bloke?"

"Fair enough, ma'am. Sorry. Still heard nothing back from Fitch on the mobile trace. So you want to hit the gym first, or visit his wife?" He checked the mirror as he indicated right into Hornsey Road.

"The gym's likely to be rather crowded, isn't it? Post-work rush. Let's visit his wife. What does she do?"

"Works at various sports centres, including *CrossTrain*. She's on the books as a qualified physio but mainly teaches classes. She's the Pilates instructor. And a bit of yoga, spinning, that sort of thing."

Beatrice glanced at Grant, irritated by his absurd mirrored sunglasses. Was he aspiring to join the CIA? "How do we know she's not at work?"

"I checked her schedule. She teaches mornings only. Bored housewives and all that."

"What is 'spinning'?" she asked, ignoring the chauvinism.

"Sort of cycling on a stationary bike. Cardio-intensive but boring as hell. Not my sort of thing."

"Nor mine. Then again, nor is rugby. All that scrumming and tackling and grabbing and ending up under a pile of none-too-fragrant bruisers."

A proud smile spread over Grant's face. "It's a man's game, all right."

Beatrice wrinkled her nose and chose not to respond. She looked out the window. "Good Lord, look at this. Crouch End is a world away from Finsbury Park, isn't it? Mothers in Birkenstocks, fathers with pushchairs, wine bars, delis, and I bet it would take us less than five minutes to find a child called Imogen."

"London's like that. Here we are. Lightfoot Road. How do you want to play it?"

"By ear. But if he's there, would you be so good as to loom?"

"No sweat. I'm good at looming."

"I can well imagine."

Suzanne Bennett's thighs were no broader than Beatrice's forearm. She opened the door wearing an all-white tracksuit, full make-up and a perky ponytail.

"Good afternoon, Mrs Bennett. My name is Detective Inspector Beatrice Stubbs, and this is Detective Sergeant Ty Grant of the London Transport Police. We wondered if we could have a word with your husband. He's helping us with an investigation, you see."

Grant turned his head to her. He'd obviously noted how she phrased their introduction, thereby avoiding mention of the Met.

The woman laughed and rolled her eyes. "Talk about the left hand not knowing what the right's up to. He's in work. They called him in last minute, 'cos someone's off sick. Again."

Beatrice did not look at Grant, but could feel him tense. "Oh that is stupid of me. I should have checked. In that case, we'll catch up with him back at base. But while we're here, I don't suppose I could have a few minutes of your time, could I?"

Suzanne Bennett stepped back and gestured inside. "Sure. But I've got book club in twenty-five minutes. It's only the other side of the park, but I have to leave in quarter of an hour."

"Thank you. We won't delay you. Which book are you discussing tonight?"

"*Kitchen Roll or Toilet Paper*. Have you read it?"

"I've not heard of that one."

"Well, get yourself a copy. It's brilliant. A self-help manual for women who can't see the difference between Nanny and Nurse when dealing with husbands, bosses, children, neighbours, friends and all that. One of them books where you just go 'Oh yeah', all the way through, you know what I mean?"

The terraced house, like most in the area, possessed an impressive depth. The spotless living room stretched all the way back to the neat little garden. White décor gave the room a spacious feel despite the fact that every surface was covered with photographs of the happy couple. Suzanne chattered away as she poured glasses of mineral water and Beatrice sensed that with some skilled questioning, they could find out a great deal from this painfully thin female. However, whether anything was possible in fifteen minutes remained to be seen.

Beatrice shifted forward on the sofa, while Grant stood by the mantelpiece. "After that passionate recommendation, I'll have to read it. Now, Mrs Bennett, not to waste too much of your time ..."

"Will you call me Suzanne? I hate Mrs Bennett. Makes me feel like something out of Jane Austen."

"Certainly. And you can call me Beatrice. I wonder if I can ask you how Nathan feels about being called into work at such short notice? You can speak freely, as I have no control over staffing rotas."

She cocked her head like a small bird. "Can't lie to you, he's not happy. I mean, once in a while is fair enough. But as he says, it's getting ridiculous. Over the summer, almost every week when he's off, he gets a call. He's not complaining about the extra money, course not, but it spoils any plans we've made."

"I see. Yes, that must be a nuisance. And this has become worse over the summer?"

"Yeah. It happened a couple of times before we went on holiday. But since then, it's been once a month, easy. Sometimes twice. This month, he's been called in three times."

Beatrice shook her head. "That's unacceptable. Not least because we cannot expect our staff to operate at peak performance if they're tired or demotivated."

"Yeah, he is looking tired. And today he left his mobile at home again. That's happening more and more. I reckon he's getting forgetful under all the pressure."

Beatrice glanced at Grant. "Listen, Suzanne, I might be able to do something to help. If you could you let me have the dates he was called in unexpectedly, I'll have a quiet word with the powers-that-be. See if we can't make this system a little fairer."

"Ooh, now you're asking! Let me have a look at the calendar. That's where I usually make notes." She bounced off towards the kitchen and was back before Grant had finished raising his eyebrows.

"Here we go. This is nowhere near all of them, but I can give you some of them in the last couple of months." She began scribbling dates on the back of an envelope. Beatrice scanned the calendar as she waited.

"That's very helpful of you. And, Suzanne, why don't we keep this visit to ourselves? So when his life starts to change, he'll never know how much his clever wife is responsible."

Suzanne beamed, Grant stared and Beatrice sipped her water.

Chapter 34

At Finsbury Park Control Centre, Beatrice and Grant showed Kalpana Joshi the matching dates against the pattern of attacks.

"He told his wife he was working overtime and went out to sexually harass other women? I just cannot believe Nathan Bennett capable of that. He's not the type." Kalpana gazed at the screen. "But he is, isn't he?"

Grant shrugged. "Seems you can't tell who's the type just by looking."

"What I find even stranger is that they're trying to have children," added Beatrice.

Grant gawped at her. "When did she tell you that? Or was it just feminine intuition?"

"On her calendar, she'd marked five little red asterisks each month. And approximately a week and a half later, a block of days highlighted in pink."

Kalpana nodded. "Ovulation. Her fertile days. In that case, do you think he's on strict rations?"

"Even if he's only allowed to hump her once a year, that's still no excuse for what he's done," Grant huffed.

"Quite. And delicately put," agreed Beatrice. "The problem we have now is how to find him. Every member of our team is on surveillance, watching Paul Avery and our police decoy. Bennett may go after her, too. After all, we can't be sure who it is that follows her on camera every night. If it's Bennett, and he does go for Karen, he'll walk right into the same trap."

Kalpana pressed her palms together and rested her chin on her fingertips. "But if he's got someone else in mind, where do we start?"

"On the street. He conveniently left his mobile at home so we can't trace him that way," said Grant.

"Our operation is all over the Finsbury Park area," said Beatrice. "Grant and I taking off in another direction is a politically unpopular move, so we can't get any more officers as support. But we hoped you might be able to provide us with a few extra pairs of eyes to search for Bennett."

"One. One pair of eyes. I can't swing any more officers, but for what it's worth, I'm at your disposal."

One. One bright, experienced senior officer on their side. It was better than they could have hoped.

Kalpana left to change, Grant went outside to make some personal calls and Beatrice rang Hamilton. She knew Virginia had his ear and would have reported Beatrice's decision to change tactic as soon as she was able. It was a wonder Hamilton hadn't been roaring at her already.

"Stubbs? What do you want now?" Even for Hamilton, the tone was especially irascible.

"I apologise for the disturbance, sir. I just wanted to inform you that the investigation has widened somewhat. DI Lowe is supervising the lure and surveillance pairs. DI Joshi, DS Grant and I are following up another potential lead."

"I understood you had your man marked and it was simply a matter of catching him in the act, so to speak. Why are you chasing another lead?"

Beatrice acknowledged her boss's precise grasp of events. No matter how many cases ran simultaneously, Hamilton had an overview of every one. She used to think he was checking up on her. Now she saw it as the mark of an excellent manager.

"Your information is correct, sir. But look at it this way: we're 98% sure of our suspect, therefore we've allocated the giant's share of the manpower to observing him. And the female officer he's been watching. Yet there is an outside chance of another man having slipped the net. Just to cover every base, sir, three senior officers are going to locate him, observe him and question him."

Hamilton's voice dropped. "Are you telling me the whole joint effort involving a staggering amount of expenditure and overtime has been barking up the wrong tree?"

"No sir, we can't be sure ..."

"You can't be sure. And did I comprehend you correctly? You don't know where your second suspect is?"

"As of yet, sir, we're uncertain of his whereabouts."

"Don't doublespeak me, Stubbs. You think you've buggered up the ID, you've set the dogs on the wrong man and now you and Lowe are haring all over North London hoping to find a needle in a bloody haystack."

"Not DI Lowe, sir. She's supervising the Finsbury Park op. DI Joshi is assisting, along with DS Grant, both of BTP. Grant's the sergeant who brought the possible anomaly to my attention."

Hamilton paused. "Can I suggest, DI Stubbs, in the strongest possible terms, that you stick to your remit? A collaborative effort with the BTP to apprehend a potential rapist. I have less interest in your relations with DI Lowe than the outcome of *The X Factor*, but I vainly hoped for professionalism, selflessness and an arrest. If you can manage neither of the first two, I'll settle for the third. Depending on the outcome of your adventures this evening, I suggest a meeting tomorrow. Good evening, Stubbs."

"Good evening, sir."

Hamilton's exasperation depressed Beatrice less than it should. He had no idea she'd split from the main team, which meant Virginia had said nothing. That could be interpreted as loyalty. She picked up the phone again.

Virginia might be loyal, but she was stubborn. Despite the strong evidence to support their pursuit of Bennett, Virginia's tone was dismissive and short. She was convinced of the target and the lure was cast. Harrison in place, all officers prepared, the two officers tailing Avery awaiting his emergence from his flat, everything was set. Nothing would dissuade her from seeing this through. After agreeing to update every hour, Beatrice wished her colleague luck with the evening's operation. With some reluctance, Virginia did likewise.

Adrian's mobile was still switched off. Beatrice didn't leave a message, trusting him to call when he had news. She wondered if they were still enjoying playing detectives. So long as they were playing it safe. And having more fun than she was. She allowed herself a fond smile.

Kalpana returned from her office wearing cut-off trousers, a long-sleeved T-shirt and her hair loose. She looked about sixteen years old. Beatrice realised how vital the severe bun, smart suits and serious shoes were to maintaining her authority at work.

Kalpana gave her a tight smile. "Ready?"

Beatrice nodded. "Yes. I still can't get hold of my men-folk, but I'll just have to trust them to keep out of trouble. Are you all sorted regarding domestic arrangements?"

"Yep. The neighbour feeds my cat if I'm called away like this. Moira's an animal-loving, widowed telly addict and he's a greedy, attention-seeking, ginger gigolo. They adore each other. I often think if it happens too often, Scaramanga will pack his catty bags and move round there permanently."

"Wonderful name for a cat."

"It suits him."

While Ty Grant patrolled the Hornsey and Crouch Hill region alone, Beatrice joined Kalpana in her Toyota to scour Crouch End. Between them, they covered the whole area between Bennett's home and Finsbury Park. Hours of tension solidified Beatrice's shoulders into setting cement. The radio informed them Harrison left 'her flat' and made the journey to Leicester Square without incident, while Paul Avery was in the Snooker Club.

Kalpana seemed tired, so the two women made little small talk, apart from enquiries as to the other's state of comfort. At five to eleven, Beatrice received a text message. Adrian.

> Got an ID for Ponytail. Eoin Connor, Lannagh Farm, Kilmore Road, Ballyharty. Elementary, my dear Stubbs. Ax

She smiled, more relieved than she'd expected to hear they were safe, but instantly began worrying about how he'd got hold of the information.

The next update from Ty provided nothing new and Beatrice's eyelids started to droop. She scrunched up her face and rubbed her eyes.

Kalpana noticed. "Me too. Shall we pull onto the High Street and get some coffee? I need a shot of caffeine."

The High Street had a selection of bistros, tapas bars and pubs, but all the coffee shops had long since closed. They drove up and down without success. Finally, Kalpana pulled over outside the newsagents and released her seatbelt.

"Right, so two cans of Red Bull instead. Anything else? You hungry?"

Beatrice shook her head. "Entirely against character, I'm not. Have we given up on coffee, then?"

"Coffee at this time of night means a nasty takeaway or kebab shop. And this is Crouch End. So we're in the wrong place." She closed the door and headed into the fluorescent-lit shop.

Beatrice's head jerked up. *We're in the wrong place.* Bennett never attacked near his middle-class home. He targeted poorer Finsbury Park. None of his victims had been glossy Jemimas on their way home from the wine bar, but exhausted Janines on their way home from a twelve-hour shift. He watched his victims carefully, selecting those he thought he could intimidate, grooming those he thought would capitulate. He wouldn't find many of those round here. Plus the fact these people were his neighbours. It would be soiling his own doorstep.

When Kalpana got back in the car with drinks and samosas, Beatrice explained her thinking. Kalpana got it right away, and drove them back in the direction of Harringay, while tearing into a samosa. Beatrice informed Grant of their change in location, but agreed he was better stationed where he was.

At half past eleven, they parked on Lordship Park. All ears strained to pick up every detail of the commentary from the radio.

Harrison had caught the Tube and was heading north. Everyone was in position and poised for action. Avery was still in the middle of a game, a fact that was relayed to Harrison. Virginia's voice advised her to delay returning to the flat. Harrison exited the station, stood by the bus stop sending a text message and finally headed towards the Snooker Club.

"She can hear us, then?" Kalpana asked.

"Oh yes. And we can hear her. One of the reasons for the title of 'Operation Robert' is because that's her alarm word. If she says 'Robert', in any context, we mobilise."

"Is that in homage to Robert Peel?"

Beatrice beamed. "You are the first person who hasn't required an explanation. Well done. The thing is, I am completely torn. If she gets home safely, I'll be delighted. And almost equally disappointed. It means he's still out there somewhere."

"I get it. Sometimes, you just get sick of waiting."

PC Fitzgerald informed them that Paul Avery had left the club and was heading in the direction of his own flat. Karen Harrison anticipated his route and walked ahead of him on Blackstock Road. He seemed to be following her and gaining. Virginia's voice warned all units that Harrison was turning onto Somerfield Road, approaching the police flat. To Beatrice, it seemed even the radio was holding its breath. However, Avery continued along Blackstock Road, heading for home and showing no interest in following the lure. No one spoke until Harrison arrived at the police flat and the applause and whistles began.

"You see, we're all confused. Harrison got home without incident. Hooray. But we failed. He didn't pick up our lure and rather than banging him into a cell tonight ..."

Kalpana picked up her thought. "... we have to do this all over again."

"You don't. You've done enough. In fact, you could head off home now, if you like. Other officers will be available to support Grant and me."

"I'll stick with you for another hour. If all's still quiet, I'll leave you to it."

Virginia's mood seemed a similar mix of disappointment and relief, but she agreed easily to Beatrice's request. She offered to alert the Control Centre to scan all footage for Bennett's presence and sent ten officers to patrol with Beatrice and Grant. Another two already stood watch outside Avery's flat. Beatrice handed coordination duties to Grant, both out of respect and exhaustion. With a guilty twinge, she remembered the sergeant had lost sleep too.

Conversation became easier after Harrison's safe arrival, or possibly due to the caffeine. Driving around the suburban streets, Kalpana talked about growing up in Hackney, in a culture of respect, obedience and cooperation. "So the police seemed a natural choice. My parents weren't keen, and I had a hard time getting accepted, not because I was Asian or female. The problem was being such a shortarse. But when I came home with my first uniform, my folks almost burst with pride. Even my brothers couldn't stop boasting, and they make a living out of things that fall off the back of a lorry."

"You've certainly made a success of it. And I noticed how much respect you command from your team. That can't have been easy," Beatrice said.

"Thank you. I appreciate a compliment like that coming from you. I fought some battles, but I was the middle girl of the family. Two brothers older, two younger. I was used to holding my own. But things were easier for my generation because of women like you. You carved a path through the force long before the words 'women' and 'career' were ever heard in the same sentence."

Beatrice inclined her head, accepting the compliment. "My turn to thank you. Although I'm not flattered by the allusion to mediaeval times. I was born in 1954, you know."

"Like I said. The fifties. Before career women. Before female detectives. Probably before fish fingers."

Beatrice's laughter was interrupted by the radio. Quarter to one. Nothing to report. Avery's lights were out, no sign of Bennett.

Beatrice turned to Kalpana. "Why don't you knock off?"

"You sure? I'm happy to hang on."

"No, Kalpana. You've been a great help. Where do you live?"

"Still in Hackney. But *not* with my Mum and Dad."

"Glad to hear it. If you could drop me at Finsbury Park, I'll join

Ty Grant and keep watch for another few hours. Bennett will have to go home then, as his supposed shift finishes at six. Once he's in his own house, I'll feel able to get some sleep."

Kalpana yawned widely, setting Beatrice off. "OK. Only because I have a meeting at half eight. But call me if anything happens."

"Fair enough. And would you let me know when you get in? Just so I know you didn't nod off at the wheel and drive into a reservoir."

"No chance. As soon as I've dropped you off, I'm going to listen to break core all the way home."

"I don't think I like the sound of that. Women my age are much more at home with a fourteenth century madrigal."

Kalpana's face creased with laughter and she looked remarkably pretty.

Quarter past one and fatigue was beginning to show. Frustrated by the lack of urgency demonstrated by the remainder of the team, Grant became flushed and inarticulate. The pairs dispersed to search the streets for Bennett, but Beatrice had her suspicions that most of them would spend the next four-and-a-half hours moaning about Ty Grant. He'd had enough. So had she. But Nathan Bennett hadn't.

She joined Grant and they drove for the twelfth time up Green Lanes.

Chapter 35

As she swung into Sutton Square, Kalpana turned down the sounds of *Venetian Snares*. Drum beats from passing vehicles were part of Hackney life, but on this quiet square, she chose to keep her neighbours sweet. She parked the car on the tiny forecourt and noted the time in luminous digits on the dashboard. Twenty-five past one. She had to be up again in five hours.

So what? There was only one decent course of action and she'd done the right thing, out of a sense of obligation to Beatrice and her team. A member of her own staff was responsible for these attacks. She had a duty to help catch him.

She locked the car and identified her front door key, glancing two doors down to Moira's house. As if she was likely to see him now. He'd be curled up in a ginger ball on Moira's bed, purring like a chainsaw.

She smiled to herself, opened the front door and reached for the light. In the few seconds before she hit the hall carpet, she registered three things. The rapid crunching sound of footsteps on gravel, a hand shoving her forcefully into the house and a strong smell of feet.

The heels of her hands suffered carpet burns as she broke her fall. Adrenalin pulsing, she rolled onto her backside, ready to defend herself as the light came on. Nathan Bennett stood smiling at her, wearing a baseball cap and carrying a backpack.

"Here I am, ma'am. Just like you asked."

The stench was nauseating. Bennett sat opposite her, forearms on his knees, peeling the label from his beer bottle, with a permanent grin playing across his face. Kalpana was tempted to take a swig from her Pilsner, just to block out the odour for a second, but needed to keep her mind as sharp as it could be. She had to work out what the hell he was thinking. He acted as if he'd turned up as a result of an invitation, accepted the offer of a beer, refused anything to eat, all with the casual demeanour of a friend popping round. Nothing about his behaviour was threatening, apart from pushing her into the house at two in the morning, and he seemed relaxed, sober and pleased to be there. Kalpana knew her best hope of getting out of this unscathed would be to talk. Tidal waves of terror made this an awkward prospect, but she had no other ideas.

"So, it's nice of you to come round. I was just wondering ... to what do I owe the honour?" Her voice sounded girlish and false.

He exhaled through his nose, a dry laugh. "I should be asking you that question. Why did you choose me?" He reddened and a jolt of alarm shot through her as she realised he was blushing.

His eyes remained on the ground. "Look, it sounds like I'm fishing for compliments, which I suppose I am. But I really would like to know. Why me, Kalpana?"

Kalpana frowned at the familiar address and her tone was impatient. "Why you what? What are you talking about, Bennett?"

His face darkened and his mouth pinched into a bitter line. "Don't call me that! I have two perfectly good first names."

She stiffened and waited till he seemed to gain control of his temper. He was muttering.

He looked up at her and sighed. "Sorry. I didn't mean to bite your head off. But seriously, what kind of relationship are we going to have if you still treat me as if we're at work?"

Kalpana's nails dug into the upholstery, as he gave her a conciliatory smile.

"It took me a while. I have to hand it to you, you're subtle. No one at work could ever have guessed. And when I did cotton on, I couldn't believe you'd pick me."

You have a choice, Kalpana told herself. Try forcing him back to reality, or enter his skewed view of the world. The risks of both are enormous. Just by using the correct form of address, he'd flared up, ugly and angry. If he lost it and hit her, she had a feeling her self-defence training wouldn't help much. Or she could play along, discover what twisted thinking had made him decide to visit her, wait for her and physically shove her into her house. She had no idea what he'd done with the key. And she wondered, as the surges of dread threatened to overwhelm her, what the hell was in that backpack?

"When did you 'cotton on'?" she asked, her voice unsteady.

His grin was shy and pleased. "It wasn't like one big revelation. More little clues. Like just recently, when you told me that with my ambition, I could go far, in *that* voice. But at first, I told myself I was imagining it."

You were, you twisted fucking loser. You were! Kalpana clamped her lips together, refusing to allow her thoughts to tip the balance.

"You know, you're the first female boss I've had. And it seemed such a cliché, the office romance. I tried not to think about it, but the tension was driving me insane. I had to do some stuff, let off steam. Yeah, that shit was all your fault," he laughed, his tone teasing.

That shit? Kalpana searched for some kind of appropriate response. None came.

His colour heightened and he shifted forward to the edge of the sofa. A foul whiff of cheese and sweat triggered another wave of sickening fear in Kalpana's stomach.

"I'll be honest, pretty soon I couldn't think about anything else. You, in your pinstriped suits. I could just imagine what you had on underneath. Those cute little heels, your tied-up hair, I fantasised, time and time again about taking your hair down ..."

His breath was short and his colour high. He was aroused. Kalpana panicked.

"But you're married ..." she couldn't call him Nathan. It would only add to his deluded sense of intimacy. "What about your wife?"

His grin spread. "The wedding. That was when I first started to believe it. You came to the evening do, you kissed me and you whispered in my ear, remember?"

"I remember kissing you both on the cheek and saying congratulations."

"I know. I got it. That was when you told me you were giving yourself to me as a present. From then on, I watched the signs. I kept a diary of all those little signals, all the little messages you sent. Every one. And finally, you made your move."

Kalpana's fear took on a new shape and tears built as she saw the extent of the psychosis in front of her. "My move?"

The phone rang, making them both start. Kalpana lost her grip on her beer bottle. It slipped to the floor and spilt over the carpet. Bennett looked at her and wagged a forbidding finger. The machine clicked in.

"Leave a message after the tone. Please speak clearly."

"Kalpana, it's Beatrice. If you are already in bed, then I apologise. No news at this end, but you did promise to call when you got in. It's now quarter past two and I've heard nothing. Could you please give me a quick call or text, otherwise I will have to come round, or send a patrol car to check that you're all right. Call me a Mother Hen, but ..."

Bennett scowled, grabbed his bag and with a jerk of his head, indicated the phone. She moved to answer it, feeling Bennett press himself against her, one arm around her waist, the other holding a large blade just under her left ear. Cold steel and the foul stench made her flesh crawl.

"Tell her you're home and put it down," he whispered, and reached down to press the speakerphone.

Kalpana picked up. "Beatrice! Sorry, I completely forgot to call. Yes, I got home safely."

"Oh, you *are* there. Good. That's all I wanted to know. I'll let you get some sleep."

She was going to ring off, leaving Kalpana alone with a mentally unstable deviant, who'd chosen to bring a hunting knife to his imaginary date. What else had he got in his bag? Her hands shook and she felt Bennett's arm tighten around her waist, pressing his erection into her back.

"Thanks for calling, Beatrice. I really appreciate it."

"No problem. See you tomorrow. Give my love to Scaramanga."

The pressure on her neck increased, bringing with it an instant of inspiration.

"I will. Give my love to Robert. Good nig..."

Bennett cut her off.

He released her and stood back, grinning broadly. "Well done. I like it when an officer obeys orders."

Kalpana turned with a tearful smile. "So, how about another drink? And then you can finish telling me how you worked it all out?"

He stared at her, eyes tracing her form, all the way down her body.

"I think I'm done talking. You didn't invite me round here to talk. What the fuck are you wearing? Those clothes are ugly. I thought you'd have made more effort for me tonight." His face was cold and hard.

She shook her head, unable to speak, tears falling freely.

He picked up his backpack. "Fortunately, I've brought you some presents."

Chapter 36

Beatrice pressed End Call and sat back in her seat, yawning.

"All OK?" asked Grant.

"Yes, she just forgot, that's all. Seems paranoia is my constant companion these days."

"That's understandable, ma'am. Where to now?"

That's understandable? Another of those comments. Beatrice decided this was her opportunity to ask Grant exactly what he knew. He had made far too many references to her condition, indicating a distinct familiarity with the subject. She would pressure him until she found out how widespread the knowledge of her breakdown had become.

"Where are we?"

"Clissold Park. Who's Scaramanga?"

"Let's do Green Lanes again. It's the name of her cat. You don't know Scaramanga? He's a Bond villain, played by Christopher ... oh my God."

Beatrice reacted as if she'd jumped into freezing water; her skin tightened, her stomach contracted and she gasped short breaths.

Grant braked instinctively, scanning the street for danger. "What?"

"Bennett's there! After I said, 'Give my love to Scaramanga,' she said, 'Give my love to Robert.' Bloody hell, Grant, it's the alarm signal, I told her about it tonight. He's there! He's got her. Drive to Hackney! Now! I have to find her address."

He executed a rapid U-turn and drove at speed down Green Lanes and onto Balls Pond Road. All sense of tiredness evaporated as Beatrice made a series of emergency calls. When she'd got confirmation of Kalpana's address from the Control Centre, Beatrice called the team. "We need all officers to 91 Sutton Square, off Urswick Road. Approach with stealth, we don't want him to know we're there."

She informed Virginia, who promised to meet them at the scene. Her question frightened Beatrice. *Why Kalpana?* Why indeed? Was she the last in the line? In which case, what did he plan for his final assault? As they drove up Dalston Lane, Beatrice felt pathetically inadequate. How to get Kalpana out of there without injury?

"What would you do in this situation, Grant?"

His face seemed pale in the occasional oncoming headlight. "Scope the place and make a decision fast. Every second we waste ..."

Beatrice scrunched up her toes, unable to imagine what a delay would mean to Kalpana. She had to get this right, first time. She picked up the phone again and requested authorisation for body armour and firearms.

Although barging in heavy-handed might provoke a disproportionate reaction to being threatened, she knew he was likely to be carrying weapons. Attempts to negotiate presupposed an ability to get him to talk. Ideally, they could get into the house silently, wait for their moment and grab Bennett with no danger to Kalpana. But how were they to get in, unless through the cat-flap?

The cat.

Kalpana said her neighbour took care of him if she worked late. Something Scottish ... Moira! In order to get the cat, Moira must have a key.

"How much farther now?"

"It's over there, ma'am. This is Urswick Road, and that's Sutton Square on the right. I'll park here."

Beatrice fumbled with her belt and scrambled out. "We need to contact her neighbour who has a key, but let's find number 91 first."

As soon as they entered the square, Grant identified the numbering pattern and indicated that the second house on the opposite side was 91. They navigated a path around the ornamental pond, keeping their eyes fixed on the modern terraced house. A light was on downstairs, but the curtains were drawn. A movement to their right indicated the arrival of PC Fitzgerald and PC Hyen. Beatrice joined them under the laburnum bush which screened them from view.

"Check the houses either side and a couple more further down. She has a neighbour, Moira something, who looks after her cat and has a key. Don't be alarmist, just explain we need access to Inspector Joshi's house, and it must be now. Grant will try to see what's going on in there, and I'll wait here to meet the others." Her voice surprised her. She sounded calm and in control, conveying no reflection of the frantic cramps in her stomach.

Grant nodded and squeezed past Kalpana's Toyota, taking care to remain on paving stones and not to tread on the gravel. He moved with impressive speed and grace for such a great lump of a man and Beatrice's admiration surfaced above the barely controlled panic. A light went on upstairs and Beatrice froze.

"Ma'am?"

Two other teams had arrived and waited in the darkness. Beatrice raised a finger for patience and returned her attention to the house. Grant stood in the porch, peering through the curtain into the still-lit front room. No one moved. Minutes ticked past. Grant moved to the front door, lifted the letterbox and craned forward, as if listening. The upstairs light went off again and the curtains moved a fraction, as if a gust of air had caught them. Grant slid back past the vehicle towards the team. Beatrice turned to see the remaining four officers and Virginia joining the group. She motioned them back behind the bush. No sign of Fitzgerald and Hyen yet.

Grant acknowledged his colleagues with a nod. "Sounds like he's in the front room and he's sent her upstairs to get something. I heard him shout, 'I'm waiting', but I didn't hear a thing out of her."

Virginia winced. "So why are we all standing around here? Let's get in there and arrest him before he goes any further."

"DI Lowe, I sent two officers to retrieve a key from the neighbour. I'd rather not go in all guns blazing, just in case the fear factor provokes him. We need to surround the house completely. Some of you will need to find the back alley which must run behind these gardens. Grant, can you allocate places for six of the team in case he tries to run?"

Beatrice took Virginia to one side. "When we get the key, I suggest we get Grant and Fitzgerald in body armour in there to overpower him. We'll follow right behind, backed up by four more officers. Everyone else remains out here as a safety precaution ... here's PC Fitzgerald."

Fitch held up a key. "Moira Hilliard. Three doors down. Hyen stayed with the old girl, she's off on one. But this is the key to the front door."

Virginia seemed to wake up. "Right. Ty, Fitch, get your kit on. You're going in first."

They left the team in position, while Beatrice followed Virginia and the two men to the vehicles. Despite her revulsion towards firearms, her training enabled her to ready her gun automatically, leaving her brain free to think. As they prepared themselves, Virginia spoke. "Listen up, we're going to brief you as you dress. Time is crucial. DI Stubbs?"

Beatrice swallowed her surprise and donned her holster. She gave in to her impatience to take control.

"Don't take any chances. Wait for the right moment when he can't get to her before you get to him. Disarm him, get him in cuffs and no more. We'll be right behind you, ready to back you up. Use of weapons, as always, only in extreme circumstances. Injuries to yourselves, Inspector Joshi or even him in this operation are unacceptable."

Two heads nodded and Beatrice handed Grant the key. Scurrying back to the house, Virginia silently pointed out the order of officers to follow. Beatrice and Virginia were two and three. The team assumed positions. Grant and Fitzgerald were already at the door, Grant turning the key imperceptibly and listening. It opened and the two men crept inside. Beatrice and Virginia slid alongside the car, ears alert for any sound.

Entering the hallway, Beatrice saw the outlines of Grant and Fitzgerald pressed against either side of the living-room door. A faint voice, almost chanting, could be heard. Grant's hand on the doorknob moved in millimetres, and Beatrice's breath had become so short it barely reached her lungs. Grant crouched and pushed open the door gently. The voice continued.

"... told you to do it slowly. Now turn round. Good. And now bend over. Bend over and touch your toes. Look at me. Look at me between your legs."

She heard Virginia exhale and an uneven shiver crawled over her own skin. Grant eased his head into the room, then kicked open the door, shouting, "Freeze! Hands in the air!"

Fitzgerald dashed after him and Beatrice heard the release of the safety catch from his weapon. Beatrice, Virginia and their support officers rushed in to see the backs of Grant and Mitchell aiming their guns directly ahead; Kalpana Joshi in underwear, standing on a heap of pinstripes on the coffee table; and Nathan Bennett sitting in the armchair, with both hands up, trousers down and a fast-deflating penis. A foul smell of feet filled the air.

Virginia holstered her weapon and approached Bennett, kicking away the knife at his feet. The movement seemed to snap him back to reality. He narrowed his eyes at Kalpana.

"What the fuck is this? How did you call them? What did you do, you dirty slut? I took your phone, for fuck's sake! How did you do it? You lying, sly little bitch!"

Kalpana stood there, half-naked, staring at him with a look of profound revulsion.

As Fitzgerald read Bennett his rights and Grant put on the cuffs, Beatrice picked up the sofa throw to cover Kalpana. Virginia informed the officers waiting outside of the successful arrest. Bennett's voice rose, insistent and ugly. Easing Kalpana from the glass table, Beatrice could feel the woman's trembles through the chenille. Bennett was shouting over Fitzgerald as Grant pulled him to his feet and yanked up his trousers.

"You can't arrest me! She fucking invited me, the prick-tease! Ask her!"

Kalpana turned to face him, her face livid. The shakes were not, as Beatrice assumed, born of fear, but of barely-controlled temper.

"Get out of my house, Bennett. You disgust me. And you fucking stink."

Grant and Fitzgerald led him from the room, still hurling abuse at his superior officer. Virginia snapped on gloves to pick up the knife and bag it, casting sympathetic glances at Kalpana's slight form.

"Kalpana? Can we call anyone for you? PC Hyen says your neighbour is outside."

"Thanks, Virginia. Could you let Moira in? I'd like to reassure her."

Virginia ducked out into the square, taking the evidence with her. Kalpana looked at Beatrice.

"Thank God for Beatrice Stubbs. I wasn't sure you'd got it."

Beatrice shook her head. "I didn't for a moment. I'm still shocked he came after you."

"It seems I was his ultimate target. The rest of them? Just him exercising his frustrations, apparently. So in his dysfunctional logic, it's all my fault those other woman suffered unwanted attention."

Beatrice blinked, trying to imagine being in Bennett's mind. It must be rather like a William Burroughs' novel.

"Had you never noticed his foot odour before?"

Kalpana shook her head with emphasis. "He wears a uniform at work and I'm strict about presentation. I assume it was those revolting trainers. And you know what? He was the one who complained about Paul Avery's breath."

Virginia returned with Grant and an older woman in a quilted dressing-gown.

"Oh God, Kalpana, I'm so glad to see you! I was worried out of my mind, the police arriving in the small hours and demanding your key, I just couldn't imagine, Scaramanga's hidden under my bed, I had no idea what was going on and they wouldn't let me come round at first ..."

While Moira was speaking, Grant reached behind the armchair and retrieved Bennett's backpack. His face, on seeing the contents, attracted Virginia's attention. She glanced into the bag and Beatrice saw her eyes darken.

The charge in atmosphere caused Kalpana to look up. Her eyes flicked from one to the other and back to the bag.

"What was it? What did he have in there? Tell me, I want to know what he was planning ..."

Virginia interrupted, taking hold of the backpack. "No, you don't, Kalpana. Not now. Trust me." She motioned to Grant and they left the room, taking the backpack.

Kalpana covered her eyes with her hand.

"How about a nice cup of tea?" Moira sat beside her and patted her knee.

Beatrice stood. "We need to get back and start processing Bennett. Do you think you'll feel up to making a statement tomorrow?"

With a bitter exhalation, Kalpana looked up. "You try and stop me."

Chapter 37

His ankle was the worst. His jaw still throbbed, his shoulders were stiff and aching from sitting so long with his hands tied behind him and he was colder than he could ever remember being. The initial vomiting caused by the constant heaving of the boat had dissipated, but it left him weak and shaky. But the pain in Adrian's wrenched ankle was searing. Exhaustion swept over him several times and he almost dozed once or twice, especially after Ponytail Man – Eoin – had draped a blanket over his shoulders. He knew how to pronounce it now. 'Owen', as in Clive. And the other one was called Sammy.

He'd learnt their names from the furious whispered conversation they'd had behind the Porthgain quarry hoppers.

After dragging him out of sight, they searched his bag, finding the photographs, the camera, Adrian's notebook and horribly, the key to the B&B. Surely they wouldn't go after Matthew? But the key didn't seem to interest them. What really caught their attention were the pictures on the Pentax. The beach, the packages, Marie's vehicle in the cul-de-sac. Sammy stood over him, demanding to know who he was. Adrian wondered why they hadn't checked his jeans. They would have discovered not only his wallet, containing ID, but also his mobile phone. That was when Sammy hit him.

The shock of the blow totally disorientated Adrian and the taste of blood made him nauseous. Sammy grabbed his jumper and hauled his face close.

"I'll ask you again. Who the fuck are you?"

He had to lie, but was hopeless at making things up under pressure. He fell back on the only pre-fabricated story he had.

"Andrew Ramos. I'm a private investigator. I was asked to watch this beach for signs of illegal activity and report back with whatever I found."

"Who asked you?" Sammy kicked out at him. His hard boot connected with Adrian's thigh. Pain radiated through his body and he squeezed his eyes shut for a couple of seconds.

When he opened them, Sammy was waiting.

Eoin, whose face was in darkness, made a small sound of exasperation. "Sammy, would you ever stop with the fists and the feet? Let the man talk."

Adrian breathed for a second, until the pain lessened. "Professor Michael Bryant. He and his wife stayed here on the Bank Holiday weekend. After his wife's bag was stolen and their cottage burgled, he suspected something dubious was behind it. He asked me to check. So here I am."

The silence stretched out. Sammy staring at Adrian, Eoin staring at Sammy.

Finally, Eoin spoke. "What did I tell you? What did I say? Trying to get the fecking photographs back is what's caused the problem. Not the pictures. Jesus, Sammy, this is what your paranoia's done."

Sammy stared into the darkness at Eoin, until the sounds of customers leaving the pub carried up to them. Sammy shook his head, like a dog with a flea, and reached into his jeans pocket. He pulled out a mobile and opened the flap. The pale blue glow highlighted his sour expression.

Eoin's voice, low and nervous, came out of the dark. "Who're you calling?"

"We have to make a decision. What do we do with yer man?" Sammy pointed the phone towards Adrian like a weapon.

"Call Marie. She'd get here in a couple of hours."

"Fuck that. I want to talk to someone with sense. I'm calling the Mammy."

Eoin exhaled through his teeth. Sammy pressed some buttons and paced away up the slope. For a few seconds, Adrian felt eyes on him. Whichever way you looked at it, he was a massive inconvenience to these men. This quiet observation from the shadows was an assessment. What exactly to do with him? Adrian heard footsteps move away in the direction of Sammy's murmurs. If they found his wallet, he was lost. Name, address, not to mention sexuality stated on various membership cards, none of which matched what he'd told them. All he could do was to leave it here in these industrial ruins, hoping it would not expose Beatrice. And it was a long shot, but someone might find it and raise the alarm. He wriggled and winkled the flat leather packet from his back pocket, leant forward and threw it as far as his roped wrists allowed. All he had now was his mobile, switched to silent since the text message to Beatrice. His head fell back against the brick wall. He'd screwed everything up.

Sorry, Beatrice. Sorry, Matthew. Sorry, Lyndon.

Whatever 'the Mammy' said provoked Sammy into an even greater rage. He dragged Adrian to his feet and searched him as roughly as possible. He found the phone in seconds, threw it to the ground with an unintelligible curse and smashed it with his boot. Once the village was quiet, Eoin guided him down to the harbour, Sammy striding ahead. The difficulty of getting Adrian on board the small boat seemed to push Sammy over the edge. He swore, this time in English, and hauled him from the jetty like a sack of coal. Adrian's thighs whacked onto the side of the boat and he was still gasping with pain when Sammy shoved him hard down the steps to the cabin. His foot caught and he fell heavily on his side, wrenching his ankle and winding himself. That was when he passed out.

When he came round, he vomited immediately. Adrian's companion in the tiny under-deck area was a slim, dark-haired, hard-eyed woman, whose arrival he'd missed. The girl sat opposite, arms folded, giving him the occasional wary look. Eoin came down and offered him water after the puking session. He cleared up without comment, gave him the blanket and untied him long enough for a visit to the toilet. Hoping for a lockable door and the chance of a few minutes alone to assess the damage, Adrian could have cried when he saw he had to piss into a bucket. But after he'd finished, Eoin re-tied his hands behind him, placing his limbs in the same agonising position. Adrian groaned in pain, and without a word, Eoin adjusted the rope so that his arms were slightly more relaxed.

Eoin's ministrations were discreet, as if it might not meet with

Sammy's approval. Without a word, he offered the girl a bottle of water and once she'd taken it, hurried to return back on deck.

Adrian tried to talk to his fellow captive. "Are you OK?"

She looked away.

"They didn't hurt you, did they?"

She kept her head turned from him.

"My name is Adrian."

Recognition lit her expression and she faced him. "My name is Katya."

"Hello, Katya. Do you know where they're taking us?"

She shook her head and waved her hands in a 'no pictures, please' gesture, wrapped her blanket around herself and curled up on the bench.

Leaving Adrian to shiver and suffer and second-guess their plans.

The unbearable night of pain, cold and misery had to come to an end sometime. Finally, the sky through the portholes grew lighter. Noise above deck focused his attention, and the movement of the boat slowed. Dull pain and an undercurrent of dread switched places and Adrian's fear tasted as real as the coppery flavour of his own blood. His stomach heaved again but had nothing left to throw up.

Eoin came down the steps and beckoned Katya, who unfolded and heaved herself to her feet. The careful movements and recognisable stance spelt out her condition even before she turned sideways, giving Adrian a clear view of the bump. Eoin helped her up the steps, which took some time. It was like manoeuvring a heifer up a ladder. As he heaved her onto the deck, Eoin jumped back down and motioned for Adrian to follow. Shuffling forward, Adrian attempted to rise but the awkward position and white heat of his ankle made it impossible. He fell backwards, an excruciating tear shooting across his shoulders as his muscles protested against the forced position.

Eoin stooped to support him by lifting his upper arm, but Adrian's ankle would not take his weight. Shoving, leaning, struggling and with gritted teeth, the two men navigated the steep steps and emerged onto deck. Sammy waited beside the girl, shaking his head with disbelief.

"Eoin, you idiot, how long does it take?"

Despite his pain, Adrian noted the accent. A hint of Russian in those dark vowels?

Eoin ensured Adrian was stable against the handrail before withdrawing his arm to wipe the sweat from his lip. "Woulda been a lot fucking quicker if you'd not twisted his ankle. Now I'm taking off the rope. Fecker can't even walk, leave alone run. So shut it, gobshite, and let's get to the car."

The release of his arms brought tears to Adrian's eyes. As feeling returned, as if to frozen fingers, the relief and the pain seemed equally torturous. Sammy leapt into the water, helped Katya down the ladder and escorted her towards the shore without a single look backwards. The light grew stronger and to Adrian's eyes, the beach seemed hardly different to the one he'd been watching the previous morning.

Eoin watched the retreating back and looked at Adrian. A downward twist of his mouth conveyed an apology as he grabbed Adrian in a fireman's lift and struggled down the ladder. It hurt like hell. Remember the details, Beatrice had said. Hanging upside down over Eoin's shoulder, he mentally described the smell. A dampness, slightly meaty, unsubtly disguised by something artificial, like air-freshener. And what good would this do him? Tears of despair, frustration and pain rolled down Adrian's forehead into his hair.

When they reached their destination, Eoin had to lift him again. Not a pleasant task. Rattling around in the back seat of a Jeep, hands tied in front of him, and wearing some sort of blindfold at Sammy's insistence, Adrian's stomach had found something after all. So when he was hefted over Eoin's shoulder once again, his sense of smell picked up nothing more than his own vomit. He never saw what happened to Katya.

Eoin yanked the material off his head and Adrian's eyes adjusted quickly. He'd been dumped on a pile of straw in some sort of stable. Stone walls and floor, a damp chill and precious little light. Through the open door, Adrian saw a rutted farm track and more outbuildings. Eoin released his hands, fetched a towel from outside the door and threw it onto Adrian's lap. The large wooden door slammed closed, bolts shot home and Adrian was left alone. He rubbed his face and lay on his side, shivering and sore, knowing that sooner or later, he had to start thinking. But not yet. Not just yet.

During his doze, the top half of the door opened several times. He squinted against the sunlight and saw backlit silhouettes staring in. The door closed again. Adrian kept his eyes closed, concentrating on his pain and the smell of sick all over him. But each time someone came to look, another stink seeped in through the open door. It was foul and rotten with chemical overtones. He'd never smelt anything like it before, but somehow he recognised the stench of death.

When he next awoke, he felt a presence. He looked around the room. Apart from some sort of hay-holder and a metal bucket, the room was empty. The sound of someone sucking their teeth came from above. The wall to his left did not reach all the way to the ceiling. It ended some three feet below, and in the gap sat a large girl, legs either side, as if astride a horse.

She pressed her fingers to her lips and whispered, "I'm not allowed in here."

Adrian stared, unable to speak.

"But they're all arguing in the kitchen, so who's to know?" She dipped her hand into her pinafore pocket and drew out a carton of Ribena.

"I brought you a drink. And a sandwich. Well, it's not a sanger yet, you'll have to put it together yourself. But I brought bread with butter on it, and some rashers. The Mammy usually sees everything, but today her head is somewhere else so you were lucky. Are you ever coming over here, or what?"

Adrian's mouth was dry and sour and he craved liquid. His voice sounded cracked. "Thank you. You're very kind. But I don't think I can move. I hurt my ankle."

"Is that right? I did my wrist a while back. I had bandages and one of them yokes goes round your neck. Maybe I can make one for you. Right so, if you can't walk, you'll have to drag yourself over here. I can't just chuck this food on the floor, there's bound to be some horseshit down there. Come here to me, like this ..."

She demonstrated a buttock walk along the wall, looking precarious.

Adrian lifted his swollen ankle off the floor and began a painful shuffle across the six feet of stone floor to sit beneath her.

"Good man yourself! You ready now? I'll chuck your drink down first, and when you finish, lob it back up here, or they'll find the packet and know it was me."

She dropped the carton down into his lap, followed by two large slices of bacon wrapped in kitchen roll, and two thick slices of bread. The latter had been wrapped in nothing at all, but simply stuffed into the girl's apron pocket. Fortunately, the buttered sides stuck together but they were still covered in bits of grey fluff. Despite the nauseating smell seeping through the air, it was the most delicious food Adrian had ever tasted. The girl kept up a cheerful monologue as he ate his sandwich and gulped down the blackcurrant drink.

"... been to the hospital that often they say I should have a season ticket. Clumsy's her middle name, that's what the Mammy says. You finished already? Jaysis, you musta been hungry. Well, I don't know your name so I think I'll call you Gannet. Suits you right enough."

"My name's ... you can call me Gannet if you like. Thank you so much for bringing me some food and drink. Can I ask your name?"

"Sure you can, Gannet. I'm Teagan. Pleased to meet you. Now would you throw that old carton back up here to me? I have to push off before I'm missed. I'll pop back after dinner, maybe. Bring you something else."

Adrian panicked, terrified of being left alone. "Teagan, can I ask you something?"

"Putting in requests now, are you? Look, I'll get what I can. Could be steak and chips, could be dog biscuits. But I promise not to bring fish, I understand why you're sick of that."

Adrian looked up at the open face, taking in her bunches, thick calves, work-boots and cleaner's pinny. This was no child. She had crows' feet, distinct jowls and a tell-tale delta of lines across her décolletage. This was a large-breasted, middle-aged woman, who talked and dressed like a child.

"Fish? Why would I be sick of fish?"

She laughed with a hoot and clapped both hands over her mouth. "Sugar! I forgot I was supposed to keep quiet. Fish!" she hissed, more quietly. "Samir and Eoin just hooked you out of the sea, so you must be sick of them. First time they ever come back off one of their trips with a catch like you. Plenty of girls, and today, for the first time, a fine-lookin' fella. But never a single fish."

Samir? What kind of name was that?

"Teagan, can you tell me where we are?" Adrian pleaded.

She cast a worried look over her shoulder. "OK, Gannet. I'll tell you where we are. But then I have to go. Don't run away, I'll be back before you know it."

One more glance behind her and she leant down further than was safe.

"We're on the farm."

She swung her leg over the wall, landed with a thump the other side and was gone.

Chapter 38

Beatrice stepped out of the shower, wrapped herself in the bathrobe and yawned. Four hours' sleep. The average woman usually indulged in at least eight. Unless she was Margaret Thatcher. Well, a *normal* woman usually indulged in at least eight. Beatrice frowned. She was too old for all this, and the only thing likely to get her through the morning was a full-strength espresso.

The machine bubbled and spat as she dressed and gave up on styling her hair. She poured the coffee, already invigorated by the smell, and added a drop of cold milk. The telephone rang. Taking her first sip, she returned to the living room and spotted the flashing light indicating messages. Had she slept that deeply? The incoming call number was unfamiliar.

"Hello?"

"Beatrice, it's Matthew. How are you?"

"Matthew. At long bloody last. I'm absolutely fine. I've been worried about you two, so it's a relief to hear your voice. But the good news is that last night we got him! He's now in custody. The nasty part about it ..."

"Sorry to interrupt, Beatrice, but the thing is, I've lost Adrian."

"What on earth do you mean by that? Lost him how?"

"He went to the pub alone last night and didn't come back to the B&B. I waited up till gone midnight, so I presumed he'd gone off with his barman. He seemed rather keen on the chap. But the young man in question came round here this morning, determined to have it out with Adrian. According to Lyndon, they arranged to meet after the pub closed. But when he got down to the harbour, there was no sign of Adrian at all."

The cold grip of dread tightened Beatrice's scalp. "You've checked his room?"

"I'm an amateur, Beatrice, not an idiot. He's not there, and we've looked everywhere we can think of. Lyndon is worried. So am I. Apparently Adrian lifted the wallet of our ponytailed smuggler last night. Lyndon thinks he may have fallen into the sea, but my fears are more prosaic."

Beatrice dropped her head into her palm. "He lifted a wallet? I don't believe it. The man is an arse. Didn't I tell him? This was such a stupid idea. Why didn't you go to the police? I should have forced you. Matthew, we have to find him, fast. If the men from the boat have him, they also have evidence they're being watched. That is dangerous for everyone, but Adrian as the messenger is in genuine physical peril. Stay at the B&B, keep Lyndon with you. I'll mobilise the local force who will interview you first. Tell the truth, Matthew, and impress upon Lyndon the importance of doing the same. I will be there as soon as I possibly can. Is this the number of the B&B?"

"No. We're at the pub. The landlord has been most helpful now he knows of our connection. Gary sends his regards."

"In that case, stay there. The police will be there soon. Have you tried Adrian's mobile?"

"Naturally. Lyndon's been calling all night. It says number un-obtainable."

"Hellfire! Stay where I can reach you and I'll call as soon as I know more."

Mobilising both Met, Welsh and Irish local forces needed authorisation from the top. Hamilton. She dialled the emergency number with unsteady fingers, her other hand clenched into a fist. Trying to get anything out of him under ordinary circumstances was like pulling teeth from a stone. She had her trump card – Bennett in a cell with a willing confession. Hamilton had his rule book – one job at a time. But he *had* to help. With a normal human being, the personal involvement would tip the balance, but Hamilton's view of emotions was similar to his attitude to foreign languages. Highly suspicious. The phone clicked and buzzed, and began ringing. If he didn't agree to providing assistance, she'd go it alone. Simple as that.

And then she'd file an official complaint against him when she got back, regardless of the consequences.

"Metropolitan Police, DI Rangarajan speaking. How can I help?"

"Ranga? Where's Hamilton?"

"Hello Beatrice! Good to hear your voice. And well done on that arrest. That was a nasty one. Hamilton's in hospital. Silly old sod wouldn't go to the dentist and now he's got an impacted wisdom tooth. They're taking it out today. So I'm his substitute."

"Thank God. Oh, that is such good news. Ranga, listen. I need a favour."

On leaving home for the office, Beatrice's mind raced so hard she was almost able to ignore her fear. But she'd forgotten she had to pass Adrian's flat. The pain of not knowing where he was, not knowing what they were doing to him, not knowing how he felt, not even knowing if he was still alive cut into her like a Stanley knife. The memory of his proud message *Elementary, my dear Stubbs* relating the Irish address twisted the blade. She practically ran to the Tube station, listing through the positives as she went. She had all the photographic evidence Adrian had sent on her memory stick. Clear images of these men and this woman, who had to be somehow identifiable. Ranga had not only authorised Met involvement with the case, but offered a senior detective to assist – Dawn Whittaker. Beatrice could have cried with relief. Inspector Howells, fully cooperative, had mobilised the Dyfed-Powys police, who were currently searching the area around Porthgain. Her apologetic phone call to BTP had resulted in both Virginia and Grant offering their services and accepting no refusal. She welled up with gratitude once more and gave herself a light tap on the cheek. Emotional exhaustion was no excuse. Next time, she warned herself, it would be a slap.

Ranga assumed the role of coordinator with diplomacy and intelligence. With typical efficiency, he rapidly indicated names and roles of the assembled personnel, before beginning his presentation.

"I'd like to say that I appreciate your being here, especially as I know some of you had very little sleep last night. As you've heard from Beatrice, two men appear to be smuggling packages onto a remote beach in South Wales. We have every reason to believe the contents of these packages could be children. Babies, to be precise. From what we already know, four locations require investigation.

"One is already in hand. The Welsh police are searching the area around the beach and the village of Porthgain, assisted by Professor Bailey and the last people to see Adrian Harvey. The next two are connected. Marie Fisher, based in Cardiff, is the woman who receives the 'merchandise'. And the couple in this photograph, who seem to be the end clients. Their vehicle ID gives us an address in Chepstow. One team could deal with both of these. Finally, the farm in Ireland, believed to be the home of one of the supposed smugglers. There's a strong possibility that Mr Harvey was taken there. In my view, the Irish farm is potentially the most dangerous. I'd recommend DS Grant accompanies DI Stubbs on a flight to Cork."

Four heads nodded, absorbing the implications.

Virginia stated facts. "Leaving DI Whittaker and myself to handle the Chepstow and Cardiff line of enquiry. That makes perfect sense to me. Dawn has an outstanding reputation with sensitive situations such as this. I'd be happy to assist."

Blinking in surprise, Dawn took a moment before agreeing. "Sound logistics, Ranga. I presume you'll be involving the Garda at the Irish location? I mean, I'm glad DS Grant will be beside Beatrice, but they're going to need backup from the local force."

Ranga smiled. "No need to worry, Dawn. You get out there and I'll make sure you've got every kind of support there is. Don't forget, I'm one of you."

In an effort to swallow the lump in her throat, Beatrice squeezed her eyes shut and vowed to slap herself later, in the privacy of the bathroom.

Chapter 39

"Gannet? You awake?"

Adrian jumped. For such a hefty female, Teagan could creep around. He'd been straining his ears for any sound and heard nothing.

"Yes," he whispered. "I have no idea what time it is."

"Nor me. I never do. It's either before-breakfast or after-breakfast, before-dinner or after-dinner, before tea..."

"What is it now?"

"Before-dinner. That's why I can't stay long, but I got you some of last night's leftovers. Let's see here. An apple, two fine floury spuds, a lump of pork, and a drink of juice. Peas are too difficult to sneak out, you know what I mean?"

Adrian's stomach had been in spasm since the last time she left, and his level of dehydration was reaching a serious stage.

"Teagan, you are wonderful. Thank you so much. Just one question, do you think you could get me some water? A bottle, a jug, or even a bucket. I'm so thirsty."

She folded her arms and leant on them to look down at him. "Water? No problem at all. We have a tap right outside here. You want it now? Yeah, I'll fetch it for you now, just in case."

He managed to haul himself to a standing position against the wall, his injured foot held up behind him as if he were a horse about to be shod. *Before dinner.* Late morning, he assumed. He'd been here since dawn, so by now Matthew must have raised the alarm. But no one knew where to find him. His wallet might be found in the scrub behind the quarry hoppers, the broken bits of his mobile might cause some suspicion, but how could anyone locate him on 'the farm'? Think, Adrian, think.

"Here, I can't lift a bucket, but I filled an old bottle. You'll be pissing like a carthorse after this."

"Thank you so much. I can't tell you how grateful I am, Teagan. When I get out of here, I'm going to buy you such a fabulous present … what sort of thing would you like?"

"A present?" She folded her arms again, leant back against the beam and swung her legs, with a dreamy smile on her face. He was no expert, but this woman had certain special needs, that was clear. But whatever her problems, she was his only hope. He drank deeply from the plastic bottle, ignoring the swirling sediment.

"A present that comes in a box, or like anything at all?" she asked, scratching at her frizzy fringe.

"Anything at all. What would you like most in the world?"

She answered before he'd finished speaking. "A babby. But one I can keep. This time I want to keep him. Or her. One of them was a little girl. I'd like a girl."

Adrian's breaths came short and shallow. "You couldn't keep the other ones?"

Her dejected face became impatient. "Course not! None of us can, that's the rule. And you know it from the off so there's no point whining. The babbies go to a better place, we know that and it's best. The Mammy told us. They all go to university and Oxford and London and abroad. They have presents all the time."

He put down the bottle, sensing the tightrope he trod. "Best for the … babbies, but it must be hard for you. For the mothers."

Teagan rocked gently from side to side. "Some takes it harder. But when you come to Lannagh, you know what to expect." She burst into a surprisingly good rendition of Abba's *The Name of the Game*. "Everyone knows the name of the game. Or if they don't, they soon cop themselves on. Are you going to eat your food?"

Lannagh. The name on Eoin's business card. So there was a possibility that Beatrice did know where he was. Adrian bit into a cold potato, savouring the dry, crumbly mouthful. "Delicious. You're a good singer. I can tell."

"It's not just Abba I can do …
So if your man is nice, take my advice
Hug him in the morning, kiss him at night

Give him plenty love madam, treat your man right
'Cause a good man nowadays sure is hard to find ..."

"Sssh, Teagan, that's brilliant, but I think we should keep quiet. You really do have an impressive voice. Who was that? Ella Fitzgerald?"

"No idea, Gannet. It's off a record, that's all I know. Your turn."

"OK, but quietly." He flicked through his repertoire and chose something appropriate to time, place and audience.

"*I dream of Teagan with the light brown hair*
Borne, like a vapour, on the summer air
I see her tripping where the bright streams play
Happy as the daisies that dance on her way."

Teagan rested her head on her shoulder and gazed at him as he sang softly. When he'd finished, she clapped with enthusiasm, although her palms never quite met.

"Is that a real song or did you make it up?"

"It's a real song, but I changed the name. Just for you."

Her smiling cheeks shone like autumn apples. "You have a voice on you, you creature. Oh, it's a crying shame. I'd love to keep you. But no. They take them all away. That's the rule."

The potato wouldn't go down. Adrian swigged more water.

"Take me away? They wouldn't do that, surely?"

Teagan's regretful expression was that of someone looking into an open coffin. "Ah, they would, you know. That was decided first thing. The row that's gone on all the morning was only about how to get rid of you once it's done. You're not exactly what they're used to. But Samir's persuaded the Mammy." Her imitation of the harsh voice was exact. "*Everything we need right here, and we've had no problems so far. I'll sort it after dinner.* Oh aye, Gannet, they're going to take you away."

Adrian swallowed the piece of potato, which felt like a house brick. "When you say 'not what they're used to', why am I different?"

"C'mon, you know yourself, most creatures are already dead when they get here."

Adrian couldn't speak, couldn't think and focused all his attention on breathing. *In. Out. In. Out.* There had to be a way of out of this.

"Teagan, I know someone who can help. Help both of us. All I need to do is call her. Or maybe you could call her for me. I think you'd like her."

Her open face soured into a pout. "Your girlfriend?"

"No, my ... boss. She's much older than me, but a very nice person. I think she'd like to hear from you. Would it be difficult for you to call a number and leave a message? I don't want to get you in trouble."

"I dunno, Gannet. I'm not good with the telephone. But I'll have a go. What do I have to do? If you don't want that pork, I'll have it. I've always got room for more."

"I do want it. I'm starving and my stomach is growling like a mad dog. But this is more important, Teagan. What you need to do is dial 999 and ask for Detective Stubbs of the Metropolitan Police. Tell her I'm here and give her this address. Can you remember ...?"

"Police, Gannet? You're a sandwich short of a picnic, you are. We can't have the Garda round here! Am I not after telling you the rules? I'll bring you something after dinner, if you're still here." She jumped off the wall, landing with a thud on the other side of the partition.

"Teagan!"

He heard her tut and sigh, before the adjoining stable door creaked open. The male voice made him jump.

"Teagan! What the feck were you doing in there?"

"Jesus, Eoin, you scared me half to death! I just wanted to have a look at your man. Being nosy is all."

"Get back to the house. Dinner's nearly ready. And if I catch you hanging round here again, I'll tell the Mammy. You know what'll happen then."

"Ah don't, Eoin. I'll not do it again. Promise. I'll go in and help with the dishing-up, will I? What you got there? You taking him some food?" Teagan's voice switched from humble to curious in a second.

"What did I just tell you about sticking your beak in? Now piss off back to the house."

Adrian stuffed the water bottle under the straw, along with the scraps of food, and sat with his injured ankle stretched out in front of him. The door creaked open, and bright afternoon sunshine lit the stable until Eoin slid in and shut the door behind him, bringing a fresh wave of the unbearable stench.

"Brought you something. You'll be thirsty enough, after all the puking, I'd say. And a couple of sandwiches, if your stomach can face it. Cheese and pickle, and pork with apple sauce. Brought you a jacket an' all. Gets cold enough at night."

Adrian took the foil-wrapped package and bottle of water. Eoin laid the jacket over his knees. "Thank you. Look, it's kind of you to bring me some food, but I'd like to know when I can leave."

"Won't be long. But when exactly, well, that's up to Samir. But I think you'll be out of here soon enough. Right, I need to get back. How's your ankle?"

"Painful."

"Good. So you won't be trying to take off anywhere."

"Unlikely. My ankle is sprained."

"Teagan had that. My sister, the one who's been poking her nose over the wall. But when she got hold of a crutch, you couldn't stop her. She was moving about fast enough."

Adrian couldn't believe the man. Small talk when they'd already decided to dispose of him. "I'm so glad she's better. Thanks for the sandwiches."

"Get them down you. And whatever it was Teagan brought you. You're gonna need your strength." His expression was in shadow as he closed the door behind him.

Adrian heard the bolt shoot home and the turn of the key in a padlock. Heavy footsteps crunched away.

So he knew Teagan had brought him food. He swigged some water and picked up the foil package. Of course, it could be drugged. Maybe he should stick with Teagan's rations. Funny how he mentioned her ankle. She'd told him it was her wrist. A shaft of light played across the straw-littered stable. Light from the doorway. Eoin had shot the bolt and padlocked it, but the door wasn't closed. He could get out.

Adrian struggled to his foot. How could he escape in such a state? He slipped on the jacket, shoving the sandwiches and water into his pocket, and hopped towards the light. The door creaked open at his touch. He surveyed the track down towards the house.

No one about. He turned to check the uphill section and saw it immediately. An upturned broom against the wall. He checked again.

Eoin had brought him food, drink and clothes, put the idea of a crutch in his mind and left the door open. He was trying to help him escape. The smell made him pause, but he knew he had to get away.

Far enough from the house, so no one would be likely see him, especially if they were all eating lunch. He reached for the broom, shoved the bristly end under his armpit and hobbled his way behind the stable block. Every single movement jarred through his leg, but he chanted encouragement to himself. Keep going, you can do it, another step, don't stop. All he had to do was make for the road, flag down a vehicle and get to the nearest police station.

He rounded the corner of the stables, peering into the forest for a path. A shadow crossed the corner of his vision. Adrian had only half-turned before the blow caught him on the back of his head, buckling his knees and snapping the broom. His face hit the ground, all squashy and covered in pine needles, and his last conscious thought was an appreciation of the nice smell.

Chapter 40

And for One Million Pounds, Dawn Whittaker, where do you think you'll be at nine a.m. on Sunday morning?

A: In bed with toast and a mug of tea

B: Doing some half-hearted yoga

C: Cleaning up after the kids

D: Driving down the M4 with the woman who wrecked my marriage to apprehend some baby-traffickers.

Virginia couldn't have been more accommodating.

"Would you prefer to drive, Dawn?"

"Let me know if you'd like to stop for a coffee or anything."

"Is the air-con a bit strong? I'll turn it off for a while."

Dawn gave monosyllabic replies and reviewed the situation several times. Virginia was out of order treating her like a maiden aunt. She was not an invalid, nor a widow, but a divorcee. A woman whose husband had been unfaithful. After thirteen years of happy marriage, at the ceremony where she was due to receive her first policing award, Ian had gone into the toilets with this woman and made the name Dawn Whittaker synonymous with sniggers for police forces across the country.

After an hour of silence, Virginia spoke. "Do you want to talk about the obvious, or would you rather not?"

"By the obvious, you mean my husband's penis in your mouth?"

"That's the one. I'm happy to apologise, take the verbals, or you can slap me in the face, if you like. Just let me pull onto the hard shoulder first."

Dawn stared ahead, wondering what she did want. "I don't think I want revenge. It's more a case of wanting to understand. Why did you do it? You smashed up a family, a marriage, four lives, and left two children with a broken home."

Virginia drove for some miles without speaking. Finally, she cleared her throat.

"I don't think I did all that. That happened, I'm not denying it, as a result of the PBA 'event'. But none of that was my intention. I didn't know he was married."

"Would it have made a difference if you had?" Dawn faced her.

"Probably not, if I'm honest. The thing is, my selfish opportunism threw a curveball into your marriage. I'm sorry for that. But the inability to cope with it, the divorce and the resultant traumas? I can only accept so much responsibility."

Dawn turned to the window, fighting the truth of the statement. Ian had tried to repair her faith; he'd wanted to work at resolving the crisis. Still did. She refused. Once a philanderer ... it was only a matter of time before he humiliated her again. And the shame of all her colleagues knowing, laughing; she had no choice but to act. Taking him back would have been the worst kind of weakness. She despised that politician's wife kind of behaviour. Forgive and forget. How could she ever forget?

Virginia's voice was low and conciliatory. "Dawn? Saying this is a pointless exercise, but I'm actually sorry. I wish it hadn't happened. I'm older now and not all that proud of how I used to behave. So despite what you think of me, can we work together, do you think?"

Dawn gritted her teeth. "For Beatrice's sake, we'll have to. And in the circumstances, what's the alternative? Shall I take the lead in Chepstow, and let you handle Ms Fisher of Cardiff?"

"Sounds good to me. How about putting in a call to Ranga, see if he's found out which car hire firm she's using?"

"OK. And I also want to know what time Social Services are meeting us. I must have some time to talk to this couple first."

Dawn dialled, curious about how easily she'd let this marriage-wrecker off the hook. Not even a pejorative name had been used in anger. Maybe it was time to move forward. Maybe it was time to speak to Ian. Three years later, she still refused to speak to him directly. It wouldn't hurt to attempt a conciliatory gesture next week. Just a call. Or perhaps a Hi-how-are-you email. For the kids' sake. The trouble with harbouring a grudge was the time and energy it took to maintain. And who knows, if she stopped seeing herself as a victim, others might follow suit.

She was about to end the call when Ranga answered.

The terrace was on a steep slope, like something out of a Yorkshire soap opera. Virginia parked the Volvo opposite and checked the names again.

"Yvonne and Gerry Nicholls. What do you want me to do? Hang about in the background, interview neighbours, or join in and back you up?"

Dawn considered for a moment. "Why don't you see what you can find out from neighbours, wait for Social Services and ask them to hang on for half an hour. Then ring the bell. If I need more time, I'll say. But if they're still holding out, you can bring in the big guns."

"Will do. Good luck."

The door opened. Dawn offered a reassuring smile, whilst taking in every detail. Late thirties, tired and without make-up, permanent worry lines, velour leisure bottoms and stained grey T-shirt. Every inch the new mother.

"Yes?"

"Mrs Yvonne Nicholls? I'm Detective Inspector Dawn Whittaker from the Metropolitan Police. Sorry to disturb you on a Sunday, but I wonder if I could ask you a few questions. May I come in?"

As Yvonne announced 'a detective from the police', Gerry Nicholls turned from his position at the window, a tense concern dragging on his mouth as he gently rubbed the back of the tiny infant held to his chest. Dawn smiled and moved behind him to look at the crumpled sleeping face. A blue Babygro.

"How old is he?" she asked, in a quiet voice. He was undoubtedly premature, probably jaundiced and should be in hospital.

"Three weeks," Gerry answered, his eyes darting from his wife to Dawn. "He's away now, so I'll put him down."

Dawn's objective was to cause the minimum of embarrassment. The tension emanating from Yvonne Nicholls told Dawn it wouldn't take much to get full disclosure. So she accepted tea and waited for Gerry Nicholls to rejoin them.

"What's your baby's name, Mrs Nicholls?"

"Liam. We liked it because it's sort of old and modern at the same time, and it has a sort of solid sound to it. We did think about Edward, after Gerry's dad, but that's become a bit common now so ..." Her husband returned and she petered out.

He shook hands with forced levity. "So, Detective, can you tell us what all this is about?" He sat opposite Dawn at the dining table, beside his wife. Another one on a hair trigger.

Actions speak louder than words. Dawn spread the 8x4s of the Welsh cul-de-sac across the coffee table and sipped her tea. Pictures of them entering the house, pictures of them leaving with the basket. She didn't need to say a word. Yvonne cracked instantly.

"Oh God, Gerry, oh God. They're going to take him away, I can't bear this, I can't."

White-faced, he rubbed his wife's back, unconsciously repeating his earlier gesture of comfort and staring at Dawn in abject misery.

"Mr Nicholls, I'd prefer to hear your side of the story. The evidence only gives us so much."

"I should have known. Nothing ever works out for us. Everything we try and do turns to shit. Every-fucking-thing." His face contorted into a rictus of a smile, he covered his eyes with his palm and his shoulders shook silently. Dawn sat opposite the weeping pair and reached for a packet of Wet Wipes from the sideboard. He recovered and brushed away the tears with the heel of his hand.

"We can't have kids. No reason why not, nothing wrong with either of us, but it just doesn't work. We've tried hormone injections, zinc tablets, fertility cycle management, ovulation tests and three series of IVF. All we got was a big fat disappointment, every time. So we faced facts and applied for adoption."

Yvonne blotted her face with a Wet Wipe and looked at Dawn, red-eyed and desperate. "We wanted to do it properly. We did try."

Gerry continued, with a nod. "She's right. We're not criminals, Detective. But I'm self-employed. The Greenery Guy. I provide and maintain plants in offices. Or I did. After the credit crunch, lots of companies dropped me and several major bills went unpaid. I filed for bankruptcy in 2009. So we gave up on any chance of an official adoption."

"I'm sorry to hear that. So you felt you had no alternative but to adopt through other channels?"

Yvonne's voice was harsh. "There was no other way! You tell me what else we could have done?"

Dawn shook her head. "I don't know, Mrs Nicholls. But I'd like you to know that I am not here to judge you. I just want to understand the steps that brought you to this situation, and if possible, try to help. Can you tell me how you contacted the people who provided Liam?"

"They contacted us!" Gerry's voice was indignant. "They got in touch after our first cycle of IVF. This woman came round one day, explained their service and gave us her card. We said no thanks. We wanted to do it properly. I have the card here."

He pulled a dog-eared business card from his wallet.

Dream-Makers: dreams can come true. Sienna Smith. Not even a website. Only a mobile number.

"I see. So when you'd reached the end of your tether, you called Miss Smith."

Yvonne nodded. "Exactly. She told us about all these unwanted babies from Eastern Europe and how people put their kids in the orphanage if they can't afford to keep them. And Gerry and me, well, we haven't got much, but we're getting back on our feet, and we'd love a child more than anything."

"I don't imagine this service came cheap."

Yvonne glanced at her husband and looked down at the crumpled Wet Wipe in her hands.

Gerry shrugged. "Fifteen grand. And he's worth every penny."

"I have to ask, Mr Nicholls. How does a recently bankrupt, unemployed man gather fifteen thousand pounds?"

"I'm not unemployed. I do two jobs. Deliveries for Waitrose and horticulture work for the Council."

"That still ..."

Yvonne broke in. "We borrowed it. My parents and his brother gave us the money. We'll pay them back."

Dawn nodded. "So you handed over the cash to Sienna Smith, and ...?"

"No, we're not that naïve. We only handed over the money when we received Liam. But we made an agreement, gave her a deposit and prepared for having a baby. We moved here, where no one knew us. Yvonne wore a pregnancy pad under her clothes for months. We put off any visitors and told the neighbours we preferred to stick with our family GP in Salisbury. All we had to do was to make sure she didn't get ill. We couldn't risk a trip to any doctor. Then we got the nod. Sienna told us where to go and when."

Dawn rested her chin on her clasped hands. "And yesterday morning, you got your little boy. Did you know the name of the woman who handed him over?"

"No, we only knew her as Scarlett," Yvonne said. "We were worried because Liam was crying so much. She was so rude, wasn't she, Gerry?"

"Downright unpleasant. Fortunately we had all the equipment with us. Dry nappy, baby food, Calpol. Poor little sod was in a right state. How could they treat a child like that? But they've got us over a barrel. Who's going to report them?"

"You are, I'm afraid. Mr and Mrs Nicholls, your child is a case of illegal adoption. Social Services are on their way and they will help you take this through the proper channels. Liam will have to be taken into care, pending an official investigation. If the parents of the child are willing and the authorities have no reason to refuse you, there's every chance you can adopt baby Liam. The fact that you've taken good care of him will work in your favour. But the proper procedures must be observed. I promise to do everything in my power to help you."

Yvonne began to sob quietly, but Gerry narrowed his eyes. "Why would you do that? We've committed a crime."

"As a matter of fact, I see you as victims, not perpetrators. Not only that, but if you can assist me in catching these traffickers, it'll make a positive impression on those who make the decisions.

Listen, Gerry, Yvonne. You seem like good parents. Why would I want to destroy that? All we have to be sure is that the birth mother gave him up voluntarily, that there was no coercion, no rape, and no associated crimes such as blackmail involved."

The doorbell rang.

"Oh my God!" Yvonne's sobs restarted. Gerry embraced his wife as Dawn got up to answer.

Virginia, slightly bedraggled after summer rain, stood with a small bald man, who was wearing jeans and an anorak. "Mr Horniman, this is DI Whittaker. Dawn, this is Jason Horniman from Social Services, Adoption Advisor. Can we come in? It's wet out here."

After leaving the Nicholls's house, Dawn retreated into silence on the journey to Cardiff, but this time for less selfish reasons. Absorbed by thoughts of what that couple and poor little Liam had undergone, anger and sympathy filled her chest. She'd call them next week and offer her continued support. The thought of that tiny little person, carried across the sea, cold, wet and hungry when he should have been in an incubator. Whoever was responsible was going down for this.

She felt Virginia glance at her as they sped down the M4. "Hey, the social worker will look after them. They might well get him back if the investigation doesn't show up involvement in a paedophile ring or anything dodgy on their records."

"I know. I was just trying to imagine what they've been through. What the baby's been through. No, I agree with you. They're in capable hands and the social worker seemed like a decent guy. Even if he doesn't live up to his name."

Virginia took her eyes off the motorway to shoot her a puzzled frown.

Dawn deadpanned. "I could have sworn you introduced him as Horniman. Well, not in my book he ain't."

Virginia laughed loudly and shook her head. "Nor mine."

And that would do as an olive branch for now. Time to get to business.

"Right. Now for Ms Marie, or should I say Scarlett, Fisher. Do we head for Docklands Rentals or pick her up at her address?"

Virginia's eyes flicked to the clock. "The rental firm told Ranga the return was due between twelve and one. We could make that easily, with time for a sandwich stop. We're going for an arrest, right?"

"Too right. This is obviously one hard-nosed little bitch and we've got ample evidence. Take her in, lean on her and find out where they've taken Adrian Harvey." Dawn yanked up her bag from the foot well. "I'm going to update Beatrice and then see how Heddlu de Cymru want to play it."

"And I'll keep my eyes peeled for food and caffeine."

Docklands Rentals had a Portakabin as its office. Virginia pulled up onto the forecourt, positioning the vehicle parallel to the front fence, facing the line of returned cars and went in to announce their presence. Dawn finished her water, observing the traffic entering and leaving the superstore on the other side of Newport Road. She dialled the number again. He must be back by now.

"Ah, hello. DI Whittaker again. Just wondering if your duty sergeant is back at his desk? Thank you. Hello, Detective Sergeant Harris, DI Whittaker here. I called before but you were out at lunch."

"Good afternoon to you, DI Whittaker. No, I'm afraid lunch is on hold. I've been talking to DI Rangarajan and DI Stubbs just now. We're happy for you to take the lead on this arrest and I've already checked we have the necessary force to back you up, if you need us."

"Oh, I see. Well, that's good of you, but we're not expecting any trouble. So if it's all right with you, we'll make the arrest and bring her to Cardiff Bay. Would there be an interview room available?"

"Not a problem. Like I say, give us a shout if you need any help."

"Thank you, DS Harris. And I think you'll be safe enough to have your lunch now."

"Kettle's already boiled, DI Whittaker. Beef and tomato Pot Noodle today. See, I'm a traditionalist at heart. Look forward to meeting you later."

Dawn ended the call with a smile and was adjusting the radio to Cardiff Eastern frequency when Virginia returned.

"Right, as I expected. The office is staffed by two adolescents who'll keep their traps shut, but I think we should lift her as soon as she gets out of the car."

"I agree. The Cardiff force is ready with backup."

Virginia rested her head on the back of the seat. "I'm so tired, I daren't close my eyes. Not even for a second. Did you say backup? Do you think that's necessary?"

"Can't be too careful. Are you OK? Do you want my coffee?"

Virginia yawned, stretching her long, lean arms over the steering wheel. "I need some kind of kick. Adrenalin, amphetamine, I'm not fussy. Don't answer that. You know what?" She jerked her head at the Portakabin. "Behind the reception desk is one of those one-way mirrors and when I looked into it, you know what I saw? Bruce Forsyth in a Boden dress."

Dawn laughed and was about to make a complimentary comment on chins when an SUV drove past, curved around and parked in an empty space, a hundred yards in front. The driver's door opened and a slight, dark-haired woman slid out.

As Dawn put on her sunglasses, she noted Virginia doing the same. "Come on then, Brucie. Let's take her."

They opened their doors in unison and the Fisher woman's head whipped around. Her eyes moved from one to another as they approached. Calmly and with no sudden movements, Marie Fisher turned and got back into the car. Dawn stopped and looked at Virginia.

"She's not ..."

An engine roared and gravel spat from beneath the wheels.

"She fucking is. In the car!"

The SUV had already shot out of the entrance by the time Dawn buckled her belt and started the siren. She grabbed the radio and alerted Cardiff HQ as to Marie Fisher's vehicle description, plates and direction as Virginia hurled the Volvo into traffic. Poor Sergeant Harris and his Pot Noodle.

"Taking a left, and again, no indication, stupid bitch, thinks she can throw me ..." Virginia kept up a muttered monologue as she threw the vehicle after their target. Marie knew where she was going, that much was clear. Racing to a junction, cutting up other vehicles, hacking left or right without warning, she certainly gave the impression of trying to outrun her pursuers.

Dawn clenched her handset, tensing herself against the seat as if it would offer protection, and relayed as much information as she could to the operator.

"Broadway, headed south west, past The Royal Oak pub."

Cars, buses, lorries, even bikes slowed and made room for the siren, which unfortunately aided Marie Fisher in weaving a determined path down the back streets. The red light of a pelican crossing indicated pedestrian priority and a mother stepped out with a pushchair. Both Dawn's feet hit the carpet but Virginia slammed her hand to the horn, causing the startled woman to leap backwards.

Passing Cyril Street on the right, another siren joined them. A patrol car pulled in behind and Virginia's momentary glance away from the road meant she didn't see Fisher's handbrake turn.

"Left! Left here! Now!" Dawn shrieked.

Virginia hit the brakes, ramming the gearstick upwards and swinging the wheel a full circle, before changing into second and accelerating once more. Flung against the door, Dawn felt sick but kept up her continual commentary.

"We've taken a left, don't know the name but we're passing Sapphire Street, Emerald Street, Copper Street ... is this some sort of joke? Taking a left. Next is ... oh shit!"

Passengers leaving a bus had just finished crossing the road as it pulled out of the stop. Marie overtook, bouncing up on the pavement, perilously close to a pair of elderly ladies, but just made it past. Virginia swung left into the bus bay, hit the accelerator, climbed the kerb and overtook the bus on the inside. The bus driver braked and honked his horn, but the Volvo was already swinging back into position, closing on Marie Fisher. Dawn's buttocks were clenched so hard, her bum took up half its usual space.

Virginia changed down a gear and the engine whined as she gained on Fisher's rear. She leant forward, neck muscles taut, forearms tensed and eyes scanning the scene ahead. Dawn compared her own stance: hands gripping the radio, whole body clenched and thrust as far back as physically possible. She realised the radio was squeaking at her and resumed her relay.

"Sorry, lost it for a moment there. Now on Splott Road, heading south. She's doing fifty, fifty-five on a residential street."

"More backup on its way."

"Suspect on South Park Road, no, taken a right, Seawall Road, heading south-east. We're on an industrial estate, and she's picking up speed. Reading sixty-five. She's keen to get away. Is there another way into this place? We might be able to ..."

The black vehicle lost it on the bend, swerving madly from one side to the next, but Marie managed to hold it and sped on. Virginia handled the curve far better, braking, turning and picking up speed all at the perfect moment. They gained several seconds and could almost see the outline of Fisher's head. Virginia flashed her lights and motioned to pull over. Marie indicated, braked and slowed and Dawn inhaled a deep breath of relief. Then the SUV took off again at speed, spitting back stones and dust. Virginia roared with rage, changed into second and Dawn's head bounced off the back of the seat.

Seawall Road straightened and as they tore past the school, Dawn gave thanks it was a Sunday. At the end of the road was a roundabout, with two possible exits. Virginia was closing the gap and Marie's choices were decreasing. Another siren joined the cacophony. A second patrol car approached from the right exit, lights flashing. Marie didn't hesitate, taking a screeching left.

"Left. Repeat. Suspect took a left off roundabout at end of Seawall Road. Second police vehicle in support."

Virginia tore the wheel to the left and Dawn's head hit the window again, before she was thrown forward into her seatbelt as Virginia slammed on the anchors. Marie's SUV was stationary, brake lights on. The road was nothing more than a track to an industrial wasteland. Ahead: a dead end. Marie Fisher had run out of choices.

They waited for several seconds. Virginia tensed as the reverse lights came on, but Fisher killed the engine. South Wales police officers fanned out around them as Dawn and Virginia stepped out of the car. Dawn's legs were unreliable, so she leant, nonchalantly, on the bonnet.

The door of the SUV opened and Virginia stepped forward to make the arrest. Marie gave no reaction. Dawn watched as two officers clipped on cuffs and guided her into the patrol car.

Virginia strode back towards Dawn with a broad grin. "Well, that woke me up. To the station for a light bout of interrogation?"

Dawn shook her head and sighed. "To think I could be watching Eastenders."

Chapter 41

Beatrice and Inspector Crean sheltered from the shower under the eaves of the Cork Airport terminal until Grant ended his call and came across the tarmac to join them.

His face looked dreadful; there were dark shadows under his eyes and he clearly bore bad news.

"Dyfed-Powys police found Adrian Harvey's wallet near Porthgain harbour. They've searched the whole area, a disused industrial site, but found nothing else."

Beatrice's last vestige of hope died: that Adrian had got lost, met someone else, fallen asleep or anything other than being taken by suspected child-traffickers.

"I see. Inspector Crean, let me introduce DS Ty Grant. The Inspector's going to escort us to the farm. A team's already there, conducting a search."

"How are you, Ty?" Inspector Crean offered a large hand and generous smile. "It'll take us around forty minutes to get there, so I can give you all the background along the way."

Beatrice nodded, hiding her impatience. She had a feeling this gentle, slow-moving man would drive like a grandma. While Adrian lay in the hands of human traffickers who treat people like animals, using them for what they can get.

Thankfully, Crean had a police driver, who was efficient and fast, albeit monosyllabic. The inspector sat in the passenger seat, twisting round to address herself and Grant.

"Now then, Lannagh Farm. Well, first thing you should know is that it's not really a farm. It's a rendering facility."

Beatrice gave Grant an enquiring glance, but he shook his head.

"I always assumed rendering was something you did to walls," she said.

The inspector had turned his attention to the road. Banners, bikes and significant numbers of spectators announced a cycle race. Beatrice dug her nails into her upper arms, noting the time on the dashboard as twelve-fifteen. The inspector finished advising the driver as to an alternative route and turned back to them.

"So, rendering. Not one of the most pleasant jobs you can do. That's why the farm is so remote. Terrible stink. They take waste products from slaughterhouses and farms; diseased animals, or the bits not fit for human consumption and so on. A rendering plant divides it into stuff that must be disposed of safely, and the rest it processes."

Beatrice clenched her jaw. "Processes into what?"

"Fertiliser, soap, animal food, that sort of thing."

Grant met her eyes and Beatrice closed hers.

The smell grew as they bumped their way up the long rough track which led to Lannagh Farm. The Inspector wasn't exaggerating; that reek was repulsive. A young sergeant waited outside the farm buildings and an ambulance stood with its doors open on the opposite side of the yard.

Beatrice's heart pulsed with fear. She released her seatbelt and opened her door before the car had come to a halt, hurrying over to the young officer.

"DI Stubbs of the Met. Is the emergency vehicle for Mr Harvey?"

"Sergeant Sullivan. No, ma'am. We've not yet located Mr Harvey. My colleagues are still searching. It's a big place, unfortunately. We've taken Brigid Connor, her family and three employees to the station. That includes Eoin Connor, your man with the ponytail from your pictures."

"Has he given you any information as to the whereabouts of Mr Harvey?"

"No, ma'am. Mrs Connor told them all to say nothing until they speak to a solicitor."

Inspector Crean and Grant joined them.

"Good afternoon, sir. I was just explaining that we've taken most of the family and farm staff in for questioning. But Mrs Connor's husband, Samir Lasku, is out doing a job on the farm somewhere. No one seems to know what or where. So far, we haven't located Mr Harvey."

Grant jerked his head at the ambulance. "So this is just a precaution?"

"No, it's for one of the girls. Look, this is a bit complicated. Do you want to come through here?"

Grant gestured for Beatrice to go inside. "You go ahead, I'll take a look around."

While Beatrice and Inspector Crean sat, the young sergeant stood at the end of the kitchen table, as if he were Head Boy about to deliver assembly.

"We've searched the farm and most of the outbuildings, but we haven't started on the plant yet. It's a huge area, full of bits of dead animals, so it'll take a while. The Inspector has asked them to shut the processes down, but they can't, so we're going to have to work around them. They're on lunch right at the moment, but the machines will start up again in around half an hour."

Inspector Crean smiled and nodded. "Good work, Sullivan. What else is there?"

"Upstairs in this house, we found four young women, all in different stages of pregnancy. Brigid Connor says they all work here. Three of them are at the station but one's still upstairs, bleeding heavily. It looks like she's having a miscarriage. I called an ambulance to take her to hospital, but she doesn't speak much English, so the crew are having some difficulties persuading her to go."

The inspector shook his head in amazement. "Do we know where she's from?"

"No clue, sir, sorry. Don't recognise her language and she has no ID that we can find."

"Were the other pregnant girls also foreigners?" asked Beatrice.

Sergeant Sullivan consulted his notepad. "No, Ma'am. All Irish girls, but none local."

Grant ducked under the low doorway, a frown darkening his face.

"Anything?" he asked.

Beatrice shook her head. "No sign of Adrian yet. The local officers are starting to search the plant."

Grant stood with his back to the window, making his expression hard to read. But his voice was tight and angry. "Let's be realistic. Why bring him back here? Because he had evidence, and they wanted to get shot of him. The most logical place to get rid of a body is in with all the others. We need to search the rendering area, but there are still trucks arriving. Why hasn't the plant been shut down?"

Inspector Crean sat back and gave a patient smile. "We've tried, Sergeant Grant. To shut the place down, we'd need a court order. Under Department of Agriculture rules, it runs continuously to prevent contamination."

His easy-going manner infuriated Beatrice. "Inspector, if there's a dead body in that factory, everything will be contaminated. I have to ask you to prevent any more vehicles entering the plant for the time being."

Sergeant Sullivan cleared his throat. "Inspector, we can actually close that first section. It's already inactive while the crew have their lunch. The first two parts of the process are only kept moving so as to minimise decay. The only section that needs a court order is the rendering equipment, where the raw material is heated and sterilised. We can halt the deliveries right now."

Beatrice turned to give Grant the order, but he was already out the door.

"Inspector, if Sergeant Sullivan accompanies Grant and myself to the plant, could you ask your men to prevent any more lorries from arriving. Is that acceptable to you?"

His eyebrows floated upwards, but he gave a gentle smile. "It is, DI Stubbs. Wild horses wouldn't drag me up there. I'll leave the best man to the job. Sullivan, let the officers know DI Stubbs has my full support."

"Sergeant Sullivan, could you walk with me? I'd like to ask you a few questions."

Receiving a benevolent nod from Crean, the sergeant picked up his notebook and followed Beatrice outside. He indicated a path curving away to the right and they began walking towards the origin of the all-pervading stink.

"You seem to know a lot about this rendering business," she began.

"A bit. My uncle has a slaughterhouse and used to bring his waste here. I did work experience with him, only for a few months, but learned about what happens to the bits we don't eat." The sergeant's high colour could have been due to embarrassment, enthusiasm or genetics. Beatrice was unfussed.

"Can you talk me through it? I'm not squeamish."

"Sure I can. Take a left here now and we're onto the main track up to the plant. This is a Category Three facility. Animal by-products fall into three categories; the first two are the diseased or toxic carcasses, which you've got to keep out of the food chain, or process them properly, as I expect you know. Category Three includes the bits of the animal we don't eat; hooves, snouts, tails, ears, guts, well, you get the picture. Slaughterhouses can only use about half a cow. The rest is sent here. This category also includes gone-off meat from shops, put-down pets from vets and animal shelters and downed animals from local farms."

Beatrice decided she did feel squeamish after all. "So to summarise, this is one of the less dangerous facilities."

"Right enough. Anything dangerous is separated and treated at another plant. They don't have the equipment here to cope with infectious diseases. So lorries deliver the bits of meat, cat corpses, poultry feathers and so on, which they call the 'raw'. It's all tipped onto the plant floor and then it's reduced before processing."

"And that would be the first two stages? Delivery and reduction. I don't think I really want to know this, but can you explain 'reduction'?"

"Ah, it's not all that complicated. Two massive rollers crush the whole lot to a pulp. After that, it's treated with the sterilising chemicals, dried out and separated into fat or bone meal. Are you feeling all right there, ma'am?"

The smell, the images and her own fragile emotions stopped

Beatrice in her tracks. Heat swelled her neck and the blood-rush in her ears made balance a struggle. Sullivan held her elbow, peering at her face.

Adrian.

She opened her eyes and concentrated on the job.

"Thank you, sergeant. We can move on now. Tell me, have you lived in this area long?"

Chapter 42

Good cop, bad cop. No one needed to discuss it.

Dawn assumed her practised you-can-tell-me-anything expression, softened with slow blinks and beatific smiles. Virginia's tiredness and impatience made itself manifest in the atmosphere, like the unease before a thunderstorm. Her scornful lightning strikes lit up the room against Dawn's calm, kindly patience.

Yet Marie Fisher, or Mairead Connor, as her passport showed, remained unmoved. A WPC stood in the corner of the room, observing proceedings. Her presence for the sake of protocol allowed Virginia to make frequent exits. The lawyer had not yet arrived, so Dawn and Mairead sat in silence. Dawn allowed her gaze to rest on the grey table and breathed herself gently into a semi-meditative state. Addressing each discomfort in turn, she acknowledged her own tensions, her fears for Beatrice and Adrian, her need for peace and emotional processing time, her hunger, and her impatience with this witness. She politely asked each urge to wait in the queue.

The door swung open and Virginia was back, pressing the record button on the monitoring device and smiling.

"DI Lowe has returned. So Mairead, you may as well start now. Your lawyer is still en route, but your family have already coughed up the story. It's a shame, but the charges are stacking up now that the foreign girl's gone to hospital. Negligence at best, but I'm pushing for attempted murder."

Mairead's deliberately unimpressed look at Virginia slid away to the wall, reminding Dawn of her own teenage son.

Virginia's eyes shone. "Not going to give us your side? Because they're not sparing you, I'll tell you that. The whole baby farm was your idea, you organised the network of recruiters and it was your decision to use your retarded sister as a guinea-pig."

Mairead's head snapped round. "Fuck you! She's not retarded. Minor learning difficulties is all. And she's never been a guinea-pig."

Dawn flashed a look at Virginia and lowered her voice from the confrontational tone. "What's your sister's name?"

"Teagan. She's forty-five but still acts like a kid. She's not developed the way the rest of us have. But we never took advantage of the fact she's a bit innocent. God knows, others did. More than once. But we're her family, so we always helped her out. Not like we had a choice."

"You're telling me she got pregnant accidentally?" Virginia demanded.

Mairead's eyes flicked to Virginia and away in contempt. Dawn tried a softer tack.

"That must have been a shock for you all. And I'm guessing you didn't find out till quite late on."

Mairead gave a brief nod. "No. She didn't realise herself till the Mammy spotted it. But Ceana, that's my other sister, she's a nurse. She was working in Birmingham back then. She knew of a couple, infertile and desperate for kids, so it seemed obvious. Teagan couldn't even take care of herself, leave alone a baby. What we did was a kindness."

Virginia raised her eyebrows. "How much did you charge them for this 'kindness'?"

Mairead didn't even look at her, but continued talking to Dawn. "It was a one-off. But our eldest sister ..."

"Can I interrupt, Mairead? I just need to get the facts clear in my mind. When did you give Teagan's baby away?" Dawn asked.

"Ninety-four. My father died the same year, before we found out about Teagan, thanks be to God."

"That must have been tough for your mother, running the farm alone."

"She had Samir. And Eoin could be useful if he just copped himself on. He's lazy, soft-hearted and no kind of asset on a farm. But Samir's not afraid of hard work. He came over as a refugee from

Albania with his daughter. One of the first out the country as soon as they opened the borders. He kept the place going all right. We owe him a lot."

Virginia slid behind Mairead and made a speeding-up motion with her hand, indicating her watch. Dawn nodded once.

"I think your story is going to be very important to this case, so I want you to take your time. The problem is, we need to find Adrian Harvey, the man Eoin and Samir abducted from Pembrokeshire. As a matter of urgency. If you can help us locate Mr Harvey, it will do you a real favour when this comes to court. A jury is always better inclined to a cooperative witness. Can you help us, Mairead?"

Mairead threaded her fingers together and pressed her forehead to her hands, as if she was praying. Minutes ticked past. Virginia shifted from foot to foot, glowering at the silent woman. Dawn held up a hand, asking for patience.

Mairead looked up. "The guy had photographs. Pictures of me, the last deal we did, the boat ... he told them he was a private detective, so we thought he was working alone. We couldn't have let him go, he'd have blown the whole thing open. So Samir decided to deal with it. Disappear him."

Virginia sat beside Dawn, her voice hard. "By 'disappear him', you mean you planned to kill him."

Mairead stared at Virginia with naked dislike. "I just said, Samir decided. He was going to do it and dump him with the rest of the carcasses at the plant."

"How can you be sure a human body wouldn't be spotted among the animals?" asked Dawn.

Mairead leant back with a sigh. "Because we've done it before."

When Dawn got back from the bathroom, Virginia was still on the phone to the Cork Constabulary. She looked up and indicated the interview room, mouthing the word 'lawyer'.

"Thanks for your help, Detective. Call you back within the hour. Bye now." She replaced the receiver. "They haven't found Adrian. And no sign of Samir Lasku either, which isn't reassuring. But seems Eoin Connor has made a full confession and claims he tried to help Adrian get away. The girls and Teagan are spilling all over the place, but nothing from Brigid. Otherwise known as The Mammy. They're searching the factory now. Rather them than me." She lifted her shoulders and rolled her neck from side to side.

Dawn grimaced. "If he's in the factory, he's already dead."

Virginia stopped her stretching and looked up. "You're right. Oh God, poor Beatrice."

"Come on, let's go and hear Mairead's side."

Dawn's headache tightened. "Let's go back. I can see how you found prospective parents, through Ceana's job at the hospital fertility clinic. But locating the girls ..."

Virginia looked like death warmed up and the lawyer was picking at his nails.

Mairead sighed with impatience. "As already I said, we have two routes. Niamh, she's the oldest, has good contacts at IFPA, the Irish Family Planning Association. They tip her off about girls looking for an abortion. She does a bit of research and approaches them with a proposition. Her code name is Sandy. All of us begin with an S. Scarlett, Sienna, Saffron. Memorable names, see."

"So one recruitment channel was through your older sister in Ireland. And the other?" asked Dawn.

"The other route was through Elira. I told you Samir and Elira came to us as Albanian refugees. Now Elira works with asylum-seekers in London and has an eye for girls in trouble. She offers them six months' work and a solution to the problem. It's like I keep saying. We're doing people a favour. The mothers, the kids, the new parents; everyone's happy." Mairead's saintly expression was nowhere near genuine.

Dawn's instinct told her it was time to puncture that smug surface. "Was Teagan happy when you sold her twins?"

Mairead's back hit the chair and she placed her palms on the edge of the table. "Do I have to repeat everything for you people? Teagan is under-developed. She can't look after anything. We had to take the twins away and give them a proper family. Of course she didn't like it, she gets easily attached. But for everyone's sake, it was better that way."

Her expression had changed. Defensive, as opposed to indignant. There was something else. "Who got her pregnant, Mairead?" asked Dawn.

"Jesus, Mary and Joseph, how the feck do I know? I live in Cardiff, I don't follow my little sister around all day, making sure no one takes advantage. How do you expect ...?"

Virginia's voice, low and deliberate, interrupted. "Who do you think it was? There's a limited pool of sperm donors on the farm."

"I don't know! I have no idea! There are up to seventy lorries a day coming in and out of the plant, it could have been anyone. As if I'd know." Her cheeks were a stark binary pattern of white and red.

Virginia turned to Dawn and the disbelief in her eyes was clear. Internally, Dawn agreed. Whoever it was, Mairead knew. The silence swelled with implications.

Mairead's voice changed from shrill to persuasive. "Look, we wanted to help people. Unwanted kids, childless parents. All we did was find a supply to meet a demand."

"The fact remains, despite your altruistic motives, you sold children. How much, Mairead? How much did Teagan's first baby go for?" asked Virginia.

"I told you already, that was a one-off."

"Apart from the twins you flogged later. How much?"

"Five grand. But that was in ninety-four. There was one other girl in ninety-six, which was more of a favour than anything. But in ninety-eight, the fallout from Mad Cow disease hit the factory and we had cash-flow problems. But we also had a way of raising money. So we put the price up."

Dawn tilted her head and smiled, struggling to stay sympathetic. Virginia folded her arms and closed her eyes.

"Yes. I hear fifteen grand is the going rate nowadays. And that's when the 'business' started in earnest?" asked Dawn.

Mairead shrugged. "Yeah. By 2000, we had a waiting list of parents. It was complicated, but we were very, very careful. The parents won't say anything because they might lose the child. The girls have a job for six months, a solution to their problem and a cash payoff at the end. No one knows what they've done and so long as they keep it shut, no one will tell."

Virginia opened her eyes. "How much did you pay 'the girls'? How much of fifteen grand do they see?"

"We take all the risks, so we keep the majority. They get five hundred Euro and should be grateful. It's enough for them to start off again."

 No one spoke. Dawn breathed deeply and gazed at the grey surface once more, willing herself to find calm. She couldn't even attempt to communicate with Virginia, who scraped back her chair and left the room. Dawn informed the recording device of the change in personnel and returned her attention to Mairead.

"You mentioned earlier that human cadavers had been disposed of at the factory. Could you explain?"

Mairead glanced at the lawyer, who scribbled something on his pad for her to read.

"In the spirit of cooperation and full disclosure, I'll tell you. We lost three babies, and one of the mothers died in childbirth. All those bodies went into the crusher."

"And no one noticed? None of your employees saw a human cadaver? No one missed this girl?"

"She was a refugee. No one really knew where she came from, so there was no one to miss her. It was a shame, a sad situation, but the easiest thing all round was to clear up any trail. And as for the plant workers, no. Look, when carcasses are unloaded onto the rendering floor, they aim for the conveyor in the middle. Two machines push the raw from the edges onto the conveyor. If something strange was on the outer edges, it's possible someone might see it. If you just make sure your waste is in the middle, the conveyor feeds it directly to the crusher."

"Detective Inspector Whittaker is leaving the room. Interview suspended at twelve-fifty."

Chapter 43

Grant advanced towards the man, his gestures short and stabbing. Dawn's urgent tones from the mobile in her ear and Grant's threatening manner towards the group of employees combined to release a thin wail of panic inside Beatrice. Closing her phone, she approached Grant and the crowd of disgruntled lorry drivers, uniformed factory staff and their stubborn-looking boss.

"DI Stubbs, we have a problem. Mr Donelly here is the foreman and he refuses to stop the plant operations ..."

Without waiting for Grant to finish, she began issuing orders. "Detective Sergeant Grant, first priority. Ensure the conveyor belt on the rendering floor remains inactive until I give alternative instructions. Clear all personnel from the floor and the crushers. Mr Donelly will show you how, or he'll be placed under arrest and charged with obstructing justice. Go, now! Sergeant Sullivan, please remove all these people from the scene and tape the area. All workers in stages one and two of the rendering process are requested to leave the premises until further notice as this is now a serious crime scene. You may all be called as witnesses."

Donelly spat behind him, several workers mumbled abuse but Beatrice was more than ready for a fight. Scanning each face with a stony expression, watching each pair of eyes slide away, she made her mark. With a brisk nod, she marched after Grant and Donelly, towards the huge ramps used by the trucks to dump their waste. The stink waves of rotting flesh, putrefying matter and decay grew stronger until it became almost physical. Every cell in her body screamed at her to flee, her stomach bucked and heaved, but she strode on, head down, into the pit.

Donelly's attitude improved in a direct ratio to how sick she and Grant became. As they donned their protective clothing, along with wellingtons, gloves and masks, Beatrice knew her face reflected the same green pallor of Grant's. He attempted a smile but immediately tore off his mask and vomited into the toilet of the staff changing room. Donelly seemed pleased. Beatrice vowed not to chuck up her breakfast, but if it proved essential, she would bestow most of it on Mr Donelly.

Detective Sullivan and PC Hegarty, similarly clad, awaited them as they emerged to climb the stone steps to the rendering floor.

"Right. When we get onto the floor, I want Grant and Sullivan on the right side of the belt, taking half each. Hegarty's with me, taking the other side. Grant, let's start closest to the crusher. We've wasted a lot of time, so that end is our danger zone. Sullivan, keep an eye on him. OK, this is not going to be pleasant, but do your best."

Donelly opened the door to the processing plant and Beatrice forced out short breaths from her nose, a futile attempt at expelling the stench. She stamped up the concrete steps after Grant and followed him through the sliding doors. The reek of decomposition instantly caused her to gag, affecting Grant the same way. PC Hegarty couldn't even enter the room, heaving and hunched over his knees at the top of the steps. She ordered him back to the changing rooms. He would be no help.

Beatrice averted her eyes from the piles around her and pressed on towards the centre of the huge barn. Grant's retching and choking from the corner continued. Observing his spasmodic vomiting, she realised she and Sullivan would be working alone. She waved at Grant, indicating the exit with her thumb, releasing him from a duty he simply couldn't perform. He held up a gloved hand, helpless, and staggered away.

Orientation was not an issue. The vast maw at the other end gaped across the mounds of animal flesh. Beatrice, battling her stomach convulsions by repeating the word *Adrian* like a mantra, made her way to the opposite side. Sullivan traced a parallel route to her right, apparently unfazed by the atmosphere. Beatrice stared at the scene. Fur, tails, eyes, ears with tags, teeth, bone, feathers, flesh, hooves, blood, supermarket packaging, clawed paws, entrails and effervescent patches of maggots culminated in a scene of utter horror. The room was eerily quiet, but she only had to imagine the noise of the relentless conveyor, the drone of small earthmovers and the cacophonous grinding of relentless crushing rollers, to envisage one of Dante's Inner Circles of Hell.

They approached the central section, bending, lifting, kicking and examining. Beatrice couldn't see. Tears flooded her eyes as she accepted the fact they were looking for Adrian's body. No one could survive this. The lachrymose taste, unfortunately, could not repel the stench of rotting death. She got to work.

Beginning at the end of the belt nearest the inert crushers, she shifted several feet of dead sheep, checking beneath each carcass, finding nothing but more dead sheep. The next section was more varied. Poultry. Feet, beaks, heads and feathers. Pure force of will forced down her bile as she recalled Adrian's chicken cacciatore. After an area of unidentifiable innards, she came across the dogs. A pile of Jack Russells, a German Shepherd tangled up with several collies, on top of which lay two Westies, one of whose paws were crossed against its chest. He still had his collar on. Beatrice's chest was already heaving as she reached for the name tag. That was when she saw the arm.

Stepping over the dogs, she cautiously batted aside a pile of feathers to reveal Adrian's face. Bloodstained, eyes closed and skin white, he lay on his side with vomit trailing from his mouth.

"He's here! Sullivan, he's under here!"

Sullivan scrambled over the landscape of cadavers and body parts in her direction, digging under his overall for his phone.

Beatrice's tears flowed over her mask as she pressed two fingers to his neck.

"He's got a pulse!" Her cry ricocheted around the room. "I've got a pulse. Ambulance, Sullivan, now! We've found him!"

"Already on its way. The same one's still down at the farm. Don't move him, ma'am, we don't know how badly he's hurt."

She lowered her face to Adrian's, listening for any sign of breath. In the fetid, foul air, the sweetest sound blew into her ear. He was still breathing!

Sullivan arrived beside her, clearing the bloody detritus from Adrian's prone form with pragmatic ease and checking him for injury. Adrian gave no reaction as the detective's hands pressed and pushed his joints. Beatrice swiped at her face and scooped up Adrian's hand.

"Adrian, we've got you. You'll be fine. An ambulance is coming. We're here, we'll look after you, but you must be strong. Adrian, listen to me, you must be strong for me."

The Irish officer worked his way down Adrian's legs, as Beatrice gently patted his face. Once Sullivan reached the ankles, Adrian's body convulsed and his eyes opened for a second.

"Adrian? Adrian! He's gone again. It must be his leg. Sullivan? The ambulance?"

"It'll be here in less than one minute, Ma'am. Coming from the farm, see? That girl wouldn't budge, so today's our lucky day."

Beatrice could remember luckier days.

The showers were communal, so Beatrice decided to leave the men to clean up while she accompanied Adrian to the hospital. After all, one person humming of dead animals is not all that different to two. The ambulance staff diagnosed Adrian with shock, dehydration, a head wound and a sprained ankle, along with minor lacerations and bruises. None of which gave them serious cause for concern. Once he'd been whisked away into A&E, the ambulance woman kindly took her to the hospital showers and provided her with a set of whites.

She scrubbed for ages. The sticky stench of death seemed to have woven its way into her pores, her hair, under her nails. Eventually, she turned off the water and stood there, steaming. Adrian was alive. Most of the traffickers were in custody. Matthew was back in London, awaiting her return. Nathan Bennett could harass no more women. Dawn and Virginia were speaking to each other. Everything was fine. Except that Adrian had been dumped into that pile of carcasses, to be crushed alive. She sat on the floor of the shower stall, so appalled by the depths of human nature she could not even cry.

Chapter 44

Keys clattering against the door dragged Beatrice back to the present. With a disbelieving glance at the clock, she saw forty minutes had elapsed while she'd been staring out the window, dwelling on the past. The front door closed and Matthew called out.

"I'm back!"

"So I gathered. What took you so long?" Beatrice forced her attention back to the computer. She was nearly there.

"Oh, just chatting, you know what Adrian's like. I don't think he's stopped talking long enough to draw a breath. Now he's demanding a celebratory glass of something because he's off painkillers. I said we'd pop down with something special in a while."

"In a while. Yes, that's a nice, vague sort of term. I'm almost done here, so let's take him some of that champagne you bought in Reims."

Beatrice re-read the document for the last time, sighed and pressed Send. All done. She stretched her arms above her head. "How's his leg today?"

"Up. He's recumbent on the chaise longue in his pyjamas and looks exactly like Noel Coward."

September clouds parted, permitting autumn sunshine to flood the room. The low light cast a pinkish glow over the room, enriching her green tablecloth to a jewel-bright emerald and highlighting the dust. Matthew clattered about in the bathroom, raising his voice as he turned on the taps.

"How did you get on this afternoon?" he yelled.

Such a noisy man. Beatrice stood in the bathroom doorway and watched him rub shaving foam all over his jaw.

"I managed to finish it, despite the disturbance from downstairs. What on earth were you doing down there? It sounded like you were playing skittles with concrete bollards."

"Jared and I rearranged the entire flat so that Adrian barely has to move. Remote controls, books, phone and a bowlful of organic fruit are all at his fingertips."

Beatrice envisaged the pampered patient and forcibly obliterated the reminder of Adrian's pale, bloodied, feather-stuck skin under fluorescent light. The urge to hurry downstairs and check on him tugged at her for the hundredth time that week.

"Why are you bothering to shave now?" she asked.

"May as well make an effort. I plan to change too, but fear not. I won't wear black."

Beatrice smiled. Matthew's 'Raffles' look was now replaced by the familiar toad-brown cords, off-white shirt and bobbled sage cardigan. And his hair would grow back, eventually.

"What a fuss. Just for a drink with Adrian and Jared. Are you sure you're not on the turn?"

Matthew laughed. "I'm not but I wonder if he is. You know, I think he's becoming a Young Fogey. He uses terms such as 'damned fine idea', 'sagacious' and 'tip-top'. Is that healthy, at his age, do you think?" He picked up his razor and scraped a clean path through the foam from cheekbone to chin.

"I think you'll find the Young Fogey will wear off when he tires of his Agatha Christie persona. What are we having for dinner?"

"Lord knows. I'll cobble something together when we get back."

He'd forgotten, again. But somehow, it reassured her. Matthew lived in the present. And from now on, so would she. The past smelt bad.

"Aren't you going to change, Old Thing?" he asked. "That pullover's still got Bolognese sauce on it from lunch."

She muttered and grumbled but acquiesced, as no doubt he knew she would. In the wardrobe was the top she'd worn this time last year. Dark blue with a silver thread running through it. It might even jog his memory. A flattering cut, but more importantly suitable for her age. She'd never had a desire to look like mutton dressed as ham.

When she returned, Matthew was waiting with a bottle of Heidsieck Monopole Gold Top.

"Will I do?" she asked. "I wonder if we should take some snacks. I may get hungry."

"Jared's taken care of all that. Umm, Beatrice?"

"Yes, I know. I'll do it as soon as I find my hairbrush."

"That wasn't what I was going to say."

Beatrice looked into the mirror above the fireplace and wished she hadn't. Her hair looked as if someone had used an electric whisk on her head.

"Oh, well. It's only Adrian. What were you going to say?"

"Nothing. You look perfect, my love. Let's go."

As soon as she opened Adrian's door, her instinct told her something was off kilter.

"Happy Birthday!!"

Beatrice stopped dead in the hallway. Balloons. Music. People. A plastic banner reiterating the message. She turned to Matthew for an explanation, but he'd slipped past her to join the crowd.

Adrian, in an armchair, pulling a party popper. Virginia, raising a glass. Ty Grant, applauding. Dawn, coming forward to hand her a glass. Jared, blowing kisses. Cooper and Ranga, lifting cans of lager. Lyndon, yanking out a champagne cork. Kalpana, bringing forward a tray of cupcakes. And Matthew, laughing.

"Speech!"

"Speech, Beatrice, come on!"

"Speech! Birthday Girl!"

Beatrice blinked. This would never work. Who invited both Dawn *and* Virginia? What was Adrian thinking, putting Jared and Lyndon in the same room? Kalpana was far too fragile to be at any kind of party. Why the hell had Matthew gone along with such a ridiculous plan? He knew she abhorred surprises. And what on earth made them all look so happy? She had a choice. To laugh or to cry, and the former was far more socially acceptable.

"Thank you. As a rule, I hate surprises. And this is no exception. However, all of you helped me get Adrian back. For that reason alone, you are forgiven. Matthew, I'll deal with you later. Cheers!"

Grant and Cooper looked around in amusement as Virginia and Kalpana whooped with laughter. Jared grinned, pleased with his punch line. The sight of Kalpana wiping away tears of laughter provoked an involuntary smile from Beatrice. Matthew and Ranga were in the kitchen, presumably still discussing Keralan cuisine, while Dawn and Lyndon had gone to open more champagne.

Adrian shifted on his cushion and Beatrice moved to give him room.

"It's fine, stay where you are. Just itchy, that's all. Matthew says you finished your report this afternoon."

"Yes, I did." The grey gloom which had accompanied her all day made a brief reappearance.

"Why the long face? Isn't it good news? Seven child-traffickers behind bars. Jared thinks I'm insane to testify on behalf of Eoin, but I'm determined. And I've already made my statement on Teagan's behalf. They both tried to help me, I really believe they did."

"If that's how you choose to see it."

"Beatrice, you weren't there. Anyway, I refuse to rehash this. Especially tonight. You should be enjoying yourself and toasting your success. That's why we're here. You know, I was still on the pills when I heard they'd picked Samir up. Even so, I had a sneaky glass of Prosecco to rejoice."

Beatrice agreed. "Me too. His violence and cruelty and paranoia may have served him and Brigid Connor well over the years, but his stupidity let him down at the end. As Inspector Crean said, he came in on a boat and was bound to try getting out the same way. All they had to do was wait."

"Crean's a classic tortoise, isn't he? Nothing flashy, but in the end, he gets his man. Rather like Morse."

"Adrian, I know that face. Don't tell me you're inventing another detective persona."

"No. Despite my natural flair, I do accept that a little training does help. Now, will you stop worrying about me and start celebrating?"

"I am celebrating. Or will be as soon as Dawn gets back with my champers. But writing up such a report forces you to acknowledge your mistakes. That hurts."

"Good job I don't have to do one, in that case. As I said, I'm not going over this anymore. I'm bored of it. And if you attempt for one second to blame yourself again, I swear to God, I'll have you thrown out of this flat."

"You can't do that. I'm the birthday girl."

"And a royal pain in the arse. Here comes the fizz. Now drink and be merry. I insist."

"Right. I'm going to chat to Dawn and leave you and Lyndon to finish your argument about Sherlock Holmes. Were you winning?"

"No. It's a well-known fact about the Welsh. Stubborn as hell."

Beatrice gave him a kiss on the forehead. "Good luck."

She stood to meet Dawn and led the way to the window seat.

Beatrice accepted her glass with a smile. "You're too good to me. But then again, I am the birthday girl."

"For someone who hates birthday surprises, you can't half milk it. Sure you don't want any more cakes? There's plenty left."

Beatrice shook her head, her attention drawn by the two men sitting at the dining table. "They were delicious, really, but I know my limits. With cakes, at least. Thank you for that. I never knew you could bake."

"Don't tell Hamilton. He hates multi-taskers. Oi, what are you gawping at?"

"Just curious. Ty Grant seems to have buddied up with Cooper. I wonder what they've got in common?"

Dawn snorted with laughter. "Apart from being early-thirties, straight, single white males who play rugger? Only the fact that Grant is angling for a transfer to the Met. I'd say Cooper is being pumped for information. He's already worked on me and Ranga."

"A-ha. What are his chances?"

"As DS, highly likely, unless Hamilton takes against him. But DI, no chance. There's a queue and no one's due for retirement anytime soon."

Beatrice didn't answer, watching Grant's large shoulders and Cooper's shorter-than-short haircut. A matching pair of British Bulldogs.

"Are you and Matthew going to take a holiday now?" Dawn asked. "It's well overdue."

Beatrice wrinkled her nose. "His term starts in two weeks, so he needs to get back and plan lectures. I might potter off somewhere for a week or so, and take a proper break with him later."

"Beatrice?" Dawn's eyes were soft and concerned. "How are you feeling?"

"Tired. Bone-weary. Despite James and a full hour of therapy. You might be right, you know. I do need a holiday. And funnily enough, I think I need some more cake. Shall we?"

Upstairs, Beatrice's laptop glowed into life, emitting a blue luminosity in the empty room. A pop-up box flashed onto the screen, where it remained for thirty seconds.

One message received.

The box shrank to a small envelope, blinking in the bottom right-hand corner, leaving the last document visible.

Dear Superintendent Hamilton

It is with regret that I hereby tender my notice.

After many fulfilling years spent with the force, I have a duty to maintain the standards of excellence for which we strive.

After careful consideration of my performance in the two most recent cases to which I was assigned, I believe I have made serious errors of judgement, endangering both fellow officers and members of the public.

I now see myself as more of a liability than an asset, and therefore choose to leave my position as Detective Inspector after the formal notice period has elapsed.

On a personal note, I would like to thank you for your unstinting support and patient interest in my development.

I wish you, my colleagues and the Metropolitan Police Force every success in the future.

Yours sincerely
Beatrice Stubbs

Tread Softly

JJ Marsh

Chapter 1

The bells struck seven. Tiago was late. Taking a last swig of *Estrella Galicia* for luck, he gathered keys, mobile, jacket, the CD and the flowers. Were roses too much? Maybe if they were red, signalling an obvious agenda. But yellow should be innocent enough. No, leave them, it's embarrassing. No, take them, it's a lovely gesture. Yellow rosebuds could signify the start of something.

Gazing into the fragrant whorls was only making him later, definitely a negative message on a first date. He ran out the door, leaping the stairs three at a time. On the second landing, Doña Llorente, complete with shopping, dogs and inhaler, blocked his path. He greeted her with a wave, the spaniels with a pat, and on impulse, thrust the flowers into her hand.

With a gallant bow, he slipped past before she got her breath back. He hit the street and recognised a smart decision. Ana wouldn't want flowers. Independent music with quirky artwork, perhaps, but no old-fashioned gestures. The right choice. Saved from cliché and into Doña Llorente's good books.

His instinct to reach for a cigarette was countered by a desire for fresh breath. At least for the greeting kisses. His smile spread as he recalled the email. Not only word for word, but every single character.

Meet me @ *El Papagaio* on Sunday, 19.00.
Let's NOT talk about work. Ax.

One extra letter. An X. Its effect was disproportionate, but still. Ana Luisa Herrero had sent him a kiss. It had taken him an hour and a

531

half to compose a reply, and another fifteen minutes debating the pros and cons of adding a kiss.

> OK. Looking forward to it. Tx

He sped up, almost breaking into a run.

The uplight illuminated a cartoonish parrot, painted in primary colours, as he approached the door. A solitary smoker stood outside, leaning against an empty table. He didn't return Tiago's *Buenas tardes*.

The restaurant was unusually empty. But Tiago only ever came in here on week nights after work, so had no idea about the bar's weekend trade. Two men sitting at a corner table looked up and nodded. The only other person was a barman Tiago didn't recognise. Strange not to see Enrique. Perhaps he didn't work weekends.

But most importantly, Ana was later than him. Relieved, he sat facing the door. He would order two beers. Or should he wait? No, he needed a drink. And maybe some olives, mainly to give him something to do with his hands. He sent her a rapid text message.

The barman approached, unsmiling.

"Two beers and a ..."

"She's in the back." He jerked his head towards the rear of the room.

Tiago glanced in the same direction and frowned.

The barman shrugged. "She said you should go in the back. She's waiting."

Tiago scrambled from his seat, confused. In all the time he'd been coming here, he'd never been 'in the back'. He didn't even know there was another room. Was it the same sort of 'back room' as the one in *Gatos*? Everyone knew what went on in that kind of place. He got up and followed the barman's louche stroll. He knew he was being watched.

The lack of clientele, the new barman, the silence ... something felt wrong. He stopped. The front door opened and the smoker returned, locking the door behind him. Tiago's pulse pounded as the barman pressed a hand to his shoulder, guiding him firmly through the door. When he resisted, he was shoved forwards, falling across the jamb onto all fours. Fear shot through his veins like acid as he tried to make out where he was.

A door opened ahead of him, blue light and cold air spilling into the dark corridor. The fridge room. His scalp contracted as he saw the chair inside, with attachments. Every nerve urged him to run, but he had no idea which way. He pushed himself to his feet and turned to face the men behind him.

"What's going on? What do you want?"

Without answering, they moved forwards. He attempted to duck past, tripped over rubbish bags and landed on the floor.

They dragged him to his feet and into the fridge. He twisted and bucked like a fish on a line, but the smoker and barman wrestled him into the chair. His arms were cuffed behind him, his legs spread and secured at knees and ankles with leather straps. Shallow breaths made small panicky clouds in the cold air as he tried to keep from shaking. He heard the suction of the closing door. He scanned the four unfamiliar faces, searching for an explanation. The two older men from the corner table were relaxed and unhurried. One had a missing forefinger, the other's face sagged on one side. A pair of tough old tomcats. The smoker and the barman, both built like bulls, wore identical tense expressions. Muscle, no doubt. But who the hell would send four heavies after him? And where did Ana fit in?

His voice was unsteady. "Look, I don't know what the problem is, but we can work something out, I'm sure. Please, can we talk? What have I done?"

No one moved.

The greyer of the tomcats spoke. His voice was hoarse and creaky, as if it didn't get out much.

"No, Tiago. No more talking. That is part of your problem. You were warned. Twice. There is no third chance." He motioned to the smoker, who handed something to the barman. A pair of garden shears. They both donned plastic gloves.

Tiago shook his head, unable to speak, blinking to clear his vision. He had no idea what warnings he was talking about. No one had tried to dissuade him from pursuing Ana. His colleagues even encouraged him. Were these men some Portuguese relatives come to defend her honour? He hadn't even kissed her yet.

"You see, Tiago, it's like gambling. Only join the game if you can afford to take the losses."

Two figures approached, but through his flooded eyes, he could no longer differentiate between individuals. As he rocked and yanked against his restraints, he squeezed his lids shut and screamed, a desperate howl bouncing off white-tiled walls and indifferent ears. When his lungs could produce nothing more than hyperventilating gasps, the hoarse and rasping voice came to its conclusion.

"When a man sticks something where he shouldn't, he must be prepared to lose it."

Chapter 2

The smell of flesh was giddying. *Chorizo*, sausage, *cecina* and air-dried hams hung overhead; *pintxos* arrayed on the bar looked like individual works of art, spiked anchovies, layered peppers, tortilla slices and salted cod vying for attention; and the glass of *Txakoli*, wearing a light coat of condensation, reflected the sunshine streaming through the windows.

Beatrice sighed with anticipation. It was very hard to make a decision. She gazed at the shoppers on Calle de Edouardo Dato and caught her reflection in the glass door. Good God, she looked almost happy! An involuntary smile; things must be improving. She showed the barman her snacks, although the quantity stretched the definition of the word, and settled into a leather banquette to enjoy her lunch.

Content to observe the patrons and eavesdrop on the intriguing sounds of Basque, she chose not to pick up her novel, her guide-book or her map. The bar seemed a popular location for workmen, who stayed mere minutes, washing down their *tapas* with beer or cups of wine. She enjoyed the respectful nods she received from each new wave of diners and began to feel quite at home.

Meal over, she lined up her toothpicks so the barman could count them and charge her accordingly. It reminded her of *Go Sushi!* in Hoxton, another 'healthy' place which cruelly tempted diners into over-indulgence. Thoughts of home swelled a dull yearning. Not homesickness. Not nostalgia. Just an ache for the familiar. How absurd. She'd only been in Spain a week.

She ordered another glass of rosé, picked up her phone and dialled the Classics and Ancient History Department of Exeter University. Hang the expense, she needed to hear his voice.

"Professor Bailey, good afternoon?"

"Hello Matthew, it's me."

"Beatrice? Are you all right?"

"Absolutely. Only phoning to make you jealous. I've just finished the most wonderful lunch in a Spanish bar. They have these *tapas* things, but bigger. I've never seen such imaginative use of anchovies."

His relief was audible. "You are a truly heartless woman. I'm sitting here, grading first-year essays, grinding my teeth and weeping. These people use apostrophes as decoration, scattering them across their texts like glitter. And for my lunch, I had tinned ravioli."

Beatrice gave a belly laugh and checked to see if she was disturbing other diners. But all heads were turned in the opposite direction. A young brunette walked through the gaggle of blue-clad workers, ignoring their undisguised ogling and semi-audible comments. She spotted Beatrice and, with a friendly smile, seated herself at the bar.

Beatrice returned her attention to Matthew. "Now I know you're lying. You would never eat tinned ravioli."

"Ordinarily not. However, I was babysitting Luke this morning and he baulked at what his mother had provided for his lunch. Seemed a shame to waste it. But now I understand the poor little chap's reservations. Hideous slop. He made short work of my carrot soup instead. You see, my grandson already shows excellent taste. How are you enjoying ... where are you now? Santander?"

"Vitoria-Gasteiz today. And tomorrow. Glorious. I've barely even scratched the surface, so I think I'll hang on for a couple of days. Rest my feet."

The brunette, quite unmistakeably, was listening. Not only that, but watching Beatrice in the mirror. Her long hair, like a chocolate waterfall, cascaded down a suede shirt. The textures lent a softness to her unapproachable air.

"Oh dear. You need to go easy on the feet, at your age. Have you seen the Artium yet?"

"It's not my feet, it's my shoes. Blisters. And anyway, I'm all arted out after the Guggenheim. The Artium's on the agenda for tomorrow. Tonight I'm meeting a connection of Tanya's, the exchange student, pen-friend, whatever she is. She stayed with us one summer, remember?"

"Of course. Andrea Something?"

"Ana Something. Lord knows if I'll recognise her. Last time I saw her, she was all elbows and knees with a mouth full of metal. She's taking me for *parillada de mariscos*."

He exhaled. "How I wish I could join you. My particular weakness is fresh seafood. But envy, I remind myself, is a deadly sin. Now, it's mid-afternoon and your calling me via mobile is ruinously expensive. Enjoy your siesta and I'll speak to you tomorrow. Are you keeping out of trouble, Old Thing?"

"Believe me, I am the picture of innocence. Everything is fine, Matthew, and I'm enjoying a rest from it all. Love to the girls and we'll talk tomorrow."

"Very well. Hurry back, in your own time."

She smiled and ended the call. Before she even replaced the handset in her bag, the dark-haired girl had approached, standing opposite. Her expression was expectant.

"Beatrice Stubbs." The accent disconcerted Beatrice, evoking more of an Irish Colleen than a Spanish Carmen. Her face, open and intelligent, bore signs of tension in the upper lip and brow.

"Correct. And you are ...?"

"Ana Something." She smiled.

"Good Lord." Beatrice assessed the soft skin, straight white teeth and elegant proportions. The laughter in the girl's eyes gave the only clue to the gauche exchange student she had met nine years earlier.

"Or Ana Luisa Herrero, if you want the whole story." She held out her hand. Beatrice shook it, still lost for words.

Ana slid into the seat opposite, rested her elbows on the table and looked into Beatrice's eyes. "Guess how I found you?"

"I've no idea. Sniffer dog?"

The girl laughed, drawing attention from the whole bar. "I'm a journalist. Getting information out of people is my speciality. It's good to see you again. Must be, what, ten years? But I remember you very well. Mainly because you didn't patronise us and enjoyed good food. And because you were a police detective with the London Met. Apart from an air hostess, I couldn't think of a cooler job."

Beatrice recovered her voice. "Well, I thought I remembered *you*, but I would never have recognised that girl ..."

"... all elbows and knees with a mouth full of metal? Ah, don't worry. Serves me right. I shouldn't have been earwigging."

"Earwigs never hear good of themselves. No, what I wanted to say is that you have blossomed into a genuine beauty, Ana. And you wear it well."

"Cheers. Anyway, I went to your hotel. A stranger in Vitoria is going to ask for *tapas* recommendations, right? I spoke to the receptionist and tracked you down."

"Congratulations. But while I applaud your skill, I can't help asking myself why you would bother? We have an appointment this evening, and I feel sure I gave you my mobile number in case of difficulties. Why did you need to track me here?"

The girl's face darkened, her focus turned inward and her whole body seemed to sag.

"Beatrice, I'm after your help. And I needed to explain to you in person. A colleague and I have been working on a particular story. We think we've found something suspicious. The problem is that he's disappeared."

"Your colleague?"

Ana nodded, her jaw clenched. "We all had a drink together after work on Friday. But this morning, he didn't turn up for work and missed the weekly update. I had to busk it on his behalf. I've called him and been round to his apartment, but there's no reply."

"Well, it's only just after lunchtime. Maybe he took the morning off."

"He'd have let me know. He's not the type to drop a colleague in it."

Beatrice considered. A young man, a journalist. Rarely the sort to inform colleagues when chasing a story, or anything else. Missing for under twenty-four hours. No police force in the world would even blink. Young people could be so very naïve.

She adopted a conciliatory expression but before she could reply, Ana continued.

"Yes, I know. I've already been to the station and the local guys won't touch it. But I know something is wrong. I got a text message from him on Sunday evening." She slid her phone from her breast pocket and focused on finding the message.

She turned the screen towards Beatrice.

"HA! Estoy aquí - EP. SM, OK? Tx

Beatrice rubbed her eyes. Surely she should be dozing in her hotel room rather than listening to a flighty female who'd had a dust-up with a boyfriend speaking in code.

Ana explained. "HA means *Hola* Ana. *Estoy aquí* means I'm here and EP probably stands for our favourite bar, *El Papagaio*. SM, OK? Is *San Miguel* OK for you?"

"Ana. He expected you for a date, you didn't turn up and he's probably sulking. Men tend to do that."

"But listen. There was no date. I spent the weekend in the mountains. We hadn't made any arrangements for Sunday night. And now, he's completely vanished. No one will take this seriously but I feel something's very wrong. Please, humour me. The first twenty-four hours are crucial, I know that from my experience on the crime desk. Time's slipping away. I need to think like a cop. And I have one right in front of me. Would you at least give me some pointers? Where would *you* start?"

The girl wasn't mad, just desperate. Beatrice recognised the conviction in the deep brown eyes. She dropped her voice below the labourers' banter and the sounds of Shakira from the speakers.

"What's your friend's name?"

"Tiago Vínculo. Hence the Tx at the end of the message. Which is also weird."

"Why?"

"Tiago never puts kisses on his messages."

"Maybe it was a slip of the thumb," Beatrice suggested.

Ana linked her hands together and rested her chin on her knuckles.

"The thing is, I get a lot of attention, from men, because of the way I look. My mum was Portuguese and my dad's Irish. Guess they gave me good genes. I grew up in Ireland and encountered more than my fair share of charmers who turned out to be chancers. So I've learnt to be suspicious of male friends, you know, alert for any hidden intentions. For that reason, I never make empty gestures, like adding kisses to my signature, telling people I love them, or anything which could be misinterpreted. My mantra is, only do it if you mean it. My friends all know that and I expect the same from them. So why would Tiago, one of my best friends, suddenly choose to send me a kiss?"

Beatrice recognised the habitual tug of curiosity. Pieces of a puzzle and the old urge to find out the meaning behind the fragments. Ideas began bubbling. Why not? She could offer Ana some advice. After all, what harm could it do?

"Right. Let's see what we can do. But first things first, I need to buy some comfy shoes."

Chapter 3

"Papí! Papí!"

Arturo de Aguirre straightened from his inspection of the young vines. He lifted his head towards the sound of his son's voice, shielding his eyes against the low October sun. Basajaun was waving from the garden terrace at the top of the vineyard. As Aguirre waved back, he saw his wife join the boy, her mobile to her ear. His phone rang, so he moved a few paces away from his waiting workers to take her call.

"Marisol? Is everything all right?"

"*Yes. Basajaun's waving goodbye. We're going into Vitoria to meet Inez for lunch, maybe do some shopping. I've left you some food in the fridge.*"

"You're taking him shopping? I thought he was home from school because he was sick."

"*He had a temperature, that's all. But he's bored, hanging around the house, so I'll take him with me to see his sister.*"

Aguirre considered his response. "You can take him to lunch today. Tomorrow, he goes to school. His education is vital, Marisol."

"*So is his health. See you later.*" She rang off.

Aguirre watched the pair of them walk towards the Jaguar XK, Basajaun skipping and hopping and jumping about with his usual excess of energy. It was not good enough. Aguirre would wait until the weekend, letting her think he had forgotten, before making an announcement. Any future decisions regarding Basajaun's attendance at school would be taken by him alone. The trouble with Marisol? She was used to bringing up girls. She'd done a good job, mostly. Paz and Inez already married and several possibilities lined up for Luz when she finished her studies. But his son's destiny lay in the business. His education must be taken seriously. Time he assumed paternal control.

Aguirre turned back to the two workers, who waited for his approval.

"OK. I'm happy with the quality here. But this section needs frost protection while the vines are so young. That must be finished first." He checked his watch. "Go and have some lunch. I'll be back by two to supervise the process."

Left you some food in the fridge. Who did she think she was talking to? He would go out for lunch and use the opportunity to pay a visit. Striding back to the house, Aguirre debated whether to call first. He decided not. Surprise generally worked in his favour.

His timing was perfect. Most of the staff at Alava Exports were already in the canteen, enabling him to enter the building unnoticed. The security guard and receptionist barely blinked at such a familiar face, simply smiled and wished him a good afternoon. The little secretary who defended her boss's privacy like a yappy chihuahua was absent. No one to warn Angel Rosado of his approaching nemesis. Excellent.

His son-in-law remained in his office, on the phone. His habit of standing and staring out the window while talking made it even easier to surprise him. Aguirre opened the door almost noiselessly. Almost. But Angel turned and recognised his visitor. His expression of alarm gave everything away.

"I have to go, someone's just walked in. Thanks for your advice and I'll call you back later."

Angel extended a hand and forced an implausible smile. He was a dreadful actor. And Aguirre had seen a few. Some of the most painful evenings of his life had taken place during Marisol's amateur theatre period.

"Angel. How are you?" He didn't wait for a reply. "Our wives have decided to lunch together, so I thought you might be lonely. I've come to take you out. We'll go somewhere nice and have a chat."

Angel looked down, his long lashes hiding his eyes. "That's a kind gesture, but today I planned to eat in the canteen. Show my face to the workers, you know?"

Aguirre nodded his approval. "An excellent idea. Good to break bread with the staff once in a while. You can do that tomorrow. Come. You'll need a jacket, the wind is sharp."

Everything about Angel irritated Aguirre. His fastidious way of dressing, his constantly miserable expression, the grateful smile he gave to the waiter who handed him the menu, not to mention his spineless capitulation to everything his wife demanded. True, Inez was a forceful opponent. Aguirre himself recalled stand-up screaming confrontations even when she was a child. But he always got the upper hand and she respected him for that. Angel let her win. That was a mistake and he would never regain her respect. Weak. No wonder everyone despised him, including his wife.

"We'll have the *Menú del día. Revuelto de setas, txipirones,* and the house white." Scrambled egg with mushrooms, followed by squid in its own ink. Aguirre handed the menu back without looking, waiting for Angel to protest. His son-in-law always had a bad reaction to mushrooms and disliked the way the black ink stained his teeth. But Angel shrugged his acquiescence and asked for some water. His every movement invited bullying. He only had himself to blame.

"By the way, you haven't yet congratulated me," said Aguirre, flicking out his napkin.

Angel's wince showed he understood, but he faked an innocent enquiry. "With so many successes to admire, where do I start?"

So slimy, so false. It was hard to believe the man was a Spaniard.

Aguirre ignored the sycophancy. "I'm to be a grandfather, for the second time. Paz is due the end of April. As you can imagine, Marisol is deliriously happy."

"Congratulations. That was quick. Surely Ramón isn't one yet?"

"No. His first birthday, as you well know, is this Thursday. Don't forget the party starts at twelve, with lunch at two. So Paz and Guido's children will only be eighteen months apart, which I believe is a very good thing."

"I'm surprised to hear you say that, when there's such a huge gap between the girls and Basajaun."

"Not surprising at all. I was determined to have a son. That took a little longer."

A silence swelled, punctured by the waiter's arrival with a carafe of house white and a bottle of water.

Aguirre sent back the wine and ordered a bottle of his own produce, *Castelo de Aguirre Blanco*. Not the best on the menu, but he was making a point. A point Angel, despite his limited intelligence, would recognise.

"As for my grandchildren," he continued, "wouldn't it be wonderful if they had cousins of a similar age?"

Angel didn't reply, looking around the room, as if the answer lay with one of their fellow diners.

Aguirre dropped his voice and adopted an expression of concern, such as might be worn by a prurient chat show host. "I mean, there's no problem, is there? You know Marisol and I would do anything we could to help."

The boy shook his head. "I don't think anything is wrong. It just hasn't happened yet."

Aguirre kept his eyes on him, waiting for something more.

Angel changed the subject. "I've been meaning to ask you something. I still don't know whether you resolved the problem with the paperwork. I haven't heard anything more from Saez, but other people have been asking questions."

The waiter placed a basket of bread and two dishes of scrambled egg in front of them. Aguirre gave him a curt nod of dismissal and tore into a roll.

"The paperwork issue is no more. A typical example of a minion getting carried away beyond his brief. The company have assured me it won't happen again. And in turn, you will promise me that next time you have an external audit, you talk to the organ-grinder. Not the monkey."

"Of course, I promise. Although I had no idea he was a trainee. What about that journalist? He told me a missing person's report was filed on Saez." Angel's eyes scanned Aguirre's face.

"Nonsense. The company relocated him, at my request."

"Relocated? Do you know where?"

"I don't recall. Somewhere out in the sticks, they said. I expect he left a young woman behind, who can't believe she's been dropped. Far more romantic, not to mention kinder on the ego, to invent a disappearance. Anyway, where he went is immaterial. He's gone and that journalist is unlikely to return. So if anyone else asks, send them directly to me. Eat your lunch, Angel, it's why we're here. Perhaps that is part of your problem. You're not eating right."

Angel blinked at his plate and dabbed at the oily, eggy mess with some bread. His voice was weak, pathetic.

"As I said, I'm not aware of a problem. I think it's simply a question of time."

"Maybe." Aguirre poured the wine, studying the colour before raising his glass to his nose. He inhaled deeply and allowed the light fruits, the clean flowers and hints of green to fill his nostrils. He opened his eyes and held his glass toward Angel.

"*Topa*! And here's to future successes. For both of us."

"*Topa*. To success," Angel responded with minimal enthusiasm, but held his glass steady for the chinking.

Aguirre sipped at his wine, pleased with the light effervescence and lively body. This could hold its own against Portuguese *vinho verde* any day. He trained his eyes on Angel.

"A question of time. Yes, it's possible you're right. So let's give it until Christmas and then we'll look at the problem again."

Angel stared into his wine, the downward pull of his mouth reflecting the rim of the glass. Aguirre lifted a forkful of mushroom and smiled. He was rather looking forward to the rest of lunch.

Chapter 4

Beatrice stood in the doorway of the Residencia, handbag over her arm, cardigan slung over her summer dress and sore feet slipped into brand new flip-flops. Ana, wearing jeans, held out a helmet.

"It's a moped."

Ana shook her head. "That's like saying an Aston Martin is a car. This is a Vespa. A design classic and lifestyle statement. And the only way to travel in the city. Shall we go?"

"I didn't realise this would be our mode of transport. I'm not exactly dressed for motorbike riding. Do you think I should change?"

"Not at all. I've ridden this in a skirt before. So long as you can get your leg over, it's just a question of tucking yourself in. Come on, let's get going. When I lean, you follow, OK?"

With a deep breath, Beatrice wedged the helmet over her head, swung her leg over and ensured she was decent. The bike's engine whizzed up like a lawnmower and she grasped Ana's waist as they sped forward into the traffic. It was exhilarating, dodging in and out of lanes, creeping between queues of cars to be the first at the lights. The limitations of four wheels did not apply to the little bike. The wide leather seat was comfortable and despite her exposure, Beatrice felt surprisingly safe. In fact, she enjoyed the sense of being right in the middle of things. If only Matthew could see her. Actually, probably best he couldn't.

Ana bumped up onto the pavement in front of an apartment building, switched off the engine and pulled down the stand with her heel.

"This is Tiago's place. He lives at the top."

"You're allowed to park it on the pavement?" Beatrice heaved off her helmet, choosing not to worry about what had happened to her hair.

"You can park a Vespa anywhere. Let's go."

Ana rang Tiago's bell first and they both waited with a strange sense of anticipation. No reply. She didn't try a second time. Instead, she pressed her finger on the bell directly beneath. When a male voice answered, Ana spoke in Spanish. Beatrice listened, clueless, but impressed at how many syllables per minute the girl could manage. The buzzer sounded and Ana pushed open the door. She stopped and looked into Beatrice's eyes.

"You're a British writer, OK? Your book is about European journalism and you're following me around to learn how it works. I'll translate and you can tell me what questions I should ask."

Beatrice responded with an obedient nod.

Ana looked back again. "And if they believe that, they'll believe anything. You've got police stamped all over you. Well, nothing we can do about that now."

Gregorio Torres opened his apartment door wearing a black T-shirt, stonewashed jeans and a bad-tempered scowl. He appeared to be late twenties, tall and well-built. His dark colouring and deep eyes could have been attractive, but a heavy jaw tilted him into Desperate Dan territory. As he surveyed Ana, the scowl lifted, only to return when he spotted Beatrice. He shot several questions at Ana and a few dirty looks at Beatrice, before leaning against the door frame, arms folded.

Ana took out her notebook and began asking questions. Without turning, she relayed the information to Beatrice.

"He saw Tiago on Saturday – talked about football – seemed normal – wasn't here on Sunday so didn't see or hear him at all."

"Where was he if not here?" asked Beatrice and waited while Ana translated. He raised his eyebrows at her, but answered the question.

"In his family's village. It was the day of the *txoko*. It's a Basque custom where all the men get together and cook a meal for everyone," Ana said.

"What a lovely idea!" exclaimed Beatrice.

Gregorio looked at her in surprise and a slow smile softened his expression. He nodded.

"Yes," he said, in English. "It is."

Ana glanced at Beatrice before firing off several more questions in Spanish. He answered with more openness but as Beatrice could see from Ana's expression, no useful information was forthcoming. Finally, Ana shook his hand and said her goodbyes. Gregorio politely extended his hand to Beatrice. She shook it and made an effort. "*Muchas gracias.*"

"You're welcome," he replied.

On the way down the stairs, Ana seemed despondent.

"So Gregorio didn't come home on Sunday and went straight to work from his village. He has no idea if Tiago was here on Sunday night or not. No one else is likely to know. Tiago's is the only flat on the top floor."

"The penthouse?" asked Beatrice.

"More like the attic," Ana replied. "We may as well try a couple more, you never know," she added, pressing the bell on the next landing. As they waited, Ana looked sideways at Beatrice.

"Guess what Gregorio does for a living?" she whispered.

Beatrice thought. "From first impressions, I'd have him down as a truck mechanic. No, maybe a cattle brander. Well, something rough and tough, anyway. The lead singer in the Spanish equivalent of Status Quo?"

"Tut, tut. For a detective, your powers of observation are shocking. Did you not see his hands?"

Someone moved behind the door and the sounds of locks rattled.

Beatrice turned to Ana. "No, I didn't. He kept them folded under his armpits. Why?"

Ana's smile lifted her cheeks into russet apples. "He's a manicurist."

"Really?"

"Yep. Hard as nails." The door opened. "*Buenas dias*, Doña Llorente!"

Dismounting the Vespa outside *El Papagaio*, Beatrice handed her helmet to Ana and tried once again to brush the dog hair from her dress. Tiago's neighbours had been little use, and the interviews, mostly conducted at front doors, had proved surprisingly tiring. Beatrice's frustration at being excluded from the conversation and having to wait for Ana to translate tested her patience. On top of which, the asthmatic woman with the dogs had the most grating voice Beatrice could ever remember hearing. Worse still, it was obvious that she rarely had a captive audience, so she'd made the most of it.

"So, apart from the fact that woman can talk faster than I ever thought possible, I understood very little of what Doña Llorente was saying. But I gather she saw him on Sunday."

"Yes, and you were right to suggest the step-by-step approach. I could literally see her remembering. She gave me a lot of details. He was dressed to kill, as she put it, he was in a hurry, tearing out the door, but stopped to give her a present, those flowers. She had no doubts about the time, either. Just after seven o'clock."

"And he sent you a text at what time exactly?"

Ana didn't need to check. "Nineteen minutes past. As you saw, the bar is a ten-minute walk from his place."

Beatrice thought about it. A bunch of yellow roses. She doubted Tiago had bought them for his asthmatic neighbour. Did he change his mind?

Ana locked the bike and turned to face the restaurant. "Here we go."

The interior was lively; groups of people chatting at tables, a crowd at the bar and half a dozen men standing watching football on a small television set high in the corner. Two young women threaded their way through the patrons, carrying trays of beer, carafes of wine and some intriguing-looking snacks.

Ana made straight for the bar, where a jowly man in his sixties was pouring a beer. She beckoned Beatrice to join her.

"*Hola*, Enrique! Can I introduce you to a friend of mine? This is Beatrice and she's a journalist for a travel magazine. I told her to talk to you." She turned to Beatrice. "No one knows Basque cuisine like Enrique."

Enrique beamed and wiped his hands on a cloth. "*Hola*, Ana. And hello, Ana's friend, Beatrice. Take a seat and I'll join you in a minute." He waved at an empty table towards the front of the room, away from the sighs and groans below the TV set.

At least ninety percent of the men in the bar watched Ana walk to their table. Some even tore their eyes away from the football. She ignored them and sat with her back to the window. She hoicked one foot up to rest on the opposite knee and dropped her voice.

"Enrique's a good guy. And when it comes to the food and drink of the region, he'll talk the ears off you."

"Sounds like we might get along. Although I do wish you'd warn me as to my undercover roles a bit earlier. Acting's never been my strong point."

"But asking questions and eating will give you no bother. Here he comes."

Enrique joined them with a tray bearing glasses, two carafes of wine; one white, one red, and a selection of tiny canapés.

Beatrice smiled. "Ana tells me you are an expert on local dishes."

"Not an expert. *The* expert. I know the best restaurants in San Sebastian, the best wines from the Rioja and the best recipes from Bilbao to Vitoria. What do you want to know?"

Ana's expression was pleasantly enquiring and innocent, a match for Enrique's. Beatrice was on her own. Enrique opened his hands, offering his knowledge to her on a plate.

"Well, for a start, can you tell me what these are?" she said, pointing to the little snacks on the tray.

"Good question. Let me introduce you to some of our local delicacies. Salt cod croquettes with nuts. You will love them. Tell me you are not vegetarian."

Even if Beatrice had been a committed vegan, the hostile expression on Enrique's face would have forced her to lie. As it was, she shook her head.

"No, I will eat anything."

Enrique's approval spread across his face. "Good. British and Americans with their fussy intolerances ..." He waved a hand in front of his face, rolled his eyes and then pointed at a terracotta dish. "This is beautiful. Prawn and bacon topped with a home-made vinaigrette. And *Txalupa*; mushrooms and cream, covered with cheese in a pastry boat. And the speciality of the house, our secret tuna mix topped with anchovy and chives. Try, please. These are for you."

"How very kind!" Beatrice's delight was genuine. Lunch seemed a long time ago. She selected the messy-looking boat, which would force Ana to take over the conversation.

Enrique poured white wine and watched Beatrice eat, nodding his satisfaction. "Ana, try something. You never eat my *pintxos* and it hurts my feelings."

Ana picked up a croquette. "Nothing personal. It's just, when we come in here, it's usually after work. I don't want to spoil my appetite for dinner."

"It doesn't seem to bother the others. Jaime, Tiago, Maria-José; they always have something. Think of it as an appetiser."

Beatrice watched Ana in her peripheral vision. The girl's manner was totally relaxed as if she hadn't even heard the name. She bit into a croquette.

"Bloody hell, these *are* good. See, you've broken the dam now. In six months' time, I'll be the same size as Maria-José."

Enrique laughed, showing long, yellowing teeth. "She has an appetite, most certainly. Beatrice, try a croquette. Save the tuna till last. You will never eat anything as perfect anywhere in Vitoria."

Beatrice obliged.

Ana wiped her fingers and took a sip of wine. "Did Maria-José come in at the weekend, Enrique? I have a feeling I agreed to meet them, but totally forgot."

Enrique's face seemed unchanged. "No. I haven't seen her since last Friday. When you all came in together. They're good, aren't they? The nuts add something special to this croquette."

Beatrice agreed. "They are sublime. I could live on this food forever." This was her kind of interrogation. Her job was eating and appreciating fine food while Ana did the tricky stuff.

"What about Tiago? Was he here?"

Enrique poured more wine and frowned. "Tiago? No. In fact the place was very quiet all day on Saturday. Everyone deserted me."

Ana smiled. "And Sunday?"

A look of puzzlement crossed Enrique's face. "Ana, we're closed on Sundays. That shows how often you come in at weekends if you don't know that. I spent Sunday with my parents-in-law. To be honest, I'd rather open the bar than drive over there, but my wife insists."

Now Ana looked puzzled. Beatrice finished her croquette, caught Ana's eye and made a tiny twisting motion with her hand.

"Does anyone else have the keys to this place?"

"*El Papagaio*? Of course not. Why would anyone have the keys?"

Ana looked to Beatrice. The girl clearly needed guidance.

Beatrice decided to trust him. "Enrique, the truth is that I'm not a travel writer. I'm a police detective from London. Ana asked me to help her find Tiago. He's gone missing and the last place we think he was ... well, Ana can explain."

Ana pulled out her phone and explained her analysis of Tiago's last message.

Enrique shook his head and rolled his eyes once more. "You women. Too many soap operas. Always searching for the dramatic. EP is not *El Papagaio*. The bar was closed on Sunday so no one was here. But EP could be *El Periódico de Alava*. It's much more likely he went to the newspaper office and asked you to join him there. And he's probably chasing some lead or other right now, while you're panicking over nothing."

To Beatrice, that made perfect sense. She hadn't even questioned Ana's interpretation of the text and accepted it at face value.

Ana set her jaw. "And *San Miguel*?"

"SM could mean many different things. Who knows what goes on behind closed doors?" Enrique nudged Beatrice and she joined in his laughter.

Ana looked from one to the other as Enrique handed Beatrice the tuna fish.

"Even if you are nothing more than a police detective, I can see you are a woman who appreciates good food. Eat. This will be a moment of revelation."

He was right about that.

The crescendo of excitement built by the football fans was soon deflated by the groans of a near miss. Beatrice, like everyone else, glanced at the screen to watch the replayed moment. The scrambling figures, high colour and garbled commentary made as much sense to her as a computer game, so she picked up the tuna and opened her mouth. That was when she saw it. A camera. She stopped, eyes fixed on the small device high in the corner of the room, with a tiny red light announcing its presence. Replay.

"Enrique ..."

He followed her eyes. "That doesn't work. I must call the engineers. It's crazy, spending all that money on a security system which doesn't even function. I should ask for my money back. Now, tell me, is that the most delicious thing you ever put in your mouth?"

Chapter 5

Rita's hair spilt over her pillow, a matt-black tangle and as light-absorbent as Guinness. Her lips released a puff of air on each exhale and her shoulders rose and fell with her deep-sleep breathing. From the other bed, Luz watched for several moments, finally turning her head to see the luminous blue digits of the alarm clock. 01.43. Time to move.

She lifted the duvet clear of her legs and waited. Rita never woke, not even in the early hours of Sunday mornings, when clubbers returned from the city. But Luz took no chances. Especially this time. She pushed herself up on her elbows and slid her feet to the floor, stopped and listened.

"Puh ... puh ..."

The rucksack was ready, hurriedly packed while Rita had been running through her Bryan Adams repertoire in the shower, and stuffed casually under the communal desk. Luz scooped up her trainers and her keys, listened for a couple of seconds, and then slipped into the corridor. The lock clicked softly behind her. She paused, scanning the corridor for movement and padded towards the bathroom to dress.

Only two windows of the residence building were lit as Luz zipped up her black fleecy jacket. Her red pea coat would have been warmer, but too recognisable in the unlikely event anyone was looking. Instead, she pulled out a long fluorescent strip to loop over her shoulder and around her waist, unlocked her bike and checked the lights. Safety first. She was her mother's daughter. *But if she knew what I was doing right now ...* She snorted a dry laugh at the thought. With one more glance around, she swung herself into the saddle and headed towards Reyes Católicos, her breath visible and her heart already racing.

Cold tightened her cheeks as she pedalled along the colonnade and through the campus paths. A familiar sense of exhilaration and guilt filled her. There was no doubt. Taking Rita and Pilar to his restaurant tonight had been a stupid, unnecessary risk. They'd spotted the attraction immediately.

Pilar had peeped over the top of her menu. "Luz, I swear that waiter's tongue is hanging out. Why don't you give him your number?"

"I noticed that too! He can't keep his eyes off you. At first I thought it was great service, but now I suspect he has another reason for being so attentive. Pilar's right. Just leave your number and see what happens. It's time you had some fun."

"Rita! Keep your voice down. He's just after a decent tip. These guys are struggling to survive on the minimum wage and he's probably got a wife and three kids to support."

"Don't think so. No wedding ring. Beautiful eyes. Is it possible to get an eyelash transplant? If so, I want his."

"You can have his eyelashes, but I want his bum. Which bit do you want, Luz?"

Luz had joined in the shrieks of laughter, blushing and refusing to look in his direction. The tension was obvious and she couldn't hope to get away with being that close again.

Traffic was sparse as she sped past the hospital, moving from patches of street light to tree shadows in a comforting rhythm. She shook her head. The freshman Luz of a year ago would have seen rapists and psychopaths in every opaque corner. Now, she'd even befriended the night. She turned into Calle Valentin Jalón, sweating and exhilarated. This battle between body and mind brought back memories of being a child. Her mother, always insisting on decorum, correct behaviour and toeing the line, while her father encouraged wildness, breaking the rules and grabbing as much fun as possible. How things had changed as soon as she'd hit puberty. Game over. Still, the imprints remained. Luz's sensible head, in her mother's voice, told her she had already taken a huge risk tonight and she must be an idiot to get on her bike and take a second. Her body ignored the dampening maternal tones of her conscience and encouraged her to hurry, filling her with expectation and the cravings of an addict. That voice didn't belong to her father, though. That was all her own work.

The apartment block was in darkness so she was careful to make no noise as she locked her bike to the fire escape. She checked her watch. If the bus was on time, she had about three minutes to prepare. Creeping up the iron steps, breathing through her mouth, she shivered with excitement and fear. This was insane. So many things could go wrong. If someone saw her, if the door was locked, if he'd been delayed, if he'd brought someone home ... she stopped, her confidence faltering for the first time. In the cold stillness of the night, three steps from the top, she argued with herself, the rational against the passionate.

He wouldn't mess about with anyone else. He loved her. She didn't doubt him. Even the girls had seen it in his eyes this evening.

But he wouldn't expect to see her tonight. As far as he was concerned, she'd gone home with her friends and he wouldn't see her till tomorrow afternoon. He was free and he was a man. Men only ever thought with their ... she shook her head. That was a stupid cliché designed to make women paranoid. Didn't she trust him? After he'd made absurd amounts of effort to see her while keeping their relationship secret.

Perhaps the secrecy was for his own benefit. If he had someone else, the two lives could easily be kept apart. Until Luz turned up at his apartment, coming face-to-face with some Turkish beauty with honey-blonde hair. Her face flushed hot with embarrassment and humiliation.

Why did she put herself through these imaginary scenarios? Even if Tunçay arrived home now, alone, surprised and delighted, all the joy had gone from the moment. She felt jealous, betrayed and mistrustful, which was as far from the intended romantic mood as she could get. She'd spoilt it. All by herself.

She turned around and silently descended the fire escape, eyes fixed on the metal steps ahead. On reaching the last, she felt in her jeans pocket for the key to unlock the bike. A movement caught her eye.

"Luz?"

Adrenalin flooded her system and she dropped the key. Tunçay stepped away from the wall, a faint light glinting off his glasses.

"What are you doing here?" he whispered. "You gave me a terrible fright. I came round the back with scraps for the cat and thought we had burglars!"

His expression was impossible to read but Luz could hear the smile in his voice.

"I was just taking out my mobile to call the police when you turned around and came back down. Not a burglar at all, but my beautiful, mysterious lover creeping around my house in the middle of the night!"

Luz dropped her head but laughed with him. "It was supposed to be a surprise."

He pulled her into his arms and kissed the top of her head. "More of a shock, I'd say. What was the plan?"

She looked up at him and he smoothed back the hair from her temples with gentle fingers.

"I was going to use the fire door. You said it's never locked. Then I was going to get into your room, undress and warm the bed for you."

"So why didn't you?"

"I ... changed my mind. I thought it might not be such a good idea after all."

His eyes searched her face. "It's a brilliant idea. Brilliant but completely crazy. Riding around the city at two in the morning is dangerous. And how did you plan to unlock my apartment without a key? Not that I care what the neighbours think, but someone might have seen you and called the police. And most of all, Crazy Lady, my number one worry is how on earth we're going to get any sleep tonight."

All the elation and desire which had propelled her out of bed returned, and Luz kissed him, drawing his tongue into her mouth, pressing her body hard against his, feeling the heat spread in her groin. He broke the kiss with a small moan.

"Upstairs. Now. Let's stick to your plan, but how about you use the conventional stairs and take my key. Leave the door open. I'll feed the cat, which will give you two minutes. Then I'll 'come home' and get the best surprise of my life. You may as well keep that key, by the way. Just in case you get the urge to surprise me again."

Luz gave him the thumbs-up and ran round to the front door, grinning all over her face.

Chapter 6

"Shit."

Ana entered the little hotel room, dumped her handbag onto the desk and sat on the end of the bed, hands dangling between her knees.

"Shit, shit, shit."

Beatrice opened the tiny window in a feeble attempt to overcome the smell of damp. "Shit indeed. And with classic misjudgement, I revealed my profession."

"Don't beat yourself up. I thought it was a good move. Until he started lying."

"Several things occur to me. First, Enrique's trying to hide something, but not particularly well. And unfortunately, thanks to my incompetence, he knows we're trying to find it. Under normal circumstances, I'd demand the weekend footage recorded on that camera, but I have no jurisdiction here. We must talk to the police."

Ana shrugged. "I've tried that already and they dismissed me as a sensationalist. Although I suppose Stubbs of the Met might carry more weight. OK, we'll give it a go. What were the other things?"

"Alibis. Both Gregorio and Enrique gave us a detailed account of their whereabouts on Sunday, including several witnesses. Possibly both are telling the truth, but such efficient accounts might suggest preparation. And something feels odd about those flowers."

"Doña Llorente's flowers?"

Beatrice pulled out the little kettle from the cupboard, along with the tiny tubes of coffee, slim selection of teas and milk substitutes. "Can I offer you a drink?"

"Have you no mini-bar?"

"Unfortunately not. I could order room service?"

"No, I'm grand. The flowers?"

"Tiago was rushing out the door, dressed well, late for an appointment, probably scheduled for seven o'clock, with a bouquet of roses. He had no idea his neighbour would be arriving home at that moment, but decided to give her the flowers he was carrying. If he believed he was on his way to meet you, for some kind of romantic liaison, he may have bought flowers but bottled out at the last minute. And Doña Llorente benefitted from his indecision."

Ana's eyebrows rose. "Jesus."

"What is it?"

"Tiago's nickname is '*Depende*' meaning 'it depends'. He's famous, so much so it's a running joke, for being the most indecisive person on the news-gathering team."

Beatrice sat down beside Ana. "Right, we need to go through every possible scenario until we work out the most likely sequence of events which fits with the elements we know. Then we test our theories, one by one."

"Brilliant. Thing is, do we have to do it here? This place is depressing."

Looking around the room, Beatrice acknowledged the drawbacks. The minuscule amount of light, the pervasive whiff of mould and the ancient furnishings combined to create a grim echo of 1960s bedsits.

Ana elbowed her. "Look, say no if you want, but I have a spare room, a big balcony and a well-equipped kitchen. You realise that staying at mine would put you at risk of questions and queries at any hour of the day or night. But it's got windows and it doesn't stink."

Beatrice considered for all of fifteen seconds. "I'll take you up on that. Thank you, you're very kind. It's only for a couple of days, as I need to press on with my itinerary. But you can rely on my full support until I depart. Do you happen to have broadband?"

Balancing a suitcase on the moped was out of the question, so with some relief, Beatrice took a taxi to Calle Cuchillería. She paid the driver and walked down the busy pedestrian street, dragging her baggage behind her. The tall, cluttered buildings either side and the spread of cafe tables outside every other bar gave the street a narrow, almost mediaeval appearance. Washing and flags dangled overhead, rippling in the wind. The walls between the shops and bars bore murals, peeling fliers, graffiti and the occasional stone relief. Music pounded out of several doorways and Beatrice looked up at the balconies and open windows, wondering how the residents got any sleep. Crowded, colourful and just the kind of place a tourist would label 'a discovery'.

Ana opened the door with a smile. "Come in. What the hell have you got in that case? It's almost as big as you. We won't both get in the lift with that. You go ahead, fourth floor. I'll come up the stairs."

She pointed to the open lift doors behind her and raced off up the stone stairwell. She was right, the space inside was tight, barely enough room for three people. Beatrice manhandled her suitcase into position, squeezed in beside it and pressed the button for the fourth floor. With a ponderous pause, the doors closed and so began the slowest lift journey Beatrice had ever experienced. On arrival, the doors eventually opened to reveal Ana waiting.

"So, let's get this inside and then we'd better shift. I've called the local police and they've given us an appointment in twenty minutes. God, this thing weighs more than my Vespa!" She heaved the bag onto the landing, pulled out the handle and wheeled it into the apartment.

"Don't exaggerate. And I'm on an extended holiday, so I brought everything I might need."

"Including your golf clubs?"

The living room was filled with brightness: a yellow sofa, lively Kahlo colours on the walls and a washed-out turquoise table, covered with magazines. The only scent in the air was fabric conditioner from the clothes drying on the balcony.

"You're in there, and the bathroom's next door." Ana indicated a door on the right, which opened onto a small, cosy room. The bed was covered with a quilt in jewel patches of ruby, gold and jade.

"It's a beautiful apartment. The décor is a delight. So cheerful. You live here alone?"

"Yeah. I bought it as an investment, planning to get a lodger, but I discovered I prefer living alone. So I'm always skint, but at least I have my privacy. Now, come on, dump your bag and let's go. You can pay tribute to my soft furnishings when we get back. First, we have to talk to the police."

The architecture of the police station was a peculiar blend of austere and pompous, giving an unwelcoming impression. Prepared for hostility, Beatrice considered her approach as she and Ana waited in the bland foyer. In the past, the knowledge that she worked for London's Metropolitan Police had raised hackles. On more than one occasion, representatives of local forces, especially those holding the same rank as herself, felt patronised and belittled by her; as if she thought them incompetent. Once or twice, they might have been right. Therefore, in Spain and not in an official capacity, she would need to be extremely diplomatic. At least she was wearing flip-flops. It would be impossible to pull rank in flip-flops.

"Good afternoon." The man standing in the doorway had only one eyebrow. Where the other should have been was shiny scar tissue, reaching up to his hairline. Probably clean-shaven this morning, his chin now showed a distinct shadow. Black hair flopped over his forehead, partially hiding the scar. His dark eyes flicked from one to the other without smiling.

Ana rose. "Detective, thanks for seeing us. As I mentioned, Beatrice Stubbs is a detective inspector with the Met in London. Beatrice, this is Detective Milandro."

He held out his hand. "You are on holiday, Detective Stubbs?"

Beatrice's first challenge. Her title was Detective Inspector, and Ana had introduced her as such. But to correct him at this stage would be counter-productive and unnecessary. She wasn't at work. She shook his hand.

"That's right. Exploring the north coast of Spain. Ana is an old friend and she asked me for help, so I offered my advice. That's why we're here – to hand over what we know to the professionals."

He cast a neutral look in Ana's direction. "Come through. I can give you half an hour."

He took them through a security door and escorted them along a corridor. An obscenely fat man came out of an office and stared at them as they passed. He grunted in response to Ana's greeting and said something to Milandro, who motioned for them to enter an interview room on the right. He spoke quietly to the slug-like man in the corridor, leaving the door open.

Beatrice dropped her voice. "What are they saying?"

"I've no clue. They're talking in Basque."

Milandro joined them and closed the door.

"Who was he?" asked Ana.

Milandro seemed amused by her blunt query. "He is my superior officer, Detective Inspector Salgado. He likes to know what is going on."

Ana gave a contemptuous look at the mirrored window, as if Salgado were on the other side. "And what did you tell him?"

"That I don't know what's going on. I hope you can enlighten me."

His expression remained attentive and he asked several smart questions regarding their assumptions. Beatrice's respect for the man grew, particularly as he seemed one of the few men who didn't appear awed by Ana's appearance.

He looked up from his notepad and directly at Ana. "So you think he was expecting to meet you? For some kind of date?"

Ana shrugged. "It looks that way. The flowers, the neighbour's description of him as 'dressed to kill', and most importantly, the text message."

Milandro made some more notes and Beatrice scrutinised the man for clues. Lean and muscular, he looked like a runner. His face, no older than forty, bore signs of stress and more scar tissue was visible on both hands. It must have been burns, perhaps an explosion. He raised his head to meet Beatrice's stare, waited till she looked away and returned his attention to Ana.

"Why would he think you had a date? You say you made no

plans to meet him on Sunday and there was no more intimacy than friendship. How did he get the wrong idea?"

Ana shook her head. "I don't know. When he sent that message, I was on my way back from Sierra de la Demanda. The bus was full of soldiers and incredibly noisy. So I didn't hear it and only noticed there was a message when I got home. By then it was after midnight so I didn't answer. But when I read it again the next morning, I thought it was weird. I meant to ask him what he was playing at when I got to work. But as I told you, he didn't show up."

"Is it possible the message was meant for someone else, another 'A'? And he sent it to the wrong person?"

"I suppose. But I know him pretty well, and his circle of friends. I can't think of anyone who begins with 'A' apart from me."

"Men are good at keeping secrets." Milandro looked at Beatrice. "If the young man assumed there was a date, he must have had a good reason. Ana says she made no arrangement, so how else might Tiago have got the wrong idea?"

Beatrice thought about it. "Could someone have sent him a message on your behalf? Someone who knew you'd be out of town?"

Ana frowned. "No one knew I was going to Sierra de la Demanda because I only decided myself on Saturday morning. As for someone using my email, they'd have to know my password. I change it every week. And my phone is always with me. So I can't see how."

Beatrice checked Milandro. He looked back but gave no reaction. His silence seemed to be permission to continue. So she did.

"How would you ask someone for a date?" she thought aloud. "Face-to-face, over the phone, by email, by text, by sticking a note in his pocket? The first two are out, as he knows you and your voice so well."

Milandro agreed. "And I assume he knows your handwriting, as you work closely together at the paper?"

"Yeah," Ana nodded, "he takes the piss out of my writing. I learnt italics at school and still write like something out of the nineteenth century. He'd know if it was me or not."

Milandro made a respectful open-hand gesture to Beatrice,

indicating she could continue. She began to like this man. A genuinely decent sort.

"So email or text are our only options. He couldn't have received either while you were in the bar on Friday otherwise he would have reacted. He must have received it on Saturday or Sunday, while you were in the mountains. Have you checked the sent folder from both your phone and email?"

Ana picked up her phone and began scrolling back through her messages.

"How long is your vacation, Detective Stubbs?" asked Milandro.

"Till Christmas. It's more of a sabbatical than a holiday. Trying to decide if retirement would suit me."

"Judging by current events, I would suggest not." Milandro pointedly looked at Ana and back to Beatrice with one raised eyebrow.

Ana put her phone back on the table. "Nothing was sent from my personal email. I'll check my work one when I get into the office. And like I said, my phone is with me always."

"So what next? You would be able to ask for the CCTV recordings. Are you going to interview the bar owner of *El Papagaio*?" Beatrice asked Milandro.

"Possibly. Ladies, please let me know if you find any more information. I have to leave you now as I must make some calls. Thank you for your assistance in this matter. Detective Stubbs, could you tell me the name of your hotel or give a mobile number? In case I need to contact you."

"You can contact her at my place," said Ana. "Calle Cuchillería, I think you have my details."

Milandro's single brow rose again.

Beatrice withdrew a card, clearly stating her identity as Detective Inspector Stubbs of the Met. "My mobile is bottom right."

Milandro read it and slipped it into his shirt pocket. "Thanks. Have a pleasant evening and thank you for sharing your information. Goodbye."

Ana seemed as buoyant as Beatrice on leaving the police station, but had to return to the newspaper offices to update her editor on the story. She dropped Beatrice off at Calle Cuchillería and sped off, hair flying from under her helmet.

After a brief visit to the supermarket, Beatrice returned to Ana's building, recited several verses of 'The Rime of the Ancient Mariner' as the lift inched upwards and won the battle of wills with the lock on Ana's apartment door. She made herself some tea and sat on the balcony with her laptop, intending to check her emails, but found herself constantly distracted by the activity from the street below. She realised, once again, that she was smiling. This break, only a week old, was proving excellent for her health. A plethora of art, fine food and awe-inspiring scenery accompanied by good wine, a ride on a moped and a little adventure was all it took to recharge her batteries. Just look at her now.

The sound of her mobile ringing brought her back to the moment.

"Hello, Beatrice Stubbs speaking?"

"Stubbs, my team are dealing with a series of major incidents involving trafficked weapons. The media are nipping my ankles over cover-ups from the 1970s, the terrorist threat has been raised to amber and the government wants expenditure cuts but improved levels of service, if you please. On top of which, I am one detective down. Because said detective is taking a well-earned sabbatical in order to rest and recuperate before getting back to work. So can you explain why, at the end of another hellish day of defensive strokes and damage control, I received a call from the Spanish police asking me to keep my people out of their jurisdiction?"

"Sir, it's not really ..."

"The question was rhetorical. Good God, woman, even when you are not at work, you cause me headaches. What the hell are you playing at? If you want to do bloody detective work, get back here. But leave the Spanish police alone, stop telling other people how to do their jobs and keep your nose out of what doesn't concern you. If I have to make another call such as this, there will be no need to discuss your future at the Metropolitan Police in the New Year. Do I make myself transparently clear?"

"Yes, sir. I wasn't trying to tell anyone ..."

Hamilton cut her off with a pantomime sigh. "You are in Spain, DI Stubbs. Go native. Eat calamari, have a siesta, drink some sangria. Run with some bulls, if you're that bloody bored. But for once in your life, stop interfering. That is an order. Good evening to you."

Chapter 7

Ripples responded to the breeze, fluttering across the surface of the water with a sound like distant applause. Jeremy stretched and yawned. He damn well deserved a round of applause for getting up at seven in the morning. Marcus would have dragged them out of their tents even earlier, had it been light enough. As it was, he must have been up a good half hour ahead of them to get the fire going and prepare breakfast. Amazing sort, really. Just the type to keep both morale and discipline on track. Five creased and sour faces had brightened up after sausage, beans and bacon, mopped up with yesterday's bread. Protein and carbs, essential for today's forty-seven kilometre route.

Lots of groans and grunts from the chaps as they took to their bikes, not to mention a fair bit of ribbing. His own backside was tender on the saddle and his calves seemed to be screaming as he massaged in sun lotion, feeling an absolute twerp as he could see his breath in the autumn air. Whose damn fool idea was this anyway?

"Lactic acid, that's all it is," called Marcus, adjusting his helmet. "Best thing is to get the muscles moving. Nice easy one to start us off and we'll tackle the hills after lunch."

Jeremy sighed and double-checked his panniers. He wouldn't make the mistake of sloppy packing and holding up the others a second time. They made sure they left their camping spot in pristine condition, dumped the rubbish in the municipal bin and headed out of town in single file.

The inlet curved away to a perfect U, allowing for a flat, gentle ride and an opportunity to take in the views. Despite the morning chill, one could see a fine day was in the offing. Cloudless sky, mist rising from the forests beyond and the sun heralded its imminent arrival with an intense white-gold glow from the other side of the reservoir. He enjoyed the rhythm of pumping legs, team spirit and collective sense of tackling a challenge. Nevertheless, his physical discomforts were not quite forgotten. It appeared he was not the only one.

"*Sometimes, I feel
Like my arse is on fire
Sometimes, I feel
Like my arse is on fire*"

Laughter spread even as far as Marcus when Laurence's hearty baritone resonated along the line. Five voices joined in, creating a half-decent harmony.

"*Sometimes, I feel
Like my arse is on fire
A long, long way
From my home*"

The pace began to quicken as they made their way towards the dam and Jeremy felt a very simple, pure kind of pleasure. He knew he would remember this, in his dotage, as one of the happiest days of his life.

"Marcus? What say we have a photo op when we get to the dam?" Simon shouted. He'd become awfully fond of sharing their activities on Facebook, which necessitated regular stops, especially when their route passed anything tourist-worthy.

Marcus did not respond, but as they passed the massive edifice, made a crisp, military gesture to indicate left. Most of the chaps stayed on their bikes as Simon fiddled about with his gadget. Marcus removed his wraparound sunglasses.

"I told you yesterday, Harris, that you are entitled to no more than four of these stops per day. That's one down, three to go. Choose wisely."

"Wilco. Best get a group shot now then. Come along, ladies, into position."

Laurence rolled his eyes but swung his bike to face Simon. The group lined up with surprising efficiency, Jeremy taking the spot furthest from the road. He attempted a kind of nonchalant smile, as if photographs were a silly affectation he could take or leave.

"One sec ..." Simon called, messing about with the camera.

Jeremy joined in the sighs, leant on his handlebars and studied the scale of the brickwork from top to bottom. His eyes registered a shape in the water, something oddly natural and yet not. Looked like a marble bust; shoulders, back and upper arms, but no visible head or lower body. Jeremy squinted and he tried to account for the *trompe d'oeil* with a logical explanation.

"OK, sorry about that. Say Camembert, everyone. Jeremy! Where the hell are you off to?"

"Hold that." Jeremy swung his leg off the bike and handed it to Laurence. He scrabbled down the slope, annoyed by the uselessness of his cycle shoes on this terrain, focusing on his progress, not his target. He reached the fence and climbed over without a second's hesitation. Now he kept his eyes on the shape. He could already see it wasn't marble, or a bust. The indigo lines were veins and the cold blue he had mistaken for stone was pale, dead flesh. A body, face down. Legs dangled into deeper water, obscured by plants and black hair floated gently around the head. He reached the edge of the water and saw a hand bobbing along with the ripples. Fingers which must have held pencils, scratched heads, typed letters and caressed cheeks, now silently decomposing in cold, dark water. Jeremy's stomach contracted.

"Jez?" Marcus jumped down from the fence. "Something wrong?"

The usual clipped tones were softer and the friendly diminutive didn't go unnoticed. Relief in familiarity unlocked Jeremy's jaw.

"I'll say. Dead body. We should call the authorities. Simon's best with the lingo. Would you mind giving him a shout?"

The sun crept over the hills in the east, adding a cheerful light to the macabre scene. Yells ricocheted up and down the slope and some of the others came down for a closer look.

"What a horrible way to go."

"Do you suppose he was fishing and fell in?"

"I doubt it, Laurence. Unless he was fly-fishing in the buff."

"Poor bugger."

Jeremy ignored it all. There was something wrong with the legs. Bodies float horizontally, unless something was dragging the ankles down. Jeremy scanned the scene and spotted a dangling branch a few yards ahead. It took seconds to break it off and return to the corpse.

Marcus frowned. "Look here, I wouldn't touch it if I were you."

"I'm not going to touch it. I just want to know what's weighing it down."

"Best leave that sort of thing to the police, I'd say. For all we know, this could be a crime scene. Jez?"

Crouching on the bank, Jeremy lowered the branch into the water and made a slow sweep beneath the body. He met resistance, as expected, under the legs. So he tried to draw the branch, and the body, closer. But something gave way, the branch broke the surface and Jeremy fell backwards. However, the momentum he had instigated continued, to the dumbstruck horror of the men on the bank. Legs freed, the body sank, rolled and resurfaced, horizontal and face up.

"Jesus Christ!"

Jeremy's eyes registered the image for only a second before he turned to heave up his breakfast. But no matter how tightly he closed his lids, he would never be able to erase the image of what he'd just seen. A siren approached.

Chapter 8

At the *Feira do Vino*, all roads lead to Castelo de Aguirre. An exhibition stand to suit his status, at last. The centrepiece, sitting at the junction of five aisles, clearly announced his importance to the world. After attending the biggest trade fair in the country for ten consecutive years, finally, he was king. He'd allowed his daughters to select the décor, on condition he had final veto. The girls proved useful in such roles. He'd suggested red and yellow; dynamic and forceful colours, an attention-grabbing logo and beautiful young girls serving the wine. His daughters turned up their noses in perfect synchrony, comparing his design ideas to the marketing of McDonald's. Now, returning after a long lunch, he acknowledged his intelligence in allowing them a free hand.

Dark green baize flooring muffled the sounds of footfalls, establishing gravitas. The much-debated backdrop, an artist's rendering of vineyards, hinted at taste, discretion and subtlety. Three wide steps invited one in, the carved stone bar, gilded tables and chairs with blood-red cushions offered a sense of luxury, and the final touch – welcoming smiles from Paz and Inez. Neither of his daughters could be described as young or beautiful, but their knowledge of the product was second only to his own. Behind the bar, two of his most respected tasters, whose ancient faces resembled the gargoyles on the granite, poured samples and advised visitors. The cumulative effect needed no shrieking logo. Quite simply, here was the real thing. Old World wine, Old World style.

The ebb and flow of guests remained constant during the day, easily managed by the four representatives of the estate, leaving Aguirre to mingle and network. Occasionally he spent an hour or so on the stand. As well as giving the punters an opportunity to meet the man himself, it meant one of the others could take a break, refill the brochure racks, open more bottles, clean glasses and rearrange the furniture. His appearance always guaranteed a swell of interest, not least from the international wine journalists, who appeared with tedious regularity to trot out the same unimaginative questions.

Paz escorted a pair of buyers down the steps, shaking hands and smiling, before turning her attention to her father. Her hair, swept into a French pleat, was a complex arrangement of blonde highlights sprayed into submission.

"Good lunch?" she asked.

"Outstanding." Aguirre lowered himself into a gilded chair, feeling sleepy and satisfied. "In the eyes of the *Denominacion de Origen*, I can do no wrong. Everything going well here?"

Paz checked the stand, her eyes sharp. "Yes. That woman over there is a British importer. Inez's English is better than mine, so she dealt with her. I took the Valencians. They placed a decent order for next year's Crianza. The couple at the bar are time-wasters, in my opinion. I'll relieve Salbatore in a minute and get rid of them."

Aguirre smiled, confident his daughter's hard-sell charm would chase off the most persistent freeloader. Paz began wiping tables, reorganising displays and restoring the stand to its usual immaculate condition. All the time he watched her, she watched everything else. Nothing escaped her attention; her father, her sister, the employees, the punters. She reminded him of a hawk, scanning her terrain, ready to swoop. They were good girls. Real assets. At least two of his daughters took after him. Luz, unfortunately, had inherited her mother's stubborn streak. An Aguirre girl at university; it was absurd, indulgent and a waste of time. Yet Marisol seemed to be as proud of Luz reading law as she was of her first grandson. Occasionally he regretted marrying such a short-sighted woman.

His phone rang. Aguirre answered, irritation already in place. As he listened to the hoarse tones relaying the latest, his frown deepened and his jaw muscles tensed. His impatience grew until he could take it no longer.

"*Basta!* Enough! Take him a case of wine. Tell him to forget it. He knows nothing and there's nothing to know. The situation has been resolved and a pair of scavenging dogs looking for scraps is no cause for concern. I'll make sure he's not bothered again. All he needs to do is keep quiet and talk to no one. Be friendly, but let him know we expect him to keep his head. In fact, say exactly those words; we hope he can keep his head. That should shut him up."

Aguirre ended the call and scowled. Paz checked his expression and obviously misinterpreted it. She stalked across to the bar, dismissed both bar staff and stretched back her lips in an alarming smile. The bird of prey was on the hunt.

"Señor Aguirre?"

Before he'd even turned his head, Aguirre knew it was a journalist. This one was typical. Too-long hair and dressed in a cheap suit, he had the eager optimism of someone new to the job. The only point of any interest was the camera crew.

Aguirre stood with a charming smile. "Yes, I'm Arturo de Aguirre. How can I help?"

Lights arranged, furry sound boom in position, cameras and faces pointing in his direction drew more attention from passers-by than usual. A shiny sheen of sweat appeared on the journalist's brow as he checked his equipment. The boy needed to relax; after all, he was dealing with a professional. Aguirre signalled to Paz for one of the cheaper bottles, and with a circular gesture, requested glasses for the whole party. Not only articulate, accessible and an excellent interviewee, but generous. An all-round good guy.

"So, Señor Aguirre, we're all set. Oh, good idea!" the journalist exclaimed as Paz set the wine on the table between them. "We should have an example of the famous product in shot."

"Please make sure *all* our guests are served, my dear," said Aguirre, nodding at the crew. He returned the appreciative smiles. His mobile vibrated silently against his ribcage, but he ignored it.

Wine served, the young man addressed Aguirre. "I'd like to begin by asking you about the product, its history and finally ask your views on how you explain its amazing popularity. Is that OK?"

"You're the boss," responded Aguirre, despite all the evidence to the contrary.

The few curious onlookers had built to a small crowd, all stretching and leaning to get a better view of one of Spain's best-known icons. The camera operator counted down and, with a quick wipe of his face, the greenhorn began.

"One of the greatest Spanish success stories of the past few years has been the rise of white Rioja. Once the poor cousin to Spain's flagship red, one vineyard has championed the white Viura grape and boosted demand, both domestic and foreign, for this fresh, citrusy wine. Castelo de Aguirre is the brand which has come to represent the renaissance of the region's white wine.

"Today, we're lucky to interview the viniculturist himself, the man behind the brand, Arturo de Aguirre. Thank you for talking to us, Señor Aguirre."

Aguirre dropped his voice to a more authoritative register. "Happy to oblige. Every opportunity to spread the word is welcome."

"Can you begin by telling us about white Rioja? What makes it so special?"

Aguirre angled himself towards his interviewer, projecting his voice past the microphone towards the knot of observers. "Everything. From nose to palate to finish, this is an exceptional wine which can stand comparison with any Australian Chardonnay or Californian Sauvignon Blanc. Not only can it compete with the wines of the New World, but it takes on French Chablis, Portuguese vinho verde and Italian Pinot Grigio."

The journalist took a breath for his next question but Aguirre anticipated him.

"You're going to ask me why? Good question. Tastes change. For the past two decades, we have seen a trend to the fruit-focused, crowd-pleasing, oaky whites. Easy to drink, higher in alcoholic content and even the driest has a sweetness on the palate. Wines such as our neighbours' Verdejo or Albariño also favour this tropical fruit robustness. Add to this accessible taste the power of New World marketing, and you understand why the traditional white has fallen out of favour."

Inexperienced he may have been, but the boy recognised his cue. "But white Rioja is now one of the most popular wines in Europe, grabbing a huge slice of market share from other white wines. Where did this sudden interest in traditional whites spring from?"

Aguirre gave an understanding nod. "Another good question. To find the answer, we must look backwards. Rioja, in contemporary public perception, stands for fine red wine. It was not always so. In the nineteenth century, the region was famous for its white wine. Have you ever asked yourself why red wine is described in Spanish as *viño tinto*? Tinted wine? Not as in other countries: *rouge, rosso,* red or *negre*? Because the majority of the region's output was white and as a result, subject to higher tax. So the wily viniculturists added a 'tint' of red to their best-selling whites, avoiding tax and spreading the name of Rioja all over the globe."

A murmur rustled through the onlookers. Not only was he an entertaining speaker, but he taught them something as well. He kept his eyes on the journalist.

"Fascinating. So why has the general public, not only at home, but abroad, embraced white Rioja again?"

"If I knew the answer to that, I would retire, right now." The laughter came, as expected, and this time Aguirre bestowed a gracious smile on his audience.

"All I can do is guess. After twenty years of the mass-produced uniformity of sunny, fruity and disposable wines, the traditional, time-honoured methods have once more been recognised for delivering depth. Open a bulk-produced Chardonnay and a white Rioja and compare. At first taste, the Chardonnay comes out fighting. Consistent to the last drop, it tells you of the maker and his methods. A reliable if unexciting wine. The Rioja, with a more savoury, green-apple note to begin, develops an earthy, mouth-coating taste, revealing its mineral sources, and deferring finally to a buttery lemon finish. A journey from first taste to last, it tells you of the soil, the climate, the land. That is not simply a wine. That is an adventure."

His rhetoric, his gestures, his passionate evocation of the sensory experience brought forth a round of applause. He spotted Inez and Paz exchanging a look of familiar admiration. Yes, they'd seen it all before. But like a fine Gran Reserva, every year he just got better.

The journalist, quite delighted with his coup, shook Aguirre's hand more times than was necessary, before finally following his crew to the exit. Or perhaps he was just drunk. Paz had ensured their guests were well-lubricated, just as soon as the interview was over, and the atmosphere was celebratory.

Aguirre slipped into the back room, amongst the wine boxes and publicity material to make a call. It went to voicemail. He smiled. So much the better.

"Tomas, it's Arturo. Arturo Aguirre. I hear the fire we put out is still smouldering. A collaborative effort is now required. For all our sakes, we must extinguish this once and for all. I know I can count on you. Keep me informed. Goodbye."

He glared at the cases of his famous product, seeing nothing. This whole business was becoming an irritant. Just like an infection in the vines, it had to be treated at source, otherwise it would spread like a virus, damaging crops, vintages and reputations. Something like this had to be ripped out at the roots. It was time to call in some favours.

Chapter 9

The front door slammed and Beatrice jerked awake. The clock read 08.13. Ana must have left for work. Beatrice threw back the duvet and stared at the carpet. She'd guessed Ana wouldn't accept this easily. The girl's lack of respect for authority had come to the fore last night, making it harder to convince her that Beatrice had no choice but to back off. A reluctant truce was reached, after arguing back and forth till gone midnight. Beatrice's hands were tied but her mind was not. She would stay in the background, advising Ana on techniques and lines of enquiry until the end of the week. Then the girl would be on her own.

To her credit, Ana didn't sulk, instead giving Beatrice the story Tiago was pursuing; a vanishing junior accountant. Sounded rather dull, but Tiago's disappearance aroused more suspicion. With everyone, it seemed, but the police. Beatrice shook herself. She would devote no more hours to fuming at that sly, two-faced, duplicitous Milandro. She stomped into the bathroom. Rotten little rat; *I have calls to make.* He wasted no time. Nasty, untrustworthy snake. To think she'd respected him, when all the while he was waiting to drop her in it. She turned the water to full blast as if to wash away her thoughts.

How frustrating journalism must be. To have almost as many facts and opinions as the police, but without the authority of the law to investigate.

Once dried, dressed and her blisters plastered, Beatrice sought the kitchen.

A note was stuck to the fridge: *Help yourself to whatever you fancy. I recommend the rashers. Coffee machine on stove. Back at lunchtime unless any developments. Ana.*

Whilst tucking into bacon, eggs and mushrooms, Beatrice made a mind-map of all she knew in pen, adding assumptions in pencil, placing Tiago Vínculo at the centre. She retrieved her tourist guide from her handbag, identifying Tiago's apartment block and its proximity to *El Papagaio*. The accountancy firm with the absent accountant sat in the central bank and finance sector. All within spitting distance. She trawled the firm's photographs, their address, and attempted to read some of the *El Periódico* archive logged by Tiago. But her poor grasp of even basic Spanish made this a fruitless exercise.

Yes, the Internet opened many doors, but there was no substitute for the real thing. Beatrice wanted to be out there, talking to the people, pressing the editor, checking Tiago's communications. Impossible. Hamilton would explode in a cloud of indignation and serge suiting if he heard the merest hint of her involvement. And Matthew would most certainly take a dim view of her detour into detecting while she was supposed to be taking a complete break.

Matthew. He had no idea where she was and intended to call the hotel today. She washed up and went in search of her mobile, releasing her hair to do its worst. The sun cast huge rhomboids of light across Ana's living room, so Beatrice settled into the sofa, tucked up her legs like a cat on a cushion and prepared to put a positive spin on her extended stay in Vitoria.

She was still thinking of the most suitable terminology when running footsteps approached the door. Beatrice got to her feet as a key rattled back and forth. Ana burst in, breathing heavily, but pale as porridge.

"Just heard – a body's been found – at the bottom of a dam – near the Ullíbarri-Gamboa Reservoir – huge fuss at the paper – water for half the province comes from there – police won't confirm identity – we have to go – come on – your boss can just swivel."

She thrust an aggressive middle finger in the direction of the telephone.

Beatrice obeyed and put on her flip-flops; her sense of foreboding and concern growing. But as they hurried down the stairs, she couldn't help practising that gesture and whispering the word 'swivel' with a secretive smile.

The morgue, situated in the same grounds as Santiago Apostol Hospital, had its own car park surrounded by trees, effectively screening it from those who would rather not be reminded of their own mortality. Ana parked the moped as far from the entrance of the low, sober-looking building as it was possible to go. Beatrice dismounted and saw why. A police car sat squarely in front of the main doors.

It would be foolhardy to cross paths with Milandro the day after he'd reported her to Hamilton. Ana obviously had the same thought and indicated the walkway along the side of the building. As they approached, Beatrice could see that the building did in fact have two storeys, but one was below ground. On this side, a deep trench ran alongside the wall. Large frosted-glass windows allowed natural light to penetrate but prevented any ghoulish curiosity. A handrail ensured no one could fall in and a set of metal steps descended to a fire escape door. Stainless steel ashtrays indicated the smokers' corner.

Ana's phone trilled an upbeat melody. She answered, leaning on the rail, muttering a few words in Spanish, but mostly listening. Autumn leaves and litter had blown into the trench and caught in spiders' webs, giving the place an abandoned quality. Beatrice moved a little further along, concerned about being seen from the car park.

Ana ended her call. "That was Jaime, the editor at the paper. He's been talking to the cyclists who found the body. Male, young, no ID, no personal belongings and the face was unrecognisable, they say. Could be anyone."

Beatrice rested her hand on Ana's arm. "So there's every possibility it was some poor hiker who took a tumble."

The girl shook her head. "I have a bad feeling about this. We'll wait for the police to leave and then find out for ourselves who it is and how he died."

"Will the coroner give out that kind of information?"

"No." Ana's attention was caught by movement in the car park. The police vehicle pulled away, followed by an unmarked car, with Milandro clearly visible in the driver's seat. Fortunately, he faced front. Beatrice released her breath and looked at Ana to continue.

"Now what?"

"Now this. Can I borrow your phone? I'm going to call Karel, the coroner's assistant, who will tell us what we want to know."

Beatrice handed her mobile over, wondering why Ana didn't use her own.

"Is Carol a friend of yours?"

"More of a stalker who owes me a favour. Hence the need for your phone." She scrolled through her own phone and punched the number into Beatrice's keypad.

Beatrice stared at her. "Why does she owe you a favour?"

Ana frowned at her for a second before her face cleared. "Not Carol, Karel. He's a six-foot four Dutch doctor. And he owes me because I didn't apply for a restraining order." She pressed the call button and her expression hardened.

"Karel? This is Ana Herrero. I want to talk to you. Outside, by the smoking area. Yes, now would be good. Tell them you need the bathroom."

Two minutes later, the door crunched open and a tall man in a white coat emerged. He stooped to avoid banging his head on the door frame and Beatrice noticed the gesture was well practised. As well as his impressive height, Karel had the broad shoulders of a swimmer, thick fair hair and strong features. His expression was wary, searching Ana's face before acknowledging Beatrice with a bow of his head.

"Hello, Ana. I was surprised to hear from you."

"I'll bet. But it's not actually you I'm interested in. I need some information."

Karel gave a sad smile in Beatrice's direction. "Unrequited love, you see. If she'd only give me a chance ..."

Ana interrupted. "She can't understand you. That's my body-guard and she doesn't speak any English."

Beatrice kept her face stony, searching for a gesture which might indicate both incomprehension and physical power. She settled for folding her arms.

"Where is she from, because I speak several ...?"

"Karel, who is it? The body they found near the reservoir."

Karel dropped his eyes. "Ana, I can't ..."

"I need to know who it is and how he died." Her voice contained no hint of a polite request, just clear determination.

"We can't even give the police cause of death with any certainty yet."

"So you know who it is and you think you know how he died. Come on, Karel. Is it Tiago Vínculo?"

"Yes." His mouth dragged down in sympathy. "I'm sorry, Ana. I know he was a close friend."

Ana swallowed once but her voice remained steady. "Thank you. How? I already know it wasn't an accident."

Karel opened his palms. "*We* don't even know that yet. His bruising is consistent with a fall. If he slipped from the top, bumping into stones and rock, it could have been the impact of any one of those that killed him. We can't make any definitive assessments till after the examination." He rubbed his eye, as if tired.

Beatrice should have known Ana would spot a liar's tic.

Stepping forward so he had no choice but to look at her, Ana stood directly in front of Karel. "What else? You know more than just bruises. Tell me, Karel. I think you owe me that."

He scrunched up his face in discomfort. "You're a journalist. Giving you any information could get me in a lot of trouble."

"This isn't for the paper, it's for me. What is it?"

He shoved his hands deep into the pockets of his white coat and glanced again at Beatrice. Ana moved into his line of sight.

"Karel ..."

"She really doesn't understand English? I mean, I'll tell you, but I don't know that woman and she makes me nervous."

"She hasn't got a clue. I promise. Look, your toilet break is starting to get suspiciously long, so do us both a favour and tell me what else you've found."

Karel's eyes flicked to the fire door. "You cannot, under any circumstances, use this in a story. OK? The body had another injury, which can't be explained by the fall."

"What?"

"Someone cut off his nose."

"Jesus, Mary and Joseph ..."

Thankfully, Karel's attempt to comfort Ana in an embrace meant that he didn't see Beatrice clap a horrified hand to her mouth. By the time Ana had pushed him away and he looked back, Beatrice had regained her composure. Arms folded, chin high and eyes suspicious – she looked every inch a foreign security officer. But inside the implications hit her like a series of electric shocks.

Chapter 10

Bells rang across the courtyard, breaking into Luz's contented doze and announcing four o'clock. Her stomach swooped with a thrill when she realised where she was. And who with. Her risk-taking was getting worse. Bringing him back to the campus, back to her room, she must have lost her mind. Perhaps that was why she couldn't stop smiling. She nuzzled against Tunçay's chest and closed her eyes. She refused to watch the clock digits count away her remaining moments of happiness. He slept on, no doubt exhausted by late shifts, early mornings and limited sleep in between. Selfishness and lust, greed and need, was she taking more than she gave? Her guilt surfaced and she pulled away to look at his face.

Without his glasses, he looked younger, more naïve, and his face had relaxed completely. She smiled. His chest rose and fell, dark hair converging to an arrow which pointed beneath the duvet. Luz wanted to follow that arrow with her fingertips to see where it might lead, but she had no time. Always the same story – there was never enough time.

She kissed his cheek. "Wake up. It's past four."

He didn't open his eyes but breathed deeply, stretching out his arm and pulling her onto his chest.

She laughed and kissed him again. "Come on. We've got to get out of here. Rita will be back in less than twenty minutes."

"No. I can't move. I'm not going anywhere."

She laughed again, but a quiver of panic limited her smile. She shoved him, a dead weight. The clock flicked to 16.10. Her panic morphed into anger. She wanted to shout at him, threaten him, even hurt him. Anything to make him move. He opened his eyes.

"Is that the best you can do?" he asked, his smile sleepy.

She pounced, tickling his ribs, stomach, armpit, back, neck, wherever presented itself as he writhed and pleaded under her attack. Finally he rolled off the bed, gasping.

"That'll teach you. Come on, we have to get dressed." She jumped off the bed and picked up her underwear. He caught her ankle.

"You won't even give me an opportunity for revenge? Come on, I'm not going to see you again for five whole days." He slid his hand up the inside of her leg.

"No! Tunçay, please don't do this. We have to get dressed and get out." She dragged on her knickers and hooked herself into her bra. "I knew it was a bad idea to come here. I can't relax and you can't take it seriously. We mustn't get caught!"

All humour dropped from his face and he got to his feet. Luz looked away from his semi-erect penis and handed him his clothes. He sat on the bed to dress, his expression tired and sullen. Neither spoke until a trill emanated from Luz's phone. She read the message and sighed with relief.

"Rita's going for a sauna with Pilar and Mariana. She won't be back for another hour, at least. Wait, I have to reply, she wants me to join them."

She keyed in a swift excuse and glanced up to see Tunçay's face unchanged. He looked as if he'd had enough. She threw the phone onto the table, sat beside him and looped her arm around his neck.

"I'm sorry for hassling you. I just get so terrified of being caught that I tend to ..."

"Caught with a Turk? Am I really that embarrassing?"

She sat back, shocked. "No! No, Tunçay, it's not you. I told you that. My parents are incredibly strict. They have plans for me, and don't want anything, or anyone, to get in the way."

He stood up and pulled his cigarettes from his jacket.

"You can't smoke here. She'll smell it. Look, let's go outside."

He lit the cigarette, opened the window and blew the smoke into the cold air. "We can't go outside. You might be seen with me. People would talk and then your family would find out and then ... then what, Luz? Would it be the end of the world?"

Luz couldn't meet his eyes. She gazed at her fingernails and thought about his question. The end of the world? No. Only the end of hers. Her father would remove her from the university overnight, her mother would take her through the express checkout in the husband supermarket and her working womb would be the only interest she would hold. Her headlong rush towards independence, a hard-fought victory of five years' education would disappear as if it had never existed except in her own imagination.

Tunçay squeezed the butt under the tap, took a tissue and wrapped it carefully, before dropping it in the bin. She smiled, letting him know she appreciated the gesture, even though she'd have to dig it out and dispose of it more thoroughly after he'd gone. He sat down beside her and took her hand.

"I know this isn't easy for you. OK, your family is traditional. You could never introduce me to your parents. You, an heiress, and me, a Turkish waiter. The shame! I understand that. If you want the truth, I would also be ashamed to take you home to my family. I'm sorry if that hurts you, but I think we can be honest now. I'm Muslim and to have a serious relationship with anyone outside my faith would cause ..." He shook his head. "I don't know what it would cause and I'd never try to find out. No matter that you are the daughter of a highly successful businessman, you are still a Catholic."

The way he said it: Catholic, as if it was dirty. Luz's eyes stung but she blinked away the tears, breathing fiercely through her nose. She sat beside him on the bed, holding his hand and wondering if this was the end of her first relationship.

"Listen to me, Luz. I feel very strongly for you and I'm happy we met. I don't know if we can plan too far ahead. Our being together would hurt a lot of other people we love. But for me, that's the future. What I want to know is – do we have a present?"

It hardly ever stopped at a kiss. Luz found herself tugging at his jeans almost immediately. And after such a dance alongside the abyss, she needed that physical affirmation of his need. His love. Quick, urgent and intense, they were dressed and saying farewells within twenty minutes. Luz opened all the windows, sprayed deodorant and took the bin to the waste disposal chute in the corridor. She stopped at the vending machine for two *espressi* – one to drink and one to soak up any odours in the room. She made her bed, spread out her books to reinforce the lie that she'd been studying and sat in the armchair staring at the ceiling.

Her eyes were in the sky but her head was in the sand. Yes, she'd won the battle to go to university, to study law. Her parents were even convinced it might be of benefit to them and their business. It had never been stated explicitly, but they'd given her five years. A long leash, but still a leash. Four years to go and then what?

Chapter 11

At the *El Periódico* offices, Beatrice sat in the meeting room, fidgeting. Ana had only gone downstairs to collect their guest, but unease stretched every second. Since the meeting with love-struck Karel, Beatrice was reluctant to let the girl out of her sight. Especially as the information about Tiago's body had galvanised Ana into frenetic activity; the threat implicit in his mutilation serving as catalyst rather than check. But she insisted the news they'd received at the mortuary remained their secret. Beatrice somehow doubted she was protecting her source and more keeping her cards close to her chest.

The activity log at the paper's server showed Ana's computer had been accessed on Saturday morning, while Ana herself was on a bus passing Logroño. Tiago's computer at the newspaper contained few leads, as he preferred to use his own laptop. Official tape barred entry to his apartment so the only trace of the original story remained in Ana's memory. Fortunately, a memory of superior quality.

"The guy's name was Miguel Saez and he worked for GFS, Gasteiz Financial Services. The company does audits, performs due diligence and generally checks the books for small to medium-sized companies. He went missing about three weeks ago, maybe more, and the police seemed to think he'd done a runner. I don't think they closed the case but they definitely weren't chucking resources at it either. So his girlfriend contacted the paper to try and publicise the issue. Not exactly a hot story, so our editor assigned it to Tiago. He resented being given such a dud, at first, but then he got the wind under his tail and you couldn't hold him back. Tiago's theory was this: Saez had accidentally found some sensitive information and was paid to disappear. Saez's girlfriend – what was her name? Whatever. She confirmed their relationship was volatile, he had few ties here and no family. Tiago believed he'd just taken the cash and gone. The girlfriend insists he would never do that, but how well does anyone really know a partner? Word of warning, though. I suggest we tackle that subject very carefully when we meet her. She's pretty scary. What the hell was her name?"

"Margarita Xarra."

A curly-haired woman entered the room and stomped up to Beatrice, her bag slung across her chest and one hand thrust forward. Short and square, she wore tight jeans and a glittery blue sweatshirt which bore the words 'Too Hot To Handle'. Beatrice estimated her to be early forties, aggressive and best given a wide berth. Ana followed her into the office and stood just inside the door, giving Beatrice a wide-eyed look of mock alarm.

Beatrice jumped to her feet, shook hands and attempted a greeting in Spanish. After that, conversation would be down to Ana.

"*Buenas dias, Señora Xarra. Muchas graçias ...*"

"I can speak English. You're the London detective?" Her tone was sceptical and her eyes were hard as she took in Beatrice's flip-flops.

"Yes. I am a detective, but I'm on holiday at the moment. My name is Beatrice Stubbs."

She dug deeply in her bag. "I don't care if you're on holiday or not. If you are a detective, you can help find Miguel. I brought everything I have. Why don't you sit down?" It wasn't a suggestion.

She yanked out a folder stuffed with papers and plonked herself opposite Ana and Beatrice. As the woman rifled through the papers, Beatrice voiced her concern.

"Miss Xarra, if you have some evidence relating to Miguel's disappearance, you really should give it to the police."

Margarita's head snapped up to face Beatrice. "I'm not stupid. The police have seen all this stuff. I tried to explain but the truth is I don't really understand it either. I'm not an accountant, but I'm not stupid. I know Miguel hasn't just left me, and I know whatever happened to him is connected to this." She stabbed a forefinger at the papers in front of her.

"I've been through this with the police, several times. I've been through it with your colleague and answered every one of his questions. And now I have to do it all over again with you."

The woman's pugilistic attitude rankled with Beatrice. They were hardly duty-bound to find her missing boyfriend. All they could do was offer assistance. And here was this female acting as if she were under sufferance.

Margarita evidently sensed the change in atmosphere, or registered the aggression in her tone. "But if it helps Miguel, I'll do it again and again until someone finds out what happened," she added, looking from one to the other, her expression no less confrontational.

Beatrice conceded. "I appreciate this is difficult, especially the repetition. Could you start at the beginning and tell us as much as you can about Miguel?"

"Miguel. We've been together for two years, almost. He's Galician. Not physically attractive at first glance but he has a good heart. He's a junior accountant with GFS. Because he was new to the company, they only allowed him to assist on most jobs, doing the boring bits. I can't give you any detail because we don't talk about his work. Boring like you wouldn't believe. Sends me to sleep. But a while back, around two and a half months ago, he got an opportunity to take over a job. He wouldn't shut up about it."

She pushed a brochure towards them. "You'll have to make photocopies; I'm not giving you the originals. The job was at Alava Exports, which handles some of the regional wine trade. Miguel was so excited and determined to prove himself, he worked extra hours at the weekend, checking and double-checking. It really pissed me off. We argued a lot around then."

Ana cleared her throat. "Very often, when a couple's relationship has been through a rough patch, the police take the easy option and presume he ran off. What did you say to convince them otherwise?"

Ana's subtle probing failed. Margarita's eyes flashed and her voice rose.

"How can I prove something *didn't* happen? Tell me! What can I say to a lazy son-of-a-bitch police officer who just wants to close the file? I *know* Miguel would never do that. He's a noble, honourable man and he loved me. We planned to get engaged at Christmas, so why would he run away? He told me he was under my spell."

Beatrice dropped her voice to a gentle reassuring pitch. "That's very romantic. He sounds like a charming man. Margarita, the first journalist you spoke to believed Miguel was paid to disappear. Think carefully. Could he, under any circumstances, have accepted that kind of offer?"

Margarita shook her head, slowly, but with absolute conviction, a faint smile on her face. "No. For money? No. His parents died some time back and as the only son, everything came to him. He works because he loves it, not because he needs the money."

Alarm bells rang in Beatrice's mind. A young man, no family, madly in love with an older woman, vanishes completely. "Do you know if Miguel had made a will?"

The question seemed unexpected. Margarita blinked, her face smoothed into a thoughtful calm. For the first time, Beatrice could see the natural beauty previously masked by defensive hostility.

Margarita pursed her lips. "I don't know, but I doubt it. We've never talked about it. We talked about a pre-nuptial agreement, though. That was my idea. He didn't want to discuss divorce before we'd even got married. But I want to sign a piece of paper saying everything he has before he marries me, he gets to keep. I'm not interested in his money."

So that answered that.

Forty minutes later, they said their goodbyes and Beatrice watched Margarita follow Ana out of the room. The short woman even managed to convey aggression in her walk: head down, shoulders back, like a prop forward. The pile of photocopies on the table sapped Beatrice's energy. All the painstaking legwork would be down to her and Ana; no detective sergeants to assist, no forensic expertise to call upon, and the strong possibility that any relevant papers were long gone. Or in Spanish.

"You must be Beatrice Stubbs."

The man resting his hands on the table wore an open-necked denim shirt, demonstrating that his tan spread further than his neck. Chestnut hair above dark, smiling eyes and a row of even white teeth flashed in her direction.

"How come everyone in this city knows who I am?" Beatrice asked.

He laughed. "I think there may be one or two who are still in ignorance. Jaime Rodriguez. I'm the editor of *El Periódico*. Pleased to meet you."

Beatrice half-rose to shake his hand. "Likewise. So you're Ana's boss?"

He shrugged and leaned his head to one side. "The word 'boss' implies I have some control over what she does. That is the total opposite of the case. But as I guess you know, she's an excellent investigative journalist, so I can live with that. She tells me you're helping her on that missing accountant story."

Beatrice stiffened. "Missing accountant *and* missing journalist story. Are you not concerned about your employee at all?" She reined herself in, recalling Ana's words. *Tell no one.*

"May I?" With a grin bordering on wolfish, he relaxed into the seat opposite and looked her in the eye. He was undeniably attractive, in that slightly rough, French actor sort of way. And close up, it appeared his eyes were deep blue. Beatrice smiled back.

"It's not unusual for a journalist to slip off the radar when they get close to cracking a story. Sometimes because their hours are irregular, sometimes because they're working undercover and can't take the risk of contacting the paper, sometimes because their minds are on other things. I trust Tiago's judgement and I think he'll be back with a fantastic exclusive in a few days."

Determined to stick to the party line, Beatrice ignored the sudden urge to put the man straight. Instead, she focused on his smile. Teeth that white surely couldn't be natural. She wondered how he did it.

"You must wonder what kind of undisciplined shop I run, Detective Inspector Stubbs. I guess the Metropolitan Police must be more rigid, no?"

"Hi, Jaime. You met Beatrice, then?" Ana returned to her seat and began stacking the photocopied papers into a neat pile.

He fixed his deep blue eyes on Beatrice. "I have had the pleasure, yes." He turned his attention to Ana. "So, any developments?"

Ana shook her head. "Not yet. We spoke to the girlfriend and now have to go through everything she gave us – this lot. I'm taking it home, OK? And I plan to visit the accountants' office tomorrow, but I'll keep you informed."

Jaime laughed. "That'll be a first. I must get on. Good luck with all the research." He waved a hand at the uninviting stack of documents. "Hope to talk to you again, Detective Inspector Stubbs. Can I give you my card?"

"Thank you. Here's mine. And please call me Beatrice. I'm off duty. Nice meeting you, Jaime."

With another flash of teeth, he wandered away. Beatrice noticed the black cowboy boots complete with faux spurs and the tight-fitting jeans. Jaime was one of those men with an impossibly small bottom.

"Beatrice Stubbs! Were you just flirting with my boss?"

She met Ana's incredulous expression with a look of outraged innocence.

"Don't be ridiculous. Just because I enjoy some civilised interaction with an aesthetically pleasing specimen, you suspect the worst."

"You were checking out his arse!"

"I most certainly was not. And one thing you should learn; making easy assumptions leads to guaranteed failure in the field of detective work. So, out of interest, is he single?"

More photographs of beautiful people. Beatrice's head throbbed and she'd long since lost interest.

"This is Angel Rosado, successful businessman, well-connected and happily married. He and his wife often attend high-profile cultural events, pressing powerful flesh."

"Handsome." Beatrice observed, with little enthusiasm. "And she's very glamorous. Although that's one hell of a nose."

"Yep. Runs in the family. Boom boom." Ana scrolled through more pictures on the gossip website, as Beatrice watched and listened to the commentary. Two solid hours of poring over the scrappy and incomprehensible notes left by Miguel Saez, followed by endless screens of false smiles. Even if she knew who these people were, she'd still be bored. As for the case, a feeling of complete confusion made logical thought beyond her.

"Ana, I think I need a break ..."

"OK, two minutes. This is his sister-in-law again. See how the whole lot are interconnected? There's no branch of the trade without one of them involved. And here he is, Arturo de Aguirre, the patriarch and champion of white Rioja."

Beatrice squinted at the screen. The man's arch expression conveyed immense confidence. "Well, you can see where Mrs Rosado got her nose from. And this bloke does what exactly?"

"He owns one of the most famous vineyards in the region, Castelo de Aguirre. It's open to the public, maybe we should have a poke around."

"I think that might be a job for me. I planned to visit some Rioja producers. But now, if you don't mind, I need to lie down in a dark room and have a glass of water."

"Are you OK?"

Beatrice considered the question. A vague panicky feeling lapped at her insides, her head pounded and she felt smothered by the foreignness of it all.

"Yes, I think so. Just feeling out of my depth. Miguel's notes in Spanish, his sums, incomprehensible numbers, and all these well-known faces I've never heard of. I wonder how much use I can be."

Ana closed the laptop and went into the kitchen. She returned with a glass of water, ice cubes chinking cheerfully. "I should apologise. I get so into all this stuff, I forget you're not working, you're on holiday. I'm being a bully. Listen, why don't you rest for a couple of hours and I'll make some food. And some phone calls. The only way we'll get any sense out of these figures is by asking an expert. This is where a large family can come in handy."

Beatrice sipped, the cool sensation spreading down her throat and across her chest. She pressed the glass to her forehead, condensation chilling her brow. The itch around her nose and eyes seemed to abate and she looked up at Ana. "Let me guess. You have three highly qualified accountants for siblings and a bank manager for a mother?"

Ana sat on the coffee table, her face concerned. "Do you want a paracetamol? You don't look good."

"I'm fine. Just in need of a rest. Which experts are you going to call?"

"All right. No, the immediate family are no good. I'm an only child and my dad is a professor of Celtic History. He's worse at maths than I am. My mother, when she was alive, couldn't even work out percentages. But I do have plenty of cousins, all of whom have done better in the professional sphere than me. Armando's not only a partner in a Porto accountancy firm, but he loves a mystery. I'll scan this stuff over to him and see what he makes of it."

A breeze brushed over Beatrice's face, a soothing feeling. She wanted to ask Ana more questions, particularly about her mother, but they would keep for later. And anyway, she was still talking.

"Then tomorrow, I'll visit the accountants, check in with Milandro and you can do the tourist thing and take a nose around the Aguirre estate."

"I'm not sure it's a good idea for us to split up. If what happened to Tiago was intended as a warning ..."

Ana hesitated. "I know. I'll be careful. If it makes you feel any better, I'll call the paper and let them know what we're up to. Don't worry about me, I can look after myself."

Beatrice frowned into her water. For an intelligent girl, Ana could be absurdly naïve.

Chapter 12

To: beastubbs@ttl.com
From: Matthew.Bailey@exeter.ac.uk

I shall begin, as is only polite, by thanking you for your previous. However, please do not think for one moment that I am ignorant of the reasons why you chose to explain via electronic correspondence. More of that in a moment.

Firstly, I found much about your communication cause for relief. Your tone sounds cheerful, optimistic, inspired and engaged, just as a tourist should. If your intention was to engender a jealous rage by detailing your culinary experiences thus far, you succeeded to such an extent that my eyes seem to have changed colour permanently. Tanya's journalist friend sounds delightful and very generous in allowing you to stay in her apartment. Both Tanya and Marianne asked me to pass on their regards.

Yet the cautious curmudgeon in me has found much of interest and concern between the lines. For the first week of your extended holiday, we spoke daily on the telephone. Yesterday, you chose to substitute our conversation for a one-sided email, with the casual aside: 'too much to tell you over the phone'. It may well be the most efficient method of informing me of the significant changes which have occurred since our last chat, but also ensures I cannot interrupt.

A further worry is your decision to abandon your plan for re-laxation and 'battery-charging' to become involved in an investigation. The fact that it is under the auspices of journalism rather than crime is a semantic distinction. You are working, Old Thing, while on holiday. I only hope Hamilton doesn't find out.

I have typed and deleted the following sentence three times: You know best. Unfortunately, our experience shows this conceit as fundamentally flawed. I trust you understand that I am not talking about the Pembroke incident. Not even I could be that crass. In a more general sense, we have agreed that you function best with your support mechanism intact. While I respect and admire your judgement and professional brilliance, sometimes, Old Thing, you make the worst imaginable decisions for yourself. I hope you understand my unease as concern rather than mistrust.

All that remains for me to say is that I wish you a wonderful adventure in Vitoria, be it culinary, advisory or artistic. I would feel vastly reassured if we could find a way of conversing in the next few days.

Beatrice, be careful. And please call James.

With love, affection and considerable exasperation
Matthew

Chapter 13

It took less than a minute for Beatrice to decide that she loathed at least eighty percent of her companions on the wine tour. Unreasonable it may have been, but an undeniable fact. A thundercloud loomed over her outlook, driven by her worry for Ana along with a general sense of isolation and loneliness. Not only that, but Matthew's email had hit its target. He should be here. When she'd made the decision to travel alone, with the aim of considering her options, she thought it was best. Now, she missed his anchoring effect and light touch on the tiller. How he'd love this autumnal light, the vivid landscape of seasonal tones, the epicurean delights, her snide observations on other travellers and most of all, he'd love the wine. But he wasn't here. All her own fault, which only made it worse.

The ill-matched bunch waited in the assembly area, a lumpen assortment wearing the universal uniform of the tourist. Turquoise anoraks, puce bum-bags and lime rucksacks, elasticated waists and bulging pockets of all-purpose beige trousers with an abundance of zips. The party, to which Beatrice contributed her own sour expression, created a startlingly ugly contrast to whitewashed walls, oak barrels and a panorama of vineyards through the window. She hated to be part of such a group, and hated herself more for being such an unbearable snob. Perhaps she should leave.

"Good morning, everyone. My name is Claudia and I am your tour guide today. OK, how many English speakers?"

Most raised their hands, excepting three superior-looking ladies with steely hair and pastel suits, the Italian foursome and a young couple who could not stop kissing and giggling. Beatrice wondered if they'd even heard the question.

"*Qui parle français? Español?*"

Claudia, after much discussion, agreed to conduct the tour in English, Spanish, Italian and French.

She led them outside and began her spiel. The sun bounced off the white walls of the Tourist Centre, as the visitors listened to the history of the Castelo. The two Italian couples continued to talk amongst themselves, pointing out objects of interest to each other as if nothing else was happening. Claudia raised her volume and switched to Spanish. The young couple paid no attention, whispering, goosing and squealing while the poor guide ran through her speech. The Frenchwomen began to scowl and tut, the sun caused Beatrice's eyes to water and her irritation reached breaking point. This was a waste of time. She would leave, forget the money she'd spent on the taxi and admission fee and go back to Calle Cuchillería.

"Claudia?" A stentorian voice echoed around the courtyard, silencing the Italians and drawing everyone's attention upwards. Even the dry-humpers took their eyes off each other for a moment. Arturo de Aguirre surveyed them from a stone balcony above. He exchanged a few rapid words with the tour girl and disappeared. Her strained expression evaporated and she broke into a genuine smile.

"Ladies and gentlemen, we have luck. Señor Aguirre, the owner of the vineyard, will join us. This is not usual."

The truth of that statement was visible in her face. Her anticipation affected everyone, so that as Aguirre rounded the corner, a spontaneous patter of applause greeted him.

"*Kaixo. Ongi etorri!* Welcome, *bienvenue, benvenuti, bienvenidos, velkommen.*" He turned his attention to an oriental pair. "*Mabuhay.*"

They nodded and smiled. He'd clearly done his research on their party.

He continued with an expansive gesture. "Sadly, that is the extent of my Tagalog vocabulary. Claudia is far more talented with languages. We're so lucky to have her. And yet, four translations make the tour hard work not only for your lovely guide, but also for you. So let's split the group. I will take the English speakers, Claudia, the rest. Come, everyone!"

He did not translate, leaving their tour guide to relay the reason why most of the party was departing. Beatrice assessed the individual striding ahead. The photograph in the gossip magazine had captured his essence. Arrogant, confident and with such force of personality, compliance seemed compulsory. She could still leave and call that taxi, if she wanted. But in the interests of research, it might be better to persevere. She hurried after the rest of Aguirre's acolytes in the direction of the vines.

Long rows of richly coloured foliage stretched into the distance; copper, amaranth, gold, carmine and rust, the breeze and sunlight creating an illusion of flames rippling across the fields. Towards the end of the ordered lines, workers moved back and forth, tending the plants. As the party descended stone steps from the terrace to the vineyard, Beatrice raised a hand to shield her eyes from the sun and caught her foot on the step. She stumbled and lurched into the young man in front.

"Hey up, steady on." He caught her arm, restoring her balance. "You all right there?" His head was shaved and he wore a white T-shirt stretched over a muscle-bound body. Normally the sort of man Beatrice would avoid.

"I'm so sorry. It's these bloody flip-flops. That and not looking where I'm going."

"Can't blame you. One hell of a view, in't it?" He stood beside her and they gazed out over the sweep of ridged vineyards and distant mountains.

"It is," Beatrice agreed. "Imagine waking up to this every morning."

"Beats the back end of Bolton Gasworks, all right. Can you see that church? Over there, on the top of that hill."

Beatrice's eyes followed the direction of his finger. "Oh yes. Looks like something from a tourist brochure."

"Or a spaghetti western. Come on, we're getting left behind." He held out his hand to guide her and she took it, the kindness of the gesture overcoming her pride.

"Do you really come from Bolton?" she asked.

His eyes creased with amusement. "Somebody's got to. Yeah, I'm a Bolton lad, but I don't live there anymore. Got a place in London."

"Whereabouts? I live in the East End."

"Nice. My flat's in the Docklands. I don't spend much time there. I'm in the army so it's only for when I'm home on leave. You can't knock the Docklands for convenience, but it's got a bit pretentious."

"I know what you mean. Same round my way. Gastro pubs instead of boozers, Italian delis instead of Billingsgate and you could walk the length and breadth of Hoxton in search of a pickled egg." Her foot met soil and she released the man's hand.

The rest of the party awaited them at the top of a row of vines, so they picked up their pace.

"I'm Kevin, by the way."

"Beatrice." They shook hands. "Thanks for the help."

Ana's patience was wearing thin. The receptionist at GFS had assured her that the CEO would be out to meet her in about ten minutes. That was over half an hour ago. She replaced the Financial Times in the rack and approached the desk.

"Sorry to bother you. You said Señor Alvarez would be here soon?"

The woman, whose forehead seemed to be laminated, tilted her head in an expression of artificial surprise. "I said he would be here as soon as he gets a spare moment. You had no appointment and he is a man with many demands on his time."

"I understand that. I'm just wondering how long it's likely to be. Can you give me a rough estimate?" Ana gave her brightest smile.

"I doubt it." The forehead obviously couldn't do frowns either.

Ana maintained the smile as she retook her seat. She'd wait it out. She had to. After drawing a complete blank at the police station, she couldn't go back to the paper empty-handed. Anyway, he couldn't stay in there much longer; it was almost lunchtime. Even Ana's stomach was rumbling, despite what she'd put away at breakfast. A sense of guilt tugged at her, in the knowledge that Beatrice's tetchy behaviour yesterday and this morning was wholly due to Ana. The poor woman only wanted a relaxing break, but she'd been bullied into working for free. Well, their agreement was until the end of the week. Two more days and then Ana would be on her own. And she'd got nowhere.

Her hollow promises to Tiago's mother rang in her ears. Yes, she would come to the funeral. Yes, no matter what the coroner said, she'd try to find out what happened. Yes, of course she would pray for them. Her eyes pricked as she recalled the devastated woman's attempts at controlling her grief.

This was bullshit. The one thing Ana didn't need was any more thinking time. Alvarez could stuff it and Ana would find the information she needed some other way. She got to her feet. The receptionist watched her approach, picked up the phone and asked a question. She listened for a second and replaced the receiver.

"I'm sorry, but it seems you're out of luck. Señor Alvarez has left for a lunch meeting. Why don't you try some other time? Perhaps when it's more convenient for our managing director."

Ana knew there would be no convenient time. "Is there anyone else I could speak to? Someone who worked with Miguel Saez? There must be someone here who knew him."

The receptionist shook her head. "It's a busy time of year, I'm afraid. Might I suggest you call ahead next time, and I'll see what I can do?" She slid her hand back to the mouse and stared at the screen. Ana suppressed her parting shot and left quietly.

The lunchtime rush created the usual jam of vehicles, all searching for the elusive parking spot. Thank God for the Vespa. Ana unlocked it and retrieved her helmet under the seat. From the open window of a passing blue Mercedes, a cigarette butt traced a long arc to the gutter at her feet. Ana glanced at the driver, but only a hand and forearm were visible. She just registered a white shirt with rolled-up sleeves and a missing forefinger, before the car turned the corner. What a tosser.

Whilst the beauty of the region left her slack-jawed with awe, Beatrice wasn't sorry to return indoors. The sun, even in October, still contained substantial force. Crouching low under the vines, she'd admired the texture of the trunk, twisted and fibrous like the ropes of a mighty ocean liner, and relished the shade.

Aguirre talked them through the harvesting process, emphasising the length of time from the earliest September ripeners, such as the Viura grape, to the latest in November. He encouraged them to taste a grape from the vine and pointed out the baskets and padded trucks used for transporting the fruit to the press house. The middle-aged British couple plied him with questions, while the Danish family and three Bolton boys limited themselves to respectful nods. The two Danish children, no more than thirteen, behaved impeccably. Their interest in wine must have been on a par with Beatrice's in Disneyland, but not once did their attentive demeanour slip.

En route to the wine press, Kevin introduced her to his companions.

"This is Beatrice, who tried to nut me between the shoulder blades back there. Beatrice, meet Tyler and Jase, two of me oldest mates. It's Tyler's fault we're here, 'cos he's getting married in three weeks. This is his stag weekend."

Beatrice shook hands with the two men. "Pleased to meet you, and congratulations, Tyler. I'm aware a stag weekend is supposed to entail alcohol and entertainment, but I'd always assumed something racier than a wine tasting."

They all laughed and Tyler shrugged with a weary grin. "There's eighteen of me mates and family arriving in Bilbao on Saturday. But it were only us three fancied seeing summat more than the inside of a bar."

Jase took over. "So we come out a week early, hired a car and headed to Rioja country. What about you, Beatrice? You one of them pilgrims?"

"Good God, no. My interests are far more secular. I'm on holiday, using Vitoria as a base to explore the region's food and drink. The only pilgrimage I'm likely to make is to the altar of fine wine. Talking of which, we're holding everyone up."

Aguirre's smile as they approached the elevated walkway remained as broad as ever, although Beatrice detected a tension in the jaw, as if he were grinding his teeth.

"Ah, finally, our stragglers. So, if you'd like to gather round, I'll explain the process and let you watch in peace for a few minutes.

First, the grapes are de-stalked before entering the press. The machine squeezes out the grape juice and here at Castelo de Aguirre, we allow the juice to rest with the skins for two hours, to allow maximum flavour. After the pressing and resting, the juice is extracted to vats for the fermentation process to begin. Why don't you spread out and have a look?"

Beatrice was about to follow Kevin to a vantage point at the end of the platform when Aguirre intercepted her. "Probably the best spot is at this end. Come."

His arms were spread in an open gesture of demonstration, although Beatrice couldn't help feeling as if her getaway were blocked. She allowed him to guide her away from the others with the distinct impression she'd been corralled.

Even the Vespa couldn't avoid every jam. Especially when the traffic was bumper to bumper. Ana rested her foot on the ground and waited as a vegetable truck, beeping its monotonous alarm, reversed into a delivery bay. Radios competed from open windows and the smell of roasting chestnuts teased across the stationary traffic, reminding Ana of her stomach. The café opposite the office always did decent *pintxos* so that would be her first stop. A sudden impact jerked her forward, causing her to slide off the seat and bang her knees against the chassis. The bike heaved sideways as her foot left the ground and she struggled against its weight. Once stable, she twisted in her seat to yell at the thoughtless driver behind.

Rather than the apologetic mother or impatient taxi-driver she expected, the occupants of the blue Mercedes were four men, all wearing sunglasses and staring blankly at her.

"What the fuck! Look where you're going, arsehole!" She twisted over her shoulder to see if the Vespa had sustained any damage. The Mercedes blasted its horn, making her jump, and was joined by several others behind. The truck had gone and the road was clearing. She flipped them the finger, revved and took off down Calle Postas, furious and shaken.

Macho dickheads! Dressed up like Reservoir Dogs and having fun by picking on a woman on a Vespa. She should have taken the number of the Merc. Too late. After dodging in and out of the lanes on Calle de los Herrán, it was nowhere to be seen. Her adrenalin levels began to settle as she took a right, muttering insults in three languages.

A squeal of tyres made her glance in her mirror. The Mercedes tore onto Calle de Olaguibel, gaining fast. The liquid heat of her anger solidified into an icy fear. She felt exposed and precarious on the Vespa, against the malevolent weight of the approaching car. They couldn't do anything, not out in the street, surely? Without indicating, Ana took another right turn and accelerated well over the limit towards the park.

They were right behind her. The Vespa had the edge on standing starts, but it would never outrun a vehicle with that horsepower. It pulled level with her back wheel. Ana's hands, sweaty and tense, reached for the brakes. She had to slow down. One nudge at this speed would send her flying over the handlebars. But if she slowed, they could draw level and broadside her. Lights changed ahead and Ana leaned to the right, braking hard. A group of teenagers sauntered over the pelican crossing to Parque di Judizmendi. The nose of the Mercedes inched closer until the wheel arch brushed Ana's calf. A half-curse, half-gulp escaped her and she made a decision. As the lights turned amber, she swung the bike up onto the pavement, spun around and tore over the crossing after the kids. She hit the squeaky little horn, which parted the group, allowing her to squeeze through and into the park itself. With one eye on the mirror, she rode as fast as she dared across to the other side, out onto Calle Errkatxiki and turned left. A supermarket car park seemed the perfect place to rest, to have a few shaky tears, but she kept going to Avenida de Santiago, which would take her almost all the way home.

Chapter 14

It was good to be back.

Until today, Luz had resented the enforced separation from Tunçay, finding fault with everything at Castelo de Aguirre; her sisters seemed boring, her mother shallow and her father insufferable. Not only that, but her return barely registered as significant, because everyone was focused on Thursday's birthday party. The Birthday Party. Her nephew, Ramón, would be one year old, and the celebrations planned were worthy of The Last Emperor. Only her little brother, Basajaun, seemed pleased to see her. Probably because she was the only one who had time to play with him, listen to his excitable chatter and construct hugely complex Lego empires.

But early on Wednesday morning, her mother knocked on her door. Luz was awake, reading *The Pelican Brief*, in an attempt to improve her English.

"Coffee." Marisol took the book from Luz's hands and handed her a cup. She read the title and gave it back with an approving smile. "Good idea. Reading should never be an idle pleasure for an intelligent mind. Now, Basajaun has gone to school, the marquee and catering people will want to set up, so I thought you and I could go into the city. I want to buy you some beautiful things. Maybe a new dress for tomorrow? And after we've given the credit card some exercise, we'll have lunch. You can choose where."

Luz looked up at her mother under her eyebrows. She wanted to refuse, to tell her that she knew exactly the purpose of the outing, and that no matter how much they spent on a dress, Luz would not be groomed and paraded in front of eligible suitors like a prize poodle. But a morning away from the Castelo with her mother's full attention was an opportunity not to be missed.

"All right. But I don't want anything colourful. Ideally, I'd like something black."

Marisol opened the blinds. "Why not? Shall we get your lip pierced as well? I mean, if you want to buy into the nihilistic student uniform, you really should do it properly. Now, I'm going to check which car we can take, and I'll see you outside in twenty minutes. Put your hair up and wear those earrings your grandmother left you. Strapless bra and comfortable shoes but bring a pair of stilettos in your handbag." She smiled. "Today, we are shopping professionally."

Two pairs of amazing heels, a silver choker, a cocktail ring and now the dress. Marisol should have been a lawyer. She knew exactly how to make you think you'd won, while she came away with every box ticked. It was black, yes. A halterneck prom dress, with diamante detail and a circle skirt. Despite herself, Luz stared at her reflection, entranced. Her mother had always had an eye. All the Aguirre girls had the classic pear shape. But this dress suggested a cleavage, while minimising her substantial hips. She twirled, imagining Tunçay's face.

"What do you think, my darling?" Marisol's voice carried pride, admiration and the slightest wobble. Luz couldn't resist.

"It's perfect, Mama. I love it."

Marisol held her face and kissed her on both cheeks before grasping her hands. She had tears in her eyes. "My baby girl. Look at you. Such elegance. You do have real poise, Luz. Your father will just burst with paternal pride when he sees you."

Luz doubted that, but chose not to break the moment. "Thank you."

"Now change, quickly. I'll pay and then we have one more stop before lunch. No outfit is complete without the right foundations. Just one moment ..." She ducked behind Luz, took out a marker pen and drew a line on her back where the dress ended. She was an expert, no question.

"Black, yes, and a flesh-coloured one but we'll take toupee tape so there's no danger of slippage. Visible underwear ..." Marisol shuddered and the assistant nodded with absolute sincerity.

"Is that everything?"

"I'm not sure. Luz, why don't you choose some things for yourself? There are some fabulous sets here. Look at this one, blush pink with either a thong or Brazilian to go with it. I'm sure you're getting to the age when you appreciate beautiful underwear. Or perhaps you know someone else who does."

Luz spotted the conspiratorial look between her mother and the assistant. The smiles. The understanding. It would be so easy to play along.

"No one apart from my room-mate. And she favours sports bras, so there's not much point. Shall we go? My stomach is rumbling. I missed breakfast, you know."

"It's only half past twelve, my sweet. And even if you don't see the need right now, perhaps you might be glad of some quality items soon enough. I'm going to look at pyjamas for Basajaun. You choose and put them on my account. See you in a minute."

The assistant and Marisol melted away, as if by an agreed signal, and Luz felt like a mouse facing a cube of cheese. If she took it, she was trapped. If she refused, her mother, with feline patience, would get her claws in some other way. So she might as well have some decent knickers. Those black high-legs reminded her of paintings by Lautrec. If they had a matching bra in her size, a private version of the can-can might be just the thing. Luz picked up the lacy panties.

By the end of their lunch, during which Luz demolished a full *Marmitako* and her mother picked at a Caesar salad, Marisol had still not pounced. They chatted about the law course, Basajaun, the imminent party, Luz's room-mate, the guests invited for tomorrow, local gossip and the advantages of small breasts for an ageing décolletage. Over coffee, the conversation became more intimate, Marisol sharing her concerns about Inez's marriage and Angel's impotence. Luz enthusiastically defended Angel, who did not fit the typical arrogant money man Aguirre preferred to cultivate.

"And I bet if you two stopped looking over their shoulders and putting on the pressure, it would happen. Sometimes, I wonder if you realise how much your children feel more like puppets than individuals."

Marisol's teaspoon stopped its circular motion and her eyes locked onto Luz.

"That's a strange thing to say. I fought with your father for months so that you could go to university. I thought, maybe I was naïve, I was trying to give you independence."

"I know. You did fight for me and I'm sorry if that sounded ungrateful. I love being there, I'm happier than I could have imagined, but I keep asking myself, am I really free?"

The waiter brought the bill and Marisol tossed the credit card onto the silver platter without checking.

"Free. That's an interesting word. How was your lunch?"

Luz blushed. "If you mean ..."

Marisol's face hardened and she shook her head. "As you grow, my dear, spoilt, little girl, you will realise that no one is free. The hawk, soaring over the fields at will, is chained by his need to find prey. The bat, roaming the night while the world sleeps, is driven by a need to survive. You have no such biological urgency. You have never had to fend for yourself. But you are part of the system. We all find ways of surviving."

Luz rolled her eyes at the rhetoric, but didn't hesitate. "Why can't I find my own way of surviving? What if I don't want to be a submissive brood mare like Paz? I can be a useful member of society, a lawyer, a professional who can earn her keep. I'm not ungrateful, it's just I have to be my own person."

Neither spoke again until they left the restaurant and headed for the car.

"Mama, thank you for lunch and all the shopping. I'm sorry."

Marisol reached out to kiss her on the cheek. "It was a pleasure. I don't get to spend enough time with you. Today was important to me." She pressed the fob and unlocked the vehicle. "But I am keen to hear about the boyfriend."

Luz opened the back door and stashed her bags. She didn't speak until her mother started the car.

"It's complicated."

"Most things are. But is he worth the pain?"

Luz turned to her. "How did you know? Please tell me the truth."

The Jaguar pulled out of the underground car park and into the afternoon sun. Two nuns crossed in front of them and Luz watched her mother nod at them piously, then break into a smile.

"You're glowing, my darling girl. Your family evidently bore you to tears, you can't wait to get back to Burgos and I haven't seen your eyes shine like this since you were six years old and we bought you that puppy."

"Bear. I loved that dog."

"He was a favourite with all of us. But he doted on you. People change when they fall in love. With a dog, with a cause, with a person, no matter. So either law is proving the love of your life or you've met someone. I suspect the latter."

"You can't tell anyone. Especially not Papí."

Marisol checked her rear-view mirror, her smile fading. "You'd be surprised, my little Luz, how much your father cares for your happiness. I think he'd be happy to hear you had someone special in your life."

Luz turned to look out of the window. It was a lie. Her father would only accept one of his own choices. Even if Luz had met a good Catholic boy, whose father was well connected, whose honour was beyond reproach and who loved her like Romeo, he would never pass. Luz had seen the list of her possible future partners. She despised every last one.

"He wouldn't, Mama. Even if I told him that there's no future for this relationship, he'd still disapprove."

Marisol slowed the car and glanced at her.

"Why? What kind of man is he?"

Luz laughed at the suspicion in her voice. "He's the most honourable, devout and loving man I know, and I'm not good enough for him."

"Is he married?"

"No. Don't worry, I'm not that stupid."

They drove on in silence until Luz blurted it out.

"His name is Tunçay. He's a Turkish waiter and a Muslim."

As the road straightened, opening up the landscape, they both instinctively looked up to see the first view of the Castelo. On so many occasions, the sight had filled Luz with pride, anticipation, impatience and even reluctance, but today was the first time she experienced dread.

Her mother began talking, facing directly ahead. "One thing you will learn from studying a subject such as law is the art of compromise. You are still young, and you should enjoy this time while you have no responsibilities. Celebrate your time with your waiter, making sure to live every moment to its fullest. Later, when you have to face the reality of adulthood, when you must use your head over your heart, when your decisions are practical rather than romantic, you will have some beautiful memories to sustain you."

Luz watched her mother's face, which seemed to shift between soft comprehension and hard certainty. "Do you have some beautiful memories?"

Marisol smiled without taking her eyes from the road. "Yes. And some of them after I married your father." She indicated left, into the driveway of the Castelo.

Luz gazed over the estate and spotted her father leading a group of tourists into the visitors' centre.

Marisol frowned. "What the hell is he doing? He's not supposed to do tours today because we've got enough to do! It's Claudia's job to look after visitors."

"Mama? You won't tell him, will you?"

"No, I don't think that would be wise. And you must give nothing away either. Be the good girl you always have been, give him no reason to suspect. You still have time, Luz. Don't waste it by challenging your father. Now, I'll take your shopping upstairs while you check the bathrooms in the visitors' centre. Toilet paper, air freshener, you know what to do. Then tell your father to come up to the house."

"I will. Thank you, Mama. For everything." She kissed her mother's cheek.

Marisol touched her finger to Luz's lips, half an affectionate gesture, half a reminder. Luz understood.

Chapter 15

"Hey, Beatrice, I reckon you're in there." Kevin sidled up as Aguirre led the party back to the assembly point for tasting. And naturally, shopping.

Jase wiggled his eyebrows and could not suppress a grin. "Play your cards right and you could be going home with more than a plastic cup. He couldn't keep his hands off you."

Beatrice laughed at their semi-salacious teasing. "He is a gentleman and took pity on me, as an older lady on her own. I have to say, he really is a fascinating speaker. Didn't you think?"

"He were all right. But we didn't get the personal touch, see? 'Look at this, Ms Stubbs. Would you like to stand here, Ms Stubbs? This is a superlative view.' Old Aguirre is on t'prowl." Kevin's impression was remarkably accurate. "Well, Beatrice, keep your hand on your ha'penny, that's all I'll say."

Tyler nudged her with an elbow. "I suppose we're dumped now you've hooked yourself a Latino, hey? Typical woman. Three handsome blokes, all fit as a butcher's dog, but no. She's had her head turned by a more expensive vintage."

The lads' protective loyalty amused Beatrice and distracted her from the obvious question. Why would Arturo de Aguirre go out of his way to be charming and solicitous to some dowdy old trout? Unless he knew, or wanted to know, something.

The tour, the sunshine and one glass of white Rioja had finished the Danes off. The British couple headed straight for the shop, so only Beatrice and the boys were graced by the presence of their host. Kevin and Tyler kept exchanging knowing looks, but Jase, with good manners and genuine interest, engaged the man in conversation, allowing Beatrice to make her own assessment.

The man had a presence you could not ignore. His voice sent vibrations through the wooden furniture, his expansive inclusion of everyone worked its charm on even the most suspicious and his anecdotes and incidental facts about the wine made the small group feel fortunate for his insight. Yet, for all his magnetism, it seemed his eyes were drawn to her. She sensed his gaze as she sipped, laughed and checked her watch.

"Señor Aguirre, I need to get a taxi back to Vitoria. Do you happen to have a telephone I could use?"

Tyler put down his glass. "Beatrice, we could give you a lift, if you like. It's no bother. We're staying in Vitoria."

Aguirre beamed at them. "Vitoria? Perfect. I have to collect some items from the city this afternoon. Ms Stubbs, I would be happy to drive you myself. And then, perhaps you and these young gentlemen would allow me to invite you for *pinxtos* in one of our most famous bars. An insider tip, I think you'd say."

He didn't wait for agreement but beckoned the barman to give instructions.

Beatrice ignored all three of the smug expressions surrounding her. "Excuse me, gentlemen. I must just visit the ladies' room."

Stone steps in flip-flops demanded careful concentration, but when a figure crossed the flagstones and disappeared in the direction of the toilets, Beatrice stopped dead. Why was Ana here? She hurried down the steps and opened the door. Immediately, she realised her mistake. The girl placing a bouquet of sweet peas in a vase in front of the mirror had long dark hair, a slender figure and a pleasant smile, but that was as far as the resemblance went. Ana's fine features and glowing skin were absent, replaced by a broad forehead and sallow complexion. Her nose stamped her unmistakeably as Aguirre's daughter, clear as a cattle brand.

Beatrice returned the smile. "*Buenos dias.*"

"*Buenos dias.* I think you're one of the English party, no?"

"That's right. The tour was most entertaining."

The girl's smile seemed to fade a little. "Yes, my father is a great ambassador for Rioja. The UK is our biggest export market, you know."

"So I hear. I'm not surprised. It's a wonderful wine. You must be very proud of him."

"Wonderful, yes. Well, I mustn't detain you. Have a nice day, Ms Stubbs."

"Thank you. You too."

Only as she was washing her hands and inhaling the perfume of the sweet peas did it occur to Beatrice to wonder how the girl had known her name.

She checked her watch as she ascended the steps to join her companions, quite unnecessarily as the growls in her stomach were already announcing lunchtime. The lapse of concentration proved unwise. Her foot didn't clear the step, the flip-flop caught the edge and tipped her forwards onto her knees, and the bridge of her nose connected painfully with stone.

She cried out. Pain shot through her face, her eyes watered and she tasted blood.

"Oh my God! Are you okay?" The girl rushed down the stairs and turned Beatrice to face her. "Let me see." She removed Beatrice's hand from her face and winced. "You have a nosebleed. Come, we need to get ice on that before you get a black eye. These steps! One of these days, someone will sue. Come, can you stand?"

The kitchen, illuminated only by a pale blue fly-killing fluorescent, was a cool and silent oasis of stainless steel. Beatrice sat on a stool, holding kitchen roll to her face while the girl dug in the fridge for ice. Her whole head throbbed, her teeth ached and her knee was already stiffening.

"The ice must be upstairs, behind the bar. Put this on for now while I get some." She handed Beatrice a bag of frozen spinach. The cold went from relief to agony in seconds, springing fresh tears to add to the mess on her face. She kept up the pressure for as long as she could stand it, and then removed the spinach. Again, relief for an instant, before the pulsing pain returned, spreading across her face and into her head.

Loud voices came from outside the door. Aguirre's daughter sounded shrill and determined, although Beatrice couldn't understand a word. The door opened and Aguirre strode across the floor, followed by his daughter.

"Ms Stubbs, I am horrified by this. To have such an accident, here, at the Castelo! I insist on taking you to the hospital personally. I will ensure you get the best treatment, all at my expense. What a terrible thing to happen!"

The girl offered Beatrice ice wrapped in a tea towel, guiding it to her face. The pain, metallic and relentless, forced her eyes to close.

"Keep it on, Ms Stubbs, even if it does hurt. You can go to the hospital, if you want. But I have studied first aid. I can check if it's broken in ten seconds. If it's not, there's no point in going to hospital. You just need to keep it clean and cold and get some rest. What do you think?"

"Luz! Don't be ridiculous." Aguirre's tone bordered on menacing.

His daughter's calm voice held a hint of stubbornness. "It's up to Ms Stubbs."

A voice came from the doorway. "That would be the best solution, I believe. Good afternoon, Ms Stubbs. My name is Marisol de Aguirre. I'm Arturo's wife. I'm so sorry to hear what happened. It must be very painful for you. Luz is right, you should keep the ice on to minimise the bruising. If you will allow her to check, she can either get medical help or simply clean you up and drive you home."

The word 'home' worked like a talisman. "Yes, I think that might be best. You do it, Luz. But please don't hurt me … I have a terribly low pain threshold."

Luz put her hand on Beatrice's. "It will hurt. But as I said, only a couple of seconds."

The woman spoke again. "We will give you some privacy. Come, Arturo."

The door closed, Luz lifted the ice pack and Beatrice whimpered.

By the time Luz had applied butterfly stitches to the cut, cleaned Beatrice's face and found her a T-shirt to replaced the bloodied twin set, the men had gone. On the bar sat an envelope containing a note of heartfelt regret from Aguirre and his wife. Propped next to it was a napkin with Kevin's number scrawled across it. He'd also written the name of their hotel, and 'Let us know how you are' with three kisses. Beatrice tucked both into the carrier bag containing her soiled clothes. Once belted into Luz's Peugeot, she replaced the ice pack against her face.

"How are you feeling?" Luz turned to her as she started the engine.

"Stupid, mostly. With a pounding headache. I need to lie down in a darkened room for a few hours, I think."

"Good idea. I could find no signs of concussion, so a sleep should be just what you need. Which hotel are you staying at in Vitoria?"

"I'm staying with a friend. In Calle Cuchillería. Do you know it?"

"Very well. It has some great bars." She pulled out of the estate and onto the main road. "Is that why you're here? To visit a friend?"

"No, I'm on a sabbatical from my job. Trying to decide if I should take early retirement. So I thought a holiday in Spain and Portugal would be a good way to start."

"Definitely. What do you do?"

Beatrice hesitated. "I'm a detective with the Metropolitan Police in London."

Luz took her eyes off the road to look at Beatrice, her expression hidden by her sunglasses. She turned to face front.

"That sounds like a great job. I admire people like you. It must be fantastic to know you are making the world a better place, every day. That's exactly why I want to work in law. I know your job can't be easy, and neither is pursuing the legal profession, but you are helping people, directly. Why do you want to retire?"

Beatrice considered her response while watching the lush colours of the landscape undulate into the distance.

"You're right. It's not always easy to see it, because I spend most of my time exploring the darker end of society. But yes, we do make a difference. And that's why I'm thinking about retiring. Because I'm not sure I'm good enough."

"Hmm. I'm not sure I'm good enough either. To be honest, law was not my best subject. The important thing for me is that I have passion. I want to help people, fight for them so they get what they deserve. I want to understand their problems and try to do something right. So I will work and work until I am good enough. You should put that ice back on unless you want to look like Rocky."

Beatrice did as she was told. "I wonder why you don't want to follow in your father's footsteps and take over his successful business. He has passion too."

Luz's tone turned acidic. "Yes, a passion for making money. My father is a great showman, Ms Stubbs. Behind the scenes, it's a different story. Now, where are you going after you leave Vitoria? Have you worked out your itinerary?"

Despite her pain, Beatrice recognised the whiff of an opportunity rapidly followed by a changed subject. But she was too tired to care.

The aftermath of adrenalin left Ana sick and light-headed. She shoved her helmet under the seat and locked the bike. The muscles in her legs felt as if she'd been sprinting and her hands shook like she'd been mainlining caffeine. She hesitated. Maybe she should go into the office, talk to people, seek comfort in companionship. Beatrice might not be back for a while. But the draw of her own balcony, her bright, optimistic flat and some peace to think this through won her over and she headed down the street.

Unusually, the constant movement of passers-by and chatter billowing from the bars irritated her. A fleeing child shot into her path. Rather than grabbing him and returning him to his mother, she side-stepped and powered on. The sun beat down, her clothes scratched at her skin and the lure of her cool, empty flat shimmered like a mirage ahead.

She unlocked the front door with a sense of reaching sanctuary and rested her forehead on the cool marble while she waited for the lift. She never usually bothered but today the creaking ascent was exactly what she needed. Had she opted for the steps, her soft footfalls may not have warned the men waiting above. Maybe she would have spotted the shadows looming over the stairwell. The smell of smoke might well have alerted her to her welcoming committee. And then she could have run, fled back out the door, escaped into the cat's cradle of intersecting streets and alleys, and lost her pursuers.

The lift ascended with stately grace, giving Ana several moments to breathe deeply, feeling her tension recede. A satisfying clunk announced her arrival on the fourth floor. She yanked open the doors and stepped outside. Her senses, already sharpened from her earlier encounter, screamed alarm signals. The smell of black tobacco and body odour, the sound of shifting feet and the shapes moving in her direction pumped a chemical reaction to danger and she jerked back into the lift, knowing as she did so, the futility of such a move.

Four of them, two older, two younger. The thick-necked younger one reached out his hand as if to cup her arm. The gesture served two purposes; invitation and threat. She came out of her own accord. One of the older men had a missing finger. Ana wasn't surprised.

She raised her voice. This was one occasion when nosy neighbours could prove useful.

"Right. I've had enough of this. What do you want? I should report you to the police for harassment. I know it was you in that ..."

Thick-neck smiled and guided her forward to her own front door with his right hand on her back and his left jabbing a blade under her ribcage.

The greying, saggy-faced older man spoke with a weary bluntness. "Let us into the apartment and keep your mouth shut."

She spent several seconds fumbling for her keys, still hoping a neighbour might intervene; perhaps an enquiry would float down from an upper floor, an act of casual curiosity could rescue her. The other young meathead took her bag, snatched up the keys and had the door open in seconds.

Thick-neck slid his arm around her waist and looked down the neck of her shirt. With a shit-eating grin, he jerked his head towards her apartment. "Ladies first."

He shoved her into the hallway. She turned to face the four men as they approached. Missing Finger was smoking. The saggy-faced guy indicated the door and the meathead, still holding her bag, locked it. Thick-neck stood openly leering at her.

Missing Finger spoke. "Ana, go back to Portugal. That's an order."

Ana found her voice. "Fuck you."

He exhaled a foul cloud of smoke in her direction. "Funny you should say that. To be honest, it's all the same to me. Go back to Portugal, stay here in Spain. I don't care. But the boys ..." he looked at the two thugs. "The boys would prefer it if you stayed. Because if you disobey me, they will be responsible for your punishment. And it seems your minds are running along the same lines."

He lowered himself into an armchair and without taking his eyes from her, nodded his permission. The saggy-faced one folded his arms and leant against the wall as the two thugs, practically salivating, approached her.

Chapter 16

Calle Cuchillería swarmed with activity. Everyone was dressed up, made up and ready to be seen. Couples, families and groups of young men strolled past the bars and cafés, stopping to greet friends, kiss cheeks and shake hands every few paces.

Luz had repeated her instructions regarding painkillers and herbal teas several times, apparently reluctant to let Beatrice go. Eventually, after extracting a promise of a phone call the following day, she got back in the car and left. Beatrice made her way to Ana's flat, passing restaurants and street vendors emanating aromas which would normally cause an inevitable delay. Today, however, she needed her bedroom, a cup of tea and a mirror to check the extent of the damage.

The lift seemed even slower than before, but four flights of stairs was out of the question. The ice pack, now soggy and uncomfortable, dripped onto the lino by her feet. Eventually, the lift released her to do battle with Ana's apartment door. This time, the door won. Each time the lock seemed to give, another barrier prevented it from opening. Defeated, Beatrice rang the bell and waited. After a full minute of silence, she rapped on the wood, already rehearsing her apology. She was reaching for her mobile when she heard a bolt withdrawn.

The door opened. Beatrice stood back to allow an ugly, grizzled individual to come out. Unsmiling, he stared at her and passed by. He was followed by a hefty farmer-like man in a white shirt, who jerked his head in acknowledgement, and two lumps practising Elvis-type sneers. They moved down the stairs, the last two throwing aggressive looks back up at her. Beatrice rushed into the apartment, locked the door and followed the sounds of vomiting to the bathroom.

Twenty minutes later, after opening all the windows to get rid of the smell of smoke, Beatrice perched on the edge of the sofa and listened to Ana's story. A sense of panic escalated as all her previous perspectives shifted and shattered. The unencumbered freedom of the scooter became vulnerability, people's friendly assistance twisted into sly observation and the sense of solidarity engendered by their collaboration dissipated like the steam off her tea. They were no safer than a pair of kittens on a six-lane motorway.

"So after you shook them off in the park ..."

"I made a massive mistake. I came home."

Beatrice stomach convulsed. "Oh my God. They were waiting for you. Did they hurt you at all? Ana? Did they hurt you?"

Ana drew her top lip into her mouth and shook her head.

"No. They came in, made some unsubtle threats and told me to go back to Portugal. If not, I have to take the consequences."

Her tone was casual but Beatrice observed the girl's demeanour. Legs crossed, or more like wrapped around one another like pipe-cleaners. Her arms crossed her chest, gripping shoulder and elbow, in an attitude of defensiveness and fear. Beatrice felt as if she'd swallowed an ice cube. She slid off the sofa and moved closer to Ana. A memory surfaced, of watching a children's counsellor interact with a frightened teen. She allowed the recollection to guide her movements and didn't attempt to touch Ana, kneeling instead beside the armchair.

"Ana, what did they do?"

The girl shook her head, rubbing her upper arms as if she were cold. "Nothing. You turned up and rang the doorbell, thanks be to God. If you'd been any later ... oh, let's not talk about it. There's no real harm done."

"Of course. I don't want to push you."

A silence expanded into the space between them. Beatrice felt foolish, kneeling on the floor in sympathy, but instinct told her to wait a few more seconds.

Ana's voice, when it came, was tight. "They didn't hurt me. Just gave me a taste of what would happen if I refused to leave. Bit of manhandling to let me know who holds the power, that's all. It was enough."

"I'll make some more tea and then perhaps we should consider our next steps." Beatrice's knee protested as she rose, so she used the armrest to help herself upright. She was surprised to feel Ana's cold hand cover hers.

"Beatrice, I've been honest. No rape, no violence, just some inappropriate touching and heavy threats. Now will you do me the same courtesy and tell me what really happened to you?"

"I fell up the steps. Honestly. These bloody stupid flip-flops tripped me and I smacked my face on a lump of stone. Clumsy, yes, but sinister, no. What happened here frightens me far more."

Ana looked at her, nodding slowly.

"You're right. You don't need this bullshit. Look, you're very good and you've been generous with your time. I really appreciate all your help, but I've held you up long enough. I'm going to take a break and return to Portugal, so it might be time for you to move on with your trip. We've reached the end of the road."

Beatrice sat in her room, or rather Ana's guest room and acknowledged her duty. Her conscience, which she'd been able to drown out by constant activity, took full advantage of the meditative silence. *Call him*. She'd left it far too long and apart from anything else, it was bad manners. With a glance at the clock, she picked up her mobile.

"Beatrice! How lovely to hear from you. I'm so relieved you called."

Bubbles of unanticipated pleasure fizzed upwards, countering the leaden pull of homesickness. She missed him. She needed him. Why had she waited so long?

"James, you're very kind. Rather than reprimanding me for missing our last session, you sound as if you're actually pleased to hear from me."

"I most definitely am pleased to hear from you. Although I

should say that I have another client due in about ten minutes, so a full consultation will not be possible right now."

"Oh, I didn't expect one. Phoning you out of the blue and expecting you to have a free hour would be downright rude. No, it's just a quick call to tell you I decided to take the sabbatical after all. Which is why I missed my last appointment. I'm in Spain at the moment and plan to travel around till I get fed up."

He took a few seconds to respond. "I see. I hope you have a relaxing and contemplative holiday. Can I ask what you had in mind regarding our ongoing treatment?"

With a grimace, Beatrice knew she should have thought about that. She hadn't and James knew it.

"Well, I was wondering if we could have chats over the phone, instead. We've done that before, remember."

"I do remember. That's certainly possible. I have a couple of practical concerns, but they can wait. I have the feeling this is more than a courtesy call, Beatrice. Is there anything you'd like to talk about?"

Seconds ticked past as Beatrice considered her reply.

James prompted her. "Any indications as to your state of mind are always welcome."

"My state of mind? I'm watching an abyss open up. This situation is complicated and not entirely relevant, but it makes me feel helpless. Exactly the problem I was facing before. I will never be able to protect all of them, so what's the point? What is the point of any of this? Right now, the world seems callous, James. Just selfish and brutal in pursuit of its own interests. On top of that, institutions which supposedly stand for truth and justice and honour are infected with the same individualistic point-scoring as everywhere else so I really don't know why I bother feeling any obligation to do my duty."

"I may have misunderstood, but I thought you were on holiday. Whom exactly is it your duty to protect? Have you adopted a colony of Catalonian cats?"

Beatrice laughed, acknowledging James's accurate analogy. "Not cats. But I offered to advise on a missing persons' case. I tell you what, James, it's no fun working a line of enquiry as a civilian."

"Which leads me to ask, why do it? I understood the offer of a sabbatical was to take a break from your routine, to use the time to reflect and consider your future."

Again, Beatrice dug deep for an honest response, but time ran out on her.

"Beatrice, I'm sorry, but my next client is due. And I think we need more than a few minutes to unpack what you've just said. I have a slot on Friday. Could you call me at eight-thirty?"

"Yes, of course. Sorry to hog your time like this."

"Please don't apologise. I'd rather know how you are than not. Between now and Friday's conversation, I'd like you to think about three things. What is the aim of this sabbatical? How is your current choice of action furthering that aim? How would Matthew and Hamilton react if they knew? And how does that affect you?"

"That's four things."

"You can have the last one for free. Half past eight UK time on Friday, okay?"

"Thank you James. It's kind of you to fit me in. I'll try to be better by then."

"You don't need to be 'better'. Just honest."

He made it sound easy.

A tap on the door pulled her from a fretful doze. Still fully dressed, she lay on top of the quilt, trying to recall her peculiar dream when the tap came again.

"Hello?"

Ana's voice came through the wood. "Sorry to wake you, Beatrice. Can I come in?"

"Of course. I'm decent." Beatrice swung her feet to the floor and rubbed her face.

The woman who entered the room was wholly altered. The tense, haunted creature had disappeared, replaced by a determined expression in jeans and a leather jacket.

She smiled as she came into the room and stood with her hands on her hips in front of Beatrice. "I heard you on the phone before. Have you made arrangements to leave?"

A warm flush crept up Beatrice's throat. "No, I suppose I should ..."

"Good. We might need to rethink this. I had a couple of calls while you were resting. The police went public with the identity of the body this afternoon. Jaime, bless him, called me first to break the news. The story runs tomorrow."

"And cause of death?"

"Accident. No mention of the mutilation. So we know the police are hiding the truth. But more importantly, Armando got back to me. Seems Miguel Saez was onto something. Come on, we're going to *El Papagaio* to eat lunch and create a smokescreen."

Chapter 17

"Ana! Beatrice! Finally!" Enrique's pleasure at their arrival seemed heartfelt. He clapped a hand to his chest. "Oh Beatrice! Your face!"

"I tripped up some steps. My own fault for wearing ridiculous shoes."

"You poor woman. On your holiday as well. Where have you two been? I haven't seen you all week."

"Sorry Enrique. You know how it is." Ana's smile disappeared so fast it might not have even been there. The girl was quite a performer.

Concern rippled across Enrique's face. "Have you news of Tiago?"

Ana nodded, her face scrunched up she covered her eyes. Right on time, Beatrice put an arm around her shoulders and pulled a sympathetic face. Enrique hurried from behind the bar, shielding them from the inquisitive stares of his other customers.

"Come, sit at the back, it's quieter. I'll bring drinks."

Ana looked up, her eyes glistening, her forehead creased. "Tiago's dead, Enrique. He had an accident and fell. I just heard this afternoon."

All animation and colour drained from Enrique's face. "*No puede ser*! Not Tiago? When was this?"

Ana shrugged as if the timing was an irrelevance.

"You need something for the shock. Sit, sit." He rushed back to the bar, snapping an order at a young waiter, who tore himself away from the TV and trudged through to the back.

Beatrice dropped her voice. "That was amazing. You convinced me completely."

"It wasn't only an act. Tiago was one of the sweetest, gentlest men I ever met. I'm going to miss him."

Shame burst over Beatrice like prickly heat. "Ana, I'm sorry. I didn't mean to be so insensitive ..."

"It's fine. I've not yet cried for him, so I may as well take the opportunity to grieve when it's most useful. See? Not entirely heartless but always practical. Here he comes."

Enrique set a bottle of red on the table with two glasses. On his upper arm, he wore a black armband. He tapped it, met their eyes and nodded with theatrical woe.

"Today, you are my guests. You will drink a fine Rioja, eat the best I can offer and say goodbye to our friend."

Ana gave him a weak smile. "Thank you. It's a double goodbye, in fact. I'm leaving Vitoria. The loss of Tiago ... I can't explain it. I just want to go home for a while."

Enrique shook his head. "For me, this is a second blow. The tragic death of that fine young man and now you, one of my favourites, go back to Portugal. Today is a sad day. Very sad for all of us."

He returned to the bar, maintaining his pained air even as he continued to serve his curious clientele. His explanations involved lots of head-shaking and sorrowful glances in the direction of their table.

Beatrice poured the wine. "How does he know that 'home' means Portugal?"

"Everyone knows where I come from. I speak reasonable Castilian, but if I get stuck, I simply use Portuguese with a Spanish accent. They call it my *Portañol*. He's not given us anything new by that."

"Hmm. Did he react as you imagined? He learns of an acquaintance's death, provides food and puts on an armband. I appreciate the offer of sustenance might be a cultural trait, but I find it very peculiar that he asked no questions."

Ana sniffed the wine, nodding. "Me too. That's not normal behaviour. Every time I've interviewed someone even loosely connected to an unexpected death, the first thing people want is the details – how. Enrique asked only one question – when. Why would it matter when Tiago died, unless it was Sunday night and so connected to *El Papagaio*?"

The young waiter approached bearing a heavy copper tureen. He placed it between them and lifted the lid. "*Paella, señoras. Buen provecho!*"

The golden rice, studded with prawns, clams, peas, mussels, peppers, lemon wedges and chicken sat in a bath of fragrant stock. Beatrice looked across at Enrique. Despite her suspicions of his various sins such as lying, dissembling and ham acting, she acknowledged his gift with a happy grin. The tragic lines fell away from his face and he blew them both a kiss before placing his hand on his chest, shaking his head and adopting his grief mask once more.

The waiter served a portion each, brought a breadbasket and returned to his spot to watch the football. Determined to devote at least four of her senses to the feast in front of her, Beatrice lent Ana her ears.

"Your cousin. What did he say about the accountant's books?"

Ana kept her head down, but a slow smile crept across her face. "What do you think of the wine?"

With exaggerated respect, Beatrice lifted her glass to the light, wafted the rim under her nose and finally took a careful sip.

"Magenta and ruby, fading to a cerise rim. No hint of tawny. Nose, a riot of summer fruits with some leather, earth and French oak. Textured and creamy with structured tannins which do not dominate the end palate, leaving us with caramel and burnt toast. A deeply satisfying glass. I suggest paella as the perfect accompaniment."

She dug her fork into the steaming mass and was about to lift it to her mouth when she caught Ana's gesture. Holding the bottle by the neck, Ana twisted the label to face Beatrice.

Castelo de Aguirre Gran Reserva 2009

Beatrice began to eat. Ana began to talk.

"Do you know how much Rioja is produced every year? I'll tell you. The region produces just under 200 million litres of red, over 100 million of white, with around 15 of rosé. It used to be around 300 million of red and very little else."

This much Beatrice knew. "So white is on the up. Largely due to Aguirre and his operation. Are you not going to eat?"

"I'm in shock, remember. I'll grieve here and get a kebab on the way home. It does smell gorgeous, though. Force a couple of mouthfuls down me and don't take no for an answer."

An elaborate Kabuki performance ensued, after which Beatrice felt she'd earned a part in any major mimed soap opera. Ana, for her part, affected great reluctance and misery while making enthusiastic noises of enjoyment.

Ana: (drops head onto fist) Jesus, these prawns taste like a fishy bicep. Pass me another, would you?

Beatrice: (opens pleading palms) Wait till you get to the clams. Melt in your mouth. Do you want some bread? (offers breadbasket, squeezes hand)

Ana: (shakes head sadly) Is the Pope Catholic? Tear me off a chunk and pass it over.

Beatrice: Grief steals the appetite but the bereaved often take to drink. Do you want a top up? It really is a divine wine.

Ana: (wipes away fictional tears): For authenticity's sake, I suppose I can't refuse.

Enrique and his punters proved an attentive audience, observing and remarking on each gesture with less than covert analysis. Many heads joined Enrique in the regretful shake.

"Right, so Miguel's figures focused on exports. Our friend," she tapped the bottle, "is the leading exporter of white Rioja. His marketing pitch makes a massive deal of the Viura grape. Apparently it forms 80% of every bottle of Aguirre white."

"Exactly what I heard on the tour. He grows almost exclusively white grapes as the Control Board permits a greater density per hectare than red."

Ana focused on Beatrice, her eyes sharp. "Do you remember the numbers?"

"No. And you look far too cheerful. Now dab your eyes and tell me."

Ana pressed a napkin to the bridge of her nose and talked almost as quickly as if she were speaking Spanish.

"No wine-grower can produce more than seven thousand kilos of grapes per hectare. Not if they want the official Rioja seal. Aguirre has just under sixty-five hectares. So his maximum output can only be around ninety million litres. Most, but not all of which is white. And out of the total yield, most vineyards sell two thirds to the domestic market. The figures Miguel found at Alava Exports showed that Aguirre's vineyard exported seventy-three million litres. Not simply white Rioja, but Viura."

"Numbers aren't my strong point. But it seems the bloke sells more of his stuff abroad than he does at home. So his worst crime is disloyalty?"

Ana dropped the napkin but kept her hands in a prayer gesture over her nose and mouth. "More like fraud. He also sells fifty-eight million litres in Spain. Numbers aren't my strong point either, but I can add seventy-three to fifty-eight. Comes to more than his maximum yield of ninety-one. Someone's getting shafted, Beatrice, and I doubt it's the Spanish."

Beatrice remembered the spotlight and handed Ana a tissue while considering the implications. She imagined the outrage of her favourite connoisseurs if they heard.

"So while you go to Portugal, should I go back to the police?"

"I'm not going to Portugal and you're not going to the police. Come here to me and listen. I've delayed you long enough. Go on holiday. I'm more grateful for your help than I can say, but I can't ask you for more."

"Without that first sentence, I might have agreed. I'm not comfortable leaving at this point. However, since I'm your guest, you could always throw me out, onto the street, like an unwanted old moggy ..."

"If you make me laugh, our performance is knackered. Thing is, I really don't want you to go, but I can't think of any good reason to keep you. If you would hang on a few more days, though, I'd be more grateful than you can imagine."

Beatrice reached for her hand, this time for a genuine reason.

Ana squeezed back. "Thing is, we have to get out of my apartment. For our own safety. Perhaps Jaime would let us stay at his place."

"There's a thought."

Ana's eyes crinkled. "You'd better behave yourself, mind. As well as being easy on the eye, he's a decent bloke and has some useful contacts. You know what, we could really do with comparing the export wine to the stuff Aguirre sells here. Do you know anyone in the wine trade?"

"As a matter of fact, I do. And he would just love the thought of offering his expertise. I'll give Adrian a ring when we get back."

"Great. Shit." Ana's shoulders shook, her face crumpled and she held out her arms. "Enrique's coming. Give me a hug."

Chapter 18

"Oh my God! What the hell happened?"

"It's fine, Jaime. My nose became intimately acquainted with some stone steps. I fell over. Nothing broken but I know it doesn't look pretty."

As if remembering his manners, Jaime leant in to kiss Beatrice. He smelt of coffee and cigarettes, a surprisingly attractive combination. She offered both cheeks and inhaled.

"Welcome, Beatrice. I'm very happy to see you again." He searched her face. "Are you sure you're all right?"

"Yes. Really. Probably because of the painkillers. It's very kind of you to put us up. I was quite prepared to book a hotel, but I must confess, I feel far safer here. It's awfully good of you."

"Not at all. I'm glad I could help. I told Ana on the phone, I'd rather know you were safe. For me, it's a pleasure to have guests. A boring bachelor doesn't often receive visitors, so this gives me a chance to practise my cooking. Have you eaten?"

"We had lunch, but that was a while back. And I'm sure Ana's still hungry. Where has she got to? She was only supposed to pay the taxi driver."

With that, something crunched into a wall followed by a foreign expletive. Beatrice and Jaime walked back along the corridor to find Ana wrestling with Beatrice's suitcase, plus her own two bags.

Jaime shot Beatrice a wicked grin. "Here, let me take that. Otherwise you'll damage the paintwork."

Ana thrust the handle towards him. "Bugger the paintwork. Your lift is out of order. And so are you, Beatrice Stubbs. I swear to God that case is even heavier than before. What the hell have you got in there?"

"Inappropriate shoes, mostly, and a few souvenirs. The Guggenheim had the most wonderful pottery."

"You're travelling round Spain dragging a suitcase full of crockery?"

They followed Jaime into his flat, a large gloomy space with minimal furnishings and a surfeit of electronics. But it was clean and tidy and smelt of furniture polish.

As if he'd read her thoughts, Jaime said, "I'm afraid the place was a bit of a mess. So I've been cleaning since you called. You should come around more often. Now, are you hungry?"

Ana dropped her bags inside the doorway. "I could eat the leg of the Lamb of God and come back for its tail. Beatrice, how about yourself?"

The sun set, filling Jaime's apartment with golden-pink light as they sat around the remains of roast chicken in sherry sauce. He listened to the whole story with careful attention. Like Ana, he seemed initially suspicious of the explanation for Beatrice's puffy eyes and butterfly stitched nose, but accepted it after Beatrice repeated her tale twice. He offered his unconditional assistance, asked dozens of questions and smoked several cigarettes. The only time his composure wobbled was when he heard the truth about Tiago. He placed his hands over his eyes and seemed to wrestle for control. Eventually, he lifted his head.

"You should have told me. Tiago should have … oh shit, this is such a mess. Ana, this isn't some scoop about dodgy politicians or footballers having underage sex. If what you say is true, Tiago was killed for chasing this story. And you two carry on as if …" He lit another cigarette, shaking his head.

"Jaime, listen …"

"No, Ana, just shut the fuck up for a second. Sorry, Beatrice. But you must understand how dangerous this situation is. If Tiago was murdered, whoever did it wants the story as dead as he is. We have to be extremely careful. Neither of you should be seen in Vitoria. If there's any further investigation to be done, we'll find another way.

The paper can't afford to make an enemy of Arturo de Aguirre, but nor can we afford to lose an exposé like this."

Lit up by the rose-coloured sky, Ana's eyes blazed in the autumn sun. "If it is fraud, it is on an industrial scale, and will have repercussions all the way along the chain. This will go national and probably international. We'd better be prepared to take some heat."

Jaime stretched his arms above his head, which, Beatrice noted, tightened the muscles across his chest. His shirt, made of some heavy cream material, strained at the press studs.

"I'm ready for that. The paper can handle it." He relaxed his stretch and pointed at them with his cigarette. "But you two, as individuals, are far too vulnerable. Now listen to me. Both of you. I want you to promise that neither of you will do anything, say anything, or call anyone without telling me first. We need to work as a team and that means no individual risks. OK?"

They promised.

He gave them a quarter-smile. "*Vale.* Now, I'd like to take a coffee. There's a nice café at the end of my street, if you ladies would like to join me."

Beatrice still found this habit very odd. Heading out into the streets at the time she'd normally be donning her pyjamas.

"If you don't mind, I think I might stay here and lie down a while. Today has been rather hard work and a beast of a headache has begun."

Jaime's deep blue eyes were full of concern. "Of course. You look really pale. Ana can take the guest room, but I've put you in my bed. I'll sleep in the study. Don't argue, there's a sofa where I often fall asleep if I'm working late. The bathroom is through the door on the left."

"You do look peaky, Beatrice. Will I get you some more painkillers while we're out?"

"No need, thanks. I have some spares in my bag. I'll see if I can sleep it off before taking any more. Jaime, you're extremely kind and I'm very grateful."

"Don't mention it. I hope you sleep well, Beatrice, and feel lots better tomorrow." He bent forward and kissed her forehead.

She sat on Jaime's bed, listening to the sounds of them leaving the building. Beautiful eyes, great cook, generous personality and the softest lips. Why on earth was he living alone?

Chapter 19

Rain lashed the panes as if someone were repeatedly hurling a bucketful at the window. Adrian stood with his hands on his hips, frowning at Boot Street. The view outside was a colourful blur, as umbrellas bobbed along the pavement like petals floating downstream. A piquant waft of *jamon iberica* from the meat platter on the table caused him to inhale and close his eyes. The doorbell rang. Even though he'd been waiting impatiently for over an hour, it startled him. He buzzed his visitor into the building and unlocked the flat door.

Wet patches darkened the shoulders of Matthew's mud-green jacket, his hair dripped down his face and his shoes oozed water onto the hall carpet. He looked every inch like an eccentric English university professor and smelt like a spaniel fresh from the river. Adrian shook his head as he reached for Matthew's suitcase.

"No umbrella?"

"Left the wretched thing on the train. I'll take my shoes off out here."

As Adrian returned with two bath towels, Matthew wiped the water from his face with reddened hands. Affection overpowered Adrian's annoyance and concern for soft furnishings.

"You need to get out of those wet things. Immediately."

Matthew nodded. "Yes. I don't want to catch a cold."

"Not only that, but the whiff would overpower any kind of accurate tasting."

The miserable expression lifted. "Oh, you managed to get some then?"

"Did you doubt I would? Now, go and change and I'll make you a hot toddy."

Some time back, a *Color Me Beautiful* consultant had identified Adrian as winter. His colouring, sharp and distinctive, apparently allowed him to wear bolder hues; black and white, berry and jewel. The system intrigued him, so he read up on it and reorganised his wardrobe accordingly. Customers who came through the door of the Hoxton Wine Emporium were mentally assigned a season in under ten seconds. Adrian took no formal training in the science of complementary tones, merely employing natural good taste and excellent instincts. He was rarely wrong.

Matthew, despite having all the fashion sense of a goat, had also discovered his true palette. Moss, rust, olive and taupe, the colours of a kitchen garden, complemented his chocolate eyes and warm skin as he sat opposite, sipping from a Villeroy & Boch mug. The lemon juice, honey and Aberfeldy did the trick and Matthew glowed with enthusiasm while Adrian explained how his Spanish ex-boyfriend had arranged for a case of Castelo de Aguirre white Viura to be delivered direct from Rioja country.

"He's the perfect one to call, because his current squeeze is a trucker who works the continental routes. Paolo's tastes generally run to rough trade, you see. I must have been an exception. Anyway, the trucker picked up a case en route and it got here in less time than it took you to travel up from Devon."

"Well done. And please express my gratitude to Paolo and his timely trucker. So if the goods are here, perhaps we should perform the experiment?"

"Why not? And if our results are conclusive, we can call Beatrice back this afternoon. Are you feeling better?"

Matthew stood. "Thoroughly restored, thank you. Just curious and a little peckish."

"I can meet both those basic needs. We have a selection of Spanish meats, a quality Manchego, roasted peppers, chilli almonds and a baguette fresh from the oven. I went for the terroir concept. But rather than sully our buds beforehand, shall we taste first?"

Matthew rubbed his hands together. "Superlative plan. I assume the wine is chilled?"

Adrian gave him an arch look before leading the way to the kitchen.

On the central island lay a white linen napkin, six Riedel wine glasses, two water glasses, two ballpoint pens and two brand-new notepads purchased that morning at Paperchase. Adrian's preparations, as ever, were thoroughly thought through.

Matthew seated himself on a breakfast stool and adopted a certain critical air. For his part, Adrian was unconcerned. In certain fields, such as wine and musical theatre, Adrian remained the uncontested expert. Even more so since opening his own emporium. Matthew took off his glasses to read the label on each bottle, observed the extraction of all three corks and studied the elderflower-coloured liquid as it rose to a third of the way up the glass.

The pair began a practised routine. Each lifting their first glass to the light, they studied the colour. Adrian replaced his on the napkin and wrote a brief description. Pale, more hay than straw, vaguest hint of green? Matthew raised his to the window, tilting it at various angles a moment longer before turning to his notebook. By which time Adrian was assessing the bouquet. Holding the stem so as not to affect the temperature, he swirled the wine around the bowl, using minute revolutions of the wrist. He passed the glass under his nose, on the inhale. Some lemon, green beans, and blossom. Cut grass? He pressed his nose deeper into the bowl. Camomile, apricot and asparagus.

He set down the wine and wrote detailed impressions on nose. Lastly, the attack. He rolled the liquid around his mouth, giving each taste bud its chance. Elegance, some honey, a whisper of apple. Pleasant acidity, light and dry. The taste developed depth, revealing more of the fruit as green apple, balanced by a floral sweetness. After swallowing, the mouthfeel lengthened into a spice. Baked apple?

He returned his attention to Matthew, who finished scrawling in tiny handwriting and looked up with a smile. "We'll compare later, of course, but that was a wholly pleasurable experience."

Adrian bowed his head in acknowledgement. "That was the original. The Aguirre white Rioja sold in Spain. Now for the exports. I have two samples; one from my own supplier, Imperial Wines and another sourced from Grapemeister."

He poured them both some water, they drank and began again. The routine followed the pattern exactly until Matthew took his first sip. Adrian, still trying to define the exact nose, had fallen behind and when Matthew placed his glass back on the napkin as if he'd been poisoned, Adrian's first reaction was offence.

"Oh, please, Matthew. I accept you might not like it quite as much, but this is a product from my own shop. I chose to stock this so it can't possibly be as rank as that expression of yours makes out."

Matthew wasn't listening, instead pulling the napkin from around the neck of the bottle and examining the label once more.

Adrian took a sip, rolled the liquid around for three seconds and swallowed quickly so he could speak.

"That could be a supermarket blend-in-a-box! There must have been a mistake."

"A little harsh, but it is far from the same wine."

"Matthew, I take my choice of stock seriously. There is no way I would have selected this. I never buy on mere strength of name. I taste. I go there and taste."

Matthew steepled his hands under his chin. "Right. One more to go. And if the gap between the two remains as startling, we may need a whistle to blow."

Adrian returned from his office with a print-out and stood in front of Matthew, raising his eyebrows in enquiry. Matthew glanced at the paper, gave the thumbs-up and returned his attention to the telephone, through which he reassured Beatrice.

"Absolutely. I think you could say we learnt our lesson last time, Old Thing. Yes, I know and we're only coming over to act as consultant oenologists. Just for the weekend, that's all. I have to get back to Exeter and Adrian's colleague has only agreed to cover till Monday. But we are both convinced our expertise will be beneficial ..."

Adrian held the print-out in front of Matthew's face, pointing out the flight times before indicating his watch.

"Ah. Now, it seems we really have to step on it if we're to make these flights. Sorry? No, no, Adrian has arranged a hotel, but perhaps you'd like to make a dinner reservation? We'll be with you by teatime. I'd lean to seafood this evening, but if you have ..."

Adrian sighed and flapped the papers.

"Must dash. See you this evening. Jolly well looking forward to it. Bye for now."

The doorbell rang.

Adrian picked up his hastily packed suitcase. Fortunately, his skill at packing for a mini-break was honed through practice. "That'll be the taxi. An extravagance, I know, but it's still raining. Come on, Matthew, Beatrice needs us."

Chapter 20

Beatrice needed to calm down. She'd taken her mood stabilisers every day, but because of the irregular routine of the past week, her timing was all over the place. And now, she was like a hyperactive child. Even knowing that this phase would inevitably be followed by a dip, she couldn't summon up any sobering anxiety. The most frustrating thing when she felt sociable, extrovert and animated was spending the majority of the day alone.

By the time Beatrice woke, Jaime had already left for work. Ana was pacing the kitchen, speaking Spanish on her phone. After helping herself to coffee, Beatrice's first priority was to check the damage to her face. Her left eye was swollen and the colour of an overripe damson. The right looked far from normal but no worse than if she had a stye in it. The bridge of her nose had bled in the night, leaving a dark dried crust around the stitches. She looked bloody awful, but apart from a constantly throbbing face and a very stiff knee, she felt fantastic.

Ana made a series of phone calls to arrange meetings for the following day and then dressed herself for Tiago's funeral. Black suited her; the sadness in her eyes less so. Jaime returned to pick her up at ten, as the funeral was taking place in Tiago's home village, near Pamplona. In a narrow black suit with shoestring tie and messy hair, Jaime looked like an extra from *A Fistful of Dollars*.

He flashed those astounding teeth and took her hand. "Be careful, Beatrice. I think it would be better if you stayed here till we return. Remember, no risks."

She saw them off with a sigh. Probably the only occasion in her life on which she actually wanted to go to the funeral of a complete stranger. Matthew and Adrian were due to arrive in Bilbao at three o'clock, but then she had to wait for the bus to deliver them to Vitoria.

Five hours and nothing to do. Jaime's apartment was the average single male's abode, purely functional and unless you liked video games, a little depressing. Like a student's flat. For the editor of a newspaper, he didn't seem to have much in the way of books. She mooched about, idly examining the few framed cuttings which she couldn't read, opening kitchen cupboards, looking out over the city from the second floor balcony and checking out the wardrobe. Denim, leather, embroidered shirts, cowboy boots; she wondered if he might be into line-dancing. Telling herself she was looking for something to pass the time, she decided to take a peek at Jaime's study. She found it locked, to her surprise and immediate guilt. *Why would he lock it, unless he didn't trust ... oh.*

Time to go out. She'd stay on the main streets, potter about in the city, keeping her head down and later find somewhere to have lunch. That could hardly be seen as breaking her promise to take no risks. Her mood lifted still further as she collected her handbag, checked she had the key and headed out into the streets.

But she'd forgotten about her face. Everywhere she went people stared, or winced, or gave sympathetic smiles; she certainly was drawing attention to herself. After a while, she began to avoid eye contact until she realised that keeping her focus on the ground would be counter-productive to remaining alert and thus safe. Her optimism for the day soured and the low sun seemed unnecessarily bright, so she gave up. The only useful thing she managed was to buy a pair of trainers and sports socks to protect her feet. Just as she turned back towards the apartment, an idea occurred. Sunglasses. They worked wonders, reducing the staring and softening the glare. Why did it take her so long to think of these things? Half an hour later, she'd purchased something suitably Jackie O which didn't hurt her nose. By which time her headache had returned.

The walk back was not as easy as she had imagined. She'd over-estimated her familiarity with the layout of Vitoria and found herself going in circles around every country in South America. Calle Argentina, Calle Chile, Calle Ecuador, and when she eventually found Calle Bolivia, it was not the place she had left that morning. She felt like Patrick McGoohan. Disorientation, heat and her throbbing nose combined to turn stress into a growing panic. She followed the street again and noticed that Calle Bolivia was not a dead-end, as it first appeared. A footpath led through to another street, also called Calle Bolivia. Beatrice still wasn't exactly sure where she was, but her instinct told her to turn right. As the road curved around, she recognised the building ahead. She'd been gazing at it that very morning, from Jaime's balcony. She lifted her eyes towards the block across the road, seeking Jaime's apartment. She wasn't the only one.

Two men stood outside the apartment block, also looking up at the second floor. Beatrice stopped. She couldn't see them clearly, but the matching hefty physiques, shades and dark suits seemed familiar. She slipped behind a tree to observe the situation. Everything fell away; the heat, the pain in her face, her dry mouth, the slick moisture of her hands on the carrier bag, as her training and experience kicked in. She focused on each detail. One of the men walked up to the door and rang one of the buzzers. He waited, listening, while his colleague kept his head tilted back, watching the apartment.

If these were the muscle-bound Rottweilers who had so frightened Ana, where were their handlers? Possibly watching her watching them? Beatrice scanned the street, her pulse rapid and her breathing short. A dark blue Mercedes, Ana had said. Most of the cars were white, with the odd silver or red vehicle. Further along, some darker colours stood out, but they were too far away to be distinguishable. The doorbell ringer returned to the street and a grunty conversation ensued. They turned and swaggered in the opposite direction to Beatrice, glancing backwards and upwards with ostentatious suspicion. She followed, with extreme caution, using trees, vans and advertising hoardings as cover, until she saw them stop beside one of the darker sedans; a Mercedes.

Of course. Anyone returning from the city would come up the street that way, passing the Mercedes first. Simply due to her erroneous sense of direction, Beatrice had come the other way. She started to retreat, pausing to check she had not attracted attention. The pair of thugs stood smoking and waiting, keeping their attention on

Jaime's building, talking to the occupants of the car. Beatrice turned the corner and started to speed-walk while dialling Ana's number. Straight to voicemail. The clock said eleven-fifty. They were probably already at the church. She left a message and looked around, wondering what to do next. Alone in a city where she knew no one.

Almost no one.

The napkin was a little worse for wear from being stuffed at the bottom of her handbag, but the number was legible. Beatrice kept walking as she dialled.

"Hello, is that Kev? This is Beatrice, the clumsy woman you met on the wine tour. Just wondering what you're up to today? Do you happen to have any plans for lunch?"

The Artium was an inspired idea. Cool, quiet and displaying so much of interest on the walls, Beatrice's face barely attracted a second glance. She pottered around for over an hour before the lads arrived, and had only seen a fraction of the vast collection. Yet one thing had already made an impression. The glaring gap between 1936 and 1940. It wasn't the only glaring gap. Her knowledge of the Spanish Civil War was gleaned from writers such as Laurie Lee and Jessica Mitford. The Artium's extensive library would be able to set her straight, but Beatrice hesitated.

Past experience had taught her the danger of comprehending history. Knowledge with the aim of learning lessons was all well and good, but exploring a tragic period in a nation's past, coupled with excessive empathy, could be devastating. One of her worst black holes since 'the incident' had occurred after visiting the *Umschlagplatz* in Warsaw. All those first names carved onto a white wall, representing 300,000 individuals transported from that very platform to the Treblinka gas chambers. The horror and enormity of scale penetrated her bones. She was unable to speak for three days, while Matthew paced corridors, called doctors and tried everything to stop her tears.

No, not the library. *Because history is more than dates and artefacts. History is human.* Instead, she chose to explore the gift shop, a place bright and lively enough to distract her from the welling blackness inside. She bought presents for both Matthew's daughters, for Adrian and for herself, but nothing seemed exactly right for Matthew. So just before two o'clock, she paid and left the shop, with a vague sense of guilt, as if she'd forgotten something. Flashbacks, gloom in beautiful experiences, self-flagellation … the patterns were familiar. A mood swing now was the last thing she needed. The sight of three strapping chaps standing underneath the enormous chandelier made of lightbulbs gave her a fillip.

"Hello Kev, Jase. Hello, Tyler. It's very good of you to come and meet me at such short notice."

Kev gave her a broad smile. "All right, Beatrice? Good to see you again."

"Yeah, we wondered how you were getting on," added Jase.

"Bit worried old Aguirre might have kidnapped you," Tyler grinned.

Beatrice looked at each of them in turn. "It's lovely to see you all. And even better, not one of you has winced or gasped or shown any kind of reaction to the mess I've made of my face."

Kev shrugged. "We've seen a lot worse than that. Right, where's this restaurant?"

A strange sense of disconnect came over Beatrice as they got experimental with the menu, encouraged each other to taste their dishes and laughed at Tyler's anecdotes. The three men appeared completely relaxed, with not a hint of awkwardness towards her, but she could find out precious little about their profession. Each time she asked a direct question, one of them would gently lead the conversation elsewhere. So far, she had established that they were stationed in Afghanistan, they'd met while on training and they all came from the Manchester area.

"And your fiancée, Tyler? Is she a Mancunian?"

"Oooh, no. Good job she can't hear you. She's from Birkenhead. It'll take her years to get over the shame of marrying a squaddie from Stockport."

"But what happens after you get married? She won't go with you to Afghanistan, surely?" Beatrice asked.

"No, no. But after this tour of duty, I'll get stationed somewhere else, most like. Don't mind where so long as it has smaller insects. Hey, Jase. Tell Beatrice about that scorpion you found."

And once again, the conversation carried her away. She didn't resist. The waiter cleared their plates and Beatrice expressed her compliments on the garlic soup. Since arriving in Spain, she had dined exquisitely everywhere she went and collected enough recipe ideas to last her months. Jase and Tyler excused themselves to have a cigarette outside, while Kev and Beatrice ordered coffees.

Beatrice tried another, blander query. "How much longer are you staying in Vitoria? If you don't mind my asking."

Kev nodded, as if considering the question with care. "We're off to Bilbao on Saturday to meet Tyler's crowd for a weekend of mayhem. Listen, Beatrice, don't get us wrong; it's not like we're being evasive. Well, I s'pose we are, but not to be rude or owt. It's not easy to get people to understand, but we're on active duty. We're part of a peacekeeping force in the most dangerous country in the world. The past isn't pretty, and God knows what the future holds, so we'd rather just talk about the here and now. Immediate plans, that's about as far as we can go. Might not make much sense to you, but for us, that's the way it is."

Beatrice gazed at him, noticing for the first time how his eyes seemed much older than the rest of his face.

"As a matter of fact, it does. To me, it makes perfect sense."

Chapter 21

The usual frisson rippled across the crowd as Aguirre and Marisol descended the steps to the ballroom. The huge French windows opened onto the terrace, which today was covered by a marquee in primary colours. The sun playing on the canvas gave the scene a sense of vibrancy and warmth, the latter assisted by outdoor heaters. Beyond the marquee, circus performers threaded their way between a bouncy castle and a petting zoo, face painters and a puppet show. Most children seemed to be running from one attraction to the other, rarely standing still for long.

The majority of adults remained indoors, sipping champagne, observing one another and occasionally glancing towards the garden with indulgent smiles. The colours indoors were no less splendid. Like an exotic aviary, the plumage made up of vibrant dresses and designer suits. Aguirre affected not to notice the covert glances and the overt stares as he took in the room, nodding at acquaintances, smiling at friends and ignoring his mistress entirely. Marisol had an unerring sense of which women caught his attention, so he had learnt not even to make eye contact. Nevertheless, his Polish beauty's platinum hair refracted light in his peripheral vision, along with chandeliers, diamonds and envious eyes.

Paz turned to look over a bare shoulder, waving her fingers in a half-greeting, half-beckon. She and Angel were talking to the handsome young CEO of Tortuga Construction, Simon Vasconcellos. A clever move, as Aguirre had him on the shortlist for potential partners for Luz. Of whom there was no sign.

Kisses and handshakes exchanged, small talk performed and Aguirre was already bored.

"And your sister?" he asked Paz, scanning the room with impunity and resting his gaze on Klaudyna, who was laughing at some frivolity. She held his gaze for a second, before focusing once more on her companions.

Paz shrugged, without breaking the flow of her monologue to her mother, a speech so familiar Aguirre could have delivered it himself. Immigrants – the scourge of Spain. Angel answered in her stead, apparently relieved to have an excuse not to listen.

"Luz isn't feeling so good. Inez has gone up to see her."

Aguirre frowned. "She's sick?"

"I doubt it. More like chronic shyness," Paz interrupted and immediately returned to her theme. "Which in turn leads to social unrest and a destabilising of the whole country merely for the sake of a minaret!"

The construction magnate's eyes were glazing over. Marisol moved with grace and speed.

"Paz, my darling, how many times must I tell you that politics interests no one but politicians? It's a good job my other daughters are less opinionated. Señor Vasconcellos, I hear you are an art lover. Did you see the piece in the hall? We picked it up at auction and I find it so intriguing. It's through here. I'd love to hear an expert's opinion."

Aguirre watched his wife do what she did best and congratulated himself on his excellent judgement in marrying her. More beautiful candidates had scored poorly in the social arena, sexier possibilities had unimpressive backgrounds. Marisol, average-looking at best, beat them all with her blend of charm, contacts and determination. And for the losers, Aguirre was generous with his consolation prizes.

A silver shift and blonde hair shimmered past, a magnet for attention. Aguirre directed his eyes at Angel.

"Any news on the German supermarket contract?"

"I think," Angel glanced at his sister-in-law, "we've been banned from talking shop. Today is all about Ramón. Inez and Paz insist."

"You see, Angel, another classic example of how you are failing as a husband. A woman never tells me what I can and cannot discuss in my own home."

Angel's posture gave everything away. He recoiled, feigned amusement and attempted to hide his blush. Such a stupid man. The arrival of Guido, his other son-in-law, diverted his attention.

"Since when is *pata negra* an 'amuse-bouche'? This catering company is run by a pretentious goat's arse! Where did you find these people, Arturo?'

An equally stupid man. Proud of his oafish disrespect and ingratitude, assuming his nationalistic hubris will mitigate any offence. A baboon. But at least this baboon wasn't firing blanks.

Aguirre rolled his eyes. "Tell me about it, Guido. Your mother-in-law attended some charity do and came back singing the caterer's praises. I decided to give them a try. Pretentious, indeed, but I have to say she was right about the quality. After all, we wouldn't want that bunch of cowboys who did your garden party, would we?"

And balance restored.

Across the lawn ran a gaudy troop of small boys, yelling at the top of their lungs. Basajaun was right in the middle, his features obscured by markings. Face paint, but at this distance, Luz had no idea what he was supposed to be. She smiled at their noisy enthusiasm, at the balloons, the stilt-walkers and the bubble-machine and wished she could join them. Just take off this dress, clean her face, drag on her jeans and run and laugh and play until she was exhausted.

She should join the party. She looked exactly as she'd hoped. Classy, groomed and a little bit sexy. But if he wasn't there to see her, what was the point? She tugged at the Cartier diamonds in her earlobe. Today, she was a show pony, with no other purpose than to be admired and offered up to whichever poor devil her father had chosen. For a second, Luz considered her potential suitor's lack of freedom. For as an Aguirre-in-law, his hands would forever be manipulated by invisible strings. In many ways, Tunçay was lucky. She should go.

A knock at the door made her start and snatch up her lipstick as an excuse.

"Come in. Almost ready."

It was not, as expected, her mother, impatient and shrewish, but her oldest sister.

"Hi Inez. Sorry, my make-up took ages. I'm just on my way."

Inez closed the door. "Relax, I'm not on sheepdog duty. I just fancied a few minutes peace. Talking of which, guess who's on the warpath again. Ranting to Vasconcellos about Spain's loss of identity to Islam, blah, blah, bloody blah."

"She should shut her mouth. She has no idea what she's talking about." Luz blushed, aware her vehemence might arouse suspicion.

Inez didn't notice, picking up pieces from Luz's jewellery box and placing them against her neck. "I know. He's quite a looker, actually. Tall, big brown eyes and dirty blond hair."

"Vasconcellos? Bland. Looks like a catalogue model. I suppose he's the recipient of my batted lashes today?"

"Yep. But you might get off lightly. Mama will be watching Papí and he'll be watching his Polish slut."

"He's lining up a new mistress? What happened to the Brazilian model?"

"Luz, you are so out of touch. He's been banging Klaudyna Kulka ever since our garden party in June. Is that dress new? It suits you. Flattering up top."

"Thanks. Yours is fabulous. I love all the pleats."

Inez sat on the bed, her eyes sly. "Yes, I'm hoping the pleats come in useful, in fact."

Abandoning all pretence at make-up, Luz turned to her sister. She'd seen that expression of cunning triumph before.

"What is it? Tell me."

A smile spreading across her face, Inez reached into her Hermès handbag and brought out a plastic bag. She unwrapped something from the tissue paper and waved it in a figure of eight in front of Luz.

A jolt of delight hit Luz as she realised what she was seeing. "Oh my God, are you pregnant?" she whispered.

Inez shrugged. "Nothing's certain till I've seen the doctor, but the test says yes."

Luz jumped to her feet and hugged her. "I'm so happy for you! You and Angel, I mean, you've waited so long. And I'm going to be an auntie again. Oh, make it a girl, will you? Paz is having another boy ..."

"That doesn't surprise me. If I didn't know better, I'd say Paz *was* a man."

Luz laughed, a little shocked. "So you must give me a little niece, so I can buy her beautiful things and play princesses."

Inez laughed and squeezed her sister's arms. "I'll try. Now listen. No one knows, not even Angel. I want confirmation before I tell anyone. And try and keep Mama away from me. She's stressed as hell at the moment, but I swear she can smell when something's going on. I don't want her to guess, I want to surprise her and Papí. I can't wait to see their faces."

"And Angel's!"

Inez took Luz's place in front of the mirror and tilted her head left and right. "Yes, you're right. I guess it will come as a bit of a surprise to Angel. Listen, they'll ring the gong in about five minutes. We should get down there. I'll go first and keep your Vasconcellos entertained till you arrive. He'll need rescuing from Paz by now."

She slipped out the door and blew a kiss.

Luz took one last look in the mirror then decided she didn't care. He could like what he saw or not. It made no difference. She had no interest in him and would tell him so.

Aguirre worked the room, expressing admiration and pleasure everywhere he went, but kept Klaudyna and Marisol in his peripheral vision. His impatience at his youngest daughter's absence grew along with his geniality. He glanced at his watch and across at his wife. Eyes as bright as a lighthouse, Marisol picked up Aguirre's intentions, excused herself and ascended the stairs. When the housekeeper appeared at his elbow to ask if she should sound the lunch gong, he hesitated, but then spotted Luz skulking along the wall in the direction of the garden. He instructed Carmina to wait fifteen more minutes. The dress Luz wore was spectacular, undoubtedly chosen by Marisol, but the guilty look and withdrawn posture showed it at its worst. He moved as fast as his status allowed, kept his focus on her and broke into a huge smile as he cut off her escape.

"My beautiful little girl!" he boomed, attracting attention from every corner. "No, no longer a little girl, an elegant woman. Look at me!"

"Papí," she moved to kiss his cheeks, partly to hide her embarrassment, he noticed.

Aguirre turned to the nearest party; a judge and two executives from the TV station who cast approving looks at his daughter. On cue, the producer nodded. "They grow so fast, don't they? She'll be breaking hearts soon, I'll bet."

Aguirre acknowledged the compliment with a modest bow of his head.

"Come, my little jewel. There's someone I want you to meet." His hand firmly on his daughter's elbow, he smiled at the ingratiating faces.

"Papí, I thought I'd find Ramón first. I haven't said ..."

He dropped his voice. "You should have thought of that earlier. There's only quarter of an hour before the gong. Didn't you see what time it is? And I'd like you to escort Señor Vasconcellos to the buffet. Your duties are firstly to our guests."

He steered her back in the direction of their group. Luz pulled her arm from her father's grasp but continued walking in the right direction. No more than Aguirre expected. Had it been Inez, a full-blown row could easily have erupted. But Luz was gentler, more malleable and always did as she was told.

According to family tradition, Marisol would escort the most senior male figure, today a French count in his eighties, while Aguirre charmed one of the influential ladies. His daughters had instructions to target some useful contact or other and the rest could fend for themselves. He expected nothing of his sons-in-law. Angel was positively dangerous when he opened his weak mouth. Guido, slow-witted and dull, would find someone with whom he could argue football. Perhaps his third son-in-law might break the pattern by being rich, well-connected *and* intelligent. Aguirre waved Vasconcellos over.

"Simon, let me introduce my daughter, Luz. The jewel in our family crown. She lives up to her name, a very bright girl. Bright and beautiful."

Luz offered her hand which Vasconcellos took but pulled her closer to brush both cheeks with his lips.

"Miss Aguirre, it is a pleasure. I've heard so much about you."
His smile was generous. Hers was half-hearted.

"Oh but you haven't heard the best. Luz is a great aficionado of
fine architecture. I'm sure she would appreciate your views on that
Calatrava project we discussed earlier. Excuse me one moment."

He wove a path to the dining room, resisting a look back until
he reached the open doors. With some satisfaction, he noted
Vasconcellos bend his head to listen to Luz, who was explaining
something with great earnestness. Aguirre sighed. If only she could
smile a little more and talk a little less.

His eyes swept over the room, checking all was as it should be
when his attention was caught by Marisol, standing motionless on
the staircase. In a second, he knew something was wrong. She stared
across the room, her jaw set and lips pinched. Aguirre followed her
sightline, almost sure the object of such livid focus would be his
beautiful Klaudyna, and began rehearsing denials. He frowned
when he realised her furious glare was directed at her youngest
daughter. Oblivious, Luz continued to lecture poor Vasconcellos.

Aguirre slid through the crowds, exuding purpose so as not to
be derailed by favour-seekers, until he reached Marisol.

"What is it?"

She fixed her stare on him and he noticed her fists were clenched.

"Marisol?"

"Come with me. We need to talk."

Chapter 22

The bus arrived five minutes early. Beatrice was already waiting. She found a free spot on a bench between a chap in a business suit and two teenage girls and settled down to wait, anticipating Adrian's reaction to her bruised face, Matthew's thoughts on today's close shave and both their impressions of Ana and Jaime.

When Beatrice called her from the museum, Ana had returned to the apartment with Jaime and reported the coast clear. Of the 'welcoming committee', there was no sign. They agreed on meeting at the hotel for dinner and strategic planning.

She shifted around and crossed her legs. A twinge in her knee made her grimace. She started to give it a gentle rub when her phone rang. She didn't recognise the number but answered anyway.

"Hello?"

A woman's voice. "Hello, is that Beatrice Stubbs?"

"Yes. Who's this?"

"It's Luz Aguirre. From the vineyard. I just wanted to ask how you are after yesterday's fall."

"Oh, how kind of you to call. I should have called you to say thanks, but there's rather a lot going on, you see. I'm fine. Surprisingly well, in fact. Your first aid was extremely efficient."

"I'm pleased to hear that. My parents would like to send you some flowers, by way of an apology. I know you're staying in Calle Cuchillería. Could you tell me which apartment?"

Uneasy about sharing Ana's address, Beatrice stalled. "There's really no need to apologise. If I received flowers every time I tripped over, I could start up a business."

"They insist. Personally, I think those steps are lethal. So I think they're lucky to get away with nothing more than a flower basket."

"I suspect the insistence comes from you rather than them, but a flower basket is always welcome. The thing is, I'm moving to the Hotel Valencia, which is in the centre. Do you know it?"

"Yes, I do. My sister had her wedding reception there. It's very grand."

"Is it? Oh, good. I like a bit of luxury."

Luz laughed. "I hope you have a lovely stay and the flowers lift your spirits. It was a pleasure to meet you, Mrs Stubbs. Get well soon and enjoy the rest of your holiday."

"Thank you Luz, and good luck with your studies."

It could be genuine, of course. A gesture from a nice, well-mannered young woman with a conscience. Or it could be an Aguirre-induced way of finding her. Happily, she hadn't needed to lie, but nor had she given too much away.

After an alarming start, the day had exceeded expectations. A hushed hour in front of Miró, Gargallo, del Rivero, Brossa and Nagel, the delicious lunch of fresh pintxos with a glass of rosé and pleasant company and a feeling of having averted a trough had brought Beatrice to almost a kind of equilibrium. Now a friendly gesture from the Aguirre family and her two favourite men in the world were imminent. All well with the world.

Someone cleared his throat, pointedly. Beatrice realised she was bouncing up and down on her buttocks, so forcing the other occupants of the bench to bounce with her. She desisted and held up her hands.

"Sorry."

The suit, the teenagers and an older woman with a laundry bag smiled at her evident impatience. Certain behaviour was universally understood and forgiven.

Seconds later, the bus arrived. Choosing to stick with the sunglasses to minimise the shock factor, Beatrice hurried to meet them.

Adrian spotted her first, but was diplomatic enough to point her out to Matthew while he claimed their bags.

"Beatrice!" He embraced her cautiously. "I've been rather worried about you. Are things really all right? Are you?"

"I am now. It's actually wonderful to see you, Matthew. Oh dear, I really am getting to be a sentimental old bat. It's not even a fortnight since I left."

"An eventful fortnight, by all accounts," Matthew said, his smile not quite eradicating the frown of concern.

"Hello, Beatrice! Hardy Boys reporting for duty!"

Beatrice beamed. Adrian, crisp as a stick of celery, wore a green linen shirt, off-white trousers and carried something resembling a cricketer's holdall. He held out his arms as if for a hug but grabbed her shoulders.

With maximum drama, he dropped his voice to a funereal pitch. "I think we'd best get it over with. Let us see your face."

Beatrice sighed, and with a shrug, removed her sunglasses.

Adrian dropped his bag and clapped both hands over his mouth. Matthew's eyes roved over her, finally meeting her patient gaze. They were attracting quite some attention in the bus station, everyone drawn to such a spectacle.

"Tell me again, and I promise to believe you. This was an accident."

"It looks horrific, I know. But the culprit was a useless pair of shoes, as prosaic as that. Matthew, and as a matter of fact, you too Adrian, should both be aware of my clumsy streak. We do have things to worry about, but I assure you, this isn't one of them. Now come on, let's get to the hotel. There are some people I want you to meet."

Despite the promised grandeur, the superb location, fine food and perfectly matched wine, the meeting was not going well. Matthew had taken against Jaime. Beatrice wasn't sure precisely why. Perhaps Jaime's casual dress: jeans, an open-necked shirt and a bandana round his neck instead of a tie, had offended him. It might have been Jaime's familiar way of flirt-teasing, or maybe he'd caught one of Beatrice's admiring looks at the editor. One thing was for sure, Matthew was unimpressed.

"I have to say I disagree, Jaime. Hard evidence is exactly what Adrian and I have flown here to provide. We have bottled proof that the export wine is something other than what it says on the label. And as two people investigating this racket have already met with a sticky end, I think it wisest to take what we have to the police. Now."

Matthew's measured tones sounded calm and reasonable. One would have to know him extremely well to detect the undercurrent of hostility in his voice.

Beatrice chipped in. "The thing is, Matthew, we've already tried to get the police to take this seriously. We know for a fact they suppressed the coroner's findings about Tiago. His death was recorded as an accident and thus no investigation will be forthcoming. Not only that, but the detective we spoke to immediately contacted London to call me off."

Matthew fixed her with a frown. "How do you know that?"

"Hamilton rang me and bawled me out. Told me to stop interfering." She returned her attention to the pork fillet on her plate, avoiding Matthew's incisive stare.

Ana took over. "In a way, Matthew, you're right. We have proof that someone, somewhere, is ripping off the British public. But we don't know which link in the chain is responsible. Or whether, which I think is more likely, the whole process is corrupt. We need to find out a little more about where this is happening and then we can point the finger in the right direction."

"Sounds fair enough to me," said Adrian, topping up Jaime's glass. "And I quite fancy a nose round the vineyard. Why don't we see what we can find out tomorrow and then have a rethink?"

Jaime smiled at him. "Thank you. Yes, I agree. With information from the DOC, the wine expert's insights and the background of the vineyard, we should have a clearer picture by tomorrow evening."

Matthew shook his head. "Jaime, Ana, forgive my being blunt, but I am concerned you are chasing a story. Whereas I see this as a criminal investigation, which should be carried out by the professionals. The *local* professionals." He glanced at Beatrice. "Dabbling in a case which involves two dead men seems at best foolhardy."

Ana put down her fork and gazed at Matthew. "One of those dead men was my best friend. The police won't investigate why someone hacked off his nose, so I will. I want to take them enough evidence so they are forced to act. And at the moment, I haven't got it. Couldn't we work as a team, as Adrian says, for one more day?"

Everyone paused; forks hovered, glasses stopped midway to lips and all eyes rested on Matthew.

He sighed. "No one should do anything alone. We must stay in pairs, or all together."

Ana gave him a brilliant smile and the meal resumed.

Jaime nodded. "I agree with Matthew. No need to worry about me. I'm going to be at the office, surrounded by people. Ana and Beatrice should go to San Sebastian together. You can take my car. And Adrian and Matthew could join an official tour of Castelo de Aguirre."

Ana's eyes widened. "Your car? Seriously?"

"I know. Trusting you with my pride and joy, I must be out of my mind." Jaime took a sip of wine. "But if I can't be there myself, it's the least I can do. Just be careful, OK?"

Ana grinned. "Trust me. I'm an excellent driver. Adrian, can I get a top-up there? I've a throat on me tonight."

Matthew caught Beatrice's eyes. He smiled but she knew there was trouble brewing. And what was worse, she knew she deserved it.

Chapter 23

The police arrived as Tunçay was spooning yoghurt onto a plate of corn fritters for the party on table six. Three burst through the serving doors, two of whom carried guns. Another two appeared from the back door, also armed. The kitchen, normally filled with shouts and clatter, had never heard noise like it. All the gunmen were shouting, making it impossible to hear any clear instructions. Tunçay put down the yoghurt and raised his hands in the air, just in case.

The only man without a gun marched up to the chef, Mehmet.

"Immigration Office. I want to see your papers. Now." In chef's whites, there was nowhere to keep documents, so Mehmet went to the cloakroom to fetch his coat. The whole time, two gunmen kept their weapons trained on him. His documents, of course, were legal and valid, which seemed to disappoint the officer. He repeated the process with everyone, glaring at each man as if he'd caught them stowing away in the back of a truck, rather than trying to serve starters for a party of nine.

Tunçay put it down to paranoia at first, but as the seconds ticked by, he knew the officer was taking twice as long to scrutinise his own work permit and passport as he had the others. He lifted his head to stare at Tunçay. Everyone watched and all four guns pointed his way.

"How do you pronounce this?" he barked, stabbing his finger at Tunçay's name.

"Toon-Jai Kilij."

"Where are you from?"

"Turkey. Sinop, on the Black Sea coast."

"Why are you here?"

"To travel. To learn Spanish and ... everything."

"When are you going home?"

"About two in the morning, I expect. We have to clean the restaurant after ..."

"I mean when are you going back to Turkey?"

"I ... I don't know yet. I have plans to travel and ..."

The man threw the papers onto the stainless steel counter in Tunçay's direction and walked back through the swing doors. Holstering their weapons, the police officers followed, casting aggressive looks at anyone who raised their eyes. Tunçay collected his documents with shaking hands and looked up at Mehmet. Normally, Mehmet took the title of the scariest person in Tunçay's life, but today he'd been reduced to the status of victim by a different kind of bully.

"What was that all about?"

Mehmet scooped the corn fritters back into the deep fryer. "I guess the old bastard didn't get laid last night and needed to release some testosterone. Put some more yoghurt on that plate then get these to table six. They've been waiting almost twenty minutes."

The last comment contained a reproach, as if Tunçay had neglected his duties in favour of being hassled by Immigration.

He dressed the starter and once the golden patties were reheated, balanced the plates and bounced his way back into the restaurant, already rehearsing his apology in Spanish. The police had gone, but Deniz the barman signalled his concern with a pointed look at the staff table. Two men sat with Bulent, both wearing dark suits. This was not unusual, as Bulent had various business activities in addition to the restaurant. But the shifty glance he gave Tunçay was certainly out of the ordinary.

Dumping the plates with a distracted 'Sorry', Tunçay leant over the bar to Deniz.

"Who are they?"

"No idea. Don't think Bulent knows them either, but I'd say his balls are in his throat. The ugly one with the wrinkles sat down, took Bulent's cigarette out of his mouth and stubbed it out on the tablecloth. So I'm pretty sure they're not from the church."

"Which is the ugly one with the wrinkles? They both look the same to me."

A bell rang from the kitchen and Tunçay hurried away.

At nine-fifteen, Tunçay took a break. Desserts had been served, so there would be a lull until coffee. He held up his Marlboros and indicated the door, just to let Mehmet know, and pushed out into the night air. The alleyway stank of urine and bins and greasy fumes pumped out by extractor fans. Still, it was quiet. He lit a cigarette and inhaled, holding his breath for just a second, before blowing a thin jet of smoke towards the sky. Tonight, he wouldn't need to perform the elaborate post-cigarette ritual of teeth-cleaning and breath-freshening. Luz wouldn't be back until Sunday. It was bad enough in a normal week, not knowing when he'd see her again, but a guaranteed absence of four days made him miserable.

She was missing him too, if the several text messages per day were any indication. And he certainly liked the idea of her new underwear. Sunday. A day off, no work on Monday, and his sexy Spanish chica all wrapped up in black lace and ribbons. Time just didn't move fast enough.

The door opened behind him. Tunçay didn't bother to turn around, knowing Deniz would be hoping to scrounge yet another smoke.

"Ah, there you are."

Tunçay had never seen Bulent in the kitchen, leave alone outside the back door. He dropped his cigarette and straightened up.

"Sorry, just taking a quick break."

"It's fine. It's all calm in there. No need to rush back. Look, have one of these." He offered his silver case, which Tunçay had often mocked behind his back as affected.

"OK, thanks."

"Turkish tobacco. I never smoke anything else." Bulent flicked open a Zippo and the whiff of lighter fuel made Tunçay feel momentarily nostalgic.

They smoked in silence, Tunçay struggling to think of something cool and Mehmet-like to say. Bulent sighed and ran a hand over his thick black hair.

"I'm sorry about this, Tunçay, but I have to let you go. The police were here tonight looking for illegal immigrants."

"What? I'm legal. You know that."

"Yes, I know that. The problem is you have made some enemies somewhere. I don't know who, but these are powerful people. Powerful enough to get the police to search my premises every single night until you leave my employ and return to Turkey."

Tunçay couldn't see Bulent's expression, but his tone was serious and regretful. This was not a joke.

"Bulent, you have the authority to fire me. It's your restaurant. But to make me go back to Turkey? That's insane."

"On the contrary, young man. That would be the wisest course of action I can think of. You're right to say my authority extends no further than this restaurant. But my concern for you goes far beyond that. I can't make you leave this country. If I could, I would. Because if you go of your own accord or if you go under my persuasion, at least you'll go alive."

The Bond baddie routine was too much. Tunçay burst into snorts of laughter.

"I'll get my stuff. You know, you could have planted a can of chick peas in my jacket or something. Most bosses would have the balls to tell me I'm not good enough instead of inventing all this bullshit. What about my wages?"

Bulent caught him by the shoulder. "If you ever had any respect for me, please take this seriously. You're a good man, and a good waiter, in fact. I'm sorry to lose you. Mehmet will be mad as hell. You're the best we have, according to him. Here. This is five hundred euros, which should cover your wages this week and buy you a last-minute flight to Turkey. Go, Tunçay. And I wish you happiness, health and peace."

He walked away, down the alley to the main street and around the corner.

Five hundred euros. He stared at the pool of light where Bulent had disappeared. A compliment from Mehmet. Something he'd always craved but now it came too late. Two silhouettes crossed the light and stopped, turning to look at him. A tiny glow indicated a cigarette. Powerful enemies.

Confusion gave way to temper which caved in to fear. Tunçay stormed into the kitchen, grabbed his jacket and walked out through the restaurant, aware of Mehmet's silent gaze.

He didn't say goodbye.

Chapter 24

Brilliant sunshine enriched the terracotta and sand of roofs and spires, the sky offered a royal blue mantle as backdrop and a cacophony of horns echoed up from the streets below. With a towel wrapped around his waist, Adrian stepped onto the hotel balcony to appreciate the view. The air smelt fresh yet autumnal, containing a reminder. All is ripe and the time is now. He stretched, wincing slightly as his back muscles complained. By heaving Beatrice's suitcase out of Jaime's flat and up the steps to the hotel, he was sure he'd done himself a mischief. One day, he would have to teach her the art of capsule packing. The phone rang.

"Hello?"

"It's me. Matthew and I are on our way down to breakfast. Are you fit?"

"Not quite."

"Well, hurry up and put a skirt on. Change of plan. Full briefing before I leave, which is in half an hour."

"Give me five minutes. See you down there."

Adrian shook his head as he replaced the receiver. Her joy and relief at their arrival had soon reverted to the usual bossy exasperation. He smiled and began the task of choosing a suitable ensemble for the day. An ensemble which was unlikely to include a skirt.

Beatrice looked like hell. The black bruising around both eye sockets, the swelling of her eyelids and the little bits of crusted blood between the stitches wrenched at Adrian's heart. He almost wished someone had done it on purpose so he could hate them. But he, like Matthew, was familiar with her lack of coordination.

She seemed unbothered, launching straight into her instructions as Adrian sat down.

"I don't think there's anything to be gained from visiting the vineyard again. You should go to Alava Exports. Take a look at another link in the chain."

Adrian shrugged. "Fine with me. Could you pass the coffee?"

Beatrice shoved the cafetière towards him.

"Ana has made you an appointment for eleven. You're posing as British wine buyers, which won't be too onerous a challenge, I shouldn't think. Ask as many questions as you can about Alava Exports' numbers. See if you can get a feel of which vineyards have a sizeable share of the market and how much. Don't limit yourselves to Viura or even to white. Be enthusiastic, be professional and be curious. But also be bland. The proprietor, Angel Rosado, is Aguirre's son-in-law, so will be alert to any excessive interest in the Castelo de Aguirre output. Matthew, you have toast crumbs on your tie."

Matthew looked down. "That's not toast. That's croissant."

Adrian poured coffee into the white china cup. "The white Rioja story is big news, though, so it won't hurt to make some general enquiries."

"He's right. If we ignored the phenomenon, it might look even more suspicious," said Matthew, picking pastry flakes from his woollen tie.

Beatrice twisted her wrist to see her watch. "Yes, yes. What I mean is, just try to be subtle. Underplay everything. We're treading on thin ground. I have to go or I'll be late. Be careful. Far more careful than ... you have ever been."

Adrian appreciated her sensitive circumnavigation of unpleasant memories. "We will. What time will you be back?"

"No idea. Ana's meeting someone from the *Denominación de Origen* Control Board at midday and I'm lunching with that wine writer at two, so if all goes smoothly, we'll be back by tea-time. Now I really must go. First I have to call James, then Ana's picking me up."

Matthew frowned. "Picking you up with what? Not that ghastly moped?"

Beatrice stood and hitched her handbag up her shoulder. "It's not a moped, it's a Vespa. And that's strictly for city driving. Jaime lent us his car to get us to San Sebastian, remember? We're going to have a whale of a time. It's a soft top BMW, you know, in powder blue."

Matthew stirred his coffee. "Hardly *Easy Rider.*"

Adrian smoothed over Matthew's obvious snipe by deliberately misunderstanding the reference. "No, it'll be more like *Thelma and Louise* meets *Sideways.* Have fun and be careful."

"It's you two I'm worried about. Remember what I said. Be subtle. See you both later." She kissed Adrian's cheek and patted his shoulder. "Look after him." She reached down to embrace Matthew. "Stay out of trouble, you old coot."

With that, she hurried away towards the lifts.

Matthew yawned. "She does worry so. Now, shall we have another croissant and discuss how to approach this?"

Adrian reached for the coffee with a grin. He'd got it all worked out.

The huge warehouse appeared unwelcoming and unattractive after the charms of the city. Two olive trees in faux cut-off wine bottles either side of a large welcome mat indicated the visitors' entrance. Adrian and Matthew slammed the taxi doors shut and, with a wave, the driver sped off in the direction they had come.

"I had no idea you spoke Spanish so well," said Adrian, as they surveyed the building. "How come you let Ana and Jaime do all the ordering last night?"

"Sometimes it's better not to let on how much you understand. You never know when it will come in handy."

"They *are* on our side, Matthew. You don't like Jaime much, do you?"

Matthew squinted at him. "I'm yet to form an opinion. Anyway, Spanish isn't all that different to Italian. You should hear my Greek. I sound like a native, if I do say so myself. Shall we go in? Only I find this sun awfully strong."

Adrian accepted the change of subject and began walking across the dusty drive. "I think I'd like Greece. You should invite me sometime."

"And Greece is guaranteed to like you. Are we all set?"

The receptionist behind the marble desk greeted them with a perky smile as they walked into the air-conditioned foyer.

"Bailey and Son, Fine Wines? You are right on time. Mister Rosado will be with you in one moment. Why don't you take a seat? Help yourself to coffee. Could I take your business cards to add you to our system?"

Adrian tensed, but nodded. He held out a hand to a blinking Matthew. "You did bring our business cards, Dad?"

Matthew ran a hand across his hair. He patted his pockets, looked in his briefcase and sighed. "I must have left them at the hotel. I'm sorry, young lady. Perhaps my son could let you have our details by fax later this afternoon."

Adrian rolled his eyes and addressed the receptionist. "I'll email you by close of play today. And your name is ...?"

While Adrian entered the details into his phone, he noticed two things. Matthew pulling out a handkerchief and taking off his glasses to polish them, and the lift numbers descending. Professor Bailey was wholly in character and ready to make his debut performance. The lift doors opened.

"Good morning. My name is Angel Rosado. You must be Mr Bailey, and son."

He extended his hand and gave his full attention to Matthew, so Adrian took the opportunity to pass judgement. Slicked-back hair and so cleanly shaven he looked waxed, Angel Rosado was polished to perfection. The cut of his suit and fall of the navy fabric made Adrian covetous. His lemon shirt would not favour many complexions, but on Rosado, it heightened the tan and emphasised the whiteness of his teeth. Black brogues, a Tissot watch and a fresh trace of Miller Harris; this man dressed the part.

Greetings exchanged with Matthew, he turned to Adrian. "Mr Bailey Junior, I presume?" His hazel eyes met Adrian's, the mildly patronising smile evaporated and they shook hands. Cool, professional and firm. And Adrian knew.

Chapter 25

At eleven minutes past eight, Luz opened her eyes and made a decision. Having debated her promise to stay for the weekend versus her will to get on with her own life, Maria Luz Dolores Santiago de Aguirre opted for the latter. She would take a train back to Burgos, the first available, and tonight, she'd go to the restaurant, wearing her new dress. She couldn't wait to see Tunçay's face. Especially when she told him what she was wearing underneath.

Her duties performed, her family appeased, she had no reason to stay. If possible, she'd avoid her father, say goodbye to Marisol and leave a present for Basajaun. She badly wanted to kiss him and hold him and tell him she'd see him soon, but his heartbreaking sobs whenever she left were more than she could take today. Just the thought of his tearful blue eyes made her bite her lip.

After a hot shower, she dressed in her old jeans, a navy jumper and black leather biker boots, an outfit to infuriate her father. She searched for her phone to check train times but couldn't find it anywhere. The Castelo clock chimed nine. Hunger gnawed at her, as she'd only picked at the buffet yesterday. Maybe breakfast first, then trains.

He would be in the vineyards. He always toured the estate after breakfast. She would be in the breakfast room, nibbling on toast and fruits, reading a magazine. Basajaun, if the gods were smiling, would be at school. The usual sounds floated through the house; sounds which, as a child, she had spent hours decoding. In the car park stood her mother's Jaguar, but the Range Rover was missing. She smiled. As she expected. Time to venture downstairs, grab some food and say goodbye.

Her smile contracted as she opened the door to the breakfast room. Her father's head rose above the newspaper.

"Good morning, Luz. I wondered when you would finally rise. Please sit down. While your mother is out, we need to talk. Coffee?"

With a nod, Luz sank into the chair nearest the door. He filled a cup and pushed it towards her with a cold blank stare. She knew that look. He was about to read the riot act. She'd ditched Vasconcellos as soon as she was able and retreated to her room, claiming a headache. Instead, she'd checked her emails, made some calls and sent more than one lewd message to Tunçay. In her father's eyes, she'd neglected her duties.

Luz added sugar to her cup and stirred. She didn't care. He could rant and rail and threaten till his arteries burst, but she was no longer under his control. And poor old Simon Vasconcellos could find some other strategic alliance. She slugged the espresso in one. All she had to do was listen, appear contrite and she could get out of there. Back to Burgos.

"You are not going back to Burgos."

She jumped, dropping her cup into the saucer.

"Your studies are officially at an end. I called the university this morning to withdraw you from the course. You are to stay here with us, until your mother and I resolve this situation."

Luz shook her head and opened her mouth but he had no intention of stopping.

"What? You expected to go back? How could you be so selfish? How long did you think you could continue like this? Our agreement was for five years. Five years in which you would study law. Which, incidentally, already put you at risk. You would have been twenty-seven by the time you completed that course, which is very late to marry. I should never have allowed myself to be persuaded. In retrospect, I was the stupid one." He stood up and faced the window.

Luz blinked. "You cannot stop me going back. I have to finish ..."

"I think I made myself clear. It is finished. Your mother has gone to collect your things and finalise any outstanding arrangements. And how did you propose to deal with your current situation? I doubt you even thought that far. I still can't comprehend this. My own daughter. To bring such shame on me, on all of us. How, Luz? How could you be so stupid?"

The caffeine buzzed around Luz's bloodstream, making her feel simultaneously wide-awake and as if she were dreaming. She kept her eyes on her father's thunderous face as she grasped the enormity of his words. He wanted to destroy her. He wanted her back on her leash. She'd always known her freedom would be short-lived, but to snatch it away already? He was right about one thing. How could she be so stupid? Her mother had unlocked the information and handed her father the key. By trusting Marisol, she'd signed her own jail sentence. She should have known. They weren't parents. Parents were people who loved you and wanted nothing more than your happiness. These two were debt-collectors.

Luz got to her feet. Shaky and cold, she made a decision. Her voice was steady.

"I am leaving now. I am going to Burgos and I will complete my studies. All I ever asked from you was financial support. But I can live without it. I can get a job and pay my own way. I am twenty-three years old and an adult. I thank you for all you have done, but I need to be my own person. You no longer tell me what to do."

Aguirre exhaled a humourless laugh. "Go to your room, Luz. You aren't going anywhere but I want you out of my sight. Tomorrow, you will travel with your mother to Bilbao, to see a specialist. We have to deal with this situation as soon as possible." He took out his mobile and began composing a message.

Luz exploded. "Situation!? What is the matter with you? I'm in love. That's all! I'm not mentally ill, you arrogant, domineering arsehole! I know there's no future in this and to be honest, wouldn't even want to bring him into such a family. He deserves better. But you will not manipulate my relationships! Not now, not in the future. I am never going to marry some chinless prick because it suits your empire-building. I will NOT be bullied by you. Not anymore. And if you try to interfere ..."

The door opened. The housekeeper peered in.

"*Señor*? Your car is ready."

"Good. Please make sure my daughter eats something. She's becoming hysterical."

Without another word, he left the room. The housekeeper took one look at Luz's face and followed.

The urge to smash something, to hurl something, to wreck his hermetically sealed world bubbled up like lava. She clenched her chunky little espresso cup in her hand and aimed for the window. Beyond the glass stretched acres of vineyard, a quivering palette of Van Gogh colours which represented so much more than grapes. She replaced the cup on the saucer. Smashing his window would be an irrelevance to him, merely proof that his daughter was undisciplined and immature. If she really wanted to cut the cords, to remove his influence, she would have to go much further.

The housekeeper was still lurking outside the door when Luz emerged.

"I'm sorry, Carmina, I'm just not hungry. In fact, I still have a headache. Maybe it's best if I have a lie-down in my room. Papí's right. I got a bit over-emotional. Do you know where he's gone?"

The relief on the housekeeper's face showed she'd been prepared for a battle.

"The airport. He's going to Madrid. He has meetings today and a television interview this evening. We're all going to watch it." She gave a proud smile. "He wants you to stay indoors till your mother gets home. I think a rest will do you good. Do you need anything?"

Luz shook her head, tempted to check the front door to see if the old bastard had locked it, but she stuck to her role and made her way quietly up the stairs. Halfway up she stopped.

"Carmina, which channel is the interview?"

"EITB. Eight-thirty."

"Great, thanks. So he'll be back very late this evening?"

"No, he's not coming back until tomorrow. He has a room in the Hotel Ritz, you know, all paid for by the TV station. He's a real VIP, your father!"

Luz smiled and continued upstairs. Father in Madrid, mother in Burgos. Looked like she had some time on her hands.

Her laptop was missing from the bedside table, where she'd left it last night. And the reason she couldn't find her mobile phone? Because it wasn't there. Luz called it twice from the phone in her room, before she realised it was probably ringing in the depths of Marisol's handbag. Her mother had made it as difficult as possible to contact Tunçay. A clean break, she would say, you'll soon forget all about him. Why hadn't she memorised his number instead of relying on technology for everything? She clenched her fists in frustration and glared at herself in the mirror.

A clean break. Yes. She inhaled deeply. Tunçay wasn't expecting her till Sunday. He might send her a text or two, but by this evening she'd be with him in person. The priority now was the break.

Clean, yet irreparable. She rummaged in her bag for her pencil case. Inside were two memory sticks, one partly filled with notes on EU Food Safety legislation for her second-year project. Notes she could afford to lose.

Back in the corridor, she checked the window. The only vehicles now on the forecourt belonged to the caterers, the event managers and a cleaning company. The household was busy restoring order after the party. If nothing had changed, the spare key to her father's office would be in his bedside table. A creature of habit, he never expected an enemy within.

Her parents' room was pristine. The bed had been made, the rugs vacuumed and the flowers changed. Just as if they lived in a hotel. Luz padded up to the Emperor-size bed and opened the cabinet on her father's side. Several business books, an English-Spanish dictionary and a tube of haemorrhoid cream. In the drawer lay a notebook, various ballpoint pens, a box of tissues and a set of keys. She released her breath. The only obstacle now would be the password. He always used the same system, so all she needed to know was how to spell it.

At 11.22, Luz plugged her memory stick into the USB port and saved the Alava Export files, copies of relevant emails, Excel accounting sheets and personnel details of people who never appeared on the payroll. She printed everything out and also emailed them to herself as attachments. Then she flicked through her handbag until she found a card. She checked the email with great care and sent everything to that address. She wrote nothing in the body text. Even if she had no opportunity to explain, any half-decent brain could work it out. And this recipient's brain was above average. Luz cleared the browser history, shut down the machine and rifled through the drawers for cash. She collected 270 Euro. Then she listened at the door for over two minutes. Satisfied, she locked the office, returned the keys, slipped back to her room and prepared to leave. She shook her head with a smile. KLAUDYNA. How could *he* be so stupid?

She emptied her room of everything valuable. The dress, the heels and the diamonds she took. Sentimental gifts from her mother and sisters she left behind. Unless she could sell it, it was of no use to her. The suitcase, stuffed with clothes, jewellery, watches, paintings and shoes, weighed three times as much as when she'd arrived. She heaved it down the stairs, stopping frequently to check no one was around, and dragged it through to the library, the least used room in the house. This place had been her sanctuary as a teenager. When she tired of her sisters' incessant bickering or her father's continual booming oratory, she would nestle into the wing-backed chairs and let the words fly her far away. And should she hear approaching feet, there was always the door into the old conservatory, where she could hide behind any number of potted plants or rattan sofas. The newer, larger 'Wintergarden' had taken prominence so that now, only she and the staff ever used this largely forgotten room.

It was approaching one o'clock. She had to get out before her mother returned. Luz watched the activity in the courtyard and chose her moment. A cleaner threw the last bags of rubbish into his two-seater pickup and wiped his hands on his overalls. Luz broke cover and approached, checking the name on his badge. Raoul.

"Hi, my name is Luz Aguirre. You've done a great job."

His eyes widened and he spoke with a Mexican accent. "You're welcome. I hope the little boy had a good party."

"He loved every minute. Raoul, can I ask you where you're going now?"

The guy's eyes widened further. "Where I'm going? To the dump and back to the depot in Vitoria. Is there something else you want me to do before I go?"

"Yes, kind of. You see, I ordered a taxi, but it's late. I need to get into the city fast. Could you take me? I'll pay you, of course."

His head retreated into his neck, like a tortoise. "In this van? *Señora*, it's dirty and it stinks."

Luz jumped into the passenger side of the cab. He wasn't wrong. It was filthy and it stank of rotten oranges.

"Seventy Euro to take me to the city. See that door over there? Behind it is a big suitcase. Can you bring it over here and throw it in the back?"

"*Señora* ..."

"If you don't argue and just do it, I'll make that a hundred. Come on, Raoul, I'll be sure to tell my father how kind you've been."

Chapter 26

Just hearing the phone ring soothed Beatrice. She sat on the windowsill of her hotel bedroom, staring out at the streets of Vitoria, but visualised James's office: cream and white upholstery, light wood and James himself, legs crossed, quietly exuding peace.

"James Curran?"

"Beatrice Stubbs, checking in."

"Beatrice, hello, you're punctual. Thank you for calling."

"Thank you for finding the time. I realise we should have discussed ongoing treatment before I left. It just all happened in a bit of a rush. But I am taking my mood stabilisers and feel mostly OK."

"Good. The medication is essential. Think of it as the scaffolding around your treatment. Whereas the building work within rests on the foundations of CBT. Are you still maintaining your journal? Or mood diary, if you prefer to call it that?"

"Not really. I mean, I'm keeping an eye on the swings, and just avoided a trough, but I'm not recording my emotional state on a daily basis. I'm not really in any sort of routine, you see."

"I appreciate that. But when you do find yourself with a couple of minutes to spare, such as just before you go to sleep, that would be an ideal opportunity to make a note of your mental outlook. Now, two things you've said already raise questions in my mind, but first, can we return to the points I asked you to consider yesterday?"

"Yes. I have thought about them." No matter how much effort she put into James's exercises, Beatrice always felt as if she were back at college, busking a tutorial on a subject she had but skimmed. "You asked the aim of this sabbatical. It wasn't my choice, to be truthful. Hamilton refused my resignation and this was his idea of a compromise. Three months away, then if I still wanted to resign, he would accept it. So in a nutshell, the aim is to find out if I really want to retire."

"If you're not sure if you want to retire, why did you resign?"

"Because I don't feel up to the job. I have endangered other officers and civilians, either through omission or incompetence, so shouldn't be in the position of Detective Inspector."

James remained silent for several seconds, prompting Beatrice to second-guess him.

"So your next question will be 'Why are you getting involved in another investigation when you don't feel competent?' Well, that wasn't actually by choice either. A friend of a friend needed some help, so I sort of rolled up my sleeves and pitched in."

"Interesting. So the situation in which you find yourself is not of your choosing. You are powerless, at the mercy of stronger wills. Forgive me if I find that image difficult to reconcile with the Beatrice Stubbs I know as my client."

In the seconds that elapsed before Beatrice composed a reply, she recognised a pattern so familiar she almost bored herself. A flare of anger at James's disrespectful tone. Infuriation at his lack of faith in her. A moment of considering a different therapist. Acknowledgement that he only ever treated her with less respect when she did likewise. Acceptance of a failed smokescreen. She was dissembling, refusing to face reality and James knew it.

"As for Matthew and Hamilton, the former joined me last night. He and Adrian have come to lend their wine expertise. And Hamilton would sack me if he knew. He's already told me not to interfere."

"Do I need to help you unpack the implications of this, or can we move on?"

"Let's move on. Fourth question. What was it again?"

"No, I'd prefer you to elaborate on two phrases you used at the beginning of this call: 'mostly OK', and 'avoided a trough'. Are they connected?"

"I suppose. I've spotted some features of rapid cycling – giddy bouts of elation, followed by over-sensitivity, an urge to recall maudlin memories, increased sexual attraction, and a tendency to extrapolate. You know, seeing one incident as reflective of what is rotten with the whole world."

"So the avoidance of a trough took what form exactly?"

"Umm ... calling you. Seeing Matthew. An awareness of other kinds of coping strategies. I feel much more grounded. Back on track sort of thing."

"Beatrice, I apologise in advance for what I am about to ask. But I believe I would be negligent in not doing so. I would like you to take five minutes to think. I will stay on the line, but I don't want you to speak until I tell you the five minutes are up. During those five minutes, you are going to think back to the months leading up to your attempted suicide. I want you to tell me the patterns you and I uncovered together, how one state of mind can give way to another and the impact those months had on you. Please be honest."

Before he'd finished speaking, the domino-effect began. Her heart rate increased, self-pity provoked tears, fear invoked resentment and her mind flailed around for a means of escape. She switched the phone to speaker, placed it on the table and put her hands over her eyes, blocking out images of what came afterwards and focusing on what went before. The circles, the cycles. Bad days, bad weeks, followed by a determination to help herself. New starts, excessive optimism, inappropriate behaviour. Three steps forward, four back. And the gradual comprehension that it would never get better. She could never evade this black demon permanently. She would fight this battle for the rest of her life unless she withdrew from the fray. The clarity and the horror of that moment emptied her of all emotion and her practical side took over. Make it painless, with as little mess as possible, organise the paperwork and get it over with.

James's voice came from the mobile. "That's five minutes. Beatrice, I know that was a deeply unpleasant exercise and I am sorry for the pain I caused. When revisiting those months, what did you observe?"

Beatrice blew her nose and picked up the phone. "Patterns. I keep thinking I can fix it myself. I keep thinking I will get better and be able to manage on my own again. But I never really managed. Not always when I was hyper and definitely not when I was depressed."

"Can we take that one step further? When you're in a cycle,

regardless of direction, how would you assess your decision-making capabilities?"

"You're talking present tense, James."

"And you're talking past. Are these patterns obsolete or something we still need to address?"

Beatrice stared at the palm of her hand. Lines she'd been born with, scars she'd added.

"No, not obsolete. I recognise paranoia and a certain amount of displacement activity."

"So we come to question four. Is your current choice of activity furthering the aim of your sabbatical, or are you seeking any opportunity to evade serious thought?"

"Why would I call you if I was trying to avoid thinking? Every single time we speak, I end up crying. I'm doing my best, but it bloody hurts, James. You bloody hurt. I know this is good for me and it is working, I suppose, but it's not easy."

"Beatrice, I think we can consider a milestone passed. Normally when you rail against the painful nature of therapy, you cite your age as a reason for sympathy. This time, you have taken responsibility. A story, if you have time. A child born with a malformed right foot. The big toe was missing and therefore so was his balance. Nevertheless, the child learnt to walk, even run, after a fashion. But he expended so much effort, compensating for that missing digit. Medicine advanced and surgeons were able to fit him with a prosthetic toe. Once he got used to it, he could do twice as much with half the energy. It didn't take him long to adapt, as he was only nine. You have a few years on him, but I'd like to think of what you and I do together as an artificial, but not uncomfortable, improvement to your life. Perhaps we can re-imagine Cognitive Behavioural Therapy as Curran's Big Toe."

Still sniffing, Beatrice expelled an involuntary laugh. "Do you use that line on all your clients?"

"No, because none is so determined to repel my assistance as you. Now, could we look at some exercises for you to try and arrange a follow-up session as soon as convenient?"

James. Inextricably linked with tears and tissues. Maybe he was right. It was simply a question of balance.

Chapter 27

By the time Ana found a parking spot in the shadow of the Good Shepherd Cathedral, Beatrice was feeling guilty. Absorbed in dissecting her own behaviour, the usual reaction to a conversation with James, she'd made barely any conversation with Ana on the journey. But her companion seemed similarly introspective.

They made directly for the seafront and wandered the wide promenade. Both gazed at the spread of sand and sea as the bay curved away. To her left rose a hill, covered in greenery, and to her right another, featuring some impressive architecture. Natural sentinels protecting the harbour. On the beach, dogs hared after one another, chased balls, splashed in the surf and barked. At the base of the sea wall, two bare-chested men worked on a sand-sculpture, their shirts spread out to catch coins from above.

"What do you say to a snack and something to drink first?" Beatrice asked her transformed companion.

Ana's hair was pulled into a tight bun and her face heavily made-up. She wore a dove-grey trouser suit with flat brogues. Her earrings were silver studs. She checked her watch, still radiating unease and tension.

"You've got plenty of time, so go ahead. I'll give it a miss. I'm going to take the scenic route to the meeting, just in case."

"You don't still think we're being followed? I thought you were convinced we were clear?"

"I am convinced. Those how-to-shake-a-tail tricks were very useful. Specially as I'm not even sure it was a tail. But you can't be too careful. Now listen, I don't think this guy's likely to give me more than an hour of his time, so I might come and lurk in the background while you talk to the Lopez woman. I won't join you, just be there to keep an eye." She opened her briefcase and withdrew a pair of black-rimmed glasses. In a second, her soft, luminous beauty developed an incisive edge, a metallic precision which could both intimidate and impress.

"I didn't know you wore specs," commented Beatrice.

"I don't. They're just glass. I used them a fair bit when I was younger, in an attempt to make people take me seriously. I thought glasses and DMs gave me an attitude."

"Did it work?"

"Sometimes." She applied plum lipstick, using her phone screen to check her reflection. "But it turns out blokes *do* make passes at girls with glasses. That's when the Doctor Martens came in handy. How do I look?"

"Somewhere between a columnist for the Financial Times and Belle du Jour. Either way, quite scary."

Ana laughed, straightened up and scanned the street. People crossed back and forth to the beach; holidaymakers, old folk, workers taking a break from the office. Children's laughter carried over the sound of the traffic. Beatrice felt a pull towards the water. Perhaps an ice-cream and a wander along the sand. She had ages yet.

Ana picked up the briefcase. "Right, I'm off. Wish me luck. And I'll join you at Casa Mimo just after two. You're sure you know where to go?"

"Lord, you do fuss. Yes. I wrote everything down. The directions, your instructions, the line of questioning we chose and even your recommendations as to what to eat. I'll be fine. Good luck, be careful and don't talk to strangers."

Ana grinned and strode off in the direction of the river. Beatrice crossed the road and spent forty minutes just people-watching. Unfortunately, people-watching, no matter how joyful, tended to put her into a fug. An affliction she couldn't shake, like being unable to appreciate a film because you can see through the flimsy sets. All these smiling faces, scampering paws, affectionate gestures and abandoned squeals of delight simply reminded Beatrice of how this moment was soon to be nothing more than a memory. One to be recalled, perhaps, beside a hospital bed, in a snowy graveyard or on a therapist's couch. She got up and headed for the old town.

On arrival at the restaurant, the waiter showed her to a reserved table near the back. It was a relief to sit down. Traipsing around the city streets was illuminating but tough on the feet. Not only that, but as preparation for a pretentious lunch, she had denied herself any kind of pre-lunch snack. In short, she was hot, tired, aching, hungry, and in a foul mood. Now, rather than enjoying her food, she could fully expect to be patronised and belittled by a snotty bloody wine expert. She ordered a glass of Rueda and a bottle of mineral water and hoped the bread basket would accompany her aperitif.

"Ms Stubbs?"

Beatrice looked up with a start. The tall woman standing at her table wore a black dress beneath a leather jacket, sunglasses and her short hair was dyed a shocking pink. She held out a hand. "I'm Isabella Lopez. Nice to meet you."

Beatrice got to her feet and recovered herself. "Nice to meet you too, Ms Lopez. Please, have a seat."

The dramatic creature smiled and hooked her handbag over the back of the chair. She sat, eased off her jacket and removed her sunglasses. "What happened to your face? You look more like a cage fighter than a journalist."

"At my age, that's actually a compliment. I fell up some stairs and hit my nose."

Isabella shrugged. "It happens. Are you waiting for long?"

The waiter arrived with the drinks. "Just long enough to order a drink. What would you like?" She remembered she was talking to one of the most famous wine experts in the region. "Or maybe we should decide what to eat first, so as not to queer your palate?"

"Queer my palate?" An enormous smile spread across her face. With a laugh, she reached behind her and pulled a gold-covered notebook from her bag. "I have to write that down. What a fantastic expression!" She looked up at the waiter, still beaming. "*Una cerveza, por favor.*"

"Beer? Oh, I assumed you'd want wine. I suppose that's a stereo-typical assumption you get all the time?"

"I do want wine. But I'm thirsty and beer is the best solution to that problem. Now, you must call me Isabella and can I call you Beatrice? You see, Beatrice, people do make assumptions about wine writers, but why wouldn't they? There is probably more bullshit written about wine than any other subject I can think of. Except modern art, perhaps. So it's no surprise that people expect us to be pretentious, precious snobs. Many of us are. But there are a few, and I include myself in this particular circle, who write about wine because we love the subject. It is a fascinating field which you must already know, as a food writer. Which magazine do you write for?"

Stunned by the torrent of rapid-fire information, it took Beatrice several seconds to remember the persona in which Ana had drilled her. "*Contemporary Cuisine.* We're independent, offering unbiased advice on quality food and drink all over Europe. We feature a different country each issue, which is why I'm researching Spain. It seemed to make sense to start in San Sebastian, and talk to the experts first." Her speech sounded rehearsed and unnatural, but Isabella was nodding.

"Of course. Where else? Have you tried any of the Michelin three stars yet? Who have you seen so far? Arzak? Andoni? Berasategui? When did you arrive?"

"Two hours ago."

That dazzling smile stretched across her face again as she thanked the waiter for her beer. He seemed pleasantly surprised by the reactions to his presence. Isabella took a long draught and smacked her lips.

"So I am the first? Perfect. You could not have made a better start, Beatrice, and you will be glad. I'll order for us today, and make a list of where else you should go and in which order. We're going to start with the equivalent of fish and chips. Today, you'll eat everyday Spanish food. Nothing special. But wait till you see how special it is. Then you will try an asador, visit one of the vineyards, perhaps one of the less famous ... what are you drinking?"

Without waiting for an answer, she picked up the glass and

sniffed. "Good choice. In fact, visiting the Rueda region is a great idea. They're overshadowed by the Rioja country, especially in recent years, which seems unfair as one of the finest wines ..."

"Yes, I wanted to ask you about that. You see, Isabella, the truth is, I'm more of an expert on food than wine. Which is why I chose to start my research with you. But should we order first, do you think? I've not eaten since breakfast."

Isabella obviously heard the urgency in Beatrice's tone and hailed the waiter. She rattled off instructions, underlined by emphatic hand gestures, and the waiter obediently wrote it all down. Then, finally, he brought the bread.

Beatrice grabbed a small roll and began buttering. Isabella studied her.

"Not too much bread. We have a feast ahead of us so you must not ... what was it ... queer your palate." She laughed and picked up the wine list. "This is fun for me, you know. To introduce someone to our food, our wine, our culture. You said you had a question."

Beatrice swallowed but before she could speak, Isabella flowed on.

"About Rueda being overshadowed, wasn't it? Mmm, that wasn't always the case. Their whites, verdejo and sauvignon blanc, have always outsold those of Rioja and built a well-deserved reputation for excellent wines. White Rioja used to be made the same way as red, in small barrels, aged for years. But then came stainless steel tanks, allowing vinification at low temperatures. Very successful move. Clean, fresh and the fruit to the fore. But the New World Chardonnays did it better. So white Rioja, once again, became the bridesmaid."

The roll had gone and Beatrice eyed the basket. At the risk of getting told off, she sneaked a slice of dark brown seeded stuff and asked another question to distract her pink-haired companion. "So what changed? How come it's the trendy wine of the moment?"

"Yes, that's what we all want to know. The truth is actually quite simple. It's a combination of a new style, smart marketing and one influential vineyard. That bread is very heavy so I suggest you only have one piece. So first, the new style. Rather than ageing it in barrels, the wine was only fermented in oak. That's what gives the stamp of old school quality to a modern wine. This showed the grape, mostly Viura, at its best. Mixed with Malvasia, the new white Rioja has a depth and richness, orange along with lemon, giving it a subtle edge over the competition. Ah ha! *Mejillones tigres!*"

An hour and a half later, Beatrice could take no more. Her appetite satiated, her notebook was as full as her stomach. She wrote the wine information in the front and details of the meal in the back, so she could gloat to Matthew later. She was also a little tipsy, in a pleasantly soft, at-ease-with-the-world sort of way. Isabella was still talking. In fact, she hadn't stopped.

"... lost his grape grower's card as a result. So no, it would be impossible to sell your wine as anything but what it is. As I said, the Control Board performs strict tests, both sensory and in the lab. If the wine is sub-standard, it cannot be called Rioja."

Beatrice saw Ana slip through the front door and take up position on a bar stool. She took a slow scan of the interior but did not acknowledge Beatrice.

"So if the wine is confirmed as meriting the Rioja label, what happens next?"

"That's up to the vineyard. They choose a winemaker and distributor and decide how much they want to sell and where. Do you want dessert?"

"Yes, but possibly sometime next week. Thank you for choosing such an amazing selection. I can honestly say that was one of the finest eating experiences I've ever had."

Isabella flashed her teeth once again. "Just a normal everyday snack for us, you know."

"So if a wine went out into the world labelled as Rioja, but actually contained something else, that could only happen at the bottling stage?"

Isabella's smile faded to be replaced by a look of puzzlement. "It's highly unlikely. I mean, the wine that leaves the vineyard has been quality tested and bears the guaranteed official label. Each bottle carries a stamp and a number. Impossible to fake."

Beatrice nodded and made a note. Nothing was impossible to

fake, but Isabella Lopez had certainly narrowed the scope. At only one point in the chain could another wine find its way into a Rioja bottle. After paying the surprisingly reasonable bill, Beatrice stood and offered her hand.

"Isabella, you have been more help than I can say. Thank you so much."

Isabella brushed her hand away, took her by the shoulders and kissed her on both cheeks. "It was a pleasure to meet you. Thank you for lunch. Please don't forget to send me a copy of the article. I would love to read it. Have a wonderful stay!"

"I won't forget." This lying lark got easier the more you did it. Not even a blush this time. Isabella turned and waved as she left, with one last burst of that incredible smile.

Ana came over and slid into the recently vacated seat. "You've lipstick on your cheek."

Beatrice dabbed at her face with a napkin. "How was your meeting?"

Ana shrugged. "Not sure. False. He was so cagey and asked more questions than he answered. I've a feeling he'd been primed. How was yours?"

"Excellent. I had seafood, the most astonishing ham, black pudding, little fishy kebabs and green beans with garlic, those Gernika peppers and three different kinds of wine to match."

Ana started to laugh. "So while you were sampling the local goodies and getting drunk, did you make any progress at all?"

Beatrice shoved her notebook at Ana. "All in there. I am a consummate professional."

Ana pushed it back. "And a lush. Come on, you can tell me all about it in the car. It'll keep you awake. Do you need the bathroom before we go?"

"You treat me like a wayward child. Actually, I think I do. Back in a minute."

Chapter 28

On the outskirts of Miranda de Ebro, the Range Rover turned into a newly developed housing estate, passed a group of gardeners planting shrubs along the roadside and rumbled into the underground car park. A navy Maserati was the only other vehicle in the extensive space.

Marisol checked her make-up and switched her phone to silent. She took the lift to the penthouse floor, as instructed. The door to the show apartment stood wide open and she heard classical music – Ravel's *Bolero* – playing within. Floor-to-ceiling windows filled the space with light. She locked the door behind her, turned and saw what lay on the dining table. A black cat mask, complete with ears and whiskers.

A note read: *Put this on. Take everything else off. Except your heels.*

She sighed. Masks. Of course. They'd done striptease, handcuffs, feathers and ice cubes; next on the list had to be masks. Why was the sexual experimentation phase always so predictable? Next, it would be role play or body paint.

She did as she was told, taking the time to fold her clothes carefully on the chair. She glanced out the window. Even if there had been anyone around, no one could see this far up. She walked to the bedroom, her skin responding with goosebumps to the cool breeze.

The room was empty. She stepped further in, to check the en-suite. Two hands caught her hips and pulled her backwards. She gasped as his lips met her neck and she felt the hairs on his chest tickle her back. The momentary adrenalin of fear transformed into an erotic charge of need, causing her breath to grow ragged. His hands moved up, cupping her breasts and pinching her nipples as she arched back against him. He kicked the door closed and turned her to face the full-length mirror.

A second electric charge shot through her. Most of his body was hidden by hers, but he towered head and shoulders above her, even with her heels. Dirty blond hair spiked over the devil mask disguising his eyes, but his mouth was visible, lips parted as he breathed into her ear. His hands moved with the grace and confidence of a master conductor, coaxing an orchestra of moans, sighs and whispers.

"Oh yes. Oh God, yes. Please, Simon, please."

Towels. Marisol smiled as she stepped dripping from the shower. He'd even remembered to bring towels this time. The man who thought of everything. Her body glowed as if in agreement. She dried her hair and reapplied her make-up, her mind already on the next phase of the day. When she returned to the living room, he had set the table for a picnic, with bread, cheeses, grapes, tapenade and red wine. He'd even brought a tablecloth and glasses. Still naked, he offered her a grape.

"Let me get dressed first."

"No, I want to watch you eat as you are."

Marisol put on her underwear. "If I do that, we both know what will happen and I'll have to shower all over again. How late is it?"

"Only two. We have plenty of time, and I know so many ways we could spend it." He gave her what he obviously thought was a smouldering look.

"Not today. Too much to do." She zipped up her dress and checked her phone. No messages. Relieved, she sat at the table and cut herself a slice of Manchego.

Vasconcellos watched her, his pretty features swelling towards petulance. "I arranged it so there would be no viewings today. We can stay here as long as we want. Anyway, I thought he was in Madrid until tomorrow?"

"He is. But I have other problems to deal with." She plucked a handful of grapes. "One of which is your ex-future wife."

"My ex-future wife – how does that work?"

Marisol took a sip of wine and studied the naked man opposite. Beautiful, needy, reasonably smart, potentially powerful, eager to please, very rich and a seriously good fuck. It was a damn shame to let him go. He'd have made an ideal son-in-law. Still, dropping him as Luz's intended meant their affair could continue for longer. Every cloud …

"You're not going to marry Luz. And before you ask, no, it's nothing to do with us. The stupid little bitch is pregnant."

"No way! Luz, pregnant? Jesus. I didn't even know she was seeing someone."

Marisol decided to limit what to share. This kind of gossip was practically hard currency and Vasconcellos would not always be in her thrall. It would be tough to find her daughter any kind of match now, but if the full details emerged, it might be impossible.

"You aren't the only one. Arturo and I only found out by accident." She sighed. "It's inconvenient, but not a major problem. This morning I took her out of university, tomorrow I'll take her to my specialist in Bilbao. All over and forgotten by Monday. Then I'll start the search for someone older, equally wealthy but slightly more desperate than Vitoria's most eligible bachelor, Simon Vasconcellos. On the bright side, you and I can continue to enjoy each other's company for a while longer."

His concerned expression softened into a smile, then his focus shifted and he gazed at the tapenade. Marisol waited a few moments, aware the vague expression on his face could mean anything from digestion to deep thought. Finally, she got bored, wiped her fingers with a napkin and emptied her glass. If that got no reaction, she'd glance at her watch. He reacted. Turning to her with an intense blaze in his eyes, he reached for her hand.

"So your daughter loves another man. For my part, I wish her joy. Why don't you find the baby's father and see if he wants to marry Luz? Life is short and hard enough, so when an opportunity for joy arises, she should take it. Maybe they'll be happy together. Happier than she and I could have ever been. What kind of marriage is it when two people swear vows to one another while both are in love with someone else? Yes, that's right, in love with someone else. I love you. So this is not just a chance for Luz, it's one for the two of us. Leave Aguirre and be with me, Marisol. I can give you everything you want and more. I've never in my life loved a woman the way I love you. I don't think I ever will. This is *our* chance."

Marisol removed her hand from his grasp and reached up to stroke his face. Their eyes locked and she saw the conviction, the determination, the foolish belief that love could conquer all.

"Simon, you wonderful, sexy, thoughtful man. Listen to me. You will thank me for the rest of your life for saying this. No. I will not leave Arturo. For someone born as beautiful and privileged as you, it is impossible to understand how some of us need to constantly shore up our positions, strengthen our defences, prepare for enemies where we least expect, and ceaselessly work to maintain our status. I will never leave my husband for you and there will come a day when you'll be grateful I did not. Nor will Luz marry whichever opportunistic little shit rutted her. She will do the correct thing and stand by the family. Because she is an Aguirre. And so am I."

Vasconcellos stared at her without moving. Marisol stood up, brushed off any crumbs and picked up her phone.

"Thank you for this afternoon. You're amazing. And if you're free next Thursday, I'm attending a charity lunch in Santander. We could book a hotel and experiment a little. I was wondering … would you like to see me in my uniform?"

His eyes changed. She walked round the table and kissed him deeply. He kissed her back with such craven desire her resolve weakened and she found herself reaching beneath the tablecloth.

Ten minutes later, the Range Rover emerged from the underground car park, nosed out of the driveway and turned in the direction of Vitoria. The driver didn't look back.

Chapter 29

"Oi. I need to get a coffee. Do you want to come in or stay here?"

Beatrice jolted awake and stared out at the car park. "Where are we?"

"About twenty minutes from Vitoria, but I'm flagging and I need some caffeine. You can carry on snoring if you like." Ana unclipped her seatbelt and reached in the back for her briefcase.

"Yes," Beatrice yawned. "That might be best. I'll sit here and keep an eye on things."

Ana withdrew her purse and shoved the briefcase behind her. She shook her head with a laugh. "Three glasses? You're a cheap date. Back in five minutes."

Her hair loose, the jacket discarded, Ana looked much more like herself as she strode towards the entrance of the motorway services. Beatrice adjusted her position. Creaky and sticky and rather puffed-up, she needed a shower and a lie-down under cool sheets. She dragged her bag from the back seat and checked her phone. 16.24. No messages. So presumably Matthew and Adrian had nothing to report. Well, she'd be back at the hotel by five-ish and a full report could be delivered over dinner.

A car reversed towards her from the space opposite. Ana had a habit of parking backwards, presumably to make a quick getaway. That girl really would make an excellent police officer. Beatrice watched a family return to their Opel Corsa, the children's whiny bleating audible. Too much sugar, bound to be. Why, she wondered, did motorway service stations all over the world attract exactly the same kind of washed-out, tetchy, badly dressed people?

Still, the journey had been worth it. Not just for that lunch, but her and Ana's information tallied exactly. The fraud could not be perpetrated from the Aguirre estate. The Control Board lived up to their name and even Aguirre's influence would not be sufficient to endanger the name of Rioja. So it had to be Alava Exports. Filling an approved bottle with another product made no sense, so they must be making fake labels for sub-standard bottles. Unless something else happened between approval and bottling. Did Aguirre bottle his own produce, or was that part of the Alava Exports service?

Beatrice picked up her phone again to call Matthew. 16.36. The phone rang before she could press a button, startling her into losing her grip. She snatched it up again. Ana's name on the display. Probably enquiring as to drinks preferences.

"Yes? Five minutes, I think you said. You've been in there almost quarter of an hour."

No response. Beatrice checked the screen. Full signal. She pressed the phone to her ear, peering at the main building.

"Ana? Are you all right? Ana? Ana!"

The phone went dead. Beatrice scrabbled to release her seatbelt while redialling Ana's mobile. It rang and rang and went to answer phone. She looked around the car park again. The bland, boring functional car park had shifted into something with shadows, anonymous vehicles and hidden eyes. She got out of the car and went round to the driver's seat. The keys dangled from the ignition. She yanked them out, locked the car and hurried towards the service station, pressing Ana's number again. No reply.

The automatic doors opened, releasing a smell of chips, coffee and fried onions. Beatrice glanced at the café, her eyes scanning and dismissing each dark-haired female in seconds. The shop, full of shouting teenagers; and the toilets, with the inevitable queue of false smiles and sharp eyes were all devoid of anyone resembling Ana. Beatrice hurried back to the main concourse and took several deep breaths, while her eyes assessed each passer-by.

Stop panicking. Ana pressed the number by mistake. Her phone is at the bottom of her bag and she can't hear it. Beatrice shook her head at her own reasoning. Ana keeps her phone in her pocket and answers on the first ring like a gunslinger. Her briefcase is still in the car. Which is locked. Where right now, Ana will be standing outside, frowning and holding a take-away coffee.

Beatrice ducked her way through a crowd of German bikers, but even before approaching the car, she knew Ana wasn't there. She tried the phone again. Her head, muddled and hot, nagged at her. She'd forgotten something. Her eyes lifted and she saw it. A large black SUV had stopped directly in front of their vehicle, blocking their exit. Two thickset men, the driver and front-seat passenger, turned to stare. The tinted back windows gave nothing away. Blood pumped in Beatrice's ears as she unlocked the car and sat in the driver's seat. A pointless exercise, as she couldn't drive. Her phone beeped. Beatrice jumped.

The message was from Ana. Short and to the point.

GO! NOW!

A car horn made her start once again. A Dutch motorhome behind the SUV expressed its impatience. The black vehicle drove forward, at about two kilometres per hour.

Beatrice looked back at the screen. Go? Where? Her hand reached for the keys. Everything was wrong. The handbrake, the gearstick, the seatbelt and there was no bloody clutch pedal. An automatic. It was insane. She rarely drove in Britain, so to take a strange car onto the wrong side of Spanish roads whilst in a blind panic was pure madness. The SUV turned left at the end of the row. They'd be back, she knew it. In as much time as it took to circle the car park. Beatrice started the car, as Matthew's voice surfaced from a half-forgotten memory.

"It's like riding a bike. You never really forget how to do it. Now, check your mirrors and indicate. Off we go."

Pulling out smoothly, without a single kangaroo jump, Beatrice followed the path the SUV had taken. Her right foot tensed, ready to brake as she cruised out of the service station and back onto the motorway. She checked all three mirrors every ten seconds as her thoughts followed a circular swooping pattern. She'd left Ana. On Ana's instructions. But was it really Ana? She should turn back. No sign of the SUV. She should call the police. The traffic was terrifying. She'd left Ana. Still no sign of that car. Or those men. She kept going. She'd left Ana. The speedometer bobbed around just below ninety kph. She stayed in the slow lane, a healthy distance behind a large truck. A blue motorway sign informed her that she was thirteen kilometres from Vitoria. A flash of lights made her check her rear-view mirror. The SUV was speeding down the fast lane, intimidating vehicles in its path by flashing its lights and driving dangerously close.

Beatrice fought back her panic and tried to think logically. The men were after her, that much was clear. The question was, why? Did they mean to crank up the level of threat so she and Ana would do as they were told and leave well alone? Or was their intention to get rid of them more permanently, in the same way as Tiago? The tension in her shoulders developed into a pain as she saw the vehicle indicate and slow to pull in behind her. They couldn't run her off the road, not with this many witnesses. They would have to get her onto some deserted back road, which was not going to happen. One alternative was to follow her into the city and grab her as she left the car. In which case, she would have to stop somewhere public. The grille filled her rear window. They were so close she couldn't even see the occupants. If she were to brake ... and that gave her an idea.

On entering the centre of Vitoria, Beatrice had no idea which way to go. The traffic stopped at a set of lights, with Beatrice on the inside lane and her pursuers directly behind. Her hands were still shaking. She looked for the handle to unwind the window. It was missing. Her heart skipped until she realised this was a slightly more modern car than Matthew's ancient VW Golf. She depressed the button and the glass rolled down. An elderly man with a stick stood waiting for his Scottie dog to finish sniffing a tree trunk.

"Scusi? Pardon! Donde é policia? Emergency! Policia?"

The old chap and his dog both looked up. The dog lost interest instantly, but the man continued to stare. Beatrice checked the lights. Still red. The old man. Still staring. With great deliberation, he pointed up the street to her right. He raised one finger and indicated a left with the opposite hand. The lights changed and an immediate blast of a horn sounded from behind. The old man continued, by holding up two fingers and indicating left again. He gave the thumbs-up just as she jerked forward from the impact of the SUV driving into her bumper. The old man's jaw fell open.

She accelerated and swung into the right turn without indicating. Her eyes flicked to the mirror. She'd gained a second or two but they were approaching fast. She indicated right and slowed, watching for a gap in the traffic. She had to time it perfectly. A motorbike zoomed past, leaving a space before the taxi behind and Beatrice wrenched the wheel to the left. The taxi blared its horn and the driver stopped to gesticulate out of the window, blocking the path of the SUV. Second left. She hoped to God the old sod had given her the correct directions. The cacophony of horns and voices receded as she followed the curve and she checked the mirror to see how much time she had. Here they were.

She sped past the first left, conscious of the black shape growing in her peripheral vision, and screeched into the next street. He was right. She recognised the street up ahead and the forbidding façade of the police station. She checked the mirror to be sure. Much too close. She took a deep breath, mentally apologised to Jaime and slammed both feet to the floor. Her judgement may have been accurate and the BMW might have halted in time. She'd never know. Because three tons of Mercedes-Benz driving at forty-three kilometres per hour rammed her straight into the wall of the police station.

The airbag released, her seatbelt squashed her ribcage and all the air seemed to leave her lungs. A second of stillness. Then a metallic squeal pierced the silence and a reverse pull bounced her forwards. She banged her face on the steering wheel, bringing tears and blood to her eyes. Bile filled her mouth as she heard shouting. The shattered windscreen collapsed inwards. Her door opened and a man said something she didn't understand. The SUV pulled past, gunned its engines and screeched off down a side street. A fresh volley of yells went up and a siren began wailing. The man released Beatrice's seatbelt and eased her out of the car. She got to her feet, bloodied and shaking, and threw up all over her shoes.

As she submitted to an examination by the police medic, she prepared herself to face Detective Milandro. She knew how he was likely to perceive this situation. The interfering Brit crashes back into his life. Literally. She had to convince him to take her seriously. This was not simply an overactive imagination and excess of alcohol. She needed backup.

To her surprise, the medic didn't breathalyse her. Instead, he squirted some clear gel onto a dressing and handed it to her.

"Keep this against your lip. The bleeding has stopped but this will prevent the swelling. You will have some more bruises. I leave you now. Good luck."

"Thank you," Beatrice mumbled. Once the door closed behind him, Beatrice reached for her handbag. What a mess. Tiny cubes of glass and brick dust lay in every fold of the leather, along with a dark greasy stain all over the bottom. Still, she should be grateful someone had thought to rescue it from the car. Keeping one hand pressed to her mouth, she carried the bag over to the bin, wincing at the pains in her chest and neck. She shook off the debris then dug around inside till she found what she was looking for. Her mobile and a business card. Jaime Rodriguez, Editor of *El Periódico*. With a glance at the door, she dialled.

"Rodriguez? *Diga.*"

"Hello, Jaime. This is Beatrice."

"Beatrice? Beatrice! How's your road trip going?"

His friendly voice offered a sense of sanctuary which swelled Beatrice's throat so that she was unable to speak for several seconds.

"Beatrice? What's the matter?"

She took a deep breath, which hurt. "Jaime, I'm afraid I have some bad news. Ana has disappeared. And I crashed your car." She blurted out the story, managing to stay professional as she delivered the facts.

Jaime didn't waste time. "Where are you now?"

"In Vitoria, at the police station. Could you come? Only I think I might need moral support."

"Give me ten minutes."

Twenty minutes later, she was still sitting alone in the medical room. The shock gradually subsided and all she had to focus on was worry and pain. She called Ana's number every five minutes, but the phone was switched off. Flicking through her address book, her thumb hovered over James, but she decided against. Too complicated. Instead she selected Adrian.

He answered on the first ring. "Aha! You're back. How did it go?"

"Oh Adrian. I am glad to hear your voice. Are you at the hotel? Is Matthew with you?"

"He's just popped to the loo. We're still in Ribera. I'm on the terrace sampling a rosé and admiring the scenery. We've got lots to tell you. When will you be back?"

Beatrice hesitated. "How far are you from Alava Exports?"

"Around a fifteen-minute walk. We were about to pay the bill here and call for a taxi back to Vitoria. We've had a marvellous afternoon. The tour was tremendous, let me tell you. And Spanish men! I had no idea! I fell in love three times today and at least two of these waiters meet with my approval."

"Adrian, listen to me, this is important. Is there any way you can safely observe the Alava Exports site without being seen? I need you to watch for any activity over the next couple of hours."

"Umm, I think so. What sort of activity are we looking for?"

"Anything. The company should be finished for the day, so I want to know what goes on after hours. But Adrian ..."

"I know. Keep out of sight, do nothing, say nothing and just report back to you later."

"I'd be most grateful. Shall we meet back at the hotel at eight?"

"See you then. Oh, how was your day?"

"Horrible. I lost Ana and I crashed the car into a police station."

His gasp was genuine. "Oh my God! Are you all right?"

"Yes, yes. Right now I'm more worried about Ana than anything else."

"We'll come back and help."

"No, you stay where you are. The police are already searching for her. The best thing you can do is keep an eye on that place. But please do it safely. Give my love to Matthew and tell him not to worry. Everything is under control."

"OK, I will. Beatrice?"

"Yes?"

"Do take care."

Detective Milandro opened the door and studied Beatrice.

"How are you feeling?"

Beatrice knew from experience the Spanish detective's bland expression was not to be trusted, but his concern seemed real. "Shaken and bruised but mostly worried. Is there any news of Ana?"

"Not yet. But I have dispatched three teams to search. Your associate is here, from the newspaper."

"Oh thank God."

"I'd like to hear the story again and this time my boss wants to sit in. Would you come with me to an interview room?"

Beatrice got to her feet and took the dressing from her lip. "Of course. Detective, I know I'm a horn in your side, but I assure you I really am trying to do the right thing."

His eyes narrowed, but his lips twitched in an impression of a smile.

"This interview, can Jaime come too?"

Milandro looked at her, his expression neutral. "Are you sure that's what you want?"

She nodded. He shrugged and led the way down the corridor.

Jaime seemed most dreadfully upset. Of course. Seeing the remains of his beloved vehicle being winched out of the wall must have come as a bit of a shock. While Milandro went to find his senior officer, Jaime's hands shook and he looked as if he was about to cry.

"Jaime, I am so sorry about your car. Believe me, if there was any other way ..."

He gathered himself. "I don't care about the BMW. It's insured. And there are more important things to worry about. I'm just thankful you weren't too badly hurt. Even so, you don't look good. You're so pale. Maybe you should eat something? Perhaps some chocolate? Did you take a coffee?"

"I'm fine, really. I know my face is a train wreck, but it's not as bad as it looks. I'm just so worried about Ana. These men, if it is the same bunch, made some very unpleasant threats last time. They frightened Ana badly. They told her to leave Vitoria."

"But she didn't." Jaime shook his head, a tired gesture.

"No, of course not. She's a journalist. She could no more leave a story alone than a child could a scab. We found out a great deal today and I'm convinced we've been looking in the wrong direction. It's not Aguirre himself who's been ..."

The door opened. Milandro hesitated, his face dark and uncertain. Beatrice's instinct screamed bad news.

"Ana?" she asked, her voice constrained.

He shook his head. "Nothing yet. Patrols have combed the site and alerted traffic police. A general bulletin has gone out across the region. But I just had news from the coroner which makes me very concerned for her welfare. The body of Miguel Saez surfaced this morning, in the lake near Garaio. The coroner suspects foul play. The cause of death was drowning, but his body had been mutilated before he died."

Beatrice clutched her hands together, her eyes fixed on the detective. "Facially mutilated?"

Milandro's eyes narrowed. "Yes. His mouth was slit to his ears."

Jaime retched and staggered out of the door. Beatrice went to press her hands to her mouth but reconsidered. Instead she squeezed her eyes shut. Tiago's nose, Miguel's mouth. And Ana?

She looked up at the detective, unable to voice her plea. He understood.

"We'll find her, Detective Inspector Stubbs. But I think you might need to tell me everything."

Chapter 30

Tunçay's chest constricted and his dry eyes opened. Shafts of sunlight penetrating the curtains showed the layers of smoke shifting around the bedsit. The connection between the smell of an ashtray and the taste in his mouth repulsed him. He never smoked in his room. It was disgusting. He was disgusting.

He swung his heavy legs off the bed and sat up. Fully clothed, stinking of cigarettes and with a hangover pounding at the door, he needed water. As he got to his feet, his lungs protested and a coughing fit forced him back onto the mattress. It also welcomed in his hangover. He stumbled to the tiny kitchenette and drank three glasses of water in succession, hands shaking and eyes watering. There had to be a word for what his stomach was doing but he couldn't describe it, not in any language.

He opened all the windows, squinting into the low sunshine, and breathed some fresh air, which set off his cough once more. With an extreme effort not to vomit, he collected the empty bottles and full ashtray and tipped them into the bin. The stench of stale lager brought acidic bile to his throat and he stood with his head over the sink for several minutes. The wave receded.

Chill air freshened the room but turned his skin clammy. Tunçay grabbed his washbag and towel and unlocked the door, putting his faith in the power of hot, steamy water.

Forty minutes later, he was dressed, the flat was cleaner and he'd begun throwing his few belongings into his suitcase. Some decisions were clear. He would not leave Luz. But he would leave Burgos. Where to go was another question. Not Turkey. He wasn't ready yet. Maybe he could get a job in Logroño and see Luz at weekends. He needed to talk to her before doing anything, but her phone went unanswered and his texts received no reply.

Maybe he should wait till Sunday and talk to her, face to face. He finished packing and ate a noodle soup. If he didn't show up at the restaurant and kept his head down, he could take action in the next couple of weeks. No need to be hasty. After all, his rent was paid till the end of October. His phone rang.

Mehmet. Tunçay let it ring. What could he say? He was washing up his bowl when he heard something outside the front door. He stopped and held his breath. Nothing. He tiptoed across and looked through the spyhole. Nothing. He unlocked the door and slowly inched it open. On the doormat lay a magazine. Tunçay scanned the corridor. No one. He bent to pick it up. A tourist brochure: *Turkey. A Country for all Tastes.*

He left it there, locked the door and called Mehmet.

"I told you on the phone, the only place I will take you is the airport. You have to get on a plane and leave. Don't piss me about, Tunçay. Listen, I've never seen Bulent scared of anything or anyone before. But this is serious. On the next flight if I have to drag you myself."

"Mehmet, you're not listening. I can't leave yet. I can't. I need to talk to someone and I can't get her on the phone. I need to tell her what's happening. I have to stay until at least Sunday."

Mehmet didn't reply. Tunçay recognised that expression of focusing on the task in hand. Whether it was mincing mutton, shelling fava beans or driving through midday traffic, Mehmet maintained his concentration.

"This is your university girl, I suppose? Yes, don't look shocked, everyone knows. Deniz's mother-in-law lives on the ground floor of your building so nothing is secret. By the way, she doesn't mind the overnight guest but disapproves of you feeding the cat. Listen to me, Tunçay. For your girlfriend, this is a student romance, a bit of exotic while away from home, forgotten as soon as real life starts. You'll get more loyalty from the cat. As soon as she goes back to her family, you'll be dropped. Don't risk yourself for a spoilt little princess. And remember, these people could make life very awkward for Bulent, for Deniz, for all of us."

Tunçay stayed silent until the traffic began moving. "All right, I will go back to Turkey. At least for a while, till things settle down. But I must go to her *residencia* first. If I can't leave her a message, I won't go."

Mehmet cleared his throat with something like a curse, but indicated towards the university. "Which way?"

"Left. Calle Francisco de Vitoria. Do you have a pen?"

Confident, loud laughter filled the open spaces as Tunçay moved through the lunchtime crowds of students. Everyone seemed to have a purpose and a right to be there. He reached into his jacket for the letter and reminded himself of his own purpose. Luz's block was quieter than the main concourse, but he still felt an interloper as he stood in the doorway. Where were the mailboxes? Exposed and nervous, he turned away. He'd call. He'd send an email. What difference did a hand-written letter make? He knew exactly what difference it would make. He turned back.

The *residencia* door was wedged open. Perhaps the mailboxes were inside. Once over the threshold, he made a rapid decision. He would go to her room. Maybe leave the letter with her flatmate. He'd come this far, Mehmet was waiting, he had to act and get out. Her voice seemed to echo in his head, giving him directions as he ran up the stairs. He'd gone two doors past her room before he realised and retraced his steps, breathing heavily.

When he'd recovered his calm, which took longer than his breath, he knocked. The girl who opened the door looked familiar. Rita. The room-mate, the giggling customer, the uninteresting background to so many photographs featuring his beautiful Luz. Her expression was haughty, but curious.

"What do you want?"

His speech facility stalled. "I came because of Luz." He indicated the envelope.

Rita dropped her head onto her shoulder and her smile fell short of her eyes. "Ha! I thought as much. Well, Lovely Lashes, you missed the boat. She's gone. Her mother came this morning to collect her stuff. She's dropped out, the silly cow."

Tunçay shook his head. "She's resigned from her course? Are you sure?"

"Sure enough to advertise for a new room-mate. Hey, don't look like that. Not the end of the world. It's a shame for me, and for you too, I guess."

"Well, I ..."

"It's even a shame for the legal profession. She'd have made a great lawyer. But we should be happy for her. She's found her Mr Right. Her mother said they announced their engagement this weekend and they're getting married next summer. Wouldn't suit me, I want a career before I have kids, but her family's pretty traditional. And her fiancé is something impressive in the building trade, apparently. Good luck to her, I say."

"Of course. Good luck to her. I should go. I'm sorry to trouble you."

"No trouble. Hope to see you again sometime. Maybe we'll pop into your restaurant one of these days, just to say hello. I'm Rita. What's your name?"

"My name is Mehmet. Thanks very much. Goodbye."

He stood in the hallway of the *residencia*, his head resting against the wall and his feelings draining out all over the industrial-grade carpet. He told himself this was a good thing. It would make him lighter. He would go home with less baggage.

Chapter 31

She told them everything. Almost. As soon as Jaime returned, pale-faced and sweaty, Salgado-the-slug joined them, with a brusque nod of acknowledgement towards Beatrice. He ignored Jaime completely. Beatrice gave a full account of what she knew and the source of her information. The only item she omitted was the current location of Matthew and Adrian. Without telling an outright lie, she inferred they were on their way back to the city, having visited a vineyard. She wasn't even sure why.

Salgado required frequent translations, eyeing Beatrice with great suspicion, as if she were using expressions such as 'trawl', 'scupper' and 'shaking like a leaf' deliberately to annoy him. After Milandro produced Ana's briefcase, she handed over all the documents. It felt like a second betrayal of her friend, but she had no choice. Salgado asked a question in Spanish. While they spoke in low, guttural tones, Beatrice got chance to talk to Jaime.

"I'm so glad you're here. I feel absolutely out of my depth. Are you feeling all right?"

Jaime shrugged. "I think I now understand the meaning of the phrase 'worried sick.'"

"Me too. I can't bear to think of those men ..."

"Beatrice, the one thing we must remember is that Ana is one of the most resourceful women I know. If anyone can find a way out of this, she will."

The senior officer shoved back his chair and with a dismissive nod in their direction, made for the door. Milandro stood, rasping the backs of his fingers against his chin.

"Detective Inspector Stubbs, I'll take you back to your hotel. Under the circumstances, I think you should stay there for the time being. I checked just now and your friends have not yet returned. Where are they?"

Beatrice didn't hesitate. "Sightseeing, probably. They'll be back for dinner, I'm sure."

Milandro's expression, blank as a snake's, still managed to convey disbelief. His black eyes bore into hers as if trying to force out the truth. Jaime broke the spell.

"I'll stay with her until her friends return, Detective. I hate to think of her being alone."

Milandro's eyes flicked away and back again, reminding her of a gecko, silent, patient and predatory.

"If you wish."

The drive to the hotel seemed interminable, as the streets were clogged with rush-hour traffic. Beatrice fidgeted in the back seat beside Jaime, who stared silently out of the window. She would bet he was wishing he'd never met Beatrice Stubbs. Milandro sat in the passenger seat, making occasional comments to the police driver. Beatrice tried to concentrate on how to proceed, but her mind replayed the expressions of the men she'd interrupted at Ana's apartment. Ugly, cruel and without compassion. She placed her hands to her temples and tried to massage away her imagination.

The hotel doorman was obviously intrigued by Beatrice's arrival in a police vehicle. He looked at them with a kind of amused respect until he saw her face.

Milandro got out. "I'll escort you upstairs, if you don't mind. I'd like to check your room." It was more of an imperative than a request. Beatrice didn't argue.

They crossed the marble floor towards the lifts, Jaime on one side, Milandro on the other, making her feel more like a convict than ever.

Once inside, she watched as the detective checked the room with methodical precision, trying window locks, testing the phone, searching the wardrobe, shining a torch under the bed. Jaime's phone rang, but he cut the chirpy tune dead. The atmosphere reminded Beatrice of the days when she had worked in witness protection. Long hours of tension, bored but alert, tuned to every irregularity. It wore her out. The sound of Milandro tearing back the shower curtain made her jump. Jaime reached across to squeeze her shoulder in a gesture of reassurance but unfortunately chose the left one, still tender from being wrenched by the seatbelt. Then someone knocked at the door.

Milandro emerged from the bathroom and Beatrice tensed as she saw him withdraw his gun. He jerked a thumb at her, indicating she should go into the bathroom. Despite her resentment at being bossed around, she knew how frustrating it could be when someone disobeyed orders. It was his investigation now and she was nothing more than a witness. She went into the bathroom but left the door ajar. She watched through the gap between hinges as Jaime retreated to stand with his back against the wall. Milandro checked the spyhole.

He holstered his gun and looked in Beatrice's direction with a half smile. "It seems we can call off the missing person search. She's here." He unlocked the door.

"Oh thank God!" Beatrice hurried across the room only to stop in her tracks. The dark-haired woman in the doorway with a suitcase and a basket of flowers wasn't Ana. It was Luz Aguirre.

Luz obviously had not expected Beatrice to have company. She looked from one to the other and her face showed more alarm than surprise. "I'm sorry. I didn't want to disturb you. But I have something for you." Her expression was hunted.

Beatrice made a decision. Whatever the reason for this unexpected visit, she needed privacy.

"Hello Luz. You're not disturbing me. Just a case of mistaken identity, that's all. Detective, I've made the same error. This is an acquaintance of mine, and she certainly does look like Ana, I agree. However, the search is still on. Gentlemen, thank you both for your support. I'm tremendously grateful. But now I think I'd prefer to have some time to chat to my friend and have a restorative gin and tonic." She pointed towards the phone. "Can we agree to maintain mobile contact and update each other when we have news?"

Milandro moved to stand in front of her, his eyes like anthracite. "If you hear anything, I want to know. And I mean anything."

She nodded, forcing herself to maintain eye contact until he glanced at Luz.

Jaime reached forward to kiss her cheeks. "Call me. Anytime. I just need to know you're OK." He squeezed her upper arms as if to underline his sincerity and stared deeply into her eyes.

Beatrice tried to smile but instantly felt her lip crack and begin to bleed. She reached into her sleeve for a tissue. "I'll be in touch. And really, thank you both so much for your help. Detective, please find her. Remember what I said about *El Papagaio*. It must be worth a try."

Luz stood back and allowed them to pass. They watched the two men turn the corner of the corridor, Jaime's mobile audible once again. Poor man. The life of a newspaper editor was hectic enough without dropping everything to hold Beatrice's hand. She turned to her visitor.

"Please, come in."

"Thank you." Luz handed her the flowers. "These are for you. Did you have another accident?"

"Yes, this time with the wall of the police station. Seems I attract trouble."

Luz closed the door behind her. "No, I don't think you attract trouble. I think you go looking for it."

Chapter 32

Take, take, take.

He only had himself to blame. Women were, always had been, his Achilles heel. They sucked him dry, took everything he had and came back for more. Aguirre stared out at the dense cloud, a black roiling fungal formation, a reflection of his emotional state. The private jet sank lower and Aguirre clipped his seatbelt before the attendant could advise him to do so. Even when it was in his own interests, Aguirre hated being told what to do.

Klaudyna made no move to return to her seat, still curled up on the buttermilk leather sofa, her back to him, sighing, sniffing and cuddling a sheepskin rug. Silly bitch. She'd dragged it out for almost half an hour now. Whining and griping all the way to the airport about their aborted evening, complaining and sniping for most of the flight about his family and then she'd crossed the line, suggesting Marisol had him by the *cojones*. His outburst sent both attendants into hiding and a fountain of tears flowed down that pretty Polish nose.

Enough.

The flight touched down at 17.20. Ten minutes late. The pilot blamed the weather. Like a gentleman, Aguirre gestured for Klaudyna to go down the aisle first. She threw a reproachful glance at him which evoked nothing more than repulsion. Puffy eyes, red nose and her messy make-up showed how far the mask had slipped. His decision was the right one and part of him already yearned for the next adventure.

They crossed the tarmac, where two vehicles waited. His Range Rover and a taxi. He motioned to his driver to collect his suitcase and signalled to the cabbie.

"Get that bag and take this lady where she wants to go. Charge it to my account."

"*Si, Señor Aguirre.*"

Klaudyna's eyes blazed. "You're putting me in a taxi? I don't believe it. Arturo, for God's sake, what is the matter with you!"

"It is finished between us, Klaudyna. I wish I could say I'm sorry, but in fact, that would be a lie. You are greedy and demanding and have no sense of your place. It's my own fault for indulging you. This is where it stops. Goodbye, Klaudyna, and good luck."

He got into the passenger seat of the Range Rover and closed the door, shutting out the infernal noise. For a foreigner, she knew some shocking words.

On the approach to the Castelo, Aguirre's phone rang for the seventh time. He checked the display and once again rejected the call. He switched the phone to silent and looked up at the house. Marisol waited in the doorway.

"Arturo, you mustn't blame Carmina. She's terrified and already had a panic attack this afternoon. It's not her fault and after all she's a housekeeper, not a security guard. Luz went out via the library and must have hitched a lift with the caterers. Carmina thought she was in her room. She had no idea she was missing until she took her lunch upstairs. Inez is on her way to Burgos and Paz is calling all her friends in Vitoria. I've been thinking. When we find her, we must send her away for a while. Maybe abroad."

Aguirre swept past her and strode up the stairs. "Arturo de Aguirre is well known for his refusal to tolerate incompetence. We never use those caterers again and ensure no one else in our acquaintance does. Carmina is due for early retirement and I will choose the next housekeeper. I think we'll have a man this time, someone discreet. More like a butler. As for your daughter, I'll decide how to handle this."

Marisol made to follow him but he held up a hand.

"If you don't mind, I'd like to see for myself."

He knew as soon as he opened the office door. The chair was halfway across the room, as if its last occupant had rushed out in a hurry. Aguirre would never leave the room that way. This place was his haven, his War Office, his operational HQ and each time he left, he prepared it with great respect for the next visitor – himself.

Years ago, he'd allowed the girls to join him for short periods. Pie charts, bar graphs and colourful graphics demonstrated their father's power and reach. Yet their tiny attention spans and irritating prattle had disappointed and bored him. Now, no one, not even Marisol, came in here. When the time was right, he would introduce Basajaun to his domain. When the time was right.

The machines booted up and he examined his work station. The mouse lay to the right of the mat. All the loose change in the drawer had gone. Two greasy smudges marred the screen. His browser history showed no activity, but recent items viewed included payrolls from the last two years, personnel data, private profit and loss accounts, and carefully worded letters to significant influential people in the wine trade.

He pressed his fingers to his temples.

Power.

His daughters were not beautiful or particularly intelligent, but they took after their father in one way. They understood power. Find it, ally with it, marry it, use it and hang onto it at all costs. Luz was powerless in the face of her father's strength and influence. So she had stolen herself some bargaining chips. She found a way into his private affairs and armed herself for battle. In a way, he admired her gall. He would win, of that there was no doubt, but Luz could be proud of herself. She put up a fight.

The battle would be one-sided, however. And the sooner it were over, the better for everyone. He reached for his phone and cursed when he saw fifteen missed calls. Eleven from Klaudyna, two from Tomas, one from Paz and the one he'd been waiting for.

He pressed voicemail and allowed his eyes to rest on a photograph. The three girls, apparent angels in soft-focus, surrounded their mother, who held a week-old Basajaun in a crocheted blanket. In the background, the Castelo de Aguirre vineyards. A family, finally complete. He would protect them with his life.

In his ear, laconic growls and adenoidal shrills told him Tomas and Paz had nothing to report. Luz was still AWOL. The final message, timed at 18.08, began to play.

"*Arturo? Call me back. We have a problem. Might be nothing, but if it's something, it's potentially ruinous. Your daughter, Luz, just turned up at Hotel Valencia. She came to see Stubbs, the British detective. Said she wanted to give her something. Call me as soon as you get this and please, for the love of God, tell me Luz knows nothing.*"

Chapter 33

The sun streamed through the open windows as Luz parked her suitcase beside a chair.

"Don't worry. I haven't come to stay. I'm going back to university this evening. But I wanted to talk to you before I go."

"Have you been waiting long?"

"Not really. About four hours."

Something about Luz made Beatrice uneasy. The girl seemed composed, determined and almost confrontational. Better to let her do the talking.

"I see. So it must be important."

"The two men that just left. Police and newspapers, right?"

Beatrice met her eyes. "Right. Do you know them?"

"Not really. I know who they are, but they don't know me. Unlike my sisters, I don't take every opportunity to get photographed with influential people."

An uncomfortable pause followed that non-sequitur.

"Luz ..."

"You're investigating my father, aren't you? On behalf of the British Police."

"Not exactly. I am a British detective inspector, yes. But I really am on holiday. Someone asked me for advice ..." She broke off as her stomach seemed to drop. How many hours since Ana had disappeared?

Luz nodded impatiently. "And?"

"This afternoon, she went missing."

"Not another one," Luz muttered. She clasped her hands together. "This is something else, something so much worse. He can't just dispose of people who cross him."

"What do you mean by that? Who? Are you talking about Alava Exports?"

Luz exhaled through her nose, a laugh devoid of amusement. "Angel? He wouldn't get his hands dirty. No, the people who killed Miguel Saez and Tiago Vínculo are sadistic, unpleasant bastards who are paid, by my father, to intimidate, wound and kill. They enjoy their work."

Beatrice pressed her tissue to her mouth. "Oh God. And they've got Ana."

"Is she a friend of yours?"

"Yes, she is. If they hurt her, I'll hound them all the way to hell if I have to."

Luz's expression of pity made Beatrice's throat contract.

"I understand. Just don't do it alone."

"Luz, if you have any idea where Ana might be, I need to know that first."

She shook her head. "I don't. I really don't. Who knows where these thugs do their thing. You've reported her missing to the police and that's the best you can do. How long has she been gone?"

"I lost her after lunch," said Beatrice, distracted. She mentally scanned every detail of Ana's life, or what little she knew of it. Her friends at the paper, that man at the mortuary, Enrique at *El Papagaio*. Could she trust any of them to help?

"So there's nothing else you can do. Why don't you sit down and I'll make you a drink. Gin and tonic, wasn't it? Mind if I join you?"

Beatrice sank into an armchair with a heavy sigh and watched Luz rummage around in the mini-bar. "Thank you. So if you didn't come here to tell me about Ana, why did you want to see me?"

"To help you. The fact is, my father is a criminal. He and his collective of white Rioja producers are growing wealthier and more powerful by committing fraud on an industrial scale. Quite literally."

Beatrice brought her mind back on track. "He's selling substandard product for export, isn't he?"

Luz raised her eyebrows. "Yes. You've got further than I thought. It's mainly to Britain, but there are other markets which are paying four times the market rate for something which contains less than two percent of the Viura grape. Here's your drink. Cheers!"

"Cheers." Beatrice took a careful sip, sensitive to her swollen mouth. Her eyes watered, not with pain but at the amount of gin. She glanced at the empty bottles on top of the fridge. Luz had used all four little Bombay Sapphires but only one bottle of tonic between them. No ice, no lemon. No-nonsense. Serious G&Ts. Beatrice approved.

"But from what I understand, the controls make it impossible to substitute poor quality wine at the vineyard. So it must be at Alava Exports."

"Not impossible, but far more difficult. Alava Exports, on the other hand, can not only reproduce labels, but buy bulk loads of industrially produced white and market it as Rioja. Not in Spain. But my father takes great delight in conning 'the country with no taste', as he puts it. I am proud of my country, and even prouder of my region. We have a brilliant reputation for food and wine, deservedly so. I used to be proud of my family, too. Now, my father has bribed or blackmailed more and more vineyards into participating, coerced my sisters and their husbands into collaboration, paid officials at every level to ease his path through bureaucracy and built himself a persona based on bullshit. He has the wine industry by the balls. White Rioja, with the right blend of grapes from carefully tended vines and made with care and respect, is a wonderful wine. What my father and his cronies are doing is pissing all over its reputation. And I want you to stop them. I'm sorry for my bad language."

The sound of a text message dragged Beatrice's attention from the impassioned face in front of her. She grabbed the phone, deflating as she saw Adrian's name.

Zilch happening. We're bored.
How much longer should we wait?

Beatrice sent a rapid reply.

A bit longer. I'll get a taxi and come fetch you.

She returned her attention to Luz. "Sorry about that. I hoped it might be news of Ana, but unfortunately not. And as a matter of fact, I think your language is entirely appropriate. So how do we proceed?"

Luz took a long draught of her drink and gazed at Beatrice, before pulling a document file from her bag and handing it over.

"I'm not proceeding. You are. You need proof and I can give it to you. The one thing I ask is that you do this through the proper channels. You must work with the police because this is far too dangerous to tackle alone. This trail goes all the way to the top and some very powerful people would do anything to stop this information becoming public."

Beatrice frowned as she flicked through the printouts of emails, spreadsheets and bank statements. Two memory sticks dropped onto the floor. "How did you get hold of all this?"

"My father underestimates me." She reached over and withdrew two pages of despatch schedules. "Call the police and get them to intercept any one of these deliveries. Tell them that according to your enquiries, you suspect the Aguirre brand of being a fake. They'll get it tested and expose it for what it is. But you and I must be well out of the way. Please don't think I'm being melodramatic. You must not put yourself at risk. You have no idea how far they'll go."

Beatrice opened her mouth and closed it again. The police. If Aguirre, according to his daughter, had 'paid officials at every level', why should the police be exempt? Milandro had been deliberately obstructive and unhelpful, his supervising officer had made no secret of his dislike and despite two dead bodies and a missing person, no formal investigation had been launched to explore connections. Beatrice made up her mind to trust her instincts. She wouldn't go it alone. But neither would she involve the Vitoria police. She looked at Luz.

"OK. I'll play it safe. But I have a question. Loyalty to the region and passion for wine is one thing, but to blow the whistle on your own father? Your own family? Is there more to this story?" Beatrice placed her drink on the table. The potent effects of the alcohol were more than she could take at the moment.

Luz glanced at her watch and threw back the remainder of her gin. "Yes, there is. But it's complicated and I need to catch my train. Here's my card, but you can only call me if it's really urgent. Remember, the trail cannot lead to me. He has no idea I can hack into his computer and if he suspected, he'd kill me. And that is not immature hyperbole. He would have me killed."

The cramping acidity in Beatrice's stomach increased. "How do you know he didn't follow you here?"

"He's not back till tomorrow. My mother has probably raised the alarm by now, but he won't give up the chance of being on television to search for his daughter. He's doing a live TV broadcast from Madrid this evening." She gave Beatrice a sly smile. "Half past eight. You should watch it. He's quite an entertainer. Listen, I have to go."

"I'll come with you. I'll walk you to the station. You don't have to tell me the whole story; we could talk about the weather instead."

An oppressive fug hung over the streets. The blue sky and sunshine of the afternoon was replaced by thick cloud cover, trapping heat rising from concrete, a lid on a boiling pan. Almost as soon as they reached the last of the hotel steps and hit the street, Beatrice started to sweat. An ashen bank of thunderhead built over the edge of the city, a mushroom cloud before the explosion. Beatrice sensed the city's inertia, leaden and in limbo, as it waited for the rain.

They passed the Parque de la Florida and followed Calle Ramón y Cajal towards the station. Exhaustion caused by heat, tension and alcohol frayed Beatrice's nerves. Every passer-by appeared suspect while Luz appeared intent on speed-walking, manoeuvring her suitcase and talking at the same time.

"My father is a traditionalist. He is of another world. He's a snob, a bigot and a bully. As far as he's concerned, his daughters are only useful for making good marriages. My brother, Basajaun, will be the heir. My father tried to block me going to university, but my mother battled him on my behalf. She was very sick at that time and he gave in, to keep her happy. She's pleased I'm getting an education, but even she knows I have no hope outside the Castelo de Aguirre network. When I finish my studies, I must get married. My parents have already chosen the shortlist. And every single one of them disgusts me. You know what, that gin's gone right to my head."

Panting, Beatrice stopped. Speech was impossible at such a pace. "That's barbaric. Nineteenth century sort of thing."

"I know, but it's true. Come on. I can get the 19.35 if I'm lucky. What makes it worse is that I've met the man I want to spend my life with. But it's a lost cause."

A flash caused them both to look up. The sky loomed lower and darker than before, the colour of dirty sheep, and a distant boom of thunder reached them.

"Why?" asked Beatrice, scurrying to keep up.

"My family ... let's be diplomatic and call them xenophobes. Marrying anyone who is not Spanish and not Catholic is unthinkable. All the shortlisted candidates check both boxes, they're mostly Basque, all rich and definitely influential. Tunçay is a Turkish Muslim whose family would be equally appalled by me. It's hopeless."

"But surely ..."

"We have another four years, until my degree ends. Then we must separate. We understand that, which is why we're making the most of every day. I can never be free to marry him, I know it. But I can be free of my father's choices. *Mierda*, it's raining. You should turn back."

Beatrice lifted her face to the sky, allowing fat dollops of rain to fall on her flushed face. "No, I'll see you onto the train. I want to know you're safe. Anyway, we're almost there."

Rain fell harder and faster, bouncing off the steaming tarmac, darkening Luz's shirt and soaking Beatrice's hair. They rushed across the street, splashing and gasping as they reached the station building. Beatrice wiped her forehead with a wet hand and shook herself. Luz pulled out some tissues and handed one to Beatrice. Her eye make-up had run, so black teardrops stained her cheeks.

"Just made it. Do you have a ticket?" Beatrice asked, mopping her eyebrows.

Luz patted her handbag. "I'm all prepared. Thank you for listening to me. I wish you luck with exposing all this corruption. Please be careful and don't tell anyone about me. I'm trusting you." She bent to kiss Beatrice on both cheeks. "And I hope your friend will be fine."

"So do I. Take care, Luz. I'll do everything in my power to bring this to light. Don't worry, I always protect my sources. I appreciate your trust."

Luz smiled, which did nothing to change her sad, stoic air, and made her own way onto the platform. She stamped her ticket at the machine, gave one last wave and heaved her case onto the train. With a sigh, Beatrice turned to look out at the weather. Glittering curtains of rain blurred the hectic scene of taxis and rushing commuters, thunder cracked away to her right and the smell of drenched streets and soggy people surrounded her. Regardless of how wet she got, she had to get back to the hotel. She took a deep breath, wrinkling her nose at the stench of pungent tobacco and launched herself into the deluge.

Chapter 34

"This is getting ridiculous."

Matthew pressed himself further against the tree trunk and looked up at the drips falling between the leaf cover. "How much longer does she expect us to stand out here in the rain? We don't even know what we're supposed to be looking for."

Adrian sighed. "This is the reality of detective work, Matthew. Long, dull hours of surveillance. It can't be all car chases and shoot-outs, you know."

Matthew shot him a dour look. "I yearn for neither vehicular action nor gun-play. A cup of tea and a warm towel, however, would be most welcome. The point is, we offered our services as consultant oenologists. Why then, are we squashed against some Spanish foliage spying on a deserted warehouse? She's taking advantage."

Thunder rumbled like barrels across a wooden floor. Water trickled down Adrian's neck and he began to have some sympathy for Matthew's perspective.

"Look, it's almost half past eight now. What with the thunderstorm, we can't see much, so by nine o'clock, we may as well pack up and go back to the hotel. I admit to feeling in need of some creature comforts as well. Thirty minutes more, and if she hasn't arrived by then, you can call us a taxi."

Matthew inhaled and released a theatrical sigh-groan. "There has to be a reason you are so unwaveringly loyal. Fair enough, I hitched my wagon to her cattle train many moons past. But why does an urbane, gay sophisticate with a taste for Rodgers and Hammerstein carry such allegiance to a woman who with the best will in the world could be called difficult?"

A brilliant flash lit the sky, allowing a glimpse of sooty plum-coloured clouds, starkly exposed trees and the bald expanse of nothing in the car park of Alava Exports.

Adrian considered. "I can't say I've ever thought about that. If I had to define it, I'd say I can see qualities in her I wish I had. But she's also very much like me in other elements. We both have gluttonous, lustful appetites and indulge them without apology. Maybe we just see enough similarities to attract and enough differences to respect. Put it this way, I've never wanted to unfriend her."

Matthew looked at him. "An eloquent explanation, with the exception of that bastardisation of the English language in those final words. It does go some way to explaining your companionship, but why do you literally endanger yourself on her behalf? You could be at home right now, watching ... I don't know ... *The King and I* while sampling something delicious from the wine rack. Why are you standing in the damp gloom of a Spanish thunderstorm watching an empty car park ... oh, hello. What's that?"

Adrian followed Matthew's sightline, as a discreet sedan eased into the yard below them, pulling up beside the raised delivery bays. Still and silent, they watched as a tall, dark-haired man exited the car and climbed the steps to the huge doors. He seemed unaware of the rain, moving at an unhurried pace. He bent for a few seconds and a normal-sized door shape appeared in the corner of the massive shutter. Adrian hadn't even noticed it before.

The figure turned and scanned the area from the shelter of the eaves. Adrian held his breath and sensed Matthew doing the same. From such a distance, it was impossible to be sure exactly where he was looking, but both exhaled as he loped back down the steps and opened the back door of the car. Another man stepped out, who could have been the first's twin from this distance; same height, build and colouring. However, number two seemed more perturbed by the weather, holding his hand up to shield his eyes as he too spent several seconds checking the empty landscape. Adrian prayed the lightning would hold off.

Satisfied, the second man ducked back into the car. He heard Matthew's sharp inhalation as he dragged a young woman with long dark hair from the interior. One man either side of her, she was bundled up the steps, through the black opening and into the warehouse. As the door closed, Adrian struggled to contain his panic and motioned to Matthew with his eyes. Retreat.

He slipped backwards behind the tree, moving as gradually and subtly as he could manage. Once hidden in deeper foliage, he spoke.

"That was Ana. And she was not a willing guest."

Matthew's face sagged. "That's what I thought. So we've found Ana, but where's Beatrice?"

Adrian hit redial before Matthew had finished. The phone rang and rang. And went to voicemail. A flare of anger superseded his nerves.

"Where the hell are you? We've just seen two men take Ana into the warehouse. I hope you're already in a taxi, Beatrice Stubbs, that's all I can say."

He rang off and stared at Matthew. "Listen, I know what we promised, but I am not going to stand here and wait for instructions while those gorillas do what they want with that girl. We have no choice but to help."

"I agree."

Busy building up a head of righteous steam, Adrian was wrong-footed by Matthew's acquiescence.

"Oh. Good. So?"

"Call the police. Adrian, we are horribly under-prepared for any kind of encounter with the criminal element. We may well put Ana in worse danger than she already is. I know Beatrice mistrusts that one particular detective, but she's not available to advise us. In the circumstances, we have to call for professional help. We saw a woman forced into a building against her will by two men. Regardless of Beatrice's investigation, that is cause for alarm."

Adrian could see the logic. He desperately wanted to burst into that warehouse and stop them, but Matthew was right. Ana's safety came first.

"We must dial 999 immediately. Or whatever number they use here."

"112. The European Union countries all use the same. Apart from Britain, of course."

Adrian hesitated and dialled Beatrice one last time.

This time, she picked up. "*Hello Adrian, I ...*"

"Where are you?"

"*Just got out of the shower. I got soaked on the way back from the train station. I'm just getting dressed and then I'll call a cab. Be with you in a short while. Are you terribly wet?*"

"Beatrice, did you listen to my message?"

"*No, not yet. It's like Piccadilly Circus here. I have five missed calls and now the bloody doorbell's ringing. What was your message?*"

"They've got Ana. Matthew and I saw two men take her into the Alava Exports warehouse. We have to do something! Matthew and I think we should call the police. Immediately."

He waited for a reply.

"Beatrice! Beatrice?"

Matthew's eyes bore into him and he pressed the headset so hard to his ear that it hurt.

"Bea ..."

"*Sorry, Adrian, I had to open the door. Could you repeat what you just said?*"

"Two men, lookalike Sopranos rejects, took Ana into Alava Exports through the delivery bay. She is in there now. With them. On her own. Beatrice ..."

"*That's not Ana.*"

Adrian took the handset from his ear to stare at it in disbelief.

"And how do you know ..."

"*Because she's standing right here.*"

Chapter 35

Beatrice stared at the girl in the doorway, transfixed. A lift pinged along the corridor and broke the spell. She pulled Ana into the room, locked the door and attached the chain. Then she grabbed her in a tight hug and felt Ana squeeze back. Somehow, the pain of squashed bruises seemed insignificant. She released her with a smile and lifted the phone to her ear.

"Ana's right here. How long ago did you see them take that woman inside the building?"

Ana stared at her, listening intently. She mouthed 'Who is it?'

Beatrice mouthed back. 'Adrian.'

Adrian sounded indignant. "*Just now! Two, maybe three minutes ago.*"

"Then it couldn't have been Ana."

"*Well, it was someone who looked exactly like her.*"

All the blood seemed to drain from Beatrice's body. Her hand felt weak and cold as if the effort of holding a tiny Nokia was too much.

"*Thing is, Beatrice, whoever it was, she was forced to go in there, so we have to call the police,*" Adrian hissed through clenched teeth.

Beatrice shook her head. "No. If I'm right, it was the police who tipped them off. I think the woman they've got is Luz, Aguirre's daughter. She came to see me today and Milandro was here when she arrived. He must have called Aguirre's thugs as soon as he left the hotel. But I put her on the train myself!"

"His daughter?" Ana's eyes were incredulous. "He'd never set those bastards on his own daughter, surely to God?"

Beatrice paced the room, searching for her shoes and talking to Ana and Adrian at the same time. "He would. She told me so herself. But he can't do anything yet, he's still in Madrid. Ana, put the telly on. Listen, Adrian, we can't call the police. They're in this up to their necks. But we absolutely have to get Luz out of there before Aguirre gets back. I'll call Jaime and see if he can't find us some reinforcements. And then I'm taking this to Interpol, to expose this bloody nasty little boys' club for the greedy, murderous cabal that it is. I'm on my way, but please don't do a thing till I get there. I'm serious. It's too dangerous."

Adrian didn't answer immediately and she heard him have a muffled conversation with Matthew.

"*OK. But do hurry. How's Ana?*"

Beatrice held the phone away from her head. "How are you?"

Ana shrugged. "Better than you by the looks of things. Where's the remote?"

Beatrice waved vaguely in the direction of the desk. "She's fine. We'll call a cab and see you in twenty minutes."

Ana flicked through the channels until she came across a panel discussion. The camera panned the table and Beatrice spotted a familiar face. Arturo de Aguirre, dressed in a deep blue suit, gesturing and posturing with typical éclat. She couldn't understand a word. Ana stood beside Beatrice and they watched Aguirre's confident, relaxed performance for several seconds.

Bored of guessing what the conversation was about, Beatrice turned to Ana. The familiar dark hair, sardonic eyebrows and suspicious frown at the television set induced a burst of affection and a genuine smile. Which restarted the bleeding.

"I'm so happy to see you. I imagined all sorts," she said, her voice muffled through bloodied tissue.

"I'm fine. Not a bother on me. But what the hell happened to you?" Ana winced in sympathy.

"To be honest, I am sick to the back feet of telling the story. Where did you go? I thought they'd got you. How did you get away?"

Ana shook her head with a laugh. "Saved by the smell. On the way back from the loo, I stopped off at the shop. As I went in, I caught the strongest stink of black tobacco. And that set off the most almighty alarm. I'd smelt it before. One of those goons who turned up at my flat was smoking that. It's rank."

"Did you see him?"

"Not at first. I ducked behind the CD racks and watched. I saw one of them come out of the restaurant. His mate joined him from the coffee shop and then they both went into the ladies' loo."

"The ladies' loo? And no one objected?"

"Sure, but they don't give a toss. They were looking for me. No doubt about it. So I was about to take my chance and run for the exit when I copped myself on. If two of them were inside, looking for me, the other two were outside, looking for you. So I sent you a message and got myself arrested."

Beatrice gawped.

"When trying to escape from men with guns, the best place to hide is behind other men with guns. I ditched the phone in case they could trace it, snatched a handful of CDs and walked out without paying. The alarm went off and the security guards marched me up to the office. I was arrested and charged and taken back to San Sebastian police station. Arsewit and Dickhead must have thought I'd disappeared down the plughole."

"Arrested!"

"Petty crime. They flexed a few muscles, lectured me a bit and told me to piss off. So I got on a bus and came back. Picked up my Vespa and rode over here. Then I watched the hotel from the café over the road, just in case. You know the police are outside?"

"Milandro?"

"Nope. But there's a plain-clothes guy outside I'd swear is a cop. Now tell me what the hell happened to you and your face. How did you get back to Vitoria?"

"I drove."

"No way! You told me you were useless behind the wheel."

"I am. Hence my face. I wrote off Jaime's car. Which reminds me, I need to call him. And I'd better let Milandro know you're here. And would you call us a cab?"

"Sure. But can I use your bathroom first?"

"Be quick. We need a plan."

Milandro actually sounded relieved to hear Ana had turned up unharmed. He made an appointment for them both to come to the station in the morning for a formal statement. He didn't exactly order her to stay in the hotel, but strongly suggested they stay in and enjoy room service. Beatrice agreed that would be best, all the while lacing up her trainers in preparation for their departure. After finishing the call, Beatrice took several deep breaths, ignoring the twinges all over her torso. Her mind attempted a logical analysis of a situation which frightened her witless.

Aguirre was cornered. His malpractice was on the verge of being exposed and the only question now was how far the corruption went. Killing off everyone who knew the details would be impossible. Jaime could run the story as soon as the day after tomorrow, tugging at the thread which would unravel the whole affair. But how to protect Luz? Beatrice had no back-up, no authority and no plan.

It would not do. Whatever was going on at the warehouse put them all at risk and Beatrice needed an insurance policy. She scrolled through her phone until she found the number of Conceição Pereira da Silva. An Interpol agent and ex-colleague, Conceição would be the perfect person; guaranteed to understand and ask no stupid questions.

As she pressed dial, she relaxed in anticipation of hearing Conceição's magnetic voice, recalling those bright eyes, her huge smile and constant air of amusement. But there was no reply. Beatrice left a brief message explaining where she was and why and asking Conceição to sound the alarm if Beatrice had not called back in twenty-four hours. Then she called Jaime, informed him of Ana's safe return and explained the situation.

"As far as we know, there are two men holding a young woman in that warehouse. My suspicion is they have Luz Aguirre, that girl who turned up here this afternoon. They're probably waiting for instructions from her father. If you can join us, that's five against two, even if we are unarmed. That should give us the edge."

"Of course. I can be there in around half an hour." Bless Jaime, the man who never said no. "So, let me understand. Matthew and Adrian are already there? Inside the warehouse?"

"No, they're watching it from the forest behind. They have a clear view of the delivery bay, which is where the girl was taken."

"I see. Have you called that detective?"

Beatrice hesitated. This was no time for double-dealing. She chose to put her cards on the table.

"Jaime, I'm afraid Milandro may well be a part of this. My priority now is to get Luz to safety and then I'm taking this investigation to Interpol. I think the police are probably on Aguirre's payroll."

"Really? My God! Are Interpol already involved?"

"I've got to assemble a case first. I believe Luz has given me everything I need. I'm just afraid Aguirre has found out what she's done. If he has, she's in trouble. We must get her out, Jaime."

"You don't really think he'd hurt her? This is his daughter we're talking about."

"I know. But I have a nasty feeling that makes the betrayal so much worse. When he gets back from Madrid, I want Luz somewhere safe and an airtight case prepared for his arrest."

"OK, Beatrice. I'll make some calls and join you as soon as I can."

"Thank you, Jaime. I'd be lost without your constant support. You've been right with me, every step of the way."

"No problem. Please look after yourself. And give Ana a kiss from me."

Beatrice smiled and rang off. She picked up her gin and tonic, took a slug and pulled a face. Lukewarm.

Then she froze, gazing into the middle distance.

Every step of the way.

Milandro wasn't the only person to see Luz this afternoon. And Jaime had shown no surprise on hearing the name of Luz Aguirre. When Beatrice was supposed to be in Jaime's flat, the gang had shown up. How had they known she was there alone? It could have been coincidence. And today, Jaime had loaned them his distinctive powder-blue BMW. Their fears about being followed on the way to San Sebastian were groundless. Of course. Aguirre's crew already knew where they were going. The hoods would have had no difficulty tailing them on the way back. She'd kept Jaime informed of every last movement. And he knew perfectly well who Luz was because he was working for her father.

She shook her head. Paranoia. She'd be suspecting Ana next. But if Jaime *was* a snitch, she'd just dropped Matthew and Adrian right in it. And possibly jeopardised herself and Ana. It wouldn't be difficult to arrange a "taxi" for them, driven by God knows whom.

Raging paranoia. But if she couldn't trust the police, Jaime or even the hotel staff, where the hell was she to get back-up?

By the time Ana came out of the bathroom, Beatrice had convinced herself. She stood in front of Ana with her hands on her hips.

"How long have you known Jaime?"

"About eighteen months or so, why? Ah, Beatrice. Tell me you're not suspecting him."

"Think about it. We've told him everything. If he's passing on information to Aguirre, we've been undercover investigating in broad daylight."

"No, he wouldn't. This is a false alarm. He was the one who put Tiago onto the Saez case." She checked her watch.

"Which was supposed to lead nowhere. Only Tiago found out rather more than expected. No one else, apart from you and Jaime, knew how much. So how come Aguirre's mob disposed of him?"

Ana hunched her shoulders. Several seconds passed.

"Jesus. That makes a twisted kind of sense. And Jaime knew enough about Tiago to use me as a lure."

Beatrice stated the obvious. "Tiago was in love with you, wasn't he?"

Ana paused. "I suppose so, yeah. I'd picked up a fair few hints. Jaime could have sent him an invitation from my work computer, knowing damn well he'd not be able to resist."

"On Saturday morning. And of course he wasn't surprised when Tiago didn't turn up on Monday. The mutilation of Tiago's face was a warning to you."

Beatrice watched Ana's expression change from horror to incomprehension to anger. In a couple of seconds, her whole demeanour changed and she began pacing the room, gesticulating in every direction.

"I can't believe this. What a piece of shit! And he went to the funeral! He stood there, expressing the most sincere sympathies for Tiago's parents, when the whole time he'd set the poor bastard up. I believed he was one of the few people I could trust. What a stupid cow! And I prided myself on not falling for his bullshit charm."

Beatrice flushed, recalling her own susceptibility. "It's quite effective, I admit."

"Thing is, if it was Jaime who gave Aguirre all he needed, does that mean we can trust the police? Should we call Milandro?"

"No. We trust no one. Where's your Vespa?" She scrabbled in her bag for her phone and began dialling.

"Round the corner. I thought we were getting a cab."

"Change of plan. And I'd like to leave the hotel via another route than the front door. Ideally, we should get out without being seen. There must be a staff exit or ... Oh hello. Is that Kev? It's Beatrice here. How's the trip going? Are you still in Vitoria? Oh good. Listen, Kev, I have a bit of a problem and wondered if you might be able to help."

"Beatrice ..." Ana had changed channels to a football match.

"Just a sec." She covered the mouthpiece. "Ana, I'm on the phone."

"Yes, but ..."

Beatrice scowled and shook her head, returning to the call. "Kev? Sorry about that. The thing is that a friend of mine is in trouble and ..."

"Beatrice!"

The intensity in Ana's voice made Beatrice turn. Ana wasn't looking at her, but at the television. She'd switched back from the match to the bunch of suits talking. Beatrice could see nothing of significance. Ana flicked to the football again and back to the panel.

"Kev, bear with me a moment, I'm sorry about this." She pressed her thumb over the microphone and turned to Ana. "What's the matter now?"

Ana prodded her finger against the screen, indicating a pony-tailed man with stubble and an earring. "That is Julio Villa, Real Madrid's star striker."

"And?"

"And, as you can see," she flicked to the football, where the crowd were leaping up and down and roaring, "he's just scored a goal against Atlético Madrid."

"The football's live?"

"Mm-hmm. People tend to prefer it that way. Which means this ..." she pressed the button to bring back the studio discussion, "... was pre-recorded. As for the current location of Arturo de Aguirre, we haven't got a bloody clue."

Chapter 36

Dusk settled over the landscape, light evaporating below the western horizon. A Hunter's moon offered an eerie monochrome illumination, when not obscured by fast-moving clouds, the last remnants of the afternoon's storm. Ana scrambled back onto the road and Beatrice gave her the thumbs-up. The scrubby bushes completely concealed the Vespa from view. In silence and with ears alert for the sound of vehicles, they set off into the forest, keeping a parallel course to the driveway to Alava Exports.

The warehouse, a grey malevolent monolith gave no indication of being occupied.

Several kilometres from the nearest village and set back from the main road, with nothing but forest around, it was the perfect place to hide something. If you had something to hide. As they approached, Beatrice could make out the white markings of visitors' parking spots and the glass windows of reception. A Range Rover and another smaller car occupied the spaces nearest to the door. The drive continued to the right with a sign indicating the lorry route. Beatrice frowned. The delivery bay must be round the back. So how could Adrian and Matthew have seen the girl taken from the car?

Ana stopped frequently to listen and check if they were being followed. Beatrice kept her eyes on the trees ahead, peering for any sign of Adrian and Matthew. She couldn't decide if the wind were help or hindrance. Trees cracked and whipped, leaves danced in Van Gogh swirls and the absolute lack of human movement both impressed and alarmed her. Of Adrian and Matthew, there was not the smallest indication. Either they were behaving as instructed, keeping quiet and concealed, or, far more likely for the two least restrained men in her acquaintance, they had already been discovered. She sped up, still scanning the forest and walked straight into Ana.

Ana jerked her head to the sedan in front of the vast shuttered bays.

"If that's the car that brought Luz here, where did those two round the front come from?"

"Just what I was thinking. I wonder if I should call Adrian. Or maybe send a text in case he hasn't switched his phone to silent."

"I'm not that stupid."

The voice made them both start and twist around. From behind a tree trunk, Adrian appeared, followed by Matthew.

Beatrice exhaled. "Thank God. Are you all right?"

"We just had a bit of a fright," said Adrian. "After I spoke to you, two cars came down the drive. No idea where they went, but a few minutes later, those goons came out of the back and headed straight for us. We retreated further into the forest, but they didn't come far. They spent a while searching around the edges then went back inside. It was as if they just wanted to scare us off. Beatrice, you look terrible. Are you OK, Ana?"

"I'm grand. How about you two?"

A rather damp and cold-looking Matthew moved towards them, his expression impossible to read.

"We're fine, although I am unconvinced by the argument for acting alone. A handful of half-baked incompetents versus who knows how many men, probably armed and in possession of a hostage, with no hope of professional back-up. Not only that, but we can't even speak the language with any degree of accuracy."

Ana stepped in front of Matthew. "I can. And I'm not incompetent. The thing is, Matthew, we must act quickly because we're pretty sure Aguirre is heading in this direction. We have to get to Luz before he does. Reinforcements are on the way."

Matthew's face, lined and shadowed by lunar light, seemed to contract into a deeper frown. "Reinforcements? You mean your editor, most likely accompanied by a photographer, just to guarantee an exclusive front-page splash?"

Beatrice chose economy of truth. "That's a good point. We don't really know how many people are in there, so it might be wiser to wait until the cavalry arrives. The reinforcements are trustworthy, Matthew, believe me. Let's approach this logically. When you did the tour today, did you see the whole building? What I mean is, how well do you know the layout?"

Adrian glanced at Matthew. "Correct me if I'm wrong, but the reception and offices are at the front. There's a middle section containing the bottling plant and packing areas." He pointed to the delivery area. "That section is divided into wine storage on the right and the warehouse section on the left. That's where they took the girl. It's stacked with boxes of wine ready for despatch in different sections. UK export was quite clearly marked."

Beatrice motioned for Adrian to drop his voice. His enthusiasm and conviction had raised his pitch. They stood in silence for several seconds, checking for any sounds or movements in the forest, from the lorry bays or in the building, before Adrian continued in a stage whisper.

"No detail is insignificant, you told me. So I watched Angel Rosado very carefully and decided he is extremely vain, seriously uninformed about his own operations and unquestionably a friend of Dorothy's."

"A what?" Ana hissed, her irritation visible. "What in the name of ..."

Again, Beatrice raised a hand for silence.

"In Adrian's opinion, Angel Rosado is a homosexual," she said.

Ana snorted. "Bollocks! Would you ever cop yourself on? The man's married to Aguirre's daughter. No disrespect, Adrian, but do you not think you maybe got the wrong signals because you were staring at the poor f..."

A torch lit Ana's face and at the same time, the unmistakeable sound of safety catches being released announced the fact they had company. Another torch joined the first, moving over Adrian, Matthew and shining directly in Beatrice's eyes. She raised her open hands to shoulder height, blinking into the glare.

A voice, rasping and low, gave an incomprehensible order.

Ana translated. "Hands in the air, turn round and start walking."

They made their way through the trees in silence, apart from the sound of a cigarette being lit behind them. Ahead, the huge shutters rolled upward and Beatrice could see the figures of three men silhouetted against walls of white cardboard boxes. They walked out onto the platform to meet them.

As they crossed the car park, light from the plant spilt out and the torches went off. Beatrice took the opportunity to glance back and recognised their escorts. Tweedledum and Tweedledee in identical black suits and slicked-back hair carried matching accessories; handguns and torches. The grizzled older man was smoking some foul-smelling tobacco, while his gun dangled by his side. He saw her look and motioned she should turn around. He used his gun as a Japanese courtesan might use her fan, in a professional, yet unambiguous gesture.

She couldn't be sure of the weapons the Thompson twins were carrying but the ugly man's stainless steel piece was a SIG Sauer, probably a P226. A favourite with police forces everywhere.

Beatrice looked past the three men waiting on the platform and squinted into the space behind them. A forklift truck, a stack of pallets and blocks of cardboard boxes filled the space, but no dark-haired girl to be seen. They stopped at the base of the steps and Beatrice lifted her head.

Aguirre stared down at her, his face resembling that of a gargoyle, his hooked nose carved from grey stone. His eyes bored into her as if she were the only person there. The second man, also dressed in a suit, seemed ill-at-ease, his eyes not resting anywhere for more than a second. Angel Rosado, undoubtedly. The final individual had a face like Samuel Beckett and he beckoned them forward with a repulsive smile. But rather than using his index finger, he used his whole hand. A classic police gesture. Palm upwards and four fingers waving inwards. Or in his case, only three.

Chapter 37

Outnumbered. Six men, at least four of whom had visible guns. Beatrice's toes curled in frustration as she watched one of the younger hoods take his time over frisking Ana, purposely groping her breast with a nauseating leer. Ana remained expressionless.

After fixing their captives' hands behind them with plastic ties and relieving them of mobile phones, the twins ushered them to sit on a small stack of pallets near the back wall. Beatrice sensed an uncertainty in their behaviour. Apart from taking liberties with Ana, the treatment of them was restrained, almost polite. No shoving, no casual violence. One of the identical macho men raised a finger and drew it across his lips, meeting each pair of eyes in turn. Then he and his fellow thug moved away to join the others. Grizzly, Rosado and Three-Fingers stood inside the closed shutter doors having a hushed conversation. Aguirre had disappeared through an internal door. Grizzly occasionally pointed his gun in their direction, less as a threat and more of a conversational gesture.

Beatrice leant forward to look past Ana at Matthew. He was disturbingly pale, an odd blue tinge to his lips. He shouldn't even be here. None of them should. The cold of the warehouse seeped into her clothes, while a hot surge of guilt flushed over her. She had to do something.

"What are they saying, Ana?" she whispered.

She felt Ana's shoulders shift against hers as she shrugged. "I'm not sure. They're speaking Basque, so I can't understand much at all. They keep saying they're shocked, that they can't believe it. But I don't think they're talking about us. And I get the impression they're debating a decision."

Adrian spoke from her other side. "Have they said anything about the girl?"

Beatrice dropped her voice still lower. "It's vital that he thinks we're just snooping, investigating the wine issue. We know nothing about any girl. Don't even mention her name."

"What do I say about Tiago?" asked Ana.

"Nothing. You're taking over his story. As far as you're concerned, he had an accident, and you are now chasing his leads. The fact that you know Tiago was murdered, probably by this lot, has to remain our secret. That's our most likely chance of getting out of here."

Matthew cleared his throat, but did not speak, as the group of men turned to look. After they'd returned to their conversation, Matthew spoke in a deliberate whisper.

"And the cavalry? Does *anyone* know we're here?"

"Yes. Firstly, I left a message with Interpol, explaining my intentions. So if anything happens to us, they know where to look."

"That's comforting," said Matthew.

"Secondly, ..."

Someone banged on the metal shutters, galvanising the men and shooting tension through the group on the pallets. One of the younger men opened the door, allowing Aguirre access.

Beatrice watched the body language of the group with curiosity. The men bowed their heads, in an oddly deferential gesture of respect. It reminded her of mourners at a funeral.

Rosado dabbed a handkerchief repeatedly to his mouth, staring at the ground with wide eyes, fidgeting and awkward, as if no comfortable position existed.

Aguirre spoke to the men in hoarse tones, indicating with his finger at every individual as he seemed to deliver instructions. Each nodded, crossed the vast space and left through the internal door. Leaving one of the twins. The young gunman moved forward to train his weapon on the seated group.

"Oh my God," murmured Adrian.

"They won't shoot us," said Beatrice. She knew she was right. The hood held his weapon in a state of readiness, not with intent. And disposing of four executed bodies without trace would be a challenge for even Aguirre. Still, Beatrice could feel both Ana and Adrian tense against their ties.

Aguirre approached to stand in front of them. His expression, that of a wounded bull, bore equal measures of pain and rage.

"Ana Herrero. It was a simple enough instruction. Was 'Go back to Portugal' so hard to understand? Detective Inspector Beatrice Stubbs. I should have known. Bad luck to spill blood on my steps. An unfortunate day, for all of us."

Her body immobilised, Beatrice had access to only two elements of her arsenal. Her mind and her mouth. Both of which had previously proved unreliable.

"Señor Aguirre, I acknowledge the fact that we have been trespassing, but I must insist you let us go. Such treatment is absurd. Feel free to call the police and have us arrested, but you cannot truss us up like so many turkeys."

Aguirre shook his head, pressing his hand to his eyes. He swallowed twice and looked at Matthew.

"And you two? Bailey and Son, wine importers who conveniently forgot their business cards? I don't think so. You are friends, or possibly colleagues, of Detective Inspector Stubbs. Which is your misfortune."

"My name is Professor Matthew Bailey, oenology expert and my colleague is Adrian Harvey, wine importer. For your information, both of us have found our association with Beatrice Stubbs to be extremely fortunate." Matthew's tone was calm, measured and a little condescending.

Aguirre narrowed his eyes. The interior door reopened and Three-Fingers returned with a carafe of liquid. Aguirre nodded once, gesturing with his forehead towards Matthew.

"No!" Beatrice jerked forward, trying to get to her feet, but bounced back onto the bench. "If you plan to punish anyone with your brutal bully-boy techniques, you can bloody well pick on me. These people are not involved. Leave him alone."

"Leave him alone? The way you left me and my family alone? I'm afraid not. We told you to go away and mind your own business. But I've noticed that women rarely listen. They can talk, oh yes, but cannot listen."

Three-Fingers knelt beside Matthew. With a certain amount of weariness, he poured some liquid into a small glass, pointed at Matthew and mimed drinking it. He nodded and gave the thumbs-up. Then he mimed refusing the glass and averting his head. With a shrug, he pulled out a flick-knife and with a total absence of drama, demonstrated slashing a face. He opened his palm, as if to ask 'What'll it be?'

Before Beatrice could open her mouth, another voice rang out. Angel Rosado placed his hand on Aguirre's shoulder, his eyes fixed on Matthew.

"No. Él no tiene la culpa. Deja-le!"

"He's saying he's not guilty and let him go." Ana kept her eyes on the two men in front of them, but muttered, "You might have been right."

Aguirre did not acknowledge the plea, turning instead to the gunman. Rosado, who up until the last two minutes had seemed practically catatonic, shrugged off the gunman's guiding hand and pulled at Aguirre. The gunman didn't hesitate, bringing the butt of his weapon with full force against Rosado's head. The pallets wobbled as all four observers recoiled. Rosado collapsed onto the concrete floor, clutching his head as he was dragged to the other end of the room. Aguirre had maintained his intense focus on Beatrice, but now turned to the gunman and yelled. The man dropped Rosado and exited via the door in the delivery bay. Aguirre barked at Three-Fingers.

"Vamos, Tomas!"

Spell broken, the man offered the glass to Matthew, the knife poised in his other hand. Beatrice writhed against her restraints.

"Stop! Aguirre, make him stop! What is that stuff? If you poison him, I ..."

"Women. Always talking. Cannot keep their mouths shut." Aguirre shook his head and walked a few paces, like a general inspecting his troops. "It's *aguardiente.* Fire water. Hooch. That's all. He might enjoy it." He stopped to observe the show.

Matthew pressed back from the glass until he could stretch no further. The glass, and knife, kept coming. Finally, after a pat on the cheek with the flat of the blade, Matthew opened his mouth.

Tomas poured a small sip into his mouth, dropped the knife to the floor and reached in his pocket for a blue-checked handkerchief. So he was ready for the inevitable spluttering and coughing. He wiped Matthew's eyes and mopped his nose, while patting him on the shoulder. He stopped short of a smile, but nodded and made the thumbs-up sign.

"Matthew, are you OK?" Beatrice asked, peering into his flushed features.

"Yes, it's like grappa. Just a bit stronger than I'm used to. Powerful stuff."

Tomas seemed pleased and raised the glass again. This time, he didn't bother with the knife, but readied the hanky.

Aguirre sniffed. "You see, he's enjoying himself. So he should. That's a top quality product. He needs to be drunk, and this is the fastest way to do it."

Beatrice understood. "You're going to put us in a car, Matthew behind the wheel and shove us off a cliff. Your men are preparing the car right now, just to make sure we go up in flames and all evidence is destroyed."

Aguirre watched the ritual once more, apparently ignoring her. A moan came from the end of the room, where Angel Rosado sat up and pressed a hand to his head. He seemed to be crying. Matthew swallowed once more, cheeks flushed, while Tomas patted him and wiped his face, as if he were a wrestling coach between rounds with a prize fighter.

Ana glared at Aguirre, her eyes black and furious. "You have no conscience whatsoever, do you? When's it going to stop, Aguirre? Six deaths on your hands already and those are only the ones I know about."

Aguirre looked at Ana. "Why is it that smart girls don't know when to shut up? You know, I should just give you to Tomas. He knows the best way to keep a woman quiet, isn't that right? *Tomas sabe callar a una mujer?*"

Tomas showed his top teeth, rendering him uglier than before, caught hold of his own crotch and gave it a shake.

Chapter 38

Four men shaking hands.
Three in suits.
Two carrying handguns.
One smoking.
Zero signs of target.
Cloud cover sporadic, night visibility variable.

Kev watched as the four men exchanged handshakes. The new arrival held something out to the older suit who took it and indicated over his shoulder. All four turned to look in Kev's direction. He dropped lower on his forearms, but they weren't looking as far as him. Their sightline was lower, towards the stream.

He tensed as he heard a sound behind him. Jase, returning from the recce. Kev squinted and frowned. They'd done their best with shoe polish but the white of his trainers still shone through the camouflage. Tyler, silent as a cat, approached from the other direction and crouched beside him.

"Nothing. She's not in this side of the forest." He looked up at Jase, who shook his head. "OK, so she must be inside. Lights are on in the depot but the rest is deserted. What's going on with this lot?" He jerked his chin at the group of men.

"The Rhinestone Cowboy down there turned up three minutes ago. In that Peugeot. Handshakes, a friendly chat and there's something interesting about that ditch."

Jase squatted next to Tyler. "Access from the front and delivery bay. Four fire doors, two either side, probably alarmed. Roof this end has windows. Too high for surprise entry but helpful for surveillance assessment via metal service ladder twenty-six metres to our right."

The three men breathed, waited and watched. A hum built in Kev. A hum born of training and experience. This situation was unknown and their role unclear. But when it came to scoping a location, identifying risks and minimising danger, he could rely on his team. Beatrice needed their expertise and anyway, he'd had enough of *tapas*.

The man in the leather jacket did the round of goodbye handshakes, but didn't get back in his car. Instead, he revved up the Corsa and drove back up the access road.

"Shit," spat Tyler. "Too dark to see the fooking number."

Kev grinned. "Already got it, mate. What are those bastards up to now?"

Each of the three men hauled something from the back of the Range Rover and strode towards the delivery bay.

Jase took a deep breath. "Petrol cans. They're gonna torch summat."

Employing his stealth training: heel-ball-toe walk, deep breathing and low crouch, Kev crept through the trees, stopping, listening, watching and waiting; Tyler and Jase moving with him like shadows. Once their sightline cleared the corner, they dropped onto their chests. Two men were opening all the doors of the black sedan, while the other removed the number plates. One picked up a can and unscrewed the top. The smoker flicked his glowing butt into the ditch and they began soaking the whole vehicle in petrol.

"Right, while they're busy, I'm having a look at what's going on indoors."

Kev checked out the route. Jase slipping through ten metres of trees, over the ditch and a sixteen-metre stretch of moonlit tarmac unseen in radioactive trainers? No way.

"Swap shoes. This is one hell of a sacrifice. Your feet have plagued me worse than any Afghani insurgent ever could. If you're not wearing Odor-Eaters, I'll kill ya."

Tyler took point, Kev followed. Neither checked Jase. His feet might be rank but he could be trusted to do a proper job. The situation was risky. No doubt the suits were busy round the back, but if one of them popped back to check the coast was clear, he and the lads were unarmed and as vulnerable as rabbits. Rabbits in white trainers.

As they reached the stream, Kev nudged Tyler and pointed to his feet. "I'll dip these in the ditch, see if a bit of mud will help."

Tyler's head scanned the area like an owl. He crouched into the scrub and Kev spotted a glint of metal in his hand. "Be quick, then. I got you."

Kev slid down the bank into the blackness below. His feet hit mud and instantly the cheap trainers absorbed water. Typical. Kev focused on dirtying his footwear, revolving his ankles to attract maximum muck. As he turned to yank himself out, his left foot caught on some weeds. He pulled again, trying to release himself and looked back at whatever was holding him. Dark fronds wrapped his ankle. He lifted his leg and the fronds came with him, dragging behind them a human head.

Chapter 39

"Where are you from, Señor Aguirre?" Matthew's authoritative tone caused everyone to turn, even Tomas.

Aguirre's eyes hardened as he turned to face the tired, pale and bedraggled man who Beatrice loved more than anything in the world.

The jut of his jaw made Beatrice simultaneously swell with pride and cringe in dread. Matthew, powerless, vulnerable and faced with armed, violent men had chosen to pick a fight.

"I would have assumed you were Spanish, until now."

Aguirre's voice was quiet, but still carried the marks of an orator. "Spanish is a big word. Each Spaniard has a complex identity, based on his country, his region, his language, his community, his family. You should be able to understand that, Professor Bailey. Being British used to mean something. Being Spanish still does."

"True. The essence of Spain, I would suggest, is about honour, about pride. You have a sense of loyalty, despite the divisions and rivalries between the various regions, to the concept of Spain. Rather like The United States. Which is why I find you as an individual rather an anomaly."

In a second, Beatrice caught up. Matthew may not have carried a SIG Sauer or a flick-knife, but his intellect and comprehension of the enemy had already exceeded hers. He stepped into the role of *toreador*, with every intention of baiting the bull.

Something flickered in her peripheral vision. Both the high walls to her left and right had windows at the top, presumably to permit natural light. At that time of the evening, internal light and external darkness made it impossible to see anything outside. But high up above Tomas's head, there was a movement. Someone was out there. Her heart pumped faster and she tried not to stare.

Aguirre laughed. "That is because you are a snob. A typical British snob. You are offended by my business proposition, which is to give people what they want. Do you want to tell me the British are unhappy with my wines? That is ridiculous. They will drink anything, if it has the right label and reputation."

Ana leant into her, applying pressure to her shoulder. She looked up and right as if stretching her neck, then returned to her previous position. Beatrice waited a second before looking in the same direction and forced herself not to jump. A face, streaked with dark marks, looked down at them. At that distance, she couldn't recognise him, but whoever it was, that was army camouflage.

"I'm afraid I disagree, Señor Aguirre. If, as I believe to be true, you export a blend of various whites and call it Rioja, how are you furthering the image of Spanish wine? I wholeheartedly applaud your successes in your domestic market, but by selling an inferior product to your chief importers, you are an embarrassment. To your vineyard, to the Rioja region and to Spain. As for you personally, you should be ashamed."

Tomas looked up at Aguirre, evidently judging by the tone of Matthew's voice that a challenge had been issued. Aguirre caught his curious expression and glared, pointing an impatient finger at the bottle. Tomas filled the glass and lifted it to Matthew's lips once more, with a compassionate pat of the shoulder. Matthew swallowed, gagged and retched, but kept it down. His eyes were wet. Ana nudged Beatrice, using her eyes to indicate the doors. Beatrice frowned. She could hear nothing and see even less. Ana sighed, shifting in her seat and indicated once more with her eyes. Tomas's knife, beside Beatrice's foot.

The trouble with this generation was watching too much James Bond. If Ana thought was any chance of retrieving and concealing the knife without raising suspicions, she was deluded. And in any case, Beatrice was far too concerned about Matthew sticking his head in the lion's maw.

Aguirre had not moved. His eyes, locked onto Matthew's, seemed oddly devoid of life. His voice creaked, as if an ancient gate had opened.

"You know nothing of shame."

Kev pressed back against the warehouse, feeling the tension in Tyler and Jase either side of him. Three heads twisted left, observing the preparations.

They watched as the older man walked away from the petrol-soaked vehicle towards an outdoor tap above a drain and gave an order. One of the sharp suits started slamming the car doors shut, while the other one picked up the empty cans and headed in their direction. Kev spotted the opportunity and whispered his instructions.

"OK, Tyler, while he's got his hands full. Go!"

Tyler, smooth and noiseless, timed his attack to perfection. He waited till the man had almost drawn level with their vantage point. Any second now, he'd see them. In two long strides, Tyler broke cover, grabbed the man by the chin from behind and pressed a knife to his throat. The petrol cans hit the ground. Kev acted fast. In his experience, a hostage was not always the best bargaining tool. He knew nothing about this bunch and their loyalties. All he knew for certain was that they were armed. Whether they'd give up quietly or sacrifice their mate – he decided not to take the risk.

He ran to Tyler's side, located the pistol tucked into the man's belt, threw off the safety, twisted and crouched. Jase remained in the shadows, their secret weapon.

They took their time. When they finally rounded the corner, the older bloke's timing worked in their favour. He was lighting a fag, the stupid bastard. The young one's reactions were slow. He saw his mate, took in Tyler's knife, then made for his gun before he spotted Kev, who knelt, arm steady, aiming the SIG Sauer at his head.

"*Me cago en la puta!*" he swore as he raised his hands to head height.

So Kev was right. The bloke with the blade against his windpipe and the curser looked close enough to be brothers, but the latter had still reached for his weapon. Seems blood wasn't all that thick.

Jase slipped out from the recess and with practised skill, removed both their guns and a vicious-looking knife from the old fella's boot. The plastic ties he found in the younger bloke's suit pocket came in handy and in under ninety seconds, he'd tied all three men's hands behind them, attached them to each other and had them facing the wall.

"Nice work, Lance Corporal. And that was a bloody classy jump, Tyler. You've still got it."

"Still got it? Bollocks. I just keep getting better. What do we do with the Reservoir Dogs while we tackle the warehouse?"

"Leave 'em here. We've got to get in there as soon as poss because whatever they ..."

Jase hissed. "At the ready, Sergeant. Three, armed, incoming at one o'clock."

Kev saw them. Three figures in night gear, emerging from the trees with no attempt at stealth. Jase and Tyler aimed their weapons at the approaching men while Kev scanned all other directions.

"Two more at eleven o'clock, two more at twelve. All carrying," he reported. They were surrounded.

As Kev watched, the man leading the first group raised his hands. He still held his gun but the gesture was conciliatory. He kept walking until he was close enough to be heard.

"Police. Do you speak English?"

"Yes."

"Drop your weapons, please. What are you doing here?"

They each engaged the safety and allowed the guns to fall to the ground. Kev answered the question.

"A friend of ours asked us for help. She and three others are tied up and held at gunpoint inside that warehouse."

"A friend? Detective Stubbs, I assume. Are you also police?"

"No, we're British Army officers."

He came closer. "I thought there must be some kind of training involved. That," he nodded his head at the row of backs, "was a very impressive ambush. But I must ask you to stand down now. This is a police operation and we can take it from here."

He moved closer into the light and holstered his weapon. Something odd about his face made Kev uneasy. It wasn't till he stepped into the floodlights that he saw what it was. The Spanish copper only had one eyebrow.

Matthew groaned and coughed. Tomas jumped backwards, just in case. He showed the bottle to Aguirre. It was two-thirds empty. This seemed to satisfy Aguirre, who jerked his head towards the doors, turned and strode off towards the main building. Tomas shoved the bottle into his pocket and bent to retrieve his knife. Then several things happened at once.

Matthew threw up a violently colourful shower, just as the door in the delivery shutter opened. Two men, dressed in black, dashed in, aiming their weapons at Tomas. Aguirre had almost reached the far door leading to the main plant when it burst open, admitting two more dark-clothed men. In a second, Aguirre ducked behind the stacks of cardboard boxes and a shot was fired, making everyone on the makeshift bench, with the exception of Matthew, jerk backwards in alarm.

Beatrice looked for Tomas but he had disappeared. However, a box on the corner had sprung a leak and white wine trickled out, staining the cardboard. The whole room held its breath.

Milandro entered from the delivery bay and shouted something. Beatrice only understood the word *Policia*, but understood the tone.

Ana muttered a translation. "Give yourselves up, no point in any further loss of life, the entire building's surrounded and your associates are already in custody."

"Further loss of life? Oh God. If Kev or the boys got hurt ..."

She sensed Ana and Adrian staring at her and assessed the situation. Four sitting ducks in the middle. A ruthless criminal, ready to go down firing, hiding in a stack of boxes to her right; his henchman, with nothing to lose, on her left. There was someone missing.

"Where's Rosado?" she asked.

Adrian was chewing his lip. "He went into the main building. His head was bleeding. Is this really the police, Beatrice, or should we be worried?"

Ana spoke. "God knows." She bunted Beatrice with her shoulder. "Get the bloody knife. I'm not sitting here while they shoot it out."

Tomas's knife lay in a pile of fresh vomit, which consisted of alcohol, fish and tomato skins. Matthew's head hung forward, a thin strand of drool hanging from his lips. He couldn't help, even if he wanted to. Beatrice shuffled closer and stretched her foot out over the pool of puke. Using her heel, she scraped the knife towards her, shoving it under the bench and behind them. Ana arched backwards, a Tchaikovsky swan, and scooped it up. She twisted sideways towards Beatrice's bound hands.

A loud rumbling began and the first shutter began to rise. Beatrice watched as the tarmac came into view and was surprised to see no flashing lights, no police vehicles, no Kev. But at least ten crouching figures, all in night combat gear. Another shot startled them all, including Ana, who accidentally stabbed Beatrice's thumb.

The shot came from behind the opposite wall of boxes. Aguirre had taken aim at the men outside. A gun battle was more than likely to erupt, with the four of them sitting like fairground targets. Beatrice breathed deeply, imposing an artificial calm on herself. Shaking hands would make Ana's task all the harder.

The sound of shattering glass and hoarse male shouts resonated from the main building. Bullets rained through the delivery bay, horrifically loud, punching into the metal doors. Aguirre was not going to run, but fight like a cornered beast. Beatrice could only hope he'd forgotten his hostages. Ana manipulated the slimy knife between Beatrice's wrists, adding the pain of nicked fingers, hands and forearm to the increasing stiffness in her shoulders. Eventually, she found purchase on the plastic tie, slicing through it in a second. Relief spread across Beatrice's upper body as she took the knife and returned the favour.

Shots could be heard from the other side of the building as she cut Ana loose and handed her the knife to free Adrian. She turned to the wretched creature on her right.

"Can you stand, Matthew? We really must get out of the firing line. Can you hear me? Matthew?"

He turned his head but did not lift it. His eyes remained closed. He looked like a blinded war horse, responding to a familiar voice. A burst of agonising empathy suffused Beatrice.

"Ana, give me the knife! And you two take cover. We'll be right there."

"Here."

She clasped the sticky handle and turned to Matthew's wrists.

Then the lights went out and everything stopped.

She felt her way carefully down Matthew's arms, trying not to tremble. She heard the stealthy movements of Adrian and Ana retreating into one the many cardboard corridors behind them.

"Beatrice, this way! Run!" Ana's hoarse whisper carried urgency. Beatrice caught hold of Matthew's jacket and attempted to haul him to his feet. A dead weight. He keeled to one side and Beatrice knew they would be running precisely nowhere. Instead, she rolled him onto his back. He didn't protest. A stack of wooden pallets could hide a comatose Classics professor until the action was over. Feeling her way, she half-rolled, half-dragged him to the back edge of their makeshift bench and clenched hold of his clothing. As she shoved him over the edge, she broke his fall by holding on as hard as she could. He'd be bruised, but that couldn't be helped.

Ana's angry voice came again. "Beatrice! Get out of sight!"

"Nearly there ..." She spent several more seconds placing Matthew in the recovery position, then hurried to join Ana.

"Where's Matthew?" Adrian whispered.

"He couldn't move. I've left him behind the pallets. He'll be safe enough there." She wasn't even convincing herself.

They hid behind the first section of boxes. Like a corridor, the path between the stacked wines cases stretched almost the length of the room. As far as she could tell, Aguirre had darted behind the stacks along the right-hand side, but by now, he could easily be at the other end of their bolthole. It was impossible to see in the blackness. Tomas must be somewhere in the left-hand stacks. There was a sizeable gap between their stacks and his, so he'd be unlikely to break cover. Ana and Adrian pressed their backs against the far wall, Beatrice as close as she dared to their left. That way, she could just see the spot where she'd left Matthew. The three of them stood in the darkness, listening.

More shutters clattered upwards, exposing the warehouse and its contents. A cry of pain pierced the air, Beatrice couldn't tell from which direction, followed by more gunshots. A silhouette dashed through the nearest doorway and disappeared into the shadows.

"Beatrice Stubbs!" She recognised Milandro's voice. "You and your friends, stay where you are. Don't move."

Ana whispered. "Do we trust him?"

"We don't have a choice," said Beatrice.

Police vehicles rumbled into the car park, turning to train their headlights into the warehouse. Visibility improved but the horizontal angle threw deep shadows across the concrete floor. However, Beatrice could see well enough to be sure that no one else was lurking in their corridor.

A megaphone screeched into life and a male voice addressed Aguirre. Even without the distortion, it was impossible for Beatrice to understand.

Ana began translating. "There is no way out apart from surrender. They're telling him to throw his weapon into view and ... what the hell is that?"

A small light had appeared halfway along the corridor, bobbing along the floor towards them. A torch. The light swung upwards and illuminated a face. Angel Rosado. He held the torch at arm's length to show he was unarmed then shone it back at the floor to illuminate his path. They froze and watched as he came closer. He waved the torch briefly over them, then stopped, shining it up at his own face. The blood on his temple and the ghoulish uplighting did him no favours.

"I don't want to hurt you. I can help, I can get you out. There is a gap halfway along here and we can get into the bottling plant. Follow me."

Beatrice stared. "Why should we trust you? The police told us to stay put."

"The police don't want you to move in case my father-in-law shoots you. But if you come with me, he won't even know you've left the warehouse. Please. I want to help. This has gone too far."

"It's almost over. They're telling him to surrender," said Adrian.

"He'd never do that. It goes against all his principles of honour. He'll stick this out to the end. I know him."

Ana spoke. "Have you got a gun?"

Angel hesitated. "Yes. Hold this." He handed Ana the torch and reached behind him to bring out a stubby pistol, which looked like a Beretta Tomcat. He offered it to them.

"Fair enough." Ana took it. "We keep the torch and the gun and we'll follow you."

"Not me," Beatrice said. "I have to stay with Matthew. But I think you two should go. Just be very careful."

The megaphone stopped and silence filled the void.

Adrian dropped his voice to a whisper. "There's no point in staying with him. He's out of it. The best thing is to leave him where he is. We can escape with Angel, get round the back and show the police we're out, then they can take the scene by force. It's the best way."

"You go. Tell them exactly where I am and where Matthew is and where we think Aguirre and Tomas are hiding. But I'm staying here. I have to keep an eye on him. Now go, and be incredibly careful."

Ana shone the torch at Beatrice's face. "Are you sure?"

"Absolutely. Do stop wasting time and get out of here."

Adrian's arms enfolded her and she noted that even after an evening hiding in the forest and tied up in a warehouse, she could still smell his lemony aftershave.

"See you on the other side," he whispered.

Beatrice watched as they crept back along the corridor and abruptly disappeared to the right. Somehow, she trusted Angel to keep his word. Now all she had to do was wait. With the intelligence the three of them could provide, the police would be able to employ much stronger tactics. This could be over within the next fifteen minutes.

A grunt snapped her attention back to the gap. She pressed herself against the very edge of the boxes and looked out at the sliver of warehouse she could see. The sight horrified her. Matthew, lit up like a Roman monument, was staggering to his feet.

The police had no idea who he was. Ana and Adrian hadn't got out yet; mere seconds had passed since they'd gone. So a marksman could easily shoot him, if Aguirre didn't get there first. Matthew fumbled with his fly and looked sleepily around for a suitable spot.

The megaphone came again, probably instructing him to put his hands up. Even if it had been in English, Beatrice doubted he would have understood. She had to help him. She dashed out into the warehouse and heard an order yelled from the car park. She caught Matthew's jacket and dragged him towards her hiding-place. A shot punched into the boxes behind her.

A silhouette appeared at the side of the shutters. "Beatrice Stubbs! Get down! Now!"

She threw herself backwards, yanking Matthew with her. They stumbled to the ground, Beatrice's elbows taking the impact and Matthew crumpled like a bag of compost. She turned in the direction of the voice. More shots rang out and Detective Milandro hit the ground.

Chapter 40

Angel loped silently between the lines of boxes, while Ana kept the torch trained just ahead of his feet. Adrian could hear nothing but their breathing and the distant sounds of police radios. Suddenly Angel disappeared into a gap on their right. Ana ducked after him and Adrian followed. This corridor of cardboard boxes was much shorter and lighter, thanks to a glass door at the end. Beyond, fluorescent lights illuminated a mechanised production line, which snaked and looped around the room like a Scalectrix track.

Angel held the door open for them and Adrian was just about to step through when he heard the megaphone. The amplified voice held a new sense of urgency. Ana stopped and opened her mouth to say something when a shot made them all jump. Another voice shouted an indistinct order and more shots filled the air. Angel pulled at Ana's jacket.

"Please, we must get out. It is the only way to help."

Ana's face reflected her fear. Adrian put his hand to her shoulder both to reassure and guide her forward. His hand shook.

"This way. Come!"

They ran diagonally across the huge room, weaving between the lines of bottles, under pulleys and tubes and past pallet trucks, their feet echoing off the tiles. Angel led the way towards a door under some steel steps and they found themselves once more in darkness.

Ana flicked on the torch, enabling Angel to locate the light switch. The sunken spots glowed into life and Adrian recognised the foyer where he'd met Angel only that morning. The marble reception desk, the annual reports on the table, the state-of-the-art coffee machine all looked the same. But rather than being greeted by a young woman with a pleasant smile, this time they faced three police officers, pointing guns.

Adrian felt frustrated and impatient. Once identities had been established, it seemed everyone except him could be useful. Angel guided the three officers back through the bottling plant. Ana accompanied a detective to the despatch bay to indicate the precise location of Beatrice Stubbs. Adrian was to wait around the corner, behind the vehicles and out of harm's way. It seemed terribly unfair, but he did as he was told. Two other men stood in the shadows, and nodded to him as he joined them. Although Adrian couldn't see what was happening in the delivery bay, he had a clear view of the driveway, and watched as blue lights from three ambulances flashed towards them. The night air penetrated his linen jacket.

One of the men murmured to the other. "Don't like the look of that. Unless the other two are a precaution."

Adrian had never been happier to hear a northern accent. "You're English! Thank God for that. Do you know what's going on?"

"Not really. We're here to help a friend out. But as far as we know, she's still in there."

"Oh, you must be Beatrice's cavalry! Yes, she's still in there. We managed to escape through the building, but she wouldn't leave Matthew. They got him drunk, you see."

"Yeah, that's what Jase said. Another mate of ours. He's up on the roof with the police now. He was watching you through the window."

"Beatrice thought they were going to put us in a car and push it over a cliff with Matthew in the driver's seat."

The two men exchanged a look and the tall one spoke. "She weren't wrong, mate. There's a Seat Toledo round the back doused in petrol. You'd not stand a chance."

Adrian's stomach plummeted and his skin cooled still further. Trapped in a car, burning to death.

Police officers directed one ambulance to the forecourt and the other two past them to park just out of sight of the delivery bay. Medical staff jumped out and wheeled out stretchers. Adrian turned to check the other vehicle. The crew remained in the cab.

The first man followed Adrian's sightline. "My name's Kev. This is Tyler. And as I said, our mate Jase is on the roof." He held out his hand.

"Adrian." He shook both hands, distractedly. "You said just now you didn't like the look of two ambulances. Has someone already been hurt?"

Tyler looked away, but Kev answered. "Judging by the shouting, someone's down in the warehouse. But that," he pointed to the inactive ambulance, "is to collect the body. They're just waiting for the coroner to finish. Look, mate, I'm sorry, I'm not sure if it's someone you know, but there's a woman in the ditch over there. She's been shot."

A sudden barrage of yells went up from the delivery bay and the ambulance crew dashed around the corner. Adrian forgot his instructions and ran towards the action, unable to comprehend what Kev had just said. A single phrase ricocheted around his mind – 'someone's down in the warehouse'.

Kev and Tyler were right behind him as he took the corner. He scanned the scene. Tomas, cuffed, being led down the steps. Police everywhere. Two clusters of paramedics bending over prone bodies. And Ana, standing with her arms wrapped tightly around Beatrice Stubbs.

Chapter 41

One ambulance raced away, bearing the stricken detective and an injured officer. The second crew loaded a comatose Matthew onto a stretcher. Beatrice kept her concentration on him, even as the two police cars drove past. She had no desire to see Tomas's repulsive sneer or the face of Arturo de Aguirre.

"*Señora?*" The paramedic came to the door of the ambulance.

Beatrice called across to where Ana was talking to a tall blond chap in a long coat. "Ana, sorry to disturb, but can you translate?"

Adrian, Kev, Jase and Tyler all gathered around her, each face full of concern, as Ana listened.

"He's going to be fine. She says it looks like alcohol poisoning and they want to take him in for observation, but she reckons that with decent hydration and rest, he'll easily be on his feet tomorrow. Do you want to go with them, Beatrice?"

"No. I'm sure they will take good care of him. I'll go in later but first I need to talk to the police. Check which hospital, though."

"I meant for a check-up yourself. You had a nasty fall."

"Bloodied elbows, that's all. To add to my collection. Just ask where he's going, because we need to get on."

Ana took out her notebook and turned to the paramedic.

Adrian placed a hand on Beatrice's arm. "It's fine. We don't have to talk to the police tonight. They agree we should go back to the hotel, get some rest and go into the station in the morning to provide statements."

"It's not about statements. I need to know what's happened to Luz."

The ambulance doors closed and Beatrice watched it roll away. Look after him, she thought, he's very special. Only then did she notice all five of her companions wore the same sorrowful expression.

Ice spread from her scalp and for the first time that day, she sensed the onset of tears.

"She's dead, isn't she?" she said.

Kev nodded. "I'm sorry, Beatrice. We found her, by accident. They took the body away before we even got you out of the building. She was in that ditch." He indicated the stream behind them, black, cold and shallow.

She couldn't bear to know but she had to ask. "What did they do to her?"

Kev took a deep breath but Ana answered first.

"I don't think 'they' did anything. From what we've worked out, Aguirre did it himself. Looks like the forest sweep for Matthew and Adrian was a distraction. Seems Aguirre's guys knew they were there. So they made a half-arsed search, checked there were no observers, and Luz was taken out front and left in the car. Then Aguirre's mob did a wider circle and prepared a trap. All they needed to do was wait for you and I to arrive. They were very well informed."

Jaime.

A rage boiled up which Beatrice controlled by clenching her jaw and fists. "I asked you what happened to her."

Ana continued. "With us tied up in the warehouse, Aguirre went out – remember – and disposed of his daughter."

"Disposed? Don't pussycat round me, Ana. How did she die?"

"He shot her in the mouth."

Adrian, Kev, Jase and Tyler all dropped their heads.

Beatrice fanned her fury. Fury was good, active and articulate. Grief was debilitating and blocked her throat. "In cold blood, he took his own daughter to a mean, lonely ditch and shot her, just to protect his business interests. The man is evil. How the hell did he expect to get away with that?"

"We reckon he planned to fake her suicide," said Jase. "The gun was in her hand when they pulled the body out. Wouldn't surprise me if there's a typed 'I have to end it all' note at home in her bedroom."

"Nor me," agreed Ana. "But that's not all. I just had a chat with the coroner's assistant. He checked out the surroundings: pockets, handbag and so on. She had a pregnancy test in her bag. Positive."

Beatrice's head reeled as she went through the options. If Luz was pregnant, it would certainly be complicated. According to her, the boyfriend would never meet with parental approval. Allowing grief the upper hand, Beatrice pictured her. Dark hair, kind eyes and her prominent nose as she dipped into her gin and tonic.

Gin and tonic. A newly pregnant woman, slugging back a G&T? Something smelt off. But if Aguirre wanted to add a reason for her to take her own life, a positive pregnancy test would convince most coroners. Despite advances in understanding, for many single mothers a sense of shame remained. Was it possible to fix a pregnancy test and plant it on someone? If so, the man was a truly twisted individual.

"But how did he work the logistics? How was Luz supposed to have got here?"

Kev nodded. "That's what I thought. Then I remembered what we saw when we first arrived. The Reservoir Dogs bunch was out front when some bloke arrived in a Peugeot. I thought it were weird. He stopped for a quick chat with his mates and left in the Corsa. My money's on the Peugeot belonging to the dead woman."

"Luz," Beatrice insisted. "Her name's Luz. What did this bloke look like?"

"Mid-thirties, dark hair, leather jacket and cowboy boots. Kind of fancied himself, I thought."

Jaime. Lying, duplicitous, venomous rattlesnake. Beatrice looked at the ditch where Luz had died at the hands of her own father.

"Right, so let's wait for the forensic pathology report and give full statements to the police tomorrow. In the meantime, there's someone I want to talk to. Where's your car, Kev? I'd like to visit Jaime."

Chapter 42

She came empty-handed. He couldn't eat grapes, and flowers were banned in his room. In any case, she wasn't even sure if they'd let her in. Generally, hospital staff took their lunch immediately after the patients, so Beatrice grabbed the opportunity and ascended three floors to Intensive Care.

The nurse held up a splayed hand. "Five minutes, OK? Is very tired."

"Of course. No problem." The trembling began again as she walked down the corridor to Room 223. A deep-seated shudder which spasmed though her whole body at random intervals. Delayed shock reaction, that's all, nothing to worry about, she told herself. All the same, she might just share it with James when she got back.

She knocked lightly and pushed open the door. A low hum from the various machines was the only response. The curtains were half-drawn, creating shadows in the corners while dust motes seemed suspended in the sunlight across his feet. She approached the bed, taking in the neatly folded sheets, the tubes piercing his bruised flesh and the bandages around his shoulder. His face, despite the intrusion of stitches and tape securing his oxygen tube, seemed peaceful and calm, a different picture from the rictus of pain he'd worn last time she'd seen him. His dark eyes opened and focused on her, sending a jolt of surprise along with the shakes.

"Good morning, Detective ..." she ran out of words.

Milandro blinked and unfolded his hand. She grasped his fingers in a simulation of a handshake.

"I know you can't speak yet. But I had to come. I want to, well, first of all ... how are you feeling, on a scale of one to ten?"

Milandro dropped his eyes to his hands, limp on the white sheets. He uncurled his right hand to display four fingers, considered a moment and added two more from his left.

Beatrice smiled with relief. "That's wonderful. We were all so worried about you. Detective, my main reason for coming is to apologise. I mistrusted you, suspected the police of corruption and thereby endangered ..."

He lifted his hand, took a moment and opened his mouth. "You were right." His voice sounded painful.

"Don't talk. Firstly because it sounds like it hurts. And secondly because I haven't finished yet."

He ignored her. "The police *were* corrupt. My superior officer was on Aguirre's ..." He coughed once, winced with pain and squeezed his eyes shut.

"Please, Detective, you must rest. I won't be the cause of you tearing your stitches or rupturing something else. I do have a few questions, because the police officers at the station will tell me absolutely nothing. It's a closed shop. But all I need at this stage is a yes or a no. Can we agree to that?"

Milandro opened his eyes, blinked and indicated the water jug. Beatrice poured a small amount into a glass and twisted the straw to the right angle. She placed it between his lips and watched as he swallowed two tiny mouthfuls. His face was grazed along the cheekbone and dark stubble with flecks of grey covered his chin. Even with the striking scar tissue, he was a good-looking man. As if he could hear her, he looked up with amusement in his eyes.

Beatrice fussed over returning the glass to cover her awkwardness.

"Finished? OK, I'll put this here in case you want some more later. Now, as I said, there are just a couple of things I'd like to know. You said Aguirre had nobbled your superior officer?"

Milandro dipped his chin slightly to indicate the affirmative.

"So it must have been Salgado who called Scotland Yard. I thought it was you. Within an hour of our first meeting, my boss phoned me and told me to mind my own business. Said I was a bloody nuisance."

Milandro nodded again.

"Are you saying yes to the fact it was Salgado or agreeing that I'm a bloody nuisance?"

Milandro twitched his eyebrow and smiled. Beatrice pressed on.

"I realise it was stupid to tackle Aguirre's people alone, but you understand I had no faith in ... well, in the force. Can I ask how you knew how to find us at Alava Exports?"

He pointed an index finger to his right eye, pulling down the lower lid.

"You watched the hotel. You didn't trust me. I suppose I should be glad, because you were absolutely right. Seems I placed too much faith in certain people. I presume you know Jaime Rodriguez has disappeared."

Milandro fixed her with a furious glare.

"I know. I feel more stupid than I can express. No wonder Aguirre was always one step ahead. Jaime and all his worldly goods have vanished, including the contents of his office."

The indignity of being played for a fool rose up in Beatrice like bile. She walked to the window, paced back to the door and back to the window, unable to keep still.

"That sly, evil, devious, two-faced, foul, ingratiating little weasel! How could anyone behave like that? So sincere, so caring! Good God, we were totally taken in! He definitely set Tiago up, you know, and would have thrown Ana to those wolves. The dirty little sleazebag! And he must have told Aguirre about Luz visiting me."

"Luz?"

Of their own volition, Beatrice's hands assumed a prayer-like pose over her nose. She stared at Milandro and spoke with a steady voice.

"The woman who came to my hotel room on Friday was Aguirre's youngest daughter. She gave me all the necessary documentation to expose him and his operation. He found out and he shot her. In the head. That bastard intended to fake her suicide, with a note and everything. He'd even planted a pregnancy test in her handbag, as if that would provide just cause. What kind of man is he?"

Milandro's mouth twisted in an expression of sympathy or disgust. He shook his head and went to speak. The door opened and the nurse bustled in with a trolley bearing pills, dressings and the suchlike.

"*Señora*, you go now. Is time. Bye, bye."

"Yes, of course." Beatrice gathered her bag and got out of the way. "Thank you for your time, Detective. I wish you all the best and a speedy recovery. And I really am sorry."

He smiled and raised a hand a couple of centimetres from the bed.

An impulse swelled in Beatrice and she knew this was her chance.

"Detective? Would you give me permission to see him? They'll never let me in without your say-so."

Milandro's eyes hardened, as if he were trying to read her mind.

His voice scratched out, provoking a frown from the nurse. "Why?"

"It's just something I need to do."

His gaze lingered a second longer and his chin dipped once more.

"Thank you."

Chapter 43

After reading two articles on Hellenic politics and British artefacts in *The Times*, Matthew dozed off. She waited several minutes before tiptoeing into the bathroom to call Ana.

"Hi Beatrice. You got my text?"

"Hello. Yes, I did. Still no trace of Jaime?"

"Nope. The man has gone up in a puff of smoke. But I have got the autopsy results on Luz. She wasn't pregnant."

"So why was a pregnancy test in her bag?"

"I think I can answer that. I went to the Aguirre estate this morning. Closed shop. Marisol's still sedated and the sisters set security on me. But I had a nice chat with the housekeeper. Firstly, Inez is up the duff and receiving medical treatment. The shock of her sister's death, father's arrest and husband's departure is seen as extremely dangerous for 'her condition'. There's your pregnancy test. I reckon she was in on this. The housekeeper also said Aguirre and Luz had an almighty row at breakfast on Friday. She thinks he wanted Luz to drop out of university and come home. And get this. Our junior reporter just got back from Burgos. According to Luz's roommate, Marisol Aguirre had already cleared out Luz's university room on Friday morning."

"So the whole family conspired to get rid of her?"

"Dunno. Nothing concrete yet, but it stinks to high heaven."

Beatrice stared at herself in the mirror and made her decision.

"Are you still at the paper, Ana?"

"Is the Pope Catholic? Got in at six this morning and been flat out ever since. But I'll make it to the restaurant tonight, don't worry. How's Matthew?"

"Asleep at the moment, but improving all the time. I think we're all going to fly home tomorrow."

"All of you? I thought you had a grand tour of Spain planned."

"I had. Still have. But I may just do it in small doses. Right, I'm going to get my head down for an hour. See you at *La Cepa* at eight."

Lying was like any other activity. The more you did it, the easier it became. Beatrice splashed some water on her face and thought of Shakespeare. *If it were done when 'tis done then 'twere well it were done quickly.* Quickly. It had to be now. Ana was at the office, Matthew asleep, Adrian distracted and Vitoria on a Sunday timetable. She packed her handbag, including Milandro's letter of permission, and wrote a breezy note for Matthew. She propped it against his litre-bottle of mineral water and blew him a silent kiss, before hurrying along the corridor to Adrian's room. He opened the door, barefoot and smiling.

"Hello. I was just about to pop along and check how he is. Did our lunch excursion wear him out?"

"It seems that way. He's got his feet up on the sofa and he's napping. A post-prandial snooze always does him good, even without the upsets of the last two days. I need to toddle along to the police station for a short while. Might you be good enough to look in on him occasionally?"

"I'd be delighted. Why do you have to see the police again? We gave them the whole story at least five times yesterday. I even dreamt about it last night. Do you need my moral support?" He assumed a concerned frown.

Beatrice waved a hand in a vague gesture. "That's very kind of you but this is boring paperwork, more line-of-reporting stuff. I'd be happier knowing you were keeping an eye on Matthew."

Adrian's face relaxed. "Rather you than me. So if he's feeling fit enough to travel, shall I see if I can find us some flights for tomorrow?"

"Yes, please do. Morning if you can manage it. Right, I'd better make a move. Back by six at the latest."

Adrian glanced at his watch. "Six? A bit more than 'a short while', then. Just remember, I'll need at least an hour to get ready for tonight."

"Is that all? Don't worry, I'll be back in plenty of time. In fact, I'm heading to the police station on foot, with the sole purpose of walking up an appetite."

And to make sure that no one knew where she was going. In quite the opposite direction to the recently damaged police station, Beatrice headed towards the medium-security custody centre at the Alava Psychiatric Hospital. To interview Arturo de Aguirre.

While receptionists, medics and nurses studied the paperwork behind a glass door, Beatrice concentrated on looking relaxed. There could be no doubt about the authorisation, so it was a matter of patience. She breathed slowly and deeply, assuming her role. In order to convince him, she had to believe it herself. She repeated certain phrases, rehearsed certain emotions and visualised her own body language. Every minute or so, a small voice would ask, *Is this the right thing to do*? A blazing roar answered in the affirmative.

"Detective Stubbs. Sorry to keep you waiting. It was necessary to check your permission and as you are not on official police business, we have to ask the patient if he is willing to talk."

Beatrice stared at the earnest young chap in a yarmulke and white coat. She hadn't even considered Aguirre might have the opportunity to refuse.

"I see. And?"

"Everything is fine. The authorisation is confirmed and Señor Aguirre seems keen to speak to you. Please follow me."

He led the way past the glass doors and along the grey, muted corridor. Beatrice grabbed her things and followed, as he was still talking.

"It's such a shame our senior clinician isn't here today. He would love to have heard about this project of Scotland Yard's. Research on empathy is his own personal area of expertise. Would you have any time to come back again tomorrow? I know he'll be disappointed if he misses such an opportunity to discuss your work."

Beatrice pulled a pained expression. "Unfortunately not. I have an early flight back to London in the morning. But look, here's my card. He can email me at any time. I'd be delighted to discuss our project with such an expert."

And she'd cross that bridge when she came to it.

His trainers squeaked as he stopped and he took the card. "A Detective Inspector? How fascinating." He tucked the card into his breast pocket with a smile. "Thank you. He'll be so pleased. Here we are. Please observe all security precautions as detailed on the wall. Also, a supervising orderly will attend your interview."

"That's not a problem. If I get into any language difficulties, he or she can help."

The young doctor shook his head as he peered through the window. "Oh no. No, orderlies are there to guarantee safety of both interviewers and patients. Juan is simply your insurance policy and in any case, he doesn't speak English."

Just for a second, Beatrice closed her eyes and beamed. Then she followed the verbose young man into the room, forcing her features into an expression of contrition and sorrow.

Jeans and casual shirt notwithstanding, Arturo de Aguirre retained every inch of his dignity, rising from his chair as they entered in a gallant gesture, as if he were receiving her in his office. He exchanged a few words in Spanish with the doctor, who gestured to a tall orderly in white overalls, before turning to Beatrice.

"Nice to meet you, Detective Inspector. Good luck with your project. Juan will see you out after your interview. Have a nice Sunday."

"Thank you, you've been most kind."

The doctor left, eventually. Beatrice faced Aguirre, who gestured to a chair. His expression was mild, with a hint of a smile.

"Thank you for seeing me, Señor Aguirre. Rejecting my request for a meeting would have been perfectly understandable, under the circumstances."

Aguirre sat and faced her, his eyes hard. "My understanding is that our conversation is to be informal. This interview is not being recorded and is therefore legally inadmissible in court. There are no witnesses who understand the lingua franca and your permission explicitly states that this conversation is not part of the current criminal enquiry. You have presented a letter of permission from the judicial Spanish police entitling you to discuss the subject of empathy with me. Under such circumstances, I find myself agreeable to a debate on the subject. I will not discuss the charges against me but can offer some insights of value regarding human motivation."

Beatrice blinked. His grandstanding had lessened not a jot since being incarcerated. She took a moment to retrieve her notebook and pen from her bag.

"I hope you can. I only have a few questions, which should take no more than fifteen minutes. Before we begin, and this is not an attempt to draw any incriminating statements, I'd like to say how sorry I am for the loss of your youngest daughter. I only met her twice but I liked her enormously."

Aguirre dropped his eyes and inclined his head but did not reply.

"My first question is about something you said on Friday evening. In response to an accusation, you told Professor Bailey he knew nothing of shame. Could you explain what you meant by that remark?"

He clasped his hands together as if about to pray. "I think that is obvious. The man attempted to berate me by invoking my sense of national pride. It was a crude effort, much like the losing poker player accusing the winner of having a better poker face. In order to feel shame, you need to have self-respect. That is what shame is, the direct opposite of pride. My point was simply that the British, in many ways, but let's stick to wine, have no self-respect, no taste and no pride. Therefore, they cannot feel the opposite. They are not ashamed of themselves."

In a moment of absolute clarity, Beatrice realised he was lying. And further, he was trying to provoke a reaction. She played it as coolly as possible, continued making gibberish notes and forming her own poker face.

"Thank you. An interesting theory. Perhaps we can pursue that point a little further. You have confessed to the fraudulent export racket ..."

"Confessed? That makes it sound as if I am ashamed, which is not the case. I regard the boom of the Viura grape and the change in the reputation of white Rioja a huge success. Not only that, but selling substandard product to the British for full price has been one of my greatest triumphs."

Beatrice smiled, observing a man in thrall to his ego. "You have pre-empted my question. I was going to ask if you felt any remorse at having devalued the image of the Spanish wine-making industry, but I can see you do not."

He snorted. "The expressions of outrage and apologetic hand-wringing you see on television are a diplomatic mask. The wine-making industry, if not the entire gastronomic world of Spain is secretly laughing behind your backs."

"Really? Well, I'm sure you're right. Although I can't say I've encountered anyone of that opinion. The word most people are using to describe Castelo de Aguirre is 'disgrace'. But you're bound to know best, as they're unlikely to tell me the truth. Now I have one last question. International wine fraud is one thing, but pre-meditated murder is another."

"Correct. While I excel at the first, I deny all charges relating to those men's unfortunate accidents."

"I will not ask you any questions regarding Tiago Vínculo or Miguel Saez, as these are charges yet to be tried in court. However, you claim your daughter's death was by her own hand. Not yours."

His eyes seemed to soften, his mouth pinched and his shoulders sagged. The impression was of deepest sorrow. He was quite a player.

"That is the truth. A tragic truth, most certainly. A parent should never suffer the suicide of a child."

"Why do you think she took her own life?"

He looked up at the ceiling for several seconds before training his eyes on her. "I think you are probably more aware of her reasons than I am. After all, you were the last person to see her before she died."

Beatrice's cue. She was ready. She dropped her head and generated a blush. For this performance, every single word must be chosen with precision.

"Yes. I admit to feeling some considerable discomfort at my own role in this sad event. But although I refused to help her, the young woman I walked to the train seemed anything but defeated. This is what I cannot understand. She intended to catch the train back to Burgos and continue with her studies, but she had no intention of giving up her battle."

Like a cat, aware of the danger but fatally curious, he watched her: suspicious, alert but unable to resist.

"I'm not sure what you mean by 'her battle'. Why on earth would she need *your* help?"

The balance had shifted and he knew it. The contemptuous emphasis sealed her conviction that he was still attempting to crack her composure with increasingly feeble blows. Beatrice gazed wistfully into the distance and brought out the big guns.

"I don't have children, Señor Aguirre. Something I don't regret. But hearing Luz use every ounce of passion she possessed to persuade me to drop my investigation into Castelo de Aguirre ... well, I realised I would never know such filial loyalty. Such fierce love. I couldn't agree to her request, of course I couldn't. But I said goodbye with nothing but admiration for her efforts. I was deeply touched by her love for you."

She shook herself and sought his eyes. "As I said, I only met her twice but I won't forget her. A true lion heart. But at that stage, we had all the information we needed and arrests were imminent. Our informant had delivered all the proof we needed to go to Interpol. We'd realised by then that Salgado was corrupt and chose to effect our operation ..."

"Stop." His body seemed frozen, all his energy concentrated in his eyes. "Luz wanted you to leave me alone?"

Beatrice feigned puzzlement. "Of course. She's not, sorry, she wasn't stupid. When she drove me back from the Castelo the first time, she asked some very searching questions. She knew who I was. The day she went back to university, she came to the hotel specifically to ask me to leave Vitoria and forget the story. In fact, she was so determined, I almost had her in the frame for the witness murders. But our contact had already identified Tomas and friends."

"Your contact?"

Beatrice gave him a reproving look. "You know I can't divulge that information. A good police officer should always protect her sources."

"But you're on sabbatical. Officially, you aren't a police officer at the moment."

And all that is left is to reel him in.

Beatrice looked at her watch. "I must go. You've been most kind and very informative. I will see you again, when the case comes to trial, naturally."

She placed her notebook and pen back in her handbag and lifted the card.

Aguirre leant forward, his arms on the table. "If not for me, for my daughter. Tell me the name of the mole."

"I'm sorry, I can't do that." Beatrice stood. "But I will say congratulations. I understand your daughter Inez is expecting her first. That must be some consolation under the circumstances. Goodbye, Señor Aguirre. Thank you for your time."

She held out her hand. He got to his feet. His eyes bored into her and she had no idea if he would spit, shout or accept the gesture. If he didn't, she'd have to find another way. Eventually he reached out and shook her hand. To his credit, he betrayed no surprise. The orderly opened the door and Beatrice exited the room.

She walked in a straight line, following the white shoes, concentrating on her breath, her steps and the image in her head. Aguirre alone, sitting at that table, looking at the business card she'd slipped into his hand.

Jaime Rodriguez, Editor of *El Periódico.*

Chapter 44

"Sorry, sorry, sorry." Ana flopped into her seat, shrugged off her jacket and brushed her hair out of her eyes. Her face was free of make-up and evidently tired, yet she looked lit from within.

"Left at ten to eight but I couldn't get a cab for love nor money so had to go back for the Vespa. I'm so shagged I can't tell you. How're you doing, Matthew? How's the head?"

Matthew raised his glass of sparkling water. "I've sufficiently recovered to try another local brew. I'm very glad you made it. I know it must be enormously stressful at the paper today."

"Stressful? I've never known a day like it. Manic from morning to night. Where's the waiter? I have a desperate thirst. What's the story with the flights, Adrian? Good God, you're looking sharp enough to cut yourself."

Adrian smiled the smile of a compliment well-earned. "Thank you. And I must say, after fourteen hours in the office, you don't look anywhere near as wrecked as I'd expect. That's the joy of fine bones, you see. We're flying out at quarter to ten in the morning. So tonight is both a celebration and a farewell."

"You have a way with words, my man. Can I have a swig of your water?"

Beatrice hailed the waiter and ordered two bottles of cava and more water. A beeping came from Ana's jacket and she snatched up her phone. Her face softened into a smile. She turned the screen to Beatrice, and then to Matthew and Adrian.

The image showed three laughing lads holding beer bottles – Kev, Jase and Tyler. And the sender and text beneath hadn't escaped Beatrice's notice.

"Looks like the stag weekend has begun in earnest," she said.

Ana looked at the picture once more. "I'd say it has. Lock up your daughters, Bilbao."

"And apparently you're joining them tomorrow?" Beatrice kept her enquiry light and innocent, as she continued to butter her roll.

Ana snorted with laughter and shook her head. "I should have known you'd spot that. You don't miss a trick, do you? Yes, all right, I'm joining them for lunch. Kev invited me. He seems like a decent bloke."

"Definitely," Adrian agreed. "Not to mention totally ripped."

The waiter brought an ice bucket and the first bottle of cava.

"Ana, you must be exhausted. Do you need to de-brief or would you rather just enjoy the food?" Matthew asked, with classic avuncular concern.

"Food first, no doubt about it. But I have updates, unless you're sick to death of the whole thing. Would you ever pass the bread over, Matthew? My stomach feels like my throat's been cut."

They ordered chorizo, quails' eggs, tortilla, Gernika peppers, kidneys in sherry, octopus, three kinds of ham, green beans and asparagus, with plenty of bread.

As the plates arrived, Beatrice saw Matthew's eyes widen and a sense of calm settled on her. Not every Beatrice-related experience meant disaster. Meanwhile, Ana ate and talked at a similar speed.

"All four of Aguirre's muscle men refuse to talk. Aguirre himself accepts all the wine fraud charges, but won't even discuss the murders. Still insists Luz killed herself. The whole guilt-over-pregnancy deal is blown, as the autopsy showed she wasn't."

"Do they know if the test belonged to her sister?" asked Beatrice.

"Haven't heard yet, but that's the premise I'm working. Salgado is subject to an internal police investigation. Word is that it's going to be a slap on the wrist and early retirement. Milandro's slated to take over. New broom and all that. God, this ham with the acorn oil – I could just roll in it. Now we're not talking just the police, but governmental organisations, media and major companies. Lots of dirty fingers in mucky pies. Everyone's likely to get splattered now the shit has hit the fan. Ah, sorry, we're eating."

Adrian bit into a tiny egg and followed it with a nibble of asparagus. "Don't worry. It would take more than that to put me off this food. You know, I'm almost looking forward to coming back for the trial. We simply must revisit this place. Every mouthful is a joy. Now what about Jaime?"

Beatrice stopped chewing.

Ana shook her head. "No sign. My guess is the Aguirre network set him up elsewhere, new identity, the whole shebang. Turns out Jaime Rodriguez wasn't even his real name. Dirty little scumbag slipped the net. If I could get my hands on that stinking heap of ..."

"You won't," said Beatrice, prodding a kidney. "Write him off and focus on the trial. The Aguirres will take care of their own."

She felt the weight of Matthew's gaze, but raised her glass as deflection.

"A toast. To a successful collaboration and justice served."

Glasses glinted and sparkled, as three voices repeated her words. "Justice served!"

They drank, met each other's eyes and returned to the spread. In the contented appreciative silence, Beatrice made another decision. Her sabbatical was over. It was time to get back to work.

Dedications

Behind Closed Doors
For Bonnie and Clive – wish you were here

Raw Material
To Janet and Terry – for being you

Tread Softly
For Florian – with love, respect and admiration

Message from JJ Marsh

I hope you enjoyed *The Beatrice Stubbs Boxset One*.
If so, there's another bundle of three ready and waiting.

BOXSET TWO
Cold Pressed
Human Rites
Bad Apples

For occasional updates, news, deals and a FREE exclusive prequel:
Black Dogs, Yellow Butterflies, visit jjmarshauthor.com and
subscribe to my newsletter.

If you would recommend *The Beatrice Stubbs Series* to a friend,
please do so by writing a review. Your tip helps other readers
discover their next favourite book.

Thank you.

Also by Triskele Books

The Charter, Closure, Complicit, Crimson Shore,
False Lights and *Sacred Lake*
by Gillian Hamer

Tristan and Iseult, The Rise of Zenobia, The Fate of an Emperor,
The Better of Two Men, The Rebel Queen and *The Love of Julius*
by JD Smith

Spirit of Lost Angels, Wolfsangel,
Blood Rose Angel and *The Silent Kookaburra*
by Liza Perrat

Gift of the Raven and *Ghost Town*
by Catriona Troth

http://www.triskelebooks.co.uk

CPSIA information can be obtained
at www.ICGtesting.com
Printed in the USA
BVHW071100280119
538839BV00004B/520/P